To

Audrey

Beyond Mercy

by

Audrey Coatesworth

Audrey Coatesworth
Oct. 2009

In memory of
Ann and Emily Kittle and Catherine Shaw
Died July 27th 1497

§

'Their spirits can now rest in peace'

'A book written in months, prepared over centuries'

A different message

Published by PLP Publishings (UK), Buckingham
Printed by Moreton Press, Buckingham
Cover graphics by Corporate Design Solutions, Buckingham
Illustrations by David S. Earnshaw, Yorkshire

ISBN 978-0-9555310-3-3

Acknowledgements

Grateful thanks

To my husband Peter, for his endless love, care and encouragement on our long journey

To my brother David, for painting the pictures for the book, which are included on the cover

To my grandson Toby for his help in designing the cover

§

The course of my life was enabled by two truly amazing people whose paths happened to cross mine and who opened gates that would otherwise have been shut against me. I was so fortunate to have been able to benefit from their foresightedness and understanding. If only there were more people like them in these days of often 'spurious progress'. They were visionaries with inspirational and practical solutions. By writing these few words, I wish to express and acknowledge my debt of gratitude to them both.

Sir Alec Clegg was the Chief Education Officer in Yorkshire from 1945-1974. The County Major Scholarships in the county allowed able students to go to University, with all expenses paid. I wanted to become a doctor, but my father could never have afforded medical school fees or accommodation for me at that time. Without this facility being available, in 1956 when I left school, I would have had to get a job. The money was not 'as a matter of course' or a grant that would land a student in debt for years to come. No, it was a result of application, study, ability and getting high marks in the relevant exams needed to enter the faculty of choice. The opportunity it gave was highly valued.

Dr Rosemary Rue, Chief Medical Officer of Oxford Regional Health Authority, came into my life at a much later stage. She was a wonderful woman who recognised the needs of married women with children to be able to work part time. She organised the 'part-time women doctors' scheme' in the Oxford Region. Women doctors could, should they wish, take a break from medicine and then join the training scheme when ready to resume work. They could decide how many sessions they could offer on a regular basis. They could progress through the levels of higher training, each phase being prolonged as necessary, to match the training and experience of those working full time. The same examinations had to be taken. I can say that without any doubt, we were a hard working dedicated group, serving, as well as we could, both the Oxford Region, our patients and our children at the same time.

I didn't 'choose' psychiatry as my specialty. It was the only post I could find when my youngest child started school. I was determined to work part time to fit in with school hours. At the time, that specialty was desperate for qualified and interested staff, and enthusiasm has always been part of my nature. So, I was appointed. I never regretted my decision. But once on Dr Rue's scheme, I could and did continue further training to become a consultant.

I met some wonderful people as patients. Many, who had great fortitude and courage in the face of adversity, were inspirational. I specialised in psychotherapy and my particular endeavour was to help patients recover lives that had been interrupted and marred by the effects of traumas. I studied the phenomenon of 'dissociation'. At an extreme level of pain or fear, the conscious mind can, as a final protective mechanism, leave the body for a time. The degree to which this happens depends on the level of the pain or fear involved and the individual concerned. This can happen in all children, up to the age of 6-7 yrs of age, and in some adults.

I have to say that without all that work, extra training and understanding I would not be writing this book now.

A book in three parts

Contents – Part 1

2009

A few brief words of explanation.

This book is set not only in the future but also in an era that is long since past – a time that was never expected to surface again.

This is the first of several books that I shall write about events in centuries gone past. I have to say that I have only been able to recall or know this information in the last few years, as if collecting the pieces of a huge jigsaw. I understand the 'why' and 'how' of the process, but this is not the time nor the place to explain. Yet, I still find it rather strange being able to do so at all. When at school, though I was intelligent and did well at most subjects, one seemed blocked to any part of my brain, namely history. My problem was that, though I understood the historical concepts and the reasoning, I could scarcely remember a name or a date. Hence, I did not know who did what or who was who, or when or where.

But now I realise that this lack of knowledge and ability, at that time, had a purpose. As I now recall past events, I do so without the clutter or preconceived notions of previous knowledge. I have **not** done any research for any of my books. The information is 'just there' in my mind, as easily obtainable as events in my present life. Have I just a very good imagination or is it true? Only time will tell. But for the purists or historians, these books are about people and what happened to them, and are not meant to be accurate social or historical documents, though they may well be so! I know only what is relevant for me to write the books.

Let me say now that I believe the events from the past are accurate. In Part 2 of this book, I have used what could have been the original historical names of the villages. Some differ from those of today but are the ones that have come into my mind. But, I have, as far as I can know, created all the names of the people in the future and the events – as one would in a story. But, the proof of what I have written about the past will be found, of that I am sure.

All I can say at this point is that, in reading this book, there will be chance for interest, challenge and future enlightenment. There are many connections between the past, present and future (in this book), linking both people and events. I freely acknowledge that in the climate of present beliefs many of these may be overlooked, missed or thought of as fantasy. If such be the case with the first reading, let me say that the book will not change and the truth will eventually be apparent. I merely ask that you keep an open, if sceptical mind. Scepticism is healthy and I have no problem with that. However, a closed or biased mind is limiting and denies opportunity.

This book is about a village which I shall call Stocksmoor. It was the village of my birth in 1937 and I lived there until I went to Edinburgh University in 1956. I studied medicine and qualified as a doctor in 1962.

Though I often visited my parents, I finally left Stocksmoor, as my home, on July 28th, 1962 when I married.

2013

» Late September

"Now, sir, can I help you? What would you like to drink?"

"Just a tonic water, please," replied Brian, "and then I'll order some food if you don't mind."

He looked at his watch. Five thirty. He decided that he would just stay a while - about an hour or maybe two. It would be his last time here, so he wouldn't rush. Anyway, he didn't like driving along the motorway in heavy rain and hoped it would have stopped completely by then. He wasn't in a hurry, so he would just 'play it by ear'. He felt 'released' from stress. It was a new and recent experience and he still savoured every minute. He actually fancied a long cool drink, a beer or a pint of coke. But it would take very little to put him to sleep, and he would need to concentrate hard if he was to travel home this evening. He didn't want to have to stop again on the way back and it would just be his luck to be stuck in a long motorway queue, with a full bladder. He wasn't neurotic, at least he didn't think so, but it had happened before - which had not been comfortable! He was used to travelling up and down the country; he had done so for several years.

He had stayed at the motel next door many times. He was glad that his colleague at work had recommended it. He had always thought that it was attached to the pub, 'The Dun Cow', but had never bothered to ask if his assumption was correct. All he knew was that each time without fail, he had been comfortable in the motel and well fed in the pub. He was now in the bar lounge of the pub, where he had spent many evenings.

"You're very busy," he observed. He had waited ten minutes before getting the attention of the lady serving behind the bar.

"Yes, we have been very busy all afternoon. So sorry for the delay, sir."

"Oh, that's no problem. Pleased to meet you. I haven't met you before."

"Oh, I'm June, a friend of Tom's wife. There has been an event in the back room this afternoon. It's been hectic and seems to have gone on for ever. It started at half past two. I think it's just about finished. I'm helping out. I live nearby, so it's easy. I usually get called in if there is something special going on. Will you order a meal? We can serve food in about half an hour?"

"Yes, indeed. I've broken my journey especially for the roast beef dinner and, hopefully, apple pie. They've always been my favourites here. Is Tom around?" asked Brian. He'd only had a light lunch at 12 noon and he couldn't miss the chance of a final 'Stocksmoor special'.

At that moment Tom entered the bar. "Brian! What an unexpected pleasure. What brings you back this way? No offence, but I thought we'd seen the last of you two weeks ago."

"So did I," answered Brian, "but Len, you know, my old boss, sent me an email. He asked me to go to the office today. His message was short but none too sweet. No please or thank you! 'Brian,' it read, 'meet me at 11.30 am, next Thursday, sharp, Leeds office, to iron out some unfinished business'. I was a little worried, as you might expect. I knew Len wasn't happy with my leaving, but I was sure that I'd left everything absolutely in order. I'd checked everything I could think of. Several times in fact. I nearly phoned him, to see what it was all about. But in the end I didn't. Sarah's response was, 'You'll have to go, you know, so I shouldn't bother. You'll find out when you get there, and that will be soon enough.' Anyway, I turned up as ordered.

"Lo and behold there was Len, all the staff – even three from the other office, and a sandwich, sausage roll, and quiche buffet, with fruit, coffee and a glass of wine. All set out ready. He'd arranged it just for me. He apologised that he'd not had time to organise anything before. He hadn't expected me to leave and he'd been away during my notice. After we had eaten, he took me aside and, out of hearing of the others, he asked me not to open the envelope he was going to give me until I had left the premises. Then, in front of the staff, he gave me a sealed envelope and let everyone know that it was a token of his respect and thanks for all my hard work Do you know, he has given me a cheque as a leaving gift? A thousand pounds! No less. Isn't that fantastic?"

"That is amazing. You don't usually get anything like that these days," agreed Tom.

"I shall give it to Sarah. After lunch, we've all spent the afternoon chatting, about this and that. I'm afraid no work was done, but Len didn't seem to mind."

"All I can say is that I am really pleased for you."

"Well, I did turn loss to profit for him, yes, a really good profit. But it's very satisfying to have my contribution to his success recognised. I was really overwhelmed at his gesture. After all, I was only doing my job and he did pay me. Quite well in fact. I've been very lucky."

"You earned every penny, considering all your long hours and nights away from home. Our gain of course, but that's not the point. But, at least he has rewarded you for the extra 'pound of flesh' that he seemed to expect, and which we all know, you gave. I recall that you always seemed very tired."

Tom went over to a table near the bar where there were two small piles of books. He picked up one from each pile and gave them to Brian.

"Here's something else for you. There are just a few left over today. Take them as a parting gift from me. You'll never forget your visits here while you have these particular books. I know you have bought this one, 'Beyond Mercy' before," continued Tom and he pointed to one of the books, "and you may by now have this other one, 'Justice'. But take them anyway."

"Thank you Tom, that's most kind. It's like an early Christmas. No, I haven't a copy of the second one."

"These are not in the same league as the cheque, of course, but you will need 'Beyond Mercy' in a moment when I take you through to the other room. I have a surprise for you. You're just in time to see someone I think you'll like to meet. She's just about ready to leave. We set the main room aside for her this afternoon. Any ideas?"

"No, I haven't a clue!"

"Think 'writing'. Writing books. Those books! Can't you guess yet?" quizzed Tom. He smiled and waited.

Brian looked puzzled for a while, then, as the 'penny slowly dropped', he exclaimed, "Oh! Do you mean Audrey Coatesworth? Actually here in the pub? June, at the bar, told me that you'd had an event here this afternoon, but she didn't say who or what and I never thought to ask."

"Yes. I asked Audrey specially. We remembered about a month ago that this week is the twentieth anniversary of when we actually took over the business from my parents. They started building the business up in the pub by cooking meals. We came to help and well, we've just continued. But, we'd sort of lost track of the time and hey presto, twenty years have gone. So, we wondered what we could do. As the book has more than trebled our trade already, we thought we would try and do something connected with it. Audrey was coming up this way today and agreed she could bring a load of books with her. We sell them in the pub and buy ours from her, anyway. So, it just sort of fitted in very well. She didn't mind at all when we asked her; in fact, she felt quite pleased to be 'signing' in her own home village. We put a notice in the local paper, and we've had queues outside the door since noon, despite the weather. I think she has just about reached the last one."

"What a stroke of luck I called in," remarked Brian, looking at the books. "Thank you so much, Tom. I'll treasure these and give them to Ben one day."

They both went through a door to a rather large area used as a dining room-cum-lounge. Near the fireplace where, even though it was only September, a log fire was slowly burning, Audrey was sitting chatting to her husband and drinking a cup of coffee.

"Audrey, there's a young man here. He would like you to sign his book if your hand will still write?"

"No problem. Hello!" She smiled up at him.

"Hello. I'm so pleased to meet you. Could you possibly just write a few words for my son, Ben? This will be his copy of the story when he grows up."

"Of course." She wrote 'To Ben, with best wishes for a healthy and happy future, wherever you travel and whatever you choose to do. Audrey Coatesworth, 2013'.

"I bought your poem book, 'Growing Up', and Ben loves it. Sarah, that's my wife reads it to him - very often. Oh, and she's found your

'Coping with Illness and Grief' very comforting since she lost a friend last year."

"I'm so pleased," she replied.

"Thank you so much." Brian took back the signed book.

"You are very welcome," answered Audrey. "Do you live round here?"

They had a conversation for a while. There was something about her that reminded him of someone. But he just couldn't think who that was. He would try to puzzle it out later.

§

"Well, that's finished. Thank you for asking me to be here, Tom."

"Not at all, it's me who should thank you for all the signing. I guess your arm will ache in the morning. We've sold a lot."

Audrey and Tom continued to chat as they walked through the bar area. "I'm really pleased. I like to think my books are being read. We're just going to walk down the village to the cemetery to pay our respects at my parents' grave. It is exactly thirty years to the day that Dad died. It seems like forever to me. I'm sure he would have loved to read my book. He wrote about the village in two small volumes, you know, just before he died. I took the map of the village from one of them and just changed the houses and names. Is it alright if we leave our car in the car park till we return?"

"Oh, of course. You have no need to ask. Can you stay for another meal?"

"No, but thanks for asking. The lunch was huge and delicious and will keep us both satisfied for the day. We'll just have a breath of fresh air and then be on our way. See you next time."

§

Tom came to his table. Brian had just finished the apple pie.

"That was very good, as usual," he remarked, as Tom took his plate. "She's perfectly normal, isn't she? Just like you told me."

"Of course!" replied Tom.

"But, you know, somehow I expected a much older woman."

"I understand her mother never looked her age either. It must be in the genes."

§

As he was about to leave, Brian could see that the car park was still busy. "It's so much busier than when I first came here. I do hope it all continues this way in the future," he remarked to Tom, who was standing nearby.

"Yes, the business has grown tremendously over this past year. Our son is thinking of joining us. He would take over in a year or two, anyway, but now he is thinking he may start earlier than we expected."

"Well. I'll be off." Brian shook Tom's hand. "Thanks for everything, Tom. Take care."

"Goodbye, Brian. All the very best in the future."

Brian left the inn for the final time. He had secretly hoped to see Bert, but there was no sign of him. If he was honest with himself, that, rather than the beef dinner, was the main reason he had broken his homeward journey by stopping at the pub. The rain had stopped. 'Oh good,' he thought, 'the sky is clearing. It should be a pleasant drive home.' As he walked to his car, he suddenly saw it. A stunning, brilliant rainbow. He had never seen one so vivid before. He stopped and stared. It seemed so near he felt he could almost touch it. The colours made a perfect arc over the valley beyond, and its end appeared to be in the upper corner of the village common land.

"Simion's corner!" Brian, spoke - aloud. "The proverbial gold at the rainbow's end. How appropriate!"

"Indeed! It is quite beautiful, isn't it?" He turned as he heard her voice. Audrey had just returned from her walk with her husband and had stopped by Brian's side. She smiled at him.

"Yes, absolutely amazing."

As he looked round the car park, he noticed that, though there were small groups of people talking and others getting into their cars to leave, no one else was taking any notice.

"How very odd! They can't possibly see a rainbow like this every day, can they?" He suddenly felt rather bemused.

"Maybe they don't see it at all," replied Audrey, as she walked away.

Time

Walking, as in a mist
Towards the new unknown
Time can never stop
And no future is she shown

Walking, at the same pace
Though, often, she would run
If she could, away from
The sound of war and gun

Walking, step by equal step
Her face is etched with pain
Will she ever find a place
Where peace and quiet reign?

Walking with a heavy heart
Why must earth be this way?
Yet, she cannot leave her task
Of creating another day

Walking, eyes full of tears
She thinks of home and love
Those with whom she can rest
In the heavenly court above

Walking, she remembers
The ones who had no voice
But, while the human race exists
She has no other choice

Walking ever onward
Her legacy left behind
Knowledge, hidden, that will change
The beliefs of all mankind

1501

» The casket is buried

Miriam and Miranda stood arm in arm, dark cloaks draped around their heads and shoulders with their silk lined hoods almost hiding their faces. Although it was warm weather, in fact, the middle of what was turning out to be a hot summer, it was now very late in the evening and there was a definite chill in the air. It was welcome after the heat of the day, but they both felt shivery.

Maybe it was their task, along with their apprehension of being back on the common land of this village, which contributed to the feeling of uneasiness and cold. This common land, once a place of fun and games, now seemed sinister in its dark mantle of recent history. Four long years had dragged past since the day they were taken from this village. The life they had known then had disappeared for ever.

"I feel scared. Do you think we made the right decision?" whispered Miriam.

"Oh yes," replied Miranda, softly, "we just had to come. Our Mamas were very brave and we have nothing to fear. Uncle Richard will look after us as he has always done. He wouldn't have brought us if he thought there was any danger for us now."

§

They had prepared for this journey since the evening when their uncle, Richard, had visited them, just three weeks ago. After they had all greeted each other, he went out to look at their horses as he always did. He could never pass a horse without checking it was fit and well. Then, before they sat down to dinner, he had taken a calico wrapped object out of the canvas bag he had carried with him.

"Inside this parcel is a book. I have recounted everything that I found out about the deaths of your mamas and aunt, Catherine. Robbie has kindly scribed it for me over the past few months as and when I have felt able to dictate to him. His hand is much better than mine and he wanted to do it as a gift to us all. I have tried faithfully and truthfully to record everything. Neither Nell nor I have ever told you the whole of what happened as you were too young and too upset to either listen or heed."

"And I shall never tell them," interjected Nell, interrupting his carefully controlled voice.

"No, I know that Nell, but we both agreed that they have a right to know. Time has stood still long enough in all our lives and needs to start to move on again."

He faced Miriam, Miranda, James and Mark.

"I have brought this book in case any of you wish to know the truth. You can all read and I shall leave it with you. It is not easy reading as you will understand, but please, just remember that your mamas and aunt are not now in any pain. Of that I am sure."

He put the parcel on the cabinet behind him.

"I shall come back in a week and tell you of the arrangements for my journey, should any of you decide to accompany me. I plan to bury this book as a memorial to the three of them. I shall put it in your grandmama's casket and then inside one of my metal boxes. Maybe in time to come, it will be discovered. I have a mind to think that one day the world will need to know of evil deeds done in the name of the Church. It will be buried where it all happened, in Stocksmoor. I have chosen 'Simion's corner'. My book is as complete as it shall ever be and I want as much as possible of my grief, and I hope yours, to be buried with it, or else our lives continue to be tormented."

During the next two weeks, they all read the book except Mark. The girls had talked and cried together, sharing their sorrow at what they learned. James read separately and silently and made no comment to Mark or to the girls. None of them knew that Mark had not read the book. All four had determined that they would travel with Uncle Richard to bury the casket.

§

Now they were here and they were finally saying, 'Goodbye'. Richard hoped that they had been helped with knowledge of the truth. He was sure there had been many unanswered questions in their young minds.

They watched as Uncle Richard and their two brothers dug a hole in the ground as quietly as was possible. Digging is not a silent event, but the three were doing their best. They did not want to alert anyone as to their whereabouts. Simion was nowhere to be seen. They had brought pickaxes to break up the ground. The hot weather had caused the ground to be compacted and it was as hard as stone. In the stillness any noise carried. They had waited deliberately until it was dark, but, in their planning, they had hoped for just such a night. It was clear and cloudless with a bright moon showing enough eerie light to let them see what they were doing without using burning torches. The people here still lived in fear. Maybe some felt guilt, some shame, and for a few, it was sorrow, but what was certain was that none had been left unscathed.

The young women had promised each other that they would not cry as both their mamas and aunt might be watching. They didn't want them to be sad. But, now they both realised it was a promise that neither could keep as, try as they may, they could not stop the gentle and continuous stream of tears flowing down their pretty faces.

They had discussed so many times where these women, whom they still loved so dearly, could be – now they were dead. They were sure that, as they were such kind and gentle people, they would be somewhere peaceful even though some people had hated them. But, they wondered if anywhere was pleasant or peaceful when you couldn't be with your children. They hoped that their mamas would be with their papas. If so, then they could stop feeling so sad. But, how could they ever know? That was the problem.

"Why don't you just rest in the wagon, lasses?" asked Richard Shaw in a hushed voice. "We will get the hole ready and then we will wake you."

"We are alright, truly, we are. But thank you," replied Miriam.

"We can only be here once. We want to watch everything that happens, so we can remember fully. It is the least that we can do," added Miranda.

§

They had not been to this village in Yorkshire, their former home, since their mamas, Ann and Emily Kittle and their aunt, Catherine Shaw, had died four years ago. There had been no funeral, no goodbyes, nothing. Just an emptiness that never ended, accompanied by a feeling of regret that they had been too young to help them to survive at the time.

The other big worry that haunted them was that they had moved away from the village and that their mamas wouldn't know where they were. It felt as though everyone was lost to each other.

The two girls were cousins and each one had a brother. Both their mamas, Ann and Emily, had been identical twins and so had their fathers, whom none of them could remember at all. But, surprisingly, the four children were very different to look at. Miranda and James were brother and sister. Miranda had dark straight hair and James had fair curls and both were tall and slender. Miriam had fair wavy hair and Mark had dark waves and both were shorter in stature. The girls were now eighteen years of age and their brothers were both sixteen. The four were, however, very alike in their natures and rarely was a wrong word or any discord found between them. They were hard working and humorous, but Uncle Richard, who had cared for them all in the past four years, knew that underneath the smiles was a very deep and unremitting sadness.

He had carried out his promise, made to Ann and Emily a few months before they died, to his uttermost ability. He would never forget the day he had visited and they had asked him if he would be the children's guardian should anything ever happen to both of them. He had since wondered if Ann and Emily had had a foresight into the events that would unfold. It was true that there had already been activities or atrocities, instigated on behalf of the Church and carried out by the Church Army, reported in several areas. At that time, he had certainly noticed a change in the atmosphere around the country as he travelled with his work. He was a journeyman who attended animals and prescribed potions. People had gradually become less friendly and he had realised that doors were not being left open as had been the case for all his previous travelling life. In Ann and Emily's case, the fears had been fully justified.

§

Uncle George, Sir George Shaw, Lord Lieutenant of the county of Yorkshire was uncle to Ann, Emily, Catherine, and Richard. He had been kindness itself in their hour of need, and ever since, and now clearly regarded the four children almost as if they were his own grandchildren. He had made sure that they were all being educated with his own son's children and by their tutor. Even the girls were taught to read and write. As he explained, what other people thought was none of his business and what he thought was none of theirs. If he wanted his daughters and granddaughters to read and write, so be it. And he did! He loved his books and had accumulated a large library on a wide range of subjects.

"I have all these beautiful books. They tell of history, places and people that we should never otherwise know about and what is the point if only half my family can enjoy them?" he asked. Up to that time, only Robert, a quiet grandson and an avid reader, had shown much interest in his library.

§

The journey 'proper' had started at the Manor House in Poppleton, near York, Uncle George's beautiful and large manor. This had been their first refuge and home when they had had to leave Stocksmoor.

They had set off at the very crack of dawn, with a horse change and a rest about half way through the journey; it had taken most of the day. Richard still lived with his family in the converted stable block of Uncle George's manor, and, at his uncle's insistence, they had left armed with bread, cold cooked meat, cheese and water from the main house's kitchen and a bag of early apples from the large orchard.

They had rested for two hours at Richard's old family home about four miles away from Stocksmoor, on the outskirts of a small village, Sheepley. Staying there had meant only a short detour. He had left his cottage furniture and taken only a few essentials and clothes when he had moved his family and the children to York. This was primarily so that neighbours would not have to lie, should questions be asked, as to their whereabouts. "The family were away for a while," "Yes, there are problems," "Bad times in the family," and, "No, we are not sure when they will be back," could be replied with truth.

When he travelled this way he always stayed in his old house, which he still owned and made a show of lighting a fire and having lanterns in one or two rooms. He visited about two or three times a year, and, as the cottage was rather isolated from the others, their absence appeared to have passed unnoticed by anyone other than the villagers. He had arranged that a neighbour would occasionally light the lamps and put a fire in the hearth, in his absence, to keep up this pretence. You just never knew who was skulking around these days.

Finally, an hour before dusk, they had set off again to travel to Stocksmoor, their final destination.

Richard, an expert in animal welfare and potions, was, formerly, well known in the village of Stocksmoor, having grown up there; but he had only occasionally passed through for the last two years. He had found out what he needed and then avoided the village completely. He just preferred to go elsewhere. It was simple really. Now, they arrived on the high road leading to the inn in the village. He decided to back the horse and his covered wagon down the narrow lane running to the village's common land. He wanted to park near to Simion's corner. There was a ditch on one side of the lane, so he had to be guided by the two boys. But he managed very well.

"We cannot take any chances in being seen," Richard had told them, when their plans were being made. "But we shall be well hidden behind the wall and there are trees at the end of the lane. If we 'back up' the lane we shall be facing the right direction should we need to leave in a hurry. Mind you, the last time I went through the village, there were still shutters at every window. The doors were closed and, I suspect, barred. I met and spoke with no one, so I'm not expecting any trouble at all. But, it's better to be safe than sorry. It used to be such a friendly, welcoming place. Now it seems cold and forbidding. It's a place of haunted memories for everyone."

He had weighed up the pros and cons of this long, purposeful trip and the possible dangers involved, but despite all, he had decided that it was time for this final pilgrimage.

§

Both girls were to be married within the next two years. He hoped that by this act of saying goodbye, as near to a burial as they could manage, that their grief may be lessened and recovery begin, at long last.

The two boys had been given land a few miles out of York by Uncle George about a year ago. Their business of growing willow canes and fashioning baskets and panniers was getting known and had started doing very well. Their sisters helped with the willow work. They all shared a house at that site, presided over and looked after by Uncle George's unmarried daughter, Ann, and their own Nell. Despite her lineage and her father's elevated position, Ann was a woman who preferred nothing more than doing homely activities. She loved cooking and was a skilled weaver of willows and taught them, gradually, all that she knew. Richard mused, 'They are all doing fine, considering everything, but sadness surrounds them like a vapour.'

Richard knew that Uncle George missed them greatly when they had arranged to become more self-sufficient. Being very wealthy, he had ample funds for all. None need work and he told them so. But the children wanted to contribute something themselves in their lives. However, he arranged for fruit and vegetables, with meat, to be taken from his kitchen for them each week. He also arranged for the two girls to be collected twice a week and taken to his manor house, which was situated only a few miles away. They helped to amuse and look after his youngest two grandchildren. He had grown used to having them around and he liked to listen to them as they read to the youngsters and showed them how to draw.

In the village, the girls also taught the young children, both girls and boys to read and to write. Classes were held in their own parlour and lasted just an hour each day. In this way, all the children in the village had some time when they were not being employed in the fields or cleaning the houses. The parents in the village could not object or they knew they would risk Uncle George's disapproval. Though a very kind man, the disapproval of the Lord Lieutenant was not something to be courted. The girls had only two rules, dirty boots should be taken off and left at the door, and only those who wanted to come should do so. All had boots, as the girls would get Ann to buy some if the parents did not do so. It was accepted that the children of this village were very fortunate when Ann and Emily's children moved to live there.

Richard knew that he could not have helped his sisters, Ann, Emily and Catherine, in those dire days four years ago as he was away from the area at the time. But, even so, continuous grief weighed heavily on him, despite having his own loving wife and children. He had worked very hard to make sure that the culprits had gone to court and they had been punished accordingly. Now that was well over and finished he too needed to say a final farewell to a disturbing and overwhelming chapter in his life – one that broke his heart and nearly broke his spirit.

§

So, the three dug silently and carefully. They had planned exactly what they were going to do.

After a couple of hours the hole was about five feet deep and three feet wide and five feet long. They needed just over two feet square; the extra length and width was to enable them to dig as deep as was necessary. When the hole was complete, as arranged, James and Mark handed down tightly woven wicker panels made by Miriam and Miranda from willow. These had been dipped in molten candle fat. Richard fashioned them into the base and four sides of a box. Fine willow ties had been left to keep the structure together. He fastened these.

Next, an empty wooden box, which Uncle George had had made out of mahogany by the local carpenter and lined with a thin layer of beaten lead, was lowered to Richard who placed it into the waiting willow box. On Uncle George's advice he had used this rather than the metal box that he had intended. Uncle George felt that the wood might last longer in the soil than the metal. Finally a casket, completely wrapped several times in waxed sacking was put into the lead lined box. The casket had been prepared at home and the wax had set solid.

The casket had once belonged to the children's grandmama, Richard's stepmother, Eve. It had originally been given to Eve, on her wedding day by her own father – their great grandfather. He was long since deceased and had been the owner of Bretton Hall. Bretton was a neighbouring village to Stocksmoor. Much of the land around the Hall, including both Bretton and Stocksmoor, was part of his large estate. The land on which their grandparents' house had been built was given to their grandmama by her father. To make sure grandmama had always enough money, her father had put golden coins in the casket along with pieces of family jewellery he had chosen for Eve, his favourite daughter. The coins had long since been spent or given away by their grandparents, but their mamas had kept and worn the jewellery. Their mamas had put their own 'treasures' into the casket. Following their deaths, these treasures had been added to by Richard.

Miranda and Miriam had both put on some of their mothers' jewellery for this ceremony. Miranda wore two hair slides of gold encrusted with rubies and Miriam wore a bracelet of simple, twisted gold and a chain, with three drop pearls at the front.

Several years ago the two girls had learned from their tutor about the customs in Egypt when the pharaohs died. They decided that, if the

Egyptians believed that dead people could use food, then they could at least try to tell their mamas how they were and where they were living. So, finally and after a lot of discussion, the two girls wrote letters to their mamas and Aunt Catherine.

"Now, if ever they can return, or can see things that we can't see, then they'll know where we are."

"I see no other way to tell them," replied Miriam. "I try to talk to mama but I never get any answer."

They had asked Mark and James if they were going to write letters. James had spoken, in a voice full of emotion, "No, and I think you are being silly. Our mamas are dead; you should know that by now. They are dead. You can't read when you're dead."

Mark had simply muttered, "No," and turned away. He never mentioned his mama, or his aunts, Emily and Catherine.

> *Dearest, dearest Mama,*
>
> *I hope you are not in any pain or suffering now. I miss you all the time and hope that does not make you sad, but I cannot help it. I try to be cheerful as you would want me to be, but it is often very difficult. I want you to know that no one hurt us after you died as Nell looked after us and then Uncle Richard came and took us all away. He and Great Uncle George have been so very kind and we are well. We used to live in the manor in Poppleton but we now live in a little village on one of the roads out of York but you can find the way easily from Poppleton where we still visit a lot.*
>
> *Great Uncle George says he is getting old. We hope he doesn't die too and leave us.*
>
> *I am going to marry a lovely young man who is Great Uncle George's eldest grandson and he is a year older than I am. I wish you could see him. I know you would like him. I love him very much and when we are married I will try not to be sad anymore.*
>
> *I hope, Mama, that you have found Papa wherever you are. Please tell him that everyone says that I have grown up to look like you. I have had a dream that you and he*

are together and smiling at me. It is like a picture in my mind.

We try to be as good as we know you would want us to be.

I have written this verse for you and have called it 'LOVE WILL LAST'.

> *Your gentleness still surrounds*
> *Like warm mantle in the snow*
> *I feel your smile, like a light*
> *With a golden yellow glow*
> *Cruel death snatched you away*
> *Yet, for me you are not far*
> *Just riding on the passing clouds*
> *And watching from a star*
> *One day I shall find you*
> *When my life becomes no more*
> *We shall spend our time together*
> *As we always did before*
> *I will tell you all that happened*
> *Since you went away*
> *Then there will be no need to think*
> *You missed out on any day*

Love in abundance,
Miriam

Dearest Mama

I can see you in my mind when my eyes are open and when the lids are shut. I see our old house from my window pane and then I have to remind myself that I am but dreaming wishes as, really, I see a field and trees.

It seems a long time since you went away, but yet it seems like yesterday that I saw you and held your hand. I have grown up now, but, in my heart a part of me stays the age it was on the day that you died. It feels as if it is frozen in time, lest should it move on, you will disappear completely and I shall forget you.

What is this life, Mama? You have children and love them and then are cruelly taken away from them? I think I can know a little of your sadness when Papa died, as now I love and am loved. I do not want anything to happen to separate us.

Please forgive me, but I was very angry with you at first, but Uncle Richard found out all that happened and he told us. Now I feel ashamed that I could ever have been angry with you. I am so sorry. I just didn't know.

I have another thought, yet another dream, that sometimes you are with us all. My memories of you are always filled with the scent of flowers and I try to believe you make that happen.

The worst thing of all, dear Mama, is not knowing where you are and if you are out of pain. How do we know if pain can go with you or not? I have to believe that someone as kind and gentle as you were must be loved by God and so he will have taken your pain away. I hope he knows and is very angry with those who caused your death.

If only you could let us know, but you can't. I shall think of you every day of my life and wait patiently to be with you again.

> *In my mind I shall always see*
> *Your kind face, your lovely smile*
> *In my heart you will ever be*
> *Separate now - yet for a while*

My love for ever,
Miranda

The girls showed each other what they had written.

"Neither of us has sent a message or any love to Aunt Catherine." Miriam broke the silence. "I want to, but I cannot write anything if I cannot write all I need to say. I want to tell her how I feel, but at the same time I do not wish to hurt her by my words."

"I feel just the same," agreed Miranda. "What do you think we can do?"

"Let us write together." After a lot of discussion, thought and tears, they composed their letter.

Dear Aunt Catherine,

We want you to know that we loved you. You were always very kind and helpful to us and we always knew you loved us. We hope you are now well and have no pain.

We think that if our mamas can know what we write to them, then you will be able to know in the same way, as we are sure you will be together, wherever that place is. So we are writing this letter to you.

We had a question that we never asked you. 'Why did you not help our Mamas when they were not able to breathe when you helped other people?' We used to see them suffering. You saw them too, and we felt angry that you never eased their distress. We wished we had asked you then, but we didn't.

We know now, from Uncle Richard's book, that you would have liked to help their breathing if you could. We both feel we were very unfair to you in thinking the way we did. So, we have decided, finally, that there must have been some reason, which you couldn't change and we can never know. But, at last, we are not angry with you any more.

We also know that you tried to stop the soldiers from killing our mamas and we want to say, 'Thank you', even though your words made no difference. You were never angry with them, like Uncle Thomas, even though you lost your mama when they were born.

But, Aunt Catherine, please can you look after our mamas PROPERLY in heaven?

Thank you for all your love to us, and we are sorry if we have upset you.

Love from us both,

Miriam and Miranda

The girls had kissed the letters, folded them and fixed them securely with sealing wax. They wrapped them together, with some added dried rose petals, in a small parcel and put them carefully with all the other articles that each decided, either collectively or separately, needed to be in the casket.

Now they were finally here - on the common. Before the lid, which was also lined with lead, was closed on the lead-lined box, both girls came forward, each with a linen bag. They contained the rose, dog daisy and marigold petals and sprigs of lavender, which they had collected and dried. They sprinkled handfuls of the fragrant potpourri over the box until the bags were emptied. They did this slowly, letting the leaves and petals float down until the top of the casket was covered. Though they knew this was a festival of delicate colour, they saw only shades of grey in the twilight. But, they had discussed this and felt it was worthwhile as they were sure their mamas and aunt would see the colours as they could not imagine them to be in darkness.

Before closing the box forever, the four knelt in their own silent thoughts, and each, in turn, murmured their final farewells. Richard, in the hole, bowed his head and let his tears fall freely. He had loved the three women, his half sisters, more than he could ever say. He hoped that somehow they would know that he had cared for their children as best he could and would continue to do so for as long as was necessary.

The box was closed with the lid and fastened with iron bolts made by their local blacksmith. The girls then put fresh leaves and the flowers, collected from Uncle Richard's old cottage garden, on top of the closed box. The garden was still blooming wildly despite not having had any attention. The final wicker panel was placed on top and Richard climbed out, helped by James and Mark. For the next hour the three shovelled and stamped the soil back into place, stamping hard to make sure that, if possible, there would be no sinking of the site later.

"I shall come round this way in a few months, just to check. Let us all now put some of those fallen stones in and among the soil. I don't think many people come this way now, and if there is any sinking I am sure this area will be overlooked and soon overgrown. But let us take as little chance as possible, though, I'm sure no one will be looking around here for anything unusual," Richard told the four, standing close together.

They put the stones and then the grass sods back over the soil, and, when they had finished, they were quite happy that no one, even if familiar with this place, would have been alerted as to what they had done.

"I think it is time for us to go now," decided Richard. "The sun will up very shortly and we should be on our way before people start to rise."

The girls got into the wagon, under the cover, and the boys sat on the wide driving seat with Richard. They had just gone about half way up the lane towards the main road when Mark spoke,

"Where is my jacket?"

Richard reined in the horse and stopped the wagon.

Turning round, Mark asked, "Can you girls see my jacket? It's quite cold out here now we have stopped work."

"No, it's not here," answered Miriam.

"Are you sure?"

"Yes, quite sure. Did you take it off when you started digging or before?"

"Oh, I've just remembered. I put it on the floor by the gate. It must be still there."

"Run back, lad, and get it and don't dally," ordered Richard, quietly.

"I'll come with you," muttered James, almost to himself. "I don't trust you to be out of sight and alone in this place."

The two boys ran back down the lane and turned left at the end of the wall and went towards the gate, near where they had buried the casket.

Mark, in front, suddenly stopped and James ran into him.

"What are you . . . ?"

Then he too saw what Mark had seen. A man was sitting where they had been digging, head in hands and rocking back and forward, but not making any sound.

This man was known by the village and around as an imbecile. He lived out in the open, wandering the common and the surrounding area, and relying on the villagers for his food. He was an object of ridicule to many people and lived a life of rejection. Then, as if he knew they were there, the man raised his head and put out his hands. For them his dishevelled appearance, the mass of long, tangled, dirty white hair and beard and his wild look merely gave recognition. They knew him simply as Simion.

Without hesitation, they smiled at him and rushed over to grasp his outstretched hands and both boys, simultaneously, started to cry. They would never forget the debt of gratitude they owed to this gentle, dumb, ungainly outcast of society. He was still wearing the voluminous cloak that Ann, Mark's mother, had made for him out of two dark woollen blankets. They knew he could understand if they signed to him, so, as they spoke out loud, they also tried to sign that something very special had been put under the ground.

But, unbeknown to them, Simion already knew. He had been dumb from birth and was afflicted with a grossly misshapen spine making his appearance a shock when first seen. Was he deaf? No one could know or tell, though most assumed that he was. He had never given any indication that he heard anything. He was not unintelligent as most people thought. In fact, quite the reverse, but had had to accept his pitiful lot in life. He had not been given any choice. The two boys noticed that he was even thinner, if possible, and that his spine seemed more bent than before. Their mamas and aunt, Catherine, had always given Simion good wholesome dinners every day while they lived in the village. The boys guessed he had not had many, if any, since they died.

Simion had been asleep in the dry undergrowth when he had been awakened by the digging. Whether by the sound, the vibrations in the earth or some other sense made acute by his problems, who could tell? However, by long practice in survival skills, despite his gross disability, he could move quietly and be totally undetected. He had been curious and had witnessed everything. He acted as if digging, then made the shape of a box, then pointed to each of the boys and pretended to rock a baby. Then he pointed down to where the box was buried.

The boys nodded.

Then he sat down once more and rocked back and forward.

The boys knew then that he would guard the area as long as was necessary so that no one would notice what had been done. Anyone seeing him rocking would move away. People in the village rarely talked to Simion.

"Thank you, thank you."

The boys both held out a hand once more and Simion held them. Rarely, if ever, did he have or allow any human contact. Then Simion let go of their hands and made a waving motion as if telling them to go.

The boys whispered, "Goodbye," – as if out of habit, and waved.

"Don't forget your coat, Mark."

Mark fetched his coat and they ran back to the wagon. As if by mutual consent, they kept silent about Simion to their sisters and, at that time, to Uncle Richard.

Later when they were well on their way home, Richard stopped at an inn he knew well. He had stopped for refreshment many times on his travels as a journeyman. They were all eating bread and cheese washed down with milk, when Miranda commented,

"I do hope no one notices and digs up our casket."

"Never worry, it will be safe," reassured Richard, "I've heard the people of Stocksmoor stay in their houses now and few if any walk the common land. No one keeps cattle there any longer. Anyway, maybe I didn't tell you but there is no pond there now for the animals to drink from, so there is no point using it for grazing. That would make too much hard work."

James and Mark looked at each other. They knew that no one would investigate that part of the common, at least, not while Simion was alive. In time, no one would even try to remember their mothers or even care to look.

Not until the twenty-first century would that land be disturbed again.

2010

» March

The smartly dressed man, in dark grey suit, pale blue pin-striped shirt and dark blue tie, was standing at the reception desk of the motel.

"Good evening, sir. Can I help you?" asked the girl, looking away from the computer screen.

"Yes. I would like a room for the night, please."

"Let me see." She looked at a chart on the wall behind her, showing the up-to-date status of all the rooms and replied, "We have one free on the first floor. Can I have your name, please?"

"Brian T," he answered, without hesitation.

The receptionist looked up at him, with an odd expression.

"Brian T? And how would you like me to spell that, sir?"

"Sorry. Brian T Woolstone," the young man corrected himself. God, would that habit never disappear? He wasn't at school now. 'She must think I'm strange, by the look on her face,' he thought.

He was tired. He had worked all day, after an early morning start and a long journey on the motorways. He was working on 'empty' at the moment and, now that he was out of his car, he had temporarily stopped concentrating properly. Her question and something about her voice had taken him straight back to his young school days. It was an automatic answer.

His father had thought he had registered him as Brian Trevor Woolstone. Only when he got home and showed his wife the certificate did she notice that the registrar had put 'Trevore' instead. She was very upset at the time as Trevor had been her first choice of name for their baby if he was a boy. She wanted to name a son after her father, Trevor Benson, who had died three years before. He had been her hero and she had always planned to love and cherish a son with his name.

She had, very reluctantly – though she couldn't tell anyone why she felt that way – agreed to 'Brian', her husband's elder brother's name. He, the former Brian Woolstone, had joined the army at eighteen years of age, but had been accidently killed when he was only twenty three 'on manoeuvres'. The family heard at the inquest that the ammunition that had been used was not 'blank' as it should have been, though at the inquest no one was blamed for the mistake. She and her future husband were engaged at the time. She had had a brief dalliance with this brother, and she believed that, had he not been killed, they would have married instead. Her husband never knew, and so, of course, she could not protest about the name without giving a reason. After five months of sickness, followed by four months of backache and a very difficult labour, she had had time to accept the name 'Brian' and had had no energy left for any argument. She agreed that 'Trevor' could be his 'middle name'. And now, not even that was right!

She had stoically adapted. She hid her disappointment, yet could never feel for her son the warmth of love that she had anticipated. She wondered if she was odd or ill. Was she frightened that he might die as his namesake had? She often asked herself this kind of question, and had many private tears, but nothing changed. Yes, she was fine with his elder sister and she tried to be a good mum to them both. She felt grateful for what she had, but was always aware that she felt unemotional towards her son and that any show of affection felt like pretence. It upset her, but she couldn't alter how she felt and hoped that he never realised.

But, Brian had turned out to be a friendly, pleasant lad and he appeared not to notice. She hoped that the saying, 'what you don't know you don't miss', was true for him. In reality, for Brian, his mother was just 'Mum' and she looked after him, and he never questioned further or deeper.

Brian was forever after 'Brian Trevore Woolstone'. He had long since decided that the year of his birth had been the year of the 'Brian', as in his class at primary school had been no fewer than three boys called Brian. There was Brian Colin Pastelle, who insisted that his father had French in his blood, Brian David Wellington, but you couldn't believe him about anything really, and finally himself, Brian Trevore Woolstone, who never talked about his father. As they were all bright lads, they stayed together in the top 'sets' throughout his school life.

So, to avoid confusion, having two of the surnames starting with 'W', they were always known as Brian C, Brian D and Brian T.

§

Having seen his room and unpacked his few belongings, he went downstairs, and was directed for 'good Yorkshire cooking' to the pub next door.

'Your typical, youngish, travelling executive,' the landlord thought to himself, as Brian entered. He went about his business of clearing the tables, for the final time that day, in the dining room-cum-lounge of his pub. The room though large, had a homely feel created in part by the open log fire set deep within the inglenook. Arranged around the hearth were a few comfortable chairs on a large and, what had once been, a bright and colourful rug, slightly worn in parts and faded through years of wear. The 'eating part' of the room had a polished dark wood floor. "It's much more hygienic and easier to clean up this way," he always told his wife who had fancied carpeting the whole room in hessian.

"No, the rug by the fire is fine," he told her. He didn't say it reminded him of his parents and his younger years in this, the only home he had ever known. His father had bought it one day many years ago from a travelling salesman who claimed that it was 'authentic' and from the actual, beautiful Indian continent. It had graced the family living quarters ever since until after him, and his wife, had taken over from his parents. They had decided eventually to upgrade the 'home' part of the pub and had fitted carpets door-to-door. He couldn't let the rug go and, when the chairs were in place the faded and worn areas were scarcely seen.

He tended to 'sum up' people as they passed through. He seldom knew if he was right or wrong, but that didn't matter; it added that extra bit of interest to his job – 'just for himself you understand'. He was never a gossip, but a 'people watching' person. Yes, that's what he was. He liked that phrase 'people watching'. It had a 'wider than local' ring to it, and he could do it right here in his own front room. 'I've no hassle and no travelling like some poor sods,' he told himself, looking at Brian's tired face, 'who spend their lives on the motorways.' Tom Richardson, owner and working landlord of 'The Dun Cow' pub at Stocksmoor, was happy with his lot in life and was grateful to his parents for their tireless hard work which had left him in this position.

"Are you ready to order, sir?" he asked Brian.

§

At forty-one years of age, Brian looked somewhat younger than his years. Tom was right. Brian was a young executive. His success was self-made. He had gradually been promoted, doing his best for a few years in one post, then moving – ever upwards. He was glad he had gained a degree; it always helped on the CV. though how much of what he had actually learned was useful in his present job, he wasn't sure. But at least he knew how to apply himself. No way would he have let his parents down. He had wanted them to be as proud of him as they were of his sister. Sadly, they would never know of his business success, nor see his four-bedroom executive style house.

Being intelligent, trustworthy and industrious, he was now manager of the northern branch of a communications company, basically a business available for 'correcting blips in computer software systems'. He had to confess to being amazed how many blips there were! He was based in Gloucester. IT was his forte, but, unlike a lot of computer buffs, whose relationship with their computer was preferable for them rather than 'face to face' communication, Brian was friendly and outgoing.

He wasn't always quite as confident as he appeared. He knew he was good at his work, and having to organise staff was no problem. In fact, he liked being in charge and could usually talk to anyone easily. But, it hadn't always been the case, as a mild speech impediment when young had made him a victim of some bullying. His pleasant personality had won through at school with most of his class mates, and he had always been popular. But there had been one or two boys whom he would not cross the road to see. They had imitated him so often that it was a mystery to him how they had avoided having the same problem. And he remembered Mr F-----, one of his primary school teachers, with something akin to loathing. Then, last but not least, there had been his clever, but very jealous, elder sister. She had spared no effort in highlighting any and every difficulty that Brian had ever had and cruelly exposed his speech problem whenever possible. His parents seemed to accept that his sister should express herself as she wished and did absolutely nothing to stop her.

Despite all, or maybe because of, the continual teasing, Brian had gained the courage to ignore and persevere. He conquered his difficulty and had basically forgotten about it. But it had left a hidden legacy behind. If he became stressed or very tired then he was prone to feel anxious and he knew that at those times his speech could be rather stilted, and he would find himself having to think about how to say what he wanted to say. He recognised this. He knew he was getting overtired quite regularly at present. He was aware, fairly often, of a feeling of apprehension in the evening when he finally finished all his work. At the same time there seemed nothing much he could do to alter his situation.

He and his wife, Sarah, had bought their present house in Gloucester when he had first been appointed to this company four years ago. Now, with the promotion and, in particular, this extra office in Leeds, he had started to wonder if that hadn't been a mistake. He hadn't anticipated the growing ramifications of his post. 'I think it will evolve', his boss had indicated, smiling as he shook his hand after the successful interview. What Brian should have realised was that his boss's words meant, 'The work will increase steadily and you will be expected to do the extra without complaining as we are paying you a decent salary!'

With hindsight, he thought it would have been better if they had rented somewhere for a year or two. He now had such a lot of travelling. But he had Sarah and Ben to consider, and he couldn't possibly uproot them now. They had both gradually settled very well into the new house and area, and the only justifiable reason would be to save his personal time and energy. He didn't want to upset Sarah by saying anything. So he didn't. She often commented that it took several years to make true friends, and the 'Jeanettes' of this world were treasures that did not appear very often.

§

It was the first time he had stayed at the Stocksmoor Motel or visited the adjacent pub, The Dun Cow. The pub apparently provided very good food at lunchtimes and evenings. He would soon find out if that was true. He was going to spend another day in the office in Leeds tomorrow. Via the motorway, this motel was only a mere fifteen to twenty minutes away, yet out in the country and away from the noise and bustle of the city. He didn't know this area at all, having never even visited before. He had only ever driven through, at speed, on the nearby motorway. He agreed that staying away from home was the best option when he was in Leeds. It had been Sarah's suggestion.

His expenses would be paid, so that was no problem. He knew he had to give himself time to get to grips with all the intricacies of the new office and its work. He was sure that it would get less confusing soon. But, he was 'up for it'.

He had to admit, though, that it annoyed him to have to stay away from home and that it was all becoming rather exhausting. He saw a copy of the local paper that was lying on a side table and picked it up. Then he decided that he was too weary to read at present so he put it down again. His brain felt as though it had gone into some degree of hibernation. He couldn't be bothered to find the 'on' switch but neither could he go to bed just yet. God forbid! He wasn't that old! He hadn't eaten since the cheese sandwich at lunchtime, so he guessed that was, at least, some of the reason for feeling so tired.

Sure enough, after a good dinner, he felt a lot better.

The local newspaper still beckoned. The information didn't mean much, but it was something to do when he had no company. It gave him a 'feel' for the place and a brief respite from his laptop. He had more preparation facing him – later. 'It's worse than homework ever was,' he thought, 'not exactly self inflicted, but if I don't do it I shall be lost in the meeting tomorrow.' Anxiety about his work performance seemed to hang over him like a dark grey cloud most days. 'But, let's face it,' he thought, 'so much really does depend on achieving my next target. Always bloody targets. I don't imagine them.' If only he did or could, life would be simple! In his mind he saw each one like a black vulture, perched nearby, waiting for him to fall. He had to face the fact – there was always someone ready to pounce on his job the moment that he failed in his commitment.

But he wasn't going to fail. Brian T Woolstone was made of stronger stuff than that, oh yes! He hoped his grandfather, the person who had meant more to him than even his parents, would be proud of him. "What young people need is a backbone and moral fibre," he would say. He was the embodiment of both, having served in the navy and seen active service during the Second World War. Brian often imagined him looking down and either shaking his head or nodding approval. Yes, he'd made an impact in his life. But it seemed a long time ago.

The meeting room had been very stuffy this afternoon. He decided that he must arrange for the windows to be mended. It was ridiculous not to be able to be open them but he guessed no one had ever tried before. He nearly cricked his back on the solid wood sash windows, stuck with many years of renewed coats of paint. There was only one that he had managed to open, but to no avail as it had a broken cord. It was a fine old building, nevertheless. First item on his agenda tomorrow was going to be maintenance. He really would need someone to oversee the repairs, put up shelves and such like. A new cloakroom was an essential. He wondered if Tracey, the chief secretary, would be able to do that, or should he ask one of the boys? He thought 'boys', as he was sure not many of the office staff were over twenty-five years of age, if that. Anyway, he would get estimates and bring up the matter with Len at the first opportunity.

He had spent the whole day at the new branch, after the early morning journey. People tended to discount the journey, especially when they lived locally in relation to the office. For him it could be well over three hours door to door, if he was lucky and hadn't to stop at all, but it could easily be more. It was mostly motorway driving. Even after a few weeks, he still thought of it as the 'new' branch. He had already told the staff on previous visits that there were to be no breaks to go outside to smoke, but each time he visited they seemed to have forgotten or, more likely, taken no notice. Pleasant he might be, but they would have to learn he was no push over. He would sort them out. Ten minutes here, ten there, first one away from the desk, then another; he had never seen anything like it. They were used to a total lack of any supervision.

No, he had decided. He would organise a twenty minute break for everyone mid morning, and another mid afternoon. All must stop work and put phones on answer mode. He would order them all to take forty five minutes for a lunch break. He decided to put this new work plan at the end of the agenda for tomorrow. He had read somewhere that the brain could not work efficiently for more than ninety minutes at a time. Then it needed a break of about twenty minutes to 'assimilate and categorise information that had been taken in' – or something like that! Right, that's what he'd implement. He wanted a happy band working for him, but efficient at the same time. He just wouldn't tolerate either laziness or slackness. He'd monitor the results, as best he could. Maybe the statistics in his degree would come in useful, after all. He hoped so. It hadn't been the easiest part of his studies, for him, that's for sure.

It had taken no time at all to realise that the office was a mess in every way possible. Sorting it was taking a bit longer than he had anticipated, but a tidy, well-organised office was what he was aiming for, not the shambles he had faced on his first visit. There were papers stacked over every desk in the room and on the floor and window sills. That told him more than any portfolio or CV. Dear me, where did they train? What had they been doing all these years? More work here than he originally thought! "Thanks, Len! Thanks a million!" he muttered aloud as he thought of his MD, Leonard McIntock's words when he had reported back after his first visit to the office. "Brian," he had announced, "I am one hundred percent confident that you are the man for the job. I hear what you say, but with your experience, expertise and common sense, I think you'll find it won't seem much of a task or a strain for you." 'You can go off people like that!' he mused. He worked hard and got on well with his boss, but he didn't call him 'Len' to his face. No, that wasn't allowed. Leonard McIntock had remarked, "Call me boss, or Mr McIntock, or Leonard, I don't mind which. Feel free to choose. I want you to feel at ease, Brian. I am sure we shall have a successful relationship, based on trust on both sides." 'Len' had not been one of the options.

§

"What hours do you serve food in an evening?" he asked the landlord as he passed by. "It's good to know - just in case I'm late coming back one evening."

"Oh, it varies. We can serve all evening from about five thirty onwards, but, basically, anytime anyone wants to order. I would say about nine thirty is the latest order we accept. We do lunches too, from noon to two thirty each day. Sundays we don't do an evening meal. Most Yorkshire people prefer their Sunday roast at lunch time and it means that we manage to have an evening off to watch a bit of telly or go out for a walk."

"Well, I have to say, it was a first class dinner. Many thanks and compliments to the chef." Brian felt comfortably and happily replete.

"Thanks. That's mainly my wife. I'll tell her.

The landlord went over to the fireplace and bent down, picked up an armful of logs and built up the fire.

"Non-smoking is a boon these days," he continued, "apart from the fire. Everyone likes the log fire but up here on the hill, well, the wind can gust down the chimney. I get it swept twice each winter, just to be on the safe side. It has a good cowl, though I have to admit that it can still smoke occasionally, usually if it's an easterly. Those dry logs are almost smoke free, you know, so I reckon they're good for the ozone layer and all that! We all have to do what we can, and still live, haven't we? But we have no time for travelling, so me and my wife have small 'carbon feet' in that respect. I store the logs neatly in an open shed during the summer, so the air circulates around them to dry them out. They're a perfect fuel really. I buy them from the local wood yard, down in the village, so it couldn't be easier."

He swept the hearth with the brass handled brush and shovel.

"Some burn faster than others, you know, but that lot should last an hour or two now. Then, the ash goes back on the garden, so recycling at its best." He went out of the room.

Brian thought he would soon get used to this lifestyle, and learn to accept it. But that didn't mean he liked it. No, not at all. The work was interesting, and he would have good meals in places like this pub, but he wanted to see more of his family. To be part of his own family was the reason why he had married and why they had had Ben. Not for Sarah to spend her evenings alone. God only knows how they would afford another child if ever she fell pregnant and couldn't work. But she had insisted, quite emphatically, that one was enough for her, and that she felt like a single parent most of the week. Being away so much reduced that chance I suppose and especially since Sarah had decided to stop the pill. Things could become a bit worrying sometimes.

They didn't have many disagreements, and Sarah kept herself very busy, what with part-time work, Ben and the four bed-roomed house to look after. Yes, he agreed with her that having some help in the house was essential. So, Sandra came two mornings for two hours each and, of course, having Jane collect and deliver all the ironing was ideal. The gardener was very reasonable and came once a week throughout the year, and of course, he never expected Sarah to wash all the windows herself. All in all, it was organised and seemed to be working out very well.

The pub was humming to the sound of friendly chatter. Brian felt very comfortable and, oddly, quite safe. He looked around. 'Small groups of friends who have arranged to meet, I suppose,' he thought. Brian instinctively looked at his digital watch, his all singing, all dancing version, to confirm the date, though quite why it mattered just now he didn't know. 'Habit, I suppose,' he mused. An older man was sitting in a chair nearby. Brian hadn't noticed him before, being so engrossed in his dinner and his own thoughts.

"I feel better now. I must have been hungry," he spoke aloud. The man looked up.

"Sorry! I quite lost myself for a moment. It must be the wine." He felt as if he should say something - though the man hadn't spoken. He added, "But I only had one glass." He smiled at the man out of politeness.

Brian leaned forward.

"I am Brian, Brian T Woolstone. Good evening, sir," he proffered.

"Just call me Bert," replied the older man. He smiled back but did not offer a hand to shake.

"It's good to meet you, Bert. Are you from around here?"

"Aye, that I am and I never stray far away. Not a lot I don't know about this place. And what about yourself? Visiting I imagine?"

"Yes, for my work. I have to travel a lot. In fact, more so now since I took over the management of an office in Leeds a few months ago. But, this is my first trip to Stocksmoor. I live in Gloucester, so have decided I want to live a little longer and stop wearing myself out travelling home every night. The stress of all that travelling must have an effect eventually. I don't smoke and try to keep as fit as possible, but I've been getting a bit unlike my normal, easy going self. At least, so my wife tells me. I hadn't really noticed anything other than feeling tired. We decided this would be best. Everything considered, you understand. It's not an easy decision to stay away, but then, I didn't get much home life anyway. I often didn't get home before about nine o'clock of an evening, and that was if the roads were clear."

"Well, it seems to me that life is being lived in the fast lane by so many of you young people these days. I have no doubt it gets you somewhere very quickly, but you may miss the scenery on the way."

"Well, everything costs money and I have to earn it and, in business and sales, you're really only as good as your last results. But, on the whole, I like the job. It's a challenge."

"Twilight living, I call it," commented Bert, quietly.

Brian didn't appear to hear him.

§

Brian was in Stocksmoor, a small hamlet in West Yorkshire set on a hill. In daylight, there are panoramic views over and beyond the Calder valley. In the opposite direction, towards the West you can just see the Pennines. The television masts for the area, at Emley and further away still, Holme Moss, can be seen on the hills, visible symbols of the communication age.

A breeze usually blows in this village, even on a calm day, directly from the hills. It used to be very quiet and quite isolated, but the road through the village is now used as a link road from the M1 to several towns of West Yorkshire and beyond, with a resulting increase in traffic. So, as the problems of isolation disappear, so does the peace and quiet.

The chapel, completed in 1910, stands 'sentry' at the top of the hill. Though still a landmark, of the typical nonconformist architecture of its day, it is now closed due to lack of a sufficient congregation attending the services to provide the dues required by the Methodist circuit. It has been converted into a house. The pub, on the other hand, flourishes. It provides a place of comradeship in the area, along with a bit of excessive indulgence now and then. It is well known for its hospitality and its freshly cooked food, and quite rightly so, as Brian had found out this evening. A motel has been built very near the pub and shares the same car parking facilities.

For centuries the simple layout of the village, basically a road with a T- junction at the top of the hill, has scarcely changed, give or take a few cottages. The wood-yard, which was the hub of the working life of the village and surrounding areas for over a century and was situated in the centre of the village, opposite the large area of common land, has moved. In its place there is now a small housing estate. The new houses were built soon after the chapel closed, though unrelated to this fact. Would there have been a reawakening of spirit and life in the chapel had it been the other way round? Who can tell?

The wood-yard has now relocated to the old pit site, hidden by woodland, except for a large notice near the road. But everyone around the area knows JOBES wood-yard and the quality of the wood and in particular, nowadays, the fencing. The coal industry has been dismantled, gradually and irrevocably throughout the country, including the Stocksmoor pit. Consequently, the focus of the wood-yard's work has altered with the changing needs. No longer are the pit props required, nor the spindles, as the woollen mills in the area have also closed. But gone, at the same time, has the grime with the subsequent smog in the area. Jobs lost but lungs protected.

§

"Len, that's my boss, has his own business called IT Solutions Inc. and is keen to expand, so hence the new office in Leeds," continued Brian, as though he owed Bert a further explanation.

"I'm surprised to hear of a small company expanding just now. It's been hard times for such a lot for a few years and so many firms have closed down completely."

"Yes, I know, but I have been very fortunate. As Len's business sorts out problems for people it has expanded, particularly as many people and small businesses have had to keep their old computers and software systems, instead of upgrading all the time. Anyway, I have agreed to include this office in my schedule. I was given choice according to Len. But there was no choice really. It isn't sensible to block anything, even if it appears 'offered' rather than 'demanded'. In my business there are always others ready to step into your shoes. Then you are out, and quite honestly, become easily forgotten."

"Aye, I have noticed a big, though gradual change these last thirty years," replied Bert.

"I commented to my wife, Sarah, 'It's as though I haven't a wide enough area to cover. I wonder if Len actually knows where Leeds is, other than a point on a map or how busy the motorways are?' You know, I already have five other offices north of Gloucester to manage. So, I spend a lot of hours driving. But, profit is everything these days."

"Your boss must think you can do your job."

The older man remained quiet, but looked attentive, so Brian, encouraged, carried on.

"Oh, he knows that, alright. Brian the beaver, that's me. The main office, coordinating the whole business, is in Reading. I have to attend management and policy meetings there once every fortnight, summer and winter – and I do! Snow or ice makes no difference. But I didn't hear Len tell us he was buying this branch in Leeds. At least it was never on any agenda that I heard or saw. So, when he announced this new addition I was really surprised. I asked if I had missed a meeting. He looked a bit sheepish, but answered, 'No, but, as boss I have a prerogative.' I suppose he meant he could make independent decisions. But it's his money at the end of the day. I really had no option but to accept and here I am. I keep in contact with Sarah by mobile phone. They are brilliant."

He took out his mobile phone and leaned over to the older man.

"See, that is Sarah, that is Ben and that's our dog, Snatch. It's a silly little thing and fits its name perfectly, but Sarah wanted it. She just fell in love with it. Of course it was a puppy then and most puppies are cute. I find that he's a bit of a yapper if I'm truthful, but Ben loves him." He showed Bert the photos on his mobile phone.

"Very nice. He looks a grand little lad. Aye, the phone helps, but absence and overtiredness do neither you nor your family any favours. What do they call you, a Class A, is it? Something like that I believe. High achievers but highly stressed? But only you can decide if the rewards are worth it."

Bert paused for a moment.

"My Father, long since dead, of course, used to say he would rather sweep the roads with a brush, as they did in those days, and be poor rather than be away from home for his dinner. He liked his dinner at noon, sharp, on the dot. He'd be home by five for his tea and had no travelling. Then, out with the dog or in the garden tending his vegetables. We had little money and few material possessions in our family, but we had each other's time and he was never stressed. He was always good natured, and always had time for his children. He was very intelligent and read a lot. He liked music and had a good tenor voice. I think he could have been a university graduate but he was never given that opportunity. I wonder what choice he would have made, or been able to make, if he had had that option or lived now."

"You may wonder why I agreed to do the extra work. Mainly, it was because I couldn't risk losing my job. And then the boss offered an extra two thousand pounds a year plus a higher bonus depending on results, and promised a new car in six months time instead of at the end of the year. What could I do but accept? After all, there are plenty of others around, waiting for the chance of promotion. He actually told me straight, 'Brian, it's either you or Justin. You have the first option. Let me know, shall we say first thing tomorrow?'"

"So, not a lot of time to decide, then?" commented Bert.

They sat quietly for a while. Brian could easily go deep into thought. 'Only as good as last year's figures', was the motto cynically put on the notice board in the main office under the picture of two mannequins. Len hadn't connected the significance or, if he had, he hadn't let on to anyone. He had looked, but not commented. But results were always at the back of Brian's mind. A five percent increase in profit expected year on year.

"You know, I hadn't really expected to spend my life driving and inspecting other people's work when I studied mathematics at Oxford. I did well and was awarded an Upper Second, though not everything was as easy for me as it may appear. But I wonder why I bothered sometimes. I don't quite know what I had expected but it was certainly not 'this'. This life style may suit some or even a lot, but not me."

The older man nodded, "We don't really know the map until we've walked the path."

"If I'm late home my meal is always ready, waiting to be heated in the microwave. Then, of course, I usually eat alone. Sarah can't wait until late for her meal and eats with Ben. He's already asleep, for several hours usually, so I don't see him to talk to or play with during the week. Then, I'm up very early, like this morning, before either of them has surfaced. It's often like being a lodger. I work all the hours that God sends to fund our home and I seem to be hardly there to enjoy it all."

"It sounds as though the week is mostly work and no play," remarked Bert.

"Yes, it is. I would say 'totally'. But now, because I'm not home, I tend to carry on with work even later. Somehow it seems to multiply, not get less. A bit like the roads. When more are built there is more traffic. It must be 'somebody's law' or 'principle', but I can't remember who! Was it 'Peter' or a name like that? We all have laptops, of course, and so we carry work with us wherever we are. I can get emails at midnight! You wouldn't believe it, would you?"

"It's quite shocking really. It means your work day never ends. No buzzer to tell you 'work is over'. But it shows others are also working late. Maybe they are too stressed and can't sleep, or have nothing better to do. Why don't you just shut off the mobile phone and your computer?" asked Bert.

"I daren't – in case I miss something important. I've tried, but curiosity always makes me switch on again, however late. Or, it could be fear, I suppose," replied Brian.

Bert shook his head, but made no further comment.

"When I stay away, the overnight bed and breakfast goes on expenses. The boss agreed provided they were within reason. He wants me 'to avoid excess, but be sensible and not lavish'. Those were his words. He sounded like my father would have done."

Brian paused for a moment.

"Despite our decision, I didn't want to do it and kept putting it off, as, late or not, I like being home. But finally I decided it was for the best. I've already stayed overnight in a few places during the past few weeks. This place with its motel and pub was recommended by someone in the office, and, from what I have seen so far, I like it and will now come here each time I visit Leeds. It seems much more to my taste than the others I have tried."

"How old is Ben?"

"He's six."

"It's a real shame."

"What is?"

"Your working life, with the long hours and you, away from home so much."

"Yes. It has worked out that I am away about two or three nights some weeks. Mostly it is only one or two. One of Sarah's friends actually commented that I was so lucky, staying in hotels, wining and dining as part of my daily work. I couldn't believe it. It really isn't like that at all. It's really lonely and evenings tend to feel as if I'm just waiting for time to pass."

"It would seem more a comment on her life and wishes rather than yours."

"Why yes, I suppose so. I hadn't thought of it like that," agreed Brian.

He read a bit more of the article in the paper. He didn't normally talk about his private life to strangers.

His work took a lot of effort and he wanted to be sure he had a decent meal, with none of the 'burger and chips' variety. He hated the motorway motels and wanted something more personal, yes, and quieter, so he could always be sure of a good night's sleep. He had told Sarah that he wasn't prepared to live his life to the constant noise of traffic. That was why their home was in the country. They both wanted to have some peace and quiet.

There had to be something more to life, but the mortgage and the school fees had to be paid. He needed the extra money. This job paid well. 'Let me see,' he thought, 'it's now nine thirty in the evening and I set off at six thirty this morning. That's fifteen hours already today and I must work another hour at least before I can go to sleep.' Computerising was now expected, pie charts of all sales, records, expenses – just everything had its own database. He'd have to keep a record of when he blew his nose next! He'd decided to give a 'presentation' tomorrow. Let them know he meant business. Nothing less would suffice. The office was a mess. It was no wonder it wasn't making any profit. He was sure he could 'turn it around', despite the many problems.

"It is the same day I suppose," he mused.

"As what?" asked Bert.

"Sorry, there I go, speaking out aloud again. I was just thinking that so much relies on my work. It's been a long day and I haven't finished yet. The roads can still be a problem at this time of year, with occasional overnight icy patches and it really makes me feel anxious even before I set off. I think your father was very wise. I was always brought up to think that academic achievement was the 'be all and end all' in life. And this is where it has taken me. But what are the alternatives? Everything is so expensive. I mean your father could still afford to have a home."

"Yes, but people then didn't expect all the luxuries in it, or out of it for that matter. Of course, there wasn't even a television when I was a lad and no car."

They sat quietly for a while.

"They want machines, not people," Brian remarked.

"Now that hasn't really changed much," asserted Bert. After a pause, he continued, "If you think about the people who worked in the factories and down the pits. In this country children go to school though I gather that quite a lot of teenagers don't value it and truant. But in many parts of the world, youngsters are still working all day for a pittance and are often beaten. Their young lives are soon gone in drudgery and need. All young life should be valued. Life is a gift and not something to be thrown away or destroyed by anyone.

"No, it's swings and roundabouts, generation on generation. But the pace of life these days is very fast. I can't deny you that. Money seems to be the driving force, but to what end? There's nothing wrong with having money. But, money on its own never made anybody happy and it never will. It's what you do with it that matters."

"I've another fourteen years at least to work. That's if I'm lucky and if I manage to survive. I just hope the pension plan, which I pay into, holds out for retirement at fifty-five years and doesn't shrink as so many have done. It's quite difficult to know how to make that provision, and I find that quite worrying. I mean, how can you know that what you do is for the best. For so many people, it is as though someone comes in the back door and steals their savings. But, work basically comes down to actually providing a home and, for me and many others, just keeping up the mortgage repayments."

"Yes, they are a major commitment. I fully understand. But at one time people would look for a house that fitted their needs and were quite satisfied. These days for a lot of people, it is the second car, the extra bedroom or two – often empty – the holidays abroad and luxuries that they perceive as essential. But, everyone has to decide, if they have the chance to do so, what their necessities are. Please don't think I'm critical of people having houses bigger than their needs. Not at all, I think that a bit of extra space is fantastic and people can buy what they can afford, of course. If funds easily run to the extra, then great, but if it causes extra stress and non-stop work, then that is when I question the priorities."

"Ours is bigger than we need, I have to admit, and I have questioned whether we were sensible or not. We saw it not only as a lovely home but as an investment. "

"Yes, there are many shades from light to dark," commented Bert.

Brian was not quite sure what Bert was meaning. But he was enjoying chatting to this man, who seemed kind and genuinely interested. Far better than just sitting alone in a strange place and wishing he was at home all evening. When did he ever have the chance to discuss anything meaningful – with anyone? He didn't like to voice any doubts or worries with Sarah and he didn't share much with her friends. They were pleasant, but well, he just didn't. He was really a private man, but Bert seemed different, somehow. He hoped that Bert would have time to stay a while, but, of course, he couldn't say so to him.

"Sorry, Bert. I didn't quite catch your meaning."

"I just meant that there are many ways of looking at most situations."

"There are always decisions to be made. With the best will in the world some are easier or more successful than others. I have plenty of those to make - all day and every day. I suppose that is what management is all about really - just making decisions. Getting the facts, and then deciding.'

"Rarely is anything straightforward and simple, Brian, in this life. But, if someone does the best they can, no one can ask or expect anything more."

"We decided that Sarah would look after Ben, while I worked. Actually, to be more accurate, it was Sarah who finally decided she would suspend her career for a few years. It's strange how things happen, isn't it. Her father and mother came to see Ben about three days after he was born. Her father surprised Sarah by saying, 'Sarah. I've never been as proud of you as now. He is beautiful.' Then, with tears in his eyes, he begged, 'Look after him well for us, won't you. This is the most important work you'll ever do.' It was his last request. He died, the day after, of a heart attack.

"Sarah always says that she thinks that somehow he had to give her that message before he died, as he knew she was a career woman. Though she had wanted to look after Ben, she had felt guilty that she was not going to use her qualifications. You know her father wasn't well off but funded her at university, and was so proud of her achievement. She hadn't wanted to let him down after all his hard work to fund her. But her dilemma vanished once she heard him say that, and her decision was easy. I'm so grateful he visited that day."

"Aye, her father was a good man."

Brian was surprised to hear that, though it was true. How could Bert know? He was going to ask him how he had known Sarah's father, but the thought went out of his head.

"So basically we have depended on my income, but that was a decision we have never regretted. We never liked the thought of our small son being with strangers. He seemed so vulnerable and neither of us could bear the thought that he might feel lost or unloved. I mean the world must look very big and scary to a very young child."

"Yes, like you would feel if you were suddenly taken from your home and put somewhere strange, with no means of leaving or knowing where you are and with unknown giants who make unfamiliar noises. Yes, I think you could say that would be scary."

"He went to nursery school when he was two and a half, of course, for a few hours a week, and loved it. Now that he's at school, Sarah works part time, just in a friend's boutique. That is, mainly, because she still enjoys a lot of time with Ben, especially in the holidays," continued Brian, sounding wistful, "and, unfortunately, I'm away a lot."

"You did right," answered Bert, "You know, Brian, whatever changes have happened over the years, with equal rights for women in pay and careers and so called progress in every aspect of life you can think of, there is one thing that has never altered, and never will. The needs of tiny children are the same as they were at the time of the doomsday book. Children need not only to be loved but to feel loved. That is the inner core of their being."

"You have a different way of looking at life, Bert, and seem to put things in a different perspective for me."

"Well, as far as I am aware, it has always been the women who have carried the child and given birth and, whatever any one thinks, they can't say different to that. Those nine months inside the mother have more importance than just physical development. That warmth and security is when and how the emotional link to the mother – and to the world – starts. It always was and always will be. So, I truly believe that there is no one who can transmit that love quite like the mother; her warmth and her sounds are already in the child's memory making the child feel not only loved but safe with her.

"To be able to love, unselfishly, is not something that anyone can be taught out of a book or by mere words. One to one, gentle loving care as a baby is the best way for anyone to learn that, I'm sure, even if that person isn't the mother. Mark my words, Brian, love in that deep and inner sense is what the world needs."

'I wonder what job Bert had.' Brian quietly thought to himself. 'He seems to know such a lot. I guess my father wouldn't have known all that!'

"Sarah certainly gives her time, willingly, for Ben," he confided, "and I love her even more for doing that, you know. When I am away, then I know she is caring for him and always thinking about his welfare."

"That's lovely. Some children have sadly to manage without love and still grow up fine and strong, and some people have to learn what they value through hardship. Some must feel that they are 'just fitted in' to their parents' busy lives. But, sadly, there are many who will never have the feeling of being loved, through no fault of their own. These are the ones who can become alienated to, and in, the world. Everyone is different, but at least if the chance to feel love is given, then that is a start in the right direction."

"Before Ben was born, Sarah used to worry whether she'd be a good mother or not. I think she's brilliant. Ben adores her. But, he's not spoilt. No, she sets boundaries."

"In my view, Brian, a mother has been given not only a great gift but the unique responsibility of passing on love from generation to generation. Tell me, what work is more important than that? But it does require unselfishness and, indeed, much effort. But, nothing worthwhile is gained easily. That's a fact of life. I think many seem to feel that giving their own child their dedicated time for a couple of years, until he or she can at least start making sense of the world, is less important than a job or material possessions. I'm glad for Ben that Sarah put his needs first and, in particular, that you made it possible, and still do, despite all your tiredness and stress. The effort is shared, it isn't one sided."

"You know, I am sure many who leave their children in nurseries when they are very tiny would like to stay at home," replied Brian, "but they feel they would lose their career and status which they've worked hard to achieve – often over many years. And then there are those who are single parents for whatever reason and have no financial support."

"Oh, let's face it Brian. Some of the youngsters who get pregnant these days could be more responsible in how they behave in the first place. I, personally, would ask 'why is this happening?' I'm not saying these youngsters are not caring mothers, not at all, in fact often quite the opposite. No, it's just not quite their time for that task.

"But, certainly, in general terms, the government could and should do much more. If the people in government fully understood the needs of tiny children, then, instead of spending millions making sure that people can find nursery care for their tiny children, as if that is the right thing to do, they could enable women to nurture their child – as a first priority. They could give mothers two or three years maternity leave by law, make part-time work available, a decent maternity grant, and a guaranteed return to work with no loss of previous status. They could insist that nurseries have plenty of staff for few children and that children are not there for long hours at a time.

"We can hope that enlightenment will eventually come. You know it is quite simple. All they have to do is to imagine a situation as seen and felt from the perspective of a tiny child. In fact, I'll bet you that most of the people making the decisions would have had a non-working mum at home when they were young, or granny down the road."

"It all comes down to money, I expect," interjected Brian.

"I see no reason why the experts could not make this a viable economic proposition. After all, money can always be found for war zones or bail outs – we have all seen that, and no mistake. My mother used to say, 'What can buy one thing could buy another.' But, if the people in power don't understand the fundamental facts, then that money is spent with the wrong emphasis. You know, health and safety seems to rear his head in most areas these days and for almost anything you can think of, often quite banal and ridiculous situations, but not a squeak is heard on behalf of the emotional health of tiny children."

"I can still remember," replied Brian, "that when I went to school, even at five, I felt quite lost for a while and didn't know what was going on for ages – I didn't know who was actually in my class or what I was supposed to be doing. And I was reckoned to be bright."

"I see, from your face that you get tired after a day's work. And you are an adult."

"Yes, I can be absolutely shattered. I often just long to put my feet up at home and do nothing," agreed Brian.

"Well, just think about the children who are away from home for long periods each day. However pleasant the environment and however kind the people, it is not the same as being able to relax in their own home. Have you ever noticed that you tend to have a feeling of alertness caused by unfamiliarity – you know, a kind of extra awareness in a strange place?"

"It's funny you should say that, as when I am staying away, as now, I always feel I have to be vigilant. You know, making sure I don't leave anything, or that I lock my car or room. Just little things, but, yes, always I'm 'watching' for anything to happen. I hadn't thought of it like that."

"Well, it's the same whatever the age. It's very hard work coping with unfamiliar situations and for long periods of time. The problem is that tiny children and toddlers often don't show the stress outwardly and if they do, they are thought of as naughty!

"I can remember that children who went to school under the age of five, when I was a lad, had to lay on camp beds covered by a dark grey blanket in the afternoon, and no argument! I was one of those and we used to be put in a row at the back of the class room. It was great except that the blankets were often dusty and made you sneeze. There's nothing like that these days."

"I didn't know that. Sarah has a lot of time with Ben. I am really glad, but I am a little envious, if I'm honest. I would love to see more of him."

"Aye, I'm sure you would," agreed Bert.

They sat quietly for a while.

"Having a child often does mean reining in your wishes," Bert eventually continued. "In truth, you know, it is only for a short while. It can be very hard work, and I can see that for many it is easier to give the child to someone else to look after. I'm told that some women find looking after their child unfulfilling and even boring. But, boredom comes from within, not from without and is very limiting. But, let's face it; we can't set the world to rights in one discussion, can we?"

"We can try though! It's very complicated, isn't it? I understand now what you meant by many shades between light and dark," replied Brian, smiling.

After a while, Brian asked, "Would you like a drink or a coffee, Bert? I can go and order something for you."

"Not just now, thanks. Forgive me, I must sound a bit like a lecturer, and after you have had such a long day."

"Not at all. It is great to have a chat. I work, I go home, I continue to work and then go to bed – well, more or less."

"It's just that I feel so strongly about the wellbeing of children. After all, a child is young for such a short time. Those years build the foundations of life. No one would stint on foundations for a building would they? They can build everything else later, on those solid foundations."

Brian found that Bert spoke with a quiet and rare sort of authority that made him want to listen and learn more. It seemed to him that, yes, Bert had very strong views, but that he spoke, not only out of kindness and true concern, but with a confidence of true knowledge. There was no blame or any judgmental attitude. No, Bert had wisdom. Brian felt he was sitting with a good man and he wanted to share more with him. So, as Bert stayed in his chair, Brian continued.

"When Ben began at the local school we found out, after a few months, that he was being bullied. A nasty girl was going around, picking on the young children. We complained and do you know what we were told?"

"No."

"That Ben should meet with the girl, along with the headmistress, and discuss the bullying with this girl and how it upset him. The psychological approach, the headmistress called it."

"There are some ridiculous ideas around these days. What did you do?"

"Well, I was away at work, but Sarah went and told her that on no account was it acceptable for Ben to have to face or to speak with the girl. He was six, for God's sake. She told the headmistress that she should accept that it was her responsibility to ensure the safety of all the children at her school. She suggested that, if she wanted psychological work done with her bullies, then she was the one who should become trained to do it, that is, if she was unable to do so at the present time. She insisted that such a duty should not be delegated to a six year old as she thought he was hardly old enough to understand the relationship between intent and action. She admitted that, though she was a lawyer, she hadn't discussed the concept of 'mens rea' with him, yet! Nor did she want Ben to even try to understand the workings of a bully's mind, thank you very much! Sarah's very intelligent. She was livid. She doesn't mince her words, I can tell you. She didn't tell me what other pearls of wisdom she delivered."

"Well done for Sarah," reassured Bert.

"Oh, she has a high class law degree and worked for a law firm for about ten years or so, till Ben was born. She was really good. She could tie anyone in knots with her arguments if she wanted to and usually won her cases. But she often says it takes more energy and thought to know how to deal with Ben, particularly if he and she are not seeing quite eye-to-eye on something. I remember one day when he was about seven months old, she moaned that she had been more intellectually challenged with Ben that day than at any time during the 'Watson v Crewton case'. That was a case which stretched her, if not quite to her limit, then nearly. She just wants to do her best for Ben, in every way. She actually helps out in Jeanette's boutique part time at present. She's one of Sarah's best friends. I think I've told you that before. That's just while Ben is at school and she has the holidays free. She is waiting until he is a bit older before deciding which direction she is going to take, but is determined to fit her future career around his school hours. And she will. What Sarah decides, Sarah will do.

"But, you will understand that we couldn't let Ben continue to go to the local school to be bullied, could we? You see, nothing was done about it, and when he started to become frightened of going to school, Sarah went again - about a couple of weeks later. The headmistress indicated that the girl had 'problems at home' so her behaviour was understandable, though regrettable. But, she still did nothing to stop it happening. Anyway, we felt we had no option and moved Ben to a private school. So, you see, cutting down on private school fees is not in any equation. He has fitted in very happily to his new school and has made two lovely friends. He is not a softy, don't think that, he just isn't a fighter."

He sat, silent again, just thinking – as he so often did these days.

'Have we got our priorities right?' he wondered. Sarah had to have transport and, well, they had to eat. Maybe they did not need to feed so many others at the weekends, but Sarah liked entertaining. She 'needed friends when he was away so much and, no, it wasn't the same if he didn't know them, so he had to meet them at the weekend. When else?' She was right. Of course she was right. And, she had to look smart and have her hair done. She liked the sports club, and after all, she needed some relaxation. But, she paid for all her own extras and Estelle, Ben's baby sitter, and bought her own clothes. There was nothing in the argument Brian could fault.

"I would give Sarah and Ben anything and everything."

"They are very fortunate to have you," answered Bert, "very fortunate, indeed!"

"The only problem Bert is that I do get exhausted. I wish I didn't, but I do." He could feel the stress build up out of sheer tiredness. It was as though his very self was being drained away, slowly but irrevocably. Some days he felt only a shadow was left, walking around, wearing his clothes and using his voice.

"If you overload any machine's capacity, it will gradually show signs of breakdown. I must be going now, Brian. Maybe we shall meet another time."

"I hope so, Bert. So pleased to meet and talk with you. Good night," he replied, "and thanks."

Yes, he had really appreciated Bert's time and interest. When did he have anyone to talk to like that? It didn't matter if he let out some of his private life and thoughts. He seldom had the chance to share how he felt with anyone. It seemed right, and somehow reassuring, even though he didn't know Bert. In any case, Bert was hardly going to tell the world about him, was he? "In fact," he talked aloud to himself later, in his room, as he thought about the evening, "I've just realised that though Bert talked about what he thought, he told me nothing about himself, his previous work or his family. He's sure to be retired. All I know is that he belongs round here. How unusual!"

» April

Brian was staying once more at The Dun Cow pub. In the past month he had seen a change in the Leeds office. Gradually it was being 'turned round' to his satisfaction, but he had the next stage in their development to sort out with them. Some hierarchy of responsibility in the office, he thought. A bonus scheme was what Len had suggested. As usual, it would be based on results. All the usual stuff, but already he had a few different ideas.

This evening the pub had again lived up to its reputation. Brian had been told originally, when the pub had been recommended to him, that it was, 'Well worth a visit. You'll find that the roast beef and Yorkshire pudding, roast potatoes and parsnips, peas and thick rich gravy, followed by home made apple pie and custard would serve a King'.

'How true,' thought Brian. 'It was really excellent. Absolutely wonderful again.' Nowhere had he tasted better. He had never been used to really enjoying his food. He always ate just when he was hungry. Healthily – he admitted, since being with Sarah, but with no sense of caring a great deal about what was on his plate, just so long as it wasn't mushrooms. No thank you! He had never really had much opportunity to learn to enjoy 'good homely and wholesome cooking'. His mother had tried her best, bless her, for years, but even she had admitted her lack of ability. Hours spent in the kitchen and the result had still to be helped down by a glass of water; and a blocked nose was beneficial on occasion. She has been a wonderful knitter, skilled seamstress, but not a cook.

Food at university? Well, nothing should be remarked about what he ate there! That was the past!

Now Sarah, she preferred the ready made varieties. She just couldn't bear to cut up meat or even touch it raw. If it was just for her, she would be a vegetarian, but, "Ben needs meat," she would say, frequently, as if to remind herself. So - she made the effort. As he had a cooked lunch prepared at school, a sandwich tea during the week was sufficient, with fruit, of course, and no junk. He was allowed biscuits and chocolate on Saturday evenings. She thought that the supermarket did some really tasty meat dishes, and provided the fish was all prepared for her, she could manage a fish pie from scratch. But there was always plenty fruit on the work top, with lettuce, peppers, tomatoes, and all the usual in the fridge. And, of course, there was the Chinese and also the Indian take-away down the road. It took all of two minutes on the phone to order and ten minutes to collect when he arrived home. He couldn't grumble. He ate quite well considering.

Sarah tried really hard when they entertained her friends. "Delia never lets me down," she would share her delight with everyone, "well tried and tested recipes for years, and always reliable." She also quite liked Nigella's quick meals, but she could not forward plan enough to have everything in a store cupboard – waiting. She often tried, but then forgot what was there and ended up throwing it away, not months but years out of date. She just didn't think like that. She would spend most of the day on a Saturday preparing casseroles and pavlovas and the like for dinner guests in the evening, while he took Ben out for a walk or to the swings. He treasured that time. It was almost worth having visitors just to have free time, alone, with Ben.

But tonight! Tonight he had feasted. He had looked forward to this stay, unlike many others elsewhere and he was not disappointed. 'Maybe I wouldn't appreciate this so much if it was my regular fare. At least it's compensation for being away from home,' he mused. 'My God, how lonely this travelling becomes. What will Sarah be doing? Will Ben be asleep by now?' He'd spoken to Ben earlier when he was just getting ready for bed and heard him read a page of his book over the phone. 'It would have helped if I could have seen the words as well, but he's doing really well for six. I'm sure the teacher is wrong about him. I don't think he has any problem. If and when he wants to read, I'm sure he will. There's never been any dyslexia in our family, so I think Sarah is right. We'll wait a while and see. He can't do everything and his ability with numbers is outstanding. And his drawing is very good. And letters are only drawings with meaning. At least the teacher agrees there. I'll phone in a while when I'm back in my room to speak to Sarah.'

He realised that he had been 'miles away'. He saw the newspaper, picked it up and started to read.

"Is it April fool's day? Or am I confused?" Brian spoke this thought aloud.

"What did you mean, lad?" Bert asked, bringing Brian back out of his reverie.

"Oh! Hello Bert. How very pleasant to meet you again. I didn't see you arrive."

"I just thought I'd pop in for a while," replied Bert. "April fool's day? Nay, lad, we're well past that, right enough."

"Sorry! You know, I didn't realise I'd spoken aloud just then. I get into such a habit of talking to myself in the car that I tend to do it at other times. Sarah is always commenting on it! It's just this news item I was reading."

"How's the new office progressing? Everything going smoothly I hope."

"Oh yes, ups and downs, but on the whole I am satisfied. I know how things tick there now."

"That's good. Makes the effort worthwhile, I suppose. Why the April Fool comment?"

"Oh, I thought this article in the paper was a spoof. It says here," read Brian, from the local weekly newspaper, The Express, "and I quote, 'The open forum style Wakefield council meeting was loudly interrupted by boos and shouts of shame, shame, shame from the public when the lack of a mains sewerage system in Stocksmoor was discussed'."

"It's not often we're in the news here."

"What on earth do they mean? Lack of mains sewerage? Everyone has mains sewerage, surely, in this country? We are not in the Sinai desert or Outer Mongolia here. It must be a spoof."

"No, it's absolutely true. Cesspits are what we have; some are quite old and haven't been renewed for years. But they are much better than the old earth closets. Nowadays, water flushing is included. They are emptied if they become blocked and overflow. Don't worry yourself. There is no typhoid and rats aren't a problem. I understand that the new estate, built a year or two ago down the road, has the very latest in cesspit technology. Oh, yes, that is bang up to date. I gather it is quite massive and with different chambers, or so I heard at the time. I didn't actually see it when it was buried, but there have been no complaints so far."

"I don't believe it," laughed Brian, thinking suddenly about his usual reaction to certain vegetables and wishing that he hadn't eaten quite so much dinner.

"Nay, don't be daft, lad. It all works satisfactorily. At least most of it does and for most of the time. But there can be a few unresolved problems."

"Like what?"

"Well now, take the old chapel. The congregation dwindled to about five or six regulars. The Methodist circuit still needed its dues and the chapel became unsupportable in the village. That's a few years ago now. So it was sold and is now a house. You know, those conversions are quite popular and there's no denying that the old religious buildings were built to stay. Solid construction and all that. It wouldn't be my cup of tea to live in, but we all have our own preferences.

"The main building was converted and a big extension was added at the back. I did hear that sewerage has been known to seep up into the field below. Maybe it has too many toilets and baths for their cesspit to manage or else they didn't upgrade it enough when the chapel was converted. I don't know. But only horses graze there and a soiled bit can be fenced off. I don't think the horses would tell the difference in the grass or be affected by foot rot or anything like that. I heard that the horses' owners were a bit worried for a time. It was understandable really."

"But, just the thought of that shit soaking through the soil is disgusting, isn't it? How dreadful! What have the council done about it?"

"Nothing, as far as I've heard. If the council takes notice, they will likely have to do something about the entire village and, of course, we're talking money here."

"You are joking!"

"No, I believe that even the environmental chaps didn't want to hear about it."

"That surely can't be right." Brian was horrified. "The owners of the field could always sue I suppose," he added.

"To sue would cost too much. But I imagine by now that it has been sorted amicably. I mean, there might be a bit of an argument or protest about who had to pay and such like, but right minded people wouldn't leave such a problem, once they knew about it, would they? But, I wouldn't live there if I was paid to do so."

"Why is that? Because it is on a busy corner? It has a lovely view, you cannot deny that."

"No. Nothing like that. It's purely personal. You see, for me it's as though there are too many ghosts around. Some we know about and,

I guess a few we don't. No, lad, you'd never get me living there. Mind you, some people don't care one way or another and many would just jump at a chance to live in a place with 'atmosphere', I think they call it. 'Ghosts?' they'd say. 'What are ghosts? Bring them on!' But I know what I mean. The new bit of the house has been built over where the old earth closet for the chapel and the boiler room were situated. I can remember sitting out in the closet in the cold as a child to avoid hearing about Daniel in the lion's den. It seemed to crop up quite frequently, considering how big the Bible is and how many stories there are in it. We all had to go to Sunday school, and the classes were always in the downstairs rooms under the main chapel. I was not fanciful, but I never liked the feeling in those rooms. It always felt spooky to me. Nothing tangible, you know, just that funny feeling at the back of the neck, like as if the hair was rising. Of course, it might just have been rather cold. Even in summer there was no sun in those rooms."

"Maybe it was all the emphasis that the Sunday school teachers put on God and not doing wrong and Christ dying and the like that stirred your imagination," suggested Brian.

"It could have been, but I don't think so. It has always been my belief that something dreadful happened in the far dim and distant past in that place. No evidence, of course, just a feeling."

"What about the rest of the village then?"

"What about the village?"

"You know – the cesspits and the sewerage."

"Well, the other householders occasionally need to call out the council to empty their pit if it starts to overflow. It doesn't happen often, but some of the things that are put down lavatories these days don't dissolve as they did when the cesspit was invented."

"Bloody hell, it's only one step on from the earth toilets my granny used to talk about."

"Oh yes, we nearly got frostbite in delicate areas in the winter when the closets were all down the garden. And there was no light when the door was shut. When you went to the lavatory, you couldn't see where you pissed. Newspapers used for you know what. Good job we all ate plenty vegetables then. Going there was not an easy task for the constipated or faint hearted, I can tell you, but something we all had to do. Mind you, all the houses have inside toilets now. But it was just part of life back then. You can use your imagination." After a moment's pause he added, "Or probably not, seeing as you have just eaten your dinner!"

"I can't and, if you don't mind, I'll try hard not to!" Brian smiled. He didn't want to offend Bert, as he feared he may have done when he laughed before. He was really fascinated. He didn't usually have such an interesting evening. It was like hearing a social history of the place.

"But here, in Stocksmoor in the middle of Yorkshire, in 2010?" He stopped and sat in thought for a while. Bert did not interrupt. "I can't believe what I am hearing. The government built that monstrosity, the Millennium Dome, do you remember? It cost millions. I know a couple of people who went and, quite honestly, they thought it was basically a pathetic lot of rubbish. Missiles can hit targets accurately a thousand miles away; computers are so advanced that video conferencing can happen between almost anywhere in the world and here. Massive amounts of money are being spent ready for hosting the Olympics and Stocksmoor people's shit just goes into the ground. I just don't believe it. How much would it cost, I wonder, to sort it all? In comparison, mere peanuts, I would think."

"Well, no one has wanted to know, so we have been stuck with it."

"Do all the villages around here have cesspits?"

"No, I don't think so. I'm pretty sure that Bretton and the other larger villages around all have mains sewerage."

"So, a few miles of big pipes to connect and maybe a small brick building to house a couple of automated pumps and that would be that. Yes?"

"Aye, but it's called having priorities, lad, and sewerage isn't high on the agendas of those who have the purse strings it would seem. They won't get peerages sorting sewerage for Stocksmoor, will they? They see the system working, with the odd hitch, and well, the money is used elsewhere. You know expense accounts and the like. But, I will say this. I have never known the council lorry that empties the pits to be delayed for long when called out. There, within hours it is. The council believes that they provide a good service without mains sewerage. So, no fuss is made, and nothing changes!"

Bert paused to reflect a while, and then continued, "Oh, yes, there are changes. I hear that many councils send members to do research in other countries – with all expenses paid of course. Forgive me. I also quite forgot the lovely, glossy, brochures with coloured pictures. You know, letting us all know what they do with the money everyone has to pay in Community Tax. They could save that money for starters. I doubt that many read the brochures. We don't use it in the toilets anymore. At least we have progressed from that. It's the same story repeating itself all over but just a different context. Money, yes, there is plenty of money, but only for what the government decides. Otherwise there isn't any. A couple of years ago I heard of just one example. An old people's home was being closed for lack of funds and the old people were being moved many miles away from where their relatives lived. Remember, Brian, these were the people who had lived through and served in the Second World War, to preserve this country. But, no, there was nothing in the coffers to help them. There's a lot of talk, but, in practical truth, little action.

"Then, bingo, a year or so later, the government found literally hundreds of millions of pounds to bail out the banks, when greed, irresponsible practices, obscene bonuses and gambling on a massive scale, as far as you could gather from the news and papers, had played havoc with the banking system. No one says where all this money has been and why it couldn't be used to help those who really needed it. What's the saying? 'Those who have will be given more, but those who have not will have taken away even that which they have.' It's been going on ad infinitum – well as long as anyone can remember anyway. Out of sight out of mind, that's Stocksmoor. Could you put some wood on the fire, Brian?" suggested Bert, changing the subject. "It will go out otherwise."

"I'll just put one log on as it's getting late. There is no point keeping the spiders warm all night." Brian prodded the fire with the poker and put a log on the red embers. "I don't suppose lottery money can be used for sewerage problems," asked Brian, as he sat down again.

Bert answered, "It's used for a lot of different projects, but I doubt that sewerage will be one of them, and I don't think it should be, either. This village was delayed getting other services, you know. Electricity didn't come to Stocksmoor until the early fifties. I know it was connected before the coronation, as I remember a few people bought televisions in the village to watch it all. Before that, apart from during the blackout of the war, everywhere around and over the valley lights could be seen. But this hillside was dark. The village was only connected, eventually, because the pit in the wood had a mains supply. Then the wood-yard, which had its own generator for the saws, was connected up and the village followed shortly after. Previously the wood-yard's machinery was driven from a boiler house which had to be kept going, fuelled by sawdust. It had a very big chimney, that dominated the village, but that has long since been demolished. Otherwise, gas was the only fuel available to the households, beside wood and coal for the fires of course. I remember the little gas mantles, and very fragile they were too."

"You wouldn't think that a place in the centre of civilisation and one that used to be a manufacturing area of importance, Yorkshire, could have had or still have problems, would you?"

"Well you wouldn't, but it had and has. Oh yes, I can remember my mother brushing the carpets threadbare to try to keep the house clean. Of course, no electricity meant no vacuum cleaners, no electric washing machines, and no immersion heaters. Lord no, all water was heated behind the fire. That meant just one bath a week, only, for each member of the family." Then Bert added, "I'll bet you didn't know that you could buy fridges fuelled by gas did you?"

"No, I didn't."

"Worked like a normal electric one, as far as using it was concerned. And my mother had to use a gas iron. I always thought they were like small dragons. Flames would suddenly flare out, but it was either that or a flat iron that was heated on a metal plate on the fire, and she had had enough of those when she was young. But, how the kids were not gassed with the gas fires in the bedrooms I do not know. Little kids these days would not be safe. The gas taps were just by the skirting boards. But children did as they were told in those days. Otherwise the hands that were calloused with all the cleaning, were hard on bums and legs. We had no health and safety in those days. Just some discipline from our parents, meaning mainly, mother. Mind you, I don't agree at all with hitting or shouting. No, not at all. But, I don't remember being smacked more than the odd time, as we just knew we had to do as we were told. We were all much happier that way."

"I left work a bit earlier today and came into the pub when it was still light. As I looked around, I could see that Stocksmoor is in a lovely position, with fine views over the valley and wood," Brian commented. He was enjoying listening to all that Bert told him. "But, I can imagine it must have been hard, especially knowing other people had power and electric lights."

"Aye, lad. But you can't live on just a view. What you didn't have you didn't miss in those days. There was no television to tell you about other folks and their good fortune, only the accumulator wireless. So, ignorance was, well, not exactly bliss but just ignorance I suppose. And of course, it was after two world wars, fairly close together, you know. If ever we complained about anything, each time we would be told that people were grateful to just be 'alive and kicking' and then reminded of someone who had never returned from the fighting. Seriously, how could anyone complain when most families had gaps at the table and sorrow that never went away? I mean, tell me – how? We were just so grateful to be together and have our mother and father, grandparents and other relatives. The war memorial plaques that were fixed on the wall in the chapel, one after each war, told their own story. Several inscriptions had the same surname you know – all had been lost from one family. Can you imagine that grief?"

"No, I can't." They sat quietly for a few minutes. Then Brian asked, "Where have they been put, now that the chapel is a house? The memorial plaques, I mean."

"I'm not sure. Someone told me that they stayed in the house, but I find that really hard to believe. Who would want memorial stones in their house? I understand that if you want to keep something, you take it out of a house, or chapel, or whatever before you sell it. So, I can't answer you one way or another. Well anyway, eventually electricity came. What a difference! I can remember the first time the lights were switched on. It was like Blackpool's illuminations. It was absolutely marvellous."

They sat quietly. Brian was having difficulty absorbing the information about the sewerage. He read the rest of the report in the paper. It seemed that the council was going to have to face up to the village's archaic sewerage system. Such systems were considered in Brussels to be unacceptable and of course EEC rulings must apply.

» May

"Can I get you a drink?" Brian asked Bert. He had returned to the pub in Stocksmoor and, on entering the bar after eating his evening meal in the restaurant, he found Bert was already standing there on his own.

"Hello. It's good to see you again. But, no, not for me, thanks," replied Bert.

"Can I join you for a while?"

"Yes, of course. How are the family and how is work going?"

"Well, both Sarah and Ben seem alright, though I don't seem to have much time with them. We've been very busy. Take this last week as an example. I'd been away a lot and even when I got home to enjoy a weekend, I had so much admin to catch up on that I had to spend most of Saturday in the study at my computer.

"Then, on Sunday, Sarah's mother came to stay for a couple of weeks. Mind you, I get on fine with her. She's a lovely woman. Half French, you know. She has spent more time in France than in England for the past few years, helping to look after her elderly mother. She's dead now. But Sarah's mother likes it so much that I gather she is going to move there permanently. You know, sell up in England. It sounds as though she has finally decided, but I'm not sure when. She now has a house in France, of course, left to her by her mother so it'll be home from home. It won't be the life changing move as it would be for most people."

"That must be interesting."

"Yes, and it's good for Ben as he is already understanding a lot of French words. She's a good teacher and makes it all fun. She loves Ben dearly."

"I'll just have a shandy, please," Brian caught the barmaid's attention.

"Shall we go and sit in comfortable chairs? There were some vacant when I was eating," suggested Brian.

They went into the dining room-cum-lounge and sat by the inglenook.

"I don't drink much, and even less away from home," he spoke again to Bert. "I sort of have this inner feeling that should an emergency happen I have to be able to jump into the car and drive home straightaway. You never know, do you? I would never have admitted that I was a worrier, but these days I think I am developing into one. Quite quickly in fact. My mind is always seeing things going wrong. It's not the work itself, which I find relatively easy. I can't say that that stresses me, as such. It's just that there is far too much and though I work quickly, it takes for ever to get through it all. But no, the worry is always about Sarah and Ben."

"Well, that's different isn't it? They mean so much to you."

"Yes, I find I have them on my mind nearly all of the time."

"I understand that. I always believe that once a parent, particularly one who really loves his or her child, you can never be single-minded again."

"I worry about Ben when he plays out but Sarah is very good. She mostly has children round. That's why I bought a house with a garden, so Ben could play in safety. In fact, as he's at a private school, he doesn't really know many of the neighbours' children, so it's really up to Sarah to organise playmates for him at home. When you move into an area, it is very different from growing up where your parents and grandparents lived, isn't it? You don't have any history to attach to people you meet. I don't know whether the world has more unpleasant people than generations ago, or whether we just hear about it more?"

"It's difficult to say, but there's been bad folk around for ever," replied Bert. "We didn't have the television when I was a young lad and wireless news was not full of individual happenings as it is now."

"You know, I can't understand how parents and relatives can have interviews on the television the same day as a tragedy. Weird I call it, just very weird."

"A sign of the times, lad. Anything and everything is other people's news, and normal feelings are put to one side for the sake of the media. But, safe or not, we played out all day over the fields when I was young, in the wood and roaming the common land. There was no one to molest us. There was poor old Happy Fred, the village tramp, I suppose you would call him. He lived in the pit pump house or in the rotted tree trunks."

"Goodness, you don't say! What a life."

"Aye, I expect social services would have been involved nowadays. Then he was free to decide his own way of life. But we were all used to his being there. I don't think even now he could have claimed the dole as he never worked. I doubt he was on anyone's register. Now that I am much older I think that he was a proud man, in his own, isolated way. Used to shout out a lot, but otherwise didn't speak much to anyone, but we always understood that he couldn't help the shouting. He seemed very old, but in reality, thinking about it now, he may not have been. To children anyone grown up seems old. What a fright he would give us when he would emerge head first from a tree trunk slowly as we went by. But we knew he was harmless. Maybe he had a few fleas, but harmless."

"What happened to him?"

"I don't know how old he was when he died, but he was found dead in the chapel coal store. It must have been before the chapel was heated by electric heaters, so that would give a date if I could work it out. Only when people realised that he hadn't been seen for a few days was there any concern. But, coincidentally, I understand that one of the chapel wardens decided to look in the coal place to see how much coal was left, and found him. He'd been dead for days, so the coroner reported at the inquest. But he was not the only one to pick the chapel either to breathe their last. Another woman from the village chose the boiler room. I remember, it was sort of never mentioned at the time, not a squeak about it, and I don't remember hearing any prayers or supplications for her. You see, she had done it herself. Aye, that she did and that was thought to be a sin."

"Poor woman, what a state she must have been in to do that! Was she without a friend?"

"It seemed strange, in a small village, but I don't know the ins and outs of it all. There are always two sides to everything. She was married and a pleasant woman as I recall. It was all put down to illness, a sudden depression or something like that, I think. But whatever - it happened." Bert fell silent for a while, thinking back to those earlier days. "Aye, I'm quite sure a few ghosts are sitting in and around the chapel," he spoke in a quiet voice, as if almost to himself. "That site seems to have some jinx put on it, place of worship or not."

"Why do you say that?" asked Brian.

"I remember something happening to one of the children in the village. She was a little girl, about six or seven years old at the time. She was quite fragile really and suffered a lot of ill health, you know, chest complaints. She had asthma. There was not much of that illness about in those days, despite all the factories and smoke. There didn't seem to be anything she could have to ease it. Well, she was beaten up by two older girls from a neighbouring village one day on her way home from school. They waited for her to get off the bus. Yes, can you imagine? It was apparently all planned. I heard it was something to do with an old score."

"Good God. So, there's nothing new today is there? I mean a scrap that just happens is one thing, but a planned attack is quite another. How old were they?"

"Oh, just young, hardly into their teens, I believe. I heard that they had been originally at the same school and had been caned a year or two earlier for bullying this same child, actually at school. I mean, we're talking about very severe bullying, unconsciousness, that sort of mindless level. One had possibly been expelled and one had been sent to a Borstal for a year or two. Anyway, they obviously bore a grudge against the little girl and were bent on revenge when the corrective sentence ended. They easily knew which bus she would travel on as there was no choice. To cut a long story short, they chose the chapel earth closet, the outdoor one I was telling you about, to beat her black and blue. No one ever knew the full details and the young girl never mentioned it at all. She was a brave little lass – quite delicate and fragile but brave."

"What happened to save her?"

"It seemed that Happy Fred, as luck would have it, was asleep at the time in the coal house and was woken by the little girl's screams and the two bullies laughing as they kicked her, almost to death. He was unshaven and unexpected. He shouted at them and scared them away. He could look very scary, though I had never seen him angry. Apparently, it became known later, he found the child lying gasping on the earth floor in the closet. She was none too clean by this time. He gently picked her up and carried her out of the closet onto the path of the chapel. He knew her mother would soon be looking for her when she hadn't arrived home and would find her there. He stayed by the child's side until he could see the mother approaching up the hill and then went back into the coal place. With, I understand, some initial disgust, as her child smelled somewhat as you can imagine, her mother found her."

"It sounds as though Happy Fred was tolerated but largely ignored. Yet, do you mean that this man, who had the strangest life you could ever imagine, had saved this child's life?" asked Brian.

"Yes, without any doubt. Mind you, don't think everyone ignored him and people were not unkind to him. His sister-in-law, who lived next door to the little girl and her family, was very kind and gave him a hot meal and let him wash when he wished. I think he could have lived there had he wanted to, but he chose his own way. He used to eat in the garden though. It made her look as though she wouldn't allow him indoors, but it was not so."

"What happened to the child and the girls?"

"It was understood by several people that Happy Fred, who hardly ever spoke directly to anyone, at least not that one could recall, went to her father and took him to the chapel and the closet. He showed him, with a few words and mime, what he had seen happen and what he had done. I am not so sure, but I think that both girls were sentenced to a term of correction this time after the father of the child reported the incident to the police. The little girl didn't say what happened. It was as though her memory had been wiped out, but she had a badly bruised arm with the bone cracked and she was ill for weeks afterwards. You see they had kicked her in her stomach, chest, just everywhere. Pitiful. At any rate, the two were removed from the area and the child was safe after that. Talk about picking on the weakest. Dreadful, it was, just dreadful. The incident wasn't easily forgotten, I can tell you, although never mentioned."

"So, the old days were not always good as some people think," remarked Brian.

"Much the same as now, really, like the curate's egg. Good in parts or bad in parts, depending how think. Times were hard then for different reasons. But people reap back what they sow. I understand that those two girls did not have happy lives. It was all of their own doing. Everyone has choice," stated Bert, not really expecting or getting a reply.

"You know, Bert, I've never been one for church or chapel. My parents are both dead now, unfortunately, but they never went to church either. My main regret is that they never knew Ben. But if there is a life after this, maybe my parents can know him somehow, who knows? Mum, especially, would have doted on him."

"They must not have been any great age."

"No. I think Mum was about fifty-eight years of age and I know Dad had had his sixtieth birthday. It was a tragedy. They were both killed on the continent whilst on holiday. They had thought it would be easier than driving through Italy in the car, so they went on a coach holiday. It was supposed to be for a month, you know, luxury hotels, seeing the sites, staying in different places, the whole works. Dad had done twenty-five years as head pharmacist at the local chemist shop, and he and Mum thought they deserved a good holiday. His bosses allowed Dad to take a month of his annual leave altogether because of his long and excellent service. Mind you, they didn't give him a day extra. It was meant to be the tour of a lifetime, a reward to themselves after all the years of work and struggle. Their last child, me, was married and was settled. They felt free. They never came back. That was just after me and Sarah had married. Of course I went to their joint funeral, but I never saw their bodies. I know it sounds silly, but I often think they are still on holiday and haven't got back yet. I feel angry about it. God worship is not for me. Never was and never will be. It was so unfair."

"Do you have brothers or sisters?"

"Yes, just one sister. She's always been reckoned to be the brains of the family. My parents always liked to think we were very close. I think it made them feel they were better parents. But, we're not and never will be. I rarely have contact with her. She is very different from me. She never visits us and we are never invited to her homes. I say homes as she has at least two, maybe more by now. So, basically, there's no contact apart from the obligatory Christmas and birthday card. Mind you, I think they're a farce. I mean, what's a card twice a year? Hardly helps with day to day life, does it?

"I am the youngest and never really felt included with her, even as a child. If you met her you would, no doubt, think her very pleasant. She has, or at least used to have, a good job, one of life's high flyers. But what she does or with whom, I don't know. She married a man she met at her work, but I never knew him. I remember I met him just once before the wedding. But, whether she still is married or how many children she may or may not have, I don't know. Her Christmas card is usually just from her to me, so she doesn't give any news away nor shows any interest in whether I have a family.

"But I didn't choose her and she didn't choose me. Quite frankly, I don't think either of us would have done so, and if I am really honest, I don't actually like her. It's sad really. I think that's why Sarah and Ben are so special to me. I have no one else. I sort of 'came along after' when Mum thought she would only have the one child. I doubt that Sarah and I will have more children, either, never mind the expense. At least Ben hasn't to share Sarah when I'm away. Sarah isn't churchy either."

"You know," continued Bert, "I had to go to Sunday school morning and afternoon followed by a chapel service in the afternoon and, believe it or not, in the evening as well. Yes, all my young life up to about eighteen years. Despite all that tuition, I have no time for religion either. Oh, I could answer mastermind on the television. 'What is your special subject?' Answer, 'The Bible, from beginning to end'. Absolutely no problem. We used to have to learn psalms and recite them. I even gained a Bible that way. They were given to us from money, donated many years before, by a man who obviously thought that the Bible was the way to a righteous life. I suppose he thought he was doing his bit to keep children on the straight and narrow. He was called Wharton, I remember. The Wharton Bible Prize. Black bound with gold embossed title. It was a yearly thing, and a big day in the Sunday school calendar of events, and 'no prompting'! Outside examiners listening to us, can you believe? They came to make sure we recited the psalms word perfect. Oh, yes, it was all very serious. Can you imagine anything like that happening now?

"But, many a day wasted as far as I'm concerned. Every week, Sunday was always the same. Best clothes on, hair brushed and no playing games. But you did as you were told when I was a lad, and, anyway it was company and community life. One thing was achieved, religion aside. It brought all the children together peacefully. That all carried over into the week, you know. There was very little scrapping amongst the village children. Of course there were many spinster women in those days. Their generation of young men had been wiped out in the First World War and in their hearts they never forgave. Lonely, frustrated lives lived without much purpose or affection, I think. So, I imagine their longing for love boiled over occasionally."

"Yes," agreed Brian. "I think religion has a lot to answer for. In my view it breeds hypocrisy and deceit. There are many professing, with emotion, from the pulpit one thing and living another. Think of the many priests using their positions and trust to molest young boys. I mean, every one tarnishes the rest. It seems to have been common practice for years and years. There are so many other dreadful things you read about these days. The Northern Ireland problems lasted for generations, and then we have the Middle East. All about religion and intolerance, yet, where does it get them? Men, all either sons, fathers or husbands killed, innocent children and women accidently hurt, houses destroyed, and lives become miserable existences. What is left? Grief and hardship. And even a few women volunteer to be suicide bombers. Now, how does that happen and for what? God can't think much of what is being done in his holy name. I imagine him up there somewhere, wringing his hands in anguish and saying, 'What on earth are they doing? Why do they behave like that?'"

The older man smiled sadly at his companion. They both sat quietly in the warmth of the room and the comradeship of the pub.

"Human nature can be of the finest or of the worst," Bert carried on. "The world needs a bit of sorting. But, it will happen, make no mistake. Oh yes, it will happen. It's just a matter of time."

Brian picked up the paper again and, after reading a headline, commented,

"Ah, I see that they are doing something about the sewerage now after all."

"Well, let's put it this way. It would seem that the subject is on someone's agenda at last, but 'seeing will be believing'. In Yorkshire there is a saying, 'When you've caught your rabbit then you can put your pan on the stove. Until then don't waste the heat'. I think that is very apt for government or council plans. Wait until it happens."

"I've never heard that saying."

"Well no, you wouldn't have, I suppose. It was one of my mother's. She had lots. She was not the brain of Britain, but she could hit the nail on the head with her sayings. I'm off now; I hope you have a good night. The landlord here, as you will have noticed after a few visits, has a good, reliable staff. His missus keeps a sharp eye on everything and she's a stickler for finding a bit of dust. She keeps standards very high.

She sees it as her mission. I've heard him tell her, more than once, that she's getting too old for any extra work besides the cooking. But she just carries on as she wants. Shoes off at the door round the back, I can tell you, before anyone enters her own private domain. And I understand that the motel, next door, is very clean too."

"Yes, it's absolutely fine."

"I must be going, lad, as my time's up. See you again sometime."

"Yes, surely," answered Brian. "I shall have to continue to visit the Leeds office fairly often, not regularly every week now, but I still need to keep a check on everything. Goodnight. It's been a great pleasure to meet and talk with you again. Thanks for your company."

The older man picked up his camel coloured waterproof jacket and departed.

'My! He must have had that a while,' Brian thought, 'I haven't seen a coat like that since that film about Harold Wilson was on the telly. What a pleasant man and so interesting. Every time I find out something different. I think he's a true Yorkshire man, open, honest and kind but calls a spade a spade. I wonder how old he is. He knows so much. I'm sure he must be older than he looks.' He observed that no one looked up or appeared to take any notice as Bert went out.

'Typical,' he mused to himself, 'all engrossed in their own conversations they cannot notice anyone else. Thank goodness I met Bert. Seems no one else would have bothered to talk to me despite the legendary Yorkshire friendliness. Maybe that's just for Yorkshire folk. But Bert is local, born and bred so everyone will know him. Oh, maybe they are all from another village. Oh, shut up Brian! Stop thinking, for goodness sake! It doesn't matter anyway. Bert doesn't care so why should you. Nearly time to go to bed.'

He looked at his watch.

'Oh God, look at the time. It'll be past midnight when I finally finish that presentation for tomorrow, then morning and another long day of work. Oh, sod it all, I'll just skim through the paper,' he continued – to himself. 'Well, it doesn't go away,' he thought, as he read the paragraph.

> 'All houses in accessible areas of the country are to have mains sewerage by 2012.'

Money or no money, it will have to be done. Europe has spoken!'

With that last thought on the subject, he put the paper on the nearest table and went to his room, hoping for a quiet and peaceful night's sleep. He prayed he didn't have his recurrent dream, where he was alone and deserted and couldn't find Sarah and Ben. He would wake in a panic and the next day he would be haunted by the dream. He hadn't told Sarah. God no, she would be so upset. At least, he hoped she would be. He loved her just the same now as when he had first set eyes on her.

His mind flicked back to that student party with just a few friends and a Chinese take-away. He had been sitting on the floor eating his crispy noodles when Sarah walked in with one of the girls from their usual group. He could still remember how his heart seemed to leap in his chest when he saw her, and a strange calmness entered his mind as he thought, 'I've found her again.' He had never made sense of that, but had never forgotten it either. His problem now was that he wasn't a hundred percent sure that Sarah still felt the same way.

How reassuring the mobile phone was; yes, more reassuring than anything else, unless, as now, you had expected a phone call and it hadn't happened. He would phone Sarah in the morning before she took Ben to school. He wondered why she hadn't phoned this evening. Unless there was a major problem during the day, which fortunately hadn't been very often, they usually spoke at length in the evenings when he was away from home. He might phone again, but very briefly, in the mornings, just to say 'Hello' and occasionally they chatted in the day time. Not as much now as they used to, of course. Sarah had sort of shocked him a while ago by saying, 'We are not children having to hold on to each other's hands'. So, since then, he often had 'second thoughts' and would postpone phoning. He had liked that contact. But he could see it could be thought of as a bit pathetic at his age, so he had kept quiet about how he felt. He checked the power of the signal. 'Well, that's alright, at least in this room. She must have been busy or maybe the signal was low in the dining room.'

He took his computer out of his deluxe leather case, a present from Sarah for Christmas last year.

'Of course, it's Wednesday. It's the night Jeanette and Susanna come round to watch the telly and have a drink. I am pleased she has them nearby. Particularly Jeanette. She's so kind to Sarah and vice versa,' he mused. Jeanette lived very near and had a grown up family; at least, her sons were both at university. People considered them 'grown up' these days. He remembered he didn't feel at all grown up when he went away for the first time. In fact, to be absolutely truthful, for most of the time he was at university. Jeanette now managed a successful career. Susanna has no children. 'Not having children makes a big difference, no ties.'

"How thoughtful, a double plug in this room," he spoke out loud. He plugged in the laptop. "I'm less likely to forget something this way."

'What did anyone do without one of these?' he wondered, as he then put his mobile phone on 'power' to recharge. 'It's more important to me than my luggage.

» September

Brian drew into the car park. He had made the reservation two weeks ago, to make sure there was a bed. The Dun Cow had been newly painted since his last visit and stood out, brightly white with a yellow tinge from the late evening sun. 'How pretty the window boxes look,' he thought, 'they add such a splash of colour and still have plenty of flowers. I think a few trees would look well, but maybe it is too windy to get them established. Thank God, though, no leylandiis in sight!' Just the thought made him angry as he remembered his neighbours back home. If they didn't trim the trees down soon he would contact the council to do something. He hadn't mortgaged himself up to the hilt for Sarah and Ben to have their lovely house and garden just to find the sun blocked. They now had to have lights on in the dining room on a sunny day, and found only dark shade in the part of the garden that should catch most of the sun. Some people were so inconsiderate. Worse – they were away from home in the Mediterranean 'swanning' around on their yacht half the time. They didn't care one jot.

But he would do something about it soon, friendly with posh neighbours or not. It would be no loss to him. But Sarah didn't want to get on the wrong side of them. Unlike her, he had no interest at all in meeting them for 'drinks and just a 'small barbie'. They didn't know the meaning of the word 'small'.

Bill and Daphne – he had been told they liked first names at all times – had spent a fortune on their so-called 'small barbie' last summer. Small indeed! God, he had rarely had such a feast. It must have cost an absolute fortune. There had been at least thirty people there, all having fillet steaks and king prawns with sweet potato, pepper and courgette kebabs. There were salads of things he hadn't even heard of, with edible flowers for goodness sake. I mean, when do people need to eat nasturtiums? Three different cheesecakes, strawberries – baskets and baskets of them, with cream, and he could have gone swimming in the wine that was flowing freely. It was great, as a guest. Sarah had taken a bunch of roses and a bottle of wine. But he had told Sarah that the wine was totally unnecessary. There was no way they could compete or would ever want to. It would take his hard earned salary for a month to pay for all that. No way!

"Of course we will get them lopped, Brian," promised Bill. "That will be no problem, no problem at all." That was a year and another six feet of sun blocking ago.

He booked in, washed his hands and face and went out for a walk. He wasn't hungry yet. He took a few deep breaths. "Oh! That feels good." He exhaled with extra effort. "I'll see the village, take a good look around and have some fresh air in my lungs first, before I eat."

He walked across the road, and, turning right, he passed the chapel. He still thought of it as a chapel. Whatever the inside was like, its origin couldn't be disguised and to be truthful, he wasn't a great fan of the architect, whoever he may have been. He was sure it had to have been a man to design something like that. Then he went down the road, as far as the new estate. He crossed the road and took the path along the top of the common, turned right again at the end, walked up the path between the fields, right again along the main road and back to the pub. It could have taken him about twenty minutes, quick walking, but sitting on that gate had added another ten minutes. Not too far and, anyway, you can't get lost in this village. 'Now for some good Yorkshire cooking,' he thought, with anticipation of his meal ahead.

"I'll have the roast beef and Yorkshire pudding, what else?" he replied, smiling, as the landlord came to take the order.

"I always like to give the 'personal touch'," the landlord boasted, regularly, to his wife who was the main chef and general pub organiser, "and make people feel welcome."

"Yes, dear," she always replied.

Alright! He admitted that she did all the cooking, but he did his bit for the meals. He grew fresh vegetables, collected and even prepared them, well – nearly every day. None of your frozen kind if that could be avoided! His homegrown carrots and beans were superb, and, of course, his favourite - rhubarb – was ideal for the puddings. He went to market and negotiated prices with the butcher. Oh, yes, he played his part in the success of the restaurant. Long days, but at least he wasn't working all the hours God sent to line someone else's pocket, like poor Brian. Poor lad, he always looks so tired, but cheerful all the same. Somehow, having your own business made all the difference.

"Very nice, very nice indeed," Brian gave heartfelt praise, after he had finished. "That was truly beautiful beef. Please send my compliments to the chef."

"Local produce is the secret and having a wife who's an excellent cook," replied the landlord. "She takes after her mother. Learned most of what she knows about food and cooking from her. No fancy courses. We have the best ingredients and well, the rest is easy. But don't let her hear me say that! Freshness and quality is everything in food preparation. And with our butcher we never have to tenderize tough meat. We think that is false economy. If we want people like you to return time and again, it has to be the best. That's what I would want to eat, you know, so I expect nothing less for my guests."

As he left with the crockery, he turned, "Coffee at your table or by the fire?"

"By the fire, please."

Brian sat in the same chair as before. Four months had passed since he had last stayed at The Dun Cow. The Leeds office was doing well and he managed, now, to organize it very well by phone, fax or email for most of the time. But there was a meeting tomorrow. For all the technology, he still needed that face to face contact. He had to admit that the extra responsibility wasn't really proving too difficult after all, once he had sorted the problems out. At least, he didn't think it was, though Sarah was dubious. She wasn't sure!

He had to trust the secretary to keep him informed and she was proving worth her weight in gold. He stopped in his thoughts and an image of the secretary came into his mind. 'Well, maybe not quite ALL her weight!' She was very amiable, did very well and he was becoming quite confident in her abilities. But it was still early days for the office as a whole, so he had decided that he would spend a full day there tomorrow and check everything out. They thought he was just going for an hour for the meeting, but no, he would be thorough, look through the files, the accounts, everything. A bit like a surprise inspection, he thought. Keep them on their toes.

An experienced campaigner, he knew what to look for. By now it should be possible to tell how they worked and any teething problems with his 'remote control' methods should have shown up by now and could be sorted out. There was the slight problem of Kevin and one or two others contacting him as and when they felt the urge. He would have to put a limit to that, and tell them that emails were not intended for passing the buck, but for communicating genuine information or queries or when they had actually done the work involved.

It wasn't fair on Sarah to have dinner interrupted. It wasn't often he could be at home for guests at seven o' clock during the week and he, himself, was annoyed last week, never mind what Sarah felt. Kevin and Winston had interrupted three times between seven thirty and nine thirty. None of it was urgent and could easily have waited till the next day, or this week even, until he was at the office in person. Yes, he'd have to sort that. He made a mental note to put it on 'his' agenda. Sarah protested that he was just too soft with his staff. Even the extra two thousand on his salary didn't compensate for Sarah's anger. "All that effort and all spoiled by one phone call after another. Penelope and Angus didn't know whether to eat or wait and you know a soufflé has to be eaten just when it's ready. I'd practiced making that so many times to get it right. It was just too bad, Brian, just too bad." He knew when she added 'Brian' in that tone of voice she was really annoyed.

'I wonder if there is anything interesting in the local paper this week?' he mused to himself.

He saw the daily Post and the weekly Express lying on the table. 'No,' he thought, 'I won't waste the daylight indoors. I'll go for another walk, maybe the same one, it doesn't matter.' He put on his jacket and went outdoors. As he was about to pass the chapel house again, he saw Bert walking towards him.

"Good evening, Bert."

"Hello, young man! We meet again. Going for a walk?"

"Yes, it's such a nice evening I thought it would be a shame to remain indoors."

"Aye, you can feel a nip in the air. But it's very pleasant. I'm just taking Mick for his evening walk. Join us if you want."

"I'd be really pleased to have your company, thanks."

Mick was a black Labrador, sleek and shiny. He fussed around Brian. Bert reassured him, saying, "No need to back away, lad, he won't hurt you. He may be rather excitable, but he's a friendly dog to those he likes. I believe dogs can tell the good from the bad. Mick makes his judgments and you know about them. He is as gentle as you could find and, with children, there is no better. He is quite non-committal, so for him to show he likes someone unknown to him, like you, is unusual. But, one day a while back we passed a chap walking along the road to Bretton." Bert pointed with his hand on the road back past the pub. "Mick's hair rose on his neck. It actually became vertical, it really did, and he growled. Sounded very menacing and the man crossed the road onto the opposite verge. Mick has never hurt anyone, but, you know he is still a dog and there is always a first time. I didn't know the man and haven't seen him since. We get a lot of folk passing this way these days since the motorway was built. I used to know everyone who put a foot down here, but not any more."

"How strange. Mick's reaction I mean."

"Yes, it hasn't happened before and even I was surprised. I thought I knew this dog inside out. I've had him a good many years now, trained him myself. This breed is very loyal, you know. You see this wall?" Bert asked Brian, touching the wall at the side of the road, just past the chapel. It was a blackened, old stone wall. "Well, they say this wall has been here for centuries. Of course, the road would have been lower. It's had a lot of layers of tarmac, and the like, over generations, but this wall shows the original direction of the road. Legend has it that there were stocks just about here, in times gone by, you know, when they punished people that way. Of course, back then it may have looked more like moorland. It was certainly an isolated place so

Heaven only knows what happened away from prying eyes. Over there is the Emley television mast, can you see it? And, in that same direction, west and way beyond are the Pennine hills and moors." Bert showed Brian by pointing to the far distance.

"I think I told you last time we met, about that spooky feeling I had in the downstairs rooms of the chapel. I don't tell many people about such things, in fact, I can't remember telling anyone else. Never enters the conversation usually. Well, it has always been my belief that some poor soul was tortured hereabouts and somehow I was picking up that fear. Now, I am not a fanciful man, but a feeling is a feeling. I can still remember what it felt like, just as it was then, so maybe I am still picking it up a bit. To me that is significant. I don't get the feeling anywhere else. Sometimes in life, certain things just stand out. I think those are significant, although why we may not know."

They sat on the wall sideways, by the bus stop that was near the chapel house, looking out over the field and over the wood to the far horizon.

"Do you remember I told you about that young girl who was bullied? Well, she must have been about thirteen years of age when I saw her sitting on this wall, just here where we are. I was just passing by and I could see she was having difficulty breathing. Poor lass, she was sitting here on her own, gasping. I went to see if there was anything I could do and did she need help to walk down to her home – down the hill there. She knew me, of course, or I wouldn't have startled her by speaking. She replied with difficulty, 'No thank you, Mr. Bert. It will ease eventually.' I asked her why she sat there on her own. She replied, quite simply, 'When I can't breathe I like to sit here if I can. I feel there is more air and I like to look over that view. It helps.' Of course, back then there weren't all the medicines to help severe breathing problems, like there are now. Poor girl, she just had to suffer until it eased. So I pointed out to her, 'There is air everywhere in Stocksmoor and your garden has the same view. Why do you struggle to get here?' "

"What did she say to that?" asked Brian.

"She just answered, 'It isn't the same and I don't know why. I feel I need to be here rather than anywhere else. Here I feel some comfort.' Now, that was the strangest thing, don't you agree? Finding comfort sitting on a wall, alone and gasping? But, those were her very words."

They walked down the hill past the common land and saw where the coal pit had been, deep in the wood on the left. This was now where the wood-yard had relocated. They crossed the road that would lead to Lower Stocksmoor, a tiny hamlet, and walked past a farm and houses. They went just past where the ducking pond had been in mediaeval times and then turned right again and walked along the path at the far edge of the common. Stopping for a while by the gate on the upper path, Brian saw a tree which had a small plaque. He went to read what was written.

"It says it is in memory of a William Smallman." he called to Bert. "Who was he?" he asked when he returned to Bert again.

"He was a man who lived in the village all his life and liked rambling. Oddly enough, he fitted his name, as he was hardly half an inch over five feet. He never liked to sleep indoors and always slept in a small wooden pavilion at the bottom of his garden. People used to say that he always took a cold shower every morning, throwing a bucket of water over himself, but no one told anyone how they knew!"

"Why would he have a plaque? Was he famous around here?"

"I never heard he was, but I might have missed something. I know he went to the chapel. Maybe he asked for the plaque, you never know. You have to admit it's a lovely, quiet secluded place."

They leaned on the gate while Mick pretended to sniff out rabbits in the grass and undergrowth by the few trees.

"I was walking round here one day and that girl I was telling you about was here, just sitting on the gate on her own. She would be nearly eighteen at the time. 'What are you doing here this afternoon?' I asked her. Again she answered with something quite strange. 'I am thinking and sharing,' she told me. 'What are you sharing?' I asked again, as she was alone and so you would have thought she had no one to share anything with just there. 'Oh, just my thoughts,' she replied. 'I do a lot of thinking. I was thinking about the people whom I meet. Do you know, Mr. Bert, I think there are more kind people who never worship at a Chapel than there are of those who do. The lorry men who give me lifts home are very kind and they never attend to listen to preachers. They know I am Dad's daughter and they look out for me in case I have missed the bus home. I am so grateful. That is a long hill, from Lower Oakington to Stocksmoor, to climb at the end of a school day, particularly if you are tired and you can't breathe easily and you have a heavy satchel to carry. And there's my Grandma. She never goes to chapel, and she is the kindest person I know.'

"'Who do you share these thoughts with?' I asked, though, truthfully it was none of my business. But I was intrigued. 'I don't know. No one really I suppose, but I like to come here. I feel that when I do then I can share my thoughts. I'm not mad, you know, I can't see or hear anyone. I don't stay long though – that might not be safe. But, for a short time it's just peaceful'. I asked her if she was worried that day. 'Oh no, not today. Today I am very happy. I just wanted to share that too. I have just got the results of my 'A' level exams and I have won a scholarship that will allow me to go to university to study medicine. Dad says he will be able to make up the rest of my money as long as I am not extravagant. The scholarship means that the County pays all the fees and gives me money for my room, travel and food, and pays for some of my books. At least, all the main ones I need.' 'That is brilliant. Well done,' I replied."

"It's not like that for students these days," commented Brian.

"No. For all the progress, some changes which are meant to make things better, in the end don't really work out the way they are intended. For the lass back then, it wasn't a case that anyone could get funding for their studies. Scholarships and grants depended on ability and application. Anyway, she continued and she made me realise just how difficult a life can be. On the surface she appeared to be fine, but inside she had just a long, worrying and tiring struggle."

"Why? What did she say?"

"She replied, 'Oh, passing the exams is the easy bit, Mr. Bert. I have always been quite bright. Just a bit of studying and I know I shall pass the exams. At least, the ones I have some interest in. You know, since Dad bought a vacuum cleaner, when we were connected to the electricity supply a year or two ago, I can breathe much better. At least, I can for most of the time. But I can still have big problems. I wonder if I shall be alright and what I shall do when I am away from home if I can't breathe. But that is my life and I will do what I have to do despite it. That is, if I can. It's just much harder work than it should be. It's always like having two things to get through, not one. Sometimes it is so bad, I wouldn't mind if I died. I know asthma is dangerous, but for me it's living through it that is so awful. I am not frightened to die, you know.'

"I asked her, 'Where are you going to study?' She replied, "I have chosen Edinburgh medical school. I was accepted at an interview, depending on my results, of course. Now I can go in October and escape from this village. Not my parents or brothers, of course, but I want to have some young life with other people the same age. I have had very little here.' 'Well, I hope you have every success.' I wished her well, very sincerely. She replied, sadly, 'I want to dance to a live band and do Scottish country dancing. I have seen it on the television and it looks such fun. I want some fun, Mr. Bert, nothing special, you know. Just ordinary, simple fun.' "

"And did she go and become a doctor?"

"Oh yes, and she married and had two children. I heard she went back to work when they went to school and then she became a specialist. I think they are called consultants. She beat her illness and, of course, in later years there were inhalers and other medicines to help her breathe. For her, 'Things could only get better', as the song says."

As they walked back on the top of the common, Bert showed Brian where the bonfire used to be every year. Leaving the common they came to the main road. As they walked across the road, Bert pointed to the new housing estate. "There was a terrible happening in one of those houses a few years ago. I can't tell you the whole story, as, quite truthfully, I didn't find out as I didn't want to know. What people get up to is their own responsibility; it is no one else's and they must live with it or die, as in this case. But I gather there was a dispute of some kind or other, linked with some kind of behaviour – I believe it was of a sexual nature. Anyway, whatever, a man was found with an axe through his head."

"God almighty!" Brian was shocked. "Who would think anything like that could happen in a small village like this?"

"Oh, I don't know. A rotten apple can develop on even the healthiest tree if a bug gets into it," answered Bert.

They walked up the hill.

"Talking about people dying. Two young lads died in the village when I was young. One was hit by an army lorry. It was either during or just after the war, I can't quite remember. I seem to recall that army lorries and tanks travelled around for a while after the war had finished. He had apparently just got off the school bus and was about to cross the road, when the lorry hit him. People wondered how it could have happened. I believe he had a brain tumour developing, which, in those days, couldn't be treated. He possibly collapsed and was unconscious before the lorry hit him. We can only hope it was so. His tragedy could be regarded as a hidden blessing if that were the case and prevented him from having a lot of suffering. It was just near where the house called 'Albion Mount' is, at the lower end of the village. He lived in the next house down. And then another died of a heart problem. Their deaths made a big impact on us considering there were not many children in the village."

Brian didn't speak and they walked on, up the hill, in silence. After a while, Bert continued.

"You see that field behind the houses, down towards the wood? Well it was literally covered in edible mushrooms in the autumn of either 1983 or '84. I can't quite remember which, but 'never before and never since'. Mushrooms were just waiting to be collected every morning. For about a week it was like a magical field visited by fairies in the night. I'm not joking, Brian, never in all my years have I seen the same thing happen."

It seemed to Brian that Bert could walk in the fields and was free to roam anywhere he wished in the village. That seemed strange to one who usually had to follow byways and footpaths. He had a local ordinance survey map at home to make sure he didn't trespass. Bert appeared to have none of these restrictions. He commented on this to Bert.

"Well, lad, when you know everyone and everyone knows you and you've been here a long time, it's very different from just visiting."

"Thanks for the tour. I've learned a lot and all of it interesting," acknowledged Brian, after they had returned to near the pub. "You're most kind. I feel I am beginning to know a lot about this place."

"Well, see you sometime else. I have no reason now to visit the pub this evening. Goodnight. Come on, Mick."

Brian watched as man and dog walked back down the road, and then he went inside. He would just get on with his agenda for tomorrow. He had a list of questions to ask in case his mind should go blank, and he must not forget the intrusive phone calls. It didn't go blank very often but just occasionally he would be lost for words. He could easily drift off into his own thoughts. Oddly, he had recently kept getting the odd wave of fear pass through his stomach as if something was bothering him. It felt to be somewhere in the depths of his mind, and he couldn't quite catch it. It was more than just being a bit worried. He was so busy most of the time that he felt he hadn't the energy to investigate what it was. Maybe it was the pressure of work and being tired.

"Bert still didn't show me where he lived," he mused. "Everything else, but not that. I suppose he just takes it for granted and never thought."

2011

» March

Brian drove into the car park of the Stocksmoor Motel.

He was rather pleased with how things were progressing at the Leeds office. It had been a year of consistent and hard work, but profits had been good despite the financial situation. He kept the staff industrious, but amazingly, not often stressed. He had always believed in rewarding good behaviour. Len had taken his advice and given them good bonuses last Christmas. Not surprisingly, they had gradually become a happy bunch.

He had every right to feel pleased – not only for the staff but for himself, as Len had recognised his success and effort and, besides the yearly bonus, he had been promoted. For this purpose, Len had created another layer of management at the end of last year, and, at that time had increased his salary by yet another two thousand pounds. Yes, the hard work had paid off and the staff had soon learned what he required of them. They were a good bunch really. He visited Stocksmoor now only about once every three months. He found he could keep track of everything via technology and had introduced video conferencing. It was very useful, particularly when the roads were bad and he didn't want to travel, but face to face was still necessary every now and then.

He was encouraged that his boss acknowledged his work, as he always did his best. He had been given notice of another rise following the latest audit, which was to take place from July onwards. "I think you have earned another increase this year," Len announced to him, via email last week. He hadn't told him how much though. But any increase was very welcome. It would help nicely with the increase in the mortgage fees since they started putting on the extension last October. It was a single, flat-roofed storey at the side of the house, and hadn't taken much off the garden. It was a bedroom with en suite and was just about finished, apart from choosing the bathroom fittings. Sarah wanted her mother to choose them, as she was going to use the extension in the future, as and when she could come to stay. Of course, Ben's school fees had increased year on year, but that was to be expected.

But, none of his success in business could hide his feeling of gradual but insidious unhappiness. He increasingly wondered if Sarah loved him. Logically, he had no real reason to doubt, but each time he was away from home overnight, he returned with a knot in his stomach. He could feel it building up when he was about ten miles from home, and by the time he pulled into the drive he felt physically sick. But, he was stuck with the long schedules. No matter how he tried, he couldn't alter anything. It was becoming a slog through life with every day the same. Never a let up, for him, with work, as he always had some extra that must be done each weekend, whatever social event or distraction Sarah arranged. He wasn't being fair to himself, to Sarah or to Ben, but it was for them that he worked so hard.

He used to enjoy his work very much and he still did in a way, but there was just too much of it to fit into twenty four hours. He was always aware of having his financial commitments to meet and realised that anxiety was a drain on his energy. Yes, he had a well paid job, but, by God, he earned every penny. Len was a good boss, but in his pleasant and, apparently easy going way, he was 'demanding'. He wanted and expected results. Brian had no doubt that he would become 'expendable' if he did not achieve the goals that had been set. He felt as if his life's essence was being drawn out of his mind and body by just keeping going day after day.

Thank goodness the winter was well past. His bout of bronchitis had done him no favours, as, after two days on antibiotics he had felt he should be well enough to return to work and did. But his cough had lingered. Sarah had been cross and asked him, "What do you expect? You have to rest your body to get better. Antibiotics cannot do everything." But 'rest' couldn't find a place in his schedule. Things can soon go wrong in business. Even when he was coughing as though his lungs were trying to leave his body, he still replied to his emails, though he couldn't quite remember what happened the day the doctor came to the house. He assumed he had sent them all to the right people, as he hadn't had any odd repercussions nor had anything major gone wrong. But, he realised it was a good job he had printed them all out – as was his habit – and filed them, as there were a few he didn't recognise at all!

Yet, where else, how else, and what else could he do? He asked himself that question until it was like a record that someone put on the turntable of his mind. It was mainly when he was tired, like now. He had been up at the crack of dawn and, after nearly three hours travelling, had worked all day in the office. But it was a record that seemed to be playing more and more these last few months. He hadn't told Sarah. In fact, he daren't tell Sarah, in case he heard back something he didn't want to hear.

He would just sign in at the motel. Then, he really ought to have some fresh air, but he felt even too tired to do that and he wanted to feel alert and rested for his meeting with Len tomorrow. It wasn't the norm for Len to come to his office in Leeds and usually it was of some importance. He wondered what was on his mind now. God, he hoped it wasn't more work. Maybe there had been a hidden reason why he had been given his latest, impending rise. 'There is no such thing as a free dinner,' he thought and Len never gave away anything without good reason. He would have dinner straight away, phone Sarah, do his schedule and have an early night. Yes, that's what he would do.

Having retrieved his overnight bag out of the car, he walked away, before pressing his remote control that locked the car and closed the windows. He realised he was behaving like a little boy, but he just loved to hear the click as the central locking was activated and to see the glass being raised as if by magic as the windows closed. Yes, some things gave him a boost. To think, he, Brian T Woolstone had a central locking, air conditioned car and a big house. But the 'boost' had disappeared by the time he had written his name in the register. He went to his room and realised he was desperate to go to the loo. 'What a relief,' he thought. He washed his hands, splashed his face and went to the pub next door for his evening meal. Now, at last, he would have some peace for a short while.

He ordered his dinner from the landlord. They were easily and comfortably on first name terms now. "I'll have my usual, Tom, if you don't mind." He loved the beef.

"Peas and carrots, with a sweet potato bake alright for veg?"

"Yes, sounds great. How long will it be?"

"I'll have it on the table in ten minutes."

"Thanks, Tom."

» July

Brian was back again at The Dun Cow. Another few months had passed by in what seemed like a 'blur' of meetings, emails, phone calls, and travelling. Would he be able to continue working or should he just hand in his notice? He managed to sleep only fitfully at night, but, God, even that was a struggle. And today, well, that was just dreadful. Should he visit the doctor? But, what could he say? It wasn't his headache so much. He was getting used to that, but he just felt sick most of the time.

Why had he answered 'Yes,' again to Len? Why? Was he really stupid? He should have known there would be something new brewing in Len's agenda for him. Sarah was cross when she knew he had accepted yet more work. But, in today's climate what else could he say? He couldn't risk losing everything. He knew many who had lost their jobs in the past few years, and their houses and one, poor John - whom he'd known for many years, even his life. Everyone, except his wife, had accepted that it had all been too much for him to bear. But she was angry that he had left her to bring up the children on her own. As she had commented, bitterly, over the phone to Brian when he had offered his condolences, "It's all stress for me too, Brian, you know. It was not just for him. Now I am alone with it all." No, Brian T Woolstone would keep going. His grandfather, if he was still alive, would understand, but expect no less!

Brian pushed his plate away. He knew he was at fault and not the food. As always the food at The Dun Cow was cooked to perfection. Today, for a change, he had chosen the chicken and leek pie with sautéed potatoes. This was no exception, it was delicious. But, it had been a bad day. No, it had not been bad it had been much worse than 'bad'. 'Thank you, Len, again,' was becoming one of his stock phrases to himself. He felt as though he was slowly sinking in some kind of quicksand and he was having real difficulty in keeping his head in the air. 'That's daft,' he thought to himself, 'get a grip, Brian T!'

The meeting with Len, back in March, had meant he had, since then, had to visit Yorkshire many times at unreasonably short notice. 'He seems to forget that I do all the travelling, not him. He doesn't have to travel up and down those bloody motorways, praying for a clear run, good weather and no accidents. I do that!' Brian thought. Fortunately, the motel always found him a room, even at short notice. But, he could not remember another day in his working life that had made him feel so depressed and physically sick.

Then it was no better at home. Sarah was constantly worrying about Jeanette. Ben was having tests at school and wondering what that was all about. Would it mean he would have to leave school and go back to the one where he was bullied if he didn't give all the right answers? Poor lad had cried himself to sleep, Sarah told him. All that stress for a young child and just because he didn't understand. Ben was too young, much too young to have these worries. God, it is bad enough when you are older.

"Was dinner not to your liking, Brian?" Tom the landlord asked. "You usually clear your plate. If you don't want it I can find you something else."

"No! It was fantastic, as usual Tom, thanks," answered Brian. He really felt 'at home' here. "No, it's not the food, gracious me, no, not at all. I've had a really bad day, and there are problems at home. It all seems to have upset my stomach a bit."

"I'm sorry to hear that. I'll bring your coffee."

"Thanks."

Brian appreciated the lack of questioning. Tom knew from experience that people told him what they wanted him to know. He picked up the local paper, to distract himself as much as out of any interest. 'Anything!' he thought as he tried to switch off the memory of seeing Guy in tears.

'Ah!' He began to read.

> The digging of the trenches for the new sewerage system, to bring Stocksmoor in line with the EU, is scheduled to begin as soon as a timetable can be arranged that is acceptable to all the parties concerned. The exact route planned can be found on the internet www. wcc.com/sewerage/ or copies can be obtained from the council office in Wakefield. Please send a stamped and

addressed envelope requesting these copies. Any objections to the route of the pipes should be lodged before October 1st 2011...

'Why would anyone object to pipes being laid? I suppose farmers could if the route passed through their fields,' thought Brian. Then he read further.

The only reason for this procedure being in the public domain is that the pipes must cross the common land, land that is inviolate and belongs to the people and cannot be disturbed without due legalities being met ...

"Good evening, Brian."

Brian looked up with surprise but was very pleased. "Hello, Bert. I thought you had decided to leave the country. I haven't seen you at all on recent visits."

"Well, there are times when we meet and times when we don't. You look particularly glum this evening, if I may say so. That is not like you."

"Oh, it's just been a really bad day. Well, much worse than bad, in fact. I have had to sack two people and I am not made for sacking anyone. I feel really upset and worried about their futures, families, homes and such like. Finding a job is not easy these days," Brian replied. "I wish I had never been given my promotion. I would have been quite happy continuing as I was. But, no, you do well and then you are noticed. But, as a result, there are more demands. You see, all the work I put into the Leeds office, reorganising it, making the 'time out' orderly, buying new furniture and plenty of storage and such like, has eventually paid off. As a result the staff members are, without exception, pulling their weight. They are really brilliant and the office is doing very well despite the effects of the recession. They work hard, and are rewarded. I have to say that Len is very fair in that respect.

"But, one of his other offices about twenty miles away, I won't say where and anyway it doesn't matter it would be the same anywhere, was becoming a disaster. They had the same opportunities but were making a big loss. I mean 'mega big'. Len announced that his business could not sustain such losses and it was either 'sort it out' or sack everyone there and close that branch down. He refused to take from one branch to supplement another as that would mean he didn't value the work put in by the successful branch. And he felt that this other branch would drain the Leeds resources if he amalgamated them. 'Brian,' he told me, 'I need you to find the drones and turn it round. You are the only one of my managers who I believe can do the job properly.' Just like that. No 'can you' or 'would you give it a go?'"

"And?" asked Bert, listening intently.

"Well, I spent some time there. At first, they all seemed very pleasant and appeared to be working and well organised."

"So?"

"I couldn't understand what was going on. Anyway, one morning I arrived early and someone had left a note on my desk saying, 'I would look a bit deeper'. Just that, nothing else, and not signed. I did not tell them anything, you know, about being sent to sort them out, just that I was on the senior management team and that this office came under my direction. So, I thought I would take advantage of the message, as someone surely knew more than was obvious on the surface. I stayed back a couple of evenings, when everyone had gone home and did a computer search. I have the passwords for all the computers and I don't think any of them knew I am quite as skilled in that field as I am, even if I say so myself. After all, my degree was not given to me. I earned it. They all thought I was just a manager, you know, with a business degree. They didn't know my CV!"

"And?" Bert was still interested.

"Well, there were two who I found were sabotaging the office and the work of everyone else. The accounts and work done by them didn't tally, but they had been quite clever. To cut a very long story and much investigating short, I found that one of the staff had been fiddling the books, to quite an extent. The other who should have been getting orders was not doing anything, basically, but playing on-line bingo and such like. I had to report to Len, who immediately insisted that they must both go. Apparently, he had talked to all the staff about five months ago and given them a warning to 'buck their ideas up – or else'. The others had pulled themselves up by the coat tails and I could see that their input/output had improved.

"But there were two, Guy and Tervell." Brian saw Bert raise his eyebrows. "Yes, odd name isn't it? I'd never heard it before either. Well these two had done nothing but had continued as though work was just a joke. Added to which, one or two came to see me. They were heartily fed up of carrying these two on their working backs and covering up for their lack of effort. I found out that they were drinking heavily, not only in the evenings, but during the day – actually in work time. They would even pop out to the local for half an hour, and after three or four such trips they are not fit for work at all."

"Was there not a manager in the office to stop all this?"

"There had been, but, I gather it was a woman who was apparently harassed and so she left. Len is still sorting out her compensation. None of the others wanted the responsibility or to be bullied themselves. Me, I don't care about being bullied, as long as it isn't physical. No, words just run off my back as I don't respect people who do that. I think I learned to be tough in that way by having my sister. Anyone with a sister like mine learned to cope with any words, or not care. She had a real tongue that could lash. I was surprised she didn't cut herself sometimes. But, sacking these two, well that's another matter altogether. That makes me feel sick."

"Brian, you work long and hard. Isn't that true?"

"Oh yes, I earn every penny and more."

"Quite. Just realise that they had the same option. Since they choose not to work or be honest or whatever, they have to face the consequences. Whether it is you that sacks them, your boss, or the drink eventually damages their health, they have brought it onto themselves. One day people will realise that everyone reaps what they sow; those two had the chance in the office to work honestly and hard, like you. They chose not to. Why feel so sick? They may or they may not learn a lesson. If they don't, then the same things will happen again and again. If they do, they might make a go of their lives."

"But one of them, who's married, told me that his wife is expecting their first child. I have seldom seen a man cry."

"Then he should have behaved differently, shouldn't he? He won't have her long either if he cares so little about her and it will be no one's fault but his own."

"Sarah is cross that I took on this extra work, but what could I do?

Times are difficult in business and I need to keep my job. But, I just get exhausted, I realise that. But, I can see what you say is right. Thanks. I feel better looking at it like that. Maybe I shall sleep tonight after all. It's very kind of you, Bert, to be interested and help me see things a different way. I must say I appreciate your wisdom"

"Oh, it's my pleasure. It's the least I can do," concurred Bert.

§

Next day, Brian returned to the 'other' office. He didn't want to go but he had to. The two men were not allowed in to collect their belongings, on Len's orders. These had been put in two boxes for them to collect outside the office door. One had left a note for Brian.

"I hope you always have enough money to pay your rent. I am not sure I would walk around this area late at night if I were you." It was unsigned. He showed it to the others in the office.

"Whose ink is this? Do you recognise it?"

"No, but I would send it to the police, just in case."

"Fine, I think I will." He phoned the police. When a constable arrived he told him what had happened and gave him the letter. He really had had enough of this branch and he would tell Len so, even if he took off the last rise in salary. Money wasn't worth this kind of hassle or worry. He had no intention of walking round that area in the day again, never mind at night. 'No, Len old chum! Money will not compensate for this risk,' he thought.

» September

Brian arrived back in Stocksmoor. On a short walk down the village, he saw the leaves had changed colour in the woodland. Where had this year gone? After his last visit and the sacking of the two men at the other office, he had kept to his decision and had phoned Len the next morning to tell him he was not prepared to listen to any more of his requests. He told him of the threatening letter. Len had accepted, but thought Brian had nothing to worry about. Brian told Len he wasn't prepared to wait and see. But, after a while, he had agreed to one final visit in two months time, just to check that everything was now working according to plan and the money drain had stopped.

So, today had been that day and he had made his final visit, at Len's special request. It had been the last time they would ever see him at that office and he felt relaxed this evening, for the first time in a few weeks. Len had not docked his salary increase as a result of his refusal to go back to that office – thank God. But, Brian was pleased that even in the short time, the office was functioning much better and the loss of money had apparently been halted. After all, there had only been two errant workers. Len was grateful for his help in sorting it all out. He had recovered his appetite quite quickly after the 'hiccough' and had enjoyed a very good dinner this evening. He decided he would read the local paper. He reached out and immediately caught sight of its main headline. He read,

PROTESTORS BLOCK DIGGERS

In a bid to save the Common Land of the village of Stocksmoor from being dug up, a group from the 'Wild life of Britain preservation society' have combined with a group from 'Flora and Fauna' to stage a peaceful, but combined and continuous protest. They have now been camped on the common land for five weeks and show no sign of giving up the fight.

After the EEC ruling that every household in Britain should have mains sewerage by the end of 2012, the county council have released plans of where the new sewerage pipes, which will serve this community, will be laid. These, in their present format, will cross the common land diagonally.

Recently, a twitcher, Mr Arthur Blossom reported seeing a very rare bird on the common. It is thought to be a golden oriel, not seen in the area for over fifty years. He is taking part in the protest, saying, "There is no need to disturb this land. There are paths across the top of the common land, and in the area that was used for the wood business there is a 'ready made' route for the pipes. They can use those areas without disturbing the wild life. It would take only a minor adjustment to their plans. The stupidity of bureaucrats is beyond belief."

Some rare species of mosses and grasses have been recorded and documented by the Flora and Fauna society. Others have stated that stoats, a declining breed, have been observed, with young, on the designated line of the pipes.

The trenches were originally scheduled to be dug at the end of October this year, but it is looking increasingly likely that progress towards a mains sewerage system for Stocksmoor may well be delayed for some time, unless the protestors are listened to and their views accepted.

The protestors are camping at the four main entrances to the common and local people, in support, are bringing gifts of home grown produce. The protestors are not acting outside the law or trespassing. The land has been used by the 'common people' since the Doomsday book, so the 'common people' actually have the right to be listened to.

The simplest way is to divert the route along the top of the common and then across the land used previously by the wood business. Mr Blossom and many others have stated this solution. That that particular area has been searched and everyone understands it has no rare or endangered species. It may possibly add a fraction to the cost, but would be environmentally acceptable. The protestors they have no objection to this happening.

However, it seems that the planners are, at present, being inflexible, intransigent or, as one protestor put it, angrily, "Bloody stupid!"

Several of the villagers were asked what they thought and their replies included:-

- "Nay, I don't care one way or t'other, whether we get t'mains or not."

- "We are fine as we are."

- "What has the EEC got to do with us and our shit?"

The general opinion was that the planners should 'get off their backsides and visit the common.' There were several other comments on a similar vane.

This paper will keep you informed of events.

'Not as simple as one would have thought then, mused Brian. "What do you think is going to happen with all this, Tom?" he asked, pointing to the article in the paper, when the landlord brought his lager.

"Oh, things always do get sorted one way or another. It's just a matter of time, but it will probably be delayed until next year now. I imagine nothing will even be done until after the deadline passes, you know, no meetings and discussions etc. In that case the protestors will still be there. Then it will be rescheduled. The protestors will be blamed for the delay, but I think that it will suit the council very well. I believe the EEC has given a 'dead line' for work to be completed in 2012, so the powers that be will feel there is no urgency. Most likely start digging sometime next year. Trust me, Brian, it will all have been decided behind closed doors. There will be more to this than we shall ever hear about, you know, getting the money and such like.

"The protestors are right of course. There is an easy way. The men who organise everything just need to put in an appearance in the village and they will see how obvious it is and all will be sorted and work could begin. But my guess is they will know already! One area, used for years for storing felled trees for the wood business for decades will lose nothing by having a trench dug. But, good for the protestors, I say. The world needs such as them. People who actually show they care about different issues and use a peaceful way to demonstrate. I take them a meat and tattie pie every two or three days, you know, a big one they can share and I have told them that they can use our 'facilities' downstairs. You know the ones for the bar. The motel next door has designated a shower room 'for the protestors' use only'. We all feel it is the least we can do, don't you agree?"

"Yes, indeed. Watch this space," muttered Brian.

Brian had decided he would not sit in the lounge area for long that evening. He looked up occasionally while reading the paper. 'I wonder if Bert will visit this evening?' he asked himself. He hoped so. Somehow he always felt better after talking to Bert. Why? He wasn't sure, but he did, without fail. He looked at his watch. Eight o'clock! He was just going to go upstairs to his computer, mobile phone and, hopefully, an early night, when Bert arrived. "Hello, Bert," he greeted. "It's so good to see you. I thought I was going to miss you."

"No, lad, I'm fine. I couldn't get here any sooner, a bit of urgent business to see to. Good to see you too. How are you faring? You look tired."

"On the whole, I am feeling less stressed thanks. Yes, better than I was. You really helped me see that we all have to be responsible for what we do and take the consequences. I told Len what he could do with that new office and I'm not going there any more. But, the other work doesn't get less."

He sat without speaking for a few minutes and Bert did not interrupt his thoughts.

"Actually, Bert, if I have to be really honest, I must say that I'm still not quite myself at present. Always worrying, you know, about silly things. However I try to relax or switch off, I get a knot in my stomach, especially in an evening. But, I don't want to burden you with my, or should I say 'our' problems."

"It's no burden, lad. What are we old folk for if not to be there to listen to the young?"

"Are you are sure you have time, you know, with urgent things on your mind."

"Oh, that's sorted out now. You just carry on."

"Well, Sarah is very worried about her best friend, Jeanette. Do you remember I told you that she's older than Sarah with grown up children away at university? She owns the boutique that Sarah works in part time and they hit it off right from day one. I don't know whether I mentioned before or not that Jeanette had had breast cancer. It's been so disappointing. She thought it was all over and done with. But, apparently, she saw a hospital consultant when she went for a check up. She had to have more tests and was finally called back two weeks ago. Sarah went with her. The consultant told her that not only had it returned, but that it had spread and she had probably only a few months to live and a further operation was not possible. He gave her all the information about the local hospice and she saw the liaison nurse and such like. Sarah thought they were very kind, but, I mean, what can you say?"

"Oh dear, problems never seem to come on their own, do they? Always in twos or threes. But I am very sorry. Everyone seems so frightened of dying."

"Sarah is devastated for Jeanette and also for herself. She has been a tower of strength to Sarah ever since we moved to our house. She lives very near and they became firm friends – literally, from day one. She's a lovely woman, wise and gentle. Ben loves her, almost like a second granny although she's a bit young to be called that. She told Sarah that she was going to close the boutique and organise her finances ready for her children, as she didn't have long left. She divorced her husband several years ago. I gather from Sarah, that he was a bit of a wanderer, shall we say. She had had enough of his excuses and finally showed him the door."

"Seems quite a common thing these days," commented Bert.

"I'm away such a lot and Sarah seems distant, and, well, I'm working such long hours. She needs support but I'm not there."

Bert remained silent.

"I think I'm just overtired tonight. You are probably thinking 'yet again', but it is the pattern of my life. I am going to try to have an early night and hope to sleep. Recently I have been disturbed by dreams that waken me, dreams of being alone and not being able to reach those I want to be with."

"I won't detain you with talk tonight. Off you go and rest. I think that everything always seems worse, whatever, when you're tired," suggested Bert.

Brian folded the paper he had been reading and put it down on his table. "Oh, before you go, Bert. What about the protesters on the common? Do you think they will be listened to?"

"Oh, yes, eventually. Nothing gets done quickly in these sorts of matters. But, it is an important issue and it would be a pity to miss the opportunity that this will bring. It may not come round again. Delay long enough and the money will go elsewhere. But, have no fear, the pipes will be laid. Europe's decisions will override a local council. The time is coming for it to happen."

2012

» July

Brian was sitting at home. Ben was in bed already asleep, and Sarah took the opportunity of Brian being back early to visit Jeanette, before going to her yoga with meditation class. She was spending as much time as possible with Jeanette. She had, so far, well outlived the 'few months'. Sarah put it down to 'her fighting spirit', but she had to accept, in these last few weeks, that she was not going to be around for much longer. Make-up couldn't hide the signs of her gradual decline.

"They shouldn't have tried to guess when she would die. It just wasn't fair. I know they have to say what they know and prepare people for the worst, but all that worry for so long. It has just ruined this past year, completely." Sarah was angry for her friend, and for herself.

They were not going to go to Spain, as arranged, as Sarah didn't want to spend that time away from home just now. Brian understood. He didn't really care and was quite happy just to spend the two weeks in his garden with Ben and Sarah, if she was around. Even the thought of making the journey and all the effort to go on holiday made him feel tired.

He had made himself a dinner of beans on toast with cheese, finishing off with some fruit. Sarah had eaten with Ben earlier. But, it was good to be at home. He put on the TV to watch the news. July 29th and the first week of the London Olympics. Summer would soon be over. Where had this year gone? 2012 was disappearing fast, and if he tried to think about it, he found that all the weeks merged. It seemed only yesterday that they were putting the Christmas tree away for another year and Ben was riding his new bike round the garden.

Despite all the Olympic hype, it was all much as usual. 'What a dark world we live in,' he thought as he listened to the latest angst. He found himself drifting off in his thoughts to the increasing unhappiness that was overtaking him, slowly but gradually, despite his ingrained resilience and determination. It would lift for a while, but seemed like a shadow, dogging his footsteps. When would he be able to speak to Sarah about how he felt? He was constantly worrying, always tired and headaches plagued him every day. He had a general feeling that he was walking a tight rope that led to a place where he would find himself alone or in danger. It wasn't the time though now, to say anything, with Jeanette so ill. Sarah really had enough to cope with, so he must just put on a smile as much as possible. There was no time for self pity in his world.

He had checked on Ben. His heart ached with love for his little boy and his eyes had filled with tears. He had to keep hoping, at least for Ben. He heard 'Stocksmoor' and came out of his reverie. 'Stocksmoor?' he thought, 'What about Stocksmoor?' He knew that the sewerage works, that had been scheduled for last year, had been delayed much longer than was thought possible. But local governmental procedures, with legalities attached, could walk with leaded feet, so no one should have been surprised.

He listened, "... yesterday, July 28th, when the digger unearthed a casket believed to date back at least to the fifteenth century. Then, just a few feet further along the track of the trench, human bones were unearthed. This is causing not only great excitement but has also triggered a major enquiry." He thought, ' At last, the sewerage works must have begun.'

Different people were being interviewed. It appeared that protestors to the common land upheaval had eventually won the day, after their long protest. The plans for the sewerage pipe channel had been changed and the route diverted to a different line so as not to disturb the common land any more than was necessary. Work had been progressing for a few weeks now and the common land had been reached. The digger had lifted out an object. A man, who happened to be standing nearby, apparently watching out of interest and thought to be a local man, observed this and signalled to the driver to stop.

The driver of the digger, talking to the reporter who was 'live' at the site remarked, "I thought I must have caught the man accidentally as he was waving his arms and shouting for us to halt. I stopped the digger immediately and climbed down to see what the problem was. Josh, my mate, came alongside to see why I'd stopped. And there it was. Though it was all covered in mud, we could see what looked like a cage of wicker canes covering a large box. It was all very exciting. We stopped digging and my supervisor, phoned the police. They called in experts who have taken everything that was found to Leeds - to the university department - for examination. Imagine, I might have dug up buried treasure! That's something to tell the grandchildren."

"Would you like to say something?" asked the reporter, turning to Josh who had been nodding violently, in agreement at everything his mate uttered.

"Well, just that it was amazing. We should have missed it but for the local man. Our supervisor photographed us with him, but oddly enough, he had gone when we had contacted the police. We didn't notice which way he went. But, without his assistance I think the whole treasure would have been crushed," related Josh, grinning into the cameras.

"And can you tell us about the report that bones, thought to be those of a human, have been dug up?"

"Yes. While we were waiting for the police to arrive, we'd put the large box safely to one side and had decided to dig just a little further before we stopped for the day. Then, the man who had helped us before appeared again, and put his hand up. He must have just gone home for a while or somewhere and then come back, as he was obviously very interested. We looked and saw the bones."

"Did you ask him who he was or where he lived? I would like to interview him."

"Would you believe me when I say 'no'? We were so dumbfounded that we completely forgot."

"Well, that is a pity, but I can understand you were not prepared for anything like this to happen." The reporter turned to the camera. "We will keep you informed and tell you more when we know more, but a find like this is quite remarkable. Let us just have a word from an expert, Dr Patricia Boreton, who I believe has travelled to the Leeds Studio. She is an acknowledged expert on the fourteenth and fifteenth centuries. Hello, Dr Boreton, can you hear me?"

"Yes, loud and clear. Hello! This is very exciting. I truly cannot wait to find out more. For something like this to happen in my lifetime is unbelievable and quite fantastic." Dr Boreton was ecstatic. "Do you recollect the book written by Dr Audrey Coatesworth a few years ago? It was printed and published in 2009. It is called 'Beyond Mercy'.

Well, this is exactly what she described, and in this very place. I personally am dumbfounded. Of course, we all thought that it was a very good story, but now we wonder whether this is that book actually coming true. She foretold that a casket would be found, but I don't think many people believed her at the time. I know it sounds fanciful and we are not prone to fancy in this discipline, but not only did she predict that a casket would be excavated, but that someone had been buried nearby."

"Let me warn you. When you read her book, be prepared to be amazed, as we all are. Facts, just facts, are our bread and butter. But, if it is proven to be true, then something very different has happened, something quite unknown in human history before. It will surely change the beliefs of the world. So, for many reasons, we are all eagerly waiting to see what the contents of the big box will be and in what state we shall find everything. At the moment it is being kept in a special atmosphere to prevent any deterioration, but it seems to have been prepared remarkably well. With carbon dating we shall know accurately when it was buried. What a find! What an absolutely wonderful find! This is an area of history where every bit of information has normally to be found by meticulous sifting through documents and such like, and to have a gift presented to us like this, well, what can I say?"

"Dr Boreton, so, you agree that this is no ordinary find?"

"Oh, as I have told you, I can answer without any doubt or hesitation," replied Dr Boreton, "Preliminary findings indicate that it is totally authentic and that it was prepared in such a way that it would be well preserved for a very long time. That's all we know at present."

"Thank you." Turning to face the camera, the reporter finished the recording, saying, "We will keep you informed as and when more information comes to light. Now, back to the studio in London."

The news then passed onto something else and Brian thought, 'I'll find out more on my next visit. Tom will know everything there is to know. Imagine! In Stocksmoor! The very place I visit. I wonder what Bert will think.' With that he looked at the clock. Ten thirty. Sarah wasn't back yet, so he decided he could wait no longer and went to bed. He had another very early 'get-up-and-away' in the morning. 'Oh, well,' he thought, 'I might get to talk to her tomorrow, or the day after.'

He couldn't do without his mobile phone, his lifeline, but if he was really, truly honest, the calls didn't really say much nowadays between him and Sarah, other than the time of day or what he had eaten for lunch. Bit of a waste really, on the whole, except for work. But that wasn't what was bothering him. He knew that, but refused to tell even himself his true fears.

§

Brian deliberately watched out for the news for the next few weeks. He was really curious to know about Stocksmoor and wasn't due back to the Leeds office for a few months, but he would go before the bad weather. Leeds was progressing very well. A video conference once a week seemed to be enough to keep them on track with the work, plus the emails and phone calls.

"We are going to Leeds now, to hear the latest on the casket from Stocksmoor."

Brian heard the announcement and took his plate and fork, and went to sit in front of the television.

"I am going to speak to Dr Patricia Boreton at the Department of Historical Research in Leeds. Hello, Dr Boreton. Can you give us the latest news of the find from Stocksmoor?"

"Hello. Yes, the covered box has been finally opened. There is a small wood casket inside. It is all in very good condition, and whoever prepared it did so with great diligence, skill and knowledge. Inside the wooden casket are many articles and a book. But the absolutely astonishing fact is that the many artefacts tally exactly with what Dr Coatesworth predicted would be found. Even the pictures are accurate. It's quite incredible. She wrote an inventory called 'Contents of the casket' in her book. By now very many people will have read it. We cannot believe it and are quite stunned. We shall release photographs of the items, found in the casket, soon so that people can see for themselves. I have been given the tremendous privilege of translating the book and really I cannot wait."

"When do you think the book will be translated and printed ready for publication?"

"At this stage that is impossible for me to predict, but I hope it will be in the public domain sometime next year. I cannot at this stage say how long it will take, but I am hoping for July/ August time – at the very latest. It could be sooner. But these things can frequently take longer than you expect. However, I shall just work gradually through the book. The priority is getting it right. It is actually quite a long book. But, I can report that the parchment is in very good condition and the ink quite legible. So far, I have managed already to scan the text, and I have to say that the story which is unfolding is a chilling reminder that brutality and suffering inflicted by the strong on the weak is nothing new. The scale may be different from our modern day atrocities, but totally dreadful, none the less. As the book was dated by the writer, a journeyman Richard Shaw, and as the carbon dating of the other treasures found in the casket matches the dates given, there is no doubt whatsoever that everything in this find is authentic and true. I have spent many years reading manuscripts in and from vaults and museums, but never did I expect to be presented with this treasure and be the one asked to translate the old English into modern idiom. I realise I shall probably have to alter the occasional word as the original no longer exists, but I shall remain true to its meaning at all times."

"Thank you, Dr Boreton." Then it was back to the studio.

Brian resumed his meal. "I was in Stocksmoor before all this happened. I have a strange feeling that I have taken part in an important piece of history."

Contents – Part 2

~ JUSTICE ~

~ *JUSTICE* ~

A search for truth written in the year of grace 1501

by

Richard Shaw

"Satan feasted on our bodies, but on our souls he never fed"
                                        (anon: circa 1100)

*"Evil crossed their earthly path, but their souls were safe in
the arms of God"*   *(Sir George Shaw 1510)*

~ *Personae* ~

Sir Henry Shaw (Harry) – father to George, Samuel, Margaret, Rosemary and Albert

Sir George Shaw, Lord Lieutenant of Yorkshire – eldest brother to Albert Shaw

Lady Gwendolyn Shaw – wife of Sir George Shaw and sister of Eve

 Andrew – eldest son of Sir George

 Teresa   -wife of Andrew

  Nicolas – grandson of Sir George, Andrew Shaw's eldest son

  Robert – grandson of Sir George, Andrew Shaw's son

  Carolina – granddaughter of Sir George, Andrew Shaw's daughter

  Anna-Marie, youngest daughter of Andrew, married Gerrard

 Oliver – younger son of Sir George Shaw

 Camellia – wife of Oliver Shaw

  three children

 Ann – youngest daughter of Sir George

Samuel Shaw – brother of Albert Shaw

Clarissa – wife of Samuel Shaw

 Margareta – daughter of Samuel and Clarissa

 Hilda – their youngest daughter – married Joseph Kraft

Margaret Shaw – known as 'Aunt Peggy', sister of Albert Shaw

Rosemary Shaw – married Harold Cecil

 Henry

 John

Albert Shaw – the father

Anna – first wife of Albert Shaw, mother of Richard Shaw

 Richard – son of Albert's first wife – Anna, deceased

 Beatrice – first wife of Richard Shaw

  unnamed son of Beatrice and Richard Shaw –died

 Rosamund – second wife of Richard Shaw

  Gerrard – son of Richard and Rosamund

  Sarah – daughter of Richard and Rosamund

Eve – second wife of Albert Shaw, youngest sister of Anna
The children of Albert and Eve:-
    Thomas (? Anna's second son or Eve's first child)
    Mary   (? Anna's daughter or Eve's second child)
    Catherine
    Benjamin
    Elizabeth
    Ann and Emily (twins)

∫

Sir Reginald Kittle – father to Peter, Richard, Andrew and William
Lady Elizabeth Kittle – deceased – wife of Sir Reginald and sister of Eve.
Their children:-
    William – engaged to be married to Catherine
    Andrew – Elizabeth's husband
        Alend Kittle – Andrew and Elizabeth's son
    Peter – Ann's husband
        Miriam and Mark – Ann and Peter's children
    Richard – Emily's husband
        Miranda and James – Emily and Richard's children

∫

Sir Christopher Cecil
Lady Matilda Cecil – his wife, daughter of a Duke
    George – eldest brother of Eve
    Sarah – wife of George Cecil
        Angelina – daughter of George and Sarah Cecil, favourite niece of Eve

    Wilfred – second brother of Eve – inherited the estate when George died
        Hannah (married Robert Crecy) – eldest daughter of Wilfred Cecil
        Geoffrey Cecil, junior – Grandson of Sir Geoffrey and son of Wilfred

Jane Cecil, youngest daughter to Wilfred Cecil
Gwendolyn – married Sir George Shaw
Elizabeth – married Sir Reginald Kittle
Anna – first wife of Albert Shaw
Eve – second wife of Albert Shaw

Harold Cecil- cousin of Eve- married Aunt Rosemary
   John – son of Harold and Aunt Rosemary
   Henry – son of Harold and Aunt Rosemary

∫

Nell – housekeeper and friend to Ann and Emily

Robbie Fairless – soldier who deserted from Church Army- becomes Robbie Cecil
Edward Fairless – Robbie's brother

Captain Stanley Lesley – captain in Church Army
William O'Connor – soldier in Church Army
Annette – follower of Church Army, born and brought up in Stocksmoor

Abraham (Abe) Knott – carpenter – husband of Mary Shaw
   Marion Knott – child of Mary
Helena Knott – Abraham's sister and sister in law to Mary
Phoebe – Helena and Abraham's sister

Joseph Kraft – husband of Hilda

Canon Matthew Crecy – father of Hannah (Ben's wife)
   Robert Crecy- eldest son of Matthew marries Hannah, daughter of Wilfred
   Hannah – married Ben Shaw, and sister of Benedict and Robert Crecy
   Benedict Crecy

Villagers of Stocksmoor

Father Simon – the first Man of God
Simion – an 'outcast', who lived on the common
Bernard – innkeeper in Stocksmoor,
Alice – wife of Bernard
David – farmer, neighbour of Bernard at the inn, husband of Dorothy
Dorothy – wet nurse to Ann and Emily
Daisy – scullery maid to Ann, Emily and Catherine
Will – faithful valet to Peter and Richard Kittle
Dorah- resident of Stocksmoor
Ebenezer- resident of Stocksmoor
Martha – resident of Stocksmoor and friend of Nell
Jonas – second man of God in Stocksmoor
Phoebe – neighbour and sister of Helena Knott
John – boy in Stocksmoor
William – boy in Stocksmoor
Tobias Trevore – resident of Stocksmoor- lived near the Mount
Lucia Trevore – Tobias's wife
Charles Trevore – son of Tobias and Lucia
Ruth Trevore – wife of Charles

~ Illustrations ~

The herb garden
The stocks
The Riders of Death
The casket is buried

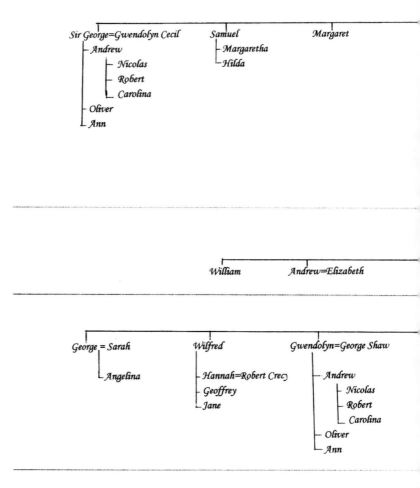

Sir George=Gwendolyn Cecil   Samuel   Margaret
- Andrew
  - Nicolas
  - Robert
  - Carolina
- Oliver
- Ann

    Samuel
- Margaretha
- Hilda

William   Andrew=Elizabeth

George = Sarah   Wilfred   Gwendolyn=George Shaw
- Angelina

Wilfred
- Hannah=Robert Crec)
- Geoffrey
- Jane

Gwendolyn=George Shaw
- Andrew
  - Nicolas
  - Robert
  - Carolina
- Oliver
- Ann

FAMILY TREES - 1497

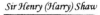

Sir Henry (Harry) Shaw

Albert=1) *Anna Cecil* = 2) *Eve Cecil*   *Rosemary*= *Harold*

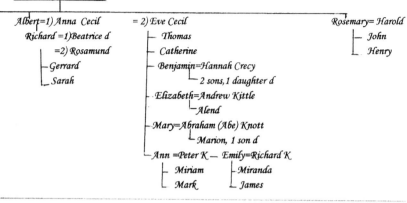

Richard =1)*Beatrice d* ├─ *Thomas*   ├─ *John*
   =2) *Rosamund* ├─ *Catherine*   └─ *Henry*
├─*Gerrard*   ├─ *Benjamin*=*Hannah Crecy*
└─*Sarah*   └─ *2 sons, 1 daughter d*
         ├─ *Elizabeth*=*Andrew Kittle*
          └─*Alend*
         ├─ *Mary*=*Abraham (Abe) Knott*
          └─ *Marion, 1 son d*
         └─ *Ann* =*Peter K* ── *Emily*=*Richard K*
          ├─ *Miriam* ├─*Miranda*
          └─ *Mark*   └─ *James*

Sir Reginald Kittle=*Elizabeth Cecil*

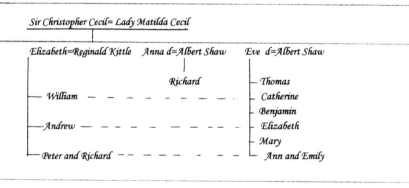

    Peter =*Ann Shaw* *Richard*=*Emily Shaw*

Sir Christopher Cecil= *Lady Matilda Cecil*

Elizabeth=*Reginald Kittle* *Anna d*=*Albert Shaw* *Eve d*=*Albert Shaw*

            Richard   ├─ *Thomas*
├─ *William* ─ ─ ─ ─ ─ ─ ─ ─ ─ ─ ├─ *Catherine*
                 ├─ *Benjamin*
├─*Andrew* ─ ─ ─ ─ ─ ─ ─ ─ ─ ─ ├─ *Elizabeth*
                 ├─ *Mary*
└─ *Peter and Richard* ─ ─ ─ ─ ─ ─ ─ └─ *Ann and Emily*

Canon Matthew Crecy= *first marriage*   *second marriage*

  ├─ *Robert*=*Hannah Cecil*   *Benedict*
  └─*Hannah*=*Benjamin Shaw*

To Upper Oakington, then on to Lower Oakington

Burial Ground

Windy Bank

Route taken by Simion with Mark and James

Trevore's house

The Mount

Charles Trevore found here

To Lower Stocksmoor

Ducking Pond

Farm of Hannah's Cousin

Martha

Joseph Kraft

Nell

COMMON LAND

WOODS

Jonas's meeting house

Phoebe

The Shaw Family

Aunt Peggy

Site of burning of the boats

Simion's Corner

Another route From west

Set of stocks

Dorothy

The Dunn Cow Inn

Lane along which wagon was seen

High Lane

To Sandal

To Bretton and Sheepley

Route from west

To the Hall

Robbie's Guide to Stocksmoor
showing only the main areas and houses

1497

~ *Introducing myself* ~

Dear Readers of this book,

It is with a sad and heavy heart that I start to write a chapter of our country's history. It is a chapter that cast the darkest cloud over my family, but which I also believe may have had an impact for the future and even on our noble country itself.

You may wonder at my title. Let me tell you that I, myself alone, and after great consideration, have chosen this word, JUSTICE, from many that came into my head. But, I implore you to read on and, if I write in a manner that allows information and understanding to be absorbed in an order which belies confusion, then you will understand this choice.

I shall write of many people. In order that you will not get confused about whom I write, a list has been compiled for your edification. I have called this 'Personae'. It is there for your perusal and advantage any time that you may wish to clarify your reading. I have deliberately put these pages at the front of the book, else you may not know that such exists, and thus read with a puzzlement which will detract from the importance and interest of the book itself. I, myself, have drawn a family tree.

I hope that these extra pages give some simplification as you read through the intricacies and complexities that you will find in this story. I would, with deference, suggest that you look at these pages; else much may well be missed. They were my family. To me all is well-known, familiar. I hope that, as much as is possible, it becomes the same for you.

This book is centred on the events which happened in a village called Stocksmoor, in Yorkshire in 1497. I have enlisted the help of a young man, Robbie, of whom you will hear more at a later stage. He will scribe this book as I relate the story to him. He has drawn a map of the village, so that you can picture in your mind where the events happened and where the significant people in the story lived.

Please forgive me if at times I get lost in description in my attempt to portray events that were, in my view, a disgrace to the very name of mankind. Because of certain beliefs and actions, dastardly deeds were done and, until the time of which I write, none could gainsay against the doers of these deeds.

I dare to write what I think as this book will be seen, at this time by very few people. These people agree with me and also know the truth of which I write and they will keep their counsel. Be assured that much of which I write is already widespread and, quite rightly and for a purpose, is open knowledge, but there are some events that others cannot know of at this time. When this book is read, as I belief it will be in a time unknown but in the far off future, then any danger will be over.

When you read it, many, many years will surely have passed, and I can only hope that my language is understood by at least one of you, should there be a change in the spoken word in the country over time. I believe this will, most certainly, be so. In my travels I visit places, even in this county of Yorkshire, where I can hardly understand what I hear. And that is in the 'here and now'. But, I write in the belief that when my book be found, it will be translated as necessary so that people in many places will read what I have written.

My own dear children believe that their Papa tells a good story and, though I have been away from home many nights during their childhoods, they still recall and relish the times spent in the glow of the firelight listening to my ramblings. It is in this rather gentle way and by my example that I wished to instil in my children the values that I hold dear. Yet, telling a story to my children, though usually based on fact, with, you will understand, a little elaboration is very different from writing that which this is intended to be. This is not make-belief but an account of events which have truly happened. I have often questioned God and his purpose, saying, over and over again in my mind, 'Dear God, if only it were not so. Why? Why had it to be this way?' But God, in his infinite wisdom, maintains his silence from mere humans and his mysteries are not known.

I ask, in preparation for your time in reading, that you know that I shall try that which is my best effort. I hope I can do this task adequately, so that you will not be made aware of any lack on my part. First, let me tell you this. I have had no training as a writer, nor have I perused much that has been written. I am a person who would rather learn by asking questions and listening to others, than being someone who sits and reads. But, suffice to say that I can read and I can write. I am assured that my intelligence matches more than a few. I enjoyed tutelage from an early age and for many years, but, it has always been my nature to want to spend time in a practical manner and out of doors, rather than to be studious. So, I entreat that you believe me when I say that, though I start this book with a compulsion which drives me on each day, I have 'some', nay in all honesty, 'much' trepidation.

My main fear in the writing is that I shall not do justice to those of whom I write. Many were people I counted most dear to me. There are others whom, if I have to put my feelings into words, I now regard with hate. That is a strong word, and one that I use very sparingly and never in jest. I would say that it did not enter into my vocabulary, except with one exception, until the events of which I write. But, I would ask that you judge those I write about, not by my own feelings, but by your understanding after you read. I shall try my utmost to be fair and truthful. That effort is necessary even though it adds length to your reading time.

My father told me, on many occasions, that I have the intellect that is necessary should I wish to change the course of my chosen pursuits. I trusted my Papa. I am now going to test his knowledge of my ability. He is sadly, no longer here to read this book, having died three and a half years ago. So I shall never know, when my endeavour is finished, whether or not he would still utter those same words. But I shall try to keep his conviction within my mind, so that my confidence is maintained throughout this task. Finally, let me say that I hope, with true sincerity, that you will be carried along with that which I have to tell you so that you will notice nothing amiss in the writing thereof. When you read, I beg that criticism of style or form is withheld, as I do not believe it to be possible that I can write a perfect book.

Why do I write this book? Why do I feel compelled to do something that is contrary to my normal way of life? You may well ask. So, before I begin my narrative, I wish to give you an explanation of how and why I have started this daunting task and why, however difficult it may be for many reasons, I shall endeavour to do my utmost to complete it to my satisfaction and in all truth as I know it.

§

January 4th, 1501 is a day I shall remember, not just for the icy coldness that pervaded everywhere and made us want, nay need, to stay indoors and gather around the log fire, but as the day I was 'given' the knowledge of what I was required to do.

I fell asleep in the afternoon, after a repast which had filled me with warmth and satisfaction, and during that short time, I had what I consider to have been a dream. I am not someone prone to a vivid imagination or fanciful, no, not in any way. But this experience was different, and so vivid and 'real' that I was made to remember and take notice. Here I will recount to you what I saw and heard.

I found myself in Stocksmoor, the village of my birth and young life. I was standing beside my dear, but departed, father. We were together in an area, on the common land of that village, known as Simion's corner. Suddenly, I heard a very loud noise and saw, to my total fear and horror, a large moving 'creature', for want of a better word, made out of what looked like metal. It was coming straight towards us. I had never seen the like before as, believe me, such do not exist, except in this dream. It was, miraculously, not pulled by horses or any other animal, but appeared to move as if it were alive and had a force within. Seated, in a glass box on what I assumed was its back, was a man holding a wheel. In front of this frightening spectacle was something that I can only describe as a large bucket with spikes which moved up and down and from side to side.

"Papa," I shouted out, being consumed by a feeling of the greatest urgency, "whatever that is, if it continues on its present path, it is going to reach us and will harm us very severely. Come, we must leave this place now, and quickly.

"Not so, son," he replied. Just stand still and watch. He walked away from me towards this metal monster, without any fear whatsoever.

"Papa! Papa! Come back." I frantically shouted so as to be heard above the noise. I was afraid for my father's safety as he ventured forth, yet at the same time, I found that I could not move to go with him, nor could I put out a hand to restrain him.

I could now see that the bucket had dug out a large trench as it had progressed across the land. Then, my father appeared to 'become part of the scene'. I could see that something had been dug up from the ground that was not soil or turf. I looked and saw that a large object filled the bucket and it appeared to be covered by wicker panels, woven and fastened together. The object had not been crushed or broken.

My father put up his hand and the monster stopped. Then, to me, all became silent. The man jumped down from the box and two other men came alongside. I could not hear what my father was saying, as though he had moved through an invisible barrier where sound was blocked from reaching to my ears, though I could see that he and the men were talking together. After a little while, my father returned to be with me.

"Papa, what is that and who are they?"

"Richard," he replied, "You have been taken hundreds of years into the future for a brief vision. That is called a mechanical digger and it carries its own power within it. It is not alive but has been made and is controlled by men. At the time you have just witnessed, such things are commonplace and used, instead of breaking the backs of men, for such heavy earth-moving tasks. I had to intervene, lest the object wrapped in the protective wicker panels would have been broken. I know that inside it there is a casket. In the casket, amongst other items, is a book. You wrote that book many centuries ago."

"Papa, you know that I have never written a book."

"I can say no more. Go back now, and believe me, you will know what you have to do. This future must be fulfilled. I will help you, as and when you need me, though you will not know. Remember, Richard, you are never alone, even though you may feel that is the case."

"Are you not coming with me, Papa," I asked.

"No, I cannot. I have one other task I must do here. But, we shall be together again, one day."

Then, I awoke. The dream, or whatever, was so real that I cried tears of joy at being with my dear Papa again, but also of renewed loss. In the next few days, my thoughts kept remembering the 'dream' and gradually clearness came to my mind and I knew that I must write this book. So, bear with any mistakes in my writing thereof, but know that I shall and must do this to the best of my ability.

§

The year is 1501, the month is now February, and today is the 13th. This day was my dear Papa's birth date and it is right and proper that, after my preamble, I now start this different and difficult journey. I may not understand the reason, but I truly believe that it will be one of the most important tasks of my life. My only hope is that I can 'do it justice' and prove myself equal to the task. Since my dream, my thoughts have been constantly on what and how I should write this book. I have now determined the path I should take and as I begin to tell my, or should I say, our story, I will tell you a little about myself.

I am a journeyman. I have, over many years, travelled around the whole of the county of Yorkshire dispensing potions, liniments and medicaments for animals. I used, in my younger years, to make detours around a much wider countryside and stop anywhere there was a request for help for an animal. I know many of the gentry, as I shall tell you. I say this, to afford knowledge, but not out of any feeling of advancement in social terms, as I need none. My particular skill and love is with horses and, of course, the gentry own many. Of all animals I think the horse is the noblest. People say that I have a connection with them and I cannot disagree, but it is wisest for me to be silent on those matters. They are not understood!

My earliest childhood is shrouded as if in a cloud or behind a veil. Whether this is more or less than other people I cannot know, and now, when I would like to be able to write what was the very truth, I have no one I can ask to verify that which I cannot remember in my mind. But, I am content in what I write as most of the detail of that time is of little significance. My mother died sometime in my infancy, but exactly when I do not know, as I shall tell you later.

She was the daughter of what I can describe as 'middle gentry'. Her father owned much land in the village of West Bretton, Yorkshire. She grew up in a large Hall in beautiful parkland a few miles from where the events, I shall eventually describe, took place. Her own mother, my esteemed and austere Grandmama, however, was from 'top' gentry as her father was a Duke. Her marriage to Grandpapa, Sir Christopher Cecil was allowed as he was a cousin to Earl Cecil, and so was deemed to have substantial social standing. Poor Grandmama, she never forgot her 'station of birth', and I have to say that she might well have been happier had she done so.

My mother, Anna, so I was told by Grandmama when I was only very young, was not a beauty but rather plain, though she had a generous and kind nature. She had three sisters. Eve was the youngest. Gwendolyn, the eldest, married our father's brother, George. Finally, there was Elizabeth, who married Sir Reginald Kittle. It was Grandmama's task to have her daughters married to suitable men, 'suitable' meaning as high up the social scale as was possible. Eventually all were married, but Grandmama was not entirely happy as you will hear. My mother also had two brothers, George, the eldest in the family who had one daughter called Angelina. Angelina had been born when Eve was only 10 years old, and she loved this little niece, more than any other.

Finally, there was my mother's brother, Wilfred, who had three children, Geoffrey, Hannah and Jane. When George died, from a kick in the stomach from an unruly stallion, Wilfred inherited the Hall. Sarah, George's wife and Angelina had then to move to a large, quite grand house in the village while Wilfred and his family occupied the Hall. I say 'occupied', as it was, in truth, a vast place and I doubt whether some doors were ever opened. I was pleased not to have to live there, particularly in the cold winter months, when even the many log fires made only pretence of heating the large, high rooms. No, I preferred a more homely life, rather than shivering in grandeur.

My father was Albert Shaw. In 'nobility terms' he was a mere 'country gentleman', though his father, also, was a baronet. When he and my mother, Anna, decided they wished to marry, Grandmama thought that he was probably as good a match as my mother would make. Despite her superior birth and views on etiquette and such like, she wanted her favourite daughter to be happy. So, she accepted what she could not change.

Gwendolyn, also had an easy time with her mother, marrying as she did our father's eldest brother, another George, and one you will hear much more of later in my book. He had a title, eventually by birth, but, at the time of his marriage, by virtue of his position as Lord Lieutenant of Yorkshire. Even Grandmama knew this brought with it not only authority but status – even beyond many of the nobility. She could ask for no more for Gwendolyn. Grandmama also admired Sir George for his high intelligence, as despite her social prejudices, she had a highly developed intellect herself and could both read and write.

After my birth and my mother's death, her younger sister, Eve, came to help care for me, though much against Grandmama's wishes, so I am told. She thought a nursemaid from the village could be found and would be quite adequate. She, apparently, would have liked me to be brought up at the Hall. But my father would have none of that. Grandmama never quite forgave him. Eve had loved her sister Anna and she loved me, her child. So, at first, she came to live with and assist my father's sister, Margaret, (Aunt Peggy) in caring for me. My father fell truly in love with her. Eve was gentle and very beautiful, rivalling even Grandmama herself.

Now, this match was not to Grandmama's liking. Oh dear no! She had very high hopes for Eve, who was 'not her most beloved but her most beautiful' daughter. Only a duke or even higher status had been on her mind for Eve, and certainly not living in a much lowlier state in one of the local villages. No, indeed! She was so disapproving that, when they married in the family church at the Hall, she had a chill and couldn't attend. I was two years old at the time.

But Eve, though compliant with most of her mother's wishes during her life to that point, did not comply with her in this. She loved my father dearly. He told me all this, many years later, when I was myself about to be married. He confided that Eve had always loved her mother and had been very sad that her mother did not visit her home and see where she and her children lived. My father had built a very good and substantial home for us all and it was nothing to be ashamed of. Grandmama never refused that Eve should take any of her children to see her at the Hall, but this was not the most practical solution for Eve. As you will hear, because of the nature of our society such matters, to my mind of trivial importance, could come between mother and daughter.

I had never known any of this as a child, as from the age of seven years, I visited the Hall at least three times a week, and oftentimes, daily, to have lessons with my cousins. Grandmama was always pleased to see me and so I never thought anything was amiss, but as a child I didn't know to think about anything other than the day or place in which I found myself.

Her father, Grandpapa, however, loved Eve dearly and, being unaffected by Grandmama's prejudices and not having the same, he used to ride to see her and her family as often as he found possible. When Eve died, he seemed to shrink, even to me as a small boy. This once big and towering man, with the gentleness that I have often noticed accompanies a large size of man, seemed somehow smaller in stature and being. I do not think that he ever recovered from her death, as he had never the same robustness afterwards.

In fact, with hindsight, I was very fortunate in my contact with both sides of my family. I would visit my father's brother, Sir George Shaw, who lived in a large mansion near York and stay for several weeks twice a year. My father would take me and my uncle would bring me back and visit his own father at the same time. I found the friendship of a lifetime there, as Uncle George had a son, Oliver, and he was the same age, but for a few months, as I.

The advantages of being part of the gentry, I have found have been threefold. I always had enough money without ever suffering need. I was taught to read and write, though in truth my writing is only decipherable by myself. Lastly, I learned to converse on any level with all ranks of society. Other than that, I have always chosen to commune with people whom I have liked, whatever their position in society, although this I know is not the most common practice. But, for me, goodness in spirit and actions are the most important and I have found those in the highest and the lowest in the land.

As a result of my learning, I have for many years kept a journal of my travels. I did this not only to recall events, but that, should it be necessary at a later time, then I have clear reference to what has happened without using the imagination to create events. I made many entries for the year 1497, the year that is at the centre of my book. I shall use these to aid me in my task of recall. I have written, before this paragraph, that I wish to ensure that I might endeavour to tell the truth as accurately as is humanly possible. That is uppermost in my mind at all times as I write, so fear not that this book is the ramblings of an errant memory or a prejudiced mind.

§

I, myself, married Beatrice, the daughter of a friend of my father, when I was but twenty years of age. To me, she was quite the loveliest creature I had ever seen or am likely to see. She was tiny, delicate and fair of face and with a nature as sweet as anyone could find. But, alas, with her she brought a fragility of body. We married at my Grandpapa's church at the Hall. Though he, by then, had been dead for several years, I always thought of the Hall and lands as 'Grandpapa's'. Beatrice came from a very wealthy family and, though my own father assured me that he would willingly provide us with our own home, her father bought us our cottage instead. Life seemed as we would ever have intended or dreamed it to be.

I still spent some time at the Hall and, though I cannot say that I was employed, I worked with the stablemen and helped in looking after the horses. I had done this as much as possible, from my twelfth or thirteenth year, when I felt that I wanted to help in whatever way I could. In later years, my Uncle Wilfred, who had inherited the estate when his eldest brother, George, died, looked upon my input very favourably. He knew that not only had I gained some knowledge, through my love of horses, but that I would want his animals to be kept in the best of health. He had little interest in, or practical knowledge of, animals other than the use thereof. In my urge to know more and never wishing to waste my hours in idleness, I travelled around to learn from anyone who could teach me about animals. My uncle provided me with my horse for my efforts on his behalf, though in truth it was my pleasure. I always found Uncle Wilfred to be a pleasant man who looked after the estate to the best of his ability, though one has to say he was not a businessman in the same mould as his father had been.

My life with Beatrice, I still find almost too painful to speak of or, indeed, to write about. Yet, without doing so I shall not complete my task as I intend.. I must, throughout this task harness my courage or I shall fail. It was for us, but a brief time spent in the company of great joy, as I shall now relate.

I have come to the conclusion that women are indeed brave to even think of wedlock. After our first year, she conceived a child. After a long lying in and with much pain, she gave birth to a baby boy. He looked so perfect that we both cried to see him. But, he never cried. We thought at first we were the most fortunate of parents having such a good child.

Soon we knew differently, as, if and when he opened his eyes or appeared to awaken, it was as though he saw nothing. He hardly moved and appeared not to hear anything. For a week or two, as this continued, we kept thinking what a perfectly behaved baby we had. However, this never altered and, dear readers forgive me for saying this, but I fear our son had no mind. He remained as if empty of anything, except he would suckle. One dreadful morning we awoke to find him dead. He was only eight weeks old.

Beatrice had never fully recovered from his birth. She had had a continuous fever and the bleeding that follows a birth never stopped. She was unable to get well. She became gradually more weak and pale, and I watched her tiny frame disappear. It was as if her life was being slowly taken from her by an unknown and invisible force. After our son's sudden death she appeared to give up her will to live. You may wonder why I do not name him. Simply, we never did. Somehow he seemed not to want or need one. However strange that sounds, it is the truth and I feel no guilt. He was loved beyond a name.

During those weeks, I called upon my sister, Catherine, who had power in her hands to help the sick as you will hear. She came several times to see Beatrice and put her hands on her and sat with her eyes shut for about an hour. Each time Beatrice smiled and fell asleep. On the last occasion, when she had completed that which only she knew what it was that she did, Catherine kissed Beatrice on the forehead. We both left the room, quietly so as not to disturb her needed rest. Catherine then whispered to me, though well out of Beatrice's hearing, "Richard, my dearest Richard, I am so sorry. Her heart is broken. Her innermost being loves you but wants to be with her son and I couldn't persuade her otherwise. But, in any event, the fever cannot be cooled as her womb keeps the source of her problem hidden within its walls since her laying in. That is something I cannot remove. She is weary and will not last for much longer. The only thing I have been able to do is to still her pain and she will be comfortable and will not suffer." Then, after a while sitting quietly, she added, "This is meant to be, Richard. Go to her while you can. She will know you are there."

Beatrice died just two days after our son, and, as his tiny body had not been buried due to Beatrice's condition, they were buried together. I had to say goodbye to these two, whom I loved beyond human words, and I felt part of my heart went with them. I was consumed with the feeling that, had I not loved her and she me, then she would have not been dead now. But nothing could bring her back.

Everyone who lost a child under two years old hung a black cross on the door at the front of the house for people to see. It was left for six months and one day. You will also understand that it was the normal requirement for all infants who died – babies under two years old – to be buried in a communal grave. But, I had spoken with the grave digger, who kept all the black crosses in a sack in his outhouse with his digging implements, and he agreed to my request that our baby should be buried with his mother. Whether this would have happened if we had not been from nobility, I do not know. Position and wealth have power, whether right or wrong, but, as you will read, this can also be an adversity. At this time I was grateful.

∫

The communal grave for children was a large hole that could contain as many as twenty small bodies, each wrapped in sacking and tied with binding. After witness to the child's origin had been documented and signed, the tragic package, for want of a better word, was handed over and laid to rest. It was then covered with earth. The hole was covered with a large, thick and very solid piece of wood, made of oak. On top were placed three huge and heavy iron weights, each one requiring three men of strength to lift. This was to ensure that no distressed mother, should she suffer any after birth and death strangeness, could possibly move the wooden door.

Women had, on occasion, been seen and heard banging on the heavy wood and screaming for their child, so the precaution was a wise one.

Eventually, time – due to a spate of many fevered deaths – caused the grave to be taken up to three feet from the surface and then it was filled completely with soil and finally grass turf was placed to cover where it had been. Only the black crosses, taken down from the doors after the allotted time had passed, were seen sticking out of the ground like bizarre flowers.

It was a sight that brought shivers to the spine of parents who cherished their children, as, at this time, many of them, even in good health, were suddenly lost to a fever. Beatrice had been adamant that she would never be able to bear losing a baby, particularly if that meant he or she had to be buried in the communal grave. Even the idea gave her nightmares.

∫

I believe now, with the understanding of hindsight, that she realised that our son was not long for this world and was determined she would go with him so he would not be alone. I can accept that, now, after these long years. I know she was so ill that her body could not survive and, I think any one would agree, truly, it was better that she wanted to die rather than to fight against something that none could prevent.

I continued to live in our cottage, which, her father insisted, now belonged to me. He decided that he could never sell it as he would always wonder if Beatrice's soul may come back looking for her son, though I believed she was with him and told him so. As for me, well, although it was painful, it was where we had been together. But, I found I had to spend most of my time elsewhere as I would sink into a deep melancholia of spirit if I spent more than one or two weeks in the cottage alone. It seemed as though Beatrice was there, but I couldn't find her. I hung our son's small black cross from a nail on the front door of the cottage and decided that I must leave our cottage and go away for a while. I truly feared for my sanity.

What should I do? Where should I go? Finally, after much deliberation in my mind, I bought a covered wagon and decided to travel the country, living as a Romany. I packed a few belongings and departed from the cottage. I did not return until the day I should remove the cross, marking each day on a piece of parchment so I should make no error in my last duty for our child. I then took the cross and placed it on the grave where Beatrice and he were buried. According to her father's wishes that grave was in the burial ground in his own village. After a few months I collected the cross and stored it, wrapped in a silk kerchief, in one of the drawers in my bedroom.

Before I set off, I decided to go to my uncle, Sir George, near York, in the first instance, to talk to my cousin Oliver. We are very alike in our nature and also in the way we look so that people would think and still do so, that we are brothers who were born very close in age. We both liked to be outdoors and, in our earlier years, would explore the countryside together, make camps in the grounds, sleep and cook outdoors in all kinds of weather. Oliver likes animals; dogs were his favourite.

When we were between our fourteenth and twentieth years, we would set off on our horses with two saddle bags and find ways to cook, eat and sleep in the open air, when the weather was fine. He can only be described as a kindred spirit. At this time, he was not as yet married and when I told him I was intending to travel, he was pleased to accompany me in my covered wagon. He brought his own horse which he rode and we had a spare. So, it was to him that I went in my distress and greatest need.

I will just say that, though, through the intervening years, we each have our own wife and family, Oliver is still my closest friend and will ever remain so. When we returned, after my first journey with Oliver had ended, even though I felt much restored, I still felt a great urge to travel as I found I could not settle in the cottage for more than a few days and nights, and thus the pattern of my life of wandering, for many years, began.

As I had, by this time a good understanding of the ailments of many animals, I occupied the days well, helping where and when I could. I sometimes stayed in inns, sometimes in the home of people who had known and liked my grandparents or father. It was a varied and interesting life and the people and animals filled my aching heart. Oliver would travel with me for a few months each year, and with him I increased my knowledge of the medicinal effects of plants. Let me say that I would recognise and remember a plant only by how it appeared, unlike Oliver, who knew and remembered their Latin names.

This was his great interest, as it had been since he was young. Uncle George had bought many books for him to peruse. He could tell me so much, that even with my limited understanding I absorbed a lot of information. As the years passed, Oliver became much respected for his scholarship, always driven by his thirst for knowledge. He was known even in the places of highest learning in London and Oxford. But, he never changed even with the adulation he received. It was, as though, he didn't recognise or care about his prominence.

Thus, I became a journeyman. I liked the way of life very much. As I went on my travels I earned a small income which I usually gave to some family who were needy. I had enough and to spare having been given some entitlements by Grandmama; these she had intended originally for my mother, her eldest daughter. She made it known quite clearly that I should have them when I reached eighteen years of age. The family kept true to her word, such had been her influence over them, that even after death she had an imposing presence. Thus, my income still continues and is very adequate for our needs.

As I went through villages, I would notice groups of women sitting quietly by the communal graves, finding solace together and sharing their common grief. I would not have been aware of these, I know, had I not felt something within me that was akin to theirs. Beatrice, nursing our son with his beautiful but empty face, is in my thoughts these many years later. It no longer haunts me nor wakes me from my sleep as it did for many years, but it is a picture on which I look as I walk down a corridor of time in my mind. One day, I hope my present tormenting images will be able to do the same.

You may think of me what you will, but, after ten long and lonely years, I met and married my beloved Rosamund. We have two children. Our love is different, maybe because I was older, but yes, different. She takes none of the love I had for Beatrice and she lacks none for herself. You see that cannot happen as a part of me died with Beatrice. It took me those wandering years to let her go completely, and then I met Rosamund. I feel complete again and Rosamund shares my life now. She is a different person. But, so am I.

When I married Rosamund, I made sure that I was home to be a dutiful husband and father as much as possible, and for most of each year I only travelled within the boundary of Yorkshire. I was unable to lead an idle *life and my work was of benefit. At the time of the events of which I shall write, 1497, our son, Gerrard, had reached ten years of age and our daughter, Sarah, was eight years old.*

§

Having told you about myself I am wondering what to tell you in the next order. I must give you information both before and after the events I am recording and find myself a little confused as to how to do this in the best way. As you read, and if I should repeat myself or labour a point in excess of which you would prefer, then I implore your understanding and fortitude as I persevere. I am determined that I shall tell this story as it was.

I assure you that you will be enlightened in a way that you did not think possible, but, even as I write that, I am not sure quite how that will come about or what I really mean. Sometimes, strangely, words present themselves as if from another mind than my own and I have to write those thoughts. Suffice to say, I feel, daily, that I am driven to write this book in a way that I have never felt about anything before.

I have enlisted the help of Robbie, a boy whose scholarly learning is well beyond my own and whose hand can use a pen better than any other I have the privilege to know. He is of our beneficent uncle, Sir George Shaw's household, and I will explain how that came about at a later time. He knows more about the English language and the written word than ever I could, despite my having years of lessons. I have had no training for this task which I have imposed upon myself. However, I hope, as we prepare this book with diligence, that, should there be any mistakes in the doing of the same, you will bear with us with patience and not be detracted from what I write. Robbie has promised to be aware of any possible lack. You will, by now, realise how important this task is to me and as you read further, you will gradually be made to understand the reason.

§

I wish to put you in the picture, before you have further reading. I have told you that Uncle George, the eldest brother of my father, married Gwendolyn, my mother's eldest sister. Let me now tell you more.

Uncle George was always a scholastic man. He studied the legal system of the land with an unrivalled intellect and astuteness and at the best seat of learning in the land. When only young, in his twenty fourth year and two years before he married Gwendolyn, he was already becoming known for his brilliance in matters of learning and in particular his interest and outstanding knowledge of the law. Some people stand out in any crowd and he did so, not by arrogance or bravado, not at all, but by achievement. Grandpapa and Grandmama were very pleased to accept him as the prospective husband for Gwendolyn. Because of his prowess, he was asked to be and became the acting Lord Lieutenant of the county of Yorkshire for many years and from a young age. His energy and enthusiasm for the causes he espoused were unequalled, and, here and now I will say that I have never stopped being grateful to the Almighty God that I was connected to him, as you will read.

Though he was well born and would inherit a title on his father's demise, his own knighthood was granted personally by the King at the time of his inauguration as Lord Lieutenant. These important men have not only influence and authority but status in the 'order' of the country. The Lord Lieutenant in any county is recognised as having a powerful and worthy position. Uncle George works very hard for the well-being of the people of Yorkshire. He has great influence in the county, but has also many connections throughout the country. By the very nature of his person, he is well liked by those who believe in fairness and generosity but, as with all good men, is hated by the mean and mercenary, of whom, I regret to say, there are many.

He married Aunt Gwendolyn in his twenty sixth year, a union of great strength and happiness. It was agreed in the family, as my father often used to say, that they were well matched. It was always recognised that Eve was the most beautiful, and her sister, Gwendolyn, the most intelligent in the family. She took on the usual role of a wife, by virtue of playing the major part in the running of Uncle George's large household, which she did admirably. But she did more. She also spent much time accompanying him around the county, putting her own thoughts into action as much as she was able. Uncle George was the first to extol her virtues in many areas.

In both my grandparents' households (I always called my mother's father Grandpapa and my father's father Grandfather) all their children were educated. This was not the common practice as many women were thought unable to have the minds that could learn to read or write. It has to be admitted, however mistakenly, that women in houses of wealth who did not need to do any menial work, were thought by most men, and even many women, to be unsuitable for book learning of any kind and would be best occupied with other activities, such as embroidery or musical practice.

Gwendolyn was a great asset and, in some ways, a guiding force for Uncle George and helped him in his work. She was not interested in the law, but in improving the lives of people, in particular their household staff and the local villagers. In addition, she travelled around the county with Uncle George. She would find out information and mix with all levels of society in an attempt to help Uncle George better the lives of those in his care. She, herself, was concerned for the poor and those who would be thought of as outcasts or not of a 'right mind'.

§

I talked to Uncle George about the book I was intending to write and what was its purpose and eventual placement. He is a man who reads on a wide and varied selection of subjects and who has a great love of books. I have indicated already that he has immense knowledge of the civil law of our country dating back as far as records can be found and has collected, over many years, a valuable collection of such books. In consequence, he has sought the best advice on how to store them to avoid damage over time to retain both the print quality and prevent staining or fragmenting of the parchment. He believes the worst culprit, in causing damage to parchments, provided that vermin are not allowed any contact, is dampness.

He instructed me that I should use only his own, very best vellum for this book as he believed it would stand the ravages of the years the best of any he knew, but that it would be most prudent to take strong actions to keep it free from any moisture. I shall remember this advice when I do that which is intended to the book. He has insisted that Robbie, my scribe, must help himself to his personal parchment store, which, should it prove insufficient can be replaced as is necessary. He has given him a key to the necessary cupboard. He has advised that we shall have quiet and be *uninterrupted if we use his own library for my dictation as few others tend to venture in that majestic of rooms. A more generous man would be hard to find. We have been truly fortunate in our uncle as you will read later.*

I am determined that I shall write this book in sections, each with its own heading, and, should you get confused by the inadequacy of my telling, despite my best efforts or the complexity of the events I recount, then you can always return to any chapter in particular and read again to clarify.

This having been explained, I will continue. Maybe you are getting the impression that, though I am giving you useful and necessary information for your understanding forthwith, there is a hesitancy, which is intruding on my actions and my will. I too feel that I am prevaricating in what I know I must write. In fact, as I search my soul, I know that I am, even though, at the same time, I excuse myself as needing to prepare you in some way. You would certainly be right if you are surmising that I am not looking forward to revisiting some of my memories, for that is, in fact, what I shall have to do. But recall in detail I must. I have explained to young Robbie, and asked him to ignore any tears he sees and just be patient with me until I can continue.

I no longer travel in the inclement weather of winter and, the next few months will be occupied with this, my self-imposed task until it is completed to my satisfaction. I realise that I have already done a lot of preparation in my mind and the facts of what I write are still fresh and clear. Now is the time to truly begin and I intend that each day shall be spent fulfilling that which I have to do. I feel I must delay no further, else I miss the 'appointed' day that is waiting to be fulfilled..

At this early stage of my writing, let me explain a little more about the people who were my family. Once this is done, then, when I narrate the rest of the story you will be armed with that knowledge and will understand who it is of whom I write. I shall, of course, tell you about many others outside the family, but that will come later as the story unfolds. For me it is so clear, but I must keep remembering that you, who are reading this book, are not in my advantageous position and lack the knowing – which I take for granted. Robbie knows very few of the people

I mention, so I have asked him to prompt me should I fail in the intention of informing you of that which you need for understanding.

As I have written earlier, there is a 'Personae', a family tree and a map to help illuminate your pathway through this book.

~ Introducing our family and village ~

Briefly and firstly, I will tell you about my grandfather's family, my father's family, as you will hear their names and need to be able to place them all in your mind, as to who they are and where they belong.

Papa, Albert Shaw, was the youngest son of Sir Henry Shaw, known as Sir Harry, and their family home was in a neighbouring village of Flockton where they occupied a large hall. He was happiest when outdoors and moved to Stocksmoor when he was only twenty three years of age when he married my mother. Grandpapa gave him the land and his own father, Sir Harry, had a house built as a gift. It was a house, not grand but neither was it small, substantial and easily enough for his needs, at least initially. He was always an active man and decided to set himself up in business. In this he was helped by his father, who ran his own estate impeccably and was very astute and honest. My father had learned much from him.

His eldest brother was George, of whom you will hear more, as you read further into the book, and all of it will be good. As I have written previously, but I will remind you at this point, he was the Lord Lieutenant of Yorkshire. It was well known that his father was extremely proud of all his children, but George was acknowledged by all, without any discord, as the most accomplished in the family. Had you, my readers, had personal contact with Uncle George, you would never have thought other than that he was the kindest and most affable of men. A different experience was found in those who had to come face to face with him in a court of law. Many strong men have quaked at his feet. He became of considerable wealth, not only by virtue of his earned position in the county, but because he eventually inherited the estate and its income.

My father had another elder brother Samuel, married to Clarissa, and they had two daughters, Margareta, the eldest and Hilda. After my father's father died, Samuel ran the family estate for George, as his duties had already taken him away to York. Though business was not really his strength he did the best he could, and Uncle George made sure that Samuel was funded very well for his efforts on his and the estate's behalf. I never knew Uncle Samuel very well, not because of distance, but because he was not a very sociable individual and he never made the effort required even should we see him. He was much more interested in literature and learning and the ways of business were not really suited for his abilities. But, he had been born an elder son and such was expected of him. My father would have been much better at running the estate. Everyone, including Samuel knew this, but 'order of birth' was 'order of birth' and none thought to consider differently.

Next in the family by age was Margaret, our dear Aunt Peggy, a lovely gentle woman who never married. She would have done, but the love of her life died in battle. She never looked at anyone else with a view to marriage, though many would want to court her. She spent many of her years looking after our family – her brother Albert's children. She moved to Stocksmoor when my mother died. When Eve also died, she helped to care for all his children, probably more than she would ever have wanted. She worked very hard for us all and we loved her dearly, though I have no doubt that we made her life wretched at times as we were not perfect children.

∫

Now I shall tell you about Albert Shaw's own family. As you know, if I repeat myself for a moment, I was the eldest and my mother Anna died in my infancy. Let me just say here and now that my father's children after me were named Thomas, Mary, Catherine, Benjamin, Elizabeth, Ann and Emily, in that order and, to all intents and purpose, we were one family of children.

I will start with the youngest, Ann and Emily as they play a central role in this book.

They were born to Eve, at Yuletide and both together in the year 1462, on the same day as the Church dictates that the Lord Jesus Christ was born. There were only a few minutes to spare between one birth and the other and Ann arrived into the world before Emily. Not many births of this kind appear to take place as rarely do you see two individuals looking so alike. I have travelled far and wide around the country and cannot recall witnessing any others that drew my attention as being as if 'one and the same'- other than two men who you will soon meet as you journey through the book. As I have grown older I fear, and am unhappy to comment, that natural causes for this lack may not always be the truth of the matter.

Anything, that is not the commonest, can be given meaning that in my way of thinking, does not attach itself by normal means. No one questions the many pups that a dog can have at the same time and other animals often give birth to more than one offspring together. So, why should human beings not, occasionally, make more than one child at a time? In my view if God intended it to be so, then who are we to question. Sadly, as I must now tell you, their mother, Eve, a kind and beautiful woman died at their birth. I was then just ten years of age and she was the only person in my life that I knew as 'mother'. In my heart she has that place, which only one can truly call their own.

I last saw her alive on that fateful morning when she had prepared mine and my younger brother Thomas's midmorning repast of a slice of bread and honey washed down with milk. This was our custom as we were hungry lads. Eve used to say that our food disappeared as if going straight into our legs!

As it was Yuletide, I had then gone, as was the custom, with my father to deliver presents of food to those in the village connected, by work, to my father. All I remember is that when I returned, Eve was lying on the long seat at the side of the front room, her face as white as any sheet and she would not open her eyes when I went to speak to her. I held her hand, which was already cold and I called her name, at first quietly, over and over again to try to waken her. I shall never forget the feeling of fear and panic that gradually rose from my stomach into my chest until I could scarcely breathe. I started shouting her name and shaking her hand, uncontrollably, until my father came and put his arm round me and slowly guided me away. When I had eventually calmed, he took me to our main living room, where I could hear babies crying. They were lying together in a crib with Catherine, the next to eldest of my little sisters and only four years of age, sitting holding each one's tiny hand.

"Eve has gone to heaven, Richard," my father spoke softly, with tears rolling down his face. "She has left us these babies as her precious gift. They are so small I fear they may not live, but if they do I ask you, for Eve's sake, to help me to look after them and love them. They will have no mother as no one will ever take Eve's place."

"I will help you, Papa and I will always love them," I whispered. I remember feeling my whole body shaking, yet even in the shock of the moment, I knew I would be true to my words from the moment I saw them. For me they truly seemed to be my Yuletide gift from Eve. Maybe that was the only way I could withstand her loss, as it felt as if she had left a part of herself behind.

They were the smallest babies who were still breathing that anyone could ever believe to see. My father told me later that they were born about seven or eight weeks before the expected date and that Eve had hoped to present him with a gift of a child, alive and healthy, to greet his birthday. Though I was not her own, but the son of her favourite sister, this gentle lady, who had now left me, had loved me as if she had, indeed, been my mother. And I loved her dearly.

I was told I looked the image of Anna, my mother, which fact of course I cannot verify but have always believed it to be true, and that I carried much of her nature. Whether it was that they were beautiful, perfect and so very tiny, or because they had also lost Eve, or because of my own nature, I do not rightly know, but, in any event, they had a special place within my heart from the first day I saw them.

I now, in looking back and knowing all that has since happened, think that from a higher place in heaven Eve gave me this understanding and love for them. She knew they would need me to care for them enough to accept what they would, one day, ask of me.

They were born weighing just over three pounds each and their survival was deemed miraculous. I have to tell you that they had to pay a harsh price for their tenacious hold on life, as they always had problems with that most natural and necessary ability, breathing. But, they never complained and led as full lives as most of ruddy health.

It was several years before I knew what had happened to Eve and this is what I found out, though the truth of the matter will never be known, as Eve took that knowledge with her to the grave. My understanding, which I will share with you, is that Eve started having pain and sent Thomas to get help from a neighbour, who lived down the road. She was a young working class woman called Nell, who came into our house each day except one day a week, to clean our home, and help Eve to cook our food. Thomas quickly met her down the road as she was already coming to the house to help Eve prepare the Yuletide feast. Normally she would have been at our house already, but she had been told to take a morning's rest and come about one o'clock when the feast would be ready. She was to eat it with us but it was her special treat not to have to work on that day – at Eve's insistence. But Nell, being Nell, could not rest and let Eve do all the preparation, so she had decided to come to our house earlier. She was, for me and all of us children, like another member of our family and a kinder person you could not have found. You see, social standing mattered not in my father's household, but the nature of a person was the only importance that we learned to value.

I was told that it was thought that Eve had gone upstairs, after sending Thomas to get Nell, to the parental bedroom to check on Ben, who was two and a half years of age and Elizabeth, who was just one and a half years old, who were having their morning sleep in their large crib. Mary, who was six years, was at Aunt Peggy's house next door at this time. But, it may be that Eve had gone to prepare the small crib for what she knew from experience was an imminent birth, though not expected to happen at this time, as there was evidence of such preparation. She had already put everything in the big oven and I can remember the smell of the food cooking ready for our feast when we returned to the house.

Whatever the truth, when Nell came rushing in, she found Eve on the floor at the bottom of the stairs and she was unable to rouse her, though she was not yet dead. Nell noticed that Eve had a small sprig of holly in her hand and that one of the paintings on the stairwell was twisted out of its usual position. She may have been trying to decorate that picture, as this was also a tradition at Yuletide, and accidently slipped while doing that task, or may have tried to stop herself from falling by grabbing the picture and dislodging the holly. But, no one will ever be sure. But, suffice to say that shortly after Nell arrived the two babies were born. Eve died from the loss of a massive amount of blood, enough that life could not be sustained. She had a cut on her head and it was decided that she hit her head against one of the steps or handrail during the fall. I was told that she never knew she had had the babies.

In such a household, with other young children around, some pretence of normality had to continue. Ben and Elizabeth were crying for their Mama and were hungry. I remember that Thomas was so affected that he could not speak and from that day onwards he often had problems saying his words, particularly if he was flustered in any way. Mary, who had been in Aunt Peggy's house when the babies were born, came to eat with us, as did Aunt Peggy herself. I remember watching Mary. She just sat on her chair, white faced and speechless. She did not cry about Eve, but neither did she eat anything for three days despite Aunt Peggy, Nell and our father's supplications.

Nell, in her practical way served all the children with their food, and sat with us at the table, helping Elizabeth who could not feed herself. In all the confusion and distress everything had become very overcooked, but Thomas and I ate our plates clean. You see, nothing as trivial, as whether food was cooked correctly, mattered any more on that day and for a long time afterwards. It was our saddest day ever, until we grew up into men.

Uncertainties are common in our lives and we have to accept that we cannot always get the answers that our inner being needs in order to make the sense our minds crave. So, we shall never know if Eve died as a result of a fall or the unnatural progress of the birth. My father told me that they had not known she was to have two babies at the one time.

Thirty five years later these two sisters were in dire straits and needed help. As you will read, only two in the village came to their assistance and you may then wonder why that could be? If two could try to help, could not others have done so? As no one else did so, the answer must be, 'No', and I can offer several reasons why that could be, but, in doing so, I offer no blame. It has taken time for me to fully understand the events that I shall later narrate, but as I proceed, I will take time to give you necessary information. To some readers what I write may appear strange and to others maybe not, but in every event what I write will be true, without exaggeration or falsification.

Sadly, I have to tell you that these two gentle, small and kind women had to face a degree of prejudice and ignorance all their lives. That saddened all those who loved them more than it appeared to affect them. If it did concern them, they made little of it. They had a self-sufficiency and closeness together that seemed to more than compensate them for their circumstances of birth, which caused such problems, and they were the happiest of girls. I will now tell you more so that you, who are reading this story, will not have to ask questions that have no answer when I am not there to fulfil that request or need.

As their mother, Eve, had died and, as they survived against every prediction, our father had to employ a wet nurse. She was called Dorothy. She was the young wife of the local stonemason. As he did much work for my father's business they lived in one of his cottages. Sadly, she had given birth to a baby girl who, having had but six months of her life, had died. She had had a fever which caused many and long coughing bouts, during one of which she had stopped breathing and had not started again. She had, to that time apparently, been thriving well. She died just three days before my sisters were born and so Dorothy had plenty of milk to feed both the tiny babies.

Possibly because my father was also quite distraught, as was she, or because of her kindly nature, she could not bear to see two more children die. She agreed, when asked, to feed them and she fed them with a willingness of a woman who only wished to be a mother. Her devotion, thereafter to my sisters, was as if they were her own. She never had any more children and devoted her life to our family. As a reward for her immeasurable care of his tiny daughters, she and her husband continued to live, free from any tithes, in their cottage in the village – at my father's decree. She was, thereafter, always welcome at our house and became part of our daily lives.

I remember clearly, one particular morning, when Dorothy told us all what I shall now recount. She had been feeding the babies in the darkness of the middle of the night, lit only by a candle, and became aware of what appeared to be a light in the corner of the room. As she looked, she saw a *lady in white, holding one small baby in each arm and she was smiling. Though bemused, Dorothy was not frightened. The lady stayed for only a few minutes and Dorothy, in her mind, heard a simple, 'Thank you.' Dorothy recognised the vision as Eve, their mother. You can believe or not. That will make no difference to the facts.*

She appeared again to Dorothy on the next Yuletide, the evening of my sisters' first birthday, when she had just put them to bed. She had put out the lamp and was sitting with my sisters in the darkness until they went to sleep. She saw their mother come through the wall into the room. She simply walked up to their large crib, leaned over and placed a kiss on each one's forehead and touched their head with her hand. Then again, Dorothy heard her speak the words, 'Well done.' She then walked out the way she had come.

Before you think that Dorothy was of a rather fanciful or deranged mind, let me assure you this was not the case. She was of a sensible nature and had a tough constitution, more than most. I know, from what I was told, that she had had a harsh upbringing. I say was, as, though Dorothy saw her beloved girls grow up to adult years, she died in 1490 of a bad chest ailment and she could not breathe. Catherine gave her as much ease as possible, but she had been destined to be called to her maker and no help would suffice. Ann and Emily in particular were grief stricken. They loved this good and kind woman. Though she was from a different and lowly station in life as governed by the ways of our land, she meant more to them than all the nobility from Grandpapa's Hall put together. Neither of them had time for what they called 'peacock feather' people.

However, to return to what I was recounting before I digressed. Enough for me to say that Dorothy talked about her experience to a neighbour who was not quite as discreet as one would have hoped. This woman was never happier than when she was telling as much information, as possible, to any who would listen. Dorothy, you understand, on the contrary, had a mind that thought no ill of anyone. But, this neighbour unfortunately happened to call the very next morning. She then, true to her nature, told another. Soon the whole village knew what had happened. It was, indeed, unfortunate that she knocked on the door while Dorothy was still bemused. As you will realise, this kind of 'appearance' for want of a better word is, at the very least, unusual.

Poor Dorothy was mortified and offered to stop coming into our home. But our father, of course, would not hear of it. He told her that those who spread malicious rumours show themselves for what they really are, and, that we all have to learn as we live our lives. He told her that we seldom know what the lesson should be until we have to learn it. I can say, with the confidence that comes from knowledge of Dorothy, that had she known it would eventually reach the man of God in the village, Jonas, she would have uttered not one more word for the rest of her life.

§

Let me just digress briefly and tell you a little about Jonas, although you will hear more at a later time. At that time, in Stocksmoor, there was a man who professed to be 'of God' and who led any worshippers in the village. He was a man called Jonas. Because they had been born on the same day and on the day that Christ himself was born, he decried their birth and refused to give his blessing to their naming. In fact, he did more, much more.

Eve had not gone to the early morning Yuletide worship at his meeting house on the day that they were born. I had heard her say to Papa that she could not risk sitting on the narrow bench in her state as she feared she may unbalance and topple off. They had laughed together, in the way that they often did. Jonas gave his opinion that Eve was punished for this lack of fervour and reverence to Christ the Lord. Not only that, but he publically blamed the two innocent babes for their mother's demise and he made sure that his attitude spread to others.

I will tell you that Papa heard what Jonas had tried to make people believe and never darkened the door to his meeting house again. No, Papa changed the day that Eve died. He remained kind, and he was always a loving father, but his beliefs in God were altered for ever.

So, dear readers, you will understand that Ann and Emily's start in life was difficult in itself and fraught with prejudice from the beginning. Despite their kind and gentle natures, Jonas ensured that many who came in contact with him, carried a deep seated 'doubt' or even suspicion about them which was stronger than their belief in their own judgement and observations. Such is the frailty of many human minds, so that fear of

God can dominate their thinking and reasoning. Jonas was well versed in creating this fear, deliberately.

Now, let me come back to Dorothy. The news had escaped our home and once Jonas had heard about the visions, he let it be known that these 'evil apparitions' as he called them, merely confirmed his view that evil had come into the village with the babies, and that is why their dear mother was taken. He conveniently forgot his prior judgement of Eve. He also let it be thought that evil must now have their mother in its power, or else she could not appear in this way. He made the whole episode last a few weeks with his 'words of holy wisdom' until no one would ever forget them.

∫

Ann and Emily also became to be regarded as 'different' for yet another reason. Believe me or not, yet I speak the truth when I tell you that, until they reached the age of four, they never spoke a word. Not one word. We knew they were able to understand as we could request them to do something, and they had no problem. They were very busy little girls and spent most of their time either with Dorothy or at Nell's ankles following her around. We knew they could hear. They laughed together, and seemed to know exactly what the other wanted – or even that which she was thinking – but not one word did they utter. Strangely, Catherine also would laugh with them without talking as though she too understood, though, of course, she talked to everyone else as normally as we did.

One day, when they were four years of age they were playing in the garden with our small dog, a lively, little creature, which we all loved. I was in the house, with our father and Thomas, when suddenly we heard loud barking, screaming and shouting. Our little dog had been savaged by a large, rough and untrained dog from lower down the village which had been roaming free and had come into the garden from the field. It appeared that our dog, had immediately tried to protect the two girls and had fought the big dog, but was mortally wounded in so doing.

The two girls, who were always silent, were screaming, "Go away! Go away!" Dorothy and our father rushed immediately out into the garden. I stood with Thomas, frightened beyond belief for my little sisters who had been knocked to the ground by the big dog, before it turned its attention on our little dog. I love dogs and all animals and my life's work has been tending to their ills and needs, but I have to say that 'rather the dog dead than my sisters'. Dorothy reached the girls first and snatched them up into her arms. The dog turned on her and took a bite at her leg leaving Dorothy bleeding. Fortunately, our father managed to pick up a gardening fork, that he had been using the day before, and beat the dog off. It ran away, leaving everyone in quite a state of shock. Dorothy had a very sore leg for several months, but in time she recovered.

Suffice to say that the people, who owned the savage dog, were reprimanded severely by Uncle Wilfred from the Hall, whose house they lived in, when my father informed him of what had happened. They were told that either they left with the dog or the dog alone left the village. Where it went, no one enquired. I have to say that I had always thought it a nasty beast. I have to admit that this one, like some humans, was an exception to my universal approval of animals. It is a fact that all the villagers felt relief when it no longer walked down our road and in our gardens. Its owner, I briefly comment, was one of the least kindly people in Stocksmoor, but I need spend no further time on him as he left shortly afterwards. None knew or enquired as to his further or future whereabouts.

These shouts were the first, but I have to say, not the last words that my sisters spoke, as following that they became very good at talking, and not so good at stopping. Please understand, I jest, as their chatter and laughter brought a fairly continuous beam of light into the house, dimmed only when they suffered the breathing problems when they had a chill or, even worse, on occasion.

§

Maybe a few words about the two men of God who lived in the village during this story will be useful at this time . Firstly there was Father Simon and then Jonas.

I wish to write this book with as true honesty as is possible, but I have to say that I loved one and disliked the other, Jonas, intensely. When you read what I have to say about Jonas and his attitude to my little sisters, not only at their birth but throughout their lives, I would be surprised should you think differently yourself about him. But, I will tell you all so that your judgment is your own.

I am a man of a kindly disposition, being much like my father, yet people have told me that my mother was also of a gentle and kind nature. If kindness is inherited, rather than learned or practised from influence and example, then I was given that quality from both my parents. Yet, I believe that I have myself made the decision about how I behave through thoughts and reasoning of my own. I hate to see suffering or pain in any living creature, though, as you will hear, even that most deep and honest belief could not be sustained in the face of certain events. I too 'walked past on the other side', on one occasion as you will eventually read. You, my readers, are free to judge me at that time according to your own self's ways, but I feel no shame in so doing.

Let me tell you that before Jonas was sent to minister in Stocksmoor, there was in the village a man of God whom I remember with deep affection. He was called Father Simon. If all men of God were like Father Simon, then people would believe in the scriptures with more ease, and, I am certain that the world would be a happier and more peaceful place, where the poor and destitute would be looked after with care and love.

He lived the life that he preached and all the villagers loved this man, and most felt as though he belonged in their own family. Many attended his meetings at least once a week. His meeting house, where he also lived, was a place where people would gather just to talk and spend a few minutes in his presence to get renewal of flagging spirits. He was given produce from the gardens and, even as a small boy I knew that here was a 'good' man. There were two men who had a profound influence in my life as a young boy, my father and Father Simon.

During the time that Father Simon was with us, there came to the village a young lad. He was maybe of twelve or even fifteen years, with a mass of red/orange coloured curls. He was small, dishevelled and dirty, his spine appeared twisted and he did not speak. Whether he could hear or not, no one ever knew and it was assumed not. He walked with a jerky step, arms flailing out in different directions. From whence had he come? We did not know and he could not say. No one in their travels ever brought back news to enlighten us. Neither did anyone ever come looking for him. But once in the village, he stayed. He would disappear for a week or more, but always returned.

There was a large area in the village designated since anyone ever knew as 'The Common' and as this belonged by the law of the land to 'the people', none could stop him sleeping or walking there, though some would try. No one could build on this land, but he had neither the will nor the means to do so. Some of the villagers were frightened and shooed him away if he came near to their cottages. He was seen as a strange young man and appeared needing of ridicule by many. He tended to stay in the far upper corner of the common and, as far as anyone knew, he spent much time there and slept amongst the plants and trees.

Now, Father Simon saw and heard all that was happening in the village; little of any note passed his watching eyes. He took food to this lad and showed him where he lived. He started putting the food by his own gate, and eventually the lad would come to his house to eat if the weather was very wet. One day Father Simon went round every house in the village and asked them to put any left over food from their pans out in a covered bowl at their gates or by their front doors so that the lad should always have enough food. He asked them to protect the food from the birds or wild animals as this would make the food unsuitable and might cause it to be wasted. "I could never eat food that a carrion crow had picked at or a pig had snuffled. So tell me, why should he?" His tone was such that they could not ignore his words.

He told them that Christ and our Almighty God would love this man as he loved them. One day he sent a message round the village. It asked, nay 'gave an order', that he wanted an exemplary attendance the following afternoon at his meeting place. Most people in the village dutifully turned up at the appointed time such was the respect they all had for him. He asked them to, "Please wait a while," and then he went out of the back door of the meeting place. Most waited patiently, though I have to say that some became a little restless, particularly the men who felt that their rightful places, at that time, were at their work and not sitting in the meeting house. Let me say that I was taken there by Eve, and, though only nine years of age, I remember what happened, very well.

We sat on one of the benches for what, to me, seemed a long time. Then Father Simon came into the room with the lad by his side. His hair and face were clean and he was wearing a coat that I recognised as one that my father had had for a few years. It was thick, long and rather too large for him in every way, at the time. However, though he remained small in stature throughout his life, he naturally grew somewhat taller, though never fatter, and, I have to say it served him well for many years after. Everyone gasped. We could hear someone at the back of the meeting place make a snorting sound. We all looked round as a woman stood up and started to walk to the door.

"Sit down in your seat, Dorah, immediately."

With no please or thank you this time, Father Simon spoke to her in a voice no one had ever heard before.

"You are disturbing the peace of this room and you will not hear what I have to say which is of immense importance to you as well as to everyone else."

Dorah, with a very red face and appearing tearful as all eyes turned to watch her, returned to her seat with her head down. No one else moved. Whether they felt the wish to leave or not, I do not know. The room was silent. I have to say, here and now, that henceforth from that day, maybe in penitence or remorse, Dorah put out a fresh loaf of bread for Simion every baking day each week until she became too infirm, many years later. She continued this practice even after Father Simon had departed this life, as if he could still observe or chide her from 'the beyond', where she was sure he would have been safely taken. At all events, she didn't take that risk.

"Dear people of Stocksmoor," began Father Simon. "It has been my calling for these many years to minister the word of our Almighty God to you all. I have loved each and every one of you as if you were my family. If my teaching has had any worth at all or been understood as having meaning, then you will all accept that which I now request. From this day forward, I ask that this young boy will be accepted as being part of this village. He is one of God's children and as such has become part of my family. I regard him now as my son. I expect you to look after him accordingly while I am here, and to continue in that service after I depart this life.

"Mr Albert Shaw has given him this coat and I have given him a blanket to help him to keep warm. He refuses to accept even my floor on which to sleep and it seems that he wants or needs to be free. But, look at these!"

He took the lad's ankle in his hand and took the boot off his foot and held it up to the people watching. It was more hole than boot.

"These can hardly be called boots. Can they? Dorah, come here. Pass this round so that everyone is sure to see and never forget," he ordered. Dorah, with fear and tears still in her eyes, took the boot from Father Simon and passed it, as quickly as she could, to the first person she came to.

"I shall expect that his feet are better shod before the day is out. I know the kindness of your hearts. And, finally, my sisters and brethren in Christ, you were all given names soon after you were born. This lad may or may not have a name. I have heard that he has been called many things since arriving at this village, which I wish not to repeat nor hear that they have been spoken again, even in jest. So, I have decided that he shall be called 'Simion', a slightly different name to mine, but sufficiently similar so that none may forget this day or my request to you all."

He took Simion, as I shall now refer to him in the book, to the door. Simion fled. Father Simon kneeled to pray at the small altar.

"Almighty God, you have sent this boy Simion into our midst. Only you know what purpose you had in guiding him to choose our village. We do not question why he must suffer the indignity and pain of his affliction, or to be as if an outcast, as that is not in our understanding. I pray you will help these dear people to accept him into their midst and may this village be his home and refuge for as long as you ordain. Bring kindness and care into his path, I pray, for the sake of your son, Jesus Christ. Amen.

"Thank you all. Simion has no home nor does he appear to want one. I think we have all noticed that he has chosen to live in the far corner of the common land. I suggest we call it 'Simion's corner' so that we all know he belongs here and has his own place in our village."

And so, it came about that that part of the common land had its own name. For a few years, though Simion continued to live his life in the outdoors, he had food and drink and the villagers would give him cast-off woollens and shoes for which they had no further use, for whatever reason. He continued to spend most of his time in his corner and, after a year or two, people from surrounding villages also knew this area by its

name. There were none of desperate means or evil intent in Stocksmoor in those days and none hurt Simion, though I have to say that gradually only a few continued to venture to that corner of the common land. So, he was left alone. The village had its problems, as had anywhere else and the people were far from perfect, but under Father Simon's guidance it had, over the previous twenty years, been a more peaceful and generous village than most.

Sadly, only a few months after this event, Father Simon died in his sleep. All knew he was of a good age, but the village mourned the loss of their guide. And, sadly, I record that over the next few years the atmosphere in the village changed. Nothing dramatic or sudden, but, as if by stealth an alien, though largely invisible, atmosphere entered into out midst. Whoever in the church hierarchy made the decision to send Jonas to replace our dear Father Simon did the greatest disservice to the village that could possibly have been done. I have to say that it was his presence that brought about the gradual, subtle change. Although he was sent by the Church, accepted and trained as a man of God, I find it impossible to attach the name 'Father' to him. So I shall always refer to him simply as 'Jonas'.

§

Jonas was a young man of about, I would suppose, twenty years when he arrived, and it was the year of the Yuletide when my youngest sisters' were born. The villagers soon made their minds up about him, and gradually, even within that first year, the meetings were attended by fewer and fewer people. He did not preach the same message as Father Simon. Oh, the words may have been similar, and the texts from the Bible the same, but the meaning never came from his heart and certainly didn't reach the hearts and minds of the villagers. Eventually only five or six would attend regularly.

I disliked him when I first saw him and I never changed my opinion of him on further acquaintance, though I have to say that I kept away from him, as much as was possible in a small village, without showing obvious avoidance. It was something to do with how he looked at me; it made my spine shiver in a fearful way. That is the only way I can explain it. I never discussed this with any of the other boys in the village or my father, but as I grew older and more knowledgeable I realised that my fear was justified and that I was not alone in my opinion.

I heard many say that he was 'unnatural' and 'different', but I did not know what was meant as no explanation went with the words and I did not care to ask. But, suffice to say that, for me, there are certain things in this life that I do not understand, and nor do I want to understand. That may be a weakness on my part, but I am who I am, and I prefer to leave some knowledge unknown. But, I mention it, not to let me be accused of an idle tongue that has nothing better to say, or that I am of a prejudicial nature nor yet that I am antagonistic to people of different inclinations. No, not at all! I comment on this information because it became of importance in what happened in later years.

I try to judge people, if I must, on their behaviour to others, and on that belief I tell you what I think about Jonas. I value kindness more than any other quality and, though I practise no religion as set out by the Church, I believe that Christ would wish kindness to be the guiding force in every being on this earth. I never knew Jonas to be kind or caring in any way. He spread dissent around the village with a quiet but obsequious manner. Words are powerful, and after he had been amongst us for a few years, the gentle teachings of Father Simon had been eroded in many ways.

∫

Let me digress somewhat and write more about Simion, who felt the effect against him of Jonas's teachings, as much as Ann and Emily.

It took time, but poor Simion gradually became an outcast again, except to a few. My family, Nell, Nell's friend Martha and Bernard at the inn and one or two others continued to give him food regularly and kept a watch that his feet were shod and he had warm woollens. These were naturally good and generous people. My sisters, Catherine, Ann and Emily carried food to him, regularly from our family dining table when they were children, without any prompting or asking on the part of my father or Aunt Peggy. Occasionally I would go with them, and saw that, if he was there, they would sit with him. They never showed even the slightest fear or revulsion at his strange appearance, though, by now, there were many whose example they could have followed.

When they were old enough and cooked themselves, they would take a bowl of food from our father's kitchen to his corner. But, in case there was food to spare or he was not there, a wooden box with a lid, left in the place where he usually sat, would keep the food safe from any animals until he had returned or the food was eaten.

As they grew older, Ann and Emily would talk together to him, as though he could understand while Catherine never spoke but sat silently as if in contemplation. Simion would, of course, say nothing, but he never ran away from them. I witnessed this many times. I was always left with a suspicion, nay almost to the point of conviction, that, though he couldn't hear a word of what Ann and Emily were talking about, Catherine managed, somehow, to communicate with Simion in such a way that he understood their conversation. I pray it may be so and can only be thankful for my sisters' kindness, otherwise his life would have been one of total isolation and deprivation. In later years, I once asked Catherine about Simion and how my sisters chatted to him while she didn't say anything.

She answered, "Not everything is as it appears, Richard."

I asked, "What do you mean, Catherine?"

"Richard, my dear brother Richard, you have a kindness in your soul. It is not so with everyone as you know. Sometimes our ears and eyes are not sufficient for our need. Do you not think that is true?"

"Catherine, my dear sister Catherine," I imitated her in return, though quite bemused, as I oft times was, by what Catherine would say. She had an intellect far beyond my own, though she never imposed such on anyone, being of a reticent and quiet nature. "My own mind is not sufficient for my need just now. Though I hear your words, I do not understand what you say. I was speaking about Simion."

"Yes, I know, but sometimes that is how it should be."

She changed the subject of our discourse, and I had had no enlightenment from her answers. I did not ask again. When my sisters left the village for the few years of their marriage, Catherine took Simion some daily food and then when Ann and Emily returned to the village, after their husbands' deaths, they all continued this kindness, each day, until their deaths. In their minds, he belonged to their family, as much as he would or could *allow. I know my father would have given him a room had he been able to accept.*

After Father Simon had cleaned his face and hands before taking him to the meeting which I have described, Simion kept himself as clean as anyone could expect, though he was always dishevelled and wild looking. As he got older, his mane of tangled hair was matched by his large beard. The red colour of both gradually turned to pure white as he entered his middle years. Maybe his body was aging more rapidly than most with the harsh life he lived, who can tell. He was seen washing at the village pump, and the sound of splashing had been heard on the darkest of nights in the pond, though that may have been one of the grazing animals or a visiting wild animal.

One day I remember clearly. I was visiting my sisters, I cannot remember whether it was just before or just after I married Rosamund, but suffice to say that their sons Mark and James had just begun to walk, yet in an uncertain manner. We went onto the common and with us we took a new loaf of bread that Nell had made earlier in the day with Miriam and Miranda, Ann and Emily's little girls. Nell was in the garden picking flowers with the girls.

We found Simion sitting in his 'corner'. As the little boys were playing around they both walked unsteadily but gradually over to Simion. Mark took hold of one of Simion's thin, bony hands with his chubby tiny fingers and James held the other. It was something that little children would do without thought, having neither prejudice nor guile. But, as they held his hands, the tears ran down Simion's face, and Ann, Emily and I, too, found ourselves weeping. This poor man had no physical contact with anyone. It seemed that he was frightened of being touched and he normally fled if any person came near to him. Even my sisters kept a few body lengths away from him. Yet, these small and innocent children had done what no one could do and in so doing had touched his heart as never before.

Simion seemed almost as though he did not notice the conditions of the elements, but in 1491, the winter was bitter and colder than that which anyone could remember. Ann and Emily were worried about Simion. He had survived all previous winters, and though he had woollens, his present coat was getting threadbare. Ann was accomplished as a seamstress and made most of the clothes of the women and girls in the household assisted ably by Emily who would decide the style, draw the patterns and cut the cloth.

So, they conceived an idea to make him a thick cloak that he could both walk around in but also wrap round himself when he slept. Emily drew a design and when both were content, they fashioned a cloak. It was made out of two layers of dark woollen blanket, an outer thicker layer and a thinner inner layer. It was made to extend to mid way between his knees and ankles, so that he would not trip over the length due to his ungainly walk, nor yet be too heavy for his comfort in wearing it. Ann attached a hood for bad weather or to act as a neck pillow if rolled up.

The next time they saw Simion, they gave him the cloak and showed him that he could put his arms through the armholes in both layers and so have his arms free. Yet, he could keep his arms between the layers when he slept, thus keeping them warm at night. When he walked he looked a little like a ship with a sail blowing in the wind, but it served its purpose very well. He thereafter wore this cloak night and day. In summer he would open the fastenings and in winter be totally enclosed. I do not think it left his back from the day it was given to him, lasting him well until he died. Little did Ann and Emily know that, by this act of kindness, they would one day help to save the lives of their young sons.

By that time Simion would, in all probability, be around his forty-fifth year. I have always thought it was something of a miracle that someone who lived his life roughly, for want of a better word, with no comfort that I could tell, should live with no illness, that anyone could know or remember, other than his affliction. Never did he appear to cough, even if coughs were causing many problems in the villages and even deaths of children. No, it is, and will always be my opinion, that Simion was different in many more ways than we shall ever comprehend. I now, with contemplation and much musing, am quite certain that Catherine knew much more about him. How or why I cannot tell, and she never spoke any words to indicate that which I believe could be true.

§

Simion became part of our village life. From remarks made by Jonas, it became clear, he considered Simion to be a freak and an abomination. I *was still only young at that time, but I have always listened well to what people say and oftentimes they would not even notice I was there to hear. But I heard neighbours repeating the way in which Jonas spoke to them about Simion when he visited their houses. I heard the men in the fields talking at their repasts while resting, when I went to help with the haymaking. Oh, yes, I heard! And so I learned to hate Jonas, not withstanding what he would say about my dear sisters.*

∫

I give no apologies for each diversion, as everything I write I believe to be of importance for the fullness and truth of this narrative. I will now return to the episode of the dog.

When the news got out, as it easily and surely did, that my sisters were at last speaking, Jonas again gave an utterance to all who would listen as he walked round the village. He decreed that he was certain, having received reassurance from his superiors following a particular discussion with them and having seen the big dog himself, that it had sensed the presence of evil. It had consequently tried to attack it. The 'it', he made no pretence or gave possibility of the misconstruing of his words, being 'within my sisters'. He was sure that in its demonstration against evil, the dog had caused the girls to speak. He suggested that he was able to see the awareness of evil remaining in its eyes.

Now, in my opinion, rubbish is and always has been rubbish, but the people fear anything that they cannot explain and the man of God was thought to have the answers from another, higher authority altogether. Why that fact itself was not also thought to be very strange, I never shall understand. But, he talked on behalf of the Church and no one dare gainsay a word against that apparent divine knowledge.

So, gradually he caused a stigma, as if from God, to be put on those lovely, gentle girls from the day of their birth. In truth I think he spoke to them rarely, and, on even more reflection, I can say without doubt that he knew them not. But such damage, if gained from words of hearsay and malice by someone of his calling, however dubious you may personally regard such a man, cannot easily be altered. On a day-to-day basis, in the early years of his residence in Stocksmoor, his talk had little effect as Father Simon's influence was still present in the hearts and minds of the villagers.

I have always thought, and that thought is still with me, that it was such a total shame, and a lack on the part of the Almighty, that Father Simon should die before my sisters were born, else a very different belief would have been born with them. I am as sure of that as I am that I have four fingers on each of my hands. Father Simon would have considered that they were a double blessing for our family and the village and the villagers would have been in no doubt.

I have to interject now that, mild tempered as is my nature, I would not have grieved for even a moment in time had Jonas been taken from this world at a prematurely young age, as so many of my family and others were taken. Indeed, I can go further and say, with truth, that I would have rejoiced.

When he came to the village, sent by the Church in York, he was housed in Father Simon's small cottage, with the meeting room attached. This was situated half way down the hill in Stocksmoor. His monk's habit gave some 'difference', an 'authority' one could say, to his speech as did his recent connection with his elders in the church, whom he continued to periodically visit. At least then, he was absent from the village for a week at a time and it was assumed he went to York for this purpose, though none dare ask. This may or may not have been the case. But, it is a surety, that as he grew older his words had more impact and he lived to a good age, so that he was at the height of his influence in 1497. I told my father what I thought about Jonas.

"Men are like most everything else that moves and breathes in this world, some are good, some are bad. In my view, Richard, the bad will not merit a heavenly space, whatever rank or position they hold on this earth and whatever their religion tells them to the contrary. So, don't waste any of your sleep time thinking about Jonas, my lad, he doesn't deserve your effort," he guided me, as usual, with his customary simplicity of speech. To me, my father was a man with wisdom. I heeded his words.

∫

Let me come back to telling you about my sisters. These 'different happenings' for want of a better name, that I have related and the comments made by Jonas were not forgotten in the village, as often I have found to be the case. This is particularly so in small communities *where any news is worthy of a mention at any time when there is a little boredom, and where little outside influence or information comes into their lives. It seems by my further knowledge that these three of my sisters, Ann, Emily and Catherine, were frequently talked about in the village, whether for good or not, and about whatever they did or did not do.*

The three of them were occupied constantly, in one way or another. No one would ever see them with idle fingers. When they walked the fields and hedgerows, they collected berries or shade-loving plants. If they saw wool tufts where sheep had caught their coats as they grazed, they would gather these. They would clean any debris from the wool, it would be washed and carefully dried and often dyed. Catherine was the spinner, Emily the weaver and design-maker and Ann the knitter and seamstress. When the villagers wanted or needed their help or knowledge, then they knew which house to visit, of that there was never a doubt. They grew herbs for cooking and for potions and they had great knowledge of the healing powers of these plants.

Catherine was their guide in these areas. I asked my father once where Catherine had learned her skill as I had not known she had visited a teacher in such matters. I shall remember his reply for ever. "Richard, sometimes it seems gifts are given but we know not the giver, just as some people are taken away and the reason we know not. So it is with Catherine. I pray that the good Lord will watch over her and her sisters."

But, readers, if you cast your mind back to what I was saying about the villagers, then I think you will agree that this kind of 'looking inwards' is merely idle gossip. It is mostly of a harmless nature and certainly my sisters showed not the slightest discomfiture from it all, and appeared to think it too trivial to be of any concern. One day, they were relating, with some amusement the fact that Dorah, of whom I spoke in relation to Simion, had commented to Nell that the hair styles of Ann and Emily were quite different on the last time that she had seen them.

"Richard, if we provide some amusement in that way, then all I can think is that there is emptiness within their heads. Do you not think we should rejoice that we are able to fill some of that space? Else, I would think it must be very uncomfortable. Would you not agree? We have no

knowledge of what such would feel like and for that we are thankful." Emily smiled as she spoke.

"And, we would prefer to fill that space with nonsense rather than it was filled with anger or comments that were hurtful to another. We have always served many purposes in this village, though, of course, some are not intended," added Ann.

You may at some point wonder about the difficult breathing that Ann and Emily would frequently suffer, particularly if they had a chill or a bad cough. At such times it was pitiful to see their struggles. This was a cruel cross they had to bear and had always been attributed to their early birth, at least by our father and family. Jonas, as you may imagine, had put forward the idea that their breathing problems were a 'kind of punishment' from the Almighty for causing their mother's untimely death at their birth. I say 'you may wonder', as it may have occurred to you that if Catherine, in particular, could visit children to help in their fevers and with times of difficult breathing, then why did she not ease her own dear sisters' breathing?

When I was older, I asked her this question, but I only asked her once. Catherine was as 'Kindness' herself would have been had she been a human being, but rarely, if ever, showed any tears or emotion about anything.

"I have done what I could have done, Richard. I cannot do that which is not possible," she answered. After a pause, she added, "If only I could Richard. Do you think I would not have eased my sisters, more willingly than I do for anyone else? Please understand that I love them more than life itself." She stopped and her face started to fill with colour, which was unusual with her pale skin. She suddenly got up from her chair, as if to stay longer was impossible, even though she would have liked to have done so. She left the room, but not before I could see her convulsing with tears.

But, whatever it was like, the input into their lives from the villagers was preferable to 'input from outside' of the sort that this village eventually experienced. I may have appeared to digress and you may accuse me of that many times, but what I have had to say will provide a backcloth for fuller understanding so that fairness will be within your final judgment.

So, now, I will continue to give more information about my father's children.

The next was Thomas. Was he the second child of Anna or the first of Eve? You may ask that question, as I also, now, ask the same. I can truthfully tell you that I do not know. In all my years until now, I have never delved into those earliest years for information. He was three years younger than me and I have no memory before that time. To me we were all one family. The important fact is what happened after Eve's death. He was only seven years of age at the time and had doted on her and, I have to say that the effect was indeed very strange. After her departure for ever and without any warning, he changed and never returned to the boy that we all knew. This had been a brother who had playfully fought with me as brothers do, had run around, shouted, laughed, and had often been a difficult lad for Eve to manage if he didn't want to be or do as she had requested. Now, he became quiet and solitary and had difficulty with his speaking, as though to speak would cause another dreadful happening.

He appeared so very angry that she had gone, he knew not where, that he never cared much for Ann and Emily, as if, in his anger he blamed them. He was forever blind to their characters and inborn kindness. He rarely talked to them as they grew older, and it was almost as though he did not see them. But, Thomas was a headstrong boy and, from an early age would only listen to what he wanted to hear. So, no persuasion or action could enter into his mind to alter it any more than we could bring our mother, Eve, back home.

My father was distressed by Thomas's evident misery, as that is how he saw it and spent much time with him. He explained that two tiny babes could not be held to account for their mother's death. But he would not listen. No, he would not or could not alter how he felt and all my father's efforts on his behalf were to no avail. I had known the same grief but have a different nature altogether and I would implore you that you do not judge this most unhappy brother. I would else wish I had not included these words in my narrative, but all I write is necessary in the understanding later.

But, it came to pass that Thomas put himself, by his own nature and, I stress, not by any intention or doings on our part, outside what the family offered. On his lonely path he found some solace, not, as you may think, in the religion that many people turn to in order to find the answer to their inner torment. No, he was tempted and walked on that which I have always regarded as a path towards more unhappiness and pain than exists already. He chose the path of liquor. At first it offered him a false happiness but, in truth, his sorrow became worse and his intelligence was drowned in his mugs of ale, until at these times, none dared or wished to speak with him. He would walk up the village hill to the inn, the one that I sometimes stayed at during the time of which I shall write, and stumble his way back home when the selling of liquor had ended and the landlord put him out to the other side of the door.

He eventually left the family home about two years after I did, when he married a woman who was more unsuited to our family than he could have found if he had searched the world for such a one. Let me just say, briefly, that her way of life was not ours and I would prefer to leave any further knowledge hidden in the annual of forgetfulness. I never stopped loving my brother, but sadly, he became more and more unknown to me. There was no power in my being that could bring him back. Eventually and with much searching of my soul, I had to accept that we each and everyone must find our own way.

He never returned, sadly, to the person that we all knew and still loved. But, he was never vindictive towards Ann or Emily and never laid a finger on them to harm them. But, neither did he do anything to assist them. He never carried or fetched for them, though he was strong and they would struggle in their breathlessness, and that did not change, not even in their hour of great need. To me, Thomas appeared as if his head was in a dark cloud and he could not see through it. I bear him no thoughts of blame, or anger, just deep regret. He had gone by himself, to a place within his mind where none who loved him could ever find him, and where I fear, he thought no one cared about him.

∫

A sister, Mary, was the next child in the family, born one year after Thomas. She was six years older than Ann and Emily, and you will hear more of Mary at a later time. I have really little to say about her at this point in my narrative. She, like Thomas and myself, had dark hair, unlike the rest of our Father's children who had very fair hair and looked like Eve. So, now, my rather different and more detailed thinking about my family makes me to believe that she may have been Anna's last child and that Anna died, in truth, giving birth to Mary. I can confide in you that these thoughts are quite unsettling in many ways. They have made me look for information that I cannot find or verify. Why did I not question before - when the only people who could know the true course of events were alive? I do not know.

I hoped that Uncle George may be able to give me the answers, but he does not rightly know either. He says that as far as he was aware Anna, my mother, had several babies and lost either one or two after me, but he is not sure about Thomas or Mary. He knows Anna died in childbirth, but during which one he does not know. He recalled that he and Aunt Gwendolyn did not see my father and his family much for a year or two, at that time, as they were all busy with young children and so travelling was not easy. But, he agrees with me that it is of little significance now and best that I do not linger on these possibilities or probabilities, lest I get distracted from or waylaid on my task.

Suffice to say that I just accepted my family as it was - and as I grew up to know it. My thoughts when awake as a child did not include the mother I never knew, only Eve. In my mind I can remember an image of Anna, but assumed it was only from a likeness I had seen in a frame on our wall. Whatever, these facts add nothing of note to my narrative, except to give you somewhat unnecessary information. Such deaths of mothers are sadly, and with great sorrow, quite common, as you will hear.

Mary was quiet, but determined. She went almost unnoticed by me when I was young and lived at home, though I am not sure why. Please forgive me, I am not perfect and with hindsight it was a mistake, but one I didn't know I was making. There were many of us and Mary made no fuss or noise. I remember that she loved to spend a lot of time with Aunt Peggy and I believe that, though Aunt Peggy loved us all, Mary was her favourite. I am pleased about that as otherwise, at least from my eyes, she became lost. When she was born only a year after Thomas, I was but four years of age and I liked to be with my father whenever that was possible.

As I grew older, from about the age of eleven, I spent much of my time at the Hall having lessons with my cousins. I would be out of the house by seven of the clock in the morning and not back home until late in the afternoon. Then I would spend time with Ann and Emily. I do not excuse my lack regarding Mary. I am merely trying to explain. But I do think that the tiny babies took whatever love I had and, as a young boy, I simply did not have much to do with Mary.

Even in a family where love dominates, everyone is different. I have a nature that can feel and show love, but even such a nature needs to receive affection back. Ann and Emily from being very tiny always liked to be with me and I knew they loved me. Mary showed little interest in me and maybe that contributed to my lack of notice of her presence, though I would not have wished any harm to come to her in any way whatsoever. So, please understand that it is now my belief, with hindsight and thought, that it was a lack on the part of Mary as well as myself. None of us reach near to perfection and I neither take nor give any blame – just some regret. We were as we were!

∫

Next was Catherine, just four years old when Eve died. You will hear more of her anon. She was a sweet and gentle girl who became totally devoted to Ann and Emily. She held their tiny but perfect hands in her own shortly after their birth and no one could make her leave their sides except for the minutes needed for her normal bodily function, or when she was found to have fallen asleep. All knew that she would be a devoted sister. She was then, even at that early age, and remained so for the rest of their lives, as if feeling they had a need for her protection. When I lived at home, which was until Catherine was fourteen years of age, I cannot ever remember hearing the three of them have a cross or bitter word to each other. Some children have ways of their own that they hold fast to whatever happens and my little sisters were no exception. Ann and Emily were sweet and kind, but at the same time very strong-willed and totally united, yet for some reason, they always accepted the path that Catherine offered.

As they grew older, all three, led by Catherine, worked together to produce herbal remedies. As I have briefly explained, they collected wild plants from the fields and woods. They knew which would ease inflammatory conditions of the body or help to reduce fevers. In hindsight, however, I believe that they, like me, used their hands to do that favour to an ill child. Children were the ones they wanted to help, and it was easy for parents to accept a potion that had a green colour or a plaster that set to a white shell. Then they did not even have to think, let alone believe, that there may be more in my sisters' ability than the herbal learning. But this was not the same for all the people who knew of their help, as you will find out.

I learned a lot from my sisters, but I shared with them shreds of wisdom that I had gleaned, and which they accepted readily.

Catherine never married and hereby is a sadness that she wore with such an uncomplaining dignity that many did not realise its presence.

We had an uncle, Sir Reginald Kittle, a minor baronet who had married our mother's sister, Aunt Elizabeth. They lived in Lower Oakington, in the valley, about two miles below Stocksmoor. He was a gentleman farmer and really a man ahead of his time, in that he believed in his workers' rights to a decent home and living. His men, who were very loyal to him, served him well and he did the same for them.

He had four sons. The eldest one, called William, was loved by my sister, Catherine. They were to be married, but just three months before the date arranged, which was to be when Catherine was eighteen years of age, on her very birthday, he was thrown off his horse. His neck was instantly broken. Dear Readers, let me tell you that her wedding dress was prepared and items collected ready for when she moved to rooms in the big house, which they were going to share with his father.

Witnesses in the field told the same story. He was hunting for deer which roamed their fields and caused damage to the crops, his horse reared suddenly and threw him off its back. His three brothers searched the area around and found a sharp metal object, like a nail, lying close by the place where he fell. They also noticed a small cut in the horse's hind quarters.

I am fairly sure that he was murdered in retaliation against his father, Sir Reginald, by a gang sent for this very purpose. There were brigands employed for many reasons; none knew their source or who was behind the attacks. However, I believe that you will also think that this is a reasonable and probably the most accurate of explanations when I tell you that his horse was one that I knew very well. It had the calmest temperament and would never have thrown William without due cause, of that I am totally certain – added to which, William was an excellent horseman.

This gentle man had been a perfect choice for Catherine. I can safely say that she was the love of his short life and he of hers. She never thought of taking another beau and never made any fuss that any of us ever saw or heard on this subject. But, her eyes held an inner sadness from that day, as the sparkle had gone and never reappeared.

∫

Then there was Benjamin, who was two and a half years old when his mother died. What can I say about Ben, the name he was always called? He was just a normal lad who, according to my father, didn't appear to notice the arrival of either the babies or the disappearance of his mother and was fine as long as his food was on the table. He was a placid boy who simply got on with his own life in a quiet, determined and kind way, yet, he showed little emotion. I recall the occasional temper tantrum before his mother died, as I was seven years and a few months older than him and have an excellent memory back into early childhood. But after that time, no emotion was shown, either great exhilaration or sorrow, until he was pushed beyond whatever allowed him to remain so phlegmatic in the face of any happening. My father, in later years, liked to work alongside Benjamin as there was never any show of anger or opposite opinion that could cause added stress in any event.

He showed an inclination and talent to draw and paint. My father encouraged him in this ability as matching his own. He married the local squire's younger sister, Hannah, and settled in that village, Upper Oakington. Let me just say here, as it will be relevant later, that my sisters and I all attended the wedding of Ben to Hannah. It was carried out at a church near Hannah's home, a medium-sized hall a few miles from Stocksmoor. Her father, a Canon, officiated. There our family was introduced to her younger brother Benedict, a member of the Church Army and someone we had not known before nor met in the years that followed. He was the son of the Canon's second wife.

∫

Let me just interject at this point, so that you will recollect later, that Benedict, Hannah's brother, looked like his mother and had very distinctive eyes. They were of a piercing, bright pale-blue colour which somehow reminded one of ice-cold, clear water. I must just say that, as with the animals that I work with, I notice people's eyes. To me they can indicate a kindly disposition or the opposite. When Ann, Emily and I discussed the proceedings, as one does after an event of this nature, we decided that Benedict was someone whose company we would never willingly seek. Humans, unlike animals, can hide their true natures by actions and words, but it is my belief that they cannot hide that which can be seen in the far depths of their 'eyes'. Maybe I am fanciful in this, or I can see that which others may not see, but I am writing that which I have found to be true for my own judgements.

Hannah and Robert were much as their late mother had been, with dark hair and dark brown eyes. Hannah was a handsome and hard working girl who kept house as well as any you could find and, if invited to a repast at their table, then it was advisable to restrict food for a few hours beforehand. They had two sons who lived and were strong, but sadly their daughter died within hours of her birth. It was as if the Almighty had presented them with a small jewel but had then cruelly decided he did not want, after all, to let them keep it. The layette, which had been prepared, was given away, apart from the tiny silk gown that she was buried in.

Hannah was greatly influenced by her father, who, by his very position as Canon, was a staunch upholder of the rules and beliefs of the Church. This caused some problems in her accepting my sisters and their herbal and healing work. However, I have noticed that it is often the case that the same belief seems to have a different meaning when different people are involved. Hannah's beliefs, while they affected her acceptance of my sisters, did not make her feel similarly about her own brother Robert's wife. Her sister-in-law, who was our Uncle Wilfred's eldest daughter and also called Hannah, openly and with a superior pride, practised the same healing art. I say 'practised' deliberately, knowing that it has two meanings!

∫

Let me now return to Ben. He worked alongside our father. Even as a small boy he liked to accompany him and, as I have mentioned before, they spent time together in their leisure time when our father would sit with Ben when he painted, giving encouragement and advice as and when Ben either needed or requested the same. I used to like to see them together. The gentle boy never argued with his father and I think my father was to him as if both father and mother. Their companionship, I am sure, sustained both of them through many of our difficult times, though it was largely unspoken. The loss of Ben's daughter was a tragedy that affected my father, causing him great sadness not only for himself but for Ben.

∫

Elizabeth, who was but eighteen months when her mother died, was a quiet girl who always seemed to have an understanding beyond her years. She was a little like Benjamin in that she too showed little emotion. This may seem a strange thing to say of children so young when deprived of a mother, but it was as if, after she died, they had no one who mattered enough again – as no one of such importance existed in their lives until they grew up. I do not mean to infer that either she or Benjamin were uncaring, not at all, but you would never have known if they felt joy and rarely would they have tears. I have to say that in such a busy household, one like Thomas was enough and maybe it was his influence that caused all the others to be very even in their temperaments.

I sometimes sit and bring back into my mind some of the 'little' things in all our daily lives together, times that have no importance to anyone other than one who does not want to forget someone dear.

Elizabeth married one of our cousins, the same family as William. You will find that Ann and Emily do likewise. It is common practice for cousins to marry amongst the gentry and our family was no exception, but they truly were love matches and not of 'convenience' to suit convention.

His name was Andrew. As William and Catherine's marriage had not occurred and Catherine still lived at home with our father, there was still room and it was convenient for them to live with Sir Reginald in Lower Oakington in the large farm house. Elizabeth was very happy and, for once, she showed it. She was a very beautiful girl, with hair that curled in abundance. Happiness enhanced her features. Soon, Ann and Emily, as you will hear, moved to live nearby and they all mixed together as usual.

Our gentle and thoughtful sister, Elizabeth, was lost to us when she died in childbirth of her fourth child. The child would have been a girl and it was hoped that this time, as there had been two in the years before who didn't live, that Elizabeth would carry the child to the end. She did, but the child died at the same time as her mother. I was told later that the birth had been too prolonged and the baby had perished and never breathed at all. There was a boy, her first born, by now aged four called Alend, who, although Andrew had a housekeeper and carer for him, much preferred to spend his time with his aunts – Ann and Emily. They loved him and he became almost part of their family, and had his own bed space in their house.

So, dear readers, if you consider for a short while only, you will understand that grief was already no stranger at our door. But, it was thus for so many families. Our young men are often slain in skirmishes, being duty-bound to answer the call of their masters, our young women die in child birth, and our children die of fevers or at their birth. Life, a mixture of joy and sorrow, is not easy and my heart feels very heavy as I recall these, the people I have loved and still love despite their deaths. Would that I had a more unfeeling nature, as I am sure that I would be saved from much pain; but that has not been the will of God, and I am as I am.

§

Our father, true to his words to me, did not marry again after Eve died, nor, I believe showed interest in any other woman, as none came to our home and he spent his non-working time at home. Even respecting my own mother, I know that Eve was the love of his life. He devoted his time, forthwith, to his family and his work. How did Eve's death affect me? You might ask. I too have asked myself that question many times. I have no real answer, except to say that I was still able to love deeply, maybe too much. That I do know. But, you see, though Eve was not my natural mother, we had a bond which death did not break and somehow, for me, she never really went away. I cannot explain more than to say *that I felt she was around, sharing the same day as me, yet unseen. Maybe that 'presence' was my own mother, I do not know, except that in my mind it was Eve. I was reconciled to have my tiny sisters as a gift from her. They grew up to look as she did and I believe that Catherine helped me greatly by her devotion and acceptance. How could I, a much older boy, make a fuss when she didn't and, I did not want to be like Thomas.*

What could Papa do with so many young children? You many recall that he had a sister, Margaret, known to us as Aunt Peggy, who was unmarried. She was devoted to our father. I think, from the conversations that I overheard, that she came with some relief to live in the cottage next door. My bedroom, which I shared with Thomas, was in that house. We all filled her life with love but without the dangers she would have experienced had she had to give birth to us herself.

As I repeat to you, a wet nurse from the village, called Dorothy, came to our home and fed both Ann and Emily when they were very small. Thereafter, she came every day to our house to help Aunt Peggy. Nell also looked after us devotedly so, all in all, though we had lost a mother, we were looked after by three women who loved us and we loved them. Our father could go about his business knowing that his children were safe. It is fortunate indeed that he had the means to maintain such help and, despite all the losses we had sustained, our household had much love and rang with laughter. I believe that Eve knew about the joy as well as the sadness in her beloved family – a family which included her sister Anna's children, as if her own.

∫

I hope you now know enough to build a picture of our family and have some idea of aspects of the village. As I thereafter relate about their lives, you will have more than a shallow understanding of what I write. So, pray continue to be tolerant if I meander amongst words that you consider unnecessary, as, after all, I am writing about the people I love and loved and others that I know and knew - for the first time. By now, I hope, it should also be quite clear why, when I left home, I liked to call to see them all when it was possible. It used to be on a regular basis and I would take Beatrice in those early, far off days. When I started on my journeyman travels, I would see them maybe three or four times in the year depending on whether I travelled far or near.

After I married Rosamund, my sisters would, at times, be driven in our father's small carriage to our neighbouring village about four miles away, whether I was at home or not, to meet and converse with Rosamund and the young children would play. We continued our lives as friends as well as family.

~ The Kittle family ~

I have explained that I was ten years older than Ann and Emily. I married and had my own cottage at the age of twenty years, and then spent many years travelling farther afield. Thus, I did not participate as much in their lives after they were ten years of age as I would have liked due to circumstances, until the time that I settled more at home when I married Rosamund.

Travelling is refreshing to the soul, but home is really where the heart belongs. I can say, with an honesty of which I pride myself, that I thought of them all at least once each day wherever I happened to be. In particular, Ann, Emily and Catherine would come as if walking and talking within my mind. I hope you do not think me strange saying that, but it is the truth.

Ann and Emily married on April 24th in the year of our Lord 1482, when they too were twenty years of age. I have to say that our father told me before they were married that, although he was delighted they had found their true loves, as no one could deny this, he felt deep and grave trepidation. He had lost two wives in childbirth by that time and he feared he would lose these daughters too. They had not, since birth, had the strongest constitutions and their breathing problems might present more problems than those that most women face when carrying their child. He was deeply worried, but he vowed to hide his feelings as he did not wish to, in any way at all, cloud the happiness which they showed so clearly.

But, we none of us knew, on the happiest of days for Ann and Emily, that that most fragile of emotions, joy, had sadness walking closely behind, as if in its very footprints. They married in a double ceremony, which included many words of thanksgiving, in the church at grandpapa's Hall. On their wedding day, which was warm and quite sunny, given the early time of the year, and a blessed relief after the harsh winter and recent heavy rain, their husbands gave Ann and Emily each a dog. These puppies were only a few weeks old, both from the same litter but of different colours. These dogs became inseparable from Ann and Emily and rarely in the coming years would they be seen without these dogs at their ankles.

I might just interject here and hasten to say that the man of God in Stocksmoor, Jonas, was NOT one of the guests. But, in future years, he let it be known that he considered that even his absence at that ceremony had been noted by his Almighty God and that, Ann and Emily, in excluding him, merely asked for the sorrow that later enfolded them.

Their husbands were the identical sons of Sir Reginald Kittle and Lady Elizabeth, our aunt and uncle, and sadly their youngest boys as their mother died at their birth. The double birth proved too much for her body to manage – as it was with Eve, the mother of Ann and Emily. The wedding ceremony was indeed a strange experience as both brides and both grooms were as alike as any two people could be and both mother's were missing. Had I not known the slightest of difference between Ann and Emily, then, I assure you, I would not have distinguished which couple was which. Despite the rareness of this event, these men matched Ann and Emily perfectly. It seemed to all who saw them on this day that God had surely provided them for each other. I can only be thankful for their brief years of happiness, as, for some divine reason they were not allowed more. It seemed that our family was standing in the full view of the black reaper who kept his eye fixed in our direction and never wavered from his grim task.

Who can tell why people believe in certain ways? These two young men were against injustice, and, though well-born themselves, disagreed with the way that society was structured. In this they were like their father. They many times conversed with me. It was their opinion that fighting was not the way to achieve a state of peace or obtain justice. They had to partake in their father's troop once they reached sixteen, though at that age they were put in the background of any action. But, though they abhorred violence they fully agreed with his cause, and in reality, they had no choice. They were brave and courageous, but no one could ever give them the name of 'fighters'. Yet, these gentle young men lived in a world where cruelty abounded. Injustice was the order of the day for the majority of people.

∫

Sadly, they met their deaths only three years after they were married. Their father, as he upheld his views against the church levies being imposed on his tenants – who already paid their dues as was required – had been taken a prisoner in the castle in Sandal, a small town nearby to Wakefield. The trial was, I understand, a travesty of justice due to corruption of the judiciary, who feared to oppose the church. The court sentenced him to death by hanging on April 27th 1485.

His three remaining sons, Peter, Richard and Andrew, determined to have justice and made a plan to rescue their father a few days before the gallows' date. Their father's troop duly made a plan, but sadly Peter and Richard were apprehended in one of those fickle turns of savage fate. They were climbing the castle wall, at dead of night, when a duty officer, whose watch had been changed only hours before, saw them and pushed their ladder from the wall. Both landed on the rocks below and died of many broken parts of their bodies. They had made careful plans and timed everything to the last minute, and could have been successful had that change not been made. Such are the vagaries of life and such is the finality of death.

Their bodies were brought back home on a horse-drawn dray, on April 24th, draped in the flag their father used when taking his troop to battle on command of the king. Their father was hung as his sentence decreed.

Yes, I can almost hear you sigh as you remember this date. It was the two couples' third wedding anniversary, but due to the circumstances of Sir Reginald's imprisonment and the attempt to forestall his execution, there were no celebrations feasible or appropriate. Such are the times in which we live. However, I had been travelling and knew nothing about this *terrible event, so I was visiting the sisters, intending to have a bite of food and a mug of ale with them on this special day.*

I was there when they received the dreadful news. I had only heard from them, when I arrived earlier that afternoon, what was happening and their fears were obvious. Neither could sit down for more than a minute, going upstairs to look as far as possible along the road, or to the door, to hear a horse more easily should their husbands be coming home. Catherine had visited to be with them and support them, but no one and nothing could avail.

They lived in two cottages owned by Sir Reginald. They had been made to be as one in a village in the valley below Stocksmoor only a stone's throw from his own large house at Lower Oakington.

I remember the scene vividly.

"What is wrong with Nell, I wonder," Ann asked Emily, as one or other was feeding their little girls at the dining table in the downstairs living area while the other went to watch for signs of their beloved husbands.

Nell, during the intervening years had married, had a son who died in infancy and by now had been a widow for several years. She had gone to live with them when they both married to help clean the house, cook and give assistance with whatever they needed. She had requested this, and, because of her devotion to his daughters, her wish had been granted by our father. Though she was now in her middle years, with her dark hair scattered with grey, she was still of a very robust and healthy nature.

"You watch the girls, Emily, I will go to see."

Before she could get far, Nell had burst into the room and her white face showed horror and great distress.

"They are dead! They are dead!" she wailed.

"What do you mean?" asked Emily.

"They are dead, look," and she pointed to the window.

Ann and Emily ran to the window.

"Oh my God, no!" they both screamed, as if with one voice. "Who are

they? Not Peter and Richard! Surely not! Surely not! But that is Will holding the horses. Oh mercy! Oh mercy!"

"Watch the girls, Nell," and they rushed outside.

"Ma'am. Ma'am. I have found them and brought them back."

Will, the trusted servant, had grown up with Peter and Richard, having been the son of one of Sir Reginald's grooms. He accompanied them everywhere as their valet and looked after their horses. Now dirty, dishevelled and covered in blood, he wept as he saw the two sisters. He got down from the dray and, lowering the side, he lifted the flag covering their broken bodies. The two sisters looked at their husbands. They were shocked beyond words. Their lovely, kind and young men, their faces now shattered and unrecognisable, were lying on the floor of the dray, their legs lying in an odd line.

Both women were pregnant with their second child at the time and both fainted to the ground before Will or myself – I had followed out of the house after them – could catch them.

Will had not been in the foray to get into the castle. His duty was to prepare food and drink, look after the horses and be ready for a quick getaway. When they did not return he and the others, as none would let the young men travel to such a task unaccompanied, scouted around the area. Eventually he found them, both already dead, at the base of the castle wall, with two others.

He was always entrusted with their money bags, so he had travelled into the market place nearby and found where he could buy a dray, while the others had taken, hidden and guarded the bodies away from the castle. He had then harnessed the horses to the dray and had travelled back as quickly as he could. He wanted to bring the bodies to their home before the castle soldiers had found them and taken them to be burned. He had known that the sisters would want it that way.

§

Thereafter, Ann and Emily always seemed to have a sad serenity beneath their kind and lively selves. This was another grievous loss. They supported each other constantly, being devoted to each other as no others I have seen, and looked after their children together. The boys were born just eight weeks later, both healthy and the mothers were safe yet again.

There followed a few weeks when the rain hardly abated. I could not travel and so stayed at home. I visited Ann and Emily and saw that although the sisters and Nell were helped by Will and others from Sir Reginald's household, they were struggling. They were never of robust health but now they had been weakened even more by grief and were tired after the births and by looking after the new babies. The only remaining brother of their husbands, Elizabeth's husband, had had a miraculous escape. He had suffered severe bruising but was found with all bones intact, though unconscious. When he recovered, which took several months, he had to take over Sir Reginald's tasks and responsibilities being the only surviving son, and was often away from home on business.

After one day of storms and torrential rainfall, the river that ran through this valley became swollen and burst its banks. Their cottages, being on the low land area became dangerously close to the water. They eventually had to admit that their breathing problems were being made worse by coughs, for which they blamed the cold dampness that pervaded the valley, and that they could not manage on their own. Our father, suggested that they should all move back to his house, which he still shared with Catherine and Mary.

So began their eventual return to live at Stocksmoor. After the flood waters had receded they returned to their home only to find that, while unoccupied, they had been ransacked by renegades. These were ruffians who roamed the countryside. This was fairly common practice. Much worse often happened should they find women alone. As you will conjecture as you read further, these are dire times in which we live, yet we are thought of as a civilized society. Our father persuaded them that living alone and with their young children was not safe in these violent days. He asked if they would, please consider him and reduce his constant worry by moving permanently to Stocksmoor. He told them that he would not rest day or night if they were known to be alone. Word travelled amongst these villains and they now knew where the cottages were. They gratefully accepted his offer and moved back to Stocksmoor with their children and Nell. Little did he know that in a few years, even this village and his home would not be the safe haven he had envisaged for his daughters.

~ May 1497 ~

Having prepared the backcloth of this book like a man preparing his ground to plant his seeds, I have determined to start my story at the point in time which, with due consideration, I believe to be the day when my life changed forever. On an every day level, I may be a little premature in saying that, but I now recognise that the signs of looming darkness were given to me when I called to see my sisters in May, 1497.

The weather in the earliest months of the year had made it impossible to travel other than in the local areas. Thereafter, I had been making good my lack of attentiveness by travelling further afield for longer than was usual once the frost and snow had given way to more clement weather suitable for my journeys. Much as I like travelling, I have no desire to be stranded out on the moors or isolated areas in my wagon, though covered, in snow or ice. Many of the farms are situated in these areas in the northern part of the county.

I had been away from home for six weeks. I knew Rosamund, my dearest wife, and our two children would be expecting me to return either this day or the next. But I decided that, despite my long absence, I would travel via Stocksmoor. Once I reached my own home I would spend two weeks resting, spending time with my family and preparing my potions for my next travels.

I always liked to visit Stocksmoor. I still knew its people well as, of course, it had been my main home for my first twenty years. I could have stayed in my father's house with my three sisters but to disrupt everyone for just one night was not necessary and the innkeeper, Bernard, was an old friend whom I had grown up with in the village. He had taken over as innkeeper when his father died. So I stayed at the inn. It was always good to see my family and hear the news and, of course, check up on their horses.

Thomas lived in the village with his wife, but, I usually saw him at the inn, and seldom, if ever, paid his home a visit. He spent as much time as was possible away from his home, so one could surmise that his marriage was not a bed of happiness, which I have to remark, was no surprise to anyone. He frequented the inn most evenings, and, I say with sadness, that he imbibed the liquor to an extent that brought out his worst character.

Ann and Emily had their late husbands' horses, beautiful, large white stallions, which had been their pride and joy. They had mercifully escaped all injury when their masters were killed, being away from the scene. They were kept in the field behind their house or in the stables belonging to our father. A finer sight than these two horses you could not see. Out of my love of horses, but also for very sentimental reasons, I checked each animal's health every time I visited. Our father had a small stables with five other horses attached to a cottage next door to his house. He and Thomas, who, despite his liquor worked alongside my father with no loss of amiability between them, used the two sprightliest mounts. My sister, Catherine, a brilliant horsewoman, had her own black mare. Our father had a small open carriage which Ann and Emily tended to use as, due to their breathing problems, they found this an easier option than riding and could share the reins if necessary. If that was not possible, then one of father's workmen would be the driver.

This time, something seemed different when I went to their house. The door was open and my welcome was just as warm as ever it was or had been, and, as usual, I was immediately included in the household as though I had never been away. However, it soon became apparent that Ann and Emily seemed a little 'edgy' for want of a better word. Never before had I seen these gentle and witty women anything other than calm and accepting of their lives, though you have read that those lives had already held plenty sorrow. They were usually chatting quickly, either to each other or anyone around and kept the house lively and their children happy. But, this time an unusual quietness seemed to cover them like a mist, hiding them from my view.

∫

As I have intimated, Ann and Emily had been living back at our father's home since the deaths of their husbands. Twelve years had slowly passed by for them since that tragic day. Ann's daughter, Miriam, was fourteen years of age and her son, Mark, was almost twelve. Emily's children, Miranda and James, were of the same ages, within a day or two, as Ann's. These grandchildren had brought great joy to Mr Shaw through the years and they loved him very dearly. He took them walking in the fields and woods, let them help with the horses and the dogs, and, in general, he was as like to a father, rather than just a grandfather, as was possible. He was more indulgent than he had been with his own children, but we all realised that they deserved the little extras that he would allow them and they never abused his kindness. On the contrary, they learned many skills at his safe side and brought him much companionship. When he was not at work, the two boys were seldom far from his side.

When Ann and Emily, with their children, returned to his home, our father asked Dorothy's husband, who was a stonemason by trade, to build another two well-proportioned rooms, one upstairs and one downstairs to accommodate their needs. In fact, despite his grief for their sorrow, he welcomed them all back with what could only be called relief. You must understand that these were uncertain times.

Elizabeth's son, Alend, a quiet, reserved boy and very much in the mould of his mother, was often staying at the house. Having no mother and with his father often away from home, the boy preferred to spend a lot of his time with his cousins in Stocksmoor rather than with his father's housekeeper. No disparagement to her, but to have his cousins' company rather that of the housekeeper was quite understandable and, as I mentioned before, Ann and Emily had always been to him like the mother he had lost.

Mary had been away from home only three years and was now Mrs Knott. At a time when she had just accepted that she should be a spinster all her life, she met and married neighbour Phoebe's brother. She was now living with her husband, Abe, short for Abraham, and his sister Helena in the next village, Bretton. It is hard to say if she was happy or not. She had already one child, a pretty girl called Marion, and I learned that she was with child again. She was Abe's second wife. His first died young, of what I know not as there were no other children in his household. Helena, I understood from my sisters, had not been the most pleasant or welcoming sister-in-law to Mary. As she was used to being the mistress in her own home, she did not take kindly to anything Mary suggested or changed.

Let me just say that, at this time, considering the number of villages I travelled through, I would have put Stocksmoor in the upper reaches for friendliness and generosity of spirit. I put this down to the comparative lack of the death of the young children in the village. As you rode past the burial ground or through the village, there were always far fewer black crosses than was normal. In fact, even the village of Upper Oakington felt very different with a suspicious wariness evident which I fear was gradually becoming commonplace.

∫

On this particular day that I mention, I recall that I did not see their children. The boys were out with their grandfather and the dogs, and the girls were visiting Aunt Peggy for some reason or other. I was, as usual, offered some food, and after I had eaten and the plates taken to the scullery, Catherine departed to visit a sick child. We sat down to talk and Ann and Emily drew up chairs, one either side of me.

In a quiet voice, Ann began, "Richard, Emily and I want to ask you a favour. We love all our brothers but you are the one who we feel really loves us and our children and so we have chosen to ask you."

"Of course you can ask me a favour," I answered, without hesitation. "Carry on and tell me what it is that you wish of me."

"It is this." Emily looked at Ann as if for confirmation that she should start. Ann nodded. "We want to ask you whether, should our children ever be left without anyone to care for them, you would take on the role of their guardian. Our father, who is sadly getting old, is often breathless and complains of pains in his chest. We are anxious that should anything happen to us after he has died, that our children would be kept safe. Please, you do not need to answer immediately, as it is something you will want to think about and discuss with Rosamund, but we had decided to ask you when you visited us this time."

"I do not need to think about it at all. I am honoured that you should ask me. Of course I promise to look after them in such circumstances and I know that Rosamund will agree. But, why do you ask at this time? Are you becoming unwell?"

"No more than usual, but we are used to our limitations. No, though the winter has been difficult at times, it is nothing to do with that."

"Then tell me what is troubling you so much," I asked with some consternation.

§

Now, I shall tell you that which my sisters told me.

Firstly, they took me back in time to the end of September in the year before last, namely 1495. They had been visiting a sick child in a house at the lower end of the village, just off the road leading to Lower Stocksmoor, and were crossing the corner of the common land on their way back to the main road through the village. It was dusk; light enough for them to see where they were going, yet dark enough to be inconspicuous in their dark clothes.

They heard a cart, drawn by a horse, coming up that same road from Lower Stocksmoor and, as anyone travelling the roads at this late hour was unusual, they stopped in the shelter of some bushes near the path to see but not be seen. From what happened, while they were briefly away from their own house in Lower Oakington several years before, they had been made aware that brigands were travelling around. Other people gave stories of similar sightings late in the evenings. So, they were very wary. But the cart did not pass them. Instead it veered to the left and took the lane at the edge of the common land that led directly to the high road. It appeared to be loaded with sacks around the sides with the centre of it piled high with hay. They thought this was unusual at this time of year and, in any event, few carts used that lane. Though just wide enough for a driver taking care, it was stony in parts and an axel could be broken in the dim light. They proceeded to walk home and then spoke no more about the incident.

Now, let me tell you some information that appertains to what they told me. There was a young boy called William who lived in Lower Stocksmoor. His father had died of an accident about a year previously. He had been a ploughman and, while bending down to correct the plough, his horse had suddenly been startled – his workmate confirmed, when questioned later – and accidently kicked him in the head. William's mother had died more recently of a fever. So the boy, twelve years of age, was now without parents and his home belonged to the local Squire of Upper Oakington, who, without considering what should happen to William or even offering him work, had reclaimed it for another tenant. Fortunately William had an aunt living nearby, also in Lower Stocksmoor and she allowed him to move into her home in return for help in her garden and such like.

Now, I think you need to know before I continue that my sisters were very kind. If ever I pointed this out to them, they simply replied, "It is easy to give when you have enough and to spare."

So, when my sisters heard of the boy's predicament, they persuaded our father that they needed some extra assistance of one kind or another – you know, a small help here and another there. So it came about that William went every other day to my father's house to tend the garden and give a helping hand with cleaning the stables. He would fill the wood basket, and sweep the paths and do any small task that was within his strength. They paid him a small wage, which made his aunt look more kindly towards him, and each day they gave him nourishing food. They watched for his needs and would find a pair of decent boots or a jacket that could be dispensed with by Mark and James, if and when necessary, to keep him dry, shod and warm.

The day after they had seen the cart, they were expecting William and he didn't arrive as and when was usual. After he had missed two further days they wondered if he was ill, though they had heard nothing untoward from anyone in the village. So, they visited his aunt. She helped the local farmer's wife, Mrs Jefferson, whose house and farm buildings were further down the lane, with her daily housecleaning. She told them that William had gone out earlier the other evening, saying he was going to pick some apples from the tree that grew where old Mr Greenwood had had his garden. When he hadn't returned she had been concerned, but, after walking down the lane to Upper Oakington and not finding him, she had gone home. She couldn't do anything except wait. Then she remembered he had been saying for some few months that one day he would go away to seek his fortune somewhere else. She had decided that he must have done just that.

Ann and Emily asked her if she knew if Mr Jefferson was selling hay at this time.

"Goodness me, no," she answered, sharply, as if they should have known that answer already. "It is all stacked away for the winter, of course, and precious it is going to be this year. Aye it's going to be a bad winter, mark my words. The hips and haws are so plentiful, it always bodes ill. But, why do you ask?"

"We saw a cart loaded with hay and sacks come by this way a few days ago, so we just wondered who could be selling at this time of year."

So Ann and Emily went home, but as William – who normally talked freely to them – had never spoken about going away to them, they were still very concerned. They told their father their fears and he had asked around as much as he could, but no one had anything to report. No one had sold any hay or sacks of anything in the past few days, not to anyone. Our brother, Ben, went around Upper Oakington and spoke to the Squire, his brother-in-law, who organised that a few men in that village should search the fields and hedgerows around in case William had suffered a fall. But he was never found.

About six weeks later, the son of the farmer at the lower end of Stocksmoor, aged fifteen, also disappeared. Several searches were made. To the shock of the whole village, he was eventually found dead at the bottom of a disused well belonging to their own farm. After much discussion and ruminations, it was surmised that he had fallen over the low and damaged retaining wall while out setting snares for rabbits. He was a garrulous lad and prone to chattering in a rather foolish way to all and sundry who happened to see him. Yet, no one had a grudge against him, so a deliberate act was discarded.

When he was found his head was much bruised and his arm broken. So, it was finally decided that he had suffered these injuries as he fell. All in the village appeared to agree except my sisters. Ann, Emily and Catherine did not believe this as it was reported that he had a cut through his chest. Only a very sharp flint or iron pointing upwards in the well could have caused such an injury and they believed he had been killed before being dropped in the well and had tried to fight his assailants. They had voiced their opinions around the village but were condemned as being 'influenced *by evil to think such thoughts' by Jonas, the man of God. From what Nell found out, Jonas had made it his duty to tell everyone that he 'expected nothing less than fanciful from such as they' and was surprised how 'the more sensible Catherine was influenced by their odd utterances'. Their neighbour, Joseph, who was married to their cousin Hilda, was scornful when he heard what they had to say. 'They must have very good imaginations!' was his retort. The villagers, of course, listened to these men rather than to Ann, Emily or Catherine.*

§

But, the story was not yet complete, and before I continue I must explain more about the village people so you will understand fully. The village had several cottages at the upper end, near the inn. Down the road, mainly on the left hand side, there were several cottages besides the enlarged one belonging to our father. There were only fields on the right side. In the village, lower down the hill from my father's house, lived Hilda, one of our cousins, the youngest daughter of one of our father's brothers, namely Samuel. She was now married to Joseph, a man who came into the village soon after my sisters returned home to live with our father. I will tell you more about Joseph later.

§

Dear Readers, please be patient with me as there are so many things of importance to write. Where to put some of the information that you will need is quite difficult for me to ascertain. I try to remember, when writing, that you are not familiar with these people as I am.

Nearby my father's house also lived Phoebe with her husband Julius and their son, John. They had arrived in the village when John was just a small baby, and when Julius was needed as a carpenter. The boy was lively but frail and Catherine had helped him many times when his breathing was very difficult. Phoebe explained that when he was born he was very weak and had breathed in some of the fluid that he was born through. He had been blue for several hours and it had been thought he would die. But, his soul was stronger than this, and, with a struggle, he survived.

As you may recall, and if not then I will prompt you, Phoebe was the sister of Abe, our sister Mary's husband, and Helena. Helena, being widowed and having no children of her own, took an interest in Phoebe's son, John. As he grew older he would spend time with his aunt at her own house. Helena was very different in her manner to John than she was with anyone else and appeared to love him, according to Mary. When he became about nine years of age, he would walk the distance to his Aunt Helena's home in the next village, Bretton, in the morning and return each evening before dusk. It was a mere thirty to forty minutes walk and he could manage this without being too breathless as most of that way was flat, unlike the other roads around.

§

The story now continues. In October, 1496, that is, a few months before my visit to Stocksmoor, John, now coming up to his twelfth birthday, also went missing. He was the third boy to disappear, and only one had been accounted for. Ann and Emily told me they were sure that he was taken in the same way as William. I asked them why they would think that as no one knew what had happened to William and he might be safe somewhere. This is what they told me.

They had been helping each other sort out the drawers in the bedroom of Miranda and Miriam. The weather was becoming colder and the heavier winter clothes would soon become needed. As both girls had grown apace, Ann, who made most of the clothes for the girls, had decided to alter, add length and whatever else was needed before making the decision to renew each item.

They were examining some material by the light of the window, when they noticed John walking along the high road on his way to visit his aunt. They also saw that there was a horse down the lane at the back of the common, which was moving towards the road. It was not being ridden, so they watched and eventually, where the field wall was lower, they saw the horse was pulling a cart driven by two men. (Let me just remind you, lest you have forgotten, not knowing the village as I do, that this was the lane up which the wagon loaded with sacks and hay had passed when William went missing.) It stopped by the road, as if waiting, and eventually, as they watched, they saw John reach the wagon. He stopped and then got up into the back of the cart. They just assumed he had been offered a lift. The cart then went along the road as if to the next village. Emily remembered, quite clearly, saying to Ann, "It's a cold air for young John this morning; at least a ride will give him ease." Ann agreed that she also remembered saying those words, quite clearly.

He didn't return home that night. Phoebe had come into their house to borrow some flour for her plum dumplings, and told Ann and Emily that she thought John must be staying at Helena's for that night as he had not returned. Sometimes he did stay and there was no way for Phoebe to know until the next day when he arrived home. So, they none of them thought any more about it. That is, until two nights had passed and John had not returned, which was most unusual.

Ann and Emily had decided to visit their sister, Mary, and her child that afternoon and fully expected to see John at the house. But, there was no sign of John. Helena was in the garden tending her flowers and they walked out to her. Ann greeted her, for them both, with, "Hello Helena, we trust you are well."

"Of course I'm well. When am I ever not well? Why on earth would you ask that rather stupid question?" she replied, with her usual acidity and her mouth expressed contempt.

"Politeness, I suppose," answered Emily, "it's how we usually behave." She raised her eyebrows to Ann, as she thought that Helena was no more pleasant that day than on other days.

"We were just looking around for John. We have a message for him from his mother who wants to know when he is returning home. Is he alright?"

"What do you mean by 'is he alright'? How would I know? John isn't here and hasn't been to visit me this week. I am very disappointed and not a little angry with Phoebe as I had prepared his favourite dinner. So what on this earth are you two talking about?"

Ann looked at Emily before saying, "But Helena, he set off as usual and got a lift. We saw him from our bedroom window. He took a ride in the back of a cart. Phoebe thinks he's with you as he hasn't been home these past two nights since he left home."

Helena went pale and leaned against the garden wall lest she should collapse to the floor.

"What do you mean? Where is he?" she asked. Then hysterically, she went screaming into the back building where her brother Abe did most of his wood work – making wagon handles, wheel spokes, carving doors and the like.

The village and the fields and woods around were searched, but, despite everything, John too was never found.

§

"So you see, Richard, should anything happen to us and Papa and our children be left alone without us, we are very worried that something terrible would befall them. They would be safe as regards sufficient means to live and would have this house, but without protection, what could happen to them?" Ann and Emily were in tears as they spoke.

"We feel very frightened, as though darkness is looming and we cannot dispel it, however or whichever way we try." Emily sighed and added, "It may seem as strange to you, Richard, as it does to us, as we are not usually afflicted in this way. But we cannot rest as we should."

"Poor John and poor William, whatever could have befallen them?" whispered Ann, as if to herself.

"Fear not. Should it ever become a necessity, and may God Almighty forbid that will ever happen, then, of course I will look after your children as if my own. I promise you faithfully, on my heart."

"Oh, Richard, we are always so pleased to see you, but never more than today." They both came to my side and hugged me close to them. "Thank you, Richard."

"Do you not think you are worrying without due cause? Is there something else?"

"We want to tell you everything. Have you time to stay a little longer?" asked Emily.

"Of course. Tell me whatever is troubling your minds," I replied.

"Well, we thought at the time that there was something strange about this cart and horse, but neither one of us could think what it was that struck us as 'not quite as it should be'. But now we know," Ann began to explain.

"We have always liked horses, even though we are not really strong enough to ride far ourselves, and, as Peter and Richard's father bred horses for hunting, we have seen many, both for work on the farms and for pleasure activities. We were actually talking about you one day and wondering where you were. We always connect you with horses. Suddenly we realised what had been amiss and what had caught our notice. We both spoke out aloud at the same time, 'It was the horse'. Those pulling the wagons were horses of note, not just large ponies to pull a cart or the half breeds that are used for such purposes. No, these were the sort of horses we have known all our lives. So, we wondered where they were from and who did they belong to that they should be used in this way as common dray horses?"

"We got our answer only the other week and it is since then we have felt so frightened," continued Emily. "You will remember that Peter and Richard both died on the anniversary of our wedding day. Well, on that day, every second year we travel in the trap to Sandal and sit for a while at the place where they died. Will takes us as he too likes to pay his respects. This year we went and while we were just standing by the wall, we had in our view the two houses that are built almost as if connected to the wall of the castle. You will know which we mean. Fairly grand looking houses but in rather a strange position, we always think, with the two being so near the wall and joined together."

Ann took over the narrative again. "A woman came out of the far door, wearing a long cloak with the hood over her head; it was impossible to see her face at all. She was carrying a large bag, a very distinctive bag. There are some things we remember Richard more than others and, as I make our bags, I'm always interested to get new ideas for patterns. This one was in a canvas with a green zigzag pattern, quite unusual, I couldn't tell whether it had been embroidered on or woven into the canvas. Anyway, it was one we could both remember and we commented on the design. The woman appeared to be hurrying away from the house, but then stopped just past the outer castle gates and waited.

"While she was waiting a man came out of the near door and you will never guess who it was. It was Joseph! Hilda's husband, can you believe? He saw us and started to walk towards us. Then, we noticed a cart being driven out of the castle main gate by two men. They stopped just by the woman and one went to the back of the cart and put down the back board. Then we could see that there were two box seats down the sides of the cart, and the man opened one and took out a blanket. He put it on one of the seats and helped the woman into the cart. She then drove off with them."

"Understand Richard," interjected Emily, "we didn't at this time know who this woman was. But, we are nothing if not observant, and we recognised the cart as the sort we had seen up the lane when both William and John had disappeared. Though this horse was different, it was of a similar breed." She stopped and looked at Ann.

"You carry on, Emily," suggested Ann. "It is much easier if we tell it in turns."

§

Before I progress with their story, let me tell you at this time about Joseph, Hilda's husband. I do not wish for one moment to confuse or interrupt that which is unfolding, but without the knowledge I now give, you will not fully understand the significance later. The man they saw was known to us all as Joseph Kraft. He seemed quite a well-to-do man and when he had arrived in Stocksmoor, about ten years previously, he had built a house of considerable size, at least when compared to most of the cottages. It possessed more bedrooms than he could use. When he first arrived he was unmarried, but it was but a year and a half later that he married Hilda, one of our cousins. She was Uncle Samuel's youngest daughter. She was great friends with Ann, Emily and Catherine and as different from her sister Margareta as chalk is to cheese.

Joseph met her while Hilda was staying at our father's house, as she often did, during the summer after he arrived to live in the village. He was out in his back garden when she walked up the field with an armful of dandelions she had gathered. He went to speak with her, and asked her why she had such weeds in her arms. From that time on they became friends and, as you will remember, after a year or two they eventually married. She lived about five miles away at the time with her parents, but used to like to stay as often as she could with my sisters.

As far as anyone knew Joseph had private means, but I have to say that no one knew a lot about him. Yet, he appeared to be a friendly pleasant man as far as anyone could tell. Not knowing his family then one could only take him as he was, without any preconceived notion of likeness to any known person.

He was a man whose bearing had some distinction. Quite why this was so was difficult to say, so I can only describe him. But whether you liked him or not, that fact had to be admitted. He was slender but strong as I witnessed on one occasion, when he had to hold a very restless horse which could have cast aside a man of less sinew. Height discernment is often dependent on one's own, and as I am quite the norm for many men, to me he was of short height – in any event, quite less than me. He had shoulder length, very fair hair and very pale grey eyes, with an almost transparent look about them, which for a reason I couldn't explain, I found somewhat disconcerting. But, as I rarely saw the man, it was of no significance in my mind other than in his presence.

He was always clean-shaven and usually wore his hair parted down the middle and fastened back with a red ribbon, which was rather unusual in the village. His 'difference' was put down to his artistry, by which he earned money – carving icons for churches. But, I have to say that no one thought this would keep him in the style of living he supported. His apparent means and unknown history made him a man who caused some curiosity in the village, as would be expected. None was ever the wiser. He was very skilled in his wood sculpturing. His name was Joseph Kraft and that was all anyone knew about him. He once carved a plaque of my sisters, of three simply dressed women, all in relief, with a basket of leaves and herbs at their feet, but no one would have doubted who they were. He thus depicted them as 'healers'. The plaque seemed as if to stand in the basket, which thus supported it.

We knew that he was often away from home, and understood that in his travelling he visited churches to work on a commission, so he was often away for weeks at a time. Hilda told us once that he even went as far afield as France, so it was obvious to all that his work was of some note. But, it meant that Hilda had much time alone and she used to help my sisters with the growing and collecting of herbs for their remedies, potions and poultices.

I will write more on this matter at this stage, though it interrupts my story of the cart and horse – to which I shall return – and which I ask that you can keep near the forefront of your minds. The information I now impart will not take long in the telling.

Joseph was, apparently, an ardent believer in religion and he seemed to agree with the Church's doctrines and, in particular, with all that Jonas preached. When home, he was noticed to regularly attend to see Jonas, even at other times than the meetings. All assumed this was for religious conversation. To be well-versed in the scriptures, I have no quarrel with, but to be friendly with Jonas gained a large point against him in my mind, disliking Jonas as I did. I heard Nell talk on this subject and she made her view quite clear. "In my mind, birds of a same feather flock closely together." I have to say that he was the only one in the village to appear to befriend Jonas. However, he was generally pleasant of manner, whether from an inner pleasantness or one created for effect. But, something happened which gave my sisters, my father and me the view that, despite being married to Hilda, he was best kept out of our inner domain. I will tell you why we thought that.

Hilda and Joseph eventually had two children. The eldest fell ill when just a few months of age. Hilda ran round to my father's house and sought Catherine. She asked her if she could help her child as she did many other children in the same feverish state. Of course Catherine agreed, stopped the task she was doing and rushed back to her house with Hilda without any delay. However, when Catherine arrived at their house, which was only a few doors away and no time had been wasted, Joseph refused to allow her in the house to see the babe. He was standing in the door frame, waiting, with his scriptures in his hand and actually raised his voice against Catherine. "You cannot use your abhorrent ways in my house." Catherine was nonplussed. But, though Hilda was screaming and pleading for him to let Catherine in, he would not move in his will to stop her. To his discredit the poor child died.

Hilda was heartbroken and so, he made people believe, was Joseph. But he was adamant that he had taken the correct action and accepted no blame, saying, "It was God's will. What God gives he can also take away. We must accept that he has taken our child to his bosom in heaven. He has gone to a better place and I fear he will be angry with Catherine for trying to intervene in his divine purpose." He then told Hilda that Jonas had told him that Catherine going to the door had been the final assault *against God's will. To Hilda's credit, knowing Catherine as she did, she did not believe this, though many villagers heard him say the same and were influenced by him.*

Two years later a second child, another boy, was born and, sadly yet again, when he was but five months of age, he started coughing and had trouble breathing. Readers, if you are of sound mind and have an understanding of parental love, you will not find this credible when I tell you that Joseph, abiding by his religious beliefs, once more refused Hilda's request to let Catherine help. Hilda told my sisters that Joseph read the scriptures over his crib while the baby gasped for breath and even prevented her, the baby's own mother, from nursing the baby to give comfort. This baby also died.

Afterwards, and for several weeks, Hilda could be seen wandering the fields and the wood behind their house shouting for her son and railing God for his cruelty. Ann, Emily and Catherine tended to her, when Joseph was away, as much as they could. Eventually, she seemed to recover but Hilda told Catherine that she could never love her husband after the second baby died. She had no option but to stay in his house, as her parents were by now dead and she had no income. I am sure, had she asked, she could have lived with my sisters or Aunt Peggy, but she never did and remained with him.

∫

Let me return with haste to what Ann and Emily were telling me about meeting Joseph, before I feel wretched at the thought of those two defenceless children being so neglected, as that is the only word one can use, neglected, and by their father against their mother's will.

"You can imagine," continued Emily, "that we do not have any inclination to converse with Joseph unless we have to, following the deaths of Hilda's two children, but he saw us. We were just about to get into our trap and set off home, but we had no choice but to wait.

"'What are you two staring at?' he asked, as we were still watching the cart and Hilda disappear into the distance.

"Against my wishes, you understand, but being polite, I answered him. 'We have seen that cart before, when John disappeared and the night

that William went missing too. It has just come out of the castle gate and we are puzzled.'

"'No doubt it was delivering goods for the troops,' suggested Joseph, in a tone that made us feel he thought we were rather simple in our thinking. 'They have to eat, you know, like everyone else. There are plenty of carts, just like that one, up and down the country. I see them all the time in my travels.'"

"We spoke no more," Ann continued to tell the story, "so that he would believe that the cart or the lost boys were of no further significance to us and were to be ignored. He then told us he had been seeing one of the church men about an icon for the chancery. We had not enquired and had no idea which chancery he meant, nor were we, in even the slightest part of our minds, interested to find out."

"But," Emily told me more, "it seemed he wanted us to know, which was quite different to his normal reticence and avoidance. He made a real point in his telling, though why we do not know. He seems ever more under the influence of Jonas and he goes to an additional meeting now each week when he is home, though he is often the only one attending. We know, as Nell sees him. From her cottage she can see everyone who comes and goes from the meeting house."

"The odd thing about seeing him, Richard," added Ann as both she and Emily were doing their best to make me fully understand their increasing worries, "is that Joseph had been away a few days at the time, and Hilda believed that he had gone North West on a commission. If that were so, then we do not think that Sandal would be on his way back home. We have discussed the routes from the north west and no, not at all would this have been on that road. We chat to Hilda about most things. She has always been friendly with Phoebe, as we have, and so we mentioned seeing the cart again and our puzzlements and conviction. Yes, what Joseph apparently thought could be right and there are, no doubt, many carts like the one we saw. But we know, deep within ourselves, that it is the same cart that took John and, we think, poor William.

"But we haven't told her we saw Joseph there. Somehow it didn't seem quite right that our cousin's husband should come out of one of those houses. We are sure that that woman was a woman of little virtue and though he came out of a different door, it is well known in that area that those two houses are connected and it is not a place where those with any decency visit. The houses are used by the soldiers to meet women, at least the ones with some higher rank and money. We have asked questions over the years since we have visited where Peter and Richard died and always we have heard the same answer."

"Anyway," Emily continued, "we set off home in our trap as we had no wish to linger any longer. After a few miles we saw the cart and the woman, in the cloak and with the bag, way in front of us, but going in the direction of one of the villages around Stocksmoor. The road she was travelling leads to Bretton and the villages further away. We turned off to take the lane that leads to Upper Oakington to visit Ben and have some food with him and his family, and so we did not find out where she was going."

Emily turned to Ann and gave a slight nod.

"Richard, that wagon belongs to the castle and the horses are army horses. We are absolutely sure."

"Let us stop just there for now," suggested Emily, "I have a feeling of unease come upon me as we speak."

"Me too," agreed Ann.

"We shall have some air and a bite to eat and we will tell you more after that short rest," promised Emily.

We went out into the back garden and examined the herbs, after which we enjoyed a mug of dandelion brew with some bread and cheese.

∫

After we had all helped Daisy, their maid, to clear the table and she had disappeared into the scullery to wash the plates, Emily continued with their story.

"Richard, we now know who that woman in the wagon was. It is very, very strange and we don't really understand, but, we want you to know all, as we think one day it may be important. We don't know why, but when we told Catherine everything, she was quite insistent. 'You must tell Richard all as soon as you see him.' She reminded us only yesterday. We asked Catherine what she thought about the cart. She surprised us by her answer. 'One day, when all will be revealed, those responsible will have to answer for what they have done. They will receive the same pain. No more but none less. True justice will be done.'

"Ann asked her what she meant. She would not answer, but her eyes filled with tears and she just walked away. We both tried again this morning, before she went out, to find out what she meant as we have never liked to feel any confusion. It distracts us in what we have to do. Again, she answered, 'I have told you what I have told you. I wish I could say more, but I cannot.' We tried again, but she became annoyed with us. 'Ann and Emily, for pity's sake, please! I must go; I have my work to do.' So we don't understand what she meant. Can you enlighten us any further, Richard?"

"No, indeed," I was forced to admit, "it is indeed difficult to understand what is happening. I have no idea what Catherine could mean. But here I must tell you that, in my travels I have, over the past four years, heard of other boys of a similar age disappearing and no one has had any idea where they have gone. In my concern, I asked questions of those around and I ascertained that each and every one was either an orphan or from a destitute home. So, you see, even if I didn't know you for the honest and true people you are, I would believe what you are telling me. Carry on about this woman of the night as you surmised that she was."

"Well," continued Ann, "about two days later, we went to see Mary as she is getting near to her next birthing. She is not sure just when, but that is Mary all over. She thinks she is about five weeks away, but it could be sooner or later. Helena was in the scullery doing some washing of clothes. As you know, she is not our favourite person on this earth, and she doesn't like us – for reasons all her own – but we are always polite. We never let her see that we sense her dislike and always behave to her as we would to anyone else."

"Yes, that is because we think that is the best way, for Mary, you understand," Emily took over the telling. "If it weren't for Mary, we would never see Helena at all, Phoebe's sister or not. But after all, poor Mary has to live in the same house. How she does it is beyond our understanding, but she loves her husband. If there is any decision to be made, Helena always wins and Abe takes her side. But, Mary knew, *when she married him, how it would be. It wouldn't suit either of us, but then, we didn't choose Abe or Helena, did we?"*

*"So," continued Ann, "I went into the scullery first to greet her and I very nearly fell over a bag that was on the floor. It was **that** bag; there was no mistaking the pattern. I just stood gaping. Helena turned round and saw me and asked, in her usual 'pleasant' way, 'Why on earth is your mouth open like that? Are you trying to catch flies or something? You look quite silly.' I pretended that I was a little shocked after nearly falling over the bag and that I had just turned over on my ankle and the sudden pain had made me gasp. By this time I could think quickly again. I just bent down and moved the bag to one side without another glance. But Richard, it was **that** bag, without a shred of doubt. As you know, Emily and I can talk to each other in our minds so I told her. After a few minutes, I went back into the main room, in no hurry and being happy to greet little Marion. Emily then went into the scullery as if just to greet Helena as politeness would seem to require."*

"Yes, there was no doubt whatsoever. The bag was the one we saw. Helena was that woman." Ann nodded as Emily spoke. They were both quite certain.

"What on earth was she doing at that house, other than what appears obvious?" I asked.

"We don't know. We didn't say anything to Mary. We have only spoken to Catherine, but not to Papa. Catherine wasn't at all surprised."

"So, now you know the full story, I think," concluded Ann.

While I was digesting all that I had been told to make as much sense of it as possible, Emily suddenly remembered something else. "Yes, but there is just one other strange occurrence. As you know, Thomas has never cared for us and we understand why as we took his Mama from him. At least that is how he has always thought, though heaven knows we had nothing to do with that decision. Well, he came to see us the other day and he was not the worse for ale, but quite sober and seemed concerned for our wellbeing. 'You three should take care. There are people snooping around who are asking questions about everyone in this village and I have heard your names mentioned several times.'"

"'Take care about what, Thomas?' we asked," Ann continued. "He answered, 'The way you see and look after other people's sick children, that's what they ask about, just that. I hear them talking, and I listen. I'm not always as drunk as they think. They are interested in no one else either. So just take care, that's all I can say.'

"'Thank you, Thomas,' we both mumbled. We were feeling very bemused. Then he left without saying any more. Do you know that Thomas has never in all our lives shown any interest in our well-being and he hasn't called, especially to see us, more than once in the past three or four years. That being so, we feel we have to take notice.

"Do you understand now, Richard, why we have asked this favour of you? A sense of dread has been growing in both our minds during these past few weeks since all this has happened. We do not know of whom Thomas speaks, but there are many more people passing through the village these past few years. Many are monks who apparently are on a pilgrimage to the new cathedral in York. We suppose some must go several times as there is a fairly constant stream of them. Stocksmoor is on their route from the west and they often stop at Bernard's inn to rest and eat after travelling over the hills."

"Fear not, I have promised. I will keep that promise to the very best of my ability and strength but God alone knows what will happen and I trust that your fears are unfounded."

I stood up and hugged Ann and Emily. They seemed so small and fragile of body, even more so in their fear. As I was about to leave, Catherine came home. We chatted for a while and then, as I was leaving, she went with me to the gate and confided, softly and out of hearing of Ann and Emily, "Richard, I cannot say more, but we all have our tasks, and some are more difficult than others. Goodbye, my dearest brother." She looked straight into my eyes and hers were full of tears. And, also unusually for her, she hugged me. Now, understand that, though she was very gentle and kind, Catherine wasn't one for any show of physical affection, unlike Ann and Emily. I loved her very dearly.

Now, I felt quite shaken. Something was not as it should be, but what and how, I could not have known. I would never understand Catherine, her quiet words and ways, but something about her this time added to my unease. I am not of a fanciful nature and thought that maybe I was tired from my travels and had been influenced to feel fear by Ann and Emily. I gave my farewells and left to stay at the inn overnight, before travelling home to Rosamund and our two children. I queried in my mind on and off, for several days, trying to understand their worries, yet all thoughts ended without any answers or any enlightenment. Little did I know that that would be the last time I ever set eyes on my three dear sisters.

§

On the morrow, I set off to my home. As the way led through the neighbouring village, Bretton, where Mary lived, I decided that I would visit her and see her little girl, Marion, who was by now almost two years of age. She was getting great with child but greeted me with her usual subdued friendliness. We chatted about her everyday activities and she, in return, asked me where I had been travelling and such like. It was just the normal conversations one would have with a sister after not seeing her for a few months. But, when I asked about Abe, her husband, then her face clouded. She told me that she did not see him much at present as he was very busy and he seemed to have something on his mind, but he wouldn't share it with her.

"Maybe he is concerned about your laying in, which will be soon."

"I asked him, and he denied that was a worry and that I managed to have Marion without a problem, so he was hoping for the same ease again."

Let me tell you. Abe is a carpenter and very skilled at his trade, in fact, he is good enough to be employed by my uncle at the Hall. Since Grandpapa died my uncle has done much renovation work and had recently built another wing to the house, though why anyone would want more rooms, than they have already, I cannot tell. The Hall is a vast building. But, if any wood work is needed to be done, then Abe does it.

"I hear Uncle Wilfred is doing a lot of new work at the Hall," I offered, as a possible explanation.

Mary agreed. "Yes, I know, but Abe is used to that. He has made a new staircase and is now working on gateposts to fit a beautiful iron gate that John has designed and Henry is making."

∫

Here, I will interject a few brief lines about some more members of our family, so that you will know of whom I write and the connections. I understand that it is my individual need to do so. However, when hearing of some event hitherto unknown, I find that information, if presented as and when relevant, always gives me the easier way to understanding. As I have suggested before, this is what I am trying to do as we progress through this book, in an effort to avoid any confusion. So I will tell you a little more about these people I have just mentioned. They were well known to us all.

John, the eldest, and Henry are the sons of Aunt Rosemary, one of our father's elder sisters, though in truth she was only ten months older than him. She lives in a rather grand, overlarge house just opposite Mary. Aunt Rosemary was married to the physic in the village. It was a match of both love and good fortune as Harold – as that was her husband's name – was a man of means, inherited from his father. I write 'was married' as Harold, at the time of my writing this book, has since died.

Let me tell you a little more about Uncle Harold. While I was growing up, I always thought that he was the brother of my mama and of Eve, that is, the son of my grandparents. Only after Eve's death did I find out that he was in fact, their cousin. His own mother was Grandmama's next youngest and favourite sister. She died at his birth, and when the baby, Harold, was only three months old, his father was killed by brigands and the boy became an orphan. Grandmama offered to take the baby to her own home, where she had many staff to assist. He was thereafter brought up at the Hall by Grandmama and Grandpapa as if part of their own family. Harold's mother, my father told me, had been a tiny person, by all accounts, and her husband was a tall man, and their union produced a large baby. He was too large for Grandmama's poor sister to sustain his birth. Harold was only a few months younger than Uncle George, the eldest son of my grandparents. When Uncle George died, Harold lost his best friend, his childhood companion and his life was diminished forthwith.

Notwithstanding her fondness for Harold, Eve used to say that he was the spoilt child in the family, being allowed more privileges than the rest. Only later, with the knowledge of his birth, did I understand that

Grandmama was probably trying to give him what he had been cruelly denied, and why she felt affection towards him different to her own children, carried and born by her own sweat and tears.

I liked him in many ways as he had good qualities, and was a good father to his sons, Henry and John. However, I cannot say that I respected him. Why? Well, he practised as a physic to all who lived on Grandpapa's wide estate. He showed great care and interest, and I have no fault to find with that admirable quality. But, he was more confident in his ability than I believe was due. He had not the gift of my sisters, yet did not seem to know this fact. If he did, he preferred not to acknowledge that truth.

He accepted their superior knowledge of herbs, potions and the like and did, on more than one occasion, request their help. However, let me say this. He would only ask for help when he knew he was sadly lacking in being able to help those who suffered and often when they were beyond any recovery whatsoever. His means of assistance, as for all physics, were very limited, though he did dispense his caring manner, freely. Rarely did anyone speak ill of him. My sisters, in their compassion and kindness, would answer his call for their help. But, then, if these people did not get well, and, particularly if they died, he would refuse to take any responsibility. Though it was the will of God Almighty, he would infer that maybe my sisters had been at fault in missing something, thus, by so doing, no ill would be thought of himself but rather of my sisters.

Now, my sisters were honest and they knew that some cases could not be helped by whatever means that they had and they would say so. They spoke rarely about Uncle Harold, except to say, on occasion, that he was not the fairest person to work with and they would prefer that he wasn't related and thereby he would be less likely to call on them. They gained a few people in the area who, in their grief, did not speak well of them, whereas he had none.

Aunt Rosemary, a few years previously, had suddenly lost the use of one of her legs and one of her arms. Though of apparently sound mind, she thereafter would find difficulty in choosing the right words she wished to say - though seeming to follow any conversation. But I was never quite sure. But, whatever, her problems meant that she could not look after herself. Both John and Henry were married. At this time, both lived in separate cottages to their mother but after Uncle Harold's death (I will tell you, later, of his death), Henry with his wife and children, decided to move back into the family home. Thereby he and his wife could look after his mother as well as their own family.

Both of these cousins, who are very artistic, were thought to have inherited that tendency from Aunt Rosemary's father, our paternal grandfather, who was quite a skilled painter in his spare time. John is a painter in oils and his pictures are well known in the area. In fact, Papa told me that Eve had asked John to paint a picture of the lake and woodland at the Hall. Her favourite niece, Angelina, her eldest brother George's daughter, was getting married and this was to be her gift to her. Unfortunately, three weeks before the wedding Eve had died. As you know it was at my sisters' birth, and the picture was never completed.

After her death, Papa had gone to collect the painting to give on Eve's behalf, as he knew she would want Angelina to still have the gift. But John, being of a headstrong though sensitive nature, had painted over the canvas, surmising it would now not be needed. It was thought, but only within the family you understand, that John would have asked for Angelina's hand in marriage. But, before he could make any move in that direction, he was told in no uncertain terms by Uncle Harold, that he had best look elsewhere rather than be disappointed. There was not one circumstance in which Angelina's mama would agree to such a union. Had Angelina's father been alive, it may have been different, but with Aunt Clarissa, no, it could never be. Aunt Clarissa had altogether superior wishes for Angelina's eventual betrothal. I, personally, thought Aunt Clarissa was rather a shallow lady, though pleasant face-to-face. She did not really contribute anything to anyone, at least, to anyone we knew about. She had never really accepted her 'demotion' in the family hierarchy after Uncle George died, despite the continued generosity of Uncle Wilfred.

Henry spends much of his time and earns his living shoeing horses and is the local blacksmith, though in truth, this is from choice not necessity. He likes to make John's designs into horse brasses and ornaments. The gentry come from miles around to buy his work and give him commissions for brasses to decorate their horses' bridles. Sometimes he is asked to make even more intricate and large designs, even in silver or pewter, to commemorate something or to hang on the walls of their mansions or at their doors.

§

After that brief interlude, I will return to my time with Mary.

"No," continued Mary, "Abe has been told he has a commission that he must complete in the next few weeks. He won't tell me who has commissioned the work or what it is. Usually he tells me most things, but I have been to look in his workshop when he is away and I can see nothing. I can't move anything, as wood is very heavy, so I cannot look properly, but he normally never hides anything. He is not himself and is not sleeping. Maybe it is just the long winter months and cold weather that has made him tired and, since then Marion has kept us out of our bed each night with a cough. We have been very worried about her, but she seems well again now."

§

I will interject just here, that my other sisters, Elizabeth and Mary, had never shown any signs of the healing ability that Ann, Emily and Catherine possess, but that is not to say it was absent.

§

"I must be going now, Mary. I pray that your confinement will be short and safe and I look forward to seeing you and your new child soon. I hope Abe tells you all to settle your mind. Give him a hearty greeting from me." And with that I embraced her and left.

I had not seen Helena, nor did I enquire as to her whereabouts.

On my way out I saw our cousin, Henry. He was standing outside to cool off, having been working in his hot forge.

"Good day, Richard, how good to see you. It's not easy in there sometimes," he pointed to the forge. "I presume you are just back from one of your longer journeys as I haven't seen you for a while. Does your horse need shoeing while you are here?"

"Have you time to take a look?" I asked, after answering his questions and voicing my concern about his health and that of his mother.

"For you, I have always enough time."

We had always been good friends when we were young and were of a similar age, but for one year difference.

"I am busy working on some very ornate gates for the Hall, but I can break off. I have just finished a scroll. You wouldn't believe it takes such a lot of concentration to get it just right. For me, it has to be perfect or I would rather not attempt the making thereof, added to which, John's designs are never simple."

He paused for a few minutes and I didn't interrupt him. I could see he was thinking about what to say.

"Richard, can I share something with you that is troubling my mind. I cannot share it with anyone else. I am so pleased to see you today, but if I can share this, then your presence is even more welcome."

"Of course," I wondered what problem Henry could be having at this time. Everyone seemed to have worries and wanted to share them with me. It was most unusual and was increasing my feeling of bemusement and apprehension, which had started with my sisters.

"I have been told to make three contraptions for the Church Army in Sandal, and I have been given this. Look!" He took a piece of folded paper from his leather apron pocket and held it out for me to take.

"I asked what they were to be used for and was just told, 'They are needed'. One soldier held out a drawing and when I saw it, I was horrified. I decided immediately that I had no intention of doing as he requested, so I replied, 'I really do not have either the time or inclination to make such items. Please find someone else.' But Richard, they would not leave until I had taken this design. They made me feel very fearful, as I have never been before. What do you think?"

I looked at the drawing with something akin to horror. 'What on earth,' I thought, 'is this to be used for?'

Before I could ask my question or reply to his, Henry continued, "Of course, I refused, but the soldier insisted, 'We have our orders and have been told to leave this with you.' They put the drawing on the side of the forge."

I had not seen its like before. It is difficult to explain, but, if I tell you I now know that it was made to hold a mouth open and the tongue down, you may be able to get into your head some idea of this design. Though I have told you of this, I would recommend that you avoid making the image strong else it may stay long in your mind. It was a hideous drawing that made my blood run cold as it obviously had done for Henry, in just the same way.

I thought that maybe I was misunderstanding Henry, so I asked again, "Who did you say has asked for these abominations to be made?"

"It was two soldiers from the castle in Sandal. They had enquired in the area around and been told that I was a skilled metal worker and hence had sought me out."

"I asked the one who seemed in charge again, 'First, tell me for what purpose and on what are these to be used?' He simply replied, without showing any feeling, though the drawing filled me with disgust, 'Our Captain's orders are that these are to be made. They are, we understand, to curb unruliness in three animals. Oh, and, he wants them ready in three weeks.' Again I objected to this task, 'I do not wish to make these.' The soldier replied, 'It would be well if you did. Accidents can happen.' I didn't know," explained Henry, "whether he was talking about a dog or a small colt that was likely to be vicious and cause an accident without the mouthpiece, or whether this was some kind of threat to me."

"What are you going to do? It is most irregular."

"I think and think but yet my mind does not give me the answer. I can't meet with an accident, if that is what was implied, as my wife and children rely on my health and ability to work. I haven't slept for the past two nights, since they came, and I haven't told anyone else."

"How can I advise? It is a dreadful thing to be asked to make." I felt great sympathy for him, but what could I say to help him? I pictured in my mind an animal forced to wear that contraption and added, "Imagine the suffering if that was put in the mouth of any dog or horse. Have you mentioned it to your father?"

"No, he has been very tired recently and I am not sure what his health is

like. As you know he carries a lot of weight around with him and, well, he is getting older. I wouldn't want to worry him unduly."

"Why don't you just wait and see if they return? If they get angry say that you have not been able to find the correct iron, as yet, to make such a delicately crafted object, or, better still, let the paper be blown into the fire and then you can say, with an honest heart, that you couldn't make them as the design which they left on the side was caught by the wind, and it blew into the fire and perished."

"That is a good idea, Richard, thanks, I'll do just that." He put the paper down where the men had originally put it, then grasped his bellows and with little effort the design was in the fire and quickly destroyed. "There, we must wait to see whatever happens next." He smiled with relief. "Your horse's shoes are fine and will serve a while longer yet."

"Thank you, Henry. I'll be gone now. Give my kindest regards to all the family."

I set off home at last, to my dear Rosamund and the children, to enjoy home comforts and their companionship once again.

~ Richard's next visit ~

I stayed at home for the following two weeks and then did one or two short trips away before starting, what I can only call my summer tour. At this time of year, it was my custom to be away for about six weeks, travelling the county, to the north, the south, the east and the west. This was before and during the harvest, weather permitting. Should a horse go lame or be affected by any illness during this time, then the consequences for some farmers was serious. The hunting horses were usually resting and so it was a good time to check them all over. I have to say that I was looking forward to when my son was old enough to travel with me on some of my trips.

That journey being so, the next time I arrived back in Stocksmoor village to call on my sisters was the fifth day of August. I shall remember that date until the day, which will surely come, when my maker calls me to rest.

I would fain not have to write more, but I must. I have found any manner of trivial excuses why I cannot meet with Robbie to continue with my task of writing this book. At the same time, I realise that, until I have completed this self-appointed task, I shall find no peace in my mind and its further purpose will not be achieved. So, I have determined to have the courage to put into words that which I know to be true, however painful to me, the writer, and to you, the readers.

§

I entered the village in the late evening and decided to rest the night at the inn. I intended to spend the next day with my father, sisters and their children. But, it took only a very short time to realise something was very wrong. As I went through the village I noticed all the doors were shut. All the shutters or drapes at the windows were closed. There were no friendly faces, and though it had been a hot day, no one was out in their garden cooling down in the evening air.

My father's house was also shuttered. I went to Nell's house to enquire where they had gone, but Nell's drapes were closed. I knocked on the door, but received no answer. Knowing Nell since I was a child, I felt able to go round to her back door without asking permission. Yet again, there was no answer when I banged on the door. I then knocked on the windows. I was, by now, getting very concerned. Never in all my years living in or visiting Stocksmoor had I found these houses locked against me.

Back on my wagon, I drove to the inn at the top of the village. Even this door was shut and locked. I knocked on the door and a voice, which I recognised as Bernard asked, "Who is there?" I answered him, "It's me, Richard, Richard Shaw." There was the sound of bolts being drawn and the door opened enough for me to enter. The landlord pulled me in and then shut and bolted the door again.

"What's going on, Bernard?" I asked.

"Sit down man. Just sit down while I tell you." He took hold of my arm and pulled me gently to a nearby chair and pushed me backwards, slowly, so that I could no longer stand. His eyes filled with tears, He couldn't speak.

"Bernard, tell me. What is going on?"

"It was the Church Army. They killed your sisters. It was on July 27th, at noon."

I felt as though I had been hit in my face and that I should swoon to the floor. I must be going down of an ague or dreaming some kind of nightmare.

"Killed? Killed Catherine? Ann and Emily dead? What can you mean? Eight days ago? Tell me it's not true, Bernard. This just cannot be."

"Aye, it is, as sure as I stand here."

"I can't believe it! I won't believe it!" I jumped to my feet and started to rush to the door. "I must go to their house and find them."

Bernard followed me and put his foot against the door. He was a strong, well-set man, taller than I. In my panic, I tried, but could not forego him. "Richard, listen to me. Would I, a friend since we were boys, tell you something like that if it was not true? Look at me. Would I?" I saw tears were now streaming down his face and I understood that he was telling me some awful truth which I must listen to. He guided me back to my chair.

"Tell me, Bernard."

"It happened without warning. About twenty of the Church Army came, uninvited and unannounced, and camped at the other end of the village, on the Mount. That same day some of the men put up a makeshift shed over the road there, and then, in the night started putting up three lots of standing stocks. We heard banging but did not know what the noise came from. To cut the story short for now, I tell you that the next morning, the officers called many of the villagers to the Mount and held some sort of trial, and immediately, the next thing we all knew, your sisters were put in the stocks. The Lord only knows what happened to them in the darkness of that first night. We heard screams on and off through the night. Me and David, from next door, went to investigate and to help your sisters, but we were held back at sword point. They were guarded by soldiers day and night. No one was allowed near, but, in all truth, few tried to help as all were too frightened.

"Their boys were driven away when they tried to get to their mothers. Nell, well, Nell can tell you about what happened to her. Only Simion managed to get near, but the soldiers obviously thought he was quite mad. We are not quite sure what they did to him. We saw them beat him but he still came back to be with your sisters. Eventually, they left him alone. At least we think they did, but we shall never know. Some were like animals, nothing less than animals."

He stopped, tears still streaming down his face.

"Go on. They surely were not killed by being on the stocks."

"Not quite, although it was very hot and what happened to them might well have killed them." He stopped for a while. "You know, they were not allowed anything to eat or drink. It was scorching hot and they were much burned. Ann especially, as she was facing the midday sun, and you know, they were very fair of skin. At one point, they were all rambling as if in a delirium. One passer-by heard Ann calling out Peter's name, as if she either saw him or had forgotten that he was dead. 'Peter, Peter, why do you just stand there? Why do you not come and help us?' But I understand she shouted only for a short while. The soldiers slashed their skirts and blouses with their swords, cutting their skin in the process and exposing it so they burned even more.

"During the three days they were on the stocks, those who live at the other end of village have now told us that the pond, at the lower end of the common, was deepened and... Oh! Richard, I can't tell you...."

"Please, Bernard, I have to know," I pleaded.

After a few moments he replied, "They were ducked, Richard, ducked. Soldiers came to take us all to watch. We were all made to stand around, under guard. Ann and Emily were held under too long and perished. We think Catherine, who was bound and had to wait, died before she was ducked. They screamed with pain as their burned legs and bodies were put in the water the first time. But then, they didn't scream again."

"The bastards, the filthy, rotten, cruel bastards. They shall pay for this, I promise, they shall pay!"

"Your cousin, Andrew, from Lower Oakington, rode here in haste, once he heard what was going on. He had been away on his estate duties. He arrived and tried to prevent their deaths, but he was too late and was killed. His son had arrived with him and he was killed too when he tried to intervene. Poor young Alend."

"Oh, my God! And my father?" I hardly dared to ask but I knew that my father would not have stood by and let this dreadful deed happen.

"He's dead too. You see, Richard, we all believe it had been well planned, so no help from any higher authority could be found in time to prevent their deaths."

"How did our father die?"

"He had left home very early, at day break, before they were put in the stocks. He had gone away for the day on business, without knowing anything was to happen. They got everything ready for the stocks, but only put them up after he left the village, then, about an hour later the soldiers went to his house. We can only surmise that his plan of action was known. Your sisters were taken without warning to the trial in the morning and straight to the stocks, which by then had been erected. Richard, believe me, it was all planned.

"When your father came home that evening, they were already in the stocks. He rushed to the Squire in Upper Oakington. We all understand that he told your father that he was going away urgently, at day break the very next day, for at least two weeks, and so would not be able to help or use his influence on behalf of your sisters. He was very sorry, but no, he could do nothing at all. We know that conversation to be true, from one of the Squire's own men, who heard the conversation. On his way back from Upper Oakington to try to rescue your sisters, your father collapsed and died.

"Richard, they were just beasts. When they found out who the dead man on the road near the camp was, they put his body on a makeshift platform. Four soldiers carried it and paraded it in front of Ann, Emily and Catherine, and then the soldiers, unceremoniously took the body to the burial ground. It was wrapped in sacking so that no animals could get to it. It was just left there. No one was allowed to leave the confines of the village to bury it. We understand that Ben buried it eventually. Your sisters must have known then that they had no hope."

"I can't believe it. I just can't believe that those dear, gentle and kind women have been killed and our father, dead. Cousin Andrew dead. Gentle Alend, dead."

I truly thought I might go mad.

"Before they were ducked and so that all gathered there could hear, the High Chief, spoke in a loud voice. He had paraded through the village that morning, coming from Sandal, you know, the main barracks. He was dressed in all his white vestments, funny pointed hat, carrying his cross on a long stick. He read out your sisters' so-called crimes, verdict and punishment. We were all made to watch the duckings. He then told us that the Church Army would never condone any blasphemy or acts that were contrary to the teaching of the Church and that divine healing belonged only to the hands of Christ, the son of God. Any who transgressed the law of God would be scourged from every corner of the land."

"What has happened to their bodies?"

"The villagers were told to burn them."

"We took down the stocks and used the wood and dry straw to make a pyre. The Church Army soldiers didn't even watch or come near until it was all over. Only the last smell and smoke lingered. They had done their bit. It was just terrible, like a nightmare."

I sat with my head in my hands for a long time. I felt too shocked at what I had heard. Yet, I had to believe it. Bernard left me alone with my anguish for a while. I felt anger when Beatrice died, but this feeling was like a fire, consuming my very soul.

He returned with food and ale.

"Have this, Richard. You cannot do anything on an empty stomach."

"The children," I exclaimed, as if suddenly coming straight out of a reverie into a panic. "What has happened to their children? Where are they?" I stood up again, feeling that I wanted to run to find them.

"Nay, Richard, sit down. Listen, we believe they are safe. But none of us know where they are. All we are certain of it that they are not in the village and the soldiers did not find or harm them. We have not been able to leave to find out. Your brother, Ben, was also away at the time on a business trip and we understand that he arrived home just before the duckings but no one told him what was to happen. He arrived in the village just as the bodies were being laid out, dead. He was totally distraught. He couldn't speak and just stood as if he had been nailed to the floor, and stayed like that for about an hour, staring into space and as if made of stone. It was really dreadful to see. No one knew what may happen to him.

"The soldiers packed up their camp and left only two days ago. Otherwise, you would not have been able to enter the village. They stopped movement in and out while Ann, Emily and Catherine were in the stocks and, for some reason, very few people have been allowed in or out of the village since. Ann and Emily's two boys went for help before the roads were blocked by the soldiers but obviously, couldn't get any aid. It was evil, Richard, pure evil. Nothing to do with God and the teachings of Christ, at least not the one I believe in. Nell has also disappeared since the bodies were buried. We all hope she has the girls with her."

"And what about dear Aunt Peggy? How has she managed to survive this dreadful time?" I asked.

"She didn't. She's dead too. It was all too much for the old soul. Again, we are not sure, but we think that she went with your sisters to the trial, as did Nell. Some say that when Peggy heard the verdict, she, too, collapsed and died while some say she was on her way back to her house afterwards. But, yet others have told me that they did not see her at the trial, so all I can really tell you is that she, too, is dead. Your sisters never knew as they were held at the camp until the soldiers escorted them to the stocks."

"They will not get away with this, I promise you, Bernard. I shall do whatever is in my ability to bring those responsible to justice."

"Nay, I doubt that will be possible. I know you are well-born, but apparently your cousin from the Hall went to intercede and got nowhere, and, he even travelled to York."

I just sat in the chair, stunned beyond anything I had ever known.

"I daren't drive the wagon in the darkness, but as soon as it comes light, Bernard, I shall set off home. Do you mind if I just sit and rest here till then?"

"Of course not. I will sit up with you."

"There is no need for you to miss your bed this night," I assured him.

"No, it's the very least I can do."

So, I sat in silent thought throughout the night. I could not sleep and spent the hours wondering about what I could do. What should I do first? I decided that I must find the children. Then I would keep my promise to my sisters and look after them. I prayed to God that they were safe, as Bernard thought. I was in such a confusion of thought that I felt I had no intelligence at all. Finally, I determined a plan of action. I would go home to see Rosamund and the children at the break of dawn; there I would leave the wagon, and I would travel to York to visit our uncle, Sir George, and ask for his aid in this tragedy. A wiser, kinder man the country has yet to find. If he was able to help then I was confident that he would.

But firstly, before going to York, I must visit our brother, Ben, in Upper Oakington to see if he knew anything about the whereabouts of Ann and Emily's four children.

∫

Next day, after only an hour at home, I set out. Rosamund was beside herself with grief, but she packed me some bread and cheese and a flagon of ale and water.

"Goodbye for now, my dearest Richard." She embraced me. "Please take great care."

I kissed her and the children goodbye. I did not know when I should be home again. I had much to do. I went directly to see Ben. His wife,

Hannah, white faced and looking very drawn and afraid, came to the door, and asked, "Who is there?"

"It is me Hannah, Richard."

"Come in, Richard, quickly," and she shut the door behind me. "Oh, Richard, what are we to do?"

"Is Ben in?"

"No, he has gone to work at the wood yard, to keep up appearances, in case the troop of soldiers comes back. Ben says the Church Army have now left Stocksmoor, but men have been riding through the village who he doesn't know and who nobody in the village knows. He thinks they may be soldiers, though they wear no uniform and have been asking questions about Ann and Emily's children. We think they may be trying to find them and take them. But, Ben says, he is assured that no one from the village is speaking to them. We are hoping that no one will betray the children. We are all very shocked, you know."

"Hannah, I am beside myself with worry. Do you know where the children are?"

"Yes, we have the boys here. We are keeping them indoors, hidden. They were brought to us by Simion, you know the one the villagers call 'Jesus'. He took them away from the scene after their mothers died and the soldiers took no notice, apparently, thinking he was just a mad man and that they would find him and them later. He hid them in the wood in the valley. The day after the burning of the bodies, he found Ben at work and took him to where they were hidden. Ben then brought them here but I don't know what we are going to do. Our children could now be in such terrible danger if the army know we are harbouring Ann and Emily's children. I live in total fear. But, what else can we do?"

"I promised Ann and Emily, at their request, that, should anything happen to them I would take care of the children. Can you keep them here until I find somewhere for them to go? I think that they must be taken right away from this area."

"Of course they can stay, but we have little room and they are very unsettled and I find them very difficult. They keep trying to leave and go

to Miriam and Miranda. Could you please speak with them and explain what they must and must not do? They are not speaking and will scarcely eat. I feel ill myself with my bad stomach. Please don't let it be too long before you arrange something. I cannot manage like this for very long," wept Hannah, the tears running down her face. She wiped her cheeks with her apron.

"I shall do what I can as quickly as I can. What about the girls? Where are they?"

"They are at the farm across the wood, you know, the one my cousin farms for my brother. Nell's sister is the housekeeper there. Nell took the girls to stay there and has returned to stay with them since their mothers were burned. They are safe for now, but it is very isolated and they will not be safe if the soldiers find out about them.

"We haven't told anyone, not even my brother, Robert, who has just come back, though he is not staying. He went away at the time, having been called away on urgent business, as the Squire, you realise. So, that was the reason he couldn't help your sisters. But, Richard, I saw Robert, just about an hour before he went away, and he told me that Ann, Emily and Catherine were 'just being given a lesson'. I don't know how he knew but those were his very words. Yes, that is what he made me believe. He told me, 'Hannah, I'm sure that it's nothing to worry about. A lesson for them and nothing more.' So that is what I also told Ben, and why Ben didn't rush straight there to try to help them. It was my fault Ben didn't go to Stocksmoor, but I didn't know. I didn't know!"

She was quite consumed by her anguish and could not stop weeping. I sat and held her hand until she could compose herself to tell me more.

"He could have arrived there before they were ducked and killed. I blame myself Richard. It all goes round and round in my head. I never thought it was serious. Surely Robert wouldn't have told a lie to me, his sister, if he had known more. He must not have known what was to happen. He is a good man, Richard, believe me, he is a good man. He is like my father."

"Maybe we shall never know, Hannah. We cannot bring my sisters back to life." I replied as gently as I could. "I like to think the best of people when I can. I will just see the boys and then I must waste no time. I must be off. Tell Ben I am going to York and will come for the boys and the girls as soon as I can. If possible, I shall be back in just a day or two. If you can go across the wood to see Nell, please let her know. But, do not tell your brother, the Squire, our plans if you see him, just in case someone hears and is not trustworthy."

I spent some time with Mark and James. Those poor boys! I could scarcely speak to them and simply held them both close. They just stared into the space in front of them but did not cry, but they knew I was there. I explained I was going to York to see Uncle George and would be back in a few days, as soon as was ever possible to collect them. I asked them to promise me, for their mamas' sake, that they would stay in this room where they were safe. They both nodded. And with that, I left with haste. At least I knew the children would be fed and safe until I could take them away. I admit to being mystified about the Squire, a man I had never liked much, but not one to whom I would have attributed any ill intent.

Later that day I arrived in Poppleton. Uncle George was sitting in his large library, poring over some documents.

"Richard, I didn't expect to see you. What an unexpected pleasure," he was smiling, then, quickly he realised something was amiss.

"Richard, what's wrong? Here, lad, come and sit down."

"Uncle George, my father …" I could say no more.

I fell into one of his wide chairs and then I wept as I had not wept before. How could I tell him what had happened to his dear brother and family?

"Here, drink this." Uncle George handed me a small glass of spirit. "You must just rest a while and, when you collect your composure, then you can tell me what your trouble is." He sat down with me and silently waited.

"Uncle George, my father is dead. Ann, Emily and Catherine are dead. Andrew and Alend are dead. Aunt Peggy is dead."

"What? How?" he exclaimed in a state of disbelief, and then he too fell backwards into his chair.

"Ann, Emily and Catherine were taken by the Church Army. They were put in the stocks for three days. Then my sisters were ducked until they were dead."

"No! No! Oh NO! The evil bastards." Sir George then stood up and walked up and down the library.

"And your father?"

"He died of shock and grief before they died. His heart just could not contain his sorrow. He collapsed and was found dead on the road home."

"My God! And my sister Peggy? Is she alive?" he gasped the words, as if to do so was an effort, but as though he had not fully heeded what I had told him.

"No. She too collapsed and died shortly after. I'm not sure of all the details yet."

"What happened to Andrew and Alend?"

"They were both stabbed. Andrew was trying to assist Ann out of the ducking bindings, as she was still just alive. Alend went to help his father."

"Someone will pay for this, if it is the last thing on earth that I ever do," promised Uncle George. "Richard, I swear I shall not rest until I have justice, Church Army or not. I shall find a way. There must be a way." He continued to first pace up and down, then he sat for a while with his head in his hands, then he got up again as if in a state of confusion, not knowing what to do. I hardly wished to interrupt him, but I must.

"Uncle George."

He lifted his head. "I'm sorry, Richard. I was overcome with your news. Please continue with what you want to say."

"Their children, Uncle George. What can I do? I promised Ann and Emily that if anything ever happened to them I would look after their children. I think they must have had a visitation of doom to ask me, but now it is necessary. It is not safe to keep them in the village and Rosamund and I are very willing to care for them all, as our own, but where can that be? We are too near to Stocksmoor and the Church Army *headquarters in Sandal to keep them safe. Can you suggest what we should do?"*

"Of course, you must all come here if Rosamund will agree. There is no question to ask. I can keep them all safe. We have so many rooms, empty and to spare and we have two of the stable cottages empty. I was going to make them habitable for the grooms and move them in, but they can wait. I can easily think of somewhere else for them. I will instruct my workmen to get the cottages ready, make them both into one for you and your family and my housekeeper can prepare rooms in the house for Ann and Emily's children. Give me just a few days. I will get everyone working today as fast as is humanly possible."

"Uncle George, we must bring Nell away with us. She knows too much as she dressed their bodies afterwards. They know her and hurt her when she tried to assist my sisters. She is the only one left in the children's lives. They love her like a second mother."

"That is no problem either, Richard. She shall look after those children as she usually does and can always lend the housekeeper or cook a hand if necessary."

Then I wept again, overwhelmed by this sudden generosity and answer to all our problems. He had not had to give it any consideration but just let his kind heart give him the answer.

"Are you sure your household can contain so many more? We are four and the children are four and Nell. That is nine more people. Uncle George, I am the only one who brings in any income," I suddenly faced that fact, and that there was none otherwise nor likely to be for some many years.

"Richard, lad, I have more wealth and rooms than we can ever use. That is not any problem, not at all. Since your Aunt Gwendolyn died, this house has lost some of its soul. I can offer my brother's family a home and education and they, in turn, will bring more life back into these empty rooms. So, that is arranged. The housekeeper's daughter is asking to work here and now she will have something to do."

"What about your son and his family?"

"Andrew? Oh, fear not, he will be delighted, as will his wife and children.

And, you are like a brother to Oliver anyway, though he is away from home now a lot. Richard, I am certain they will all welcome you equally as much as I shall. They have their own quarters. Maybe you don't realise just how big this house is. We have rooms I haven't seen for years. Here is ample room and provision for all. Let me see, I shall appoint an extra cook, we shall have another scullery maid and shall need one or two extra housemaids. That will give more work to the villagers. We can employ more if necessary."

"I am truly overwhelmed by your kindness. I will travel straight back home now, collect the children and then we shall all return here, probably on the third or fourth day from now. Will that be alright? I am frightened to stay longer in that area, as, though the soldiers have moved away from Stocksmoor, I understand their spies are still passing through the village and asking questions about the children. My friend, Bernard, who is the innkeeper, is very astute and says that he has had a spy visit the inn each day. He says he can pick them out. They may well be after the two boys who are now orphans."

"Really, why would they bother with them?" asked Sir George.

"When I return I will tell you everything that my sisters told me and what I believe is the true reason they were killed. I know it was the Church Army, but how did anyone know that they had the information that they told me? There is even more to tell you. I am going to work with you to bring those villains to justice, make no mistake. They should not be able to do such dreadful deeds without retribution. There is more to the Church Army than seeking to eradicate witches, as they apparently called my sisters."

"Witches? Your sisters? Witches? Oh, what utter madness. Richard, this time the deaths have affected people who have some authority and knowledge. Fear not, I may be getting old, but with age comes many contacts, influence and knowledge. I will study to find the best way forward. Rest for a while. Take one of my best horses. Bring them all back safely, Richard. I am going to ask Oliver to go with you. He's at home at present. You will also need two carriages, each driven by two of my men. Even the Church Army would not dare to touch my carriages or anyone in them. It sounds as if Stocksmoor is still being watched."

"How can I ever thank you?"

"There is no need for thanks. They were my family too. I am shocked and very saddened. I loved them all, you know. Take great care, Richard."

"I shall," I promised. "I will ask Oliver to take one of the carriages to my house. He can help Rosamund pack up the clothes and any household possessions we shall need. I shall go with the other carriage to Ben's house to collect Ann and Emily's children. Ben can go to Hannah's cousin's farmhouse if Nell and the girls are still hiding there and fetch them to his home. The boys are already there. Then, I shall go with Nell to my father's house to obtain whichever belongings they will require to bring with them. She'll know. I can go back to my house at a later time for my wagon. I shan't be using it for a while. I think that will be the best solution. Would that suffice?"

"Whatever you think is the best way, Richard. Any help you require is there for you. Just take what you need."

"I will find Oliver and we shall arrange our plan. I shall never be able to thank you enough, ever," I embraced my dear, kind uncle.

"Your father would have done the same for me, God forbid, in the same circumstances. Now leave me, Richard. I need time alone to try to understand my great loss. I thought when your Aunt Gwendolyn died that the most important part of my life had gone with her. She was ill and suffering and her end had to be – as a natural course of events – however sad. But now I am beginning to realise that I am to have a further importance in this life," he paused for a while.

"This is so unnecessary and unjust that I cannot at this time make any sense of it in my mind. So dreadful, it is so utterly dreadful. If only Gwendolyn could still be here to be a helpmate in this time of trouble. She was so good with children."

§

I had arrived at Ben and Hannah's house and found that all four children were already there in one of the bedrooms. They were clean, and well fed, but very pale and silent. All were sitting, in the corner on the large bed in the room, and the two girls had their arms round the shoulders of their younger brothers.

"Hello," I greeted them softly, but heard only whispered 'hellos' back. I simply leaned over and put my hand on each one's shoulder for a while, in turn. They were not ready or able to talk to me.

Downstairs was Nell, helping Hannah wash clothes in the scullery.

"Nell, I am so glad to see you and to know that the girls are safe. I was so worried about your whereabouts until Hannah told me where you were. None of the villagers knew. Will you excuse me Hannah, while I have a word with Nell, if you please?"

"Of course, Richard."

We went out into the garden.

"Nell, thank you for saving the girls from what could have been a terrible fate. Ann and Emily would be eternally grateful to you."

"For all their brute force, those soldiers couldn't beat me. I know all the woods and paths around Stocksmoor. I feared for their safety if they stayed in the village while those animals, called soldiers, were still there. They only know that their mothers are dead, but know no details. I just can't bring myself to tell them, Richard. They are lost, but, just now, I can't tell them. I wish I could, but I can't, as yet, speak the words they need to hear. The boys haven't told them what they saw. Maybe they never will."

"You did so right, Nell. We shall have plenty of time to let them know, but gradually is the best way I think."

"After I took them, I came back and went to the stocks, you know, to try to help my mistresses, but the soldiers stopped me and hurt me before making me leave."

"Nell, I am so sorry."

"Nay, it was nothing to what they did to them. I cannot speak of it now, but I will tell you in due course, as I hope some justice will be done."

"I am taking the children to York to our uncle, Sir George. He is going to give them a home. I'm going to move there with Rosamund and our children. Uncle George has offered this refuge for us all."

"That is a great blessing and he is a very kind man. I shall miss them when they go with you." Tears filled Nell's eyes. "But, you are very right. It's the only place. They cannot stay unprotected in your father's house, even if I was with them. I'm strong and would wield a sword if necessary, but I know they are better away from here for every reason it is possible to think about."

"Nell, I want to ask you a favour. Would you consider leaving your home at Stocksmoor and coming with the children? I have arranged with Uncle George that you could continue to look after them. He agrees with me and insists that that is where you belong. That is, of course, if you will accept to do so."

"Me, come with you all and live in Sir George's house with the children? Oh, Richard, I cannot think of anywhere I would rather be. Since I lost my child, I thought of their mothers as my own children. Now, their children mean everything to me. If you are sure, then yes, I don't need to think about it, not at all. I will come with you and be most grateful for Sir George's understanding."

"I will tell Ben and Hannah what is decided. Ben must do what is necessary about our father's house. I am the eldest, I know, but I shall not be here and having that house does not concern me. But, I must visit Stocksmoor before we go to York. I don't want to, but I must."

"I will go with you and help you collect the clothes and other things the children will need."

We told Hannah where we were going and asked her to put a bite of food ready for the children and Nell for their journey to York.

§

I think going back into the empty house of my father and my three sisters was one of the hardest things I shall ever be called upon to accomplish. Nell had a key to the back door and we entered into this house, no longer a warm and welcoming home. We left the front shutters closed. Nell went about her task of collecting clothes for the children and the small things that she knew they would want to take with them.

"Master Richard, here is the casket that Ann and Emily treasured. It was *the one that belonged to their mother, given to her by her father when she was married. You must take this. Ann and Emily would often look at it and wonder that their mother was like. I used to tell them that Catherine was her image, and that they were also very close in looks to her. I cannot believe they are gone and not just out in the garden or visiting someone. I cannot believe what has happened. If only someone would say, 'Wake up, Nell, you've had a nightmare,' and I could open my eyes and it was all back to how it was before."*

Her tears fell, as did mine. To have to accept and understand that those gentle, loving, intelligent women would never walk in these rooms again was almost impossible at this time.

"The girls will one day want to have these," Nell spoke, almost to herself, as she picked up some jewellery from the top of some drawers. "If we leave them, then they will be stolen when vandals realise this house is empty."

She put the pieces carefully in the casket. We went from room to room. Nell collected those clothes of the girls' and boys', that she thought they would need, to take with us. But we did not linger in the house. The sadness was overwhelming. Nell closed the back shutters that we had opened. We went out and locked the door. Nell carried a piece of cloth in her hand.

"This was a piece of Ann's skirt which had been torn. Can I take it with us?"

"Of course, Nell. Please bring anything you wish. Do you want to visit anyone before we leave the village?"

"No, it is better that no one knows where we are or where we are going. One day I will come back and visit my friend, Martha, but for now, no, I don't think it is yet safe for her to know where we are. I have asked Ben to have a word with her, just to tell her that I am safe and with the children."

"I just have to do one more thing. I want to go to where their bodies were burned. Will you come with me?" I asked her, as I put the things in the small wagon that belonged to Ben. I had borrowed it for the short visit to Stocksmoor, as my horse was resting and it would be less noticed as Ben travelled to the village most days.

We drove the wagon onto the common. Then Nell and I walked slowly to where the bodies had been burned. It was now only an area of white ash. I bent down to touch it. This was all that was left of my sisters and would itself soon blow away. There was nowhere to pay respects to them. It was desolate. Circling round the ash I found a piece of charred parchment, about the size of half my palm. On what had obviously been a scripted document, I could distinguish just one word 'granted'.

"Nell," I exclaimed, holding out the fragment in surprise, "look at this. Why would there be any parchment here?"

"Oh, Richard, imagine that piece not burning! When the bodies had been burned and the pyre was almost gone, your cousin Geoffrey from the Hall arrived. He was waving a piece of parchment in front of him as his horse galloped up to the fire. He got off his horse, tears streaming down his face, and went to face the Captain. 'What have you done? This was their pardon,' he cried, 'their pardon. Look, it is signed by the Archbishop.' He turned to everyone and shouted. 'All here, listen to me and witness, they were pardoned! They were pardoned!' He fell to his knees weeping. But it was too late. The Captain went over to him, where he was still on the floor and grabbed the parchment out of his hand. 'Signed by the Archbishop, is it? Let me have it.' He took the parchment and, with his sword, cut it into pieces and threw the pieces into the fire.

"Geoffrey had obtained a pardon for your sisters, but his horse lost a shoe which delayed his journey back. That meant that he did not arrive in Stocksmoor until the day after they were killed. He was distressed beyond words and quite exhausted with his efforts. He thought he had won but then found he had failed."

§

I then noticed a piece of wood that had not burned. It was at the very edge of the area of ash. It must have been part of the stocks as it had a curved edge to it. I realised from its size it was one of the arm holes. One of my sister's delicate wrists had been held by this piece of wood. I picked it up and as I did, anger hit me as if a blow had been struck at my very being. It felt as if the flames which had surrounded this wood were suddenly ignited in my heart and a dark red cloud enveloped my brain. I felt as I had never felt before, not even when Bernard first told me the news, or when my beloved Beatrice and our son had died. I knew from that moment that I would avenge their deaths. They would not die in vain. My whole being changed in that instant. I too will never be the same again.

§

All was soon packed into Uncle George's carriage and Nell set off with the children for Poppleton, near York, with the protection of Uncle George's men. Though York is the centre of the Church in the north of the country, with its magnificent, newly-finished Minster, and the headquarters of its army, it was deemed much safer for the children than anywhere else. Uncle George, as Lord Lieutenant, was a powerful authority and his protection would be adequate, whatever happened thereafter. I knew that no one dare hurt anyone in his care.

I continued on my journey, to my own house, to help Rosamund pack up our personal belongings. Oliver had taken the second carriage onward to my home and had been helping her. But, as she had already been preparing for leaving while I was away, we all soon completed the task and put everything we needed into the carriage. I had told her of my promise to Ann and Emily before they died. She knew we could not stay in our house and neighbourhood with their children and was confident that Uncle George would help us. The carriage was waiting to take us to our new life.

~ What happened in Stocksmoor ~

Nell was able to tell me, eventually, what she knew of everything which had happened to my sisters. It did not make for easy telling or, dear readers, will it be easy reading. But, it happened and I must make this record as accurately as is possible. I could not bring my dear sisters back, and, what happened I really would have preferred not to have in my mind, as I was tortured by the loss. But, I needed to find out in detail what happened as Uncle George wanted me to collect evidence to bring the villains to justice. He had determined to find a way of prosecuting the Church Army, something that, up to this time, no one in the country had accomplished or, in fact, dared to attempt.

One evening, about a week after we had all settled in to Poppleton Manor, Uncle George and I were in his library.

"Richard," he spoke, in a subdued voice, "I shall keep my word, however much effort it takes or even years of my life. They have picked on the wrong people this time. The deaths of my dearest nieces will be avenged. My brother was brought to an untimely end as was our dear sister, Peggy. Andrew was a good man, following in Reginald's footsteps, and Alend was but a lad. I will use every ounce of my energy and knowledge to search for a way in which to find justice. I swear that I will do what I can to stop this march of terror and intolerance. I will not stop until I am successful in my quest. Would you be prepared to help me further in this?

"Of course, Uncle. I have a fire raging within my heart which nothing can quell. Like you, it is not vengeance but justice that I want for them all. I will help all I can."

He told me that he had already heard from his contacts around the country. They told him that other women, who were kind and knew of the healing properties of plants and herbs and who helped people who were sick, particularly those having a fever, had been hanged, or ducked, and that others had mysteriously gone missing. In the course of his duties, he visited different parts of the country. He met up with other Lord Lieutenants and those whose responsibilities were to try to bring order to the communities through the laws of the land. He was able to send letters to them for help and information and, above all, he knew whom he could trust.

There was a lot of concern but no one had ever taken any action, believing that the Church Army was untouchable and unpunishable, other than by the orders from the Church itself. As it was the teaching of the Church that all infidels and blasphemers should be scourged from the land, then no action was ever taken by the Church leaders. They believed that these women were evil and hence could be lawfully killed in the eyes and the name of God Almighty and so members of the hierarchy of the Church appeared to turn a blind eye to, or even condone, how the Church Army behaved in its appointed tasks.

§

Let me explain that the King's army is made up of villeins, common men, workmen, labourers, all who owe allegiance to their masters. They are called from their duties to fight when necessary. They are immune from the civil law if they are fighting in the name of the King's cause, and they are only answerable for their actions to their commanding officers, those being the Dukes, Squires and the like. That is, put another way, providing they are fighting for the King and his causes, soldiers are immune from prosecution for their acts. The Church Army use that same protection though carrying out their scourging, not for the King, but for the Church alone. No one has questioned that right in law, so the Church Army carry on their actions free from civil justice and retribution.

No one knows much about the Church Army. However, there is common knowledge of an elite section within the army. These are known to wear white, distinctive attire which hides their faces. They are present at all the final destructions, such as the hangings, duckings and other atrocities inflicted on the so-called infidels. They are known around the country as the 'White Army' or, more commonly, 'The Riders of Death'. They are feared beyond any other men in the country.

§

I wish to continue with my narrative, yet, I feel justified in writing all my digressions as I believe that they will be necessary.

Once the children had settled into the manor and Sir George was satisfied that all was in place for my family, and to our satisfaction in our new home, he decided on a plan of campaign, with as much fire in his soul as I had in my heart. He gave me the task of finding out the information of what happened in Stocksmoor that resulted in my sisters' deaths. He determined that he, himself, was going to search the laws of the land, and would trace records as far back as was necessary to find, somewhere and somehow, a lawful means of bringing the culprits to justice, Church Army or not. He determined to go to London to the high courts and libraries where the books of laws were kept, to other major cities whose archives held important historical papers, and to visit others highly versed in the law. He would make use of everyone he knew and involve them in his campaign, so that, whatever the outcome it would be well known around the country. This was 'war' of a different kind, and one that was, until now, uncharted ground. Fired up with a desperate need to get justice while any evidence was available, he departed within four days and we did not see him again for three weeks. Meanwhile, my quest for information began.

§

It is difficult to know where to start, but I think I must tell you, at this time, that which Nell recounted to me. Then I will tell you what else I found out for Sir George. I had told Nell that I needed to know what happened, and asked her to let me know when she was ready and able to tell me. We had been living in Poppleton for about three weeks, when Nell came to me one evening.

"Richard, the children are all asleep. Can I unburden my mind and my heart and tell you all that you want to know? I cannot rest until I do so, though it will be very painful. But, for my dear mistresses' sakes, I will share with you that which I saw. No one else will be able to tell you things that only I can recall."

"Yes, Nell. I do not relish having to hear what you will say, but hear it all I must. I shall make notes in my diary for the day and record what you tell me. In that way I shall remember everything, and be able to give Uncle George the information when the time is ready."

"Richard, two weeks before the Church Army came to the village, I asked Ann and Emily if something was troubling them. They just couldn't sit still, were very pale under the effects of the sun, and they were not eating as much as they usually did. They answered, 'Yes, Nell, we are both so much troubled that we cannot sleep.' I asked them could they tell me. I thought that maybe I could help, as I hated to see them looking so full of worry. I wondered if they were ill of something and not telling me. It was Ann who finally expressed some of their worries. 'Nell, if anything should happen to Emily, to myself, or to us both, would you take the girls to safety to your sister, at the farm over in the wood?' I answered, though bemused, 'Why, surely, if that is what you would want.'

- 234 -

"Then Emily carried on, saying, 'We have been wondering about the boys in such circumstances. Would you send Mark to the Hall? James must go to his Uncle Andrew at Lower Oakington. You cannot take all four together. We are sure that Uncle Wilfred and Andrew will keep the boys safer than anywhere else.' I felt quite shocked. 'Ann and Emily, you must surely be suffering from your lack of sleep to have such thoughts of danger.' Ann replied, 'Whatever, Nell, our thoughts will not stop and reason of any kind will not prevail, so please will you agree to do that which we ask? We have asked our brother, Richard, if he will be the guardian of the children if that should be necessary, but he is often far from home for several weeks. We feel that anything could happen should he still be away when, or if, his help is required.'

"They were both talking with tears streaming down their faces, and there was nought I could do, Richard, to comfort them. The tears were not shown in front of the children, who would not have known anything was amiss. And, then it all happened, so suddenly."

Nell then told me all that had happened and I wrote it down as she spoke.

A group of about fifteen or twenty soldiers, with their Captain and his Second in Command, arrived in Stocksmoor, in the latter days of July, and made camp on the Mount at the lower end of the village. No one knew then why they had chosen to stay in Stocksmoor. She was not quite sure of exactly the number, but they all belonged to the Church Army.

But, it has to be noted in passing, that one of their 'followers', a girl called Annette, was born and had grown up in the village. These 'followers' were women who travelled and lived with the soldiers and served their needs. No one ever asked what 'needs' these women served, but all surmised it was more than cooking their food and washing their clothes. Of that fact there was no mistake. The only oddness about this was that there were no children with them, and people had their own thoughts as to the reason for that lack.

§

Nell's story about my sisters started just after everyone in the household had eaten their early morning repast, on the 24th July, 1497. Miriam and Miranda were at the far end of the garden picking herbs with Catherine and Mark and James were in the field feeding the fowls. Nell was busy upstairs with the household chores. The front door was wide open, as was the custom, to let in the morning sun and a slight breeze to freshen the house after the night.

There had been several children with fever and coughs in the village and in the farms around. Ann and Emily were busy in the scullery collecting together more potions and poultices. These would then be ready should any parent call for help for their child. They had taken little notice of the Church Army camp. Having never been accepted into the Church, then the Church, its missives, teachings, rules and regulations were irrelevant to them. They lived by another faith entirely and, despite their long grief, they were serene as if they had an inner peace.

The calm and tranquillity of this household was suddenly rent asunder by a loud banging on the door. Three Church Army soldiers, dressed in white jackets and black trousers, burst into the house. Catherine heard the commotion and, after telling the girls to continue collecting the herbs and not to come into the house for any reason whatsoever, rushed to see what was happening.

Each of the soldiers grasped one of the sisters and, without any explanation, dragged them outside and escorted them from the house. The children heard the protests and shouts for help from Ann, Emily and Catherine, and rushed back to the house. Nell would not let them go out of the front door and told them to stay in the house. She bolted the door lest they tried to reach their mothers. She asked them to please remain quiet, so that the soldiers would not know they were in the house, and she would return as soon as possible to let them know what was to happen. They promised and then Nell left to follow the soldiers and my sisters down the road.

Once the neighbours heard the commotion they looked out of their windows, but, when they saw the soldiers, they shut the windows, the shutters and the drapes. Only Aunt Peggy next door, who had heard my sisters' cries, came rushing to see what was happening and arrived just after Nell had left the house. She started running down the road after them, shouting for the soldiers to stop, but the soldiers simply ignored her entreaties, as if she didn't exist. Just opposite the common land she collapsed and it is thought she died a few minutes later.

"Bernard thought Aunt Peggy had possibly been to the trial and had died as a result of what she heard. Is that true?" I asked.

"No, she never got there, poor Miss Peggy. As you know, she had been ailing in the recent few months. She didn't complain, but we all noticed that she had some shortness of breath. The extra effort and shock just killed her. But, Richard, I am glad. She just could not have survived watching or hearing what happened."

"Sorry for the interruption, Nell. Please carry on."

As soon as she had reached my sisters to protest about what was happening, Nell had been knocked down by one of the soldiers and winded so she could not breathe or stand for several minutes. She looked back when she realised that Peggy's shouting and screaming had stopped. She saw her lying in the road. She managed to get back to her and found her dead. She gently lifted the body and placed it out of sight behind the low stone wall, which ran by the left side of the road, keeping the woodland trees at bay. Later that same day, before she took Miriam and Miranda away from the village, she found two of the village men to help her. They buried Peggy in the communal burial ground lower down the village. It is thought that the sisters never knew that anything untoward had happened to their beloved Aunt Peggy. Her death at that time has surely to be seen as a blessing. She had not to witness or even be aware of what happened later. At least she was spared that anguish.

§

The three sisters were taken up the short slope to the Mount and into the camp. There they were made to stand, each one two arms lengths away from each other, so they could not touch each other or hold each other's hands. They stood thus, in the ever increasing heat of the day until noon. By now, Nell, having moved Peggy's body from the road, was standing as near to them as she was allowed. Other soldiers had been through the village and knocked on the doors to tell everyone who could walk to go to witness the trial. They were then made to stand in rows either side of the Captain's table. This was a trestle table with two chairs set out with a jug of ale, under a canopy to shield the Captain and his Second in

Command from the strong sun. Nothing was offered to Ann, Emily or Catherine.

Nell heard Ann say, "My legs are shaking beneath my skirt, Emily. What are they going to do to us?"

"I don't know. I also cannot keep my legs still. I fear I may fall. Who has put us in this position? What are we thought to have done wrong?"

"We shall keep our faith. They are evil bastards and are under orders which they will obey whatever we say. But we know what we are and what we do," announced Catherine, bravely, but so that Ann and Emily could hear her.

The Captain banged three times on the table with a small wooden mallet.

"Silence for this court."

They were all three taken to face the table. They were to become victims of a mock court in a trial that would blacken the name of justice, and must rank among the shortest and most unjust in human history. The fate of three beautiful lives was decided in a few minutes of prejudice and hate. All present were silent, the villagers waiting with dread in their hearts.

"We have been told that you are witches with supernatural powers, and that you are evil women. Each one of you is living a life doing deeds against the laws of Almighty God and his sacred word. We have witnesses who swear that these accusations are true," denounced the Captain in a loud voice.

He looked at the three women. "You," he pointed at Ann, "what have you to say in your defence?"

"We are not witches, nor would we know what such people are or do," replied Ann, in her quiet voice, though everyone standing round could hear her words clearly. "We simply love children and when they are ill we visit them when their parents ask us to do so. We put our hands gently on their backs, or chests or stomachs, wherever they have a pain. They are soothed. We give herbal potions and apply plasters. We do nothing more than that. We do not mention God or profess to do anything in his holy name. We never blaspheme. We do nothing of which you accuse us."

"You next," he pointed at Emily. But, before Emily could speak, Catherine stepped forward.

"You need ask only me. I am the one who has the power to heal. It was a gift I was given from God. With that gift I saved my sisters' lives, even when I was a little girl. I did not ask for this. I was given it and no one has the right to take that gift away. I use it only to help the sick to heal and the dying to die without pain or fear. I am sorry you are not so blessed, but that was not my doing.

"My two sisters are innocent of all your charges. They merely help me and each possesses warmth of nature that children feel. They grow and prepare herbs and potions and accompany me in my work. They give support and comfort for the children and their families. Take me. Do what you will to me, but release them. I say again, they are innocent of all your accusations. They need not nor should endure your cruelty. They have had enough suffering by having to live in their breathless bodies, which they do with courage and determination. Yet, despite all, they have a love for others. I have wished many times that I had not this gift as they lived only because I loved them, else they would have died at birth and been saved much suffering. But, that is something I have had to live with, though it was not my will or understanding at the time as I was only a child. No one can do God's work. There is another power at work determining a healing action, another which is altogether different."

"Silence. You blaspheme against God's holy name. I will not listen to more of this. Yes, the devil is at work here, but in you. No Christian or God-loving person can even think such thoughts nor say such diabolical words. Only Christ the redeemer, who died to save us from our sins, could ease pain and heal other people. I have gathered evidence over several months and I have been told such actions take place here in Stocksmoor. This is why we have travelled here, to scourge this village of your evil. The information that has been given to me already and what you say makes me believe that all is indeed true."

Emily faced the villagers.

"You all know that what Ann and Catherine have described is the truth. Can none of you speak up for us? Mary?" Mary turned away. "Dorah?"

Dorah turned away. "Ebenezer, your son is still alive when you thought he would die." Ebenezer shook his head and looked down at his feet and uttered not one word on their behalf, nothing.

"You speak in vain, Emily," interjected Catherine. "Please, my dear sisters, both of you, say no more. Our fates have already been arranged by these men. None or our villagers ought to speak alone to try to save us else they will surely receive punishment themselves."

Catherine then looked round the assembled villagers.

"Only you can decide which path to follow. If we die, there will be no one to heal, no one to give potions and no one to sit with your children. The burial place is waiting for them down the road, as it always has been. Our house will be empty and you will feel the pain of loss. You have a choice. You can stand together and speak on our behalf or remain silent. But, understand, once their deed is done, I fear you will have no choice again. These men have not made all this effort to merely chastise us for some kind of misdemeanour. They are serious in their quest and mean to kill us, make no mistake about that."

Everyone was silent, shocked beyond action and frightened to move. Then Nell stepped forward to speak.

"No, Nell. Please say nothing unless others move to stand with you. One, alone, will have no voice," begged Catherine. No one else spoke. But Nell held her ground.

"Please, Nell, keep quiet unless others join you. Our children will need you," whispered both Ann and Emily together, so that only Nell and Catherine could hear their words.

Before Nell could speak or any of the villagers get the courage needed to act on the sisters' behalf, the Captain nodded to one of his soldiers, who hit Nell across the head, then grasped her by the arm and pulled her to one side.

"Hold her there while I finish what is necessary."

One of the villagers standing nearest to the soldier, told Nell that she heard the Captain, in a very quiet voice meant only for the soldier himself to hear, say, "We have only prepared for three to go into the stocks. Those *were our orders. Any more and we are in trouble.*" *Nell didn't hear this as her head was still spinning from the knock she had sustained.*

"*Time is being wasted,*" *the Captain then spoke to all assembled.* "*These three women visit houses, put their hands on children and when the fever eases, a connection is made with their visit. Now, the eldest says that she is a healer and that what I have heard is true. She believes and says that her healing is a gift from God. This is blasphemy of the highest order possible. I have made my decision and I shall now pronounce the sentence.*"

He stood up and then took a few minutes to walk round the gathered villagers, staring at each and everyone standing there, as if to remember their faces and so put fear into all their minds. Then he returned to the table.

"*Attention. You will all bear witness that on this day, the 24th July 1497, I, Stanley Lesley, Captain in the Church Army, and hereby answerable to my Chief and the highest authority in York, held the trial of Ann Kittle, Emily Kittle and Catherine Shaw, who abide in the village of Stocksmoor. I do now give my verdict. GUILTY.*" *He shouted the last word, so no one could be in any doubt.*

"*No! No! NO!*" *was heard from some of the villagers whose fear had been temporarily quashed and who had, in their horror, found a voice.*

"*Silence!*" *He looked directly at my three sisters as he pronounced their sentence,* "*Ann Kittle, Emily Kittle and Catherine Shaw, you have all been found guilty of the actions of blasphemy against God, Christ and his holy name. You will be ducked three times in the ducking pond. It will take three days to get the pond ready and you must stop all these evil acts from this moment onwards. If you survive, then we shall know that you are not evil. If you do not survive, then you will die as evil witches. The world will then be well rid of you and this evil force which you carry within you.*

"*Have you anything you wish to say?*"

"*Yes,*" *replied Ann, defiantly. Despite their desperate situation, she was true to herself and could not give in without trying to get understanding, however futile her efforts should be.* "*I cannot help if a child feels that their pain eases when my hand rests on them or that the fever cools. I was born and God granted me life and my sister, together at one time. We did not ask or choose, either to be born or to have this ability. But we know that there are children who are suffering even as we attend here."*

The villagers watching gasped.

"Why does she say anything?" asked one of another.

"Are you saying that you defy my orders to stop your evil actions?"

Ann answered, "I am saying that we cannot stop doing something that we do not do. We are not wicked nor do we perform any evil actions. We have never done so. But if any child needs our help, we will do what we can to relieve the suffering. That is what I am saying. The evil actions come from you, not us. We are god-fearing people, but it would seem that we believe in a different God to you. Ours is a God of love."

Emily and Catherine were asked similar questions. Their answers were the same. Everyone watching, soldiers and villagers alike, saw Catherine smile at the Captain as she answered, and that there was no fear in her face. It was a smile of pity, not anger.

"You think to answer to your own High Chief who has given you the authority and the right to use your power against us this day. But, be assured that you will answer to a much higher authority one day. Oh, yes, you will answer to God himself, as will all men and women on this earth. You will die one day and then be judged by your actions. At that time, you will have to answer for yourself and your High Chief will not be there to help you. You have made your choice as we make ours. At your final judgement day, you will answer for your actions and yours alone. I pity you."

Nell thought that, from the paleness which came into his face, she believes the Captain would have wavered, after hearing Catherine's words, had he not been too frightened to disobey the orders that he had been given. But he could hear his own men jeering and laughing at the women and rather than appear weak himself, though he was indeed the weakest of men, he continued to say what was to happen.

"The ducking is the last part of your punishment. Firstly, you will be put

into stocks where everyone can see you, at the upper end of the village. You will be an example to all who pass by. You will remain there until the pond is made ready. You will be guarded by soldiers day and night and you will have no shelter, no food or anything to drink. Should you at any time renounce your ministrations as those of the devil, you will be released from the stocks. However, the ducking will continue as planned, whichever way you decide. That is the verdict of this court."

No one in the crowd uttered even a word.

"To be fair and just, it is customary for the defendant, in this case all three of you, to be asked one last time, 'Is there anything you want to say?' After this mallet falls the judgement and punishment will stand and cannot be altered." He held the wooden mallet in the air and pointed at Ann.

"You mock us. There is nothing fair or just in what you are doing. You insist in twisting and not hearing what we say," persisted Ann. "How can we renounce something that we do not profess or do? We have never claimed to have supernatural powers, nor have we ever blasphemed against the name of our true God, the God that we believe in. In our understanding of the scriptures, Jesus Christ told us to love children. That is all that we do – nothing more and nothing less. We are simply obeying the teaching of the scriptures."

The Captain turned to Emily.

"Have you anything to say further in your defence?"

"Any words of mine would pass without notice or effect. My sister has stated clearly that which I also believe. I need not repeat it. If you haven't listened to her, or have the wherewithal to understand, then there is no more that I can say."

He asked Catherine the same question.

"Yes," Catherine nodded in his direction. "I have something to say to my sisters that I want all those present, including you and your soldiers, to hear." Then she turned to Ann and Emily.

"Fear not, my dear sisters," she spoke in a clear, strong voice that showed no fear. "They can only hurt our bodies. They will never touch our minds

or our souls. Those are safe, whatever happens. God will make the final judgment about us, not these wretched, weak men. But they would do well to hear my words and understand, as they will one day have to face the reckoning and justice of that same God. Whatever pain they make us suffer they will receive back, either after death or before. I would rather be us a thousand fold than be any one of these pathetic creatures. They will all regret this day. Oh yes! And for all eternity."

The Captain looked as if about to choke.

"I will hear no more of this blasphemy. This court is ended. The verdict has been made and the sentence given. Now everyone must leave."

The villagers were stunned, but none dared to say a word. The message was quite clear to all.

Readers, Nell assured me that the stocks were ready for my three sisters as soon as the so called trial was over, and, once the villagers had dispersed to their homes, they were taken up the road to their torment. That to me, as I interject here, means that the verdict was all prearranged and there was nothing any one of my sisters could have said or not said, done or not done, to alter the course of events.

Nell did not move and waited, hoping she could do something to help the women. But, to no avail. The soldiers took hold of them, roughly, and dragged them away. Ann, who was nearest Nell as she went past, whispered quickly so that only Nell could hear.

"Nell, remember. Please take the girls and don't let them come back until it is all over. Send Mark and James to safety. And thank you for everything. We shall always love you."

"I will," whispered Nell, "I promise."

"Hey, you! No talking to these creatures. Get on with you," a soldier shouted. He approached and pushed Nell to the floor with a sudden swing of his arm.

ʃ

The stocks were placed in such a way that the sisters could not see each other. Anne faced the valley, Emily, the direction of the moor land in the

far distance and Catherine looked down towards the village and common land where preparations for the ducking had already been started.

The stocks were 'standing stocks' rather than 'sitting stocks'. The 'standing' stocks were the truly cruel stocks as the occupant had to stand all the time and when tired, all the weight of their body would be taken by their necks, wrists, arms and shoulder joints. There were semi-circular holes, in the two cross beams that joined together. These were for the wrists at either end, and in the centre a hole for the head. The head was bent forward as the neck fitted into the hole, and I have heard that many who survived their ordeal of being in this type of stocks were never able to hold their heads up comfortably again. At the base of the stocks was a chain, fastened to the right brace pole. An iron ring was attached to the chain, for fastening round the ankle to stop any attempt at escape. Nell described seeing a very small iron ring on a chain fastened very tightly round their right thumbs. This chain was attached to the cross beam, to prevent escape should they manage to free their wrists from the holes.

I asked Nell, in one of our long and painful talks, "Why do you think that my sisters did not simply say 'sorry' and agree that they would not use their skill again rather than deny any skill was different from normal? Do you think that they would then have avoided death at this time?"

"No, Richard, I am convinced that the stocks had been made ready just for my mistresses. You had only to see the size of the holes in the stocks for the wrists, which were very small, and the height being such that their feet were just not able to rest flatly, to know that. It was as if someone who knew them very well had given the exact measurements to whoever made the stocks. And," she added, "as I have told you, I know that they started putting them up during the night before your sisters were taken to the trial. When the trial was over they were ready. If that's not forward planning, then nothing is.

"I was awake for some reason that night. I think I had eaten too much fruit. There was a glut of it in the garden. It always has an effect on my inside, yet I never learn, so I was out in the privy several times. In the silence of the night, I heard men's voices and noises up the hill. I now know, but I didn't at the time, that it was the soldiers digging and

finding that their spades were hitting stones. Afterwards I noticed that there were many stones littered around the stocks as if they just threw them aside."

"But how would the Church Army have known that which my sisters did?" I asked her. "I mean, they went about quietly and I know they never spoke about their healing, not to anyone, not even to me. You know, I remember one time when I was visiting them last year. Ann was in the scullery. I can hear her now saying, 'No, Daisy, like this', and when I went into the scullery I saw her slicing root ginger very finely for a ginger poultice and was showing their maid, Daisy, how to do it correctly. Herbal knowledge, yes, they would discuss all that, but healing, never."

"Richard, I have just had a thought, when you talked about Daisy. We have been so occupied that I had forgotten about her. She will have to find some other employment now. She lives at Windy Bank corner with just her mother since her father died. Her mother is too old to work. Do you think that Ben and his wife could give her some work or she and her mother may well go hungry and be cold? Poor Daisy, she is not of the brightest, but has a good heart. Your sisters always made sure that she faired as well as possible."

"I will ask them the next time we travel that way. Please make sure I don't forget, Nell. My sisters would want her to be taken care of, I know."

∫

Nell and I would find, in our talks that we digressed quite frequently, though usually entirely without planning to do so. But we both realised that it was the only way that we could continue, me with the information gathering and Nell with the recall. It was very painful for us both, but it had to be done.

∫

"But, you know, Richard, there were a few people who hated your sisters and despised them, for reasons all their own."

"Yes, I know. They would occasionally mention someone or another whose paths crossed theirs most unfortunately. I believe one man in particular did so, whose daughter died at her own hand, though my sisters had tried to comfort her and help her to think differently. I had heard about two years ago that he went to Uncle Harold and complained about my sisters 'healing', saying that they had killed his daughter. His daughter was one of those that Uncle Harold asked my sisters to see. They talked at length to me, so sad were they that they had not been able to change this girl's mind, but the girl had told them that she would rather be dead than live with that man as her father. Why? My sisters never let out confidences. I wonder if he went to the Church Army or talked to any soldiers that passed by. He certainly had venom in his heart towards them. I knew the man, nasty as they come. I wonder?"

"Whatever and whoever, Richard, I am sure the Captain knew everything that was needed to be known beforehand, and nothing will ever convince me to think differently. They had no chance, none. Some people must surely be having bad dreams as the soldiers didn't find out without being told."

I had to agree. This would also confirm that the trial was a sham with the verdict already made. It was a make-belief attempt at justice to convince the villagers, as if they are of inferior intelligence. In my travels I have lived amongst many different folk, and though most may not be able to read or write I believe that that is about lack of opportunity and inequality, not about lack of ability. Nell is convinced that no one could alter the path that those of top rank in the Church Army had destined for my sisters. But, why such a dastardly sentence? Why so harsh?

Nell told me that she managed to visit the stocks on that first afternoon, soon after they had been fastened there. She had had a brief word with Ann, who was nearest the roadway up which she walked, before the soldiers saw her. They were eating their meal by their hut and, for the one and only time, were facing the opposite direction, away from the stocks. She captured a few minutes before they looked up.

"The villagers do not care about their children as much as we do or they would have spoken in our defence. It feels as though all our work counted for nothing, Nell, nothing. We were useful, and that was all." Ann's eyes closed, as if finally, she admitted defeat. "Nell, we shall not get out of this *alive. We know that. Please take care of our children until Richard knows and then he will look after them. Thank you, Nell, for everything."*

Nell managed to kiss Ann, but by that act of comfort, Nell was caught and taken to the small hut that the soldiers had erected to take 'watch' at night, and she simply, without emotion, admitted, "I was raped by two of them."

"Nell," I felt I should apologise for the actions of those men, "I am so very sorry."

"Nay, Richard, it was nothing to what they endured. As Catherine pronounced, 'God will be their judge', and I am sure they will find no mercy. And for that I am very glad."

Nell told me that the cruelty to my sisters seemed to have no bounds. On the first night, the villagers at the upper end of the village were awakened by screams on three occasions. Nell, who couldn't sleep, heard them and it made her blood run cold. Even during the day, passers by have told her that they saw the soldiers hitting or handling my sisters in ways no women should be handled, for no reason other than they were near to them. One villager described to Nell what saw happening when he passed the stocks, on his way to taking his horse to be shoed in Bretton. He saw that Ann, who was nearest the soldiers' make-shift hut and hence the one they noticed the most, was being tormented by one of the soldiers. He was as near to her as was humanly possible. She used her free leg, as the other was fastened by the iron ring. She bent her knee and hit the soldier where it would hurt most. He doubled up, but Ann paid for it with a bloody mouth as he swiped her with his hand as he stood up again. The villager told Nell that he tried to approach to help Ann, but was himself beaten back by two other soldiers.

If anyone even tried to help the women, it seemed that they were rewarded by having to watch my sisters suffering more grievously. All who had that intent soon learned not to try as it seemed that any show of caring for the sisters inflamed the soldiers' wrath. It was obvious to all that my sisters were doomed.

Nell told me of Simion's actions. As I have written before, he was known by many merely as the half-wit who lived in the woods and common land, almost as a wild man, and the soldiers clearly regarded him as such. But, he was brave enough to ignore the soldiers and their threats and, although he couldn't unfasten the stocks or help the sisters to escape, I am sure he did give some comfort. Nell saw that he sat by the base of Ann and Emily's stocks almost continually, alternately, for an hour at a time each day and each night after that first night. He left only to fulfil his bodily functions and to obtain nourishment at the inn.

She found out that Bernard offered Simion meat and other foods but, despite the heat, he would only accept bread and water once a day. The soldiers kicked him, and one has to question whether they did more to harm him. We shall never know. But, whatever, he did not move and eventually they ignored him. He sat with Ann, then Emily but, I am led to understand, never with Catherine, as though she did not need his aid. My sisters had always been kind to him and this was his way of repaying their kindness, although, as you will find out later, he did much more.

∫

The three days, until the pond was ready, were very hot. The country was in a heat wave. The sun burned down relentlessly. One can only imagine what it was like to stand out in the hot sun, being fair of face and skin and being denied water. Each day Nell observed as much as she could, from a different place, just in case she could find a time when the soldiers were less vigilant. She carried a flagon of water with her, and tried to find a time when she could administer water or assistance to my sisters. But, despite her watching for many hours of each day and night, she could not manage to reach even one of them.

She told me that she was standing by the inn on the second morning when she noticed Uncle Harold arriving at the scene on horseback. But, surprisingly, though he was a physic and must have seen their dire state, he did not approach the soldiers or my sisters, but turned his horse and rode away. She watched and he went along the road that led through the park to the Hall. She assumed that he must have been going to try to get help from Uncle Wilfred. She watched out all day, but no help came.

"He came and then went away again, without a word? Uncle Harold? Are you sure it was he?" I asked.

"Yes, Richard. I saw him with my own eyes. I know him as he has called many times at your father's house when I have been there. I saw him and so did Bernard."

"I cannot believe it. Would the soldiers have hurt a physic, do you think?"

"Well, they killed a monk who approached them and tried to help."

"No! Tell me."

Apparently one monk, whose name she never knew, had travelled over the hills to stay at the inn on his pilgrimage to York. He had seen the stocks and the appalling state of my sisters and he had gone to them to unfasten them. The soldiers had seen this and without any warning, a sword was driven through his back. Not even a man of the cloth was immune to their cruelty. Nell heard he died immediately. His body was merely collected and disposed of by two soldiers.

Another incident that Nell related showed that brutality was like a black cloak which covered everything that related to my sisters. You will remember that Emily and Ann had a dog each – given to them by their husbands as gifts when they married. These were now in 'old age', but were still well and went everywhere with their mistresses. Nell had kept them in the house, but, on the morning of the third day the dogs managed to escape from the scullery when she had had to quickly run to relieve herself in the privy at the end of the garden, without thought of the open door. They were not in the scullery when she returned and Nell, at first, did not notice and gave the matter little thought. The dogs had the freedom of the house and garden.

She now realises that her thoughts were with my sisters, and the days were passing as if she was in a kind of black despair. When she found that the dogs were not there, she thought they must have gone out into the garden to relieve themselves and she just hadn't noticed. She knew that the garden fence was secure. As they were old, she did not even think they would be able to jump over the fence, nor had they ever done so before, so at first she felt no concern. However, when the dogs did not return, she went out to search for them.

But, only when she visited the stocks after the three sisters had died, did she accidentally find the remains of the dogs. Each had been bludgeoned to death and their bodies thrown into the ditch on the other side of the wall by the field. Only Nell's decision to walk that way instead of directly along the road, allowed her to find these poor devoted animals. They died wanting to be with the people they loved.

Nell picked up each little corpse and carried them, one in each arm, tenderly back to her home. On the morrow, she wrapped them in sackcloth and buried them together, at the bottom of my father's garden, underneath the shade of the apple tree where they had so loved to shelter together.

As an animal physic, who loves all animals, large and small, I was sick to the pit of my stomach, that these small defenceless animals should have suffered this fate, simply out of love and without any understanding. I can only be relieved that their deaths would have been rapid, and Nell assured me that there were no signs of torture on their small bodies.

We continued and slowly I was piecing together the last three days of Ann, Emily and Catherine's lives.

§

On 27th July, at 12 noon, the soldiers took the three women out of the stocks. Nell was watching as near as she dare go in case the soldiers became angry and were more brutal towards the sisters as a result. It had become quite clear that they were vicious and any attempt that was made to help the women ended in more hurt to them. Apparently, they had demanded not only food from Bernard at the inn, but many flagons of ale and spirits, both day and night. He had to give in to their demands under threat of death. There is no doubt that the ale and spirits clouded their minds. But being inebriated by the liquor does not, in my opinion, take the blame from them. It may explain such appalling cruelty, but it was their choice to lose their finer wits completely in this way and they will be accountable, of that I am sure.

Nell noticed that not one of my sisters could stand at first when released from the stocks, and just slumped to the ground. She had some water in a leather bottle secreted on her person and she tried to reach them again, as she had done many times during the three days. But to no avail. On each occasion since the time she was raped, she had carried a carving knife to protect herself and the soldiers did not go near her again, yet kept her *away by wielding their swords. She knew that if she died she would not be able to help the children.*

The soldiers made the women walk alone and unaided down the road. For Nell, the image of Ann, staggering down the hill, her long, fair hair dirty and dishevelled and trying to pull her torn clothes about her person, is something she will never forget as long as she lived. Because of being in the stocks, they could not hold their heads up for more than a very short time.

Down the road was Joseph Kraft, standing at his gateway and reading aloud from the scriptures. Ann moved nearer to him and rasped, but as clearly as she could,

"Joseph, take Hilda away."

He appeared not to hear but continued with his prayers.

"God forgive these women. Our Father in Heaven, grant them mercy. May you wash their souls clean in your eternal grace and forgive their grievous transgressions."

A soldier who was guarding that stage of the route to make sure no one aided the women, heard Ann speak, and gave the order, "Do not speak. You are not to speak to anyone."

Hilda, Joseph Kraft's wife, as you will remember, had helped them in their work and could well be the next woman to be taken and punished. In fact, Nell wondered why Hilda had not been included, but then let that thought pass, that is until we were talking together. That thought then puzzled me as the Church Army did not let any one escape their web.

Ann finally struggled to the path leading onto the common land, and Nell, who had been walking as near as she could, then put her arm round her to support her. By now she heeded not the soldiers' demands. Nell heard her whisper, "My children?" Nell told her that her girls were safe. She didn't tell her that her son, Mark, had returned and she feared that he may be somewhere in the crowd. He had returned from the Hall after trying to seek help. Nell knew he would try to reach his mother if he could, but she could see no way of preventing it. She did not want him to be noticed by the soldiers. She later spied him at the side of one of the monks, being held tightly by one arm. I will tell you more of Mark later.

She noticed that there were many monks in and amongst the villagers, and, in passing, thought that fact was very strange. Why had monks, who normally passed through the village, stopped to witness what happened, yet without helping or assisting the women? As they were nearing the flat part of the lower common near the ducking pond, Nell saw Ann put out her hand and heard her say, though in no more than a harsh whisper, "Catherine, may this torment finally end. I wish to die. Help me, please, and help Emily." She turned to look in Ann's face, but Ann was not speaking to her.

Nell looked behind and she could see that Catherine was still way behind, struggling down the road.

"Richard, let me tell you that Ann could not see Catherine, nor could Catherine hear Ann. But Ann was talking to someone she could see, someone else who she believed was walking with her. Someone she thought was Catherine."

'Catherine was the image of Eve,' came into my mind and I spoke my thought aloud, then asked, "Do you think she saw her?"

Nell had known Eve well.

"I have thought long about this, Richard and I think you are right. Do you remember that Dorothy saw Eve, when Ann and Emily were but babes? Well, I am convinced, in my mind, that, yes, Ann saw Eve, her mother, on the last part of the walk. I am sure that she came to her in this time of great need and helped her to endure the dreadful fate. I don't know about Emily, but they always were alike in what they thought."

"Of course, I think I understand what you are saying. You mean that Ann had never known or seen Eve, so she believed that this was Catherine walking at her side."

"I think so. She was too ill and confused by now, poor, dear Ann, to realise that Catherine was behind her on the road."

Nell couldn't be with Emily and Ann together, and kept looking round to see where Emily was. She heard a scream, a piercing but forlorn sound.

She turned round and saw Simion standing, in his jerky, noisy manner, just by the path to the common land. He had seen Emily stumble and fall. She saw the strange flailing sight as he tried to run across the grass to the path and put his arm round her. He helped her to rise and assisted her for the rest of the way. One can only surmise what the other villagers, who had been told to watch, felt as none of them dared to do likewise.

Nell believes that no one helped Catherine and when she arrived at the pond her face was covered in blood. It was thought that she must have fallen and banged her nose. No one saw a soldier hit her in the face, but we shall never know. Would I have aided them had I been there? I like to think I would have had the courage, but in reality, would I? That is something that disturbs my sleep, as I always now wake as if from a nightmare. Each and every time, one of my sisters is calling for my help and my feet are fastened in solid clay and I cannot move.

§

Please understand that Nell told me all this in small amounts, as and when she felt able to speak about it. One day Nell then told me something that I can hardly believe, but know to be true.

"Richard, you want to know everything that happened for Sir George's evidence, so I must tell you this. I didn't tell you before, as I thought I could not speak the words to do so. But, I thought long about it last night and couldn't sleep because of my thoughts. I realise now that for me to speak the words is nothing when compared to the action I describe and what your sisters had to endure. So, I will tell you.

"About the time that I knew your sisters were to be released from the stocks, I went up the hill, walking in the field and hoping I would not be seen. To my sorrow, I could not get near to help. I was standing behind the wall and looking through a gap where one of the stones had fallen away.

"Your sisters were nearly unable to stand or walk. They couldn't hold their heads up. Ann and Emily could scarcely breathe. Yet, they were taken, roughly, one by one from the stocks and dragged into the small hut, the one I mentioned previously. Despite their desperate state, they were each in the hut for many minutes. Richard, I fear that the soldiers raped

them before sending them down the road. They all left a trail of blood. The villagers will bear witness, as, being such dry weather it remained where it fell. All who walked up the road later saw the same."

"My God, was there no limit to their vileness?" I felt nausea to the bottom of my stomach.

"But, not only that hideous behaviour but something else very terrible was done to them before they were ducked. Something that all the villagers were made to see," continued Nell. Nell put her head in her hands, "I can say no more just now, Richard."

∫

I have asked Robert to just scan the pages so far to see if we have made any confusions or mistakes that he can rectify. I must wait a day of two to recover my spirits to be able to write more. I am overwhelmed with the sadness and injustice of such pain. Yet I have much more to write and my courage must recover that I may be able to do so. I am determined to complete this task.

Two days passed and Nell came to our quarters in the stable block saying that she was ready to continue. If I could face to hear more, then she would make herself recall and tell me what I needed to know.

To give a complete picture, we must briefly retrace our steps and return to before my sisters were released from the stocks. If in so doing, and to get a complete and true account of the happenings, I repeat any part of the narrative, then please forgive me.

~ The ducking ~

Preparations for the ducking had proceeded apace during those three days. The entrance of the water from the spring had been temporarily blocked and the water had been helped to drain away by a channel dug into the side of the pond. The pond had been made sufficient in its depth for the three women to be ducked. Then, in reverse, the channel had been blocked, the spring water was released and soon the pond had filled with clear water.

On the morning of the ducking, Nell was looking out of the upstairs window of my father's house, where she had been living to keep guard over their belongings and to be there in case the boys returned. Because of its position, she could see what was happening along the high road, which led to Bretton. As she watched, she saw a procession coming along this very road. She waited, to see which direction it would take once it reached Stocksmoor, and sure enough it must have turned right at the junction where the stocks were, as it eventually came down the road and past the house. She hid behind the drapes. She could see but not be seen.

Ten horses, dressed in white from ears to tail, carried ten soldiers slowly down the road. The soldiers, also dressed from head to toe in white, wore high-peaked, conical-shaped hats that covered their faces. Only slits for the eyes and a mouth hole were visible. One rode slightly in front, flanked on each side by two outriders. All, except the one in the centre front, carried triangular pennants.

She knew this man must be a very high-ranking officer of the Church Army, with his body guards, who had come to witness the ducking of the three innocent and fragile women. All wore white flowing cloaks over their uniforms, which were plain except for the one in the centre. His was intricately and lavishly embroidered around the hem in scarlet and gold thread, giving an extravagant and opulent appearance. He carried a slender but ornately carved wooden cross. The cross itself was painted in gold with a large red stone in the centre.

I ask, has cowardice no shame? He could let fragile women face degradation, torture and death, alone, with none to protect them, yet he needed to hide his face, and have men with swords near to his person to keep him safe from harm. Such is the absent bravery and great fear of those who cause pain.

It was a sight that would surely instil terror, even in those with exemplary courage. Nell felt a cold, dreadful weight descend upon her. She knew she had finally to accept that her dear mistresses were doomed. She now could only hope for a speedy end to their torments.

The men Nell saw were those of the 'White Army', who I have briefly mentioned before. Their role was to attend the execution of whatever punishment was ordained at the trials, with the sole purpose of making

sure it was carried out to the finality demanded. In simple words, they attended to witness death and hence they had another name around the country, namely, 'The Riders of Death'. It has been my fortune never to have witnessed the same.

Dear readers, if ever there was an abomination in this fair country of ours, then Nell saw its face as the riders passed by. It was a sight that she will never forget to the end of her days.

∫

Three ducking stools, which now we also know had already been built in preparation for what was to happen in Stocksmoor, were erected. A pole was fastened into the ground. Another long pole was connected to this fixed pole, and at its end was a makeshift seat with a back rest. This, I know, was not intended for their comfort, but was there to fasten their upper bodies and arms securely. When the pole was turned, the seat would swing over backwards and the women would be ducked in the water, head first. Nell says that two of the seats were fastened facing the opposite directions, so that when they were turned, the arrangement made sure that Ann and Emily could see each other's fate. Is there a level of evil to which these men did not reach? I doubt very much that is the case.

Nell described the scene exactly as I have asked Robbie to write.

A low wooden platform had been built about six tall men's distance from the edge of the pool. On this now sat the High Chief. He was surrounded on both sides and behind by his nine bodyguards along with three other soldiers from the Captain's troupe who were standing in a tight semicircle a little distance from his chair. He could be seen, but at the same time, he was safe. In his pathetic fear he needed such protection, yet the small and harmless women, that were my sisters, had none. Because of the hats, none could see the Chief's or his bodyguards' faces, nor identify them afterwards, which, of course, was the very reason why this very strange looking uniform was worn. Neither could their horses be recognised at a later date, being covered, all but the lower part of their legs, in white canvas.

My three sisters were collapsed to the ground together between the platform and the pool, so exhausted and ill that they could not stand. No one was now allowed near them, Simion and Nell having been pushed aside, roughly, by the soldiers.

Then the Captain of the soldiers who were camped on the Mount told three of them to bring the women forward. Each grabbed one by the arm and dragged her to her feet and they were brought to stand in a line. If any one of them sank to the ground, they were pulled to their feet with no thought of their condition.

The High Chief stood and spoke, "It is customary to hear a last request. Our Lord God Almighty will decide your fate. Your lives are in his hands. He will send you to the everlasting fires of hell, or he will give you forgiveness." He pointed to Catherine.

"As the eldest, I ask you first. Have you a last request?"

"I am not afraid to die but I would wish to embrace my sisters," she asked quietly.

"Request denied."

"And you," he was now pointing to Emily.

"My request is the same."

"Request denied."

And finally he asked Ann.

With great difficulty, she drew herself up with as much strength as she could muster and slowly, and with great difficulty, she replied, "I have nothing to ask of evil bastards like you, and I will not give you the pleasure of denying me also. You are the scum of the earth. You have to hide your faces for fear of being recognised. But, you cannot hide from God. I am not afraid," her words came from her mouth in a hoarse whisper, as she could hardly speak. Then, the shocked and frightened crowd, in the still silence that had come upon them, heard Ann shout out in a loud voice, "I curse you to hell and eternal damnation." The villagers and the soldiers gasped. How had she the strength to speak like that?

(I have asked many people and all say that this was not the usual 'voice' of Ann and all are mystified.)

- 258 -

No one moved for a few minutes, being stunned by what they had heard. Then the High Chief recovered his composure and stepped down from the platform and went over to Ann. As he stood in front of her, Ann lifted up her head, with great difficulty as her neck was very weak from the stocks, and looked directly into his eyes which were hidden behind his head gear. All heard her say, "YOU?" It was very clear. "I have questioned many and they agree," Nell told me, "that Ann recognised him when she looked at his eyes. Of that we are all quite sure."

"Ann recognised the High Chief of the Church Army? How could she? Surely you are mistaken."

'No, Richard. Ask any of the villagers. There is no mistake."

"How very strange, but I shall remember that in my search for the truth."

(I shall write more of this later.)

Then the High Chief bent down so he was very near to Ann. Only those nearest, including Nell, heard what he hissed into her ear,

"For insolence to the high command of the Church Army, you will be ducked four times."

Ann looked directly into the High Chief's eye holes and slowly, with great difficulty and dignity, despite her state of undress and filth, and told him, "You are a coward."

Nell thought, 'My God! What will happen to her now?' She was soon to find out.

He turned away and gave a signal to the Captain.

"Proceed," ordered the Captain.

Readers, do you remember my telling you that our cousin, Henry, the blacksmith, had been asked to make a mouth brace for the use, he believed, to control vicious dogs? Well, now Nell told me the answer to that puzzlement. The mouth braces for want of a better word, were not for dogs, but for my sisters. They were put into their mouths, and from what Nell tells me, the women, despite being already frail from the stocks, put up a struggle. These hideous, black iron contraptions were ordered to be made for just this occasion. Another reason we now know it was all planned.

These were designed with the express purpose of making sure the women could not close their mouths when they were ducked, so that the water would flow into their lungs. But – and this was even more the work of a devil – the tongue flap, which fitted on top of the tongue holding the tongue down, then snaked upwards, ensuring that though water could easily flow into the mouth, it was difficult for the water to flow out again.

If human nature can be so vile in the name of God, then the Church has nothing to recommend it. This God that they worship cannot be the divine being that I believe in. These are not the actions designed by a god of love, no never. They are the actions of the devil. Nell told me that when she cared for and cleaned the bodies after their deaths, she noticed that many of my sisters' teeth had been broken by these mouth braces.

The villagers started to shout their protests and move forward, as if to stop what was happening, when the mouth braces were being painfully and brutally inserted, but the High Chief stood up and shouted,

"Stand back. Anyone who interrupts these proceedings again will be punished accordingly. These ducking stools can be used more than once," and then sat down. Everyone went very quiet and all watched in total horror. All, that is, except the High Chief and his bodyguards. They were used to scenes such as these, and, Nell thought that though no one could see his face, she and many others were convinced that the High Chief relished all that was happening.

Ann and Emily were to be ducked first and together. They turned to reach out to each other, but the soldiers stopped them, roughly pulling back their arms and holding them tightly behind their backs.

All three were prepared together. They were put in long white garments that had sleeves extended well beyond their arms and at the end of the sleeves were straps. Then they were made to sit on the ducking stool, I say 'made' but Nell says they gave no further signal of protest against what would happen to them. Their knees were bent under the stool and the long arms were first crossed and then tied under the legs, fixing both, so that neither arms nor legs could move. Then a long piece of rope was fastened in a knot which was slipped over the bent legs and then wound up and round the chests as tightly as was possible and round the upright pole behind them at the same time. The villagers gasped. Surely this was too much, but what they did not realise was something that Nell discovered later.

It is a well known practice that anything that needs to be kept free from water is covered in wax, and ropes are customarily treated in this way. I purposely check the waxing on all the ropes around my boxes or bottles that hold my medicaments. Nell noted that the rope had been used without any waxing, and loosely twined, so that, on contact with the water its fibres would quickly swell, so constricting my sisters' breathing even further. Nell discovered this later. When the ropes were cut away deep grooves were left in the bodies. The soldiers cut off the rope and merely discarded it, leaving it lying on the ground. Nell managed to secrete a small piece and I determined that this would be shown in court when eventually we could bring these villains to justice.

Now, please remember, though I have not stressed this very often, that my sisters, Ann and Emily, had breathing problems since their very early birth. We have always believed that their bodies were not quite ready to be born, but cruel fate dictated it should be so. It was as though their minds were strong and their bodies weak. It is Nell's opinion that they would have succumbed to the ducking without the tight ropes. But they were fastened and then they had no chance – not from the very first ducking. Yet, such was their strength and love of each other and their children that their spirit resisted to the end.

"You are an abomination and always have been," the High Chief almost spat at Ann and Emily. "As you were born together, causing the death of your mother, so you will be ducked together and first, before your elder sister."

"You," he pointed to Catherine, "can watch. Then it will be your turn."

He made a big sweep of his arm so that his ornate cloak flared out behind him as he turned to Jonas, the man of God who was standing on the platform with a book of scriptures in his hand.

"Jonas, would you begin?"

§

As Nell was recounting these facts, I had many thoughts, nay, and questions.

Firstly, who was the man behind the mask whom Ann had recognised? Then I thought, 'but she could only see his eyes'. Where could she have met him?

Secondly, how did the High Chief of the Church Army who had arrived only two hours before and was so superior and 'hidden' behind his tall hat, know a local, I hesitate to say 'ordinary', village man of God, such as Jonas? Nell was absolutely sure that he didn't say 'Father Jonas' as one would expect of someone who had enquired of the man of God's name beforehand to use as necessary. No, it seemed he knew him so well, in fact, as to be able to call him by his first name. I posed these questions to Nell, while she was recovering from being overwhelmed by telling me her memories.

"I don't know, Richard. But I heard Ann myself, honestly and truly. Oh yes, she knew him but in what connection I do not know as I did not recognise even his voice. How did Jonas know him? How strange, I hadn't thought of that before. I know that Jonas was believed to be of an unnatural nature by most of the men in the village, though I never heard anyone in particular speak openly about him. We just avoided him, as I recall. He often left the village on horseback and no one knew where he went or who he visited. Though, to be honest I do not think that anyone enquired or even cared what he did. You know, he lived in the village for as long as I can remember, but few knew much about him. He wasn't liked and, in my way of thinking, did no good service to God or to anyone in the village. He did nothing other than pose as a devout man and spread discord."

"That's not like you to speak of someone with such venom."

"No, well I didn't like him before and I hate him now as I am sure he was linked with what happened to my mistresses, those dear, kind lasses I had loved since they were but babes." Nell wept.

"You know, Richard, from my house I used to see soldiers attend his meetings and usually one would stay behind for," she paused, "well, for . . . who knows what? It was certain that none of the young men in the village would ever be in his presence alone. I don't go in for gossip, but *that was common knowledge. Some of the soldiers visited him at other times and we thought, that is, my friend, Martha, and I thought that they went to see him for reasons other than the scriptures. Not only have I disliked the man but neither have I trusted him." She stopped for a moment. Richard waited.*

"Richard, I have thought of something that had quite vanished from my mind until just now. Some of the travelling monks would meet with Jonas and we all thought this was to share religious prayer or 'something'. But, a group of three had been to the village, a few times, during the space of two or three weeks before your sisters were taken. They seemed to be very friendly with Jonas and stayed in the village a few days. As you know you can't tell one from the other because they keep their heads covered by their hoods. We rarely if ever saw a monk's face. But these three, who always came and went everywhere together stood out as two were tall and thin and the other small and fat. I know these three called to see Jonas and that he knew them.

"The first time they were seen to arrive in the village, I happened to have visited Martha who, you will remember, lives near Joseph Kraft's house and I was walking back home when I saw them go into the meeting place. Jonas, who couldn't see me, his view being blocked by the monks and a hawthorn bush, greeted them like lost brothers. You know, in a different way to how you would greet strangers. He knew them, alright, I am sure of that. I never thought any monks were anything other than men of God until we have been thinking and talking about what happened.

"Anyway, for what it's worth, I know these same three monks visited the village on other occasions and, on the second day when your sisters were in the stocks. Unlike everyone else, they were actually allowed to speak to them. In other words, the soldiers must have known and recognised them too. But, unlike the monk whom the soldiers killed, they never tried to help your sisters. The farmer at the top of the village told me that he and his wife saw one of the three talking to Ann. She spat at his face. So God only knows what he was saying to her to make her do that."

"If he was trying to make her confess to heresy, then he had chosen the wrong woman," I replied. I knew Ann well.

"But at that time," confessed Nell, "everyone thought that monks were holy men and therefore good and if these monks thought that Ann, Emily and Catherine were evil, then no one expected them to help them. But, the one who was killed was different. He did try. There is so much we don't understand."

"The Church Army is indeed very devious in its ways, and I am sure there is much more to find out," I agreed with her.

After a pause Nell continued.

"I believe that Jonas gathered information from the villagers about your sisters by merely asking about their sick children and such like, as if interested, and then he passed on information about them to the soldiers. Do you think he did it by talking to these monks? I mean, he let everyone know that he thought your sisters were evil and he made no pretence on that score. He hated them and always had done so, though those kind, gentle women had done nothing untoward to Jonas, except possibly made the villagers doubt his ministry. Though by actions, not words. I never heard them speak anything amiss against him to anyone other than each other, did they? But, as we are talking I think that maybe he also knew some of the soldiers before they arrived in the village."

"Whatever, Nell, it is now quite clear that someone certainly informed the Church Army officers long before they arrived, as everything was already prepared for their deaths, even down to their correct height. That has become quite certain."

∫

Sometimes, by digressing, both Nell and I found that we could more easily talk about these dreadful events. So, I make no apology for these interruptions and I pray that it will give you, my readers, time to recollect your thoughts and absorb that which I am sharing with you. The further information, which I interject, from general knowledge, will help you to have more understanding, as you are not living in this time or with us.

∫

I will now carry on with the events of that terrible day, as Nell told them to me.

Jonas started intoning in the monotonous voice that was used by monks in their evensong, "Lamb of God, that taketh away the sins of the world, hear our prayers. Lamb of God......." He recited over and over as the ducking stools were lowered.

You will remember that the punishment was that they should all be ducked three times. The crowd were instructed beforehand to count up to ten to the bang of a drum, the time being beaten out by one of the soldiers.

As their heads went under the water, the counting began. At the count of ten, the women were to be brought to the surface and they should stay there to the count of ten. Then the counting would begin again. The Captain who had sentenced them was standing between the four soldiers, two to each pole of the ducking stool. They were watching his hand and had been secretly ordered to obey him, whatever the crowd counted. These were men afraid for, not only their livelihoods, but also their lives, as disobedience was punishable by death.

Jonas, the man of God, started at the beginning of his incantation each time the sisters went under the water.

Nell told me that the water was so clear that those villagers, who I must add were made to stand round the side of the pond, could see the horror of what was happening. She, herself, had been dragged by one of the soldiers and her head held down by her hair at the very edge of the pond. She was so concerned for Ann and Emily that, though she wished to do so, she could not shut her eyes.

"Look. Those are your friends. What can they do now?" he asked, his breath smelling of old ale.

The sight of the staring eyes, the fair hair streaming out around the heads underneath the water, and their mouths open and appearing black due to the mouth brace, is another image that haunts Nell day and night, and I fear, will continue to do so for a long time to come. Nell wakes from her sleep, feeling horror and with her arms stretched out, as if trying to reach them. But, of course, she never can, as she couldn't at the time.

When the two sisters had been ducked three times, Ann was still coughing when she was brought out of the water. Emily made no further noise after the second time and it was thought, by all standing by, that she had succumbed and been drowned. Though no one had helped the sisters, most of those watching had silent tears rolling down their faces. As though distracted, though we believe in reality he had been instructed by the High Chief after Ann's outburst, the Captain put his arm down again. The soldiers, watching him, ducked Ann for a fourth time.

At this time, Emily was cut out of the ducking stool and her body thrown onto the floor and landed on its side, facing the High Chief. Now the villagers were screaming "NO!" "NO!" "NO!" "Three!" "Three!" "Three!" The Captain took no notice. Jonas intoned yet again, and the drum beat the regular rhythm until ten beats had passed. The villagers tried to count faster in an effort to bring Ann to the surface sooner, but to no avail. My sisters were murdered in cold blood in front of people who could do nothing to assist them. Ann's stool was then brought to the side of the pond, she was cut free of the stool and she too was thrown on the ground. Still the bindings that encircled their chests remained intact and tight.

The High Chief gave an order, "Bring that one over here to me," pointing at Ann, who, unbelievably, had again started to cough. A soldier grabbed hold of her garment and dragged her roughly, bumping over the tussocks of thick spiky grass towards the platform and left her lying on the ground in front of him.

"See if the other is dead," the High Chief shouted to a soldier. The soldier went over to Emily and kicked her violently in the stomach.

∫

Nell noticed, even in her despair, that when Emily, who was thought to have succumbed and died, was kicked in the stomach by the soldier, her body just moved with the force as if a sack of potatoes had been kicked or the like thereof. But, at the very same time, Ann's body reacted as though it was she who had been kicked in the stomach. Her legs and body bent and her face showed pain. A few of the villagers, though many did not know where to look during all this harrowing procedure, were watching Ann and screamed out loud when they saw her writhe with the pain. Even the High Chief himself went pale as he knew that no one had touched Ann at that time.

But, I know that Ann and Emily, throughout their lives, felt each other's pain as if their own, such was their closeness. We had, as a family, witnessed this on very many occasions. Once Ann, as a child, trapped her finger when a cupboard door in the scullery closed against it, and Emily screamed and sucked the offending finger, though she was in the garden at the time. There were very many incidents of that nature.

I tell you this, as it would appear that Emily was not quite dead as everyone thought, though she was so nearly dead that she could not let anyone know the truth. It seems to me that people know very little about the human body and mind, nor indeed about death itself.

∫

I will return to what happened next. There was a sudden commotion and the noise of someone shouting, "Stop! In the name of the King. Stop!" All present heard the sound of horses galloping down the road to the pond. But, rescue had come too late.

∫

All were so horrified by what was happening that it appeared that none paid attention to Catherine, who was waiting, strapped onto her ducking stool. But Nell loved all my three sisters equally and looked from one to the other throughout their ordeal.

She told me that just as Ann and Emily were to be ducked, she saw Catherine shut her eyes and her head dropped forward. She noticed that her face was very blue and she is convinced that Catherine died of suffocation. I will tell you a little more of that later. I believe Nell completely, and I am very sure that Catherine was dead before the ducking and hence not drowned, and I can only feel thankful for that.

As though ignoring the two sisters, and without any incantation from Jonas, the soldiers, as if instructed beforehand as to what they should do, were about to go ahead with ducking Catherine. Nell shouted out, "Stop! She is dead. She is dead," and kept screaming for them to stop. They took no notice and carried on but everyone noticed that Catherine never coughed, even after the first immersion. Nell had no doubt that Catherine had made no attempt to survive but had gone to be with her sisters.

With the clatter of horses' hooves and shouting, the first horseman arrived. It was the sisters' brother-in-law, Andrew. He had been away from home when James had hurried to Lower Oakington to find him. But his son, Alend, was there, and had managed to send a trusted workman, one of their best riders, to find him. He had hastened back, collected Alend, James and three spare horses, hoping to take the sisters away from the village. He had ridden, with all speed, but had arrived too late to save them.

He jumped off his horse without thinking to take his sword with him. It was in its sheath attached to his saddle.

"Give me a sword," he demanded of the Captain. Andrew could see that Ann was still just alive and that the bindings were restricting her breathing. They needed cutting immediately if she was to have any chance of recovery and he saw and realised that the mouth brace was preventing the water from escaping from her lungs.

"A sword? You want a sword? Well, here, have one!" The Captain immediately thrust his sword into Andrew's stomach. Then he pulled it out and drove it straight into the right side of Ann's chest. "We'll finally have done with this one," he muttered as if to himself. Alend had arrived by this time with the spare horses. He jumped off his horse and rushed to his father's side, sword in hand.

"Father! Father!" he cried, but his father was already dead. He knelt by his body and shouted, "You will answer for this one day. Everyone of you. You will answer, not only to Almighty God, but to the King."

The High Chief was seen, by Nell, to nod to the Captain. The Captain gave an order to his Second in Command and Alend was attacked while still kneeling by his father's dead body. He just had time to swing his sword to protect himself and caught one of the soldiers behind his heel, severing the very part of the leg that upheld its movement. The soldier fell, but the Second in Command, who was close behind, put his sword through Alend's heart. Father and son lay in pools of united blood.

∫

As I told you before, Mark, Ann's son had been sent by Nell, on his mother's orders, to the Hall. He told me, "I was sent to get help." That is how he interpreted the orders, but in reality, I know from that which Nell told me, that he was sent there for safe keeping. I have spoken to him, as gently as is possible, and he told me what he tried to do and where he went.

"James and I went together to see our mamas and to try to help them but a soldier grabbed me and another one held James, both by our arms. 'Let our sons go,' cried Mama. 'You have us, you need not our children.' Then she turned to me, 'Mark, go home. Do whatever Nell tells you.' Aunt Emily told James to do the same."

The boys were allowed to leave, no doubt because the women were proving more difficult than expected to be put into the stocks and one can only think that the soldiers saw 'no hurry' in taking the boys. As I learn more, I am certain that the boys could have been in dire danger.

"We went back home and Nell was there," continued Mark. She was very upset that we had let the soldiers see us. She gave us some bread and cheese, and then told us what we had to do. She had Miriam and Miranda ready to take across the wood. So, I set off running. I went down to the top common path, past Simion's corner and then turned right to go up the lane, and through the parkland. I arrived at the Hall, and finally found Great Uncle Wilfred in his library and told him what was happening. He listened to me and seemed very worried. I was certain he was going to help Mama and my aunts.

"I remember just what he told me, 'I shall discuss what to do with Geoffrey as soon as he arrives back later this evening. You shall stay here as I am sure your mother would expect that. The housekeeper will show you to a room for the night. I will see you in the morning. You have done well.' He then rang for his housekeeper and told her to take me to the kitchen for some food and to prepare Eve's old room for me to sleep in. Eve was Grandmama, wasn't she?"

"Yes," I replied, listening carefully but saying very little.

"Uncle Richard, I found out that the room I was given had really been Grandmama's old room. Do you know, it was just as she had left it?

Nothing had been changed, and there were even some of her clothes in the clothes closet. I couldn't believe it. And, on her dressing table with her powder, brush and comb, all really fancy, and with a mirror to match, there were two pictures, standing in frames. I thought at first one was of Aunt Catherine, but then I saw written on the back 'My dear daughter, Eve' signed by Sir Christopher Cecil, Baronet of Bretton. The other was of three small girls. They were my Mama, Aunt Emily and Aunt Catherine. I know because I turned it over and saw 'My three dearest granddaughters, Catherine, Emily and Ann', signed C C. I wondered who had painted them and why were they in this room and not in the main rooms downstairs with the other portraits?"

"I will tell you about the portraits, when you have finished telling me everything," I promised, which I did.

∫

Let me say here, that your information about the portraits is written elsewhere, and you will surely find out more, but to write what you will learn at this place, will detract from Mark and his bitter ordeal.

∫

Mark told me more, "I stayed at the Hall all night and then in the morning I went to find Great Uncle Wilfred again. I heard him and Cousin Geoffrey shouting at each other in the library, and I have never heard anyone shout at each other like that before. I couldn't understand. But, I daren't go into the room and just listened at the door. I heard Great Uncle Wilfred say that he would not send anybody to help Mama and my aunts after all. I couldn't believe it. So I thought I had not heard them properly. Then Cousin Geoffrey told Great Uncle Wilfred that he had decided that he was going to go to Stocksmoor and Sandal and even York if need be. I just hid behind the side of the big clock in the corridor when he stormed past, slamming the library door behind him. He didn't see me.

"I then found my way out. It took a while as I became lost many times. I don't really know the Hall. Then I ran through the grounds and went to Great Aunt Rosemary's in Bretton. She was really sure that Great Uncle Harold would do whatever he could do to help Mama and Aunt Emily and Aunt Catherine, but that he was out at that time. She asked

me to stay a while until either Great Uncle Harold or Cousin Henry came home. So, I waited for an hour or two but neither returned. I felt desperate, so I set off for your house. But you were not there. As you know, Aunt Rosamund made me some food and wanted me to stay as it was getting late and I couldn't get back to Stocksmoor in the light. She thought it was very dangerous for me to travel alone in the dark. So, I stayed all night, hoping you would return on the morrow. But by mid morning, there was no sign of you, so, I went back to the Hall to try and persuade Great Uncle Wilfred again.

"He saw me. I asked again for his help for our mamas. He answered, 'I can do nothing and I am very cross that you are roaming around the countryside, alone. You look like a common urchin. You should stay here at the Hall where you are safe.' But, I couldn't. I left straight away and I ran back to Stocksmoor. I tried to get to see Mama, but one of the soldiers stopped me. I thought Mama was dying as her head was bent over and her eyes were closed and I started crying, but then I felt very frightened of the soldiers, as the other soldiers were coming near to see what was going on. I managed to slip away from the soldier when he tried to grab me. He was rather unsteady on his feet and I think had been taking liquor. I ran away behind the inn, up the hill towards Flockton and then back down into the wood. I know all the paths and I hid until it was dark. I then made my way back home through the field. I had decided to get my father's old sword that hung up in the back scullery.

"Uncle Richard, I wanted to save Mama, I wanted to save her. I tried everywhere I knew, everywhere and everybody. I could not find any help for her. I couldn't stop what they did and I... couldn't... save... Mama."
He then started sobbing, saying to himself as he cried, "Mama... Mama... why did you go? Why did you leave us all? I tried! I tried to save you."

∫

Sometimes you are at a crossroads and do not know which direction to take. This was one of those I encountered with Mark, and I was uncertain what to say to him. He went through such a lot of anguish to try to get help, believing that is what his mother wanted him to do. I felt he had to have a pride in all his effort on her behalf. Did I do right not to tell him the truth? Should I have told him that his mother did not expect him to do anything to prevail against the Church Army, but that she just wanted him to be safe? Would he feel that all his effort had been more in vain and even against his mother's wishes, or would he have felt that she had tried to look after him even in those circumstances? I did not know. I too was overwhelmed with emotion, and, in any event, at that time, I did not have the information I now present to you gradually in this book.

∫

I will continue his story, but now, as told by Nell.

By now, it was the night before they were released and Nell heard Mark return.

When he entered the house, he dropped, exhausted, to the floor and sobbed in despair and desperation, his heart truly broken. He told her all he had tried to do, but when he could not do more, he had returned to try to save his mother. Nell persuaded him to have a little food. He then fell asleep where he lay, on the floor. Nell put a cushion beneath his head and put a blanket round him. She stayed in the house most of that night, only walking cautiously up the road to see my sisters occasionally. She felt she was best helping them by being with Mark. When she left the house to be on the road to aid my sisters next morning, he was still asleep. She had hoped he would remain so, but no, he had woken up as she left and raced out of the house, down the garden and arrived at the ducking area by avoiding the road and without being seen by the soldiers. Nell saw, with horror, Mark standing, holding his father's sword and being held back by a monk. He shouted, "Mama! Mama!" but either Ann did not hear or deliberately ignored his cries so that the soldier following close behind would not take any notice of her beloved son.

Nell felt that everything happened very quickly after Andrew had arrived and to give a very timely account, in the order in which it happened, is not easy for her nor for me to relate. But, I will this as well as I can.

When Mark saw his mother brought from the pond and during the commotion caused by Andrew and Alend's arrival and deaths, he finally managed to break away from the monk who had been standing by him and who had been restraining him.

He rushed over crying, "Mama! Mama! It's me, Mark. Please don't die! Please! Mama! Mama!" His cries became louder as his desperation grew stronger. He cradled his mother's head in his arms. Only Mark saw her open her eyes and, very briefly, she looked at him. Then her eyes went glazed...

∫

Ann saw in the blue sky a brilliant, white dove. It seemed it was talking to her.

"Come with me, my child."

"No, I cannot come yet. My son is not safe. I must not leave him."

"Come my child, you cannot survive any longer, not even for your beloved son."

"I cannot..."

(I have asked Robbie to add this comment. I spoke these words to him to scribe without prior thought, yet I feel I must retain them in my narrative. He says I seemed a little vague for a few minutes and he thought I must be either weary or upset. As I write this book, I do, on occasion, have what I can only describe as 'strange moments in time', as just now. These pass quickly. Yet, I am made to feel even more convinced that this book must be completed and that there is a purpose, more than I can know of, to the writing thereof.)

∫

... and she was dead.

Nell thought that Mark, too, would be slain particularly as she thought he still had the sword in his hand and shouted, "Mark! Mark!" But Mark, overcome by his grief, had dropped the sword when he put his arms about his mother's head. He was crying out, "Mama! Wake up, Mama! No! No! Don't go away. Come back! I am here, Mama. Come back to me! Come back to me!"

James, who had returned on horseback with Alend, and arrived just after his Uncle Andrew, also jumped off his horse. He raced to his mother, Emily, who by now had been cut out of her ducking stool.

Nell cried as she described the scene. It was the most pitiful sight possible to see these young boys cradling their mothers' heads and weeping. I too was in tears listening as she spoke. Dear readers, if you knew these boys, you would do the same. They are such gentle boys. Having known them all their lives, I can feel they have both changed since that day. They are still kind and gentle, but, behind the sadness is a hardness of purpose that was never there before.

§

I spoke to Mark on many occasions to hear the whole of his story, as and when he felt able and wanted to speak about his mother and her death. At the final time, he told me, "I tried to pull away from the monk who held me. I wanted to be with Mama. She didn't even hear me or see me, until just as she died. She will never know how much I tried to save her. She will never know." He wept, uncontrollably, and all I could do was put my arm round his shoulders. Since then, much time has passed. Mark has not spoken any further to me about those days and never, in my hearing, talks about his mother. Maybe when he reads this book, he will talk to me about how he felt and then I shall have a further opportunity to enlighten him.

§

Let me now return you to what happened after the ducking. The soldiers took no notice of the two boys, though they surely would have done in a few minutes, when the calm had been restored. The commotion caused by Andrew and Alend had finally allowed the villagers' anger to be expressed and the soldiers formed a line, all with swords at the ready, prepared to withstand any attack. But, the anger gave courage. The villagers were shouting and waving their fists, yet all now knew that the soldiers would not fear to kill any one of them who moved a foot in the wrong direction.

Yet, it seems, though without making a knowing intention to do the same, that by creating the disturbance, the villagers helped to save Mark and James from being taken by the soldiers. As Nell watched, she saw Simion waving his arms and cloak around as the mad man he always appeared to be. Then, slowly but surely, he moved gradually to where the two boys were bent over their mothers. The soldiers took no notice of him. During the confusion, turmoil and anger, Simion took first Mark who was nearer to the platform and then James, secreting them as if within his cloak, and took them away from the scene.

I have written about Simion, so you know that he was dumb and had never been known to speak to anyone. Not even one word had ever been heard from his mouth. Now, it is interesting to note, and I will tell you at this time, that when recounting how they escaped, both Mark and James were convinced that they heard Simion speak. Both say that they heard, "Come with me now. You can do nothing more. I will keep you safe. Quick, come with me." Both agreed that they simply obeyed as though they had no choice and did not think his words were strange in any way. They only remembered later that he was dumb!

What I know from my later investigations makes me realise how very fortunate they were to have Simion. I am sure that their mothers would want to thank him from the bottom of their hearts for saving their boys from a fate, probably worse than death itself. A fate, the knowledge of which, both Uncle George and I believe sincerely, had played the major part in the killing of their mothers.

As Simion was taking the boys away, Nell had started screaming out and had made a great fuss going over to Ann's body. This was in the hope that the soldiers would be distracted also by her noise, and thus away from noticing Simion and the boys. As she knelt down, wailing loudly, to cradle the body in her arms, one of the soldiers came over to her and knocked her sideways then kicked her in the stomach. She lay, unable to breathe or move for a few minutes.

~ The bodies ~

Up to this point, Nell had spoken very little about what she believed happened to my sisters while on the stocks. She explained that she would rather not have to mention the degradation and pain she knew they must have suffered, but she felt that Sir George would need the information for any trial he may be able to instigate in the courts of law of the land. We all knew that hearsay was not counted in court, and that women were not *allowed to give evidence. But, we both hoped it would have some bearing on what happened.*

After the women were finally cut free from the ropes and the garment, which had fastened their arms and legs, had been taken off, Jonas finally pronounced them dead. Some degree of order had now been restored to the scene. The High Chief stood up.

"You, there," he shouted, pointing at Nell, who was still lying on the floor where she had been kicked, but at last able to breathe, "You! Take the bodies of the women and burn them. They must be burned by nightfall on the morrow."

§

When the 'Riders of Death' had left, in procession, and the Captain and his soldiers had retired back to their camp on the Mount, the villagers were just standing around, as if stunned and unable to do or say anything of any sense. When she could, Nell asked the villagers if anyone would go to Upper Oakington to find Ben and tell him what had happened. A man called Peter Farrier, a farm labourer offered to fetch Ben and asked Nell if he should use one of the horses that Andrew had brought. She told him to take them for Ben's safe keeping, but to leave one, as she would need one to pull the dray which she would need for the bodies. However, before he could depart on his mission, Ben arrived. When he saw what had happened, he was distraught and totally unable to speak or move for a considerable time. Two of the villagers went to stand, one on either side lest he should fall, yet dare not disturb him by touching him. Nell observed that he appeared not to notice their presence being so affected by the sight before him.

She asked if someone would go to find Thomas. All the villagers were shocked, but there was work to be done before the magnitude and effects of what had happened that day could be allowed to permeate their lives. Nell did not trust the soldiers not to come back and dare not leave my sisters' bodies, just in case. Thomas had not been seen by anyone throughout the time his sisters had been in the stocks nor had he been present at the ducking. But, Nell thought, he must surely still be in the village. It was only right that he should be informed, whatever his state or feelings about his sisters.

The follower, Annette, who had been watching in horror at what had happened, told Nell that she would find and bring Thomas to the scene. Annette was the follower whom I mentioned earlier who had grown up in Stocksmoor and whose family still lived there. She came back to say that, though she had knocked at length and loudly on the door, no-one had answered the knocking. She had not found Thomas. It seemed that neither he nor his wife could be contacted.

I have sadly to recount that my loved, but increasingly inebriated and distant brother was never seen alive again. His death was apparently discussed in the village and it was generally thought that when his sisters were taken he despaired when he could do nothing to help them. Nell, knowing the situation rather better, thought that he realised and regretted the mistaken belief that he had harboured within him all his life. Whatever, he was eventually found dead, two days later, in the wood across the field behind his garden. His clothes were in a dreadful mess. It was decided that he had imbibed a great amount of ale over the previous few days and had sought refuge from the village happenings by going into the wood. He appeared to have been vomiting. Whether he drank so much then from shame and grief or accidentally, so that he was unaware of what he did, no one would ever know. But what seemed certain was that his life ended the day his sisters died. I have to say that for me, even in my grief at his death, the time of his dying had a certain irony, because, in effect and in many ways, his life ended when they arrived into his life. As I have mentioned before, I always felt that I gained two sisters but lost my brother that day.

Will, the faithful servant of Peter and Richard, who had often helped the sisters over the years in many ways, and who had been retained by their brother Andrew, arrived about ten minutes after the High Chief had left the platform. He had been delayed because of his duties. He had left as soon as he received the message from Squire Andrew saying why he had been called away and where he had gone and the request to follow as soon as possible. He was stunned to find his master and his master's son, both dead. But, at the sight of my sisters' bodies, he fell to his knees and wept openly. Because of his devotion to their husbands, he had always had a special place in their lives. Nell put her arm round him and asked him to help her with the bodies.

Before Will took the bodies of Andrew and Alend back on two horses to Lower Oakington, he lifted the small bodies of my sisters, one at a time, and he carried them carefully to their home. Nell waited with the other bodies. It was to be her final task to clean and dress them all before their burning. Though in reality it wouldn't have mattered, yet for Nell it was of supreme importance. It was her last duty and service to them. As one of the mature women in the village, she had taken on the role of 'laying out the dead' when Aunt Peggy became too old for that task.

"Will, could you bring the dray to carry the three bodies to the funeral pyre? It is fitting that we use the same one as carried their husbands' bodies home from the castle."

"Nell, I shall be with you as soon as I possibly can," promised Will, and he set off immediately to Lower Oakington to fetch the dray.

"And so it came to pass, Richard. That is what happened. I have not spoken to anyone about the state of their bodies. I must tell you. But, on another day."

"Nell, you have told me so much and also given me many questions that are still to be answered. Tell me, how is your stomach now since the soldiers kicked you so viciously?"

"For about a week I could keep nothing in my stomach and had very much pain. I went to my sister's home after the burning of the bodies, where Miriam and Miranda were hiding, to check they were still safe. The next day but one, I managed to walk to Ben's house along the paths through the wood and found out that the boys were being cared for at his house. Then I went back to my sister's and was able to stay in my bed for a few days to rest and recover. Thank you for asking, Richard."

"Nell, you suffered so much trying to help my sisters. We can never repay you for your devotion."

"I loved them, Richard. I need no thanks or repayment. My sadness is that I couldn't stop anything that happened and my memory tortures me. But, I can, at least, look after their children as they would wish."

"When I have written down all this information in some order I shall inform Uncle George," I continued. "He has asked Oliver to travel with

me, as he used to do when we were young, and we shall go back to Stocksmoor and the surrounding areas to find out whatever we can about the Church Army. He feels that, somehow and somewhere, there are pieces of information that we need and can find. Tell me when we can finish your witness and then I shall make arrangements with Oliver."

"Of course, Richard, maybe on the morrow, I shall be able to tell you and I have something that I want to show you which, even though I cannot bear witness in court, will be evidence which Sir George will be able to use."

"Till tomorrow then, Nell. Thank you so much for having the courage," I paused as I felt choked by my emotion, "and for everything." I finished, lamely. No thanks were adequate to give to this gentle but strong woman, who devoted herself and her life to my sisters and suffered so much because of her love for them. I felt humbled by her selfless devotion.

"It is not courage, Richard, which fires my soul these days. It is anger. Anger such that I have never known before, not even when my dear Sam or when our only child died. I am so grateful to you for bringing me to Sir George's house with the children. I can never repay you, or him, for that kindness. They are, and will always be, my life."

§

The next evening Nell met me, as arranged, in Uncle George's library which he had told me to use whenever I wanted to do so. Though Nell was 'officially' one of the domestic staff, Uncle George knew that I regarded her as one of the family and also as a dear friend. He treated her as we did and held her in great esteem. He allowed her the freedom of his house, as I did of ours. But, she never overstepped the mark or intruded on our privacy.

We sat down at one of the small tables set by the big bay window.

"Nell, tell me what injuries you think had been inflicted on my sisters."

"Richard, when your sisters were pronounced dead, there was still a commotion because of the deaths of Andrew and Alend. As I bent over the body of Catherine, I saw immediately that the tooth-breaker was still in her mouth. I call it that name for want of a better one. I know not what *else I can call such a brutal piece of crafted metal. The soldiers had removed the ones from Ann and Emily as soon as they were taken from the stools and they took them away. But, with the commotion, this one went unnoticed. So, I took it out myself and put it into my pocket. Richard, what I found confirms my belief about Catherine being dead before the ducking. As I tried to release it from her mouth, I wondered where her tongue was, and then I saw that it had been forced backwards and was blocking her breathing. She could not breathe through her nose as that was full of blood from the fall or fist that bruised and damaged her. So, how would she breathe Richard? How could she breathe?"*

"From what you tell me, Nell, she couldn't. At least she was spared the drowning."

"Here it is," Nell took the metal guard from her skirt pocket. I gasped. I recognised it as having been made from the drawing that our cousin Henry had shown me. A more hideous contraption has yet to be seen.

"Do you know where these came from? Did anyone say in the village, as everyone must have seen my sisters wearing them?"

"No, no one knows. I have asked everyone."

"I think I know, but I will not say until I can be sure." I was thinking to myself that I must visit Henry on my travels. If he made it, he may have another drawing which could be used in court, but in any case this was evidence itself, as many people had seen it, even if Nell was not allowed to swear to its origin in court.

"They had lost several teeth," continued Nell. "Dreadful force was used by the soldiers when putting this contraption in their mouths and each one of them suffered similarly. Their necks were bruised very badly, back and front from the pressure of the stocks. Their faces were bruised as if they had been hit. Ann's right eye and Emily's left eye were swollen, like you see when bitten by a horse fly.

"You see, the stocks were placed where the farmer's cattle graze and, oft times, his horses. Though they had been taken from that place while the stocks were standing, there were cow pats and piles of horse manure all around the stocks. (As you know, that kind of material is a breeding place for horseflies particularly when the weather is very hot — as it was then.)

Do you remember, Richard, that Ann had had a bite from a horse fly the previous year which had swollen up very badly? You were visiting at the time, as I recall. Well, this looked much the same.

"Will carried the bodies to their home still in the ducking garments. I decided to leave them on, for privacy, you understand. I asked my friend, Martha, to help me and she will tell you the same as I do myself, should you feel the need to ask her. She has promised that she will tell no one what she saw, but I will go with you should you wish to see her and tell her she can tell you. I started with Ann and when I took her body out from this garment I just screamed. I could not contain what I felt. Let me try to tell you all, though it is truly dreadful. Richard, you will need to know.

"Where the iron ring had been fastened around her left ankle, for the three days in the stocks, was a raw area showing through to the sinew itself. No wonder that she couldn't walk. I found all three of them had suffered the same. It appeared that there were many horsefly bites to the legs and they were so swollen that the ring had become embedded in the flesh, and it was all as if rotten, even in that short few days. I cannot imagine the torture and pain they endured."

I had the thought then that I have had, oh so many times, day and night. 'If only I could have helped my poor sisters.'

§

You see, I make a liniment for treating such bites in animals and it would have soothed their distress, but was uselessly lying in my wagon many miles away. I use a mixture of sour wine and camomile gathered from the hedgerows in spring. I bottle this when it has stood for a few weeks, and after I have strained it through a fine cotton fabric. How I wish so many things, but, forgive me, I digress.

§

Nell continued.

"I lifted one at a time and laid the body on the table in the living room. I bathed each body. Richard, all their private parts, back and front were torn, swollen and bruised black and blue. It was so dreadful. Both

Martha and I just couldn't stop crying. To think of the agonies of pain they must have endured.

"Not only was the unthinkable done time and again to them, to make them so bruised and torn, but the whole of their lower stomachs and upper legs were red and swollen. I thought this looked like very bad nettle stings and when I went to search for answers, I found a large bed of mature nettles down the side of the nearby wall and many strewn around the stocks. Richard, believe me, they tried every torment and torture possible.

"It is no wonder to me that they screamed that first night, and I think that when the same happened again, they were too far gone to scream. I know that sometimes pain that is beyond normal pain does not produce screams as I remember when I was giving birth. My child would not move. It became stuck and had to be brought out in such a way that he could not live. My pain, which was totally unbearable, went on for two days and two nights. I wished to die but I didn't. I heard from the lady who attended me that it was touch and go whether I survived. She told me that I screamed a lot, which I remember, but that, for the last half a day, for which I have no memory, I was silent. I think it must have been the same for them.

"Their skirts and blouses were all torn so that their bare flesh showed through. As you know the sun shone relentlessly during those three days, and the skin of their arms, legs, chest, and face were burned so badly that blisters had formed and become burst. Richard, there were many small cuts all over their legs and arms. I can only think that the soldiers just stabbed them with the point of their swords or knives as they passed.

"The injury caused by the iron rings was not the only injury to those poor legs. When I washed Ann, I saw there were cuts on both her legs that had very deep middle parts, all blackened round the edges. Let me tell you that I wanted to know what had caused these cuts as I could not think what it could be and they were only on Ann's legs. Emily and Catherine did not have these cuts, so I was anxious to know more.

"When I searched, after the burning of the bodies, I found bones, meat bones, strewn round where Ann's stocks had been. I went to the inn to talk to Alice, Bernard's wife, who had been made to cook food for the soldiers on duty at the stocks. She told me that she had prepared meat-on-

the-bone for them as she had been ordered. Those bastards ate the meat off the bones and then it seems that they used Ann's legs as targets to aim at. This was their kind of amusement. I am sure of this, Richard, as, do you remember I told you that Ann's stocks were standing facing the valley and looking straight at the makeshift shed that the soldiers had built for their shelter. They ate at a trestle type of table outside the shed and she was within easy throwing distance.

"Ann's shins in particular were also black with bruising. I found out from a few who passed by, but couldn't, or didn't, help them out of fear, that one soldier seemed to dislike Ann more than the others. A few saw him kick her shin when he went near her or hit her with his sheathed sword or staff. I think that Ann got the worst somehow simply because she was directly in front of the soldiers, and, even in her agony, we know from the time of the ducking, she was defiant. It was always her nature to stand up for herself and for Emily, in her attempt to protect her dear sister.

"Ann and Emily had both damaged their thumbs badly as they had tried to break free, but it was impossible. It seems that Catherine made no attempt to get free and her thumbs were not swollen. Richard, other parts of their bodies were cut and their breasts were bitten. It was a dreadful, dreadful sight. I could not eat for five days, not a crumb and I do not think it was just that I had been kicked so badly. I could not stop my thoughts of what my poor, dear mistresses had had to endure. Those soldiers were animals, just animals, and that makes me sad to say as all animals would behave better than they did. How can the Church allow such happenings in their name? Do they not know what these soldiers do to those in their charge while awaiting their punishment?"

I was listening, silent and shocked. Finally, Nell, with tears streaming down her face managed to tell me more. "You know, Richard, their tiny bodies had deep grooves from the ropes of the ducking stools. I am certain the High Chief and his Captain had determined that the three should die. Though they had endured the stocks as they did and were very weak, even then the cruelty knew no boundaries. The ropes round their bodies had tightened so much. Deep, deep grooves. And the bruising, oh, Richard, the bruising." She rocked too and fro as she told me of all these dreadful injuries which she could still see so clearly in her mind. She kept repeating these words. "They were always so kind and gentle. Oh, I cannot believe *it. I cannot believe what I saw. The soldiers were not human to do those things."*

After a while she continued. "I know Bernard at the inn well and after I had spoken to his wife I spoke to him. Every evening, the soldiers on duty would invade the inn and, under threat of being run through with a sword, they demanded spirits, mainly rum. They would then just take at least two bottles from the store as well as a barrel of ale, which they carried on their backs to the shelter. Both he and his wife heard them laughing and shouting all night, under the influence of the ale and spirits. We can only assume that your sisters suffered from their drunkenness."

Nell went quiet and we sat in contemplation for a while.

"There is nothing I can say, Nell, except that Uncle George loved his nieces and the culprits will be brought to account. Thank you so much for all your care of them, Nell. You were such an important part of their lives. I think they must have known something was going to happen as they asked me to look after their children should they ever be left without a parent. I look to you to help me in that task. I know no one who can do better for them than you."

"Fear not, Richard. They are, and always will be, as if my own."

∫

Later, when I visited Stocksmoor, and here I digress to interject, Bernard told me that which disturbed me greatly. He mentioned that Thomas, our brother, would talk freely and answer any questions put to him by monks or soldiers alike when he was drunk, and when he had passed the level where he knew what he was saying. Did he in drunken error and with no intention, tell the soldiers about our sisters and their activities? Does drunkenness take away guilt or shame? I don't know but poor Thomas is dead and will be answering his maker. I can feel no anger, just pity, for my brother. I did not share these thoughts with Nell, out of my brotherly respect for Thomas. She would think what she would herself, and neither did she speak of him to me.

You who read this may wonder why I write in so much detail. I think it is important to know what happened to innocent women in the name of

God at the hands of the Church Army. One has to say that not only did the Church collude with its army and encourage them to scourge the land, but turned a very blind eye and deaf ear to what they did while doing the same. All the detail I have told you, apart from that about my brother Thomas, was eventually handed to Uncle George. It was all included in the dossier of evidence presented at the trial. But there is still much to tell.

§

Nell was walking in the grounds around the Manor, which was now her home. It had a beautiful garden, the present form having been created by our late Aunt Gwendolyn, and was surrounded by parkland. It was now September and the leaves of the trees were beginning to change into their winter vestments. I had been taking one of the horses whose fetlock had been inflamed, but I am pleased to say was now recovered very well, for a short walk in the evening warmth. I met up with Nell and after a few moments she asked, "Richard, when you go back to your house, could I possibly go with you and, please, could we visit Stocksmoor? I feel I need to do so. I have a very strong feeling as though there is something there that I have left behind. I have thought and thought but I do not have the slightest notion of what it is."

"Yes, of course. I shall have to visit our old home a few times to collect more of our personal belongings, clothes and such like. It's just that I have wanted to make sure that all the children and Rosamund are settled here first. I had, in fact, thought to go in two days time. Would that be suitable for you?" I tied the horse to a small tree and sat on the ground.

"Indeed, Richard, I will arrange with the housekeeper to supervise Ann and Emily's children should they need anything. I can say that, already, they are very able to do most things and know their way around very well."

"That's settled then. Can you stay in Stocksmoor for a day or two while I do a few visits? I want to call to see my sister, Mary, in Bretton, talk to Cousin Geoffrey at the Hall and see Cousin Henry at the forge. I think my cousins will both be only too pleased to be witnesses. Geoffrey will I'm sure want to report as to the manner in which his request for help was received, both in Sandal and in York. I shall confide in him and Henry our eventual purpose. I am confident that they will assist."

"Yes, I shall stay at the house of your father and make sure it is made into good condition in case Ben's wife has not found the time to do so. I don't now know quite what its condition will be. I know my mistresses would be upset if their home was untidy, even though they are no longer here to see it."

"Nell," I changed the subject of our discourse. "Tell me about the burning of the bodies of my sisters, so that I can complete my narrative for Uncle George. He is likely to return soon."

Nell sat down on the ground next to me.

"After I had washed the bodies, I combed their hair and put some powder on their faces to hide the bruises. Martha continued to help me and, she will verify on her own, without my prompting, that which I have told you. For one person it is difficult when the bodies are so cold and hard as theirs had become. She was of great help to me. I dressed them in their best dresses. Will had returned with the dray as I had requested of him.

"Several of the men in the village offered their help, including Bernard, who closed the inn until after the burning. The pyre was built at the upper end of the common. The soldiers did not come near or interfere. The men, with axes, chopped down the stocks which were used to lay the bodies on. We had a lot of dry straw as harvesting was well over by now, it being such a hot summer. It had all been collected into stacks in very good time and the farmers brought bundles fastened by strong bindings. These were placed under the wood, leaving plenty of space for air to make sure the fire did what was intended. Then spirits, given by Bernard from the inn, were poured over the straw and wood.

"When all was prepared, we took the bodies and placed them on the pyre later that evening. I sat there all night. In the early hours, as if from nowhere, I was aware that I was joined by Simion who had brought Mark and James with him. It was a starlit night, but Simion knew how to avoid being seen. Once I had met with the boys and hugged them close to me, he took them to sit in such a place, in the shadow of the hedge, where most would not have noticed that they were there. Gradually, in ones and twos, the villagers came. Only a few young women who had very young children stayed in their homes, but there were two who brought their sleeping child in their arms, wrapped against the chill of the night. All had collected flowers from their gardens and the pyre was covered in branches and blooms. Then we spent the night in a silent vigil, broken only by the sound of crying. Richard, I beg that you do not have anger for the villagers. They could not help your sisters and what they saw will live with them forever, as it will with me. Even those who were not the most helpful to your sisters when they were alive, I know, now feel shame and grief. As the sun started to rise, Will set the pyre alight, almost ceremonially, with a flaming torch.

"The soldiers stayed away most of the morning, so that by the time that they marched up the village to stand around and watch, with their Captain at their head, the bodies had burned. Most of us sat there until noon, when only ash was left and the smoke had stopped. We saw them coming. Simion had taken the boys away, out of sight and again to safety before day break. You know, I have no notion of how Simion knew what we were going to do, but he did. No one in the village spoke to the soldiers, and nor will they, unless at sword point.

"Richard, I would swear on my life that, as we kept our vigil hours, over the pyre were three coloured lights, pink, blue and mauve. I know that Simion and the boys saw them as I did, because the boys have since asked me if I knew where the lights came from. But, maybe our grief made us fanciful."

~ Richard and Nell return to Stocksmoor ~

As we finally arranged, the next Monday morning we set off and I left Nell overnight in Stocksmoor. She stayed at my father's house. We went into the house through the back door and Nell commented that it looked as if it had been damaged and repaired. I entered into the house with her, but all seemed to be as she remembered, except that a chair in the living area had been overturned, and the door to the stairwell was open. I straightened the chair and Nell shrugged her shoulders.

"It looks as though it has been searched for someone," I commented. "Do you think they have been looking for the children?"

"I don't know, but someone has definitely been in here," answered Nell. "Would you go upstairs please, Richard, and check that there is no one in the house? This is not as it was when we left, and even if Ben has been in the house, he would not have damaged anything or upturned a chair."

I checked everywhere. All was safe, but a cupboard door upstairs was open, which I closed.

"Do you want to ask Martha to stay with you?"

"No, Richard, it is best I stay alone. I shall not let anyone be aware that I am here. Fear not, I shall be fine. I have plenty of work to do as there is still much to sort. Believe me, I shall protect myself should that be necessary, though God forbid that anything untoward will happen."

So, I arranged with her that she should stay there just two nights and then I would call to collect her for the return journey. She had brought food with her from Uncle George's kitchen to suffice her needs. I then went onto Bretton, which was on the way to my own, now unused house, and intended to call to see my remaining sister, Mary, and her children. I say 'children' as I knew that by now her baby would have been born. To my utmost dismay I saw that her place looked forlorn, the door closed and the drapes pulled across the window. Although I was getting used to seeing most of the houses in Stocksmoor looking this way, I still felt my heart take a jump. A familiar, dark feeling of dread came upon me. But, I must surely be thinking the worst of everything.

I decided that I would visit Henry first and leave my horse with him to be shoed. It was not quite necessary, but I had a lot of travelling to do. Henry was the best blacksmith I knew, so I went straight to the forge. But the doors were shut, with no sign of any activity, and I soon realised that he wasn't there.

Next, I walked to the house of Aunt Rosemary. I knocked on the door and waited. After a few minutes, the door opened and Cousin Henry appeared. I have to confess I have not seen such a change in any person in a short time as I saw in him that day. He seemed to have shrunk. His face was white and haggard, with eyes that appeared sunken and encircled in black rings. It was but a few months since we had met. At the time, you will remember, I told you that he showed me the drawing of the mouth piece. I was taken aback with shock, "Henry, you look very ill."

"Come in, Richard," he answered.

Aunt Rosemary was sitting on her rocking chair in front of the fire and rocking backwards and forwards. She looked up. She had been weeping and dried her eyes with her apron.

"You come at a dreadful time, Richard." She waved her hand to Henry to carry on.

"More has happened and we can scarcely sustain our waking days," Henry's voice cracked with these words. He was like a broken man, and I noticed that his hands were shaking. Here was not the cousin I knew, the calm man in charge of his life, enjoying his work. But, I continued with my purpose, not knowing what else I could do.

"I came to call on Mary, but she is nowhere to be seen."

"No, nor ever likely to be again," answered Henry.

"What do you mean?" I asked, and a cold shiver went down my spine. Something was indeed very amiss and I was shortly going to hear of it.

"Did you hear that she had a baby boy two days before Ann, Emily and Catherine died?" asked Henry.

"No, I had not heard, though I knew she was with child and that she was progressing well through her confinement when I was here that last time," I replied.

"Well, she had a difficult time as she was so small and the baby was very big. She had a long labour, lost a lot of blood at the birth, and, as a result, became very weak. Soon after this, despite our efforts to shield her from the dreadful news, she heard of the deaths of her sisters. She became very quiet and would neither eat nor speak for a few days. Then, even worse, we all heard how they had been killed. Only then did Abe realise, with horror that the stocks, which he had been ordered to make, had been used for them. He was distraught. He tried to keep the truth from Mary, but it soon became common talk in the village and someone told her, though we never found out who that was. We suspect it was Helena, but will never be sure. After that, she did not sleep and none of us could reach into her mind to help her. She still fed the baby as though she was aware of him, but did not appear to notice little Marion most of the time. Her neighbour, Sarah, was very kind and spent a lot of time with her."

"Oh dear! Poor Mary." I was shocked. "She never had much time for Ann and Emily, but, you know, when people are alive it never occurs to them to be different or change. Look at Thomas, dead of the drink, yet he couldn't look at Ann and Emily without anger because of losing his mother."

"We think it was Catherine's death that hit her the most," continued Henry. "Anyway, soon after she was up and about again, and without confiding to anyone where she was going, she took little Marion to her neighbour, Sarah, in the early afternoon. She asked her if she would care for the child until she returned. She was still weak and very pale. No one would have thought she could even manage to walk to Stocksmoor at this time, let alone carrying a baby. So Sarah never thought to ask where she was going. Abe was away for the day, thinking that she was improving sufficiently to be left alone.

"Please try to understand, Richard, we feel very bad about this, but we knew nothing extra was amiss that day until the evening. We live opposite. We would have looked after her, if only she had let us know she was feeling so bad. We have been rather keeping to ourselves since everything that has happened, and we are all still so very upset. Mother has been unable to do anything since our father's death."

"Uncle Harold, dead? Your father is dead too? When? How?"

"Yes, he died while your sisters were on the stocks, but we did not find out until after they had died. Me and John were together, but not at home, busy working out the design and construction of some gates. Mother told us that when Father came home from his visits to the sick and heard that Mark had been asking for help, he went straight to Stocksmoor to see what he could do. I think that, though he was a physic and used to people being ill, the shock was too great. He was found *apparently on his way to the Hall. We think he was going there to enlist help. We knew he had gone with the express purpose of interceding for them and so we assumed he had stayed, maybe in your father's house, to take care of them as best he could. So we didn't worry for two nights. Then, his horse was seen wandering in the park by one of the stable lads, the one who usually brings the horses to me from the Hall for shoeing. He recognised it and brought it home. We went to look for him. He was near the gate to the park, dead. He was buried at the Hall the next day, after arrangements could be made."*

"Oh dear, I am so sorry."

I didn't tell him what Nell had told me. I didn't want to risk tarnishing the image of his apparently sacrificial father.

"But, coming back to your sister, Mary," continued Henry. "Mother cannot do anything without help and, as you see, she is very distressed. But even so, she would have sat with her. I was working all day. Abe came back home and, when he couldn't find Mary he came to us to see if she was at our house. We admitted that we had not seen her all day and thought she must have a chill or something and had stayed indoors. Helena was away from home as she often was and we had no idea where she went as she never spoke much to us. She didn't pay much attention to Mary or little Marion, at any time, though they lived in the same house.

"Abe went to all the houses around. He found that Sarah had Marion. Sarah told him that Mary had left Marion with her, simply asking her to look after her until she returned. By now, she thought it was time Mary was back, as the little girl was tired and crying for her mother. She had given her some food, but, really, it was too bad of Mary to be so late when her little girl needed her bed. She was as good a friend as anyone could ever have, but she felt that Mary was being unfair this day.

"Mounting his horse, which was still saddled after his return from work, Abe set off for Stocksmoor as the likeliest place to look for Mary. It appears, from what was discovered, that she had decided she wanted to take a posy of flowers to where her sisters had been burned. Abe found the posy and the flowers were just the same as those in their garden. But Mary was not there."

Henry stopped for a while.

Then Aunt Rosemary, with a big effort, spoke, "Mary walked into the pond with her baby. Both were found. They were dead."

"No, I can't believe it. And with her baby?" I put my head in my hands. "Whatever will happen next?" I sat down, stunned. My other sister, dead? Now, all had gone. I wept.

"Then where is Abe now? I must see him."

"Nay, that cannot be either," replied Henry.

"Why not?"

"He was found hanging in his work shed, the very next morning. It had weighed heavily on him when he found he had been the one to make the stocks for your sisters, and the ducking stools. He spoke of nothing else. He came over nearly every day and would sit with his head in his hand and told us, time and again, how he had been forced to make both lots. He had been visited every other day by two soldiers and the stocks had been checked by them each time. He had become very fearful for Mary as they threatened his family if he did not do as he was asked. Then, after he had made the stocks, they demanded that he should make three ducking stools. When he told them that he did not agree with ducking anyone they knocked him down. He explained to Mary that his bruises were from a fall in the yard.

"But he told us how he had thought to fool them. He made the back fixing false, by putting dried cow dung in the hole first to make it appear fixed. Then he whittled off a sliver of wood, unnoticeable really, but enough so that water would reach the dung. Once the dung became wet, it would liquefy and run out, and the tightness of the ropes would be lessened. At least that was his hope. He didn't know who the stocks or ducking stools were intended for when he made them. But, afterwards, when he heard that they had been for Ann, Emily and Catherine, he was in total despair. He also heard that the men had tested the ducking stools and so the dung had been dissolved. His plan had been to no avail."

Henry stopped for a while, overcome with emotion. Richard waited.

"Finally, when Mary and his son were dead, he could bear no more," finished Henry.

I could barely speak. For a while we all sat in silence, deep in our own thoughts. Then, as though prompted in my thoughts, I suddenly remembered Mary's little girl.

"Where is Marion?"

"She is living with Sarah at present as Helena is unable to look after her. Since her brother died, she has been incapable of anything. She has been drinking rum as often as not and scarcely been out of the house. And she lets very few past her door. Neighbours have tried but to no avail. You see she arrived home the next afternoon and went to look for him as the house was empty. It was she who found Abe hanging. We just heard screaming and went to see what was wrong. I cut him down, but he had been dead many hours," related Henry.

"Goodness, I cannot believe what you are both telling me, yet I know it to be true. It is as if I hear the words but cannot understand what you are saying. What is to happen to little Marion? Is Helena going to be able to look after her?"

"We don't know. Nothing has been decided, but Mary's friend, Sarah, has two small children of her own and another one on the way. Her husband is a gardener at the Hall and their funds are low. He has just been off work with an injured back. They cannot keep her for ever. What should be done?"

"I will visit Sarah and recompense her well for her help. Then, I will go and speak with Helena if she is home, though as I passed the house looked deserted."

"No, she is there. She has just not opened the drapes since Abe died. Anytime we have tried to speak with her she refuses company, saying that she wants to be alone."

I stood up. Henry came with me into the hallway to open the door to let me out. "Henry, about the mouth pieces. I must ask you, though I would rather not. Did you make them, in the end?" I had not wanted to speak of those monstrosities in front of Aunt Rosemary.

"Yes, I had to. But, Richard, I am tormented. I see them in my mind day and night," he replied. Suddenly unable to keep his emotion to himself, he became convulsed with tears. "Do you remember that design? Well, the soldiers came again. I told them that I could not make such instruments of hurt for any dog, however savage and, as we agreed, I told them the truth. The piece of paper with the design on it had blown into the flames. They came back, yet again with the design redrawn and this time made me make those mouth pieces. One soldier watched all day and another came back the following day. I had to do as I was bidden, Richard, for fear that my wife and children would be killed if I did not. What was I to do? They threatened me, as they had threatened Abe. But, I cannot recompense those dear women. I made what I did, and without knowledge of the true nature of what I made. I would that I had been anywhere else but here. I would prefer to have been a labourer in the fields, a cow hand, or gardener; anything other than what I was."

After a short pause to recover himself, Henry managed to say, "I have given up the forge. I can never wield a hammer or shape a piece of metal ever again."

I thought again of Marion. It was obvious to me that this was no place for a little child of but two years to stay. Aunt Rosemary was now old and needing full care. Henry would need much time to recuperate as I could tell from his haggard face that his thoughts were tormenting him and he had a wife and family to care for. No, it was not possible. Neither could I let Marion be taken away by people who would collect orphaned children if Helena refused to care for her. I was very glad I had stopped in Bretton that day. So, I went across the road to see Helena. At first she did not come to the door, but I went round to the back of the house and called into the small scullery.

"Helena, it is Richard, Mary's brother. I need to talk to you about Marion."

After a few minutes a dishevelled, dirty looking Helena, but without her usual dismissive demeanour, came to the door. She smelled strongly of ale. I asked if I could go into the house. She nodded. I went into what was usually a well kept, tidy living room. It was, unbelievably, the same place but I will not defile the memory of my sister Mary by telling you what it was like."

"Helena, I am truly sorry about your brother."

"Why did he do it? He had me, his sister. He has left me. I always looked after him, even sharing my house with him and Mary. Why? How could he, Richard? Did I, his sister, mean nothing?"

"I don't know, Helena. Where is Marion?"

"Marion? Oh, the child. I think she is at Sarah's house, up the road. She's a friend of Mary. I cannot look after a child and I don't want to look after a child. Richard, will you take Marion with you? Rosamund is a good mother. Please Richard, please," and she stood up and held my coat fronts in both hands in a desperate way. "Please, Richard, take the child. I cannot look after a child. I cannot."

"Yes, I will take her with me," I wanted to back away as soon as possible from the smell on her breath. 'The poor child, not only left orphaned but rejected,' I thought. I spoke no more except to wish her farewell. Helena was obviously in her own distress and I was not going to add to it by unnecessary comments.

For some reason, I did not tell her that we had all moved to Poppleton. I do not know why, but instinct told me to merely tell her I would take Marion off her hands. I left and never expected to see Helena again, but I did, most unexpectedly as you will find out.

I returned to see Henry and Aunt Rosemary.

"I will take Marion back to Poppleton. Uncle George will expect nothing less. He has money and staff, rooms and food. A more generous man you cannot find. I will speak to Sarah and ask her to keep the child until I call with the wagon, probably on the morrow or, at the latest, the day after. I will take her with us. I have not told Helena where I am taking her. I believe she has no idea that we have moved, so please can I ask you not to tell her or anyone else where we all are? I fear for the safety of Ann and Emily's children, especially when we start a court case, as we surely will. Will you bear witness, Henry, if you are needed, as to the plans for the mouth braces and the threats of the soldiers?"

"We shall not say a word, and yes, I will bear witness, though the distress will be great. Those bastards will answer for their actions."

I was just about to leave, when I suddenly thought of Geoffrey and his horse's lost shoe.

"Henry, have you seen Cousin Geoffrey recently?"

"No, he is at home at the Hall, I understand, but will speak to no one at present. A state of melancholy has come over him, just two weeks ago and he cries all day. He will recover I have no doubt, but that is the reason I have not seen him."

"Did you know that he travelled to York and obtained a pardon for my sisters, but arrived back too late?" I asked. "I am told that his horse shed a shoe soon after leaving York."

"Lost a shoe? No that cannot be true, Richard. Geoffrey called here before he set off and told me that he may have to ride to York to try to collect a pardon if no one would listen to him at Sandal. He took a risk even calling here as there were soldiers up and down the village. But, Richard, I shoed his horse. I assure you that I was very careful to angle the nails so that no amount of galloping would loosen the shoe. His mission was of the utmost urgency. If his horse lost a shoe, then it had been tampered with. I will swear to that in court. I know my horses and their shoes, as you know."

§

I stayed the night in my own cottage, and then on the morrow, I decided that I had one more visit to do. I was going to see Ben, my remaining brother. I must see how he was faring and tell him how Ann and Emily's children were, as I was sure he would want to know. I travelled a route to his house that missed the main village of Stocksmoor. I went down the far side of the common and through the lower lane which passed through Lower Stocksmoor to Upper Oakington. There were other routes I could have taken, but I wanted as few people as possible in the area, other than in Stocksmoor, to see me pass by.

This lane took me very near where the ducking pool was, and I was drawn to visit this site, a place where, out of cowardice, I had avoided. But, if

I was to be strong for my family, my sisters' children and do my duty, I had to face that which I would rather avoid. I did not want to look at the place where I now knew that not three but four of my sisters had perished. I feel this was a natural inclination, but for me to keep that fear and my grief to such an extent would not bode well for what was ahead of me.

I turned my horse and proceeded the very short way through the trees to the pond. At least, I say 'pond' so that you will know where I was, but there was no longer a pond. The spring now ran into a small stone basin, big enough from which to collect drinking water, but then the water that overflowed ran away into a short ditch and eventually disappeared into the ground. The pond had been filled in and was now no more than a shallow dip covered by sods of grass. Nowhere could be seen the places where the ducking stools had been fixed, nor where the platform had been. No one, who had not known what was here before or what had happened would be any the wiser for looking at the place now. In many ways I was relieved.

I found Ben in his garden. He was a quiet man, and, in all the years that I had known him, he was always pleasant. A man who, up to the present tragic events had accepted life as it came, day by day, with a calmness of purpose showing neither anger nor great joy. I loved my brother dearly. Truthfully, I can say that there was nothing, and never had been anything, that could make me not love him. He smiled when he saw me and put down his spade. We sat on a bench at the bottom of his garden and looked out over the valley beyond. After the usual greetings and sharing of information about his family, mine and the nephews and nieces in my care, I informed him about my visit so far, "I have been to Bretton and heard about Mary and her baby and her husband."

"It is just terrible, Richard. Yet more dead. We did not know anything like that could happen." His eyes filled with tears as he spoke. He wiped them with the back of his hand. "We were trying in our own way to understand our loss, but never thought that Mary would act in that way. But, as you know, Mary never shared her thoughts. We had assumed that she was quite strong, particularly being able to live with Helena as she did. I think we would agree that few women could, or men for that matter. I had been to see her with Hannah about three weeks after the baby was born. She

- 297 -

seemed to be reasonably well, though pale and, of course, very upset. A grand little lad he was. He reminded me of our youngest when he was born." He did not speak for a few minutes and we sat in quiet reflection together, thinking about a life that had not been given time to live.

"Did you know that Abe made the stocks?" Ben continued. "I visited Aunt Rosemary after Mary was found as I wanted to know what she knew of the circumstances. I was told that Mary had changed, but, you know, no one came to tell us or seek our help. Apparently, she was weak after the birth, but even so, she seemed not to be able to believe it possible that Abe could have made the stocks and the ducking stools for our sisters, her sisters. She had told Aunt Rosemary that the soldiers 'paid him well for enabling them to torture and kill her sisters'. She could not reconcile this with the fact that she loved him and I think that fact equally as much as their deaths unhinged her mind. Who knows what goes on in a mind intent on ending its life, but, sadly, she took her son with her. Aunt Rosemary told me that Mary kept saying, 'He's the image of his father,' over and over again, and maybe that was connected in her way of thinking. We shall never know, but it is so dreadful to contemplate."

"We buried Mary and the baby together, in the same grave and next to Mama's at the Hall."

"What about Abe's body?" I asked.

"His body was buried in the local burial ground. It was Helena's decision."

"I have determined to take little Marion back with me to Poppleton," I told him as he needed to know of this plan. "Helena begged me to do so and was sure that she could not, nor did she want to, look after that small child. And she is not at all suitable, in any event. I know Uncle George would insist on the same if he was privy to the facts and that he will welcome another to his household. I shall ask Nell, who, by the way, is at Papa's house just now sorting the last of Ann, Emily and Catherine's belongings, if she will take her on board along with the older ones. Miranda and Miriam, I know, will be a great help as they are very good with children, as we have all seen with Uncle George's youngest grandchildren. Are you quite happy if I do that?"

"Of course. We had talked about having her here, but Hannah is not as well as she might be. Rather than her having no one, then, of course, she would be welcome here. What else could we do? But if you can take her then that would be the best solution."

Then, after a while, I related my discovery, "I have called by the pond. It has gone."

"Yes, the villagers decided that. The work was completed only last week. There were a few very ill people in the village, you know, unable to keep food in their bodies and with fevers. They thought that they should remove any evidence of what had happened. I think they thought that our sisters were bringing bad luck to them in punishment. Something like that, I heard, was circulating around. The men gathered soil from each and every farm and every garden, except from Papa's, and each took a turn to empty the soil into the pond as if to make amends. Gradually it has disappeared.

"One of our workmen, you know him, Dorothy's husband, a stone mason, made the bowl to collect the spring water. He showed me that he had engraved our sister's initials on the base, though the villagers have not seen them. He thought Dorothy, God rest her soul, would be pleased he had done that. I took a plant of camomile from Papa's garden and planted it near the spring. It's a hardy plant and will withstand the ravages of any weather."

He became quiet again. We sat silently, both having our own thoughts, with much to fill our minds.

"Why was I not home, Richard? When I did come home, why did I not realise the danger our sisters were in? I didn't think anything like that could ever happen to them. Why did I not take more notice? I cannot forgive myself. You were not there, I know. You were miles away. But me, I returned home the night before, and though very tired, I could have tried to do something. I heard Papa was dead and that his body had been put somewhere in the burial ground. I was grief stricken. I intended to see the Captain the next morning, and find out just where his body had been put and give Papa a proper burial. I thought no further than that.

"Hannah informed me that her brother, Squire Robert, had called before he left to go away on business urgently. He told her that he had heard that *our three sisters had been put in the stocks to be taught a lesson, but that they would be released the next morning. He did not mention anything about being ducked afterwards. I have asked her so many times. She is distraught about it and says, 'No, he told me nothing else, nothing.' I haven't as yet seen him as he has been away from home ever since, on business somewhere. His wife is living at the Hall, where she was at the time it all happened. But I shall ask him, brother-in-law and Squire, or not. I don't care. I want to know. Our cousin, his wife, was very fortunate, considering she practised the very same way with herbs as our sisters did."*

"Yes, and don't forget her own sister, Jane, also. I mean everyone knew about the Squire's wife and her sister, and that the Squire was always very proud of his wife's ability. Yet, nothing happened to them. I am glad, of course, but it seems very strange."

"To be honest Richard, I didn't think it was anything serious. I mean, when did anything serious ever happen in Stocksmoor before?"

"Ben, I know how you feel as I feel the same. But I think that if you had tried to interfere, then I would not have any brother left and Mark and James would have had no home to stay at and been in dire risk until I could take them to Poppleton. Look what happened to Andrew and Alend. I think also, 'Why did I not return early from my journey that time?' But I too did not know what was or could be happening."

"Do you think we shall ever understand what happened?" asked Ben.

"Indeed we shall, if it is the last thing I ever do. Ben, I mean to know the truth of why they were put to death and by whom. We know it was the Church Army and that they were killed as witches, but who was behind it and why? They were not witches. No one in their right mind, however religious, could ever have thought that. Different in their skills, I agree, but never involved in any kind of witchcraft. It was a sham, a made up accusation, but by whom and why?"

Hannah had come to the back door to tell us that food was on the table.

§

After a very tasty repast, we went outside again. Both of us felt more at ease outdoors. Why, I do not know, but it had always been so. Ben continued.

"Do you remember Tobias, Tobias Trevore, you know the man who did all the money accounting for our father's business, and who lived in the cottage just beyond the Mount? He was married to Lucia, our cousin twice removed? He died about four years ago after some kind of accident. Why it happened or, in fact, what actually happened, never became clear, but it was rumoured he had a bad fall while making a repair to his roof. The ladder slipped or broke or something akin to that."

"I think I do, though I had never seen him for years. Wasn't he a tall, gaunt man with a swarthy complexion?"

Ben nodded.

"Yes, I remember him now. Didn't he have a son, Charles?"

"That's right. Well, Charles was also killed."

"No! I never heard that. When and how?" I asked.

Ben then told me what he knew of what had happened.

"No one knew until two days after our sisters were dead and burned. You know, Charles and his wife, Ruth, lived with Tobias's widow, Lucia. They were both too scared, with the soldiers in the field by the side of their garden, to go out of the house, except to visit the privy with cloaks round their heads. The Church Army had a 'reputation for women' that went before them.

"Apparently, late that evening, Charles had been walking in his garden, just to enjoy some fresh, cooler air after the heat of the day. His boundary was very near one of the tents of the soldiers. While there, by the hedge where he could not be seen, he heard them laughing and speaking very loudly, in their ale, I suspect, and he listened to their conversation. He heard them saying that the stocks had been delivered to the camp ready for the three witches who would be put in them when the trial had been heard. He heard one say, 'Captain laughed when he was told that they had been measured to within an inch'. One man was saying he hoped they were standing stocks, as they gave them much more chance of fun. Raucous laughter had followed. He was horrified. Back indoors, he told

his mother, Lucia, exactly what he had heard. These men had made his spine freeze.

"I have spoken with Lucia, but not Ruth as she is still beside herself with her grief. Charles had a sense of urgency quite unlike his usual self and told her, 'Now I know why they have come to this village. I must go immediately to warn Mr Shaw and his daughters. They must flee.' He had no doubt whatsoever whom the soldiers were talking about.

"That was the last time that they saw Charles alive. Lucia thought he was maybe delayed helping our sisters to pack up their things to escape. She daren't go looking for him, but by next morning he had not come home. Though frantic with worry she dare not leave their home, until some of the villagers were made to do so to hear the trial. Living so near, she and Ruth were some of those called to stand and witness what happened at the trial. Then she did not go out of her house until, again, the villagers were made to watch the ducking. She had no idea what was delaying him, but never thought he might be dead.

"Eventually, two days after the ducking, Ruth heard a knock on the door and went to answer. Two of the men who worked on the farm, down the road near the pond, called at her house carrying the body of her husband. It was now in a state that made her swoon to the floor. He had been killed and appeared to have been thrown behind the hedge, without any real attempt at concealment. He was found so close to home that she and others must had walked past his body going to the trial and the ducking. But, because that hedge is thick and strong they had not seen it. The farmer's men saw it when they had been given the task of clearing the side of the field ready for cutting the barley."

ſ

Let me just interject that it was the farmers' custom to harvest round the outside edge of the field first and work inwards in ever decreasing circles. In that way they drove any small animals and birds into the centre, making them easier to catch. So, prior to that, they made a first cut by hand, a few feet wide around the field ready for the horse and scythe to be able to pass by.

ſ

"One of the dogs was barking and would not return when they called. It was making such a fuss that one of them, while going to see what was wrong, found the corpse. Apparently, he had a deep wound through his back and his head had been cracked open. It has been surmised, though without any proof, that he was run through by one of the soldiers after first being hit on the head, and then his body was simply thrown over the hedge. It lay unnoticed until the farmer's dog had found it."

"How many more are going to die in the village? This is dreadful. I fear I cannot take in the carnage that has happened to those we love and those we know. He died trying to save our sisters. Let us pray that God in his wisdom will reward him, somehow, sometime, for his sacrifice."

"There is no end to sadness. Ruth gave birth to a baby girl only two weeks later. The child died at birth. Hannah, who knows Lucia, says that poor Ruth is in a sorry state. The Trevores were a small family you know, and I understand that they came here from southern parts – following work I suppose. I imagine the family name, Trevore, has now died out – certainly round these parts." ·

"Well!" Ben had even more to tell me. "It seems that yet another man has died as well."

"Ever thing beggars belief. It really does." I was still trying to understand about Charles Trevore and did not fully appreciate what Ben was now saying.

"Sorry, Ben, did I hear you aright? Another? Did you say 'another'? Who was that?"

"No one we know, but actually one of the soldiers. I started back at work, for the sake of the workmen, two days after the burning of our sisters. Although in truth no one had any heart for any work or indeed of even being in the village. But, that morning all the soldiers, other than the Captain, were seen scouring over the common and all the fields around. They even went into the woodland behind the village. All had their swords out and were swinging them at random from side to side. We all wondered what they were doing and decided that they appeared to be searching for someone. Then they knocked on every door in the village and even broke into our father's house. You may have noticed that the back door has had to be repaired."

"Yes, Nell pointed that out when I left her there," I recalled, "and there had obviously been someone rummaging in the house."

"Well, the villagers eventually found out that two soldiers, new recruits poor lads and only young, had deserted from the army after the duckings and the killings of Andrew and Alend. One was caught almost straight away and had to suffer the punishment of desertion. His intentions had been obvious and, as you know, in the Church Army there is no compassion. He was hanged. Some say he was hanged from a tree in the wood, others that it took place in the farmer's barn. What is clear is that he is dead. His body was buried in the village burial ground with only one soldier present and his uniform was cut into strips and put on his grave. No blessing, nothing. They say that the soldier was only twenty years of age and had been in the army only six months. So tragic."

"Poor lad. And the other?"

"As far as we know, he was never caught. The Church Army left the village, but still no one has seen him and, if he is not dead, then he must be somewhere. It is assumed by everyone that he has moved far away. We can only hope that is the case."

"It has all been too much Ben, for everyone. Now, we must part again, as I must be on my way. I shall call at Stocksmoor on my way to stay at my house in Sheepley this night, just to check that Nell is well and safe. Then, I shall collect Marion in Bretton and Nell at Stocksmoor on the morrow. I shall be coming back occasionally, next time probably with our cousin, Oliver. If you learn anything else of use, or if we need assistance in any way, I will contact you." I went to say farewell to Hannah.

Before I left, Ben asked, "Richard, lest it is a while till the next time I see you, what do you wish to do about our father's house?"

"I shall not come back to live anywhere near here again, so do with it what you will."

"I have been thinking. What if I keep our father's house, in his memory, and when my sons are old enough, one of them uses the house as their home? Does that meet with your approval?"

"Yes, of course. I may use it if necessary, when we are back and forth, but only for the next few months. I shall always make sure that it is secure. I am going to find out everything I can for Uncle George. He is determined to bring the villains to court. But I am more likely to use my own home most of the time, as I prefer it that way. Nell should be sorting our sisters' possessions as we speak, and we shall take whatever she feels the children will want. Take good care of yourself and your family. Farewell, till the next time." I gave him a warm handshake and embraced him.

"Farewell to you, Richard. May God speed you on your way and keep you safe."

§

"Did you find what you thought you had forgotten?" I asked Nell when I reached my father's house.

"Yes, Richard. I knew that I had to go back, but it was more than to sort my mistresses' clothes. Before we left last time, your brother, Ben, asked me if I would do that, rather than ask his wife. I had not quite completed clearing the bottom drawer in Ann and Emily's bedroom at that time, so yesterday I took everything out of the drawer, then sorted and folded them into what we would take back to Poppleton and what I should leave with your brother, Ben, to give to Martha. She will know if there is anyone needy of such things in or around the village. As I was emptying the drawer, look, I found that and I can see that my name is on it." She pointed to the table on which I could see a small parcel.

"It is for me, but I cannot read, Richard, other than my name. I have not opened it as I do not know what the other words say. Can you read them for me?"

I picked up the parcel and read "NELL," in large capital letters. Then underneath was written "For Richard to read."

Nell opened the parcel and inside was a letter, and another smaller parcel. Nell handed them both to me.

"Nell, these are both for you. Open the inner parcel and then I will read the letter."

She did so and gasped. "OH! OH! Richard, see what it is!" A beautiful ring made of gold, with three diamonds embedded in the gold, which I recognised as Eve's wedding ring, was in her hand.

I read the letter out to Nell,

> *"Dearest and faithful Nell,*
>
> *When you find this, we shall be no more. We are forever in your debt for all the loving care that you gave to us and our children. We love you dearly. The ring in the parcel belonged to our mother. We are sure you will be as a mother to our children for as long as you are able, and we ask that you wear it, every day until your own death, in our memory and for the sake of our children.*
>
> *Please tell Miriam, Miranda, James and Mark that we have given it to you and show them this letter. They know how much that ring meant to us and will understand why we want you to wear it. Please let them know that we could not stop or change what was to happen, but we shall meet them all again one day in heaven. God will bless you, dear Nell. We shall be with you all in spirit.*
>
> *Our love will never die, though we must depart.*
>
> *Ann and Emily."*

"Oh, Richard. Do you think I should accept it? Will you make sure that no one thinks I have stolen the ring from the house? Will you be my witness to what has been given to me?"

"Of course I will, Nell. Why else would my sisters have written on the front of the parcel for me to read the letter, knowing you can read nought but your name?"

She put on the ring and as she did so, she wept into her apron and could not be comforted. I decided to leave this dear woman for a while. She had been so strong but now was another time for her to weep. I spoke quietly,

"I am just going into the garden and for a walk into the wood for a while, Nell. Will you be alright?"

"Yes, Richard. I shall. God knows I cannot stop weeping."

"Weep, Nell, and be comforted by so doing."

§

I walked down the garden, looking at the herbs which would be no longer harvested, the flowers which would not grace the centre of the table and the apples on the trees, which would never now be picked. With no real thought or purpose, I walked out into the field and down to the wood, only a stone's throw away. Why did I take that walk, I shall never know, but I did. I have thanked the good Lord God, in whom I believe, many times that I did. I will tell you why.

There was a small valley in the wood and a path passed through, alongside a stream, where I used to go as a young child and take Thomas or Ben. There we would build a hiding place of bracken and branches and play hide and seek. It was a different life from many children. I knew that, even at the time, and always felt privileged that I was my father's son and also had my mother's family. Papa was a man who, as I looked back from my older years, I realise encouraged freedom from convention for his children. We had to help plant and gather, unlike most children of nobility, but we had freedom. Because he had money, enough and more to spare, we were spared having to work all day in the fields.

I had known many of this wood's creatures, and had seen small deer walk past at close quarters and watched rabbits go in and out of their burrows. I had observed where birds nested and counted the young as they hatched out. Yes, from an early age I had liked to be out in the middle of wild nature, for why I do not know. I too knew a lot about the medicinal virtues of different plants, as did my sisters.

I went to this place now as if drawn by a thread to a place of memories of happier times and sat by the stream, in deep contemplation. I had never had any fear in this wood. I had been there for about fifteen minutes when I was aware of an eerie feeling that suggested to my mind that I was not alone. Suddenly, making me jump and almost falling from the *log on which I sat, I saw Simion approaching up the path. Behind him I could just see a fearsome looking man, a mass of tangled hair, torn clothes and dirty, so dirty that I could scarcely see any features of his face. He was almost hiding behind Simion as though to do so was to avoid detection.*

Simion put up his hand. I held out mine and he came over to me. He turned and motioned with his hand to the man to come forward. I could now tell he was only young. He pointed to his mouth and then to the man.

"Who are you?" I asked, though I thought I knew already.

"I have deserted from the Church Army along with my brother. My life is in danger but I have stayed around rather than travel far away from here as I cannot leave my brother. Each day I search the woods for him with this man, who everyone thinks is mad, but we cannot find him. I know he would never leave without me. This man has kept me safe. He knows all the paths and we have managed to hide. He has fed me these few weeks, though I have lost any notion of what day it is."

"If, by your brother, you mean the other soldier who deserted with you, then I have sad news."

"Have you heard of him then?"

"I am afraid so. He was caught soon after he deserted. The soldiers hanged him."

"No! No! Surely he can't be dead."

The young man hid his head in his hands and fell to his knees. "Edward!" he cried "Edward!" He looked up, "Oh, sir, he can't be dead. He is all I have. I have no one else. I have no one and nothing now, in the whole world. Edward!" He wept tears of such anguish that both Simion and I wept with him. I put my hand on his shoulder and waited until he had calmed enough to hear what I had to say.

"You are safe with me. Simion knows that, otherwise he would not have brought you to me. I cannot save your brother, but I can save you," I told him. But, I had to ask one question. I had to know the answer.

"I must tell you. The three women who died were my sisters and I grieve

for them as you do for your brother. Tell me, truly, did you, yourself in person or in any way, harm the three who were put in the stocks and ducked?"

I was sure that Simion would have known, as he knew so many things, had this been the case and would not have cared for anyone who had hurt them. Simion loved my sisters.

"No, sir, I can swear to that. They are the reason my brother and I both left the Church Army. We were only recruited a few months previously, after both our parents died suddenly. I did not know that such atrocities happened, but I know plenty now. I am shocked beyond words at what the soldiers do, mostly without any thought or care. After I had to witness the ducking of your sisters and the killing of those two innocent men who came to their aid, I could not remain in the army. My brother felt the same. Sir, I am not a common deserter. I am an honourable man and well born, but one who could not live with himself if he remained one of them. I too would rather be dead than back as one of the Church Army. They are led by cruel, evil men and the God that I believe in is not the God of the Church that they hold allegiance to.

"But, I must confess Sir, that, though I didn't hurt them, neither did I help them. I could have tried, but I was too frightened. We had been told that, should we help any one of them, we would suffer the same fate. I was a coward. I let them pass by me on the road and I never helped them."

He bent down and wept, saying over and over again, "May the good Lord forgive me." Gradually, the young man calmed down and looked at me, and I could see innocence and much pain in his eyes.

"Lad, I have found out enough to know that no one could help them or they would also die. Now, listen carefully to what I say. If I take you away from here to safety, will you bear witness in a trial that my uncle intends to bring against the Church Army? Will you tell us all you know, in recompense for what you could not do?" I asked him, hoping he would trust me.

"Yes, I can tell you that without any thought. If I stay on the run, the army will find me and kill me eventually. They do not let anyone escape from being in the ranks. You see much information is known by even the lowest order. But all know that should they say anything or desert they are soon going to die or else have their tongue cut from their mouths. They find them, I know that. They will probably think I will remain in this area looking for my brother. They will come back sooner or later for me. That is why they killed him so quickly, without any court. They knew we were very close as brothers and loved each other.

"I know things that they would not want me to tell to anyone. The army you see is only the face that they present to the country. There are many spies who travel around, disguised, mostly as holy monks. Sir, I know it is but a matter of time till I am found. I shall be killed. If I stay here with this man over the winter, I shall die of exposure as I have nothing but what I stand up in. I will go with you. I promise, on my brother's soul that I will bear witness and tell you all I know. I am an honourable man."

"Then, pray say nothing more now and wait with Simion until dusk." I turned to Simion and by using many gestures, pretended to lead him away and pointing. In this way, I let him know to take the man to my father's house. I suddenly realised that, till this point, I did not know the man's name.

"What is your name?"

"I am called Robert Fairless, sir."

"Then, let Simion bring you to my father's house when the light has gone. There is a lady there, called Nell, a trusty lady who cares for my sisters' children. She has accompanied me to collect possessions from the house. I have other tasks to do, but tomorrow I shall return to my father's house with my wagon and horses, and we shall depart. Keep hidden in the house, do not look out of the windows or let anyone know of your presence. I shall tell Nell to expect you. Take care and do exactly as she asks."

"Sir, I cannot thank you enough, but I am too dirty to enter any house. Yet, I would like a little food."

"Robert, that house has no one left to bother whether any dirt is there or not. Will you do as I ask? I cannot risk Nell being in any danger while I go for my wagon. Else I must leave you here."

"I will take every care, sir. I promise you that, on my life."

§

Next morning, *I returned to Stocksmoor, going through Bretton to collect Marion. And so it came about that little Marion went back to Poppleton with Nell and myself to be cared for and grow up in the arms of her remaining family. I asked Helena to accompany me in the wagon as far as just before the inn so that she could care for Marion. I needed to be sure that she sat in the wagon, and that she be out of sight should anyone pass, nor did I want any fuss or noise. Poor child had only seen me a few times in her life, and, knowing my children when they were that age, strangers could be frightening. However, Marion fell asleep before we reached there, so Helena left the wagon by the crossroads before the long and almost flat final stretch of road to the village.*

I arrived at our father's house and I only had to knock lightly on the back door for Nell to answer, "Richard, is that you?" in a quiet voice. She had been waiting and watching through a very narrow gap in the upstairs drapes. As we had discussed everything before I left the previous day, she knew what to expect. She drew the bolts and let me into the scullery. To my amazement I saw the back of a young woman, with fair, wavy hair, clean and well brushed and wearing a white shirt with long sleeves that showed at the wrists under a dark blue travelling cloak, with a hood. She had a long skirt that reached to the ground.

"Who is that?" I whispered to Nell.

"Roberta, would you please turn round?" Nell asked, quietly. There in front of me was Robert, dressed and looking, for the entire world to see, like a young woman. Robert smiled. "It was Nell's idea. She has been busy sewing these clothes most of the night to make them fit me, whilst making me scrub myself in the scullery until I nearly took my skin off. Your sisters were so tiny that she has had to use two skirts to make one to fit me."

"And sew about half an arm to the sleeves, and use another skirt to increase the length," added Nell. "But it does the trick, don't you think? And, the bonnet is very fetching!"

"No one would know any different should they see him."

Nell nodded. "When you told me that you were bringing Marion, the idea came into my mind. I thought, at a distance, if it should be necessary, Robert could pass as her mother. Then he will go unnoticed, and no one, even if he is caught sight of, will suspect we have a man in our midst, a wanted soldier."

"Nell, you are very clever."

"When you have the need it is surprising what you can find, Richard. I may not have had any opportunity to study books, but I was born with much sense and practical ability, which, in my life serves me well. You know Robert is just the age that my boy would have been had he lived. I will care for Robert should he need any care, being as he is eighteen years of age. You can tell Sir George that, if you would."

"Of course. Let us go now, Marion is asleep in the wagon and I don't want her to awaken, and, not knowing where she is, make a fuss."

Making sure that no one could see Robert leave the house, we set off back on our journey. I had collected two more for Sir George's household, but I was sure he would welcome them both, such was his nature.

§

I must interject that as we write this, despite all our angst as we relive these memories, we have to smile when we remember that day when Robert travelled, dressed like a comely young woman.

§

He rode in the wagon with Marion on his knee, so that if and when she woke, it was as if she were his own little girl. Since that day, Marion has been a bit like a shadow to Robert. Whenever she is able to, she is with him. I tease him sometimes, but only in good nature to bring a smile to his sad face. He sorely misses his brother, Edward, but he would agree that Marion has filled a deep hole in his heart as the sister he never had. Now, as time has passed, he has already taught her to read and write and she will soon join in the lessons with the other children in Uncle George's household. Robert is determined to become versed in the law of the land and studies each day in Uncle George's library. Then, in the intervening hours he helps the tutor to educate Uncle George's grandchildren, often with Marion playing with a charcoal and parchment on the floor by his side, as quiet as a mouse.

I rejoice daily that I brought Marion to be with us, as she is loved and happy. I doubt very much whether she has any recall of Mary, her mother, or Abe, her father. I have never heard her mention either. When she may, in the future, ask about her parents that will be the time to explain to her what happened. Until then, she belongs to 'all of us', and is in 'her own' home and free from danger.

~ Robbie's story ~

It was, by now, mid-October, 1497. My three sisters had been dead for two weeks and two long months. During that time, I had ensured that Rosamund and my own children, Gerrard and Sarah, had settled well into their new home as well as Ann and Emily's children. I felt that they were all now becoming well used to their new surroundings. They seldom spoke of Stocksmoor or Sheepley and whether that was a good thing or bad I do not know. I have to say that Uncle George's men had worked very diligently and well. My own family had more than adequate rooms with good and comfortable furniture, all provided by him. It had been decided that our home in Sheepley should remain as it was when we lived there, then no one should be any the wiser as to the fact that we had left it, as a family, for ever.

Ann and Emily's children, along with my own, had begun lessons with Uncle George's grandchildren. They all were living together very amicably, even though Miriam, Miranda, Mark and James, were still very subdued. One can only say, they were still very shocked and sad. Nell was their strength and, willingly, devoted all her time to and for them. We longed to see them laugh. The girls had never wished 'goodbye' to their mothers and Aunt Catherine. They had not kissed or embraced them, being taken to safety by Nell before the direst events happened. They had been cut off suddenly from the women they loved so much. The boys had seen more than they should have done, and in all truth and honesty, more than anyone, young or old could forget.

We tried to help and comfort them as best we could, giving them love and understanding. A kinder home, other than their own of course, they could not have had, and they knew that Uncle George had welcomed them all with open arms. Apart from his study, private bedroom and living room, they had the freedom of his house. The manor house was very large, and, since Aunt Gwendolyn's death, Uncle George had taken to spending his leisure hours in the large room on the first floor at the front of the house. In that room he had a very good view over the large open space in front of the house into which the wide pathway from the gates led. He liked to know who came and went, and noticed even the tradesmen bringing goods.

He wished only that all in the household asked permission to use the library, his pride and personal joy. This was not to restrain them, not at all, but simply because he loved to know when anyone wanted to read his books. If they had wanted to spend many hours a day doing so, he would have been very delighted. Though they had become settled and at home, being of polite natures and having a natural reserve, the children would always knock before entering a room and never interrupted Uncle George if he had visitors.

When Nell and I returned after our visit to Stocksmoor, Robert and Marion's arrival caused great surprise. Uncle George was away at the time and not due back for a few days. When the girls heard that their aunt, Mary, and the baby had died, they were very upset. Since then, all the girls have been as if little mothers to Marion and played with her as much as she either wanted or needed. They have had to vie with Robert to have her attention and time. Marian slept in the Manor in Nell's room so she would not be alone at night, and it was decided that for the time being, she would do that until she was older. It was such a big house that we all felt she may feel lonely and lost in a room of her own. When Nell went away with me, then one of the housemaids, the housekeeper's daughter, would sleep in the room instead.

For the present, Robert had a room in the attic. It was warm and dry, clean and comfortable and very roomy. He had been given men's clothes on arrival, to his great relief, although it has to be admitted that he played his part as a young woman very well. One of Uncle George's grandsons was a tall lad of sixteen. He immediately donated a set of clothes to Robert, which fitted him without a problem.

∫

We had been back but a few hours, when Robert found me and told me that he wished to talk with me urgently, as he had information that he wanted me to know. I told him that on the morrow he could speak with me when he had had time to realise he was safe. He was to have a good rest and eat some decent food. It followed that on the next day he was as good as his word and came knocking on our door early in the morning. I have to say I was dumbfounded by what he told me.

First of all, Robert told me about his family. His parents had died, both of an epidemic of a fever only a short while ago. Miraculously, he and his elder brother, Edward, had avoided becoming ill. Up until that time, they had lived with their parents in a large cottage on the estate of the Earl of Leminster. His father had been the Earl's youngest brother and had been a man of letters and a teacher of the classic languages, often times at a place of prestigious learning. He had been considered, on the estate, as a man of God, though both Robert and Edward knew that was not his interest at all.

It was the Earl, his father's elder brother's, idea that they should go into the Church Army. It had been suggested by the Archbishop of that area, who was a friend of the Earl, at an ecclesiastical meeting. His father was told by that same uncle that having his sons join the Church Army was a privilege, and that he must, without a doubt, accept this position for them. When their father had related this to his sons, he was very angry. "Not on any account will you join the Church Army. It will have to be over my deceased body!"

But, in the event, that is what truly happened. His parents were scarcely cold in their grave, when their uncle summoned them to his presence. For some reason that Robert did not know or understand or really believe, they were told that their father had changed his mind and agreed that they should both serve in the Church Army. This was supposed to be during the week before he died, but neither Robert nor his brother believed that to be the case. Having had a quiet and protected childhood and later years, both Edward and Robert were very ignorant of what it all implied. But, notwithstanding, they had not at all wished to follow that path, being peaceable lads with no wish to fight anyone. They did not even fight each other. But, they were given no choice; such is the power of the nobility. Robert was in no doubt that his uncle wanted both him and his brother out of his way.

The two young men, aged now eighteen and twenty years, found out that their father's cottage was to be transferred to a man of God who would minister to the Earl and his family. Without any consultation, they were told to vacate the cottage added to which their uncle was not prepared to give them a room, even to share, in his large house.

Needless to say, it was obvious, as I listened, that Robert was not overly fond of this uncle. Understandably, as he continued, he expressed quite the opposite view and, it seemed, was still fearful of his uncle's power and position. One has to wonder why this man wanted his nephews 'out of the way' so to speak. I asked this of Robert who surmised it was something to do with their grandfather's will, but that his father had never explained fully and now it was too late. But, he was eager that his uncle did not know of his whereabouts now. He was sure he would inform the Church Army and would not stand up for him should he face punishment, as he was sure would be his fate.

I had to ponder that he certainly needed to have some good friends if his family were like that. To avoid any confusion with Uncle George's grandson Robert Shaw, a boy of but fourteen years, Robert Fairless was always called Robbie, and so I will, in future, refer to him as such.

Again I made notes, to give to Uncle George, which Robbie signed. He told me that he had learned to read and write as a child, but I found out very soon, he had a quite exceptional scholastic prowess. His father, being a scholar himself, had recognised his ability and taught him as much as he could.

This is Robbie's story, about Stocksmoor, as he recounted it to me.

∫

A few days after the company of the Church Army had arrived in Stocksmoor and the night before the trial, Robbie was on guard duty, standing outside the tent of the Captain for several hours during the late evening.

He had to guard the rear of the tent, so he never saw who came or who went from the tent. But, unlike everyone else who had to leave a distance between themselves and the tent, he was told to stand very near the tent in case of need. And so it happened that he could hear the conversation quite clearly. He heard a man talking whose voice he did not recognise. The man was speaking as if with authority. "Stanley, I rely on you. They must not survive. Do you understand? I know from my own information that they know far too much and are becoming dangerous. I am pleased that they are doing what they are doing else we would not have an obvious reason for killing them. It is much better this way. Removing one when necessary is easy, but three would otherwise pose a problem."

"They shall not survive, sir. I will ensure that."

"You are a good man, Stanley. Now, about the stocks. Were they made to the correct measurements and style as I advised?"

"Yes, sir."

"Get your men to erect them as soon as the trial begins, though the preparation should be started during this night, so as to be ready. Standing stocks will give your soldiers much more opportunity for some, what shall we say, enjoyment. They will test their ingenuity somewhat, but I'm sure your men are up to that."

Robbie heard him laugh, a crude laugh that made him feel nauseous. He wondered who it was and what they were talking about. Only a handful of soldiers appeared to have been told what the purpose of this stay in Stocksmoor was and Robbie had not been one of them. A chosen few, those of the troop who, because of their behaviours, Robbie despised more than most, were to supervise the stocks. He didn't know who was visiting the tent nor could he see him leave, as to move his post would incur a grave punishment.

"Sir, I reckon it was the same night that the man from the village must have been killed. He was thought to have been dead about five days when he was found. I think this man, who knew so much and seemed to give orders, may have been the one to kill him. All the soldiers, except those putting up the stocks, were in the camp overnight under orders, so as not to cause any suspicions or problems for the morrow. No one would dare to

leave the camp without permission. I read everything on the Captain's table, and I know that no permission or order to kill was given that night."

"Robbie, before you continue. Please just call me Richard, and not 'sir'. You are one of us now." I spoke as I felt.

The following day, Robbie wasn't at the trial of my three sisters, but had been sent to patrol the village, walking the perimeter of the common. His duties did not allow him to go to the stocks so he was not aware of what happened. However, he was told to stand half way down the hill while the women walked from the stocks to the common land. He was standing there when he heard Joseph, Hilda's religious husband, reciting words from the scriptures as Ann went past.

"That was the voice I heard talking to the Captain. It was the man reading the scriptures at a house further down the road."

"No, it couldn't be. He is married to our cousin, Hilda. He has always been a religious, upright man. He is a carver of wood and makes icons and memorials for the Church and anyone who has need of such ornaments. I have to say he is not someone whom I like, but he knew my sisters well. His wife even helped them with their herbal growing and collection. No, I cannot believe it could be him that you heard. He and Hilda left the village before the ducking and have not been seen or heard of since. No one has any idea where they have gone."

"Sir, I mean Richard, it was he. I know it was he. I know he is not wholly English."

"What do you mean, not wholly English? His name is Kraft, as English as you could list, I would think." I was nonplussed at his words.

"To my ear he pronounced some words differently. My father studied language and he used to explain much to me. I would say that that man came originally from France or somewhere over the channel and had learned to speak English very carefully. He did very well, yet there was a hint of something different."

"Do you know his name?" I asked.

"No, of course not, but I wished I did. And, what is more, he knew the Captain very well. He called him Stanley."

"I appreciate what you say, Robbie, but I fear you are mistaken."

"No, sir, Richard I mean, I am most certainly not mistaken, with the greatest respect. I learned from my father who was a true scholar. He claimed that I had an ear for language better than anyone he had met. Had he lived, I would have followed a similar scholastic career. I do not wish to appear uncivil to you in any way, and am very grateful to you for all you have done for me. But I know what I know and I cannot say different. Believe me. I am not wrong in this matter."

"I shall tell Uncle George everything you have told me, and, let me say, I appreciate your courage in doing so. Although I cannot connect my cousin's husband with my sisters' cruel deaths, I promise that I will not dismiss or exclude anything that you have told me. Thank you, Robbie." I shook his hand.

"Richard, there is something else I want to give you." He put his hand in his pocket and took out a small, cross, made of pewter. It hung on a piece of black cord, tied with a knot. He held out his hand for me to take the cross. On one side it was smooth, but when it was turned over, it had an eagle, in deep relief, as if stuck on the long aspect of the cross.

"What is this?" I asked, not having seen anything like it before.

"It is the sign of the Order of Sorro. Every soldier who becomes a member of the Church Army is given one of these and is thereby part of this society. Most soldiers merely sign with a cross as they cannot write. In fact, unintelligent men are warmly welcomed by the Church Army. They are merely fodder to be killed or do the dirty deeds, like watching the stocks, but as a reward can be as cruel as they wish. All that is required is obedience. All of its workings are secret except to those of high rank.

"This," he informed me, holding up his pendant, "is for the lowest rank being merely pewter. But depending on the rank the cross becomes more valuable and ornate. The next order up has silver ones, then gold, then precious stones are added. No one outside the army knows what these pendants mean and very few have ever seen them. Soldiers must wear them at all times, but underneath their shirts and with the eagle to the underneath, that is facing the skin. That is why I know they will come looking for me, as I have this and the information that goes with it.

"Though I am only supposed to know what a junior rank soldier would know, I know much more. You see they didn't know I can read or write. I even signed my allegiance paper with a cross like most of the others. Likewise did my brother Edward. We had arranged beforehand that we would, as it were, not be known. We were both skilled in different ways of speaking and so, all the time we were in the Church Army we spoke, not in our usual manner, but as if we were yokels and not of the nobility. We behaved like the other soldiers and did not wash ourselves as often as we would normally have done. In that way the Captain thought us no different from most of the soldiers, other than the officers. We kept this up, even to each other, lest someone could be listening. The Church Army is a very unwholesome company.

"So, I was given menial tasks. One was to clean the Captain's room and his tent when we travelled. Luckily, Uncle, in his infinite beneficent wisdom, merely sent us to the Church Army, but omitted to tell them that Edward and I were wellborn and versed in literature and letters. I imagine he thought we were better suited to the lowest ranks and, I believe, hoped we would thereby be killed. We never knew why he hated us, but it is of no importance now."

"Thank you, again, Robbie. I think your information will be invaluable. Oliver and I are going to try to find out as much as we can and forewarned is forearmed. I shall show this to Uncle George on his return. In fact I have very much of importance to tell him."

"One other thing I know, and I think it is wise that you understand and remember at all times when you and Oliver are abroad in the country," continued Robbie, "There is a select, elite group in the Church Army. Some of these travel around the country dressed as devout monks, usually in twos or threes. They are called 'scouts' but are really spies, finding out about people in the countryside or towns whose behaviour is contrary to the ways the Church want them to behave or who are becoming too curious for some reason. These scouts report back to the local headquarters and our Captain was sent reports. I noticed the names Ann Kittle, Emily Kittle and Catherine Shaw many times, and I was only there for a few months. Without any doubt, they had been watched, information collected and their deeds reported during that time." He stopped as if recollecting his memories.

I thought suddenly of what Nell had told me about the three monks in Stocksmoor. I realised they were indeed spies and Jonas was implicated, though no proof would be possible. It fitted not only with Robbie's information that they went around in twos or threes and reported back to the Captain but with Nell's doubts about their 'goodness'.

"The pendant I have given to you is worn at all times, and a soldier or monk can just say, 'Show me your throat', and when the habit or uniform is opened at the neck, the pendant is seen. The monk or soldier just needs to turn the pendant very slightly to show that the other side is not flat. He is then left alone. It is an offence to harm another member of the order unless instructed by the head of the sector, or someone deserts, like we did."

"Goodness me." I exclaimed. "Your information is truly amazing. But, please be sure to keep within the manor grounds at all times, Robbie. There is plenty to do and you will be safe here. Nobody would dare to trespass on Uncle George's land. No one will know who you are or where you came from if you do not tell anyone. Only Nell, my wife Rosamund, Uncle George, his son, Andrew, and I are aware of you real identity. I have told the children that you are an old friend's son who is good at his letters. I didn't lie as I am sure your father was someone's 'old friend' and I did not say he was mine, even though that might have been assumed. I added that I brought you back with us so that you can help me in whatever way I need, and that Uncle George agreed that I needed some assistance now that we all live here."

§

I received an early message three days after we returned from Stocksmoor. Uncle George's valet arrived, knocked and put his head round the open door.

"Mr Richard, Sir George is back and wishes to speak with you. He will be in the library at 10 o' clock this morning and can you please meet with him there?"

"Tell Sir George, that I will be there, promptly at that time. Thank you, Norman."

I duly presented myself at the library where Uncle George was already waiting.

"Richard, welcome."

"Good morning, Uncle. I trust you are well."

"Never better, Richard. I have a fire in my belly, which is like the horse in my carriage, which is pulling me towards what I need. I hear that our household has been extended. I have heard from Norman. A child of two years, Mary's daughter and a young man of eighteen I gather," he smiled as he spoke. "I am pleased you realised that I would welcome them. Tell me about them."

I explained about Mary, and that Helena was unable and, probably, incapable by now to take care of her. I had thought the best place was here with her cousins in the circumstances and so brought her back with us.

"Quite right, quite right," he nodded, "and the young man? What about him? Where did you find him and who is he?"

Again I explained. I told him that Robbie had told me many things about the Church Army which I would tell him at length when he had the time.

"I am eager to hear what he has to say. I think he will have just the sort of information we need. You did well, Richard. I always believe that, if you go with your instinct, then if you are a good soul, it will lead you to an open door, whatever or wherever. This seems to accord with my belief. I have to say though, that, try as I may, as yet I haven't fitted in the rest of the family who have been killed to that belief. But we do not know the ways of God and must just believe there has been some purpose either here or in the hereafter.

"Before I tell you what I have been doing and where I have been, or hear more from you, I would like to meet this young Robert, in person." He pulled the bell cord by the large marble fireplace and in a few minutes Norman presented himself.

"Norman, would you go and fetch the young man, Robert, who has lately joined our household and bring him here, directly?"

Very soon, Robbie was brought into the library. He looked round and gasped in amazement. His face broke into the first grin I had seen. Uncle George did not miss his look of sheer delight.

"*You like books, young man?*"

"*Oh yes, sir. I was brought up surrounded by books. My father was a scholar and interested in languages. I am the same as he.*"

"*So, who was your father, lad?*"

"*His name was George Fairless, the youngest son of the Earl of Leminster, sir.*"

"*I'm not acquainted with that family. And your mother?*"

"*My mother was a Lacey, sir, Margaret Lacey.*"

"*A Lacey? Margaret Lacey? Do you know any more about her?*"

"*Only that she met my father when he was studying at the school of learning in Oxford. Her father was one of the men who taught him. She always told me that her family came from the North, but that her father had little time or money to visit and the contact was lost. Soon after I was about three years of age her father had died and that was that.*"

"*Do you know the name of your grandfather, your mother's father? The Lacey connection?*

"*Oh yes, sir. His name was Edward Lacey. My brother who was killed was named after him. But I know nothing else.*"

"*Robert, Richard is my nephew. My mother, Richard's grandmother, was a Lacey, Matilda Lacey. I know we had an uncle, Edward, whom we never saw. I have no doubt your mother was called after my sister Margaret. Richard, I think you have found a young and distant cousin. Robert, Richard tells me that you are to be known as Robbie, to avoid confusion. Robbie, welcome to our family, your family.*"

§

"*I met Oliver in London,*" he continued, when Robbie had left to continue his lessons with the children. "*He is coming home for a visit in six days time. I think, come the spring, that you could both prepare to go spying for me. I have discussed this with him. He is his usual enthusiastic self and has got it in his mind that you will both dress as monks. God alone knows how he is acquainted with such a variety of people, but, suffice to* say, he has many contacts. Anyway he reckons for a small fee he can find someone to make or even acquire authentic habits, for you both. Then you can travel in the area of Stocksmoor and Sandal in disguise. I know there are many travelling monks traversing across the country from the west to York, so your presence will go unnoticed. Just look pious, say your rosary, enjoy your food and eat plenty. Hide your faces and then no one will be the wiser.

"Collect the evidence and find the information, Richard. I haven't found what I need yet, but I shall. Did you know that the elite ranks are known officially as the White Army?"

"Yes, and I am told that they also go by the name of the 'Riders of Death'."

"Yes indeed! That is a much more appropriate name. Black would be a better colour for them. We shall crush the menace of the Church Army. Oh yes, I am determined of that more than anything in my life before. I have friends in the highest positions in the land. We are of the same mind. They have all declared that they will help me as much as they can. The killing of my nieces, Andrew and his son, and indirectly my brother and sister, was the final straw. Just too much. I cannot stand idly by any longer. But, preparation will take much time.

"Incidentally, I met the Archbishop of York, while I was in London. For a reason I have never discovered and neither have the others, the Archbishops and their high dignitaries always attend the meetings of the Lord Lieutenants, and have done so for as long as any of us can remember. That being so and knowing of my future intent, I told him, in the presence of several of my fellows and in a very loud voice, that I and others shall bring the Church Army to account for some unlawful killings that I knew about. I let it be known that I would not tolerate such happenings in my county. I had been given the responsibility for the well-being of these people. Atrocities had been committed and must be addressed.

"No, no, lad, this time they will be brought to justice. No one can go around killing innocent people like that. My sweet, gentle, caring nieces called witches? What absolute rubbish! These sorts of killings – there are hangings as well, you know – and other cruel practices, have been talked about amongst the Lieutenants for several years now. But none has been involved sufficiently to collect the evidence, nor do we yet know quite the way to do it. The church is very powerful, make no mistake and the leaders think that in the name of God, they are above the law of the land.

"Richard, you and Oliver must be very careful. People go missing when they dabble in such matters. Of that I also have evidence. No, we need to proceed with stealth and present every shred of evidence we can find.

"But I have many searching the law libraries and archives up and down the country. We shall find what we are looking for and I am certain that what we need to use must exist. It is merely a question of time and endeavour."

I just had a thought, so lucid and clear, that I had to speak it.

"Uncle," I asked, taking the pendant that Robbie had given me out of my pocket, "have you ever seen one of these?"

"Let me see, lad. No, I can't say I have. Let me just think a while." He sat with his eyes closed. "No, never. What and whose is it?"

I then told him what Robbie had told me about the Order of Sorro.

"Uncle, if we are to travel around as monks, would it not be a good idea to have replicas of this pendant for us to wear? I have looked and there is no mark or name on it to distinguish one from the other. I gather from Robbie that different ranks wear different metal pendants, the more valuable the metal, the higher the rank. He says that anyone wearing a pendant is safe. No one can know all the Church Army members as they travel around the country, not even all those from one section. Our identities would not be questioned."

"What a brilliant notion!" he smiled with enthusiasm. "Give it to me and I will take it to my own personal jeweller to have two copies made of it. Discretion is his middle name. He has every need to have that quality and he will not let me down. I will have them ready for when you decide to set off."

After a pause, while he poured us both a glass of his best wine, I continued, "I have written here what Nell has told me happened to my sisters, and what my sisters had already told me about what they saw in Sandal and in Stocksmoor. They made observations about some boys in the village who went missing. I have also written that which I had already personally found out before they were killed, but which I now know is related to that event, though I didn't know at the time. I am sure now that their deaths were planned beforehand and I believe it was for a much more sinister reason than a few herbs and a comforting hand. They knew too much." I handed him the sheath of papers, "There is also the information that Robbie has told me so far."

"Thank you, Richard. I shall read it all and if there is need for clarification, I shall call for you. I shall be reading it as a man of the law, to see what evidence we shall be able to use. The people you write about, do you know them?"

"Yes. When I went to Stocksmoor while you were away, I spoke with many of them."

"Hmm, so you could question them again yourself if necessary?" he asked aloud but as if almost to himself. He turned to look at me, "Do you think they would bear witness and swear on oath?"

"Yes, if they knew they were safe from being victims themselves as a result of their witness. When I rode through the village that first time after my sisters were dead and when I had not known, I was immediately struck by the silence. No one was outside. Doors were barred, windows shuttered. They are very frightened. When I went last week, it was still much the same, though people did talk to me. I'm sure they would again if you have any particular question of someone. What happened is not something that anyone will easily forget.

"Robbie is prepared to stand witness to what he heard and saw. But Uncle, he could be in danger, not only because he deserted, but he is the nephew of the present Earl of Leminster. It was he who put both Robbie and his brother into the army, against their wishes. It seems that he wanted to be rid of them. Why, I do not know. Do you know of him?"

"Not as yet, but make no mistake," assured my uncle, "I shall be thorough. He probably just wanted them out of the way so that his estate or money is not under threat. His grandfather probably left them some income, knowing that their scholarly father wouldn't be able to do so, and he greedily wants it for himself. It happens fairly often. I doubt he has anything to do with the Church Army other that it being a convenient way of getting unwanted young men out of the way. There are many people like that, who only care for their possessions. By the way, does Robbie still have his uniform?"

"I imagine so, but I can ask him. Why?" I asked.

"Just that it would be a good idea if a body had been found, don't you think, somewhere near to Stocksmoor? A body, a deer or a couple of rabbits if necessary, could be wrapped up as if a man and buried and the so-called deserter's uniform placed on top of the earth. Broadcast the news around a bit and then wait and see what happens."

"Yes, indeed. Ben doesn't know of Robbie, but he would help. What a good idea."

"Could you just look at my horse, the black stallion and the carriage horses?" he asked, as if changing the subject gave him time for inner thought. "They seem fine, I may need them at short notice, anytime."

"Of course, I will do so directly."

∫

On the morrow, I asked Robbie to meet me in the library at 10 o'clock. It was a regular time to meet, being after the morning repast but before any lessons had to be accomplished.

"Good morning, Richard," he greeted me. "You asked to see me."

"Yes. Tell me, Robbie, do you still have your Church Army uniform?"

"It is in my room, in a box. I have not wanted to dispose of it, in memory of Edward, yet I do not want to see it. Why do you ask?"

"Uncle George and I have been discussing your future safety. It would seem to be safer for you if a body is found and buried."

"But I am alive," insisted Robbie, with an odd expression.

"Of course! I don't mean yours, just 'as if yours'. Would you mind giving me the uniform? I will tell you the plan."

He agreed and two days later I set off again to Stocksmoor. This time my first call was to see Ben.

§

To cut a long story short, I told Ben about Robbie, what was needed for Robbie's future safety and the need for total secrecy. I stayed the night at his house. The next morning we walked around the fields and woods between Upper Oakington and Stocksmoor, where, as expected, we eventually alighted upon the body of a young deer. Ben had known that the hunters had been out in the area the week before and knew their normal routes. As was usual, a few young deer had been made motherless. Most did not survive. There was the smell of dead flesh, enough to make the carcase appear genuine, and, as the soldier was supposed to have died a few months previously, then it figured that all the body may not be there.

Ben put it into a sack along with a few clods of earth from the overhanging banking of the stream to make it appear bigger. Then he tied string around the sack to close it completely. We carried it between us back to his house. It was certainly quite heavy, as we soon found out. As it happened, we were lucky and met not a soul. Hence no one saw us to query our actions.

Ben then went to two of his workmen's houses. These were men who had been loyal to our father and were now loyal to Ben. Whatever they thought, they would say nothing. Ben told them nothing, other than there was a body which had been found and which needed burying as soon as possible because it was not in a good condition. As it was not a working day they were both at home.

All three of them went to Stocksmoor to the burial ground in his dray and the sacking bundle with the uniform went with them. There, they dug a usual sized grave. The body had been arranged at Ben's home by the two of us to assume roughly the shape that would cause belief that it had been a human at some time. Though deteriorated and bundled in sacking, it now appeared as was to be expected for a man without any position or wealth. I did not take part in the burial, as I could not appear to be involved in any way, and waited at Ben's house for his return. I was pleased to see that Hannah was less fraught than at my last visit.

Having put the earth back in to the grave, Ben told me that he had recited, seriously, and as if authentically, "God take this body as a gift of thanksgiving for the life that has gone. Amen." Later, he confided, "I told no lie. We were thankful to find the deer, so I could say it all sincerely."

"That was very appropriate. I am very grateful, Ben."

As we had arranged beforehand, they chose to dig the grave very near to our father's and Aunt Peggy's graves. In that way, I could say I had noticed it without arising any suspicion."

Ben had folded the dirty uniform. Fortunately, Robbie had made no attempt to clean it. Ben told his men that it had obviously belonged to the deserted soldier, "May he have peace now," he had bowed his head as he spoke and had placed the uniform, as if with respect, on the grave. He said to me, "I reckon when the Church Army hear about this body, we shall find that the uniform has been cut into pieces. Then we shall know our mission has been completed. At least I have been able to play a small part. Thank you, Richard for asking me."

After Ben had left home on this mission, I set off for my home, travelling the back road so none from Upper Oakington or Stocksmoor would see me. It was good to see my old home was as we had left it, and no vandals had entered or damaged anything.

Next morning I went to Stocksmoor to the inn, greeted Bernard and then had a bite to eat. I asked him for any news. He told me that they had seen the occasional small group of soldiers ride round the village and that the monks were still passing through. Then I explained to him that I was going to visit the grave of my father, make sure his house was kept safe and that I would pay my respects at the burning site. I agreed I would call to say 'goodbye' and have a bite to eat when I had done so. When I returned, after an hour or so, I went first to the rear of the inn to fasten my horse and to find Bernard. He was sorting the barrels of ale. I told him what I had found and that I wanted, for reasons I didn't want to tell him, to let it be widely known. He knew me well enough not to ask any questions.

"I guess the uniform will be shredded, don't you? And fairly soon I reckon. You will find there are two in there just now," he spoke quietly, miming a hood over the head. I understood him completely. We agreed what we should both say when I went into the public room.

Then I went round to the front of the inn, and, as if entering after fastening my horse, I walked into the main room of the inn. I noticed the two monks sitting silently and separately, heads bowed in the two corners, near by the fire. I had a drink of ale and spoke in a loud voice to Bernard, who, as arranged, was at the far end of the room. Thus the monks had no choice but to listen to what we talked about.

"Hey, Bernard, I've just been to the burial ground and there is a new grave, but I don't think it can be someone from this village or Upper Oakington as there is a very dirty soldier's uniform on it?"

"Yes, I know. I, myself, heard about it only either yesterday or the day before. I can't just recall which," he replied.

"I was paying my respects to my father and Aunt Peggy. It is so near their graves that I really couldn't miss it.

"Most people, whom I have spoken to here in the inn, seem to think it must be that young lad who deserted," continued Bernard. "You remember. It was soon after the duckings. There were two. We heard that one was caught and hung. We all thought the other one must have escaped. I gather the body was in a very bad state but the uniform told its own message."

"Poor boy," I sounded sad, "to have had such an untimely and dreadful death. But nothing can now undo what happened."

With that, Bernard came over to talk to me, as if we were merely exchanging village news. I was sitting facing the monks, but as Bernard was in front of me, my face was virtually hidden from them, unless they deliberately turned. But, let me say that within five minutes I saw one monk slightly nod his head. He stood up and left the inn, followed a few minutes later by the second. Bernard and I, in silent understanding, exchanged a glance. It was better to keep quiet, but I am convinced that these two were Church Army spies. I had originally asked Bernard to let me know what happened to the uniform. He promised to do when next I visited, he was sure it would be found and destroyed quickly.

∫

Back in Poppleton, I recounted my mission to Uncle George.

"Well done, Richard," he sounded pleased and relieved. "Now we can proceed with my next, more pleasurable task. I have determined that Robbie's name shall be changed. He will have Gwendolyn and Eve's surname and will in future be a Cecil, a deceased cousin's boy. I have had the papers written. I have become his legal guardian. He should now be safe, don't you think? Let's tell him. Andrew knows and accepts Robbie into the family. I have put him in my will. He will share the legacy from Gwendolyn, which is the Cecil legacy. Andrew and Oliver, of course, inherit from the Shaw side and Andrew will take my title and the rest of the estate. They fully agree that they have wealth enough and to spare."

"That is very generous, Uncle. I am sure Robbie will be overwhelmed."

"Well, he is denied his own inheritance. Those bastards, including his uncle, will not win. Never!"

He rang the bell over the large fireplace.

"Norman, please would you ask Andrew, Oliver, Nell and young Robbie to come here now?" He turned to me, "Oliver is here and ready for action. He can't wait to set off on an adventure. I don't think he will ever truly grow up!"

When they had all arrived and I had greeted my dear friend, Oliver, Uncle George asked Andrew and Oliver to stand either side of him. Then he asked me and Nell to stand either side of Robbie, facing them, about six feet away. Robbie looked bemused and not a little anxious. He looked at me. I smiled and put my hand on his arm to reassure him.

"Robbie," began Uncle George, "I have taken a decision on your behalf. I am now your legal guardian and representative until you reach the age of twenty-one." He held out a piece of parchment for all to see. "This parchment is legal proof that you are a member of our family. I have taken the liberty of having your name changed to Robbie Cecil, the name of my dear wife's family and that of Eve, the mother of Ann, Emily and Catherine. Now, belong in my family and understand that you are one of my heirs. No one shall know who you were originally, as only the people in this room have any of that knowledge. The old Robert Fairless, to all intent and purpose, lies in the ground in Stocksmoor under his Church Army uniform."

Robbie, with tears streaming down his face, bowed to Uncle George, then to Andrew and Oliver.

"I am most fortunate. Thank you sincerely, Sir, for this unexpected honour. Never will you regret your most generous decision. I shall for ever do what I can for this family, of which I am unbelievably proud to be a member."

Uncle George walked over to this fair young lad and put his arm round his shoulder. Robbie put his arms round him and hugged him so hard that Uncle George was almost without breath. He cried out, "Nay, lad, I shan't live long if you don't let me go. Robbie, the world will survive as long as there are young men like you."

"We are as proud and fortunate as you." Andrew echoed Uncle George's acceptance of Robbie into the family.

"Cousin Robbie. You have already proved yourself to be a true gentleman. Your parents and your brother would be very proud of you, very proud indeed. We are very pleased you have joined us, welcome," Oliver, embraced him in his turn.

~ The quest for information begins ~

It came about that, come the spring and better travelling weather, Oliver and I set off in my covered wagon, looking much the same as we had done on our past travels together, several years ago. Though, one has to say that someone would need only little discerning skills to realise that we were older. I could advise them that we were also wiser. In bags, hidden under a selection of my normal medicaments were our monks' habits along with replicas of the pendant, made in gold. Uncle George had spared no expense having decided that the more costly pendants would provide the most security to us in our quest. I would swear that none but the sharpest eye and armed with the knowledge that they were not authentic could possibly have even guessed their origin.

We had determined to be away for about four weeks. We went directly to my old home, in Sheepley. I knew that none in that village would take any more notice of my wagon arriving or departing than they had done at any previous time. The story we had told our neighbours, who were the essence of reliability and never indulged in gossip, was that we had, as a family, decided to visit relatives who were needy of our care. This was in essence true, but not as other people would necessarily interpret the words. As it was of no concern of theirs, we left their ignorance unblemished.

∫

On the first day, it was decided that I should take my horse and ride to Stocksmoor, while Oliver would stay at my house and be intent on working out a plan of our future actions. He had a great love, interest and vast expertise in knowing about all aspects of plants. He liked being outdoors, and as I knew he had been confined in London for a few weeks, I suggested he should spend the day tending my overgrown garden to make it look more presentable, while at the same time planning what we should do.

I wanted to question, as would be seen as my right and duty, as many of the villagers in Stocksmoor as would talk to me. Obviously, I did not wear the habit on this occasion. Firstly, at the inn, I heard what Bernard had to say and made notes for every conversation in case I lacked some memory later. I called at every house. All the versions, though put in different words, were the same as Nell had told me of the order of events.

Just to add a short word before I progress, something that I am sure you will want to know. Bernard told me that within only one week, it was reported to him that three Church Army soldiers were seen in the burial ground. One villager saw them and noticed that they went straight to the newest burial site. One soldier picked up the dirty uniform and held it out in front of him while another cut it with his sword. The pieces were then unceremoniously thrown onto the grave.

Bernard told me that forthwith there had been only single monks in the inn and no soldiers had paraded down the road. It seemed that part of our mission had been successful. I was quite sure that the Church Army had accepted that Robbie had died.

~ Simion ~

As I walked down the road, I decided to pay my respects to my sisters by walking on the common top to stand and meditate a little by the ashes of the pyre. It had rained heavily the previous week and, in truth, little was left except that the ground appeared to have a burned scar.

Thereafter, I walked further along the common top, out of sight of any houses or passers by, to Simion's corner. I wished to recollect my thoughts and emotions before meeting anyone else, not expecting for a moment that Simion would be around when I arrived at that place. I felt empty of all my being, as if I was fatigued beyond my strength. It was a strange feeling. I sat on the ground with my back resting against a gate, eyes closed against all comers.

Suddenly, I became aware of a noise very near me and, before I had opened my eyes, I felt a hand on my left shoulder. My mind was already feeling very unsettled at the thoughts which Stocksmoor reawakened and the task that Oliver and myself had been set. At this unexpected touch, I jumped out of my reverie with a shock. It was Simion. I did not know how he knew I was there, having told no one of my intentions. He could not speak so could never tell me how he knew to be in just the right place at the appropriate time, as he had been when he brought Robbie to me. At this time, if he had ventured there just fifteen or nay, ten minutes sooner or later, I may well have either not arrived or already gone on my further way.

He left my side and went a few paces away, standing in front of me. He dropped the cloak from off his shoulders and as I watched, he started to mime. I can see him still, so vividly in my mind's eye, though I would rather not. Yet, I know of no way to erase that memory. Maybe when I write what he did, it will start to fade. I think you will understand that since my sisters died I have had little inner peace, if any.

He stood as though fastened in invisible stocks, arms lifted out to each side. His head was bent forward and hanging down. He held his wrists on a level with his head. He showed that he could move his left leg but the right leg he merely jerked in very small jerks. He moved to another place and did the same, then to a third. There was no doubt what he was trying to tell me. He went back to the first place and pointed to that spot. Then he sat nearby cross-legged on the floor. He moved his head violently to one side, several times as though being hit, and put his hand to his head, moaning.

He looked at me as though to ask if I understood. Having been told by Nell that Simion had sat with each of my sisters in turn when they were on the stocks, I understood perfectly and nodded.

Then, he stood up, made the sign of being on the stocks in the first place again. He then put his arms down and deliberately moved in a half circle round, so that he was standing facing the same direction but just a little way behind. Then as I watched, mesmerised, he made the movement back and forward from his waist downwards, and had his arms as if round some imaginary person. There was no doubt what he was telling me. I need write no more in way of explanation. I think you who read this, will understand his meaning, as I did. If not, it is best that you only know that at least one of the soldiers behaved to my sisters as dogs would behave to each other. I watched in ever-increasing horror as he moved round to face the opposite direction and did the same thing again, and then, yet again. I knew then that all three sisters had suffered the same fate.

Finally, with his hands punching, grasping, and nipping and with a biting action with his teeth and bending forwards, he mimed other atrocities. It all fitted in with Nell's description of my sisters' injuries. He needed no words or voice to tell, as I need add no further words of description.

Simion then went to each of the other two places and did the same. I could not bear to watch, yet could not close my eyes. I was as if transfixed in a nightmare. These had been men of the Church Army, supposed to be employed to uphold the Church and teachings of Christ. Their behaviour had defiled the human race.

When he had finished his miming, he collapsed on the ground and howled.

The most eerie and haunting sound ever to reach my ears. He rocked backwards and forwards with tears streaming down his distorted face. His heart, that of a courageous man called 'idiot 'and 'Jesus' and many more names of abuse, was truly broken. When I could I went to him and kneeled on the floor by his side. I put my hand on his shoulder and he did not run away. We wept together. Through his apparent madness was an understanding of grief, his own and mine. I thanked him, by mime and, though he couldn't hear, by words, for his love of my sisters and for saving Mark and James, and finally for telling me this knowledge. I shook his hand in true friendship. Never could anyone have had a truer friend than my sisters and their children had in Simion. No one can deny truth as if it never happened. By now, he had calmed. He stood, picked up his cloak and without looking at me further he ran away with his jerky, bent movements and disappeared through the trees and undergrowth of the common land.

Sadly, and after a time, I walked back to the village, passing again the place where my sisters had been burned. This time I kneeled to pray. I promised God that I had a resolve to do my utmost to obtain justice against those whose actions I had seen played out in front of me that day. I felt a new strength come into my being, a strength that I had not felt since my sisters had died.

The soldiers, like many, had mistaken Simion's silence and apparent idiocy within a misshapen body as ignorance. They had not realised that he was aware of what they were doing, or could, by mime, give evidence of such actions. Nothing was further from the truth. Though his evidence would not count in court, Uncle George could and did use, to the full, that which I described of Simion's actions. I decided that when I returned to Poppleton, I would not share with Nell what Simion had shown me. She was an astute woman and well versed in the ways of the world. If she had wanted to put into words what she presumed from seeing the bodies, then she would have done so. She had just described the injuries, saying nothing of what she believed they had happened. I would respect her wishes.

Again I shall write no more for the present. The sadness and pain overwhelm me, yet, I promise that I will eventually finish my recounting. I must, lest the grief destroys me.

~ Disguised ~

Let me just once again, to avoid confusion, digress from our purpose for a little while. More information of the background is needed, and you cannot decide the correct cut for a coat until the weave of its fabric is studied.

At the time of which I write there was a scathing religious fervour throughout the land. There were those who were powerful enough to impose their ideas, seemingly without redress. I was not influenced by the ideas which abounded, nor was my lack of ardour for the Church altered by the atmosphere of fear that pervaded the country. If anyone could be so affected, then it should have been me who had suffered so much at the hands of these, who could only be called zealots.

Many would have been seen to study the scriptures more diligently and attend the Church meetings to avoid further fears and atrocities. But I could not, as the ideas permeated were alien to my very spirit. I imagine there were many of those who piously attended the churches or Church meeting places who sought only to avoid the fear that the Church Army caused them to feel, rather than for the worship of God Almighty. I have to admit, that in my heart I think that many merely sought a feeling of security and attended accordingly. They hoped in this way to protect their homes and their wages rather than having any true belief in what was being preached by the men of God, appointed and distributed by the hierarchy of the Church.

But, who knows the true inner workings of their own mind, let alone those of another? That which people profess may not be that which they think at all, but only that to which is given lip-service. I suspect human nature will never change nor has done so over the centuries that have passed, nor even are yet to come. Who can gainsay that which someone says in apparent good faith? But I would ask the question? 'Who has the authority to dictate another's beliefs?' Are we not all equal in the sight of God? I believe so. Did he not create us all as individuals?

Think not that I believe there is no God or that I write from this viewpoint. Nothing could be further from the truth. But the God I believe in is a God of love, not hate or prejudice, not cruelty or violence. I feel sure that my dear sisters knew the same God that I believe in.

Cathedrals are being built to celebrate the birth and death of Christ and have become places of, what can only be called, pilgrimage. York Minster, finished around 1481, has brought worshippers to within its walls from all corners of the country. Stocksmoor is on the direct route across the spine of England from the west to the east. Many monks and other travellers have passed this way of recent years.

It has to be acknowledged, however, that the actual building of the cathedral has given much employment for many men over many years. Monks have been present to minister Christ's teaching and to give confession to any of the workmen who requested this service. Others travel across the country to worship at the new altar, give penance or to pray. But, they themselves give work for victuallers and innkeepers, and those whose households could accommodate an extra mouth at table or offer a bed. But understand this; the extra ministration is not the blessing that a reasonably minded person would suppose. On the contrary, we hear that the monks rarely, if indeed ever, pay for either food or accommodation, and that none proffer payment and none is now expected. I would question 'Why?' But it seems others, even the ones having to give that service, do not do so, either believing in this 'superior' breed of men, or out of fear.

§

Ale, bread and cheese had been placed on our table.

The previous week we had travelled around the many inns, in our normal attire, to watch and find out what was the practice of travelling monks. We found that they all sat with their deep hoods pulled well over their heads and covering their faces so none could recognise them should they be seen again. Their faces were always as if in a dark shadow. Whether this was deliberate to avoid being known or the custom in their chapter, we never knew. It mattered not, except that we should follow suit.

We found that, indeed, innkeepers did not make charge to monks for their victuals. We decided we must follow suit, though against all the principles that made us lead honest and caring lives, or else bring notice upon ourselves. I made a pledge to myself that when the trial was over, I would travel this way in my normal attire when I again visited my house. It being only a short detour, I would then leave as if an accidental oversight, a sum of money to cover our victuals for this time of disguise and information gathering.

§

Let me say now, that I have since fulfilled that pledge, yet no innkeeper has been any the wiser and, I suspect, thinks the money has been an oversight on a traveller's part. I would rather it were that way than the other, which made me feel I owed a debt or had been a sort of thief. Seemingly that feeling does not affect monks, which makes for interesting conjecture.

§

We had determined that we would sit in the darkest corner of this particular inn each day for a week. It was the inn closest to the castle in Sandal and which Robbie had told us was where the soldiers would visit when they were off duty. We listened as if in silent prayer, and waited. We stayed together, for extra safety, and we always wore our pendants. I thanked God for letting me find Robbie, as one morning in this inn we were accosted. We were in difficult territory in dangerous times. A soldier entered and came over to us. "Show me your throat," he ordered, very quietly though clearly so that only we could hear, bending over the table but holding his sword ready to draw. Obediently, but saying not one word, we opened the top of our habit to show our pendant. "Sirs," he muttered, and walked off.

On the fifth morning, when we had almost decided that we should gain nothing on this particular quest, a clean-shaven soldier, possibly about thirty-five years of age, though it was difficult to tell, came into the inn. He had black rings under his eyes and looked as though he had had a fist in his face or, yet, may have fallen causing the large bruise that was apparent. He stood by the door for some time as though deciding what to do, and then, after looking in our direction, he slowly walked over.

"Can I sit a while at your table?" he asked. "I feel the need for some peace in my mind and I can find none, nor will sleep come to me. Could you maybe pray for me?"

We had practised our monks' voices, I have to admit with some amusement, at my house and when travelling together out of earshot of any person. Being with Oliver was nothing if not refreshing as he had a wit and humour as none other I have ever known. Even in the darkest of hours, he could bring a flickering light. As the one with Latin and some ecclesiastic knowledge gained from his mother, my Aunt Gwendolyn, he thought of words that we could intone as necessary, as if in prayer or meditation, that sounded authentic. Though we never sounded as obsequious as Jonas, yet our true voices were hidden completely.

"Sit down with us, my son," I offered, and picked up the wooden cross I wore attached to my leather belt. I held it, as if reverently in my hand. Oliver did the same, but with a bowed head. "Why are you so deep in distress that you can find neither peace nor sleep?"

The soldier looked around. He saw that the inn was almost deserted, apart from a monk sitting on a table set along the wall, a few feet from where we were. He looked as if in deep contemplation of the mystery of God and his heaven. The soldier took no notice of his presence and neither did we, except to remember to keep our voices pitched very low for him to be unable to hear our conversation. Though I had no reason to suppose he was one of the church spies, I had by now become suspicious of everyone dressed in monks' clothes.

"Can I confess to you, Fathers?"

"You can, my son," I replied. Oliver spoke not a word, but just nodded.

"I let a man drown in the sea, without any attempt to save him. He was my commanding officer."

"God forgive you," I held my cross to my chest, and decided it was time to intone in as authentic manner as I could muster.

"Agnus Dei... patria... custos... omnipotens... opus dei... adestes fideles... mirabile dictum... peccata mundi... domini ... dominorum,"

I was intoning the Latin words and mumbling sounds in muffled tones between these rather more distinct words, as if entering into communion with God on behalf of the soldier and what he was about to tell us. Please understand that the words meant nothing to me, my Latin studies having been totally unsuccessful despite a fine tutor. I always had a good mind for most areas of learning, but sadly the Latin language made its way into a part of my brain where the meaning disappeared totally.

Just as my pretend prayer was coming to an end, as I thought I had nothing more of our practising to recall, a few further words came to mind, "Digitalis... prunus... cum gratias," I continued.

Suddenly, I heard Oliver appear to choke in the chair next to me. I opened my eyes, but, apart from coughing a few times, Oliver appeared to be deep in prayer with his head bent very low.

"Amen," I added, rather hurriedly.

I hoped, sincerely and fervently that the soldier was not a Latin scholar and that there appeared to be meaning to it all. I had a fleeting suspicion that Oliver had been averted from the seriousness of our mission and had played one of his pranks and that I had spoken one or more of his beloved Latin plant names in error. I would find out later. For extra effect, as though from the effort of praying so deeply, I bowed my head further for a moment and took a deep breath before speaking again to the soldier, thus giving Oliver time to compose himself again. When I sensed, as I knew him so well, that Oliver, from within his hood, was again ready to take notice of everything, I continued.

"But why would you not try to save him?"

"I have witnessed many things over the past ten years since I was recruited to the Church Army against my will. I was made to join by my step father, a man I despised. He is dead now and will not 'rest in peace' of that I am sure. I moved up in the ranks through obedience and my natural diligence to tasks, but not from desire. How I wish now that I had done less in my duties. In the event, I became one of three most

senior and regular bodyguards for a commanding officer whom I cannot name.

"We three were his special guards, who had access to his quarters, but I was one who was called upon to fetch and carry to his every whim. I have never been a fighter, but I had to ride with him wherever he went. I hated it! All of it! But, as such I became one of this company's 'Riders of Death'. We were part of the 'White Army' section of the Church Army, the most powerful but the most to be feared. People quail when they see us approaching in our uniforms and headdresses. My commander relished that fear. He was not the High Chief of the Church Army, but head of our section. It was his pinnacle of success. We had to wear white conical hats to hide our faces and ride with our officer to witness any punishments given out in the communities and to protect him should the crowds become difficult. Though only bodyguards without any authority, we were counted amongst those who meted out the so-called justice. I have seen atrocities. I am ashamed of being part of what happened, even if an observer without any voice."

By now, I was listening intently. I knew that Oliver was doing likewise. He was making indistinct sounds in such a manner as to imitate deep prayer and supplication for this poor soul. Occasionally, I could hear his voice as he raised it slightly for effect, "Domini ... dominorum... peccata mundi... " using much the same words as I had done.

"Last summer, we had to visit a village some miles away. To my horror we passed three very small women who looked almost dead, in standing stocks. Understand, we never spoke when on duty. We had to guard our commanding officer, and if we had strayed from that duty in any way we would have been dead. We were the silent men behind masks. We had to ride past. Later in the same day they were killed in front of the villagers. I will not go into details else I might vomit as I have done many times when I have recalled what I witnessed. Suffice to say that these three women were drowned. One of the women spoke to our commanding officer as he was bearing witness to the duckings. He became very angry and changed the sentence. He ordered that this woman, who may have survived, was ducked an extra time. Confusion broke out, and to cut a long story short, two other innocent men were killed.

"This was the worst I have, personally, had to witness. Maybe I have been fortunate but, for me, it was the final straw. I would like to leave this army. It is impossible to do so. In my position, you obey or die. I am only just returned from travelling, but not on a Church Army mission as I thought. No, my commanding officer feared for his life, as there are rumours about that retribution will be sought for these deaths. The women were well-born and not of the common people."

"From whom would he have heard that?" I asked, almost without thinking.

Once I had spoken, I couldn't withdraw the words, though my shin stung from Oliver's sharp kick. But, I need not have been concerned, as the soldier did not notice and carried on.

"One day, I was standing on guard in his room. He was a man who needed his bodyguards near at all times unless he had a woman with him. He opened the door and a monk was outside. No words were spoken, but he handed something to the commanding officer. Forthwith, during the next two weeks he prepared in the barracks as if to we were going on another foray. He arranged to see his mistress, which was his usual pattern and we thought nothing was changed, except that I observed she was very upset on leaving, which was very different from her usual smiling face. Then he finally asked me to prepare his 'Rider' clothes, as usual. He always left these as the last things to pack. We thought we were going on another usual trip, or to be present at a hanging or something similar, but no, we kept travelling south until we reached a port. We had never travelled over the sea before.

"Taking our horses on board a ship, we put them in the hold and waited on the deck until the boat set off across the channel. You understand it was not in our way to question, we just obeyed orders. We were called together by him and told that we were going to France.

"I have to say that I always thought that the relationship between our commanding officer and the other two was not that of a commanding officer to his men. It was not of the natural nature that I know about or practise. I was very glad not to have been one of his chosen ones, or I would have found another way out, I can assure you. He told me that I had to return to our barracks in Sandal and tell our officer here that the three of them had met with death in a skirmish somewhere south of Winchester, which is a town on the route we had taken. I was supposed to have been fortunate and survived. This I have done."

"May God forgive all who trespass against him. Agnus dei ... peccata mundi... ," I intoned anything that came into my head and my ecclesiastical words were indeed limited as you can read. "My son, continue," I encouraged him to tell more. By now I could scarcely sit in my seat. I was absolutely certain that he was telling me about the man who had been behind my sisters' deaths.

"It was very strange. This man, a commanding officer and our Captain, a man able to make innocent women and men quail and die, was inside still a little boy. As we all four stood on deck, he pointed to the many ships at harbour and, quite out of the blue, he asked, 'Have you ever heard of 'flaggy patterns?' We looked at each other and all sort of mumbled, 'No.' He continued, 'When I was a young boy, in a wealthy household, my father had a library which contained books about ships and the sea. He had inherited them when he took over the house. I used to study the messages that ships give to each other at sea by arranging coloured flags.' He pointed ahead. 'See that one with several ropes strung with flags? That says, 'Glad to be here, pirates off West France'. I used to call them flaggy patterns. Yes, that was my name for the messages. It fits very well, doesn't it?' 'Yes, sir,' we agreed, to pander to his need for a reply. What else could we say? He smiled for a while and I wondered whether he was losing his right mind. Then he went on to tell us that he had wanted to go to sea but his father stopped him and he was put into the Church Army instead."

'It may have been better for many had he gone to sea,' I thought to myself, but dared not to show any emotion outwardly or sound eager for information. I had to remember I was a monk, taking confession.

"The other guards eventually went below and I followed. The Captain went to his own room on the deck above ours. But it was a stormy night. I could not stay in the lower deck, being thrown about by the boat's movement and I was concerned for the horses. I left the room, leaving the other guards asleep on the floor, and went on deck. There, I saw this man, who commanded others to their deaths, vomiting over the side of the boat.

My first thoughts were 'maybe his father knew best' but I felt no sympathy for him, just a coldness. I saw that he was quite incapacitated as if a child by the sea's motion. The ship suddenly jerked and he was thrown overboard.

"I was by the edge of the deck and I leaned over the rail and just watched as his body hit the sea. There was plenty of moonlight shining on the water. But no one else was around to be aware of what happened. I did not call for help for him, nor did I throw him a rope. I saw his cloak flare out behind him. He went under four times before his cloak gathered enough water to sink and pull him under. I just stood and counted the times his head disappeared, as he had done for those poor women.

"I spoke to no one about what I had seen, but went down into the hold to be with the horses and stayed there until morning. After day break, I was accosted by one of the other bodyguards who came down to the hold. He asked if I had seen our Captain as he was not in his cabin. I simply answered, 'I have been here, looking after our horses.' No one questioned that, as I always took good care of the horses. Horses are my passion. I could have tried to save him or even call for help. But I didn't."

"And what about the other two bodyguards? Did they return with you after their commanding officer had died?"

"No, when the ship reached France, they merely collected their horses out of the hold and suggested I should stay on board. They went on shore and they did not come back. I went to look at the luggage, and found that the Captain's belongings had been rifled. Don't forget that I packed all his clothes. In his baggage were his vestments and his own cross of office, as Second in Command. Well, the vestments were there, but the cross of office and his bag of money had been taken It had all been stolen by those two once they knew he was dead. I hope they rot in hell, along with the Captain."

"Heavenly Father, hear our prayers and may our cries and supplications find your grace," intoned Oliver, as though waking up from a deep contemplation to the Almighty.

"Is this why you don't sleep?" I enquired, but inwardly thinking he had done the world a good service by his ignoring. In truth, the sea had claimed its victim without his help. It sounded as though rescue would have been impossible even should he have tried.

"No, Father, it is not. That may be another sin, but it is not the reason. It is that, against my will, I have been part of a cruel society, from which I cannot escape and in which I played a loyal and obedient part. No one can leave the Church Army. Some try and are either killed or their tongues are cut out before they are dismissed. But, I cannot put the sight of those three limp, tiny sodden bodies out of my mind. They haunt my waking hours and appear as if in nightmares in the night, should I ever close my eyes and sleep, waking me in an instant. I have had enough and I don't know where to turn."

I was just wondering what Oliver and I could do to help this soldier. Although he had taken part in the killing of my sisters as a member of the Church Army, yet I could not think that he was entirely culpable and was showing great remorse. Just then a soldier of a different breed altogether came into the inn.

He came straight over to our table. The soldier who had talked with us put up his hand in the salute we had noted was customary. The other, looking at me and Oliver, demanded, 'Show me your throat'. We had no choice. But, when the one who had talked to us saw the other side of our crosses as we slowly turned them to show the eagle, he went as white as a sheet, stood up and stumbling, knocking into the tables, he fled. The other, seeing the crosses, merely nodded acknowledgement and walked round the inn, as if inspecting the place, before leaving.

The monk, who had been sitting almost unnoticed in the darkness of the inn, as I have related, stood up and left. We thought nought about it and, like us, he had his hood drawn well over his face. But, strangely, neither Oliver nor myself heard him being accosted, as we had been. We only realised this later.

"Oh dear," I murmured quietly to Oliver as soon as I could, "let us go and see if we can find that poor man." We walked slowly and deliberately out of the inn with a nod to the innkeeper who was wiping the tables, holding our wooden crosses and heads bowed.

There was a small commotion about fifty yards down the road along which we were to walk. As we neared we saw a soldier lying in a pool of blood and several bystanders in a circle around him. We saw there was a monk kneeling by his side. The monk was holding the soldier's hand which held a dagger, dripping with blood. We walked even closer to approach the body as would have been expected of monks; we crossed ourselves and started intoning a prayer. The monk let go of the soldier's hand, stood up, shrugged his shoulders, made the sign of the cross and walked away quickly down a side street. It is odd how thoughts can pass through the mind even when occupied with a task in hand. I noticed, in passing that there was something slightly different about the monk. It was nothing of any magnitude, but somehow the picture of him walking away lodged into my memory. But, there was nothing we could do to help the soldier on the floor. He was the one who had spoken to us. He was now dead.

Our discussion that evening was centred on several questions. Had the soldier killed himself? Had the monk, who was holding his hand, been pulling the dagger out or had he just put the dagger into him? Was he the same monk who had been in the inn and, having heard him tell us what he knew, decided the soldier should die? I mused, 'Shall we ever know?' But, at the very least, the soldier was out of his torment and would never have to witness or be part of violence again.

We had learned much during these few weeks and that night, we both decided it was time to return to Poppleton to give Uncle George all our information. On the morrow, after cleaning and fastening my house, we set off back. Having travelled for well over an hour, we stopped, to stretch our legs and have a bite to eat, by the road side.

"Richard," Oliver called from a short distance away, "come here will you. I have something to show you." He held up a plant which I recognised from its leaves to be one that commonly grew in the garden and hedgerows. I knew it as Foxglove. Though it enhanced the land on which it grew, having pretty pink flowers on a long stalk, it was thought to have poisonous qualities and certainly you would not think to feed the leaves to any animal.

"Digitalis!" He laughed. "This is called Digitalis. Oh, I'm truly sorry,

Richard, I nearly gave the game away. You have done well not to reproach me. But how could I know that you would ever recall that name? I remember meeting your tutor once when I visited Grandpapa's Hall with you. He told me, though he shouldn't have spoken about you out of the classroom, that teaching you Latin was like attempting to prise open a locked drawer when the key was lost. Thank God the monk sitting behind didn't hear you or we may now have been dead with a knife in our backs."

"Do you think he killed the soldier, then?"

"I don't know, but I don't believe he was a monk."

"Why do you say that?"

"I've been thinking while we have been travelling. No one could walk like he did when he walked away if he was wearing your typical monk boot. The ones we are wearing were made at my request at the time I had the habits made. They are much lighter than normal, though looking the same. Most are very heavy and made for lasting a long time and walking over rough roads and, I suspect, contain an element of penance."

"But, if he wasn't a monk, what or who was he? As I know from Bernard, the spies who are monks are very authentic in all respects other than their beliefs and motives. I noticed the very same that you did, but thought maybe I was in error, due to my apprehension and hence did not mention it. I thought my heart would beat out of my body in the inn. I will do my best to remember such detail and now I am sure I shall, as I have other memories to attach to it. Digitalis, indeed! Let's be on our way, I shall be glad to arrive back to Poppleton."

We travelled amicably back with a feeling of a task accomplished.

"Oliver, you are a true friend. I am so glad we had our disguise and the pendants or we would have been in grave danger. I am and always shall be grateful for your company, at this time especially."

"No, Richard, think not to thank me. It was the very least I could do. They were not my sisters, but I loved them all and am eager to see justice done. They were so gentle and kind, yet frail. I too feel a great anger and want to assist you in any way I can. Father will do his best and I'm sure

the information we have to tell him will be very useful. But, never shall I forget your fluent Latin." He was still very amused on that subject and by now, as the danger had passed, so was I. "I think it may lighten father's heart for a few moments when I tell him." I can tell you readers, in truth, it did!

~ About the trial ~

The trial of the Church Army soldiers involved in the killing of my dear sisters on July 27th, 1497 started in September 1498, a year, a month, a week and a day after my sisters were killed. It lasted eight gruelling and exhausting weeks. Many tears were shed. Ann and Emily's children were kept informed, but they never attended at court.

I had accompanied Uncle George on his own personal visit to Stocksmoor He had read all my notes and I had explained anything that he questioned in the writing thereof. Armed with all this information, he met with and requested the villagers to have the strength and courage to stand up for what was right and to bear witness in court.

He carefully avoided seeing Jonas and asked that the villagers say nothing about his visit to either Jonas or any monks that might travel through the village. He told them that, should they stand witness, then such action would redress their consciences and give them peace. He assured them that he understood that they had been unable to go to the aid of my sisters, but now they could at least help prevent the same happening to any other kind and gentle women of such ability.

The villagers agreed to stand witness and it is my belief that they were relieved to be able to, at last, help fight the scourge of the Church Army. After what had happened at Stocksmoor, I knew that no one would speak to either soldier or monk again, unless about something totally trivial. No one in their own country should suffer such atrocities or, in general, live in such fear.

§

Uncle George, as clever a man as he was generous and kind, personally led the case against the soldiers of the Church Army who had been involved in the death of my sisters.

He decided, at a late stage in his preparations, to visit the Archbishop of York. He arranged a meeting with him, as if out of duty and consideration, though in reality, it was part of his strategy for the trial. Since giving the bombshell at the meeting in London, he had purposely had no contact with the Archbishop.

When he was ready to do so and three weeks before the trial began, Uncle George called me and Oliver into the library and proceeded to have us dress in black leggings, black jackets and cloaks lined with grey silk. We had to wear curled, short grey wigs, as befitted men of the law. He had spared no expense. We even wore gold signet rings with a seal pattern engraved in red. We were to stand either side of him, whether he was standing or sitting. He instructed us thus, "Just look as though you know what I'm talking about and nod appropriately. But, whatever happens or whatever you hear, you must not utter a word." Then as a thought obviously crossed his mind, he looked at Oliver and added, "Nothing at all. Oliver, do you understand?"

"Yes, Father, perfectly," Oliver replied, with a smile at me and a shrug of his shoulders. His father knew him well!

We arrived to see the Archbishop in Uncle George's best carriage, the one he used when discharging his duties as Lord Lieutenant of Yorkshire. The Archbishop was waiting in his chambers, with several dignitaries around him. Uncle George told him quite simply and clearly that the family he represented had suffered unbearable distress as a result of the deaths of three sisters. He stated that they had been the victims of unbelievable cruelty and degradation and had been killed at the hands of the Church Army. He did not, at this time, mention the deaths of Andrew and Alend. Those deaths were to be one of his trump cards. He had no doubt that the Archbishop knew of those deaths, from the Church Army reports, but wanted him to think that they were no part of his brief regarding justice for my sisters.

He explained to the Archbishop that several members of the regiment who camped at Stocksmoor were going to be brought to trial. He then suggested that the Archbishop should look into another matter himself to unravel and stop some dreadful activities the Church Army was doing in his and the Church's name. He went on to mention the disappearance of the boys at Stocksmoor and that he had evidence which he was to include in the trial. He let it be understood that he knew, without any doubt whatsoever, that members of the Church Army were abducting vulnerable boys and dealing unnaturally with them and that he knew of some deaths.

I have to say that on that day I felt in the presence of a master of both language and purpose. Uncle George spoke clearly, simply, but his words were like arrows hitting the centre of a target.

The only thing the Archbishop, who by now had become rather pale, could do after hearing what Uncle George had to say, was to agree to attend the trial and appear to be horrified. In so doing, he could successfully distance himself, his clergy and cathedral from such heinous behaviour. You will later be the judge of whether in truth he had known about the boys or not, or been colluding with the behaviour. I have promised at the outset, that I would write only what I believed to be the truth and not rely on my opinion, though I have many. Sufficient to say at this point, that to keep his position and the cathedral unsullied, the Archbishop had no alternative but to take some action against the culprits.

We found out later, that the men involved with collecting boys were sifted out by the Church, led by the Archbishop and spent the rest of their days in Sandal Castle, safely locked away where they could do no further harm. No one outside the Church or Church Army knew who had abused the boys or for how long and that aspect was impossible to discover. One can only conjecture that it involved those who can best hide the truth.

I now knew that the Commanding Officer of the 'Riders of Death' who visited Stocksmoor was the Captain of the soldier who had spoken to Oliver and myself in Sandal. I also knew that he had left the country well before the court case and that he had perished. This strengthened my belief that he had had information passed to him from a higher level. Who was it? I will say, for your reflection, that the Archbishop was the only one made aware of Uncle George's intentions until the ones involved were called to court to answer the charges against them. I checked the dates very carefully. I found that Uncle George had spoken in London to the Archbishop **before** the day that the soldier in the inn had given as being the day when the Captain received the warning note. I can put it another way. We now know that the Captain was warned and absconded soon after the Archbishop knew of Uncle George's intentions. At this time, I say no more and you can think what you will.

§

Let me take you back in time to when Uncle George was trying to find out a way of taking the Church Army to court, something that, until this point in time, no one in the country had even attempted, being either unable to obtain evidence or not trying to do so because of surety of failure.

When Robbie told me about the Order of Sorro, I made notes of every detail. I had given them to Uncle George, who asked to speak with Robbie.

Later in that same week, I was enjoying an evening repast with Rosamund. The children were asleep in their beds, when there was a loud knock on our door and Uncle George burst into our parlour. He could rarely be called a quiet man, and in this he was very like our father. But today, Uncle George was exuberant, and his energy could be felt in the room, as if it was being emitted from a forceful fountain. He was red in the face and his eyes were sparkling. "I have got it! I have got it!" He was almost shouting in his excitement. "Richard, we shall win. I have it! I have found the missing link." He was waving a piece of paper about.

I looked and smiled at this genial man, whose intelligence was like a rapier and who was putting so much energy into this endeavour, for his own sake, but also for the children's sake and the memory of all his dear relatives who had died in so untimely and in such cruel ways. Ultimately it would be for his country's sake.

"Richard, did you know that Robbie can read Latin? What a find that boy was and is! What a God given find! Do you know that once he reads something, he can remember it as if he is reading it again in his mind? Not only remember, Richard, but he has it with each word perfect, exactly as it should be. And in Latin, would you believe! How he does it I do not know. It is bewildering, but he's just absolutely amazing. In all my years, I've never met anything like it!"

"No, Uncle, I didn't know, nor thought it was possible to remember like that."

"His father must have been a very learned man and taught Robbie well. What a talent! Extraordinary! Let me explain, Richard.

"You know the Order of Sorro pendant that the Church Army members wear? Well, when they are each given one, they must sign a form of allegiance to the Church Army. Then they are committed for life to the Church Army. That form is in Latin, so the church believes that none of the soldiers will be able to read what it says or what they are signing. Are you following me so far?"

"Yes, I believe so," I answered, but I must admit that I was rather bemused as to where all this was leading.

"Young Robbie can remember word for word the order of allegiance, even though it is in Latin. He told me that he wanted to read what he was meant to sign before doing so, and dallied a while before putting his cross. His Captain just thought he was unable to understand what to do and eventually pointed with his finger where he was to draw his cross. But, he could actually read very quickly and only had to see it once to remember it all and look, here it is."

He gave me the paper. I have already told you in this narrative that, not only do I not know the meaning of any spoken Latin words, but neither do I read Latin. I had a good education and can read very well in the English we speak, yet Latin is something I never mastered. Please understand I was diligent in my studies but I was born with limitations. Uncle George could both read and translate Latin, as if it were his own language of birth.

"I cannot read Latin, Uncle." I handed the paper back to him.

"Never mind, I can explain. Robbie has written that which is on their form down on this piece of paper. No where in this document is there anything stating an allegiance of the soldier to the King or the state. No where. Not one single word. Do you see what that means, Richard? They are killing people in the name of this Order and the Church. The only people who are exempt from trial or punishment for killing in this country are soldiers in the cause of duty, whose allegiance is to the King and whose actions are in direct support of the King. The Church Army soldiers are no more or less culpable for their actions than common vagabonds and thieves."

"I think I understand you, Uncle, but how does that help us?"

"How does it help us? How does it help us? Nay, Richard lad, think. Do you not see? Robbie not only knows the words, he knows how it is written, what thickness of pen stroke, and what colour and thickness of parchment is used. I have many parchments but if I do not have the correct one that the army uses, then I shall procure the same. Robbie is going to create one of these papers identical to those used by the Church Army. I am going to 'call their bluff'. It will be so like the real thing that they won't know the difference.

"I shall ask them in my best legal voice, which has been known to put dread into villains, 'Have you ever seen a paper like this? Have you ever signed the same?' Then I shall ask the Captain of the troop which visited Stocksmoor, as he is the one who asked the men to sign or put their mark on the paper, to read it out aloud. I shall ask him if it is accurate. Has anything been missed out in the wording? I shall ask him quite clearly, 'Is the King mentioned in this document?'

"They will have no idea why I ask that question, what we know about the paper or how we obtained it, but will believe it to be genuine. Consequently, they will not know how much else we have or know or what my purpose is. Robbie says that they are all kept by the Captain in a locked cabinet. When the time comes, I shall ask to see the papers of the Captain and his Second in Command, the real papers, you understand, and signed by them. They will then bring them, as they must because the Archbishop will be in court and he will not dare tell them to refuse. We shall read each one and then make the statement that 'the soldiers involved in the deaths in Stocksmoor have unlawfully killed'.

"Incidentally, the Archbishop won't dare miss a day in court as he has no idea as or when I shall bring the 'other evidence' about the boys into court. Oh no, he'll want to know what I say, have no mistake."

"I understand now. Uncle, you are truly brilliant."

"Well, I cannot deny it was always so Richard. But it was none of my doing. It was something I was given and have always felt I must use, to the best I possibly could. But, never have I needed or wished to have that ability more than at this time, believe me. Robbie had the answers. I only had to put two and two together."

"Do you think someone will try to harm you?"

"No lad. I have written to the Archbishop to inform him, just in passing you know, that all my colleagues who are Lord Lieutenants know about the case and are being kept up to date with everything and that I have their total and full support. I just mentioned the uncertain times we live in, but should I happen to have an accident, then they would know exactly where to point the finger and they have vowed to continue the case in my absence." He smiled and his eyes twinkled. "I didn't want to upset him, did I?"

He could see his way forward now. He laughed for the first time since I had brought the dreadful news to him.

"And, Richard, not only did Robbie read his own paper when he had to sign, but, without the Captain's knowledge, he also read and remembered any papers that were lying on the table in the Captain's tent when carrying out his menial duty of cleaning. So, he has named names and what part they played and has been able to give us a lot of inside knowledge. He knows the names of the ones who handled the ducking stools and the names of the Captain and his Second in Command. But he does not know the names of the ones who were called the 'Riders of Death'. What a miracle you found him."

§

At the trial Robbie attended, dressed in my 'monk's habit', with his hood pulled well over his face. As he was skilled in language, he could speak and did so, with what could only be described as a different voice, as though from a different part of the country. His new name, R Cecil, was written rather than spoken, so no one could know who he was or where he came from or anything about him. He was always accompanied by either me or Oliver, dressed throughout in our 'lawyer' outfits and wigs. We looked very legal and authentic.

The evidence had taken several months to prepare. The Church who had men working for the defence of the Church Army wanted first one delay and then another, but eventually it came to court. Many long and difficult weeks followed when evidence was given by all the men in the village, who at last had the bravery to play their part in the convictions. Some asked to give their evidence from behind a screen. Uncle George personally sent his carriage to collect them and return them safely to Stocksmoor after their evidence. So being, there was not one who didn't attend and none was harmed in anyway afterwards, I am thankful to say.

Jonas assumed that he was being called as a witness against the Church Army, though no one had informed him one way or another. He arrived looking very self assured, but that soon changed when Uncle George accused him of being a participant in the Church Army campaign against my sisters. He appeared horrified and in his sanctimonious voice, decried what had happened. Uncle George called other witnesses, who all agreed that Jonas had intoned the blessing at the ducking, and had continued with the intoning at the fourth ducking of Ann, even though that had not been the sentence at the trial, but merely added by the High Chief at the time. He had said and done nothing to help the women while in the stocks. He answered that he had been under Church Army orders to offer no help them, but he had felt that in his soul it was a travesty of justice.

Uncle George suggested that he had been implicated in their deaths by giving information to the soldiers beforehand, knowing that they would use it against my sisters. He accused him of making sure that the villagers were suspicious of my sisters over many years, and that he made no secret that he disliked them. Jonas claimed that he had only ever tried to bring my sisters 'into the arms of the Church and to love God'.

Though Jonas had done nothing punishable by the court, he was reduced to a gibbering state of fear by Uncle George's questioning and comments and in front of the villagers of Stocksmoor. This was deliberate on Uncle

George's part and never again did Jonas hold any sway in the village. In fact, I heard that he was subsequently seldom seen outside his own house. None, except monks passing through the village, ever went to his meeting house after the trial.

$$\int$$

I think that here is the place to tell you of something in court that caught my eye during the questioning of Jonas, but it was one of those happenings that become catalogued away in the depths of the mind. Something that, standing on its own makes no relevance, but is there to surface at a later date when other events allow it to make a sense out of a puzzlement.

Oliver and myself stood either side of Uncle George throughout the trial and so were standing thus when Jonas was being questioned. My mind wandered every now and then and, on this particular occasion I was watching the Archbishop. He was listening intently to what Jonas was saying and at one point I distinctly saw him look up and stare at one of the monks in the public gallery and slowly nod his head once or twice. I followed his gaze and was made aware of a slight nodding, as if in reply, of the head of this monk.

I put this down to a coincidental happening, yet I did not forget it and remember thinking, 'Could the Archbishop have been signalling to a monk?' I decided to share this with Oliver later.

On this day there was something else that was unusual. As Oliver and myself were standing outside in the air, during one of the breaks in procedure, I happened to have in view anyone who either entered or left the public gallery. We were talking and suddenly something caught my attention. I grabbed Oliver's arm. "Look at that monk," I hissed into his ear. Oliver was just too late to see what I had seen, as the monk disappeared round the corner.

"What did you see?" asked Oliver.

"That monk. His walk. It was the same as we saw when the soldier was killed. He has been to the trial."

"Are you sure?"

"*Absolutely. Same walk, same build.*"

Only when we were home did I tell Oliver what I had seen in court.

"*Do you think it was that monk who the Archbishop was nodding to?*

"*I don't know. All I know is that it was during the time that Jonas was talking freely when questioned by Uncle George.*"

I would ask you, dear readers, to remember this interjection, as I shall later write of it again.

§

Women were not allowed to give evidence and so Nell's description of the injuries was read out by Uncle George. I am sure that, though regarded as hearsay, what she had described had an impact. Uncle George asked that this be so and that, if necessary, he would delay matters and go to a higher authority to request an exception for Nell, so that she could bear witness. It was not necessary. The Archbishop and the Church Army now knew better than to open up yet further problems.

Simion, could have been the most reliable witness had he been able to talk, but, as he could only mime, he was not called into court. His miming however was described by Uncle George with gestures that left no one in any doubt what was meant.

Uncle George had learned from both Oliver and me, and Robbie, that a soldier would be asked to 'Show me your throat' by another soldier of the Church Army when they met. Relying on this being an order that a soldier would obey without thought, Uncle George asked for those on trial to be brought to stand together, in a row, on show to those witnessing the trial, before the individual trials began. This was an unusual step but no one knew why this should be and so no one from the Church Army or the Archbishop gave any objection.

"*Please turn to face the public.*" *The soldiers did as they were bidden. He then, in what sounded like an order, barked, 'Show me your throat'. Taken by surprise, all the soldiers in the dock did so and all were wearing their 'Order of Sorro' pendant. That was the time when Sir George brought out the allegiance paper that Robbie had prepared. Uncle George walked to stand in front of the first soldier.*

"When you received your pendant, did you sign this form?" he asked the first soldier.

"Yes, your honour," he whispered.

"Speak up, man," ordered Uncle George, "all those present in this room must hear what you say. I will ask you again. Did you sign or put your mark on this form when you joined the Church Army?"

"Yes, your honour," the first soldier shouted out.

All thereafter were asked and all answered, so that they could be heard in the court. It had exactly the effect that Sir George had anticipated. The Archbishop went pale. He knew then that the Church Army was beaten.

He then read out the allegiance paper, first in Latin and then translated into English.

'Does this, anywhere, mention an allegiance to the King or the state?"

All in the dock answered, "No, sir."

The Captain, Stanley Lesley, was asked to stand forward. Uncle George asked him separately if he agreed.

The Captain, who had held the trial of my sisters and sentenced them, in fact to their deaths, was accused of having unlawfully had my sisters killed without evidence against them of any wrong doing against the law of the land. The Church's rules, regulations, and obligations belonged only to the Church and were not the law of the land. In the law of the land, Uncle George explained, in many words and in many ways, there was no felony in picking herbs, making potions and medicaments or comforting children. In fact, if more people had that knowledge and cared about children, then certainly, the country would be a better place.

However, Uncle George knew what he was doing and that the Captain would get his 'just deserts'. He agreed to the plea that there were extenuating circumstances due to the fact that the Captain had been under the orders of the Church and its law.

For the crime against my sisters, the Captain was to be imprisoned for ten years. The Captain obviously thought he had escaped with his life intact and no doubt believed that the Church would free him from gaol *earlier than his sentence demanded. But, just as we all saw a trace of a smile cross his face, Uncle George intervened.*

"Captain Stanley Lesley, please stand forward."

The Captain went deathly white as Uncle George spoke these words, "Stanley Lesley, I now charge you with the unlawful killing of Sir Andrew Kittle."

Uncle George then pointed out that Andrew had committed no offence, had had no trial or sentence of any kind and, what was the crux of the case, being a Squire with land and villeins, he was a 'free' man in the eyes of the king and the state.

Sir George had done his research to the last detail. He read out the law dating back to the Magna Carta which stated, put into simple words, that a 'free' man could not be harmed, unless he had had a trial in a court of law and had been convicted for committing a felony. So the Captain served only a few weeks of his prison sentence for the killing of my sisters, which was during the time of the trial, but when found guilty, he was hanged for Andrew's murder.

His Second in Command, one William O'Connor, all witnesses agreed, had been the one who thrust his sword into Alend. Uncle George again proved from witnesses that Alend, being a free man as he was Squire Andrew Kittle's son, had had neither a trial nor sentence nor had he committed any offence against the law of the land punishable by death. William O'Connor was sentenced to death by hanging.

It seems that time and justice often produce final ironies as Stanley Lesley and William O'Connor were hanged together, as was appropriate, at Sandal castle on the very place where Andrew's father had suffered the same fate, though he had been an innocent man.

The soldiers who raped my sisters on the stocks were let off any punishment, as, though the injuries of my sisters were not disputed, all had happened in the darkness of night and none could be proven to have been done by any one individual. Only Simion knew who had done what, and he couldn't be a witness.

However, Uncle George obtained agreement from the Archbishop, in front of the assembled court room, that these men were deemed to have acted in ways unbefitting a soldier in the Church Army and would be disciplined by the army itself, as the injuries had to have been caused by someone. The Captain had earlier agreed the names of those he had sent to guard the stocks. All the witnesses agreed that the soldiers prevented anyone from being near my sisters, so, by default the blame for the injuries lay with the soldiers guarding them.

§

There is some information which I found out and will recount to you. You can think of it what you will.

The four men, who guarded the stocks and behaved with the abomination that I have intimated, were discharged from the Church Army, but as I have explained, no one left the Church Army who could subsequently tell what they knew or had seen.

I was travelling in the southern end of the county about half a year after the trial had finished, and I was staying in a village which I did not know and had not stayed in before. I was walking down the street to familiarise myself with the place shortly after I arrived, when I heard a dreadful noise coming from a tumbledown, apparently derelict, cottage. Not a shout, not a scream, but a mixture of the two, a very odd noise indeed and as if some person or an animal was in dire distress. People were walking past as though they could not hear. I stopped one man and asked did he know what the noise was.

"Oh that, yes, it's a man who was a soldier in the Church Army. He has a bad pain somewhere, but there is nothing anyone can or would want to do to help him," he told me.

"But, why does he make such a dreadful noise?" I asked. "It doesn't sound human."

"Oh, that's because he had his tongue cut out before he was dishonourably discharged. We don't want anything to do with him. He won't live long and after what he did, he doesn't deserve to either."

"Why was he brought here?"

"Because he was born and grew up here. But he was always in trouble.

He raped a girl who died in childbirth so then he ran away. It seems he joined the Church Army and now he's been brought back. But, believe me, no one has forgiven him. She was a lovely, innocent child. Only twelve years of age and loved by all in the village. We hate him and always will. None of us will lift a finger to help him."

"How do you know what it was that he did that made the Church Army give him a dishonourable discharge, if he can't speak?" I asked.

"We were told about his actions in detail, by his commanding officer when they brought him back here. The officer called a meeting of the villagers. Scum doesn't change. We don't want him and no one goes near. What he did this time was even worse, if such were possible. Three sisters were raped while they were fastened in the stocks, the officer informed us, and all died. He was one of those who did the raping. No, we don't want anything to do with the likes of him. Once he's died it has been decided that we shall fire the cottage as no one will want to live in that building. We want to erase him from the face of the earth."

I began to think that we can probably assume that justice has or will be done to all those involved in the deaths of my sisters. Had the noise come from an animal, I would have tended to it to the best of my ability, but not to him. My kindness and generosity of spirit towards humankind does not extend that far. Oh, no. I was certain the three sisters were mine. They received no mercy and I had none for him. Readers, on this occasion and for the only time in my life, I 'walked past on the other side'.

§

If I visited Bretton and the area around, I would stay at my house on my way to the Hall, where I still examined the horses, and travel to the surrounding villages. I usually avoided Stocksmoor but on this occasion, about a year after the trial had been completed, I decided that I would pass through the village. I called to see Bernard at the inn and had a bite to eat. I asked, in general, about the village. We chatted for a while, and then he surprised me by saying, "We have no man of God now."

"Why? Has Jonas left?"

"No, he's dead. No one saw him for a few days and, I have to add, no one wanted to. The villagers have been very different since the trial, you know. They lost their fear of him and his teachings and few ever spoke to him. Anyway a monk was travelling through and stopped by here, at the inn. He asked me if there was a man of God in the village as he wanted to pray. So, I directed him, saying, 'Yes, just go down the street there,' and pointed down the main road. 'His worshipping place is on the left, just past that first lot of cottages. You can't miss it. You will see it has a cross on the door.' Well, off he went, after eating a good repast and I thought not to see him for an hour or two, as once they start their prayers or mumbling, they lose themselves, you know. But, within ten minutes he was back, bald head showing and in a right state, I can tell you.

"He was talking so fast and in such a way that I couldn't make sense of him, at first. But, apparently, he had found Jonas dead, on the floor in a pool of blood, but with his hands tied behind his back. You won't believe this, Richard, but Jonas had an axe stuck in his head. The monk was shaking like a leaf, I can tell you. Poor man, I thought he would suffer an apoplexy. He sat doing his rosary all evening but it didn't seem to help him. He never had a drop to drink neither. Shocking really, though I haven't seen anyone shed any tears. But, who could or would have done it?"

"What do people think?"

"Well, it's hard to say. Since many heard him in court, none of the villagers have been to his place to worship and only a few passing monks have called in to see him. The general opinion is that one of the soldiers who had been dishonourably discharged after the trial came round this way and took his revenge. If you remember, we all saw him point to those who had been the ones guarding the stocks to confirm to Sir George who they were. Considering what would happen to them after the trial, it wouldn't be surprising, would it?

"There are one or two findings that are against that explanation though. We think that Jonas must have known whoever it was and let him in himself. He certainly wouldn't have let someone he bore witness against in to see him would he? He'd be too scared. He might believe in his God, but not to that extent. Like us all, he still kept his door locked. The monk insisted that the door was not damaged, or as if broken into by force. He *apparently called out, but when no one came he tried the door, and it opened. Then, there was the matter of the boots."*

"Boots?"

"Yes. Apparently, Jonas was found without any clothing. Nothing a stitch!. I don't like to dwell on that picture. Oh dear me, no. Anyway, to give you the full picture, his clothing was thrown into a corner of the room and underneath his habit was a pair of boots, which had cuts in the leather and blood inside the boots. Richard, you will remember that Jonas was a bigger man than you or I. Well, these boots would not have fitted him. No, the boots were too small and what's more Jonas did not have any cuts to his legs to account for the state of these boots. His own boots were found later at the bottom of his garden near to the field boundary and with blood in them."

"How odd," I mused.

"A knife was found, you know. The villagers decided that now Jonas was dead, they could clean the house of any connection with him. All his belongings and the furniture that he used were collected together and we had a bonfire in his garden. When we were covering the still smouldering ashes with soil, to make them safe, one of the men's spades hit something metal. It was an unusual knife with a polished handle, shaped for the fingers to hold without moving, and a sharp short blade. I have never seen the like before.

"It is a testimony to the villagers that, though a large quantity of money was found in a box in a drawer in Jonas's living room, not one villager wanted even a coin from the box. No, not even for a child some new shoes."

"What did you do with it?"

"What indeed! It was decided that the box and coins should be sent to the Church headquarters, you know, the ones who kindly sent Jonas to the village. A letter was written and signed by all the villagers. Those who can't write put a cross and someone wrote their name for them by the side of the cross. The letter informed them that Jonas was dead and that this was his money and hence belonged to the Church. They added that there was now no room in the village to house a man of God. We are all hoping that they get the message that we don't want another Jonas. No thank

you. We are still waiting to see what happens, and feel that as every week passes, we are going to be blessed by being forgotten."

"I think that may well happen, considering the trial and its effects. I hope so, for all your sakes. But have you no idea who killed him?"

"No, not at all. But, someone did it, and it must have been someone who knew the place and how to come and go without being seen and someone whom Jonas recognised. We have wondered if that would apply to any of the soldiers. I doubt any one of them knew any of the paths around here or indeed the neighbouring areas at all. Those we had to give food to at the stocks were ignorant beasts and wouldn't have known east from west," concluded Bernard.

"Nor would one or those who were punished," I added, "Partly because of Jonas's testimony at the trial none would be in any fit state to travel far once the Church Army had let him go," I replied. "I heard one in the south of the county. He'd been one of the soldiers guarding the stocks, of that there was no doubt. He had had his tongue cut out, and was howling like a dog. It was a dreadful sound."

"Aye, you're right there, Richard. It wouldn't have been one of those. Maybe we shall never know."

ſ

We all agree that we owe a debt of gratitude in so many ways to Uncle George. Had it not been for him then nothing would have been done about what happened to my sisters, Andrew or Alend. Did we ever find out who put the knife or whatever sharp instrument into Charles, Tobias Trevore's son, the lad who was killed when he was going to warn my sisters, if you remember? I have some more information on that matter which I will share with you at a later time. But, in truth, we did what we could and more than any others to stop these atrocities. Other dreadful acts had been committed in many areas of the country over the past several years and none had been brought to trial before. But we were very fortunate indeed, to have been connected, both by birth and friendship, to a man so renowned, intelligent and with as much influence as Uncle George.

Though nothing would bring back all who died, at least the trial had the effect of precipitating the removal of the Church Army from its headquarters in Sandal. It was moved to York where the Archbishop could have closer supervision, or so it has been stated. Its fanatical rule appears weakened as far as we hear from reports that circulate from town to town. So, West Yorkshire can rejoice. One can only pray, with some trepidation, that our gain is not someone else's loss, but that its activities will be modified on a permanent basis.

Also, for some considerable time one hopes that vulnerable boys may receive help and not abuse, at least in the county of Yorkshire now that the practice has been brought into the open. Sometimes ripples on a pool travel further that you would think and we surmise that this might be the case in this instance. At least some of the culprits were punished. But, on that matter I am very sceptical and would ask everyone to keep vigilance for unfortunate young lads who have no one to care for them. Practices, even when brought into the open, can find other hiding places. Closed orders and high authority can keep doors locked that would be well to be opened.

The trial in York, I am sure, will become even more widely known in the next few years, even throughout the country, involving as it did, by default if nothing else, the Archbishop of the magnificent, recently completed cathedral. The last thing the Church wants is adversity connected with its awesome precincts. Knowing this would be so, Uncle George summed up by saying that he would make sure, by all the means at his disposal, that notice of the trial passed well beyond York's boundaries. He promised, to all in the court, that before he hands over his governance to his son, Andrew, he would personally make sure that all the Lord Lieutenants, either by word or by written information, would know what had happened and the outcome of the trial. He has already been active in preparing to pursue that final duty.

The Church's decree had been that any persons of mature age who claimed to, or were deemed to, heal by the laying on of hands were charlatans and infidels. All those practising these evil arts should be scourged from our country lest the fabric of our society became tainted by these people. But the fervour of the men in the Church Army who visited Stocksmoor, in the carrying out of their duties, had been beyond any reasonableness. Those kind and gentle women never professed anything other than to be kind and helpful and they had a love of children. In fact, it was the very people whom they helped who gave them the title of healers. God will be the final judge of my sisters and of those who hurt, abused and killed them.

The Church has had to distance itself from such behaviour and the Church Army has no choice now, thank God, but to comply with new orders. When they hear of women who heal or work with herbs, they must offer only caution and advice. So maybe there is a small cause for optimism. If that is so, then the deaths of my three sisters, along with Andrew and Alend will not have been totally in vain. As for our father and Aunt Peggy, I can only be glad that, as they could not alter or stop anything that happened, then at least they did not have to witness the same.

In my humble opinion, it is not within humankind's own ability to heal and that all such power must come from a holy God working through any particular person. If others find benefit from a gentle hand on their afflicted body, then who are we to question where that benefit comes from? Who knows the mind of God or how he works? I know, myself, that I can calm a fevered horse when I place my hand on its neck or ease a pain in its swollen leg. The way the horse behaves makes this, not a claim of fantasy, but an observation that any who love horses, as I do, could see. The same happened to the children who felt the energy from my sisters' hands and whose fevers calmed.

Dear Readers, my sisters did nothing but show concern, kindness and love for children. If healing happened as a result, then it came from beyond their power. It was the compassion of God for the children and a means whereby his presence in heaven and his connection with mortals was able to be shown. It was the choice of God, not of my sisters. That is my true opinion. Why were they chosen? Well, all I can say is the answer to that question is far beyond my mind's capacity. I cannot even contemplate the reason.

~ Helena's story ~

The trial of the Church Army members involved in the killing of my three sisters had taken place against all expectations and practices prevalent in the country at the time. The verdict had been given and the punishment meted out as deemed reasonable and fair by the court. Yet, I still suffered a feeling of frustration and failure that I had not fully understood the reasoning, the motive or even the identity of the person behind the killings. Conjecture, yes I had plenty, but evidence, no. Was it, in fact, the High Chief of the Church Army, himself or yet another, though powerful but of inferior rank, who had drowned at sea? In other words, was he behind it all or was there someone else? Within the secrecy of the Church Army lurked many unknown truths.

This uncomfortable feeling, which was no longer guilt or sorrow, did not leave me, try as I may to put it all behind. Rosamund and my children, along with my sorrowing nieces and nephews, advised me that justice had been done as much as justice could be done and that it was time for us all to remember Ann, Emily and Catherine as they had been to each and every one of us – gentle, kind and loving. In my mind I agreed, but somewhere inside of me was a sense of incomplete work or unanswered questions. Such is the way that my mind works and I give no apologies, just comments. But I was not the only one to think on these matters in this way, as I know that Uncle George thought the very same. He has told me, on more than one occasion, that he hated unfinished business.

No one had appeared at court who could rightly be accused to being the authority behind the action. Yes, we knew the ones who took the mock trial and sentenced my sisters, those who fastened them in the stocks, put them in the ducking chair and followed instructions and killed them. Truly, they were identified and punished. But, the Church Army works in secret. Its highest leaders wear uniforms that hide all features of recognition. No one knew who they were. One, who had been the High Chief at their ducking had died, who ever he had been. His death had also been by drowning. We knew that, but two questions kept coming back into my mind. Was he the blackest villain of them all? Dead or not, I wished to know who he was. And if he wasn't, then who was?

As you know, I had spent many months searching for as much knowledge as possible to put before the court. But, I had failed to find out the identity of he, or 'those', should there be more than one, who were truly responsible. I had not and, indeed could not, find out the names of the ones who organised the killings. What to do now? Well, to be honest, I did not know. All I knew was that an inner part of my being needed to find out, if it was humanly possible and that part would not rest until my self-imposed task was completed. Those who have lost loved ones without full knowledge of the cause will understand this need.

But, one day, without searching further, part of the answer was given to me.

§

Before I carry on and become engrossed in what I have to tell you, let me discuss with you one other matter that was puzzling me. You who read this book may be wondering in the same manner as myself – or, possibly, maybe not. But, in any event, I will write what I have to say just in case you too pose the question as I did myself. You may understand that as I write I am always concerned as to where to interject information, in an attempt always to enlighten but never to confuse.

When my sisters died, I had to decide the best action for the safety and wellbeing of their children and you now know the course I took. Uncle George in York was the person whom I trusted to accept and look after them, though even I did not, at that time truly appreciate the full extent of the generous nature of this wonderful man.

Why, you might ask, did I not take them to the Hall of their mother's family? I accept that the Hall was nearby and that was, of course, part of the reason as I wanted to move the children as far away from Stocksmoor as was possible and feasible. But, there was a much deeper reason than that. I asked myself over and over again why Uncle Wilfred, who had shown himself over all my years to be a good man as far as I was concerned, had not mobilised his villeins? Why had he neither ridden himself nor sent Cousin Geoffrey to Stocksmoor to actually rescue my sisters from the clutches of the Church Army?

I am not a coward, but, other than talking to Cousin Geoffrey, who had ridden so bravely but in vain to York, I have not spoken to Uncle Wilfred on the matter. The main reason I have not done so is that his wife, Aunt Penelope has become ill and has taken all Uncle Wilfred's concern. I had asked Geoffrey the question, and he answered, simply, "It was Papa's decision, and I could not make him see other reason." I asked further, "Was it because he is a believer and attends his church meetings regularly and so accepts the Church's decisions about those who can help relieve pain and illness?"

"No, Richard," Geoffrey replied, with a certainty in his voice. "It has something to do with Hannah and Jane and what Robert told him. That is all I know, and Papa will not tell me more. I have asked him several times, as I love Papa and never thought to think ill of him for any reason. But, I have to tell you this. They were not sufficient reason, in my mind, for his lack of action. Papa's position made him able to protect them whatever should happen. I told Papa so before I set off for York and we had many cross words. But he was adamant. We would have outnumbered the Church Army in Stocksmoor had they tried to fight us, but at least our dear cousins would still be alive. I couldn't make him listen. When I, myself, think about it, as I still do, I cannot understand. He wanted Mark to stay at the Hall, you know, but when Mark knew that Papa wouldn't help he just ran off."

So, for a long time I was in ignorance of the reason behind what seemed at first sight as a betrayal by Uncle Wilfred of his sister, Eve, when he declined to help her daughters in their hour of need. Yet, somehow I could not feel the anger towards him that I felt I should have. What I knew, from fact, had happened did not fit easily in my mind when put alongside my long knowledge of and affection for Uncle Wilfred. It was more puzzlement without answer.

But, many things were to become clear as I shall relate later in this narrative. All I can say just now is that it is human nature to err, but sometimes to make good an error is not possible, and living with the result is a cross to be born by the strongest and the weakest.

§

As was my habit, I went into the city of York from our home at Uncle George's manor, about once every four weeks. I always went early in the morning, the reason being to obtain the medicaments needed for my potions and plasters. The apothecary expected me before his business opened so as not to interfere with his own preparations. We had known each other and had this arrangement for many years, long before I moved to York. Any time I was passing through I would stock up on essential items. Nothing untoward had ever happened, until this particular morning.

It was a very cold morning with a bitter wind blowing into town from along the river. As a result of much recent inclement weather, the river was in full spate, with the water high and flowing very fast. Fears that its banks might overflow were causing great concern around the town and in the lowest lying areas. Fortunately the roads that I had to travel that day were all passable.

I had completed my purchases and was carrying several packets to my covered wagon. I had left it in a small road parallel to the river where my horse could be tethered. As I approached my wagon I saw a woman, in a cloak and carrying a large bag, walking towards me. She had her hood well over her face and was bent over, as if struggling against the elements. She looked dirty and dishevelled. Her cloak was torn. The poor woman looked destitute. As she reached my wagon she leaned against the side for support, clutching her cloak around her.

"My good woman," I spoke to her, as I reached my horse, "do you need assistance?"

She looked up and, to my utter amazement called my name. "Richard Shaw, is that you?"

I still could not see her face, but I answered, "Yes, that is my name. How can you know me?"

I have, at this stage, to say that she was obviously a 'woman of the night'. I do not frequent such places or have any dealings or association with such women. I wondered how she could possibly know my name. It was painted along the side of the wagon, but it never occurred to me that she could possibly read it, and, moreover she spoke as if I were a familiar person to her.

"Don't you know me, Richard? I am Helena, Mary's sister-in-law."

I have written about Helena before and you will remember that she gave me Mary's surviving daughter, Marion, to look after as she did not want to be burdened by her after Mary's untimely death.

"What on this earth are you doing here and in this condition?" I asked her.

She did not speak.

"Here, have some bread, cheese and water," I offered, reaching into the wagon for my daily provisions, which, though not elaborate, were adequate for my needs during my day away from home. I could see she looked very thin and near to collapsing to the ground from fatigue and, I suspected, from a dire disease, if my surmise of her way of life was accurate.

"Thank you. You were always kind."

"Come, sit a while in my wagon and put this blanket round your shoulders. It is bitterly cold today and that wind feels to go right into the bones. Tell me what you are doing in this place at this time and in this state. Why are you not at home in Bretton?"

Then, as we sat in my covered wagon, she told me a long story which filled me with not only sadness but anger. From her I gained extra knowledge that led me to believe that, had we known what she told me, we could have pursued the dreadful abducting of young boys much further. But, we cannot alter the past and hindsight is always very knowledgeable.

Let me tell you what she told me.

∫

She took me back many years to the time when she had lived in a village about eight miles from Bretton. She was the daughter of a well respected man called Ebenezer Knott. He worked for the estate of Canon Matthew Crecy, a well known senior in the Church. She had been beautiful. I knew that fact was true from my own observation, having known her over many years since our sister Mary married her brother.

When very young, she had worked at the Hall as a lady's maid to the Canon's second wife. She had grown up on the estate and had known and fallen in love with the Canon's youngest son, Benedict. She believed, despite the difference in station, that Benedict truly loved her. Whether he did or not is a different matter. I am sure that despite my best endeavour, I would be biased in my comments if I now give my opinion. He was not the Canon's favourite son and that was the reason he had been sent by the Canon to be a member of the Church Army. But, Benedict was a man who, apparently, took advantage where he could. He was tall and fair with startlingly clear blue eyes and of an appearance that many women found pleasing. She was flattered by his interest in her and her love for him had blossomed very early in their acquaintance.

§

Now it is interesting to note, in passing, and here I digress to tell you about the members of the said Canon's family, as told to me by Helena. I, personally, had surprisingly little knowledge, despite being related through two marriages within my family.

I knew that the Squire of Upper Oakington, Robert Crecy was the Canon's eldest son. Robert's mother, a beautiful, gentle but high-spirited woman died tragically when he was a small boy. The small open trap she had been travelling in on one of her frequent forays into the local villages overturned at a corner and the occupants were all thrown out. It was thought that her horse must have been disturbed by something, and reared suddenly, unbalancing the rather unstable two-wheeled craft. She had Robert with her and his nursemaid. Her other child, a baby girl, Hannah, (who later, you will remember, married my brother, Ben) had fortunately been left at home. Robert landed in a hedge and sustained only a few scratches and the nursemaid was alive but unable to remember what happened. But sadly, his mother landed on a stone. She was found dead with the small boy crying at her side, and the nursemaid was wandering, as if in a dream, along the road nearby.

The Canon married Benedict's mother soon after. Although she never knew the Canon's first wife, not being as yet born when she died, Helena understood that Benedict's mother was a woman of a very different nature. She worked for her and she hated her. It seems that she passed her worst qualities onto Benedict, being cold, cruel and arrogant. But Helena had no choice in her employment.

(In due course, Robert married and his wife, also called Hannah, was, in *fact, our cousin, by virtue of being the elder daughter of our Uncle Wilfred. She was, of course, brought up at Grandpapa's Hall in Bretton, when her father inherited the estate after his eldest brother, our maternal Uncle George, died.)*

§

Let me digress here to add to your knowledge, as I otherwise would not know where to put this information. Having the same Cecil family origin as my sisters and being Eve's niece and our cousin, Hannah (Squire Robert's wife), liked to think she was equal to the task of knowing herbs and even having the healing touch. She thought herself to have quite the same skill as my sisters. She was a beautiful woman, a year older than Ann and Emily. She liked people to know of her 'gift'. She distributed her presence around Upper Oakington with, what could only be called 'pride mixed with condescension and superiority'. Now, as you have gathered, my sisters were not of that nature, but never once did I hear them comment on Hannah's avowed blessing or on their own abilities.

Hannah's younger sister, Jane, also liked to practise in the same way and had as much, or lack of, natural ability as her sister Hannah. She spent a lot of her time at Upper Oakington with Hannah and her children, being as yet unmarried herself. They had a large walled garden with a gardener and grew many herbs for their potions. They did not take much notice of Ann or Emily, but they learned a great deal from Catherine, whose skill they admired.

You may wonder, as Nell, Uncle George and I did, why then, with their quite 'open' activities, Hannah and Jane were not included in the scourge of the Church Army? How did they avoid being put into the stocks or submitted to the duckings? Let me say now, that I am very glad that they escaped that fate, of course I am, but the questions 'why and how' have been ever present.

Ben told me that Hannah and Jane, both, had gone to stay at the Hall in Bretton, two days before the Church Army arrived in Stocksmoor and had taken Hannah's three children. Now, I am sure that on Hannah's part it was an innocent wish to visit her father and mother and spend some time in the lovely grounds in the warm weather, free and with her children.

Jane was merely 'going home'. But, it was very coincidental that they were under a safer roof and in a safer place when the happenings of Stocksmoor took place and I do not have faith or belief in coincidences. In general circumstances, the Church Army could not trespass on private property belonging to the gentry, and, you may remember, Grandmama had been of the 'highest gentry'.

I can understand prudence but not without reason. So, I had to think that someone gave them prior knowledge that the Church Army was to visit and kill in Stocksmoor, or else they would surely have been included in the scourge.

Suffice to say that following my sisters' deaths, I never heard tell of Hannah or Jane being interested in healing powers or herbs again. I saw Hannah on just a couple of occasions at the Hall subsequently, when I was requested to tend Uncle Wilfred's horses and not one word did she say about Ann, Emily or Catherine. Not even a word of condolence. It was 'as if' they had never existed in her life; not even Catherine came into her conversation. In fact, my cousin and her children never went back to live in Upper Oakington and within less than two years following my sisters' death, Robert Crecy with Hannah and their three children moved well away from the area to another part of the country entirely.

I heard that Canon Matthew Crecy's eldest brother lived in the east of the country and he – very conveniently, I have to interject – needed a Squire in one of his villages. His only son was otherwise engaged helping his father on their estate and did not want that extra responsibility. So, Robert went to that part of the world and Upper Oakington lost its Squire.

Hannah, Ben's wife, who, if I need to remind you within these complications, was Robert Crecy's sister and half sister to Benedict, was indeed deeply upset when they moved. She heard that her brother, Benedict, had been lost on one of his forays, but Robert was her favourite brother. She missed him sorely. Benedict's death had little sign of sadness attached to it.

Hannah, Ben's wife, did not understand the reason that Robert should move his family away. Ben told me that, though Robert knew how his family's move would upset Hannah, he never explained to her why he left Upper Oakington. Robert had made a perfect squire, and had fully enjoyed his authority in the village. He had held a position more elevated and important than he could really have expected had he not married my cousin. So his move away from Upper Oakington caused many questions. But, I am totally certain that Ben's Hannah did not know the facts that I shall relate as I tell you Helena's story in a little while, else she would have told Ben.

But I will continue on these matters for the present. As you know, when Ben returned home from his work, having been away for a few days, he was not informed that there was a serious risk to his sisters and merely thought they would be mildly punished on the stocks. Hannah had told him that they were being 'taught a lesson', according to Squire Robert.

One has to wonder. How much did Robert know? Why did he tell Hannah that there was a lack of seriousness in the situation, even though he felt it imperative to send his own wife and children to the safety of the Hall and then went away himself very speedily so that he would not be involved? He knew something that made him take action in his own family, but how much? Did he tell his sister the truth or did he withhold information from his sister so that Ben would not know and take no immediate action? All these questions had been in my mind for a long time, though I did not want to think ill of Robert.

I confess that I do not care much for the Squire. I have always found him to be someone whom I could never know even should I wish to do so. It surprises me that two people can speak in the same language and have a conversation that is not complex in any way and yet not convey mutual understanding. I have met him for many years now since he married my cousin, Hannah, and lived near his sister, Ben's wife. But I have to say that I know no more about how he thinks or what he believes now than when I first met him. He never asked me to see his horses, though he had four that he used regularly. Why? I do not know.

I now dislike him because he didn't help my sisters. He was in a position in which he could have done so, but he chose to remove himself from the area at the time — for whatever reason. But, in the circumstances, none could have been needier of his input on their behalf than my sisters were. Whatever he is like, I cannot make myself think he deliberately went out of his way to cause problems for my sisters. Notwithstanding, I must remember the fact that his wife and sister in law practised in a similar way to that which the Church Army was opposed, and which was the declared reason for my sisters' deaths. In conversations when I have heard him speak in the past at family gatherings and the like, he always seemed not only pleased that Hannah and Jane were ministering to his village people, but also manifested a little knowledge himself. So, something is not making sense to me at this time.

But now, as Helena told me her story, small pieces were being found that had been missing. I suddenly realised that the Benedict who she spoke about was in true fact, Hannah, Ben's wife's younger step brother. Benedict Crecy, no less! It was as if a door had been opened and inside was a light, shining to let me see that which I needed to know.

Though my sister-in-law Hannah knew that her half brother, Benedict, was in the Church Army, I do not think for one minute that she knew of Benedict's position and power in the Church Army or anything about its hierarchy or the elite section or really anything that Helena was telling me. At all events, Hannah saw little of Benedict. But I am sure Benedict would not tell his sister Hannah, Ben's wife, about his progress in the Church Army for fear she would not keep her council, in her desire to spread his achievement to any who would listen.

I believe that Benedict would have told his elder brother, Robert, of his position in the Church Army. As a younger brother trying to impress, I cannot believe he could keep such information, of his elevated rank, from his elder brother. Benedict must also have known of his sister-in-law, Hannah's claim to the same talents as my sisters. I think that there is no doubt at all that Robert inadvertently passed on information to Benedict about my sisters, even if only in the conversation that is held in homes and families about events and actions in the local neighbourhood.

When you hear what Helena has to say, you can do your own thinking but I believe that you will agree with me. If not, then I acquiesce to your decision, as it makes only for interest now, and nothing will change what happened. All that is important to me about this particular matter is that I am absolutely certain that Hannah and my brother Ben were totally innocent and did not know the truth of what was likely to happen. But, I cannot with a clear or honest heart say that Squire Robert was the same.

Whatever, I am sure that he was warned beforehand, yet did not warn either my sisters or Ben and actually told my father he could not help. For those reasons, I cannot forgive him.

I hope you do not think I have laboured this point. I myself feel that this may be so, but that has not been my intention. But, please understand that I am trying to put everything in its correct place and not make any dreadful insinuations or accusations that are not valid. I have no wish to put a slight onto someone's memory, which will be stored for posterity in this book, should those facts not be true. When you read that which I write, then think what you will about Robert Crecy, Squire.

∫

Let me continue now with Helena's story.

Helena's father was opposed to her having anything to do with the Canon's son, knowing that this could only lead to disaster. She had heard him say that Benedict was above her station, but more importantly he believed he was 'not wholesome'. She could not ask what he meant, yet she did not know his meaning without asking. Would she have altered her passion, had she known? Life is full of 'ifs', but with hindsight, all actions are easier to decide.

When he went away into the Church Army, Benedict was firstly posted to York. During those years she saw or heard little of him until he was moved nearer and became permanently stationed at the headquarters situated at the castle at Sandal. The relief felt by her father was short lived as Benedict contacted her and their liaison continued. The years between only had the effect of increasing Helena's love for Benedict. Within a year of his return to the area she had become his mistress, conceived and bore his child.

When her father had found out, he was going to disown her there and then. However, she had confided in her eldest sister, Phoebe, who stood by her on the understanding that when the child was born he or she should be given to her and become as if her own. Phoebe was married but had never been with child, though six years had passed. By coincidence, she and her husband moved to Stocksmoor close by my sisters, soon after the child was born, so I knew Phoebe well, even before I had ever met Helena.

The arrangement was that Phoebe would gradually appear as if getting larger with child and when the time came for Helena to have her child then Phoebe would go to her father's house, at his apparent command, to have the best lying in possible.

Meanwhile, during the preceding months, Helena should remain at her father's house, not communicating with any one or leaving the house. Should anyone of her friends ask where she was, the message was merely that she had gone to visit a young aunt to help her look after her children as they were proving too much for her. Helena had no choice but to obey, or else be destitute. In this way, none but the family knew of her being with child.

Her father requested that Benedict should visit his house to tell him of his decision. He told him that once the baby was born, he would renounce his daughter, though for her sake and his, he would not make his decision public. Neither would he tell Benedict's father, but, and he stressed the 'but' so that Benedict was in no doubt of his meaning, only on the condition that the Captain should provide accommodation and food for his daughter and child, henceforth. Should he not do this or fall back on this arrangement the Canon would be informed forthwith and he would make sure that Benedict was publicly disgraced in the eyes, not only of his father, but in the Canon's public domain.

Her father told him, in no uncertain terms, that, though the Canon was far superior to him in rank, his own acquaintances ranged far and wide through his work and many were well-born. He knew that the Canon gave Benedict an allowance each month, despite his wages in the Church Army. Benedict knew that this exposure was not only possible but certain and so he agreed and was allowed to meet Helena once more, before she became secluded.

"He had agreed to support me, but only if I would call the child, if it was a boy, John, after his grandfather. If it was a girl I should call her Mary. So, my son was called John." At the mention of her son, Helena wept.

So Benedict, who Helena always believed truly loved her, had rented the house for her in Bretton and agreed that her brother, Abraham, who later married Mary, should live with her to help look after her and, in part, pay for her upkeep. The secret was kept and her story was, as you will already know – that she was widowed early, her dear departed husband had been tragically killed in battle, and that he had left her enough money to live comfortably in the rented house. Everyone believed her as, though she had only lived about eight miles from Bretton, no one in Bretton had ever either heard or seen her before. It was oft like that, as most people did not travel far afield in the course of their day to day life. Should anyone ask her father about his daughter, the story was to be, 'word for word', the same.

She had been faithful to Benedict and had never had a relationship with any other man during those years. Rather was she a 'kept woman'. Being beautiful and appearing refined, and wearing clothes that the village people would not, normally, wear, everyone had believed her story. No one surmised or ever wondered that 'her nephew John' could actually be her son.

"Richard, please believe me when I say that Mary never knew who or what I was. When I went away, to fulfil my obligations to my 'master', for want of a better word, I told Mary I was going to stay with a friend who needed me. I didn't lie, really, but it was a long way short of the real truth. I could not keep Marion. How could I, a 'kept woman' keep the child of an innocent well-born woman? I never allowed myself to get close to that child, though my yearnings to be a mother never left me."

Her father, true to his word, threw her out, though only her sister, her sister's husband, her brother, Abe, and Benedict knew. No one else was ever privy to the truth, until she told me at this meeting.

Phoebe, though not endowed with Helena's beauty, had a quality of kindness and loved her younger sister, and always allowed her to visit their house in Stocksmoor to see and play with her son. Helena loved the boy, but she never broke that trust. So, everyone in Stocksmoor thought John was Phoebe's child, and that he was merely very fond of his aunt in Bretton. Once he reached nine years of age, he would walk the two miles to Bretton, quite alone. He, himself, was never to know who his real mother was.

As you know from previous pages in this book, this boy went missing when he was ten years of age and was never found. She was heartbroken and, when he wasn't found after a few days, she went to see Benedict at his accommodation in Sandal to tell him of their son's absence and her worries for his safety. She always met him in a house by the castle walls; she never asked any questions about his rank in the army or about the house that they 'used'. She thought they were his living quarters. She now realised that she had been both blind and deaf to him and what was happening.

But readers, in defence of Helena, love can make even the best amongst us blind so that we cannot see what others see; added to which anyone, with position and no conscience, can take advantage of someone of lower station.

She continued with her story, telling me that Benedict was often away from the headquarters in Sandal as, by now, he had the control and command of a special platoon of ten men who travelled up and down the country. She never asked what he did or where he went as that was army business. He happened to be stationed at home when she arrived in great distress, and he promised that his soldiers would search for John. A few days later, a soldier visited her home to say that John had not been found.

The disappearance of John broke her sister Phoebe's health completely, and she never recovered from the shock. Whether this was related or not no one knew, but Phoebe collapsed and died in her small garden two months later. Helena knew that my sisters, who were collecting herbs rushed to her when she was seen to fall, but that nothing could be done. Fortunately, she had died instantly, and all hoped that she was able to be reunited with John. Most thought it was from a broken heart, yet others agreed that she had lost the will to live. The result was the same in the end. She had not eaten much since his disappearance and had been seen standing on the common land in all weathers, sometimes for hours in the night despite her husband's entreaties, calling John's name, as if to find him.

§

Helena knew nothing of the court case. This is not surprising as there was no reason for anyone to tell her. After her brother Abe's death, she seldom saw anyone in the village. No one knew she could be connected in any way to the Church Army and she certainly had never taken any interest in Ann, Emily or Catherine.

From what she told me, and I have tried my uttermost to put the dates in order, it seems that many weeks before the court case started, a soldier rode to Helena's door and gave her a message, asking her to visit her lover, Benedict. Though she had always known he was in the Church Army, she still believed him to be a Captain, though more senior than before. She did not know that he had worked his way up through the ranks to be in a position of some senior command. All she knew was that he was now away from barracks a lot more of the time. A soldier bringing a message was the usual way, in the four past years since his higher promotion, for her to know when to visit, and, hence, when he was 'in residence'.

She put on her best dress and coat, packed her overnight bag and made the well-travelled journey. This was the bag that I mentioned before and which my sisters had recognised in Mary's home. I might just interject that, as I sat talking to her in my covered wagon, that same bag, tattered and dirty, now carried all her remaining worldly possessions.

At this, her last visit, she saw the true and different side to the man she had loved since her teenage years; the one and only love in her life. She went into his room. He greeted her and had his way with her, as was normal. Then afterwards, they had some repast and chatted. She suspected nothing.

Up to this point she had no idea that her world would be destroyed, in a few minutes and by a few words. Certainly, she had realised that she could not feel the same towards him, or anyone, since her son, sister and finally her dear brother had died, but she always pretended to him that she was the same as ever. She admitted that the death of Mary and her baby had not affected her very much and my sisters' deaths even less. No, it was the loss of John, Abe and Phoebe that had broken her.

However, she still believed Benedict to be kind and generous and true to her. Whatever she felt or, more truly, didn't feel, she could not risk being any different as her livelihood and home were totally dependent on his generosity. By this time her father had also died. Her father had been a man sorely saddened at the loss to him of his beautiful and most loved daughter, as her sister Phoebe always told her, but he had remained resolute in his disownment. He left her not one penny. He died a melancholic man, being even more deeply saddened after his son, Abe, hanged himself. Since Abe's death, she had been very aware that she had no one but Benedict to support her. Without him she would have nothing.

As she was telling me her story, at this point she faltered again and for several minutes could not speak. Her tears fell freely. After a few minutes, she wiped her eyes, and in doing so, pushed back her hood. I saw for the first time the ravages that had taken place to her once beautiful face. Whether you had liked her before or not, there had been no denying her beauty. Now, not only was her skin sallow and ingrained with dirt, but there were dark hollows in her cheeks and the skin round her eyes was blackened. The once shining, thick hair was hanging in dank, thin and greasy strands about her face. I sensed that here was a woman who was very ill and possibly dying. It was truly a sad sight.

"Are you in pain?" I asked.

"Yes, Richard, I have much pain in my body, but nothing matches that within my heart."

The story continued. ·

Her long time lover had eventually pushed his chair back and gave her this devastating news, "This is the last time you will see me. I am going away directly and I will not be coming back."

As she was about to speak he held up his hand and looked angrily at her.

"Do not interrupt what I have to say. I have supported you at your father's behest, lest my own career be ended, but that is now no more. I have heard that your father has gone to his maker and well pleased they both should be."

Helen asked if she could go away with him. She told him that he was all she had now and all she cared about. He had laughed in her face.

"Of course you cannot go with me. But, I feel somewhat obliged to tell you the truth about what happened to your son. You would do best to listen and keep quiet, else I shall stop and you will never know."

After his first few sentences, her blood ran cold and she thought she would swoon to the floor. But, she needed to know and made herself listen. As if through a mist, she heard that John had been taken by two soldiers from the Church Army on his way from Stocksmoor to Bretton – when he was going to visit her the day he disappeared. Benedict had been very angry with her as he knew that he had given John protection. When John had reached nine, the Captain had presented her with a silver cross on which an eagle was attached. A black cord was threaded through a hole so it could be worn round the neck. He had told her it was his gift for John and to make sure he always wore it if he was out and about away from the confines of his home, though he had never explained its significance.

"He was angry with me, but I told him I always insisted that John wore it. And he did. But, until that day, I did not know the reason or its meaning. I thought it was just a keepsake, a gift, for our son.

"Richard," she stopped and lifted her head to face me. "Richard, he told me that he was not only in the Church Army, but the White Army. You may not believe me, but I had to ask him what he meant as I did not know. He snapped at me and told me that he would explain, all in good time, if I did not interrupt. I swear, Richard, that until that day I had seen not one trace to make me think he was anything other than an ordinary captain in the Church Army. I was ignorant, yes, ignorant of it all. But, I am going to tell you now as much as I know. It isn't much, yet it may be useful and you can pass on what I say if you wish to whoever may be able to use it."

I couldn't bring myself to tell her how useful and important it would have been had we known this information before the trial. But, even so, Uncle George shall know all, and do with that knowledge what he thinks is best.

Benedict informed her that the eagle that he gave to John was the emblem of the Church Army and the soldiers should have looked at his neck. That particular eagle had been his, when in the lower ranks. He explained all about their use and how they were worn, and that, as soldiers made their way up the ranks, the eagle became more ornate, with stones set in gold with the chain of the top ranking men also made of gold.

(Of course, you understand, I did not tell her that I knew these facts already from Robbie.)

However, as John was so young and not expected to have a pendant, and as no one knew that he was the son of the Captain, the soldiers had omitted to look and only when he arrived at the camp was his eagle found. He then told her that John had been put into the space under the seats in the wagon, but must have suffocated in the wagon. In any event, he was dead on arrival at the Church Army quarters.

('So, my sisters were absolutely correct in their reasoning about the wagon,' I thought.)

She then realised that the wagon that he had organised to take her nearly home was the same wagon in which her son had died. Horrified and shocked she had slumped to the floor. He did not even attempt to help her, but simply waited until she recovered.

She asked him, "Why would John be taken and why would he arrive at the Church Army? How can the Church Army be connected with John's disappearance?" Then he laughed.

"Richard, it was truly a cruel sound. I wonder that my life was literally given to such as him. My father was so right. God rest his soul. I was so foolish, so very foolish. I have wasted my life on a monster."

It seemed she had urgency in her mind. She needed to tell me what she knew, despite the cold and her ill state. After a short pause, I learned more.

Benedict had told her, with some bravado, 'My dear, don't be so simple. The soldiers have to have amusement and some prefer the young boys to women, and some – and I count myself one of these – like both. You would be surprised at how the terror on a young boy's face increases the excitement. So we oblige as best we can to keep them happy. Do you seriously think that our camp followers merely look after our uniforms and cook our food? Come, come, Helena, I had thought you would realise why we chose women, not men, for those tasks. A happy soldier is, indeed, a good soldier I have always found.'

Helena could not believe what she was hearing. She felt as though a knife had been pushed through her heart and all the breath had been taken from her. But, she now felt a sudden and wild hate for this man, a hate that kept her asking for more information. One day, she would find someone to give that information to. She promised herself that on behalf of her son.

Sometimes she recounted the story, but at other times she told it as if it was happening then and now, as if she were talking for them both. I sometimes felt that I was listening to a play and both parts were being read by one person.

∫

"But John was your son," she had wept as she spoke, but Benedict was unmoved.

"I know. Be assured that the soldiers made a mistake but did not live long to regret it. Let me see, yes, I remember, one was found in the river and strangely, apparently, the other had a spear through his heart and was found at the base of the castle walls. And, you know, my dear, they had thought they were doing so well."

Helen had looked with horror. Who was this man? As if reading her mind, he answered her thoughts.

"Yes, I can tell, you are wondering who I am. Well, as I am going away I can let you into my secrets."

He then told her much more and about the section of the Church Army called the White Army. This was a special branch. Its main roles were getting information, organising the timing and outcomes of the trials, and carrying out the sentences against infidels. They were the ones who wore the white uniform and attended all the hangings, beatings, duckings and the like.

"We are an elite troop known around the country as the "Riders of Death". Something to be proud of, don't you think? Not many people can say they cause terror just by sitting on a horse! I am the Second in Command of the White Section of the Church Army, which is why I am often away. You can now know that the women in Stocksmoor died at my command, though, you understand I, myself, was under orders."

Distraught as she was, she managed to hold herself together to find out more. As you will know, this was a woman of some practised hardness.

"You are bluffing, telling me lies so that I shall not want to go with you. What could those three innocent and gentle women ever have done to you or your army that would justify their deaths? They did no harm and professed nothing, and I knew them well."

"How did you know them?"

"They were Mary's sisters."

"Really? I didn't realise that. I should have done as I saw them at Hannah's wedding. I just thought they were local women of no significance. You couldn't really miss the abnormality of those two being so alike, now could you? I did not even think to enquire further about them. Though one of them was an insolent little bitch, as I recall, and didn't know what could be good for her." Helena saw a dark look pass over his face, and then he smirked, as if he was remembering some incident that gave him pleasure. *"But, I took my revenge on her. I never forget an insult. Oh, yes, I always win and the men had fun. A pity but, my dear, they knew too much about the boys who disappeared. They were very astute you know and had started interfering in something that was none of their business."*

"But how did you find that out?" Helena persisted.

"Oh, we have spies everywhere, so don't think to tell anything I have allowed you to know. Not to anyone, you understand, or you will be the next to be found in some dark gutter. One of our women followers came from the village, you yourself talked about the three and, I assure you, your information filled in a few gaps. But mainly they talked to someone close to the highest in our command and so information was collected without any difficulty whatsoever. Of course, they had no way of knowing about the one to whom they spoke." He laughed. *"If only they had known."*

"Who was that?" I asked. But he wouldn't tell me.

"Despite the fact that I am going away, I cannot tell you who received that information. There are only two men who know the identity of our High Chief, our highest authority in the Church Army. I pride myself that I am one of them, and, though I might be many miles and a different country away, believe me, I would be found if it was ever known that I had spoken his name. We knew all about their so-called healing for a long time, but the information about the boys, was much more recent, and dangerous to us and our cause. They had to be killed. But, they had given us the perfect reason which fitted in with our orders about infidels."

"Who is the other who knows the name of the Highest Chief of all?"

"I cannot tell you that or my life would end very shortly, I assure you. Even the walls would appear to have ears to pick up that name being spoken."

"What about Robert's wife, Hannah, and her sister Jane? They have practised as healers these many years. You knew about them. Why did you not include them? No one touched them, though they practised the same as Ann, Emily and Catherine."

"Come, come. Helena, family is family after all. Whatever else, blood is thicker than water. No, I sent a soldier to call on Robert with a message to take Hannah and the children to the Hall and make sure that Jane went home too. I had told Robert about my promotion to the elite section and what that entailed. He was sworn to secrecy, so our sister Hannah did not know about it. He knew that we had a mission to scourge the land, but we had a secret word that only Robert knew.

"I had promised him that if ever it was urgently needful that he took Hannah to safety, then I would use that word. Which I did. He didn't actually know what was to happen, other than 'stocks can be used as a lesson'. That is all he knew as I guessed he would pass that on to our sister. I have to say that Robert is not without guile or intelligence. But, for his own sake, he was not directly informed of the duckings. I couldn't trust even Robert to know that. I don't think that he would have agreed to keep silent on that had he been told directly. But he actually loves his wife, so I did not think he would risk her death."

"But what about his wife's father, Sir Wilfred? Why did he not arm his villeins and send them to rescue his nieces. You couldn't stop that, could you?"

"You are really a simpleton, Helena, much more than I have ever realised. I have never questioned my assumption that along with your beauty came some amount of intelligence. I see I am sadly mistaken, but it is of no consequence now as our paths divide and will never cross again. Of course I could. If Sir Wilfred had sent men against us, we would have fought him. I had sent a good troop to Stocksmoor for that eventuality, twenty well-armed and very good fighters they were too. Rough and uncouth maybe, but they could fight. His labourers would have stood no chance. Oh, no, I sent my best. We would have sent just empty horses back, and Sir Wilfred would have lost his heir, that rather foolish son of his, Geoffrey.

"In my message to Robert I told him quite clearly, 'Tell your father-in-law to keep out of this, for the sake of you all. I know that Hannah and Jane practise the same, and I can use that as or when necessary and your father-in-law's position will not be able to stop their punishment. I have influence in the highest places.' My orders were to kill Ann Kittle, Emily Kittle and Catherine Shaw. But, in his defence, I did not tell him the details. I don't think he would have expected the three of them to die.

"So you see, Sir Wilfred could do nothing nor could he say anything or else Robert would have been implicated by default. Although he only knew we were going to 'punish' but not kill, he still had prior information. But, had he used it, then his wife would have been punished in the same way as the other three. Oh, and her sister. I made sure he realised that. I was not bluffing. He knew a few days before, hence he took his wife and sister-in-law to her father's hall.

"Oh yes, I am clever, Helena, much more than I have ever been given credit for. There is no love lost on my side, you know, I care for none of my family or his. And Robert is weak and always has been. I knew which path he would take. I only warned Robert to keep Sir Wilfred away from interfering or trying a rescue. I had my orders. I was told to kill the three sisters, not anyone else. But, in truth, three more would have made little difference. Just more pleasure for the men!"

Then, he started laughing. Helena stood and waited.

"Oh, I have just realised. My dear brother Robert would have been in quite a dilemma about Sir Wilfred's nieces!! I thought at the time that they were just village wenches and that neither he nor Sir Wilfred would have been much troubled at their demise. Ha! Ha! What a pleasure to find I have probably caused my brother more angst than I thought. Ha! Ha!"

He paused for a moment to savour his glee.

"In fact, my dear, I pride myself that it all went very smoothly, apart *from those two idiots at the end, who got themselves killed. I suppose they were related as well, silly fools, to think they could stand up against the Church Army and with the Riders in attendance. Then, we had just a slight annoyance that took a bit of last minute organisation. Yes, Sir Wilfred's stupid Geoffrey. He ignored Robert. But his horse was.... how shall I put it? Let us say it was 'delayed."*

(So now I knew the truth of why Uncle Wilfred had ignored my sisters. He had to live with that decision, but in truth, what would have been the result of a different decision? Just many more dead? And, I knew for certain that Geoffrey's horse had been tampered with.)

Benedict had continued. "Everyone in the family has underestimated me from when I was a child. Robert was always the favourite son. Well, I have shown Robert at least, that I am superior, at last. My dearest Helena, what had to be done had to be done on highest orders. It was quite a spectacle, believe me."

"I can't believe this. After all these years of knowing and loving you, to find you are a beast, an animal, a murderer. What would your father think if he knew?"

"Well, he put me in the army, so he is responsible for that, if nothing else. You are not going to tell him, are you?" He grabbed her wrist, cruelly twisting it as she tried to get away.

"You must be having a cruel joke. You are lying. Oh! My son! My son!" She cried and backed away towards the door as if she, herself, was to be a victim.

"This is not make-belief on my part or my imagination. See for yourself!" He grabbed her shoulder roughly and dragged her over to a large cupboard.

"I will show you."

He felt around his neck and pulled out a string on which was threaded a key.

"I never leave this key anywhere. I carry it on my person," he informed her. "But soon it will be useless as I shall not need this cupboard in a few days time. And our High Chief will not use it again either."

Helena interrupted him, "Why? Why are you going away?"

"Simply, my dear, to save my life. I am too young to die. Those dullards, my spies, could not think that well-born women would ever live without their finery and servants and it never occurred to them to even ask a question. I have found out, and I won't tell you who has informed me, that their uncle is the Lord Lieutenant of Yorkshire, no less. Their grandfather was a Duke or Earl. **You** knew, you could have told me all this. Robert could have told me. Sister Hannah could have told me. Nobody, just nobody bothered to tell 'young Benedict', did they? Oh no! Young Benedict had to find out, didn't he? But they don't know who I am now. Oh no!

"I hear that this meddling old man, the Lord Lieutenant, is to hold a trial and bring those involved in the deaths to account. He will not be able to do so, I have been assured of that, but I have had, shall we call it, a warning. I have been advised to go away until a few months after the trial. It is not quite an order, but I listen to a message from such a source. I have been relieved of my duties until I should return. See, this is evidence for you that I speak the truth."

He suddenly turned on her. "You didn't tell me, did you? You talked about Ann and Emily and Catherine, but how was I to know they were well-born? How did I know your precious Abe had married someone well above his station? Where were the signs?" Out of the blue he swung his hand and hit her across the face, first one side and then the other, eventually knocking her over onto the floor.

It can only be assumed that out of sheer bravado he told Helena all this information. When she had recovered, he ordered her to stand up. He took out a small piece of paper from his pocket, unfolded it and read, "Trial. Beware. Go immediately. Do not return until summoned. Suggest Rouen. Find Anton."

He threw the paper down on the table in front of Helena and continued to open the two strong doors of one of the very large cupboards that stretched across half of one wall from floor to ceiling. Helena had only ever seen this cupboard closed before and had never even wondered what could be contained therein. Now Helena gasped as she saw the finery.

There, hanging inside, on wide hangers covered with white silk, were what looked like two white cloaks or vestments. She could see that one was embroidered in silver and blue around the hem, but the other was much more elaborate and ornate, with much gold and red embroidery. On a hook, at the back of the cupboard, was a gold chain hanging from which was a large, ornate gold cross which had a large ruby in its centre. She then saw a large, carved wooden cross painted in gold, of the same shape as the pendant on the chain, at the end of a slender wooden pole and resting up against the corner of the cupboard. Benedict moved the cloaks around so she could not miss any of the splendour.

"Whose are those?" she asked, with disbelief and awe.

"That one there is mine," Benedict pointed to the silver and blue embroidered cloak.

"And the other?"

"That belongs to the High Chief of the White Army, our superior, the leader of the 'Riders of Death'. He keeps it here. This room, which we have always used for my, what shall I say, diversion with you, my dear, is his dressing room. Remember, only two know his face. That is how important I am. I am his dresser. You may as well see everything, before you leave. That big cross on the chain is for the public to see when he rides to an execution. His personal pendant with the eagle, which he wears next to his skin under his clothes, is the biggest and most ornate of them all. You should see it. It is truly magnificent. But, he keeps that himself. Again, there are just two of us who know about that or have ever even seen it." He was unable to hide his pride.

He pointed at the most ornate cloak. "I wore that in Stocksmoor to the duckings. I shall remember it, always. It was a magnificent day. The pinnacle of my life's achievement, so far. Other than becoming High Chief one day, I could not ask for more."

"Why was that you instead of the High Chief?"

"Well, dearest Helena, let me just say that he was unable to attend, for reasons that I, sadly, cannot divulge. Enough for me to say that he was occupied otherwise with duties related to his person, and could not, in such circumstances, wear the vestments or actually witness what

happened. So, I was given that honour. These particular duckings would have given him great pleasure. I know as he told me, but it was not to be."

He touched the Chief's vestment, running his fingers gently over the embroidery as if caressing it.

"Yes, I wore that. Just look at this intricate work. It is quite beautiful, isn't it?" He lingered over the vestment, tracing the gold embroidery pattern, before he turned to face Helena. At the sight of his once loved face, she felt only disgust and fear.

"They and you make me want to vomit. They are revolting, dreadful, evil," answered Helena, and a shiver went through her body.

The next thing she remembered, she was lying on the floor for the second time.

"How dare you? How dare you? That was my finest hour," she heard, as Benedict screeched in rage.

"Now, you will see it all. I insist." He was a big man and lifted her onto her feet by holding the clothes on her back and half carried and half dragged her to the other side of the room, before letting go of her suddenly.

As she was picking herself up, Benedict went to the far door of the nearest cupboard. Helena was stunned further by what she saw. Before that day, she had never even heard of, let alone seen, the 'Riders of Death', and had no notion of the hoods they wore. Benedict took one out of the cupboard and put it on. Helena had to hold her mouth shut tightly with her hand, lest she screamed in the sudden dreadful fear that overcame her. She hadn't really believed him before. The finery she had seen could have been clerical vestments. Now, she was left with no choice but to accept that he spoke the truth. He paraded around the room to give the full effect. As she looked away, she saw a square-shaped cushion, about the depth of her hand, on the floor of the cupboard. It was of a brilliant blue, heavy silk and embroidered with an ornate cross, the same shape as the one on the end of the pole.

"Why do you keep a cushion in the cupboard?" she asked, to distract him as much as possible. He had taken the headdress off from his head and was putting it carefully away again.

To her surprise, Benedict gave a scornful, cruelly cold laugh. His mood had suddenly changed.

"Oh that! Let me tell you something most amusing. My dear, the most important man in the White Army, the leader of the Riders of Death, one of the most powerful men in the country who instils terror into the hearts and minds of people, has a problem. Oh yes, a big problem. Ha! Ha! Ha!" he laughed. "Or, really, I should say a small problem!! Guess what it is? Go on. Try to guess."

"I can't imagine," replied Helena, feeling more afraid of this 'laughing' Benedict.

"He is short. Helena. Can you believe that? He is small, short, little, a man of modest stature!" And he laughed again. "He knows that if he sat on a saddle without that cushion, he would not cause the same fear in the hearts of anyone, no matter what hat he wore. It is beautifully made, don't you think, and stuffed very firmly with horse hair. Yes, no one else is aware of that but me, his dresser. In his unshod feet he only reaches up to here." He put an arm out, the hand being just below the level of his shoulder. "He sees it as his duty to instil as much terror as is possible, and so he fastens the cushion onto his saddle. See!" He pointed to the buckles on either side of the cushion. Helena had not noticed these before. "He fastens the cushion on securely with those and his cloak covers the cushion."

He reached into the back of the cupboard and pulled out what appeared to be short black boots.

"And, look at these! These go into the stirrups first," he told her, with continued glee, holding up the short boots, "and then he puts his own, further lengthened but smaller, boots into these. You understand, he needs to have longer legs because of the cushion. He never gets off his horse when on duty. In fact, he can't get off his horse. He needs my help. Ha! Ha! Ha! I have to keep a straight face when I dress him. No one but me knows." His voice changed again, and he hissed, "But you know now, Helena. If you know what is good for you, you will not say a word to anyone about any of this."

"Of course not, Benedict. Why would I?" Helena asked, trying to appease him.

"I shouldn't say this but I felt superior to him on my day of glory. I am tall and need nothing to increase my stature. I don't need a cushion or extended boots. I could dismount from my horse, walk around in the uniform and still cause terror. And I did! It was very satisfying, indeed it was. I suited that position, Helena, yes, I suited it very well."

(Now I knew a most important fact. The High Chief was short in stature.)

Despite being distraught and her head aching from the blows, Helena kept her wits about her. When he was busy putting the head dress away and then making sure the folds of the vestments were straight before shutting and locking the cupboard doors, she quickly secreted the paper warning, which he had read to her, into her bosom. She then fell to the floor weeping, hands to her head to distract Benedict.

"I see you are sorry, Helena. Admit, you are in awe of my position."

Not daring to outrage him again, she had to appear to agree. "Benedict, I accept that you have achieved a position of command that truly befits you."

"Why, thank you, my dear," he answered, not realising that her real meaning was hidden in the words.

Hardly able to breathe and frightened, she wanted to leave, but she had to know something else.

"There were another two boys from Stocksmoor and Lower Stocksmoor who went missing? Do you know what happened to them?"

He forgot about the paper, and arrogantly and coldly replied, "Well, yes, of course I know. Do you doubt me? I can tell you, as it now makes no difference. The same men took the younger one and in the same wagon, under the guise of having bought sacks of grain and hay. He survived but before the men could enjoy their pleasure, he died at his own hand. They were very careless. You see, there is a ritual to cleanse each boy, some of whom have lice and all seem to be dirty. We are a bit fussy, you could say."

As Benedict, with bravado and evident delight talked, Helena listened in total horror. When would she wake from this nightmare? At least she knew that her son had not had to endure any of the ordeals that were practised *on those they caught. As she listened, she knew that death was preferable for her son and for the first time felt a relief that John had died.*

"Each boy is stripped and walks into a deep trough of water with a line of soldiers dressed up in long robes and the pointed hats with only the eyes showing standing at the side, each with a bucket of water. The water is thrown over him while they chant. Ingenious really, it all appears very religious, heightening desire in the soldiers and terror in the boys. I feel quite proud to say that it was my idea. Each boy is then dressed in a white tunic and sash and sent back to his room to wait. The lad from Upper Stocksmoor must have guessed what was to happen next or heard the soldiers talking. They usually argue as to who will be first and who will do what. By the time they went to him he was dead. He hanged himself from the bars on the window, using his sash."

"And the other who was found down the well?"

"Yes, I heard about him. He had talked to the two of my men with the wagon. They were dressed as monks that time and had been walking around the village collecting news. He told them about the other young lad going missing and that he had spoken to two men with a wagon and thought they may have taken him. He didn't know they were the same men, of course. They thought he just talked too much. They didn't trust him to remain silent about the wagon. He was a year or two older so not suitable to be brought here. I told them to go back and that 'he had to disappear'. It was just bad luck that he was found."

By now, he had closed and locked the cupboard doors. Helena was truly frightened, but tried not to show it. She did not know what was to happen next, but knew she had to appease him, agree with him and even smile at him – anything that was necessary to keep his violence at bay. He had never hit her before. But this was a different Benedict whom she had not known existed. She knew he could kill her and would not care.

"But, even with fool proof plans, there is always a mystery. But it is of no importance."

"What do you mean?" Helena had been curious, as she did not know of whom he spoke.

"Captain Lesley told me there was another youngish man killed in the

village just before the stocks were erected. He had questioned all the men, one by one, but none of them were responsible. Now that was rather irregular, but, it really is only a minor puzzle and of no significance whatsoever. One death, more or less, does not matter."

(If it wasn't the Church Army who had killed Charles Trevore, then who had? I pondered on this as Helena continued.)

"I cannot believe that I have loved you for so long and with all my heart," confessed Helena, when she could eventually talk. By now she felt totally numb.

"Well, you did it very well, my dear. Yes, better than most I have to say."

Only then did Helen fully understand that she had not been his only lover. If only she had listened to her father. He carried on, ignoring her distress.

"If you ever breathe a word of what I am telling you to anyone, you will be killed. I am going away so it is no longer any concern of mine and neither are you. By this time tomorrow I shall be many miles away and will not be found. Only my three bodyguards know who I really am. Most think I am just a Captain with a troop. When we are 'The Riders' no one sees our faces. Why else do you think we wear those ridiculous headdresses? They can be really hot. So, basically, my dearest Helena, I shall no longer provide you with a home. The rent is paid until the end of this week only. I didn't want to alter anything until I had disappeared. To everyone else, me and my troop are simply off on another sortie in a more distant part of the country and expected to be away a few weeks. By that time, I shall have disappeared for good as I have decided that I shall not risk returning. Enjoy the rest of your life, Helena. Thanks for the pleasure."

"You bastard! You evil, filthy bastard!" she murmured under her breath so he couldn't hear. Out loud she asked, "What shall I do? I have no one to provide for me."

"You will have to continue in your profession. No one can ever say you are other than brilliant at that."

"I have never been with anyone else, only you."

"Well, I'm sure you will soon learn."

He went to a drawer and pulled out a cord with the silver eagle emblem hanging from it. It was the one that her son had been wearing. "I think the least I can do is to give you this. Sell it. It may pay your bills for a week or so till you find work."

She clasped it to her breast and tears fell for her son.

"Go now, I must be on my way."

He grabbed her arm and placed her bag over it, then picked up her cloak and threw it to her. Finally, as she was putting her cloak round her shoulders, without ceremony or further words, he pushed her out of the door. Bewildered, she had slowly walked the many miles home to Bretton and her cottage. Within the week, she had been evicted and homeless.

∫

Taking out the silver emblem fastened on its cord, she showed it to Richard. After she had eaten some more bread, she continued.

"Richard, this is the piece of paper that Benedict received with the message about the trial."

(I did not know what Uncle George would be able to do with this, but was sure he would find some way of making Helena's brave deed in secreting it from the room have meaning.)

Helena had decided to go to York to tell what she now knew but for a long time she had felt too frightened. But, gradually, as if slowly pulled by an invisible hand, and after months, days and endless nights she had arrived here, just a few days ago. She knew she would die soon. She had been determined to speak before that happened.

She told me that she had earned her food and occasionally a night's accommodation, by the only means available to her. Otherwise she had slept in the doorways or hedgerows. She had offered her services as a cleaner in one or two inns, but soon her appearance made people shut the doors against her. Now in York, she wanted to find out where her lover had gone. So far, she had twice attempted to gain access to the Archbishop to tell him what she knew, but each time she was refused. After these past few months sleeping out in the wind and weather and having to sleep with many dissolute and diseased men, she was ill.

She continued with her story.

"*I spent a lot of time at Sandal after he had left, hanging about the barracks and earning some food. I wanted to find out where Benedict had gone, if that was possible. Only Benedict's three main bodyguards had ever known me or that I was his mistress, so, to all the others, I was just another 'available' woman.*

"*One night I saw a man coming towards the corner where I stood. I recognised him as one of those three and, if anyone knew about Benedict's whereabouts, then I thought that he would. He was befuddled and had been drinking a lot of ale and smelt to high heaven. But I went to his room and when he was satisfied he started to talk, as though he didn't know I was still there. I clothed myself and before I left, I stayed very quiet and sat down next to him. He was, by now, very far gone with ale as I had kept giving him more from a flagon on the table and after a while he had not noticed. I heard him muttering and I listened. 'Ah, he thought he'd leave me once he reached France, did he? Clever he was. But I was cleverer than him.' I decided then to stay in his room some time longer and to go along with his ramblings in case I found out anything useful. And I did! Oh yes, I did!*

"'*Who are you cleverer than?' I asked. 'Him, my Captain, of course,' he replied. 'Do you mean Captain Benedict?' I asked again, 'Of course, whoever else? Thought he was going to France and leaving me, did he? Me? As well trained as any soldier could be? Me? Who did all his dirty work for him?' 'So what happened?' I asked, this time as quietly as I could, though my heart was pounding in my chest.*

"*I know he was drunk, Richard, but I believed his story. Though I'm sure he wasn't aware that he was sharing his ramblings with me, he told me this story. 'It was a rough sea and him, you know, the Captain, was spewing his guts over the side every few minutes. The other two were inside. 'Luke,' he rarely spoke my name, 'if and when we arrive in France, I have told you already that only two will go with me. Remember, you must return to the barracks when this boat turns round. You will tell everyone that we met a skirmish near Winchester and the three of us were killed. Then no one will be the wiser. In France no one will know who we are, what we have done and where we go. Then you will continue in the*

Church Army and join another troop and forget us. Do you understand?'
'Yes, I do.' The soldier stopped speaking and I thought he was going to sleep, so I prompted him further, 'Go on,' I murmured, hoping to encourage him to tell me more.

"After a short pause, he continued, 'Well, the sea was rough. Very rough. The Captain was not bold now as he leaned over the side of the boat letting his inside flow out. No, he was feeling very ill, but I didn't care about him. He may have been clever, but he was no sailor. There was no one around and it was dark. I am not a vicious man, but I was not going to be treated like that. I was wondering what I could do. I didn't need to do anything and I don't believe I could have. Anyway one big wave made the ship sway suddenly and over he went. I didn't tell anyone and went back inside to see to the horses. He was discovered missing in the morning.' The soldier then fell asleep.

"I left the room quietly. I am certain he was not aware at all that I had heard what he was rambling about. So you see, Richard, Benedict is dead, and dead by drowning, the same way as he killed Mary's three sisters and, indirectly, Mary herself."

The story which Helena recalled, you will have realised, was the very same as Oliver and I had heard from the soldier who later died of the knife wound. It appeared that Helena had had an assignation with the same soldier who had, some time later, spoken to us. I had to wonder if someone else, like Oliver, myself and Helena, had been watching and listening, at that time, for information about Benedict. My mind went back to the monk sitting in the inn, his strange walk and the death of the soldier. I felt more certain than before that the soldier had been killed by the monk rather than that he had killed himself with the knife.

Notwithstanding, it seemed that, at long last, we had the name of the Second in Command. He must have been Benedict Crecy and he was no more. But, there is one further piece of evidence which I now realise makes this fact definite.

§

Let me digress for a while. You will remember that Nell told me that Ann recognised the High Chief in Stocksmoor just before she was ducked. The only way she could have done so, we ascertained, was through the only part of him that he could not hide behind the uniform, his eyes.

As Helena spoke about Benedict Crecy, for a short while, my mind flittered to a scene in the past. I have a mind that forgets very little, though it may need encouragement to recall. Now, I was taken back in time to our brother Ben's wedding. As you will remember, he married Hannah Crecy. Benedict Crecy was her youngest brother. He had attended the wedding.

After the wedding, Ann and Emily were talking in angry tones about 'someone' and I asked them what the problem was and who was it that they were talking about in such voices. It was memorable as being very unusual for them. They were of lively but equable natures, and I rarely heard them speak ill of anyone. They preferred to ignore that person instead, as they did with Jonas. They were incensed because Hannah's brother, Benedict, even at the marriage of his sister, had made very suggestive comments to them and, that he would not leave them alone, even trying to drag one of them outdoors.

Finally, in order that he would leave them both in peace to enjoy meeting the wedding guests, Ann had spoken directly in his face, "Neither my sister nor I like arrogant young men, nor those who think themselves more handsome that they really are. You would serve yourself best by looking in a gutter. Yes," she paused for a moment, "on reflection, I have no doubt that you could be quite suited there and more able to find your likeness or someone to match your desires."

His face had gone a dark shade of red. "You should watch what you say. One day you will regret opening your mouth to speak like that to me."

Both agreed that they would not like to meet him in a dark alley and neither would trust him. They thought him objectionable and his eyes were the coldest blue, piercing eyes they had ever seen. I remember Ann saying, "If I were a man, I would not like to draw swords with that one as I am certain he would not play fair."

Now, I understood. Not only had Ann recognised Benedict by his eyes, but he had remembered her and her insult to him. Though Ann had suffered so much, he needed his revenge and, from hearing Helena's story, he acted accordingly. May God forgive me, but I couldn't help thinking that drowning had been far too easy for him. I believe that there is a God and a Heaven. But I also trust that there is, or, at least, will be, a Hell for the likes of him, a place where the pain he caused will be returned to him in full measure. I am not a vicious man. I believe in true justice, not revenge. I am certain in my mind, though I don't know how as I have no proof, that death is not the end of existence or a way to avoid retribution.

§

"Have you any idea at all whom the Number One in Command is?" I asked Helena.

"No, Benedict was not confident enough to let that out, and this man, Luke, didn't know."

"Will you come with me now to see Sir George and tell him what you know?"

"Goodness me, no! Not just now. No, Richard I do have some pride left. Give me time to clean myself up a bit."

"Here you are." I took some money from my bag. "Please go and buy a hot meal, a new dress and cloak, have a night's rest and I will meet you here on the morrow, about eleven o'clock in the morning. Fear not. Helena, you will henceforth be provided for."

"No, Richard, I thank you," she replied, with tears streaming down her face. She pushed my hand with the money away. "I shall manage. To have found just a few moments of kindness has meant such a lot and to be able to tell you all I know."

When I was reaching far into the wagon for more food for her to take with her, and at that moment when I was not watching, she must have dropped the emblem and its cord onto the floor of the wagon between two of the packets that she had seen me carry to the wagon. She knew that I would see it, but not until it was too late. When I turned round she was no longer sitting in the wagon, but standing on the road.

Just in front of her was a monk, of smallish stature, looking in the window of a shop that sold artefacts for the new cathedral. But where he had come from I do not know, other than to think he had passed by

while I was delving in the wagon. Maybe I had been so engrossed in what
Helena was saying that I had not heard anyone approach. I usually notice
what or who is around. It comes from long years of having to keep a safe
watch on myself and my belongings while journeying alone around the
country. I have rarely been surprised, as I felt at this time. I have to say
I was somewhat bemused, though not alarmed, but that very bemusement
ensured that the incident entered my memory. I thought, 'Monks walking
around York are commonplace. I must just have been preoccupied talking
to Helena not to notice him'.

"Goodbye, Richard."

"Helena, you have told me so much more. I am very grateful to you. Where
shall I meet you on the morrow to take you to see Uncle George?"

She didn't reply. The next moment she was on her way before I could say
anything or offer more assistance. Considering she was so ill, she was
walking very quickly up the road, having been revived by the food, but as
though she had a purpose. I called out to her, but she took no notice and
disappeared down a right turning, heading towards the river. I noticed
that the monk stopped looking in the window of the shop and quickly
followed Helena down the same road.

Though it was only a fleeting view of the monk, there was something
rather odd about the way he walked and it reminded me of something or
someone. At that moment, being immersed in my thoughts about what
Helena had told me, I did not think to bring the reason or person to my
mind. I just remember thinking that I had seen someone walk like that
before. As I have written previously, when people such as monks are
dressed from head to toe in their habits, then neither hair nor face can be
seen. It is only stature and movement or mannerisms that distinguish one
from the other to an observer.

§

Can I just interject again, for a moment, a few words of understanding?
In any profession or any kind of work certain skills are learned – some are
taught and others acquired. So, over the years, it has become one of my
habits, for want of a better word, to notice the way people walk. It is
quite on an unknown level, nor done with deliberate intent. Not at all and

the information is stored, whether I wish it or not. I know it comes from my years of studying the legs of horses. Horses can get a heat and inflammation in their sinews and the only way to know how to treat and what the animal needs of my potions, and ease through my hands, is to observe how the animal walks.

§ -

So, I dismissed the slight uneasiness that the monk had caused me to feel and thought I was just being rather fanciful. I unfastened my horse and started on my journey to see the friend's sick animal. As I turned my wagon right at the end of the road I heard and then saw a commotion on the bridge ahead and had no choice but to stop.

Climbing down off my wagon, I went to see what was happening. A man was pointing over the bridge parapet towards the river. The fast flowing water was carrying the woman away very quickly. Had she jumped into the water? No one knew as apparently no one had seen anything and I have sadly to say, that, though there was a commotion, no one appeared to care. A reflection, for you readers, of the times we live in. Her cloak floated over her body like a large protective shield. Only her head could be seen, face down in the water. The water was flowing too fast for any boat to be manned and so there could be no attempt to rescue her. Very soon she disappeared under the water.

I recognised the bag floating in the water close by. Had Helena found her final solution? Had that end been her purpose as she walked away, having fulfilled her mission by telling me what she knew? We shall never know. But, since then, I have wondered, had someone else decided that she presented a danger and should not be allowed to tell anything again? The monk was nowhere to be seen. Had he been following Helena? Had he been listening, silently and unbeknown to us, out of our sight by the side of my covered wagon? But, Helena was dead, the monk had gone and I had no idea who or where he was. There was nothing to be done. I was left with only conjecture.

§

I continued on my journey. At my friend's house, as I lifted out the medicaments, I found the silver eagle on its cord. Never could I sell it, I didn't wish to keep it and decided to put it in the casket that held the 'treasures' of my sisters and those artefacts that are part of the memory of Stocksmoor's darkest day. John had also perished at the hands of the Church Army. It was appropriate that he be remembered in this way. Yes, that is what I determined to do.

But first, I must tell Sir George what I knew. When I arrived home later that day, I sent a message to him in his room and took the emblem and the piece of paper with the information that allowed Benedict to get away before the trial. He listened attentively and made notes so that he could pass on the information, particularly about the boys, at the appropriate time to the right people. He had contact with and the trust of many people in high and influential places. Even after he retired, he would not let the reins completely leave his hands until he was taken to his maker.

Now, I know that my sisters were right in their observations and that their fears for their boys were justified. We had had no proof before, just my sisters' observations, which Sir George had used to the utmost advantage, but Helena's story told even more. The unprotected, in particular the orphaned, could still be in danger.

§

About four days after I had met Helena, I was sitting at my desk writing up my journal for the week. Sometimes I found time to write each day, but more often than not I would be too busy and then would have to recollect with a bit of effort. My only 'fault' in doing so, is that on occasion I omit the day and the date. This is only important if I do not find time to write for a week or two as I do keep the pages together. But, should you find, in this writing, any minor discrepancies in time, then please understand that the importance is in the happenings, all of which are the truth. There was the advantage however, that in this way I often found that something that had puzzled me became clear when I came to write it. This often applied to an animal I had treated and been unsure at the time what the complaint had been.

I suddenly remembered that Helena had distinctly told me that Benedict was 'Second in Command' but that he had also let out the information that the 'First in Command' used to dress for their processions in that house in Sandal. Who was he? And why could he not be in the parade in

Stocksmoor? I believe that you may be getting some conjectures for yourself, as I was, but I needed proof not imaginings. So, though my mind was forever reasoning, still the question remained. 'Who was behind it all?' Yes, I was having thoughts in my mind that I kept dismissing as far fetched, yet they would not disappear. But, I thought never to find this, the last truth, and decided I had better become resigned.

~ The missing pieces ~

Sometimes in life, being true to oneself and doing something 'extra' that is not in the order of your present normal life, but that you do out of the kindness of your heart, brings with it its own and unexpected rewards.

Little did I know when I set off, one bright autumnal morning in 1500, to visit York at the urgent request of a friend, that the last pieces of the 'jigsaw' of information about the deaths of my sisters would be given to me and which I can now, fortunately before I complete my task, write into this book.

I had never been able to find the name of the main person behind the atrocities. Secrecy was the key to the Church Army and till this day, I had drawn a blank, both at the trial and with subsequent searching. With regret, as I like to complete whatever I set out to accomplish, I had decided that it was time to let it all rest.

I stopped being away from home on long journeys. Rosamund was not as well as I would have liked or expected. I wanted to be at home to look after her, if and when necessary, along with Sarah, our daughter. Uncle George let us have one of his housemaids to assist, but we wanted to be with Rosamund as much as was possible. Her decline was gradual, long and slow. But, despite everything and my resolve to stop all my work, I could still never say 'no' to a request to see a sick horse. A friend had contacted me. He had a young foal which appeared not to want to take any food. The poor animal was becoming very weak. Would I see it?

So it happened that I was visiting the same local medicament store in York to collect what I thought I might need for the foal. As I no longer travelled far, I did not keep medicaments ready as I had found that they lost their restorative properties over a period of time.

I often mused that women who had the power to heal were called witches. No one seemed to consider that men could possibly do anything of this nature. So, it was always assumed that the 'power' was passed to them at birth by their mothers. However, I knew my step sisters had the same power as myself and had used it for children and died because of it. I had always used my ability for animals. But, my strongest connection with them was having the same father, not mother, though our mothers were sisters. So, I considered the 'power' could come from either men or women. I am nothing if not logical in the way I think and I had often thought it strange, rather than fortuitous, that the horses and dogs that belonged to my father all kept remarkably free from any ailment. I cannot remember him even once, in all his years, asking for any assistance. I now believe he 'kept them well', either deliberately using his skill or did so while being unaware of his ability. He certainly never spoke of such to me.

I left my horse and wagon, in my usual place and I walked along the cobbled streets to the store, to buy my purchases, when I saw a woman, with a shawl wrapped around her head, coming out from the doorway of a jeweller. She looked bemused and stood outside the door, as if not knowing quite where to go next. I, with some surprise, recognised her. It was our cousin, Hilda, the wife of Joseph Kraft from Stocksmoor. I had not seen her since before Ann, Emily and Catherine had died and, though I knew Joseph and she had moved away, quietly and without being observed, on the day of the ducking, no one had since had any idea where they had gone.

I quickened my pace and touched her arm. She jumped and turned.

"What ...? Oh, Richard, you gave me such a fright!" she exclaimed.

"Sorry Hilda, but what a great pleasure to see you. We never knew what had become of you. What are you doing in York?"

"I've just been in that jeweller's shop. Joseph has died and left this," she told me as she held up a box and a piece of parchment. She was obviously distressed.

"Hilda, let's walk on the path by the river and you can tell me."

She put the box and parchment in her bag and we turned. As we walked, she slowly explained and I pieced together some of her life in the past nearly four years.

She talked about her life in Stocksmoor. Then she asked what had happened to my sisters after they were released from the stocks.

"Don't you know?"

"Why, no, Richard, how can I? I have had no way of finding out, as I have been nowhere. We have stayed away from anyone. This is the first time I have ventured far from the village but I have had to do so out of necessity."

She asked me to tell her. I did not go into details, but simply explained that they had been ducked and had not survived. She was very upset. We sat quietly for a while on a seat.

"I cannot believe that Ann, Emily and Catherine died as they did, Richard. Why, when I helped them so much, was I not included by the Church Army? It really is very odd. Joseph only arrived home the night before the trial; it was already very late. I saw him unsaddle his horse, give it some water and oats and then he went straight to his work shed before he came indoors. I only saw him do so as I had been in the garden taking some cooler evening air as the day had been so hot and the house had not cooled down at all despite the windows being left ajar.

"He had come up the road and thus passed by where the soldiers were camped on the Mount, but he showed no real concern. I don't know why, but he went straight to his shed. It may seem strange my saying anything about that, but I remember it very clearly. He was a man of habit and he had never done that before. Usually he came straight indoors to greet me. I asked him, 'Are you going straight away on another commission without time for a few days respite? Surely not! Why, you are only just home and your coat is not hung up yet'.

"He had replied, 'No, my dear, I am just preparing a few things.' But he didn't say what or why and I didn't think to ask. Then he merely commented, 'I have seen that the Church Army have arrived since I was away.'

"I answered, 'Yes, indeed, and we are all wondering why they have chosen to stay in Stocksmoor. But, Joseph, you shouldn't be riding around at this hour. It is so late and cannot be safe. I didn't think you would be home this evening.' He replied, 'I walked the horse the last few miles, I needed the exercise after the long ride.'"

Hilda continued to tell me what had happened as I will now narrate.

Three days later, she learned that when Ann, Emily and Catherine were in the stocks, her husband had prepared for them both to leave their home. He had made her stay indoors, so she could not try to visit them on the stocks. When they were taken down the road, he told her not to even look out of the window in case the soldiers saw her. When the coast seemed clear, he took her out of the house, through the woodland which was just a short distance behind their house and away from the area. He had had the horses saddled and tethered in preparation for their departure and they were already hidden in the wood. Though a slight man of small stature, he was very strong and he easily carried their bags. Hilda followed. No one saw them as all others were at the ducking. As we know Thomas was unable to observe anything at all.

They wandered the countryside for many weeks, and, stayed in a different inn each night. During the day they travelled further away from Stocksmoor, until one afternoon they saw an empty farm cottage on edge of a village some miles north of York. Her husband enquired about this and later bought it. They had lived there ever since. He had carried on with his carving work, as usual, as though being in a different place had made no difference. He had travelled away as before, sometimes being away a few weeks at a time. But she had known or seen very few people except those in the nearby village from whom she had bought various victuals. Joseph had told her she must say nothing about themselves, where they came from or even their names as it was not safe to do so.

She had been overwhelmed with fear for a long time in case she should be found. She was very frightened lest she would suffer the same fate as her cousins in the stocks. She had not known that they had been ducked and had died. She only knew they had suffered on the stocks. But time had passed and she had realised that there was no one searching for her. They had had a little girl, but she too had died when only a few months old. She did not know why or how, except that she became covered in spots and had a high fever. Her husband had been away at the time. Sadly, she had been unable to get any assistance for her baby.

Then, about seven months ago, though it could be longer as she had lost sight of time passing, her husband had been returning home one evening, when it appears he was thrown from his horse, suffered a broken leg and a bad head injury and eventually died. He had been away from home for a week and a day. She had been expecting him to arrive home. But, as he came home when his work was complete, it was not something that could be arranged or for her to know in advance. However, when he didn't arrive home during the next week, for some reason she suddenly started to feel very alone and frightened. Visiting the inn in the village, she told the innkeeper her fears. He promised that he would ask men to look out for him.

Joseph was found on the moor about a mile from home after another three days by one of the local men, out hunting for rabbits. It was thought he may have suffered a great deal as the leg was in a very odd shape when he was found. He had cuts on both his legs, which they surmised must have been caused by bites from a wild animal, a wild boar or even a fox, but which they could not tell. There was a gash and bruise on his head. He was dead. His body was brought home and buried. Now she was left alone.

"I am so sorry to hear all this, Hilda."

"Everyone around here is sure that his horse must have reared so that he fell off. But, you know, Richard, he was a very good rider. He has ridden for years and never had an accident before, and some of his horses, as you have witnessed, could be quite wild. This one was my favourite, being of a gentle and calm nature. There was something very odd, Richard. For a start, when I washed his body I noticed that there were no teeth marks and that the cuts were quite straight and deep. I wondered if he had been in a fight, you know, and been attacked but escaped. His axe which he always carried with him was missing as was his whittling knife. He always carried that knife in its sheath on his belt round his waist. You may never have noticed, but he had had it made shaped to fit his fingers so that his hand never slipped while doing intricate carving."

∫

My mind suddenly returned to Stocksmoor and Jonas. Could it have been what I thought? But I didn't say anything to her.

(Later, when I returned home, I worked out the timing of Jonas's death according to what I had heard from Bernard. I reckoned, as well as I could, that it was just before Joseph was found on the moor.)

Then, I thought of Charles Trevore and what Robbie had told me about hearing someone, whom he identified as Joseph, talking in the Captain's tent the night before the trial at the Mount. That was the night that Joseph had returned home late. I was now wondering whether the same person who had killed Charles had also killed Jonas. Did he meet Charles on his way to warn my sisters? Charles would have told Joseph his fears, thinking he was a friend of my sisters, through his wife, and would have expected his help, but instead...

But I have no proof about Charles, other than Hilda's passing remark that Joseph had gone immediately to his work shed without entering the house and then had started packing things into two large panniers as soon as he had arrived home from one of his trips the night before the trial.

Was it Joseph's knife which had been found at Jonas's house after his death? Was it Joseph's axe in his head?

In my mind, I could not still those thoughts...

∫

Hilda continued with her story.

"At first, I was so upset that I couldn't open his drawers or sort through any of Joseph's personal belongings. I had no money but, even after I had sold my few possessions of any worth, that money soon ran out. I had no choice but to search for any funds. Never had I had to wonder or worry about money.

"Firstly I emptied his large panniers that came back with his horse.

Believe me when I say, Richard, that never once in our married life have I had cause to look at what he put in those panniers. They always stayed in his workshop, which I rarely entered. When he had finished a carving he would always bring it into the house to show me. He would bring his dirty clothes for me to wash and I never thought any more about them.

"I couldn't believe my eyes when, at the bottom of one pannier, folded very carefully as was his way with everything he possessed, was a monk's habit. I still can't make any sense from it, even though he has been dead these past many months. He was always a devout religious man, as everyone who knew him was aware, but I never knew he was a monk. Never! He was legally married to me! I couldn't believe my eyes. He took his religion to the point where he could not accept Catherine's help for my children. I loved him but God knows I have never, nor yet will ever, forgive him for that. But, Richard, why would Joseph have had a monk's habit in his pannier?"

"I don't know." I was being honest with her, though my thoughts started working again. And I began to wonder if I would eventually know the answer to that last question, instead of just having possibilities that could or could not be valid.

"I shook the habit to open it out," she continued, "and even then I couldn't believe it belonged to Joseph as it seemed too long. But, I had to accept it was in his pannier. But a small leather purse fell out of the folds." She fumbled in her bag and lifted out a fine, small leather bag with a draw string.

"Here, Richard," she offered me the leather bag. I opened the draw string and took out a gold pendant with an eagle. Two rubies were, as if, the eagle's eyes. The pendant was threaded on a thin leather strap tied in a knot. I recognised a gold 'emblem of the Order of Sorro'. I remained silent. Hilda carried on talking about the habit, but my surmising about Joseph was getting more strength. I was sure that I was correct in my thinking.

"Joseph never wore anything fancy nor wished me to do so either. He never saw the two necklaces that my mother gave to me and I never wore them if he was at home. He was convinced that such frippery was 'the way of the devil'. He never even had decorated or bejewelled buttons or embroidered material for his jackets. So, I couldn't believe that this gold pendant could be his. But it was in his pannier. I swear to that.

"Anyway, I just lit a fire, then cut the habit into pieces and burned them. It may have been able to be made into a warm coat for a future winter, being as I have no funds to buy any other, but I decided I didn't like it in my home. I don't know why. I just hated to see it.

"But, there was something else very strange. When they found Joseph's body, they brought him home while the grave was being dug in the burial ground of the village. The innkeeper decided that I would most likely want to see Joseph, despite his awful condition. He was right, I did, just to say goodbye. It was dreadful, so dreadful." Hilda wept. After a short pause, she could carry on with her story. "But Richard, Joseph was wearing boots such as I had never seen before with heels that were higher than usual. Indeed, it was most strange. His other boots, the ones that I knew he wore, were nowhere to be found. Now, why would he have boots that I have never seen before? And, where were his other pair, the pair he left home in?" She stopped speaking and looked puzzled.

"Carry on, Hilda. Tell me the rest."

"It was painful to do so, but, after a week or so, I sorted his belongings drawer by drawer. Eventually I decided I must tackle his private papers and such like, which I never, normally, would see. He wasn't coming back and so I had no other path to take. I knew where he hung the key for the oak chest, in which he kept his account books and papers. I opened the chest and took them all out and fully expected to see money in the chest. There was none. In fact, the chest was all but empty. I could easily have missed what I am going to show you. I found the chest had a false bottom and I only noticed that when I saw a piece of silk black material, at the side. I pulled it and the bottom started to come away, it was obviously kept like that for this purpose. This may also seem odd, Richard, but I swear I had never seen inside the chest before. I just never intruded into Joseph's possessions. Inside the base, wrapped in black cloth I found this box and this piece of parchment. See what is inside."

She opened the box. Just under the lid and concealing what was underneath was a further parchment.

"Read it Richard, please," she asked, handing me the inner parchment.

I opened it and read,

> "This is the cross of the High Chief of the Order of Sorro. By my decree it must now pass to my successor. The lady who brings this to you is my lawful wife. Provide her with sufficient funds for twenty years of comfortable living. This is an order. Let no harm befall her.
>
> Signed on March 13th, 1497, by the High Chief of Sorro.
>
> Josef, Marquis de Vere"

(I could but recollect that this was written and signed just a few months before my sisters were killed. It seemed like a letter of preparation. The letter had been written by one hand and signed by another.)

"Josef, Marquis de Vere? What on earth are you reading, Richard?" She took the parchment from my hand as if to verify it was the same as she had given me, though I have no slight of hand.

"That is what it says, Hilda. I swear to that. But, I thought his name was Joseph Kraft."

"Of course it was. I have always been Hilda Kraft since we married. But this did come out of Joseph's drawer. Richard, I promise you that I am telling you the truth," she insisted.

"I believe you, Hilda," I reassured her.

I then took away the soft hide, covering whatever was inside the box, and gasped. I couldn't hide my amazement at what was enclosed in this simple box. There, lying in blue silk was a gold chain and a large pendant. The pendant, of solid gold, was in the shape of an eagle with closed wings holding a large diamond in its clawed feet. It was as if fixed to a cross, and the wings were covered with embedded rubies. It was beautiful, yet *wholly grotesque at the same time, and immensely valuable. As you will know, I had learned a lot about the Church Army and I knew the members had allegiance to the 'Order of Sorro' whose emblem was an eagle on a cross. The higher up the chain of command, the more ornate and valuable was the symbol. This was absolutely priceless in more ways that one.*

"My God!" I exclaimed aloud. I was so shocked at the opulence before me that I was unable to hide my feelings.

My thoughts again became very fast in my head. So, he was French. Joseph de Vere was a Frenchman. I was in no doubt at all now about the man in charge of the Church Army. Robbie was correct. It had been Joseph's voice he had heard. Joseph had killed Charles Trevore. At the same time I remembered what Helena had been told by Benedict, 'The High Chief dresses in his vestments, here, in this house.'

My sisters had been puzzled when they saw Joseph come out of that house, of low repute in Sandal when they saw Helena and her bag. That was when Hilda thought he was away. He had been away, yes, as chief of the 'Riders of Death'. He was often away. His carving work had been a very good excuse for such occasions and forays to different parts of the country organising and witnessing the dreadful deeds. Presumably he had disrobed in that house before leaving to go home.

My God! Another thought came rushing into my head. That was why Benedict had to ride through Stocksmoor in the most ornate vestments as if he was the High Chief. On that day he had to take Joseph's place, while he took Hilda away at the time. Hilda had not been taken to the trial nor put in the stocks, even though she helped my sisters and worked alongside them. Now I understood why. It was Joseph who had stopped that from happening. My sisters had spent much time with Hilda, talking about herbs but also sharing their ideas and thoughts. That was how Joseph knew about their knowledge and concerns for the boys who went missing. Hilda's innocent chat with her husband had given him that knowledge. I was so stunned by my thoughts that I could not speak and had just stopped in my footsteps. I was standing, looking in such a way that Hilda asked,

"What is it? Richard. Why do you look like that?"

"I think it best you do not know. Let me see what the other parchment says."

Again, I read out aloud that which was written,

> "My desirest Hilda. This you will find when I have met my demise. But, know this, though terrible troubles have been with us, yet I have loved you. Belief me. Whatever happens PLEASE DO NOT open this box. Take it to the Archbishop in York. He will give you gold for your needs and comfort, enouf for the rest of your life.
>
> For ever, Joseph."

I noticed the errors in the spelling of certain words, but made no comment. As Hilda couldn't read, those mistakes mattered not.

"Did Joseph not know that you couldn't read?"

"Well, no. How could he? We have no books and it wasn't ever something I thought about until now."

"Well, then, you know now what to do with the box. He left you this message."

"No, Richard. I want to know what it is and why it has caused the jeweller and you to behave in this strange way. And, more than anything, where would Joseph find such pendants and why haven't I seen them before in all the years we were married?"

"I would rather not say."

"Richard, I trust you as Ann, Emily and Catherine trusted you. Please tell me. I thought to sell them for funds. I have now insufficient for me to continue to live in the cottage. I do not know what I shall do otherwise. I always thought Joseph had plenty of money as he provided, without question, everything we needed and more. But now, I have searched the cottage and find there is nothing there to account for the means we seemed to have. I have lifted floorboards, looked in the rafters, and searched everywhere except there is one cupboard under the stairs that I cannot open, though I have truly tried. But I think that Joseph put only boots in there. It is one of those places I had never bothered to look in. So, when I saw this I thought I was secure. But, I took it to the jeweller and he went pale and snapped at me, saying, 'Take that out of here. I will not touch it.' He was most rude. Why? I don't understand. That is where I had been and why I was bemused when you saw me."

"Hilda, it is best you do not know."

"Very well then, I shall have to find someone who can and will tell me. I shall go to the Archbishop and find out the truth." She made as if to walk away from me.

I decided I had no choice. If she went that route I doubted she would be alive in a few days time, whatever Joseph had written. He was dead and his commands would now count for nothing. Only a deluded man would think that what he demanded in such a letter would have any power after his demise. We had plenty of evidence that those who were suspected of having any real knowledge of the Church Army were doomed. Maybe it was time she should know who her husband was.

"Hilda, I have found out that all members of the 'Order of Sorro' are in the Church Army. The High Chief of that Order is the High Chief of the Church Army. That pendant belongs to the one who holds the very highest office of all, and it belonged to Joseph."

Hilda went ashen and her legs started to fold under her so that I had to support her. When she had recovered enough I told her what I had found out about her husband.

"No! No, this cannot be." She spoke no more just then, but started to weep. I sat with her and put my arm round her shoulder.

"Hilda, I have told you what I know to be the truth. You can believe me or not."

After a while, she recovered enough to say, "Richard, you know that your father had left the village early on the morning of the trial. Well, I remember him talking to Joseph about two weeks before. Again, it is quite clear in my mind as it was unusual. Your father was passing the garden and both Joseph and I were tending the plants. Your father stopped by the wall and spoke to us. Joseph had asked your father if he had any pieces of a particular sort of very hard wood as he needed some for two orders of his sculpting. I remember your father saying no, he hadn't, but he was going to a place somewhere beyond Wakefield shortly and he would bring two pieces back for Joseph, if he told him just what he wanted. He knew someone who obtained that sort of wood from another country.

"I can remember Joseph asking your father in some detail when he might be going and, as if just interested, he asked him what sort of time he needed to leave home if he wanted to go there and back in one day. You see Joseph always stays away if he travels and never makes the return journey the same day, so it seemed a normal question to ask. But now I realise that he was collecting information for the soldiers to arrange for your sisters to be killed and to make sure that your father would be out of the village at that time. Oh, Richard, what shall I do? I cannot contain this in my mind. I loved an evil man, a man who organised the murder of my best friends and many more. Ann and Emily meant more to me than my own sister. I thought Joseph was god-fearing and good. I should have known when he wouldn't let Catherine help to save our baby boys. I should have known."

She was becoming distraught.

"How didn't I know, Richard? I should have known."

When she had settled, after a while, I spoke the only words I could think to say; words that were not of comfort, but of practicality. You see, though I had had many thoughts on this matter, I was still stunned with this final enlightenment. Hilda was and always had been a good and kind woman. She had not deserved this. Though we did not particularly like Joseph, we did not know that we had all, my sisters and my father included, been fooled by this man. Yes, he was truly evil.

"You have choice, Hilda as to what you can do. Only you, the jeweller and I know of this pendant. Take it to the cathedral, ask to see the Archbishop as Joseph suggested and he will give you the funds. Or make a different decision using your own heart and mind. One word of advice, don't show this to anyone but the Archbishop, himself as that would not *be safe. But, take care. Joseph is not here to protect you and you must now realise that the Church is not benign as you imagine."*

They had now reached a bridge under which the river flowed strong and deep. Hilda leaned against the railings.

"Richard, I cannot live on blood money."

First she took the gold pendant from the leather purse and then she lifted the gold and bejewelled pendant out of the box and with a wide sweep of her arm she threw them both as far as she could and watched as her future life's funds sank out of trace. She then threw the purse into the water.

Then she tore the letter from her husband, and threw the small pieces into the river.

"Richard, please would you take this parchment. I don't know why I want you to have it, but I do." She handed me the parchment addressed to the Archbishop and signed Josef, Marquis de Vere. She put the empty box into her bag.

"Of course, if that is what you want, I will take it and show it to Uncle George. Hilda, what have you now left for your future needs?"

"I have nothing. I must go home. I need time to think." She seemed calmer and resigned. Then she added, "And I have many tears to shed, Richard, and I prefer to be alone for that."

"Firstly, tell me the directions to your village and cottage. Give me just two weeks and I can travel that way to check how you are and tell you what has been arranged for you. Do not worry. I promise you that I will find funds and a home for you. Uncle George will help you as he has assisted all the rest of us. Be assured of that. Believe me, whatever or whoever Joseph was, you are innocent. We were all fooled by him, not just you."

She told me where she lived.

I reached into my bag and took out ample money for her to buy food for the next two weeks. She then put her arms round me.

"Thank you, Richard. You are always so kind. I wish there were more good men like you. Are you sure Uncle George will welcome me as he did your family and the children, and Nell?"

"I am certain, Hilda. Uncle George will be mortified that you have been so distressed and alone. There is plenty of need for another person who loves the children. Little Marion is loved by all, but has no one special, you know, just for herself. Maybe she can be in your special care?"

"Oh Richard, I would so love to look after her and be part of the family again, as I used to be in Stocksmoor. My happiest time was with your sisters."

"Would you come back with me now, instead of waiting until I and someone else can return to help you?

"No, Richard," she declined, quietly. I have withstood so much grief, loneliness and fear that another two weeks will be as nothing when compared to that. I shall look forward to a different time. I will sort out the house and be ready."

"Farewell for now."

Before I could say anything more she had disappeared.

§

Two weeks later, true to my word, I made a journey northward to the village Hilda had mentioned. I had told Uncle George. He had offered a small cottage in the next village for Hilda to live in, rent free, and she could help our household in many ways to keep her occupied. He thought that Marion would be very happy to have 'someone just for her' and so all was arranged. Fortunately, nothing was mentioned to Marion, and you will understand why I say 'fortunately' when you read further. I was on my way to tell Hilda the good news and to collect her. Her belongings would require further arrangements but it was necessary to know how much there was to collect.

I had never passed this way before. It was a pretty, but bleak, part of the moorland but the village was off the main road and set in a sheltered valley. I followed her directions and found the cottage, dismounted from my horse and knocked at the door. You can always tell when a place is empty of life and this was the case now. I had a premonition that something was not as it should be. I went round the cottage looking into the small windows but saw nothing, and then to the small garden at the *back, filled on one side with many different herbs. No one was there. I called, "Hilda! Hilda!" at each window and at the doors, both front and back. After no reply at all, I retraced my steps back to the main part of the village and went to the inn.*

"I've just been to the cottage down that lane to see Hilda, but she is not there. Do you know where she is?"

"Aye, she's buried in that burial field outside the village, with her husband. Why do you want to know? Who are you?"

I sat down, dismayed beyond immediate words.

"Dead? When and how?"

The innkeeper didn't answer but came to sit at the table nearby. After a while I told him, "I have always known Hilda, since both she and I were young. She was my cousin."

"Well, it appears she had been walking on the moors to where her husband was found. Did you hear about him?" asked the innkeeper.

"Oh yes, I know about that dreadful event. Hilda told me herself."

"Well, it seems that she was revisiting that place, as her body was discovered, face down, in a stream only a few yards from where his body was also found. It's a week ago now. It seems that she meant to do it, you know, as a dam with stones had been built to make the water deeper. There was no sign of any struggle, but oddly an empty box lined with blue silk was in her hand. We think she may have slipped and fallen along her journey as she had a bump on the back of her head which had been bleeding."

"No! Oh, I can't believe it. Poor Hilda!" I felt a great pity for my cousin. "Please, tell me in which plot she is buried so that I may go and pay my respects. I had hoped to take her back with me to where my Uncle, Sir George Shaw, Lord Lieutenant of the County had found a cottage for her. Oh dear. Oh dear, poor Hilda." These were the words he heard me speak, but the thoughts in my head were saying, 'Again I am too late'.

The innkeeper gave me directions, and then asked, kindly, "Before you go to the grave, can we provide you with some victuals? There is nowhere else around here where you can buy either food or drink."

"Why, yes, that would be very welcome."

"Tell me, who owns the house now? Do you know?" asked the innkeeper, as he put the bread and cheese on the table.

"Yes, I know. But none of the family have any need of it and, I can assure you, will never want it. In fact, they have no knowledge of it. Hilda and her husband disappeared from our view, for a while, when they came to this area. It's a very long story. I, sadly, only met her again, just by accident, two weeks ago. Hilda was from a wealthy family despite her appearance while living here. Have you a family in the village that could use it?"

"Yes. That was the very reason I asked the question. We do not know what we can do to acquire the house for a family in the village. We are honest here and could not take or use it without permission. I am sorry to ask you when you are in distress but times are hard."

"I shall visit the grave and then go to the cottage and, if one of the men in the village will assist me to break in the door, I will clear anything that is personal. Then your village can have this cottage as a gift for your needy family. I will get Sir George to write the necessary legal papers and I will ride here again to deliver them in a week or two."

∫

Having eaten the repast, I went back to Hilda's cottage and picked some flowers and herbs. I took them back to the grave yard and put them on the mound of earth. I kneeled and bowed my head.

"God, please let her find rest for her soul. She was innocent of any knowledge of the real man who was Joseph and she loved my sisters. May she be reunited in spirit with them and those she loved," I prayed silently. "It will be without Joseph, that's for sure," I murmured, without previous thought. Not knowing the mind of God or what governs the hereafter I wondered if she would have to choose. But then I thought, no, by her action, she has already chosen.

I knew that she had felt a sense of betrayal and shame at having been her husband's wife. She had, in all probability and in all innocence, provided Joseph with information for the Church Army against Ann, Emily and

Catherine as she had chatted of an evening about their activities together during the day. They would have discussed their fears about the boys who disappeared. But you will remember that my sisters had not made any secret of their views in the village or about what they did, so that information was easily obtained by Joseph from any source.

But, had finding out about Joseph been sufficient cause for her to end her life? That was a puzzle I determined I would speak of to Uncle George. I had known Hilda most of my life and I knew the grief she had had to endure. She had lost three children and her best friends. She had been moved away from her home and anyone she knew other than her husband. She had survived for several months without her husband in an area where she had nobody close to her, or in whom she could confide. She was resilient. She wasn't someone who one would have ever thought would take her own life. But, it seemed that she had done so.

"It seems in the end he also killed her," I mused to myself.

"It certainly appears to have been connected," I heard in the silence. I tell you, dear readers, that I heard those words so clearly in my ears that I turned round to see who was by me. But, I was alone. You may think that it was an afterthought of my own making, but in all truth it wasn't, though where the words came from, I cannot tell.

I spoke aloud, "Joseph died, Captain Benedict drowned, yet we did do nothing to bring them to justice."

Then the words, 'Justice is mine, saith the Lord,' came into my ear. Had I heard that too or were those my thoughts? I decided it was high time to leave this place to the departed.

§

I will just tell you further some information, as to me it shows that inside an evil and cruel but powerful person can be a truly pathetic individual. These people are not the strongest members of mankind that they are given credence for, but, to my mind they are rather the weakest of the weak. They obtain glory and status from creating fear and inflicting pain and suffering on those unable to protect themselves. Maybe this is true for all of that nature, I do not know. However, what I found out about Josef de Vere, puts him truly as one of those. I can only hope that the devil has taken another 'of his own' into hell. And, moreover, this information gives me the answers to my remaining unsolved questions, as you will find as you read further.

§

I returned to Hilda's cottage with one of the innkeeper's men, the strongest. He it was who wielded the barrels of ale at the inn and the bales of hay for the travellers' horses as though of little weight. He had no difficulty in opening the heavy wooden door of Hilda's cottage.

I went inside and found that the place had been ransacked and was now virtually empty of furnishings of any kind. All the furniture, which I assumed Hilda and Joseph would have had in this cottage, had gone. What had she done with it? There was nothing left of Hilda's belongings or those of her husband. There was evidence in the hearth that fires had been burned – of paper and of cloth. I went round the rooms. All were bare. All the cupboards fitting the alcoves and the only two chests of drawers remaining in the house were empty. The larder had no food and even the plates and dishes had been smashed and left where they had been dropped.

It appeared that Hilda had left nothing.

I saw the cupboard under the stairwell and could see that Hilda had been unable to open it. I asked the innkeeper's man to break into that cupboard for me. He easily kicked the door in, then went into the scullery while I looked into the cupboard.

What I saw caused me some surprise.

Lined up on the floor were four pairs of riding boots, made in leather and of a quality that most men could never afford. But something was different. Because of the skill in the making of the boots, it took me a few minutes to realise that the soles were thicker than was customary and the heels were heightened on the outside by about a large thumb's width. There was a row of buttons along the side of one of the boots, which I undid and put my hand inside the boot. I found that the inside of the heel was also raised by a wedge of soft padded leather. On a cursory glance it looked like part of the boot, but I could lift it out. I then noticed several pairs of these wedges in a small pile on the floor. Put together, the heel heightening and wedge would make the wearer of the boot seem *taller by a good two large thumbs' widths. How vain was this man? How cruel and how vain, yes, and how truly pathetic!*

I called the village man, "Come and see. Here are four pairs of riding boots. Take them for someone in the village who could use them."

He looked at the boots and then looked at me. After a minute or two, as though thinking what to say, he replied, "Nay, Sir. Those are not for us. None in the village would wear such as those. Our nature is not like that."

I nearly asked, 'What do you mean?' But I think I knew and so I kept quiet. In the event, the boots of good, undamaged leather but with dubious meaning, sufficient that an honest village man preferred that they were burned rather than wear them, were put out in the garden. He agreed to burn them later that day in my absence. I was not staying any longer than necessary in this village or this cottage. I had done my duty to Hilda and there was no need for delay in going home.

As I rode back home, into my mind flashed two pictures. The first was of the monk who walked past in York, just before Helena died in the river. The other, the monk who walked off after the soldier died in the street, killed by a knife wound. 'It was the walk,' I thought to myself. It was the same in both monks. Then I remembered that Oliver had observed, 'No one wearing the usual heavy boots of a monk could walk like that'. The effect of the higher heels had caused the slight oddness of the walk. Under the monk's habit the boots could not be seen. But, now I knew that both Helena and the soldier had been killed by the same man dressed as a monk, Joseph Kraft or rather, Josef de Vere. Then, thinking how the villager had reacted to the boots, another thought crept into my mind.

'Had there been more to the relationship between Jonas and Joseph than religion?'

Now was the time when I remembered the trial at the time when Jonas was giving evidence. In my memory I saw the Archbishop's nod and the monk with the odd walk.

We know now that Joseph was the monk with the odd walk, due to his high heeled boots and that Joseph and Jonas had a close relationship – based on religion or not, I will not conjecture. However, it beggars belief that Jonas had to be stripped naked, as Bernard related was the case, just to be killed, but, that he was another of Joseph's victims I now had no doubt whatsoever. But, I wish to think no further on any activities they may have shared.

However, the responsibility for obtaining the truth about the abduction of the boys was firmly put on the Archbishop by Uncle George at the trial. Therefore, only the Archbishop knew about the inner workings in sifting out those who abducted and abused the young boys. It is my belief that the Archbishop gave a signal to Joseph, who he knew was at the trial and which monk he was, to indicate that Jonas must be 'got rid of' in case he shared too much information about the abduction or even the treatment of the boys. In other words, Jonas knew too much to be allowed to live with that knowledge. My sisters were killed for far less knowledge than Jonas.

It was without doubt Joseph's axe that was found in Jonas's head and Joseph's handle-shaped knife that was found in his garden. They had been the weapons used to kill Jonas. Hilda had noticed that they were missing.

To me, these facts implicate the highest in the Church in the practice of the abductions and abuse and that Joseph, as High Chief of the Church Army was working together with the Archbishop.

Now comes the question. Was Joseph himself killed? Had he met someone to tell of his success in taking Jonas out of the picture? Did he simply have an accident after being weakened by the loss of blood or maybe his animal was spooked by something? Maybe we shall never know, but something happened later that I shall recount which indicates that he was killed.

§

I had one more question in my mind. Was Hilda also killed?

My opinion was that Hilda had had many reasons for total despair during her life, and that this was not the worst of them. In fact, Joseph's death, whoever he had been, could have been the gateway to a new life, a life where love abounded and where she would have had freedom again. She would have been welcomed into our family life again.

I had discussed these thoughts with Uncle George and he was in total agreement with me, but we had no definite reason to suspect foulness in her death. That is, until I returned with the legal documents for the transfer of Hilda's house to the village in which she had lived.

I was sitting with the innkeeper and a few other men from the village. I took the documents out of my bag and was just going to explain what Uncle George had written, when one of the men spoke,

"I don't think she killed herself, I think it was murder."

"Nay, Amos, why on earth would you say that?" asked the innkeeper.

"Well, I have been thinking about that monk who I saw the day before she died."

"Which monk? You've never mentioned anything about a monk before," continued the innkeeper.

"No, I have been pondering. Let me tell you. I was by the gate of one of the fields taking tangles of hawthorn from my horse's mane. I feared they could possibly cause some damage. This monk came alongside me, creepy it was I tell you! I hadn't heard him and he didn't half make me jump. There he was, suddenly beside me, his face hidden in his hood and a staff in his hand. 'Do you know where the widow of the man, who was found dead about seven or eight months ago, lives?' he asked me. 'Yes, but why do you want to know?' I asked him. 'I am a monk and we give comfort,' says he, but I was sceptical about him giving comfort, I have to say. But he persisted and insisted that he had been sent to help her in this time of great sorrow.

"What could I do? Just because I don't personally believe all their preaching, I couldn't deny someone the right to have help. So I told him. He must have stayed around, as the next day I saw him again, but he didn't see me. I was taking hay to the horses. He was holding Hilda's arm and they both walked towards where we found her – away from where I was. I just thought he was helping her as she was dragging her feet as though finding it hard to walk.

"But, now I think that for some reason he took her out onto the moors to near where her husband died, then he hit her on the back of the head,

causing that bump and the blood, built the dam himself and drowned her, making it look as if she killed herself."

"But, why would a monk kill her and what makes you certain?" I asked.

"Well, when her husband died, we buried him, didn't we? A few of us here, in the village did it. We didn't call any monk or church man to do it. Do you not agree?" he asked the innkeeper.

"Aye, you're right there. His body was getting into a bad shape fairly quickly and we wanted it buried as soon as possible," replied the innkeeper.

"Now, tell me, when do any of us talk to monks or anyone? None of us told a soul about him. His wife went nowhere, except when she went into York that day a few weeks ago, when I gave her a lift in my cart. How did that monk know that any man had been found dead – unless he, or someone he knew, had done it? And, what is more, he knew when it was and, as he went onto the moor, he knew where to take her to.

"I think he was looking for something. Do you remember that box lined with silk. Now, that was a box to contain a cross-shaped valuable wasn't it? Do you remember? Well, why would anyone hold an empty box when they were killing themselves? It doesn't make any sense. But, if the monk was looking for whatever was in that box, and didn't find it, it makes every sense.

"Another thing. There was a cart came that same day, about an hour after they had gone out together. No questions asked of anyone, but I saw it arrive. It was loaded up with her furniture and then it left. This was in broad daylight. Whoever sent it must have known that Hilda was going to be dead and that no one would bother about a cart removing her belongings."

I sat listening, and Hilda's death as murder made sense. With Joseph dead, then his cross of high office had to be found. It was priceless. I knew. I had seen it. I wondered if the jeweller had been to the Archbishop and told him of Hilda's foray to his shop to try to sell it. That we shall never know. But, she would not have told the jeweller the details of her husband's death. No, they were known by some other means, by direct involvement.

"So we now know why the place was so empty when we went to sort it out and found nothing," I confided to the men sitting around. "I was truly surprised. If Hilda had been going to kill herself, she would never have even thought to remove furniture. There would have been no reason to do that heavy task. My cousin Hilda was going to leave and live amongst her family again and I would never have expected her to take her own life. Never! We shall never know for sure but I have to say that I agree with you. No one can recognise one monk from another, hiding their faces as they do. Thank you for your concern and any help you gave to her while she was living here. Here are the keys to the cottage, and the legal documents. I hope that some family can make good use of the cottage."

I stood up and shook those present by the hand.

"Good day to you all and I wish you all good health." Then I left the inn. I went home, thinking that the events of life can be very different from what we expect.

∫

Uncle George listened intently to what I told him on my return. He sat quietly, eyes shut for several minutes after I had finished relating the facts.

He then stood up and went to his desk and took out two pieces of parchment. He brought them to me. First was the piece that Helena had retrieved from Benedict's room and the second was the letter that Hilda had asked me to keep and which I had given to Uncle George on my return to the manor.

"Richard, I gave Robbie these two pieces of parchment and he is of a certainty that both the words on the note and the letter are on the same kind of parchment. He also believes them to be written by the same hand, but not the signature on the letter. I sent Robbie to the Cathedral in his monks outfit and wearing a pendant to be safe. He says the parchment matches the parchment used in the Cathedral. He had a certain name for it, but I cannot recall. However, it has something to do with the weave, which is quite different and special. Richard, have you by any chance kept the bit of parchment which you rescued from the fire?"

"Surely, Uncle, I will fetch it for you directly, though it is charred."

"And, on the way, can you ask Robbie to come here?"

Ten minutes later, Uncle George, Robbie and myself were sitting together with three pieces of parchment on the table in front of us.

"Now Robbie, tell us what you think," asked Uncle George.

Robbie studied the parchments near to the window.

"I still believe that these two are of the same weave. Yes, of that I am sure. I would say that the charred parchment is also the same. There is not much to go by and it is damaged. I am still of the opinion as before, that the writing of the words of the letter, apart from the signature, matches, the writing on the note. And I believe it also matches the word on the charred paper. People have a distinctive way of writing letters, just the odd curve or where they cross the 't's and such like. The words may look similar to the untrained eye, but my father's particular and peculiar interest was writing styles. He studied every bit of writing possible and taught me all that too. In other words, the three parchments are the same, and the writing is by the same hand, other than the signature. That is my considered opinion."

"Your father was a remarkable man, Robbie. I would have been much honoured to meet him. Thank you. Once again your expertise is truly valued."

Robbie left the room and we sat together, deep in thought.

"Richard, we know that Josef de Vere was in Stocksmoor when Geoffrey went to York to collect the pardon for your sisters so he could not have written the pardon. No, the Archbishop wrote and signed that pardon, and we know that Geoffrey's horse was tampered with or else Geoffrey would have been actually helped to return in time. He wasn't meant to do so, despite the pardon. Geoffrey can bear witness to all of that.

"As to the note. It is my view that the Archbishop sent the note to Benedict or even took it to his door himself, dressed as a monk. He was the only person connected to the Church and the cathedral, where the parchment came from, to know about the trial. I know, as it was me who told him.

"Richard, these facts point to the Archbishop being responsible and behind everything to do with the abduction of the boys and, of course, directly involved in your sisters' deaths. I can come up with no other explanation. Let's think this through.

"Now, with Benedict out of the way, he couldn't risk Jonas or Joseph telling what they knew in any trial. Somehow, I believe he knew Jonas well, and did not trust him to keep quiet. How could that be?

"Uncle, I think you are right and that Jonas had a bigger part in the abductions of the boys at Stocksmoor than we have previously thought."

"Why do you say that?" asked Uncle George.

"As you have been talking, I have remembered a time when I was travelling – before I married Rosamund. I would be about twenty five or twenty six. By that time Jonas would be somewhere in the region of nearing his fortieth year or maybe a year or two either side of forty.

"I was visiting York and searching for medicaments. I was in one shop when I heard two men talking as they sauntered slowly past. I recognised the obsequious voice of Jonas. I knew that voice well and hated it. Being curious, I excused myself from the shop keeper and left, saying I would return. I wondered what Jonas was doing in York. But, though I heard his voice, and in that there was no mistake, there was no monk around. Jonas wore his monk's habit in Stocksmoor, always. So, I followed the two men who went into a house very near to the Cathedral.

"When I returned to the shop I asked the shopkeeper did he know anything about the house up the road where Jonas had entered. I took him to the door and showed him which I meant. His tone altered as he answered my question. 'I know the house but have no wish to know the people who enter into it or what they do. Decent people round here would tell you the same. Now, Sir, what can I get you?'

"We often wondered where Jonas went when he was away from Stocksmoor for a week or more, and, as he had no horse, how he travelled to wherever he went. But, he was not 'as a monk' when I saw him. I never trusted that man. If he was involved more than we think, then that would explain why he had to be killed."

"Coming back to the Archbishop. Let's go over the facts again. He would know from the Captain at Sandal, who had been told by the only one of Benedict's three soldiers to return, that Captain Benedict had perished. So he was out of the way. Then, during the trial, he arranged with Joseph to kill Jonas. That was two out of the way. Then, did he arrange with one of his colleagues to kill Joseph? You see, he didn't know whether or not I, with a few colleagues might ask to be in the court when he investigated the boys' abduction and abuse. I would have expected no less than that the High Chief should be called to answer questioning. I had left that possibility open in my correspondence with him. That being the case, he had to be rid of the only three who could connect him to the abductions, to keep himself safe. That makes me feel that if he couldn't trust his High Chief of the Church Army, then he wouldn't trust anyone else – only himself.

"And, only by being aware of the death of Joseph could he know to find Hilda and achieve the return of the High Chief's pendant. He would know that Joseph had signed that letter to Hilda about its return on his demise as it was written, I would think actually at the Cathedral, by him for Joseph to sign, and on his own parchment. In fact, we now know that Joseph was French, so even more likely that the Archbishop wrote the letter and Joseph just signed it. Joseph may have been able to speak English perfectly, but may not have been able to write it with the same correctness."

"Uncle, I have just remembered the other letter that Joseph wrote to Hilda. It had been written in writing that matched his signature, and so I would think, quite rightly, that it was his own handwriting. And, yes, I remember it seemed rather strange and that some words were spelled wrongly. That would now make sense."

"At all events," continued Uncle George, "when the pendant didn't arrive he took steps to regain it. It could be that the jeweller told the Archbishop that a woman had been into his shop with the pendant, but, that being so or not, in any event, he would think that Hilda still possessed it. But Hilda beat him in the end. Never would they expect their most valuable jewel to be lying somewhere in the mud in the bed of a river."

He was silent for another few minutes, and so deep in thought that I did not speak to disturb him.

"Richard. You knew Joseph. Was he a strong man? Would he have been killed easily, do you think? Or, would he have fought back?"

"Oh, he was very strong, though of smallish stature. I once saw him hold his horse when it would have floored another of less strength."

"Then he must have known whoever killed him. Not expecting any danger, he therefore did not defend himself. My train of thought is unusual, to say the least, but I have come to the only logical answer. Listen and tell me what you think.

"I think the Archbishop killed Joseph and, a few months later, he also killed Hilda. In both cases dressed in and hidden by his monk's habit and deep hood. I would suggest that Joseph arranged to meet him, well away from York, following his mission to kill Jonas to tell him it had been successful. Let's face it Richard, there must be no one who the Archbishop trusts with his deepest secrets if even Joseph has to be killed.

"Joseph must have been well enough to travel that distance, despite his leg cuts and any loss of blood. I think he dismounted from his horse to greet him and was killed by a blow over the head with a staff and then his leg broken by that same staff. It would then look like an accident. But, he did not have his bejewelled pendant on him, hence that had to be recovered afterwards. There was no hurry. The Archbishop knew about the letter, presumably written for just such an eventuality. So, not knowing that Hilda couldn't read, he expected Hilda to take it to him after Joseph's death.. When she didn't, then he acted."

"I think your logic is sound, Uncle."

"Think again, Richard. Who could recognise the High Chief of Sorro?" asked Uncle George.

"Helena told me there was only Captain Benedict, who was his dresser but is now dead, and the Archbishop. I understand your thinking, Uncle. I cannot better it with mine. We have no direct evidence," I replied. "What can you do?"

"Nothing. This is a case where even I cannot proceed further. Whilst we know it is likely to be the truth, for any one else it will be seen as wild conjecture and totally outrageous and even worse, as directed against the Church. We have no proof other than the parchment and writing, which could easily be denied, and we cannot obtain any other evidence. But, hopefully now, that particular and dreadful evil behaviour has been halted, for a while at least. Without the High Chief and Captain Benedict, then the Church Army must surely be weakened and, we hope, for a long time.

"As we know so much about the boys and the Archbishop knows that we do, then I doubt they will dare proceed with any further abductions. I don't think we can be optimistic enough to imagine it is gone for good, but at least we have done something. I shall make sure that the other Lord Lieutenants talk about these issues in front of their own Archbishops, just in case!

"And, believe me, each time I see our local Archbishop I shall ask him regarding his success in his task of finding the culprits, and keep my interest in the outcome uppermost in his mind. I shall also tell him that I have been given the most unusual evidence, which though it sounds improbable it is also fairly conclusive, that points to a single mastermind behind two unsolved murders of people found on the moors, even involving a blue case, which appeared to be for a cross. I will ask him if anything special and valuable to do with the Church has gone missing. That will occupy him, I think."

"Take care, Uncle."

"He will not dare to do anything, and as nothing will happen except that our vigilance as Lord Lieutenants will be obvious, he will feel secure yet cautious. But, Richard, I am so glad that we took those precautions for Robbie's safety. I always knew we had to take great care in our mission for justice, but I don't think that even I could perceive that the ramifications of evil were as we appear to have discovered. They have been like the tendrils of a poisonous fog stretching out and reaching into every corner. Poor Hilda, at least her grief is over. God rest her soul. I think there are many aspects of this that we shall never know. But, I have not quite finished. I mean to restrict the Church Army activities against innocent women like your sisters, even more. I am evolving plans."

~ Uncle George's final tasks as Lord Lieutenant ~

It is July 1ˢᵗ 1501. My book is gradually coming to its completion. Now, as I write, I am telling you about events that have just recently happened. The past ordeals are over and I believe in my mind that I have given those events due consideration in all honesty and truth.

A few months ago, Uncle George called me into his library.

"Richard, I have been thinking long and hard recently. I decided last year that some of the duties of being the Lord Lieutenant do not now fit well with my advancing years. My brain is as active as ever, but I have, recently, found that the extensive travelling around the county and the country to attend meetings has become more tiresome than I would ever have imagined. I have proudly held this office for well nigh forty years and now, I think, the time has come to let Andrew take over. He has accompanied me for the past ten years; he is well known and loved by the other Lord Lieutenants. We have discussed between us and his appointment in my place has been approved in all circles. All are pleased that I shall be able to help him for a few years yet, without all the onerous tasks."

"I am surprised Uncle, but not a little relieved. The body and the mind do not seem to be as much in unison as the years pass and you are, sadly, no exception. No one can replace you, but Andrew has qualities of his own to bring to the task and he always listens to your wisdom. He will be very fortunate, indeed, to have you here to discuss and advise."

"Richard," he told me, "I have yet two tasks to accomplish before I hand over, and in each I would appreciate your help."

"Of course. My help is always there for you, Uncle. Tell me what you want me to do."

He told me about his first task.

"I was sorely troubled by the events of 1497 when your sisters died. The court case has certainly taken toll of my energy. It could be that," he admitted, with a smile, "which has made me accept, finally and long overdue, that I am, in truth, growing old. But, I would like you to travel with me for one last visit to Stocksmoor, Lower Stocksmoor, Sheepley, Upper Oakington and Lower Oakington. There, in each place, I shall meet with the villagers and agree that, should they wish it to be so, then the name of their village shall be changed to a name of their choice. They have suffered loss, great fear and humiliation at the hands of the Church Army. I know this is rather irregular and at least unusual, but I have sought advice and those learned people have pronounced that it is within my jurisdiction to do just that."

"What about Uncle Wilfred? Are these villages not part of his estate?"

"Richard, the Lord Lieutenant is responsible for the welfare of all the people in the county. I think in this case your uncle will say nothing, don't you? I am not altering the 'ownership'. I am merely letting it be known, in this way, that I disapproved of his lack of leadership, for whatever reason. After all, if he believed the soldiers could not enter his own gate, he should have realised that he could have sent them off his land outside his gate. At least he could have tried. I doubt whether your grandfather Sir Christopher would have been so intimidated, whatever reason. But what is done is done. None of us knows how we would have reacted to such a sudden situation, with no prior experience or preparation. Notwithstanding, I understand that the law has been uncertain in the matter of the Church Army and I have no doubt whatsoever that he would have been in ignorance of his true rights. But we have, as a group, now studied the powers of the landowners and clarified it, and the word has been taken to most parts of the country.

And so it was that we went together, in the early spring of this year, to accomplish this matter to Uncle George's satisfaction. Those residing in each village involved decided, and the names were changed excepting Bretton, a village where the stocks, ducking stools and mouth braces were made and from which Uncle Wilfred chose not to send armed men to rescue my sisters. Uncle George made it clear that he did not feel inclined to offer them the same opportunity for change despite having no ill will against those involved. However, he felt that Sir Wilfred should have been able to be approached by both our cousin, Henry, and by Abe, to get obtain advice when they were bullied by the Church Army soldiers. But the culture was not such that that course of events would be contemplated. So Bretton remained Bretton.

In Stocksmoor, the village returned in name to that which it had been called in the Doomsday book, except for one area of the village. Uncle George agreed with the villagers that, as a memorial to my sisters and the others who died on the common land, the common land should retain the name, 'Stocksmoor' and should hereafter be known as 'Stocksmoor Common'. It was also decided that the main road through the village, along which my sisters were made to walk from the stocks on the way to the ducking pond, should hereafter be known as Stocksmoor Road. The changes came to pass, legally.

However, I have decided, in this book, to leave all the villages' names as they were, else there would be increased confusion in the reading.

"You know, Richard," chatted Uncle George, as we journeyed back home, "I am, in so many ways, glad that your Aunt Gwendolyn has not been here these past few years. I never thought I would ever say that to anyone or even to think it. She would have been devastated not only by what happened but, because of her compassion and intelligence, it would have surely made her question the church. She loved your sisters deeply. We saw them each year as you know, often more than once, as they came to stay at the manor. Not as much as you yourself visited us of course, as you had the advantage of your older years. But she knew them well enough and never would she have thought ill of them, whatever anyone in authority in the Church might believe or dictate. She knew of their herbal work and healing and was interested in what they did. She did not understand it nor had she any aptitude that way, even though she was Eve's sister.

"We have to face the fact, Richard, that your sisters were different to most. But, I know for a surety, that had Gwendolyn been here, then she would have questioned her beliefs, however deeply felt. She would *eventually have had no choice, with her intelligence and sense, but to lean more to my way of thinking about God and cast off her staunch allegiance to the Church. She knew I had little time for doctrine and, sadly, I have to say, that that was the only discord we had between us. But, she honestly believed as she did and I believed equally as honestly, but differently. No, the God I believe in would not allow the intolerance and cruelty of the Church, but I have to be true to my inner self and admit, Richard, that even God has shocked me. I always thought your sisters were, in their way, working for him and, sort of, with his blessing."*

"Indeed, Uncle. I have puzzled this very fact many times. How can we reconcile what my sisters could and did do, with what happened? I can only think that God has a higher purpose and they had to die for a reason that we know not of. We do not have minds that are allowed to know his ways."

We were driven in silence, the only noise being the clatter of the horses' hooves and the wheels travelling on the hard road. I thought Uncle George had fallen asleep but he must have been thinking with his eyes closed.

"I have been shocked by what has happened. I may not have shown it on my face or by my manners, but, yes, very deeply shocked, more than about anything else in my entire life before. I know that Gwendolyn would have been shocked even more than me, if possible, as the deeper the foundations, the higher the building and the more damage can be done by an earthquake."

"You are very profound, Uncle."

"I wonder if I shall see her again, Richard. You know, my dearest wish would be that we can meet and be together after death. She was the love of my life, Richard. I was so fortunate to have such happiness; her love gave me such strength and that has not faded with her death. It has carried me even through this last storm."

$$\int$$

The day after we returned from carrying out Uncle George's first task, he called me into the library.

"Richard, do you remember I told you that I had two tasks to complete

before Andrew takes over? Have you time, just now, to hear of my further plans?"

"Indeed, Uncle, I am eager to hear what you have now in mind to do and for which you wish my assistance. I am sure it will be nothing if not interesting."

"I vowed that your sisters' deaths would not be in vain. Justice, as much as was possible, has been done. But, I want a more lasting tribute to them, something that will have far reaching effects for the good of this country and its people and the scourge of the Church Army be weakened as to be totally ineffectual. I have given my plan much thought." He stopped, and after a few moments, as if of recollection, added, "Indeed, much thought, day and night.

"Richard, the Church with its message telling people about what it believes and what they should believe is, in my view, relatively harmless, if and while the clerics keep to mere words, organise days of penitence or celebration, dress up in their frocks, swing their incense and such like. Those happenings don't hurt anyone, and give people something to do while keeping the clerics busy. But, when those beliefs are given such credence and importance that any different beliefs result in torture and death, by the kind of actions which we have learned, then the Church is not an amiable force for good, but, in my view, is working for the devil.

"Come now, let me show you my plans," and forthwith he laid out parchments with his fine handwritten instructions and diagrams on the long table by which we stood.

I was given my instructions and when I had understood what was to happen, in detail, Uncle George pulled the bell-cord by his large fireplace and requested Norman to bring some repast for our nourishment.

∫

Uncle George told me that, as far as the archbishops and high dignitaries of the church were aware the next meeting of the Lord Lieutenants was to be held on May 27th, in the present year, 1501. I have explained previously that these men thought they had the right to attend the Lord Lieutenant's meetings, and did so, out of curiosity so as to be informed of none ecclesiastical decisions. In this way, the Church knew enough to remain as powerful as was possible. So, they had heard this announced at the last meeting. At the time of that last meeting and, out of respect for Uncle George, the Lord Lieutenants had unanimously agreed that this meeting, when Uncle George would hand over his stewardship to his son Andrew, should be in York. Their meetings, held twice a year, unless important matters required extra gatherings, were usually held in different counties.

Uncle George told me that the meetings, of Lord Lieutenants with good communication and relationships, tended to be harmonious rather than contain much discord. This was so, in particular since Uncle George had been a senior member, as with his great skill, intelligence and humour, he could influence even the most belligerent of men. Uncle George did not want the archbishops to be aware of what he intended to do.

At his request, I asked Robbie to scribe and send letters to all the Lord Lieutenants. We sent instructions about the arrangements and their accommodation but asking them to attend at the manor on May 26th, rather than on May 27th, underlining the change of date, and asked that they be prepared to stay for two days, at least, in York. In the letter, they were requested to bring their full ceremonial robes and their coats of arms.

He had asked that they should arrive in the area in twos and threes the previous day and use only plain carriages, so as not to cause any awareness in the surrounding countryside that many important people were arriving into their midst. He did not want the Church dignitaries or the Archbishop to be aware of their early arrival in the area. And so it happened that on May 26th 1501, the Lord Lieutenants dutifully arrived at the manor. Twelve of the most senior members were to lodge at the Manor overnight. Uncle George had requested several of the nobility in the area to accommodate the rest for that night - again in twos and threes.

Uncle George, with plentiful fresh produce and excellent cooks, gave them each a sufficiency of food to feed a king. One could call the main repast a 'banquet'. Then, when the table in the large dining room had been cleared and wiped, the actual meeting of the Lord Lieutenants began. When all the issues had been dealt with satisfactorily, Uncle George described what was to happen on the morrow. There was a ripple of excitement and an element of awe at the audacious plan, but all were united in admiration and acceptance.

On the morrow, the 27th, it had been arranged that the Lord Lieutenants, dressed in their most magnificent regalia, ceremonial chains and carrying their county's coat of arms on long carved wooden poles and hanging from cross pieces, should meet near the castle at eleven o' clock in the morning. They were to process slowly, with due pomp, through the town to the room at the Guildhall, the same where the trial of the Church Army soldiers had been held.

As expected, on a busy morning in town, they caused quite a stir. Uncle George was at the head of the procession and Andrew, without regalia walked behind him. The rest followed in twos. Oliver and I, dressed in our 'legal' outfits kept step with each other, either side of Uncle George. He had declared, with a smile, "Richard, I cannot have you or Oliver missing the best action, after all your work. Stay by my side, be silent, observe and enjoy."

In the large room in the Guildhall and under Uncle George's instructions, I had had built a platform along three sides, leaving a sunken area in the centre. The platform was about two hands high. His plan was to sit all the Lord Lieutenants on this raised area, thus increasing their appearance, that of a united and powerful force.

To refresh your memory, I will tell you again that the senior ecclesiastics had heard at the last meeting of the Lord Lieutenants, that this meeting was to be in York and on May 27th. (In fact, as you will by now have realised, should you be feeling a little confused, this was the day after the 'real meeting' was held at Uncle George's manor.) Knowing that these church dignitaries would arrive to attend the meeting, Uncle George had let it be known around by word of mouth, for their benefit you understand, that the meeting would start at eleven of the clock in the morning. He and the other Lord Lieutenants were going to arrive thirty minutes later, thus allowing the churchmen to think that something was amiss with the arrangements and become a little agitated as to the time and place of the meeting.

But, he had sent two of his trained footmen to the room for a quarter before the hour of eleven, to seat the archbishops in the 'well' that had now been made in the centre of the room, to apparently reassure and so that none would leave but merely be bemused. It was a well known fact in the county and among anyone who attended meetings with Uncle George that he liked proceedings to happen 'to the minute'. So, it would seem unusual.

Just as the Lord Lieutenants were arriving at the Guildhall at half past the hour of eleven, one of Uncle George's footman, well rehearsed, walked to the front of the hall and shouted, "Please be upstanding for the worshipful Lord Lieutenants of the Counties of England". All the churchmen stood. Uncle George led the procession with Oliver down the right side of the room, between the raised area and the dignitaries, and Andrew and I led them down the left. The Lieutenants then took up their places, standing, on the platforms.

Wearing their full regalia of black velvet breeches, coats with white ruffled shirts, long, black cloaks, lined with coloured silk, and wearing large black hats of differing shapes with gold chains and such like round their necks, and carrying their county's standard, they appeared as an awe-inspiring spectacle. When they stood on the raised platform there was no denying they looked a powerful force which quite overshadowed the dignitaries of the Church. This, of course, had been Uncle George's intention. He wanted to set the tone of the meeting from the very beginning.

Uncle George stood in front of a kind of throne, with Oliver and I standing either side of him. He faced the gathered church men, who, as you will realise, were now flanked by the 'raised' Lord Lieutenants.

He addressed the gathering.

"Dear friends and colleagues, who share in the service of our country, please be seated. Today, it will be my great pleasure and honour, to hand over the Lord Lieutenant stewardship of the County of Yorkshire to my dear eldest son, a man of integrity and astute intelligence.

"It is my intention that I shall be around for several years and I will assist him, as he needs or wishes, in this, his august and demanding task, to the best of my ability. Experience does not have to be dearly bought, but can be passed on." He then sat down.

Andrew, thereafter took his oath of allegiance to the King, from the Officer to the Lord Lieutenants, and was duly inaugurated into the high office. At the end of the short ceremonial, Uncle George stood up and told the company present,

"Sirs, my son has this day been honoured with the title Sir Andrew Shaw, by order of the King, on becoming the new Lord Lieutenant of Yorkshire."

He held Andrew's left hand up and announced, in a clear and proud voice, "I now present to you all Sir Andrew Shaw, from this day he shall hold the high office of Lord Lieutenant of the County of Yorkshire."

Amidst much cheering, clapping and smiles from the other Lord Lieutenants, Andrew, now wearing his ceremonial robes, walked to his place and sat in the chair left vacant for him in the centre of the second row on the left.

When all was quiet in the chamber again, Uncle George began. "Sirs, let us now continue with the meeting and the concerns that face us this day in our care of this our country."

He brought to their attention several trivial topics, designed to fill some time and give the appearance of an authentic meeting.

Then, he asked me and Oliver if we would please lift the large sack from behind his throne to the front of the platform. No one had noticed it, as it had been hidden behind his seat. When it was opened, he informed everyone,

"I have here a parchment for each and every Lord Lieutenant. Be it known to you today and forthwith that this parchment is an exact replica of the paper that all members of the Church Army are obligated to sign as they enter the army. It is their paper of allegiance. You can read it in Latin and on its reverse side I have translated the same statement into English so that no one can be in any doubt as to what the statement says. Nowhere on this form do they sign an allegiance to the King.

"Therefore, and henceforth, you all have power to bring anyone, who has signed such a form as a member of the Church Army, to justice for any atrocity committed against any person in this land. They are simple miscreants and punishable in the same way by the same laws. This was used to convict and hang those responsible for the murder of my innocent family members.

"Be it known this day, that the full length and breadth of the country is now armed against these men by virtue of the law of the land. Only those soldiers swearing allegiance to the King, and fighting for, and on behalf of, the King, NOT the Church Army, are immune to punishment.

"My men," he turned to me and to Oliver, "please distribute one of these scrolls of parchment to each and every Lord Lieutenant." Then he sat down.

We walked around to total silence in the room, taking only a few at a time, as we had been directed previously by Uncle George. "By the time you have distributed them all the impact of the message will have sunk into the archbishops and their dignitaries." I have to say that they all appeared taken by surprise and even stunned. Not one word was spoken. Uncle George told us later that, as he sat watching, all were a pale shade of normal.

But, Uncle George had not finished yet! Oh no!

Uncle George now stood. I have to comment that he looked very dignified and imposing in his regalia.

"As you know, my knowledge of the law is second to none. That has been an abiding interest of mine since I was a young student of learning," he continued.

"I have researched the rights of ownership of land and what that implies. Every landowner knows that land within his gates is not only his responsibility but he has a right to determine who stands on that land. I have found that the same responsibility and right applies within estate boundaries to all land, whether including villages, woods, common land or river. Land that is owned by the King is equally so governed.

"My fellow Lord Lieutenants, I know that, already, owing to the serious implications involved, you have taken it upon yourselves to inform all the landowners in your county. I understand that you have told them that they must uphold this right on behalf of and for the future safety of their tenants. In this respect, there is no longer any confusion. It follows, thereafter and forthwith, that there must be and can be no camping of the Church Army on any of these owned lands without written prior permission. I trust this will never be granted. The Church Army must henceforth own any land on which it sets up camp, or be treated as common trespassers."

The archbishops and church dignitaries started becoming very fidgety and whispered to each other.

"Silence in this meeting! I will ask anyone who talks without permission to leave the premises."

He had warned his fellow Lord Lieutenants on all these points and it was obvious to Oliver and me that many were trying hard to contain their merriment. Never had they seen or heard Uncle George in finer form.

But, he wasn't finished, not even yet. He had saved his best blow for the end.

"Finally, my friends and colleagues," he continued to smile around to the Lord Lieutenants as though nothing untoward had happened so far and that this was just a normal meeting flowing as a matter of course, "there is one other matter."

He stood up and slowly walked first to one side of his platform and then to the other. (I had constructed the platform on which his throne was placed to be the same height from the floor as his fellow Lord Lieutenants.) He came back to the centre and told his expectant audience,

"For this further matter, which is a resolution with future legality, it is deemed only fair to allow an open and free vote of all the Lord Lieutenants and in front of all who are today present in this chamber. As we know from our very many years of service to our country and through our stewardship of its counties, it has become customary for the archbishops and their chosen Church dignitaries," and he waved his arm around in an exaggerated movement, "to attend our meetings.

"I have spent months, as have some other learned colleagues versed in the finer points of the law of governance, searching the volumes of laws, reaching as far back in time as it is possible. We have been gathering information as to the rules and constitution of our meetings. We have left no stone unturned in a wish to be accurate in this, as in everything else appertaining to the law in which we are involved. At no place can we find of any permission having been given for the intrusion of our privacy in this way. The Church sets itself apart from the state, with its own rules and regulations, whether legal in the context of the state or not, they make it so.

"We have, till now, accepted, if not exactly welcomed, the interest of the Church in the affairs of the country. However, after the appalling and continuing behaviour of the Church Army, under the Church's jurisdiction, then something has to change. The senior members of our august stewardship have discussed these matters at length, and we have decided to put to the vote of all our members a resolution, which I shall now read.

"Resolution: That in future, following the meeting dated May 27th 1501, in York, no archbishop or Church dignitary is welcome or allowed to attend any meeting of the Lord Lieutenants of England and must, hereafter, be excluded from knowledge of the procedures and decisions taken in those meetings."

There were gasps of disbelief from the floor of the room, and one or two archbishops stood up briefly to protest, but were pulled to their seats by their neighbours.

"Would all members of our august stewardship register their vote by raising their right hand above their heads if they agree to the resolution?"

As expected, all hands were raised.

"Thank you," he accepted the decision with a totally straight face. "Now, would all members who disagree with the resolution, please raise their right hand above their heads?"

He waited a short while, before saying, "All in this room can bear witness, that not one hand has been raised against the resolution. I can declare with honesty and clarity that the resolution has been passed with unanimous approval. It is now therefore, you will all agree, my solemn duty to ask that all archbishops and Church dignitaries leave this room." He then added, for further effect and in his sternest judicial voice, "Immediately!"

Later that night, when all the Lord Lieutenants had left York and proceeded home, Uncle George came to talk to Oliver and myself in the library.

"Richard and Oliver, my hearty thanks for your support and effort. It worked perfectly. All those years of work have been worth every minute to be able to take part in and witness this day. We have defeated them at this time and may God allow it to be a victory which lasts a long time."

The strain of years of work, concern and grief all suddenly seemed to be behind him. He sat down suddenly in his chair and tears of relief streamed down this kind man's face. His nieces had not died in vain, but had probably helped to save the lives of very many more gentle and gifted women. We both went and put an arm around his shoulder and wept with him.

§

I know now that I have obtained the information that I searched for. The story, to my mind, feels to be complete. I have now determined that it is time for us all to move on. I hope by reading this book, that my dear sisters' children will have the chance of some life of their own, instead of living in the shadow of their grief. Only then can the memories of their mothers bring not only sorrow but, hopefully, some lasting joy.

Though my search for truth and understanding is complete, yet there is something further I wish to tell you about. It involves other objects that I have decided to place into the casket.

~ The pictures ~

I will go back in time just now to the early spring of 1501. I made a trip over to my house in Sheepley, as was my custom every few months. I had thought to travel last autumn before the leaves were cast off for another year and before the cold weather set in. But, events prevented me. So, I visited as soon as the weather permitted and it was towards the end of March when I made my journey. I usually made the detour to Upper

Oakington to see Ben and his wife Hannah. He seldom visited the York area and I felt I wanted to keep contact with my only remaining brother, of whom I had not only great fondness but true respect.

On this occasion, we had just returned from a short walk in the woods on the outer boundary of the village and were about to eat a repast before I left for my home.

"Ben, let me tell you that I am chronicling the events about our sisters and putting them into a book, I kept notes and I have writings about what happened, the trial and what was discovered about the Church Army and anything else that was relevant. My firm resolve is to finish this book and bury it in a casket, as a memorial to them, this summer in Stocksmoor. I have planned that it shall be complete and packaged ready for burial on the fourth anniversary of their deaths, in July. I shall prepare it so that it will withstand the ravages of time. At least that is my intention and Uncle George is giving of his advice, freely."

"That is a wonderful idea."

"It is a task that I feel I have been given," I told him about the dream when I was, as if with our father, in a time of the future.

"Would you let me contribute to that memorial in some way, Richard?" asked Ben. "It would be my dearest wish to somehow pay tribute to them."

"Of course. I would be most grateful."

"I will think what to do and I will visit you. Let us make an arrangement. Let us decide the day so that we shall not forget and I will surely have time to think about and complete my task to my satisfaction?"

After a few moments thought, Ben suggested, "If you do not visit here beforehand, then I will visit with my offering on June 6th. How would that suit you?"

"That would be perfect."

Before returning to Poppleton, I decided to call on our cousin, Henry, to enquire as to his health, while hoping that he was able to be in good spirits once more. The deaths of my sisters had taken a heavy toll on his wellbeing.

We were sitting down to a repast of venison stew and bread, when Henry suddenly hit his forehead, making us all jump.

"I have a parcel for you, Richard, from the Hall. I will get it directly lest you ride away and I forget."

"A parcel from the Hall for me? How strange. Whatever can that be?"

"Did you know that your Uncle Wilfred had died?" asked Henry.

I shook my head.

"No, I don't suppose you would have heard or have had contact or else the parcel would not be here. He died a few months ago. I heard that he caught a chill, after being soaked to the skin in an expected downpour of rain, while in the far reaches of his parkland, with no shelter. He developed a fever and succumbed about three weeks later. Geoffrey is in charge now, and seemingly, in his present unsettled state wants to empty certain rooms of the Hall. He has never fully recovered you know and is still rather morose."

He got up from the table, though we had not completed our meal.

"Here it is, Richard." He handed me a small but quite bulky parcel wrapped in sacking and tied with string.

When we had finished eating, I opened it, and could not believe what I was seeing. There, painted as near lifelike as you could see, was a portrait of Eve and another of my three sisters – Catherine when she was about seven and of Ann and Emily, in their third year. I just looked and my eyes filled with tears. This is the only representation that I know about of those dear people. All other is in my memory.

"I know these portraits," I explained, "but I never thought to see them again."

"Geoffrey delivered them himself, and made his request. 'Would you give these to Richard, should you ever see him? They belong with him and the children, not in the Hall. They belonged to Grandpapa and were always kept in Eve's room. That room was like a shrine to Eve. Do you know, even some of her clothes were still there. There were several silk gowns, with ruffles and lace and in beautiful colours. But I don't know why. I

had never been in the room before Papa's death. It was a room no one visited. But, though it was flooded in sunlight when I entered, it filled me with gloom and seemed quite ghostly. I have had the room cleared. Papa once told me that Grandpapa always used to hope that Eve would come back and stay occasionally at the Hall. He kept her room just as she left it, and then when she died, no one dared to touch anything. She did stay occasionally after her marriage to Uncle Albert and Grandmama didn't make her very welcome or something like that. But I don't know the truth or any more about it. It is ancient history.' Did you know any of that, Richard?"

"Oh, yes," I replied. I was taken back in my mind to a memory which was as fresh as when the incident happened. I think it will be stuck in my mind for ever.

"Did you know," I asked him, "that Grandmama, your great aunt, was of very noble birth, a Duke's daughter?" He nodded. "Well, she liked the Hall to reflect that. She was very beautiful and rich. She entertained the high and mighty whenever she could, whatever Grandpapa thought about it. He wasn't like that, you know. He would have been quite happy with a much simpler life. But she brought a lot of money into the coffers of the Hall, so had quite a lot of say as to what happened there. I remember one evening hearing Eve say to Papa that she had neither inclination nor time to be fastened into gowns that made her life so difficult. She wanted simple clothes so that she could feel much freer and help keep the house as she wished it to be. So, she left most of her gowns at the Hall and only had two, hanging and covered by sheets, in a corner of her and Papa's bedroom. She wore these only to visit the Hall. If she stayed at the Hall she wore the ones that were still kept in her room there.

"But, once she had had both Thomas and Catherine she could no longer fit into the tight boned bodices, either the ones at home or the ones at the Hall. So she had the elaborate gowns at home cut up and made into simple dresses for herself and Catherine and trousers for Thomas, so they could wear them when she took them to visit their grandparents. There was enough silk in one dress to make it possible for her and the two children to wear the same colour silk clothes at the same time. Eve, who thought they looked lovely, told them so and had the two parading round the drawing room to show Papa.

"But Eve was not Grandmama. Oh no. when Grandmama saw Eve and the children as they entered the Hall, in these much more simple clothes, she was very angry. I had gone with them so I heard it all, and I understood, though the little children didn't. She told Eve that she would not countenance that anyone dressed in such paltry clothes should enter through her front door. Eve, who could be angry herself, had made a lot of effort that day, as I heard her telling it all to Papa afterwards. But, she turned us all round, and, without entering the Hall, we walked straight back home through the park.

"The next day Grandpapa came to the house trying to persuade Eve differently. He thought that Grandmama was very wrong to say what she did. I know that Eve was very upset as she was crying and Nell took us all outside. I never heard how Eve replied to her father. I do know that she never stayed in her room at the Hall after that. I continued to attend the Hall as usual for lessons. I was there one day when I saw Eve enter through the servant and tradesmen's entrance. When she and I were at home that evening, I asked her why had she entered her old home by the servants' entrance? She answered me quite carefully, I remember. 'Richard, though I believe my Mama is very wrong in how she thinks, I must still respect her wishes. But, at the same time I will not change what is best for me just to have her approval. I, too, have my wishes, and it would be better for both Mama and me if she respected mine. You love your grandparents and that is how it should be. Your Grandmama loved your Mama very much and she loves you, and I am very pleased. Now, let us hear no more.'

"As far as I can gather, hearing her tell Papa again, as was my habit, she had decided to cut up another of her gowns, one from the Hall, and had visited the Hall on the day that I speak of, for that very purpose. She went to her father to ask his permission to go to her room. He went with her and suggested that she should choose the gown or gowns and he would have them delivered to our home. Then, Eve saw her portrait, this one," I was holding the portrait of Eve in my hand, "in the room and asked her father why it was kept in there.

"Now, apparently Eve had not had cause to see the portrait since Grandpapa had been given it as a gift, and did not know where it had been put. She obviously thought it would have its proper place with other portraits, in the large drawing room or somewhere similar. He rightly explained, but later I understand he greatly regretted his honesty, that Grandmama would not allow it to be sited anywhere else in the Hall. Grandmama had decided that the portrait was such a good likeness that it was obvious that anyone could, nay, would, recognise it was of her daughter Eve. She had been adamant that she would not have a portrait of her daughter shown to anyone when she was wearing clothes that a common housemaid would wear. She felt that the painting showed this disgrace and lack of taste, even for posterity.

"I don't think Eve ever visited again. Her father called to see her and her family regularly, most weeks unless he was away from the Hall. One day I was in the scullery when he was talking to Eve in the drawing room. I heard him say 'Eve, please come and visit the Hall and bring the children. It should be part of their lives too and not only Richard's.' Eve replied, 'I will, with pleasure, Papa, once Mama has visited my home. I love Mama, but only then will I go back to her home.' Sadly, Grandmama could never allow herself to do so and they never saw each other again.

"Fate, as we know, Henry, can be so cruel. Angelina was to be married on New Year's Day and Eve, being her godmother, had surely to be at the ceremony. I can remember Grandpapa bringing Grandmama's dressmaker to our home with swathes of beautiful silk cloth and Grandpapa asking Eve to choose one for a dress to be made for the wedding. Of course, Eve would not upset Angelina in any way, so she agreed. It was to be a beautiful dress but Eve was with child again, and, I remember it had to keep being altered. But, in the end, Eve died before the wedding, and her chance of seeing Grandmama didn't happen. As a sign of respect and grief, Angelina postponed her marriage until the summer time.

"Grandmama visited our home a few months after Eve's death, you know. I was there. Papa was quite blunt to her. 'I wish you could have visited when Eve was alive, rather than after her death. She loved you and so wanted you to see her home, the place where she was happy.' She had answered, 'Albert, an understanding of my loss, like a lightning bolt to my heart, has been my punishment. I pray that God may forgive me for my transgression. I made a mistake, a very big mistake and I am the one who will have to live with that till my dying day. I only realised once Eve had gone how much I loved her. But I can change nothing now. I have come today because I have the need to know where two of my daughters died and where Eve spent these past years. Believe me, I am now content. She didn't even stay for any refreshment or talk to any of her grandchildren and neither did she see Ann and Emily, who were in their crib asleep during her visit. She never visited again. Papa was always rather angry with Grandmama, but never with Grandpapa.

"After Eve's death Grandpapa continued to visit each week, until his own death. I have to say, Henry, that to me Grandmama was always very pleasant and welcomed me, but then I was Anna's son. I never understood the full impact of all this until much later. But, it is possible to see why Uncle Wilfred, who was always close to his mother, could be rather distant and not distraught at Ann, Emily and Catherine's fates; though I don't think he would have expected their deaths."

"I never knew any of this," admitted Henry.

"Well, no, you wouldn't. Eve never spoke ill of her Mama and I know she loved her. When people believe that clothes and appearance are more important in our lives than love, so much so that they can come between a mother and daughter, then, Henry, society is quite sick, do you not think?"

"The other portrait is obviously of Eve's three girls, Catherine, Emily and Ann, the ones who looked like her. You can tell that they are obviously done by the same artist though I don't know who he was," confessed Henry. "I asked Geoffrey who the artist was, but he had no idea."

"I can tell you. They were painted by my father."

"Really? I never knew that Uncle Albert could paint."

"Oh, yes, he was very skilled in painting likenesses, but these are the only ones left. Eve didn't see this picture of her daughters, of course, as she died when Ann and Emily were born. But Papa had painted it especially to give to Grandpapa. I understand that Grandpapa showed it to Grandmama and she decided that it should be with the other one, as these children looked like common villagers, dressed as they were. Despite her grief, it appeared as though she hadn't changed her views. So it was left in Eve's room as if to keep companionship with the one of Eve. But, you know, I knew Grandmama quite well and I have a feeling that the portrait of my three sisters was actually too painful for Grandmama to look at and that is why she hid them away. I know that Grandpapa loved these granddaughters."

"Geoffrey told me that his father, Uncle Wilfred, was of such a nature that he made many new alterations, though only after long and tedious deliberation, but he rarely sorted out anything that was old and never threw anything away. So Eve's room remained, untouched. Geoffrey, of course, told us what the pictures were but didn't show them to us and, as they were for you, we would not dream to unwrap to look at them, though we have been very curious."

"When you were young and visited us occasionally, you would see there were portraits around the house of Papa's children, and many of my Mama and Eve. Do you not remember?" I asked Henry.

"Now you come to mention it, yes, I do. I didn't know that Uncle Albert had painted them all. But that must have been a long time ago as I did not see any for many years and so I had forgotten until you just told me," recalled Henry.

"This one of my sisters was the last one that Papa painted. It was a special present for Grandpapa. I remember very well when he stopped painting. I took this picture to the Hall and Grandpapa was so pleased. I think it was his birthday. When I returned home, Papa was in the garden behind the house, tending a fire. I thought he was burning garden rubbish, but no, he was burning all his portraits.

"I went into the house and all the portraits were missing. The walls, that had been covered, were empty with the marks showing where the pictures had been. I felt quite sick for a while. I was horrified that Papa should destroy such beautiful portraits, especially of Eve. 'Why are you burning all your paintings?' I asked him, in tears. 'Richard, don't weep lad. Understand I love you all dearly and have no wish to upset you. You are here with me, but when I see the portraits, I am so easily sent back in time in my mind, to be with either your dear mama or with Eve. I loved them both, very much.

- 454 -

"'I have to live, however long that may be, without either of them. I live with you all, in the present, I have so many to look after. I must do so for your mama and for Eve also as they are not here to help me. Now that I have given Eve's papa the likenesses of the girls, I need paint no more. I have not burned my easel, my brushes or my parchment. No, I shall give those to Ben, who shows a good aptitude in painting. I shall help him. But, for myself, I shall never paint again and I no longer wish to see any of my paintings. So I am burning them all.' And, he kept true to his word. He told me, 'I still see beauty, but I no longer wish to capture it, as when it disappears it has gone and cannot be brought back. I must accept my losses, Richard.'"

"Poor Uncle Albert, such talent, and such grief. I didn't know Ben painted either."

"Oh, yes, and he's very good. My father taught him all he knew, even though he stopped painting himself. You know, Henry, I did not understand Papa then, and the house felt different without all his paintings. Only on that day did he weep in front of me, or any of us. He told me what a sacrifice Eve had made, in his eyes, to be his wife and that she gradually stopped seeing any of the young women whom she had thought of as friends. They kept to the 'social order' and did as their mamas dictated and could not possibly be seen visiting a humble home, as ours was – in comparison to the Hall – you understand. But, neither had she anyone in the village of the same social standing and, though she was friendly, most of the villagers, except Nell and Dorothy, kept their distance. So she didn't fit with them either. She had Aunt Peggy, and that was all. But, he felt sure that Eve had no regrets. She always insisted that his love and the children were all she ever wanted.

"But, after Beatrice died I could understand Papa and why he would have destroyed the paintings. He was very brave all his years after losing my Mama and Eve. You know, I could not even stay in our house, where Beatrice had touched everything, and walked everywhere. Only when I loved Rosamund, so many years later, did I feel comfortable in the house again, as if her fingers and feet had not erased Beatrice but merely covered her traces with those of her own. I am most touched to the heart by seeing these again."

"Did you know that my brother John has left his home?" asked Richard.

"No, when and why?"

"It happened a few months ago. He just called in one day to say goodbye. He had decided that he couldn't stay in Bretton. He wishes to paint by the sea. He has gone alone. He too was very distressed by Ann, Emily and Catherine's deaths and has, since that time, seemed to be very restless. Mama is not sure where he is, as her mind is wayward much of the time now. She seems not to understand that he has gone away for good, or how long it is since she saw him. So we don't tell her," explained Henry.

"And his wife? Do you mean he has left her here?"

"Yes, she remains here, in Bretton. We see her and she visits our home, but I gather that she and John were not on the best of terms for some considerable time. She appears not to be distressed that he is not with her."

§

On the very next day, I decided that I must visit Cousin Geoffrey at the Hall and thank him for the portraits.

"You are very welcome, Richard." We had greeted each other and heard each other's news. He told me that his Mama was unwell and he thought it best that we did not meet together with her. She seldom saw anyone, particularly since Hannah and her children had gone to the east of the country and Jane had decided to go with her. Everything had seemed to change in the last few years, everything.

"Richard, I am glad you have come this day, as I have something I wish to share. I thought very badly of Papa for not allowing our villeins to go to the aid or your sisters, and we were not on good terms since that time. But, one day, which I now realise was the beginning of the end of his life, he called me into the library. He was coughing badly, but he managed to confide in me his distress. 'Geoffrey, my soul has been in anguish since that day when I let Catherine, Ann and Emily die that cruel death. You were right at the time. I should have sent help for them. I cannot excuse my actions but I can explain them. Geoffrey, you know me well and you will realise that all my life I have had to think hard and long before

- 456 -

making any decision. I think it was the influence of Mama as I did not want to do anything that would make her angry. I saw how she excluded Eve and, to some extent Elizabeth when they married beneath their station, as she saw it, though in reality they both married well-born men. Anna was not included in that despite doing the same. I think Mama felt that, as she had not the beauty of the others, then she was fortunate to have her married at all. I did not want Mama's wrath and I actually believed at the time that she was right. How, I do not know now.'"

He was quiet for a moment. "Richard, I know that Anna was your mother, but I am just telling you what Papa told me."

"I never knew my mama, Geoffrey. To me, Eve was my mama, in all but birth and I loved her, not Anna. Please continue to tell me about Uncle Wilfred."

"Papa explained, 'I had lost my dear sisters Anna, Eve and Elizabeth, all in childbirth, Gwendolyn was far away in York and we saw her only rarely, and my only brother George had died. Because of Mama I did not visit Eve as often as I should have done. I helped young Richard but none of the others. I had lost so many people whom I loved, and I could not bear to lose my children. On that day, I had no time to think clearly what to do, and my first thoughts were to keep my daughters, Hannah, her children and Jane safe and that you should not be involved in any fighting. I did not want Hannah's husband to be implicated as that would have affected Hannah, and the good name of my, and your, family. Hannah's husband, Robert, told me that he had been told that Hannah and Jane were only safe if they stayed at the Hall. But, should I interfere in the justice of the Church Army then they too would find a trial waiting for them.

"'I did not ask any questions as to where and from whom he had received his information. I now know I should have done, but I didn't. Believe me Geoffrey when I tell you that I didn't know what was to happen. I never thought for one moment that they would be killed. Never. But, I heard they died a most cruel death and they have been in my nightmares ever since. I know that my decision was so very wrong. I should have been strong. Why was I not strong, Geoffrey? Why? I have asked myself that question so many times these past years. If only I had had more time to think what to do. I could have asked for help from the squires around.'

"He was so upset, Richard, that my anger with him, at last, disappeared. He went on to say, 'I am frightened to die. I am ashamed to be me. I cannot believe that any good God will forgive the ill that I have done. I want to see my dear sisters in heaven, but I do not think I shall ever be allowed to go there and I am frightened of ever meeting Eve again. Oh, Geoffrey, my time is coming to an end. I cannot undo anything and I am so frightened to die.'

"He cried as I have never seen Papa cry before. I could not comfort him. I do not know how he could be comforted, not even in heaven. His illness was short and he was taken within the month. I was able to sit with him in those last days with a great feeling of love towards him. I felt so sorry for him, that a decision, made in haste, should possibly affect him for ever in eternity.

"My prayer is that God in his almighty wisdom will pardon his weakness, which came from the strength of his loving nature for his family and his other, old and many grievings. Surely Richard, there is forgiveness for such as he. He was a good man."

We both sat silently. I thought about my sisters. Would they understand Uncle Wilfred? Would they forgive him? Would it be their task to listen or forgive him? We cannot know or tell what is to come in the hereafter, only have faith and do what we believe is right. I have always believed that the quality of kindness should be our key virtue. But love and kindness to his children guided Uncle Wilfred's footsteps every day. I was left with a lot of thinking and rethinking to do as it seemed that even love and kindness were not sufficient in the face of such evil.

"I am glad I came to see you this day, Geoffrey," I eventually replied, "as I too could not understand that lack on the behalf of my sisters. I had always thought of Uncle Wilfred as a good and kindly man, until that time. Now, I can understand better and I can forgive him, if my forgiveness can mean anything."

I left with a lighter heart, and knowing that I had been right in not judging my Uncle harshly, despite what seemed, on the surface, to be the truth. I send earnest prayer to God that I may not be asked to make that choice between my duty to someone or other and my love for my children. Which would I make? I have no doubt. I know that answer for myself, but, dear readers, we must make our own decisions, as all men and women have to do in this life. We shall stand or fall by our actions when we finally answer before God, of that I am certain.

§

On the very next day after I had returned home, I took the pictures to show and offer them to Miriam, Miranda, Mark and James. I left the parcel with them for two days and then called back to see them.

"You are very kind, as always, Uncle, but, thank you, no, these pictures belong to you." Miriam handed the package back to me. "Eve was the only mother you knew and we never knew our mothers or Aunt Catherine as little children. No, these are yours, please take them."

I was made to understand that Miriam spoke for all of them.

§

A bleak and very cold winter had given way to a warm spring and early summer sun. And so it came to pass that on June 6th, 1501, Ben arrived at the Manor, much to Uncle George's delight and that of all of us. We had mid-day food at Uncle George's ample table.

"I have brought this for you, Richard, as I promised. It is my contribution to the 'casket of remembrance' dedicated to our sisters," announced Ben as we strolled round the grounds to aid our digestion. He handed me a small parcel, with hard sides, from out of his bag. Some things are as familiar as the people who own them and this bag was one of those. Ben always carried it with him if he travelled away from his home. It had been Papa's when we were children, and when he had had another made for himself as a replacement, Ben had acquired the cast-off bag. It was old and tatty even those many years ago, but Ben did not care how it looked. It was his link to Papa. He still used it for his needs.

"Maybe you can wait and look at them in the house, when I have gone home," he suggested.

"Would you wish to be with us when we bury the casket?"

"No, Richard. That is a time for the children and for you. I can and do walk on the common land. I take some of Hannah's cooking to Simion's corner each week and I visit our father's house. No, I will not meet with you at that time." He was a good horseman and I checked that his horse was in travelling condition, as was always my habit. He left soon after to be home before it became too late or dangerous to travel.

On entering the house, I opened the parcel. I saw, to my amazement, four beautiful paintings. These were Ben's way of remembering our sisters and the tragedy. As I looked I wept, not only for my sisters but for my dear and gentle brother. The first I looked at was of our three sisters, amicably picking herbs, together in their garden. The second was a portrayal of one of the grim stocks standing starkly in a picturesque open, peaceful landscape, making the contrast very apparent. The third was the casket being buried in its lonely isolation. Finally, the 'Riders of Death', painted in such a way as to instil fear in the very looking thereof.

Ben, rarely showed or spoke how he felt and always presented his pleasant and sanguine nature to the outside world, yet he could express and evoke such beauty, emotion and meaning in his paintings.

As I had to ask people for the information for my book, so Ben, not seeing either the stocks or the Church Army's 'Riders of Death', had to do the same for those two pictures. I know how it has felt writing what happened. To paint those pictures, he had to see them clearly in his mind, and to do so, indeed, needed much courage.

§

The pictures painted by my father take me in my memory, to the times I played games with my little sisters, or made up stories for them on winter evenings. I can remember talking with Catherine, wise even at a young age. I can hear their laughter. As I sit looking at her picture, I feel Eve ruffling my hair as she would when she walked past me, when, as a boy I would be seated at the table and eating some of her newly baked bread. The pictures have given me much comfort for a time, but are of such a likeness that they have also given me a deep longing to see these dear people again, just as they did for my dear Papa. I, too, fear I shall stay in my grief should I keep them in my house. I cannot live in the past. I have much to rejoice about with my own family and theirs, in the present, though I must live with a foreboding about Rosamund. No one knows what the future will bring, but I cannot add to any sadness by keeping the pictures. I have finally, but slowly, decided to let them go, though that doing will be a wrench to my spirit for a while at least.

Therefore, dear readers, as I finish this book, after much inner deliberation, I have placed the pictures of Eve and my sisters in the casket along with those which Ben painted. When the casket is unearthed, as I believe one day it will be, then those who read the book will have images about whom and what I write.

Now, you can not only read about but see a representation of their younger lives, a symbol of their middle years and the means of the end of our dear sisters as depicted so beautifully by Papa and Ben. As Ben's pictures are the same size of parchment as my book, I have been able to put them safely, without creasing, in the relevant part of the book. In this way we have remembered them for posterity, together.

§

Dear Readers, I now digress briefly, as I wish to tell you about three items that I shall place in the casket. Items that are mine, and mine alone.

You will remember that, when the baby born to Beatrice and myself died, I had to hang a cross on the front door of the house for six months. When I took that cross down I found I could not throw it away, so I placed it in one of my drawers. Neither Rosamund nor our children have ever seen it and never shall they do so, though it is with me in Poppleton. That cross shall go into the casket, a memorial to a life that, as it came and went so quickly, left nought but a small shadow in my heart.

With that cross, and in the same drawer, is a small brown leather purse with a draw string fastening. Let me tell you what is in the purse, lest you think I pass this by.

When Beatrice and myself were to be married, my father decided to give her a personal gift from himself and my brothers and sisters. Ann, Emily and Catherine went with my father to a jeweller, well known and respected, to choose the gift. They chose to have a pendant made to wear on a gold chain. It was beautiful and simple. The jeweller had many stones, some very valuable and others of less worth, and they chose one, not for its value but for its colour. It was the very colour of Beatrice's eyes, and called a turquoise.

The jeweller shaped one piece into a tear shaped drop and fastened it onto a gold claw through which a gold chain could pass. When I saw this, I then could not resist, and went separately and had a matching ring made. I have to say that Beatrice loved these pieces and wore them constantly, though she had much jewellery of greater worth given to her by her own father.

When she died, she was buried wearing her wedding ring and one of the necklaces from her mother's collection, at her father's request. I gave back to her father all the jewellery belonging originally to their family and kept the turquoise necklace and ring for my own keepsake.

But, you will understand that when I die, these items which are precious and sentimental to me will have no meaning to anyone. My children scarcely know that I was married to anyone before their own Mama and that is how it should be. My grief does not belong on their shoulders.

So, I have determined that these shall be put in the casket, a memorial to Beatrice and our son, but also they are a link from me and Beatrice to my sisters and my father.

§

Robbie has made a list of all the contents of the casket.

I thank Robbie, here and now, for his entire valuable input. With great diligence and patience he has sat many long hours scribing this book to make it as perfect as possible. He has shown in this task, done always with quiet determination, a willingness which speaks more than words.

~ Contents of the casket ~

<u>Book</u> – JUSTICE, written by Richard Shaw 1501

<u>Four pictures,</u> painted by Ben Shaw

The three sisters

The stocks

The hidden casket

The Church Army – 'Riders of Death

Two pictures painted by Albert Shaw,

1) Eve

2) Three of Eve's children, Ann, Emily and Catherine

When I told Ann and Emily's children and Nell my plans to bury the casket and its contents, I asked them what other items they wished to place within it, along with my book.

These are what were decided.

Letter written by Miriam to her Mother, Ann Kittle

Letter written by Miranda to her Mother, Emily Kittle

Miriam and Miranda wrote letters to say a final 'goodbye' to their mothers. The last time they saw them was before the soldiers took them to trial, They never saw them in the stocks. I never believed that either of these two girls, both devoted to their mothers, ever truly believed they had died. Miranda, in particular, would go outdoors, even later when they moved away from Uncle George's house, and stand by the fence at the end of the field near their cottage, looking longingly, as if she expected her mother to appear – one day.

Letter written by Miriam and Miranda to Catherine Shaw

The letter from Ann and Emily to Nell packed with the ring as she found it

Nell asked permission of all the children to put the ring and letter that Ann and Emily had left her into the casket. She was concerned to keep it safe. "What will happen to it when I am dead? It is likely one day to be misplaced or lost. We never know what will happen."

Ann, Emily, Mark and James agreed and so the parcel was remade and included in the casket.

Nell opened the envelope which the children had never seen and showed us the hair inside.

I have written, 'This is the hair of Ann and Emily cut from their heads by Aunt Peggy before they were married. She thought she might lose her 'children' when they got married, but after their husbands' deaths she continued to fuss over them as before. They never minded, and loved her for her sweet self and her continued and constant concern.'

Two small bottles containing strands of the hair of Ann Kittle and Emily Kittle

I took these from the same source as above, just in case preservation is not sufficient in the cloth. I had small thick glass bottles in which I used to carry my potions, if not needed in large amounts. I found empty ones, made sure I cleaned them completely of any previous contents. I then put in the stoppers and sealed them with wax.

Poem written by Ann Kittle after her husband's death

This was already in the casket. I asked Robbie to scribe it at the end of this book, in case the paper on which is was written should become damaged or the script unreadable, as I notice that the paper is not of the quality of parchment Robbie is using from Uncle George's store. I hope the original keeps in good condition for as long as necessary, but, if not, then the copying is a measure that I have taken in an endeavour to preserve and protect to posterity.

The poem made me weep, as I could feel that deep anguish. It brought memories from deep inside my soul of the same that I had felt when Beatrice died, a feeling I thought had gone forever in my happiness with Rosamund. Neither Ann nor Emily made any moaning of their loss. But, to someone who knew and loved them as much as I did, there was a sadness surrounding them from the day their husbands' cold and stiff bodies were brought home on a dray. It was like a soft cloud that they could not be aware of, nor could alter.

Inside the folds of the poem were strands of hair, which I knew from the colour were not her own but from Peter's hair.

Peter's hair

I put it in one of my small bottles and sealed it with wax.

There are other items which I have now put in the casket, but which I never let Miriam, Miranda, Mark or James see. Even if or when they do indeed read this book then they will not know about them. This page is not for their eyes, and I have added it after their perusal of the book. I did not want to awaken any memories of horror for the boys and the girls never saw these items at the time.

Mouth brace used by the Church Army and taken from the body of Catherine Kittle on July 27ᵗʰ, 1497

Part of stocks left after the bodies of Ann, Emily and Catherine were burned on July 28ᵗʰ, 1497

Piece of rope used to tie Emily Kittle to the ducking stool on July 27ᵗʰ, 1497

This rope shows that it was unwaxed. It absorbed the water and swelled very quickly.

Piece of cloth, bloodstained – taken from Ann Kittle's skirt after her death by drowning

Nell had cut this cloth from Ann's skirt, as evidence that blood was caused to flow by the soldier's injuries.

The Church Army pendant belonging to Helena's boy, John – with cord.

Two gold-plated pendants – those which Richard and Oliver wore when dressed as monks.

Piece of charred parchment

The word 'granted' can be seen. Found on edge of funeral pyre ashes. This is part of the pardon written by the Archbishop of York.

Piece of parchment – which Helena had retrieved from Benedict Crecy – showing that he had received a 'warning' of the impending trial. Uncle George suggested that it should be placed in the casket, as further information to verify that which I have written.

The letter signed by Josef de Vere to the Archbishop

Turquoise pendant with chain and ring – those which belonged to Beatrice

Wooden cross – which denoted the death of Richard's baby son

The cross would not quite fit into the casket, so it was wrapped in sacking, tied with ribbon and covered completely in wax. It was placed on the top of the casket but inside the mahogany box.

The casket and its contents have become the only 'coffin' or memorial that my dear sisters have ever had. I pray that all our endeavours to preserve it will be proved to have the efficacy that we all desire. Only those who read this book at some time in the future will be able to know that truth.

§

Lost love – April 24th , 1485

Written by Ann Kittle, in 1486, a year after Peter's death

What made you the way you
were?
You were never born to fight
You left only desolation
When life ended for you that
night
I understand the reasoning
For another's life you died
And in so doing, for such a one
Another's meaning is denied
My love for you is still as strong
Though you are gone for ever
A lifeless face can smile no more
Since cruel fate doth sever
But I have now to live each day
Without you by my side
My work is not completed
So here I must abide
If we meet again one day
(I ponder if that could be)

A different face, another place
An inner me you'll need to see
I will not keep this anger deep
It spoils dear memories true
But the sadness I cannot lose
As it belongs, my love, to you
It will go with me each day
This empty, lonesome pain
No years of life can erase
My loss is heaven's gain
Our lives were joined together
For this brief time on earth
No other person living could be
A match to meet your worth
I had to say, 'Goodbye,' my dear
Your body was white and cold
Taken from this mortal's door
Without you, I now grow old
Grief, shared with many more
What cruel lives we lead
People all should live in peace
This is not the way we need
I must face what has to be
Without your arm, so strong
Shall I be equal to the task?
Will my waiting time be long?
But you are not my future
You will never share my woe
I pray your soul can never feel
Nor yet my anguish know

~ Final preparations ~

Uncle George requested that I should take him the pages of the book, once complete. He knows of an excellent book binder whom he has arranged shall put them into a cover. He has chosen and approved the material as being of a sufficient quality to stand the test of time, given the precautions and care we are to take in preparing for its internment in the casket.

I had arranged to meet him in the library. He spent many hours there, alone and reading. Though a very active and sociable man (you will by now understand his nature) he always assured me that he felt content and found solace amongst his books.

When I arrived he was pacing about with a small, old and rather tatty book in his hand. At first he did not notice I had arrived, so I sat down on a chair by the door, watching and listening. "...never fed," "...did not feed," "...never fed," "...did not feed". I could hear quite clearly that he was reading the same few words in Latin, though what they were I could not tell, and then ending with these two different ways, but in English.

After a while he spoke aloud, but as if to himself, "Oh, I don't know which is the best to use." Then he looked up, saw me and smiled.

"Welcome to my recital, Richard. You will no doubt think me a little astray in my normal sobriety but, no, I am just puzzling over something of importance. You see, I too would like to contribute to your memorial to my dear nieces. I have given much thought as to what I could add to your excellent book. I think a few words, say a quotation at the beginning, would be suitable, if you agree.

"I have been perusing one of my favourite old books of Latin verse and found a couple of lines from one of the poems of an unknown sage, probably from about the twelfth century, though no one knows for sure. I feel is it very apt as it relates a story of souls who have been released from their bodies after being cruelly killed. Listen, I will translate some of it for you and then you can help with my decision.

<u>The Cavalcade Of Souls</u>

The horses passed by silently
Carrying the halt and lame
As I watched the cavalcade
There had clearly been no game

On their faces anger showed
In lines the pain was etched
To the fields of healing
They had all been fetched
'Where have you come from?
I asked from hour to hour'
Always the same answer
'Where evil released its power
We became so injured
We are now amongst the dead
Satan feasted on our bodies, but
On our souls he never fed
We escaped, by death released

"*And so it goes on, telling the story of those who died. The word 'etched' is an expressive word, but 'fetched' lacks that same beauty, don't you think. But it is the best I can do to both suggest the meaning and at the same time find a rhyme. I know you are not a Latin scholar, Richard, but the words 'he never fed' could be translated with equal correctness to 'he did not feed'.*"

"*Now, consider a moment, Richard and tell me. What would be your preference? Should I put 'Satan feasted on our bodies, but on our souls he never fed' or 'Satan feasted on our bodies, but on our souls he did not feed? I have been trying to solve my dilemma for this past half an hour.*"

"*I think I prefer the latter. But, Uncle, why don't we ask Robbie for his opinion?*"

"*A brilliant idea.*" *He summoned Norman to ask Robbie to meet us in the library.*

Uncle George told him about his dilemma and the choice I had made.

"*I shall be better able to advise if I see the original,*" *commented Robbie. He read the words from Uncle George's tatty book, and, after walking the length of the library several times, he then gave his reply.*

"Richard, I, myself think as you regarding the words, and I, too, prefer your choice. But, with all due respect, I do believe, having scribed your book and understood the qualities of your sisters, that '... on our bodies he never fed,' would convey the meaning you both require better than '...on our bodies he did not feed.' My reasoning is that the word 'never' has an absolute quality, whereas 'did not' could possibly mean 'did not now but does not necessarily rule out some time later'. It is only a mute point, but that is why I would choose the words 'never fed' so that there is no room for conjecture.

"That is a brilliant way of solving the problem, Robbie. So it shall be," said Uncle George. "Thank you. You have saved an old man much disturbed thought." When Robbie had left the room Uncle George continued, "I have told you many times, Richard, that boy was a find of gold, pure gold."

"It is good and right that you put that in the book, Uncle. It could have been written especially for them. Thank you so much."

"Then I would also like to add my own sentence, which is my way of giving the same meaning" he smiled, then added, "and I need no assistance in this."

Uncle George went to the table. He picked up a solitary piece of parchment and wrote the lines from the poem. Then underneath he wrote, 'Evil crossed their earthly paths, but their souls were safe in the arms of God'.

As I read the words, my tears flowed.

"I think God is absolute enough, don't you?" His eyes twinkled as he spoke. "I believe this to be true, Richard and would like Robbie to inscribe these words at the beginning of the book, under the others, but on the same page, if you agree."

This wonderful man, to whom we owed so much, had given this thoughtful tribute to my dear departed sisters, knowing their kind and gentle spirits. I could ask for nothing more suitable and agreed instantly and with gratitude.

When Robbie has finished scribing the following few lines, this book will be complete. It has been a task which has been done willingly, with much heart-searching and effort, but with love. Uncle George will now have all these pages along with Ben's pictures and do what is required. I know with true confidence that the cover will be of the very best.

I shall make the necessary plans to visit Stocksmoor. I have already decided that the casket shall be buried in Simion's corner, the most appropriate and, somehow, I believe, the safest place.

When you, dear readers, find this book, we shall be long since buried and our bodies but grains of dry dust. Yet, our souls will live on. That truth I know and share with you. My dear departed Papa and my family have shown me and left me with no doubt. I know not how or when the finding of the casket will come about, but that 'dream' will, of a surety, come to pass.

I will leave you with the fervent hope that any who read this book may be granted health and happiness. I pray to God that in your time, if not in ours, there is sufficient truth and love on this fair earth so that people can live together without pain and suffering being inflicted by the strong to the weak. It is my belief that even one life blighted by evil affects all, in one way or another.

Farewell, dear readers, and may you abide in peace.

Signed: Richard Shaw, 1501

Scribe: Robbie Cecil (previously Fairless)

Contents – Part 3

2013

» February

'I feel I am old enough to retire,' thought Brian.

He was just home after yet another busy day. Yes, he had interesting days, but he just wished they weren't as long. The road had been icy. Thank goodness he wasn't due in Leeds for a while; at least the weather should have improved by then. His December trip there had been a bit nerve-wracking to say the least. He certainly wouldn't have set off in the morning had he known the storms were going to be so ferocious later in the day, Len or no Len. If there was one thing he liked when driving, it was to be able to see the road in front, and that tree blocking the road, apparently only a few minutes before his arrival! Phew! God, he'd been scared. But Len had particularly requested that he should have an unscheduled 'face-to-face' meeting with the staff. "It will keep them on their toes for the winter months." It wasn't really Brian's way of working.

The time, 21:55 – why did Sarah always set the time this way? It was on the microwave clock as he was just about to put his prepared plate in the microwave. To him it was 9:55.

"I didn't realise I was so late." He shouted to Sarah's deaf ears. She couldn't hear as she was watching the TV. "No, I can do it, no problem." He had declined her offer to warm up his dinner.

"Bloody Hell, I am so tired," he spoke, aloud. 'I am sounding like a record that is playing the same track. Even to myself I moan. What must it be like for Sarah to listen to me? I do it now without thinking. I talk to myself aloud,' he thought. "GOD, I AM EXHAUSTED," he almost shouted this time, as if he hoped God would eventually hear him – but at the same time that his Grandfather wouldn't. He could hear him saying, "Brian, swearing shows a lack of the intelligent use of words, it's unnecessary and, let's face it, very limiting." 'Yes, Granddad,' he thought, 'but you are not here, feeling as I do, and I am bloody tired!'

"Brian, come and listen to the news," Sarah called. "It's about that place where you stay."

He picked up his plate and went into the lounge, just in time to hear the end of Dr Boreton's interview.

"Yes, the book is now complete. I have translated the text in such a way that modern day readers can enjoy and understand, yet I have tried to keep some concept of an older way of expression. Readers may find that this form of writing takes a little more effort and time to read, but I found it to be a most beautiful book that was obviously written with love. The author writes in such a way that I feel I have been privileged to share the lives and, sadly, the deaths of the people in the book. When its true value is realised, it will be seen, not only as a gift left for us to savour, but as enlightenment for every human in our modern world. For me, this was a privilege of a lifetime. It should be on sale in four to eight weeks, if all goes to plan and no last minute problems. I will let you know."

"Thank you, Dr Boreton. Now, back to you, John, in the studio." The rest of the news followed. Sarah shut off the television.

"It is a most unusual find, isn't it? In fact, quite unique. It's a bit like the Dead Sea scrolls. When do you go back there?"

"About April or May, I haven't booked anything yet. The Dead Sea scrolls? What have they to do with this?"

"Well, nothing really I suppose. But, as far as I recall, they were old information that was found and read, and with a message."

» May

The pub was unusually busy when Brian arrived, and he had to use the overflow car park. "What a good job I had the sense to book a room in good time," he mused, to no one in particular. It had been stifling hot all day. These last few days, though only mid-May, had been a bit of a heat wave, and though there was air conditioning in the office and in his car, for some reason he was weary. He felt absolutely exhausted and it was still only Monday.

True, they had had their usual sociable weekend. He hadn't enjoyed any of it really, if he was honest. All he ever wanted when home was a quiet time with Sarah and Ben, but he and Sarah had grown like chalk and cheese over the past couple of years. Sarah's heart just wasn't in anything, other than looking after Ben. He could tell, though she made every effort. But, he had not been able to speak to her. How could he? She had had enough to cope with. He realised that Jeanette's death had saddened Sarah very deeply. But, as time went by, she didn't seem to be improving. She was very quiet and subdued. He thought that was probably the reason for her appearing 'distant', if that was the right word.

With the finality of death had come a relief – in many ways. The last few weeks had been very difficult for all concerned, although they had been reassured by the hospice that Jeanette had been comfortable and without pain. Jeanette, Sarah often remarked, had faced death with a calmness that was quite amazing. She had cried with Sarah many times about leaving her children and never seeing them married or with children of their own, but had been quite sure that she was not afraid of death itself, as she had always done her best and been kind. It was her view that if God was there, and was a loving God, then he would understand. She was sure there was 'something' after death. She had questioned why she had to die so young when there were plenty around, living to a ripe old age, whom quite honestly, she felt the world wouldn't miss and would be a better place without.

Sarah confided, unusually, that for the first time in her life she had really thought about these things and that she now did not have the same fear as before. He had known how much Sarah had had to rely on Jeanette for friendship and that all important and sensible type of advice that someone with a bit more experience of life could give. But he knew that his long hours working and nights away had not helped. It wasn't his choice that he wasn't around. He would like nothing better than to spend much more time at home. Breast cancer was still a killer for many, he realised, though Sarah had two other friends who were in remission. They were perfectly well and appeared to have put their illnesses totally behind them.

'I'll go for a walk down the village,' he decided, 'before I have my dinner. Yes, that's what I'll do. I'll enjoy it better when I've had some fresh air and given my mind a chance to forget that meeting. How banal it all was. Len really should not interfere when he had already sorted everything. After all, it was he, Brian, who had ensured the profits, not Len. He had managed the staff so that the office ran smoothly and efficiently. Not Len! Today just wasn't the right time to put in his 'two pennyworths' as he put it. Two pennyworths indeed! Not the time at all. I'll just give Sarah a call, then have a quick shower, change my shirt and go for a walk.'

He heard the phone ringing, but Sarah didn't answer. 'She's either busy or out,' he thought. 'Let me see, it isn't cubs tonight or gym practice for Ben, and her 'girly night out' isn't until tomorrow – when I'm home. Where can she be? Oh, well, I'll phone later.' He couldn't be bothered to shower or change. He left the room, pocketed his key and went out of the pub by the front door. 'I'll have a shower later, before I finish my work. Bloody computer! Like being chained to the office.'

"I'll be about three quarters of an hour," he called to Tom, who was in the bar as he went out. "Is it OK for me to eat about seven thirty? I need a bit of fresh air and exercise first."

"Of course," replied the landlord. He thought well of Brian as, without fail, he was always a most polite and appreciative guest. "Just take your time," he added. He thought Brian looked pale and very tired this evening. He had noticed a definite change in the past two years in particular. His observations were still part of the 'bonus' that went with his job.

Brian turned right out of the pub to walk down the hill. He passed the common land and continued up the incline at the end of the village, where the house, called Albion Mount, stood – as if watching over the village. When he reached the next corner, called Windy Bank, he decided he would turn back and retrace his steps. One day he would take the walk back behind the cemetery and through the wood, but he didn't want to explore anywhere new this evening; he just couldn't be bothered. His mind felt tired and weary, but yet, at the same time it would not be sensible and switch off from work. Why was he worrying so much? Thoughts, useless thoughts, kept going round and round in his head. Stupid thoughts that he had no answer to. Why had Sarah not answered the phone? How could he know until he could ask her! As he walked he made a conscious decision to think of what he fancied to eat for his dinner.

He never had any qualms about presenting his bill for B&B with evening meal to Len for payment each month. He knew he had value for money. God, why did he think about Len, bringing work into his mind! Where could she be? She hadn't told him she was going out anywhere. Was Ben ill? Oh God, maybe she had had to take him to hospital. Stop being so silly and stupid! She'd have phoned you if anything was wrong with Ben. He must check his bank account when he went home. He'd had a few extra bills this month. Money, money, money, always the worry about money. Targets. He lived with targets, dartboard targets where he was always having to try for a 'bull's eye'. It really wasn't fair of Len to put yet another target on the agenda today. He could just feel the atmosphere change in the office when Len spoke. There must be something better to life than this. Yes, he was really angry with Len. What was that all about? He thought he would continue his tradition of having the roast beef dinner and started to picture a big white, unusually square china plate with roast potatoes... which vegetables would Tom have gathered? Then, in his mind, he was looking at the chart that Len had presented. Another f-ing chart. Oh, sorry Granddad! And now still more targets to meet ... God, there has to more to life than this.

"Oh, bloody hell! What the ..." He had just passed Albion Mount and was nearing the small road that led to the wood-yard, when, apparently out of nowhere, came a feeling of fear. 'I must leave here quickly,' he thought as the anxiety increased, rapidly. 'How odd, how can I be in danger?' He felt suddenly panicky and tried to turn to see what had frightened him before the strong urge to run took over. He was stopped by a sharp and intense pain in the left side of his chest and thought someone must have stabbed him from behind. He reeled with the shock and then felt as though his head had been struck with something big and heavy. "Sarah! Ben!" He cried out but then knew nothing more as he collapsed to the ground.

How long he lay there, he had no idea but the next thing he registered was Bert's voice. He heard a dog sniffing near by.

"Nay, Brian, what are you doing on the floor, lad? What has happened to you?" asked Bert. "Did you trip?"

"Hello, Bert." Brian sat up, slowly, on the pavement. "I don't know. God, my head hurts. I just remember feeling very anxious as though I had to go somewhere quickly and it was very important. I suddenly felt this bad pain in my chest, as if someone had stabbed me and then had hit my head with something really hard. Next thing, I found myself on the floor and I heard you. What's the time?"

"I don't know, lad, I never carry a watch," replied Bert. "Can you stand up yet?" Brian stood up without needing his support, which, oddly, Bert didn't offer.

"Staying at the pub again, are you?"

"Yes, just for tonight. Fortunately I'm going home tomorrow. I am very tired. Let's face it, Bert, I'm always tired." Realising he was still wearing his own watch, he looked at the time.

"Good, I haven't missed dinner. I don't know how long I was on the floor. I've no idea. Did you see me fall?" he asked Bert. "It couldn't have been long as no one stopped their car to see if I was alright."

"No, you were on the floor when I arrived. You'd best phone your wife about this funny turn you've had and arrange to visit a Doctor when you arrive back home, unless you feel you want to see someone tonight. But, that would mean a trip to the local hospital. There are no doctors visiting these parts after five o'clock, but an ambulance can be here within half an hour."

"No, no. I shall be alright, I'm sure. Still, I will tell Sarah and see my own GP, Dr Gibbs tomorrow, if possible. It has given me quite a scare. I have no actual pain now, just a bit of a headache. Nothing like this has ever happened before."

"And I'm sure it won't again," muttered Bert, more to himself than Brian, but as if he knew.

Together they walked slowly back up the hill towards the pub.

"I noticed when I arrived that the pub is busier than I've ever seen it before," Brian remarked.

"Yes, ever since a casket was found last summer on the common, many people have been coming to the village. It's a bit like a pilgrimage. Do you remember my telling you about the little girl who grew up, became a doctor and is now a writer? Well, she wrote a book called 'Beyond Mercy'. It was published in 2009. It's quite clear that she wrote about this very village, though she gave it a different name."

"Oh, yes. I heard about that on the telly. I understand that in 'Beyond Mercy' the author writes all about a casket being found with a book in it - written in the fifteenth century.

"That's right."

"So, is it all true?"

"Yes, every bit of it, right down to the last detail."

"No, that's not possible. Nobody can do that."

"Well, she did. Everything - the casket, its protective covering of woven willow and the contents have been carbon dated and all are from the fifteenth century.

"That is just incredible! I don't suppose these people make mistakes, do they?"

"No, it is all correct. Dr Audrey Coatesworth, because that is her name since she grew up and married, told, not only the story in the old book in the casket, but what personal things would be in the casket, what they all are and to whom they belonged. And, would you believe, where it would be dug up. Dr Boreton, the expert, has confirmed that everything in Dr Coatesworth's book tallies with what has been found. She is still reeling from the shock of this discovery and its implications for everyone. She expects the impact to be like a slow but growing wave overwhelming old beliefs.

"Dr Coatesworth's book is selling like hot cakes now and worldwide. I expect the old book will do likewise – so that people can compare and contrast for themselves. I understand there is shortly going to be a film too; one of those famous film makers is interested. I mean, no one before has ever written a book like this about a life that is long since past. And there is so much detail. It's quite unique."

"It's really hard to believe, isn't it?" Brian felt rather dubious, despite what he had heard.

"Well, a book is a book, tangible, solid. It's not pretend or a trick of an illusionist, it is real. Her book was registered with the copyright people, you know, like all books have to be. It was deposited in the legal department of the British Library in 2009. So, no one can deny anything about it. I imagine many people will be sure to try to rubbish it. But, they can't dispute that facts are facts, can they? Dr Coatesworth's book has been for sale for over three years, and the chest has been dug up less than a year ago? Mind you, it will affect religions everywhere as she writes accurately about people who have died a long time ago, and people will have to ask, 'How can she do this? How can she know?' I mean, humans are human, wherever they are born or live, whatever colour, race or religion. All are humans. But no one has ever written a book like this, never, over all the centuries since mankind could write.

"It's in all the book shops and on the internet. She has her own website where the books can be bought. She's made an e-Book and an audio book. I gather that she's a lover of technology I gather! But, just ask Tom at the pub. He has a supply. He receives them straight from the horse's mouth so to speak, Audrey brings them up to him when she and her husband visit their family in Yorkshire. Aye, she just delivers them in boxes, has a chat and a coffee in the bar. Often the pub is full of people on their pilgrimage to the site, and no one knows who she is. And she never enlightens them! She's not interested in being famous. She just wants people to read her books and understand the message behind them."

They walked up the hill in silence.

"Bert, would you call writing that book a kind of miracle? I mean it's out of the normal sphere and let's face it, people from the fifteenth century can hardly come back and tell us face to face."

"Well, it certainly something that people will have to consider, whether they care to or not."

"I shall certainly buy one of her books and read it."

They chatted as they slowly went back towards the pub. By now Brian felt much better, quite relaxed and calm. He always liked talking to Bert. Was it his reassuring voice or what?

"Do you know, Bert, I feel as if I'm in a world of work and know little else. It's like being in a little bubble that is being blown somewhere and I don't want to go in the direction it is taking me. Sarah's been very sad and distant, and it feels as though she is outside this bubble and I can't reach her. I think, or at least I hope, it is because her friend Jeanette died and her Mum is now in France."

"Poor Sarah."

"Yes, Jeanette was her best friend and only comparatively young. They say the good die young. It doesn't seem fair."

They walked on a bit, quietly.

"I mean, you can think about many people, with great prospects who die young in all walks of life. The obvious one is Princess Diana, I always thought she was 'good' and look at what happened to her."

"Well, things aren't always what they appear."

"What do you mean?"

"If you travel in your car, do you wear your seat belt?"

"Of course. That was something strange, wasn't it? The reports indicated that Princess Diana wasn't wearing a seat belt when the car crashed"

"Why do you wear yours, Brian?"

"Well, just in case I have an accident. I'm responsible and I have Ben, in particular, to think about. Sarah as well, of course, but Ben is the one who is immediately in my mind when you ask. He is so young and vulnerable and not old enough to care for himself yet."

"Quite."

"What do you mean?"

"What do you think of first when you think about Princess Diana?"

"Her kindness, her beauty but, mostly, her love for her children," replied Brian.

"And she was always a responsible mother, whatever else people say. She may have made mistakes; who doesn't? But none can say different to that. I think her boys would feel better if they knew that their mother acted responsibly, don't you, and that her death wasn't her own fault, whatever caused it? I knew a boy once whose mother was killed and he remained angry with her for years as he believed she was to blame, partly at least, and she wasn't. Not at all. It was very sad."

"Would you ever go into a car with a drunken driver?"

"Of course not!"

"Then why would she? She wasn't in the least stupid. She was used to dealing with the paparazzi. For years she had lived in the limelight, even courting it. She loved life and she was no one's fool. So tell me, why would she do something quite so crazy? No one meant more to her than her children."

"What are you saying, Bert?"

"Just what I'm saying – nothing more, nothing less. I am merely saying what I think and the same questions that many others have asked."

"So you think she wore a seat belt and it had been tampered with?"

"I am saying nothing. But, I understand that they are very easy to replace, or alter. I didn't hear. Did anyone study those?"

"I don't know."

"I don't suppose anyone ever will, either."

They walked on amicably for a while. Then Brian spoke again, "The other thing that I can't understand, you know, is that the papers all mentioned that there was a very long delay in getting her to hospital. Why was that? Was it the ambulance people or what? I don't know about French ambulances, but I am sure they are limited in their equipment just as ours are. I know of someone who collapsed and nearly died of a hole in the lung. She was deeply unconscious when the ambulance men arrived. But the paramedics were second to none, had her on medication and oxygen and everything, and in the ambulance in no time.

"They raced with sirens whining, and rushed her to the hospital, which was about seventeen miles away. They arrived within twenty minutes. I understand that that is the 'critical' time. They couldn't do what was necessary in the ambulance. It was their duty to make sure she received treatment at the hospital as quickly as possible or she, too, would have been dead. So, why would it not be the same for Princess Diana?

"I mean, I didn't read the reports on the long inquest, but, if there was a delay, did they say why? Had anyone given specific orders? No paramedic would ever have taken on that responsibility. Such a decision had to come from a higher source, hadn't it? How could a paramedic, however senior, make the decision to delay anyone from racing as fast as possible to a hospital if there was no hope otherwise? That is against all they stand for. I mean, for anyone, never mind someone as famous as Princess Diana. You know, it's never made any sense to me."

"Maybe there was a very senior doctor in the ambulance who made the decision."

"I hadn't thought of that. Is it common practice in France?"

"I don't know, but I doubt it."

"I don't believe in coincidences, you know."

"Very wise," agreed Bert.

"Still, it's all wasted breath really. Nothing can make the dead come alive again. What happened is over. The inquest is finished. The verdict has been given. I think it's really just a waste of breath to talk about it all now, don't you?"

Just then, Brian felt the need to sit down. They rested on the wall just before the chapel, near where the buses stopped.

"My, that hill seemed steep tonight. I'm quite breathless."

§

"Yes, on this plane, for and about Princess Diana, it is all over," continued Bert, "But, Brian, what people don't realise is that a memory of all a person's actions and intent, and any action to, with or against them, goes with them when they die. Life on earth is just the lowest dimension of existence. That is something people don't seem to understand yet."

"What do you mean? I have never heard anyone say that before."

"Just that what happens on this level of existence is where it starts, but not where it ends. Go down the wrong path and you reach the wrong place. Ask the wrong questions and, on earth, you receive the wrong answers. But, all truth is known, accurately and in full detail, where it is needed to be known and that is where final justice takes place," Bert informed him. "It's a pity more people don't know that. The world would change, I assure you, dramatically! Bullies are cowards. People who deliberately hurt others would not do so if they knew that one day, either in this world or the next, they will get that hurt back. There is no 'perhaps' or 'maybe' about that, just 'certainty'. If someone did harm Princess Diana, then they will pay for it eventually, fear not."

Brian didn't understand, though he had heard the words correctly. How could Bert know something that no one else knew?

"I've heard of an 'eye for an eye, and a tooth for a tooth'. Is that what you mean?" he asked.

"Oh no. Not at all. That implies retaliation. No, no. The truth is that 'what you sow on earth, so you will reap'. What someone does while alive determines where they go after death and what they experience in the 'hereafter'. I assure you, there is no vengeance, only justice. A priest's instruction, for example to do three 'Hail Mary's' and such like, to release a person from the consequence of his or her actions, doesn't have any authority or clout outside the earthly plane. It may make them feel a bit better on this plane, but that is the limit of its power.

"It's a bit like balancing energy, you know, equal and opposite forces. What you give out, so you will get back. Those who give out pain deliberately to hurt and harm, will have to accept it back, in full measure. No one can stop that happening whatever anyone of any religion or belief says. Everyone has choice on earth as to how they behave. It is human to make mistakes and people can learn and redress their beliefs or amend their ways and understanding. But there are those who do things purely out of cruelty and hate, you could say 'evil', and for them there is no forgiveness and no pardon. All could be kind and caring, whether rich or poor and whatever the race.

"You know, Brian, Audrey Coatesworth in her book, Growing Up, wrote a poem called 'Judge me not'. If I can remember it correctly it goes like this,

Judge me not

Judge me not by my face
The colour of my hair
Judge me not by appearance
As that would not be fair
I came to earth as I am
No discussion of my look
I had no pattern to study
No choice from out a book

Judge me not by ability
To read, write, or understand
Let it be by all my effort
The use put to my hand
The courage in hard times
Endurance getting through
Kindness to another
Judge me by what I do

"That's a lovely poem,"

"Yes, it is simple but so true. Everyone will meet their own justice irrespective of race, colour, intelligence, status, and whether a member of any religion or not. But, you know, where more is given, more is expected. But for some, life's experience is very tough and just getting through it is a marathon task in itself and takes all the energy available and just to cope is all that is required of them. Life is a mere fragment of time, but so important. It should never be wasted or thrown away recklessly."

"We hear that there are so many young people drinking heavily and taking drugs. They're not going to be able to use their abilities to the full if they carry on and damage their health and brains, are they?"

"No indeed, and that brings a great sadness. They are not going to be able to make the choices as to how to behave or how to change their ways when their brains are damaged. If this life is wasted in such ways, for no reason other than having pleasure, there will be no second chance. After death it is too late for anyone to decide to change their ways. Everyone will have to follow the path they created. Of that, there is no choice. Those who say there is no life after death will find the truth and finally know their mistake, as all mankind must die. For some, there will be no life after death, as that has to be earned by their lives on earth. Some will have another chance, to try again, so to speak. It's quite simple really. But, those who are evil go to Hell.

"There are many who lead others down a path of false belief via religion and that itself will carry a penalty," continued Bert. "When people are very clever or learned or hold high positions, they are thought to speak correctly on these matters. In actual fact, they have no extra knowledge of the truth. I don't know whether they actually believe that they have or whether they are deliberately fooling people."

"I heard that there is more than one scientist, well known for views on the universe based on physics and maths or philosophy, saying that there is no God. Do you know, Bert, that I read a few years ago that one man actually paid a lot of money to give that message to people by having a slogan painted onto buses," remembered Brian.

"There is a lot of nonsense around and always has been. It seems to me that those who protest that there is no God are hoping that what they believe is actually true, for whatever reason. Fear maybe? I do assure you that God is above earthly statements, wishes or calculations! That big magnet, you know the 'collider', wasted, and may well still be wasting, billions. All that money should have been used on this earth for humanitarian needs or useful research."

"I read the paper every day and listen to the news," Brian told Bert, "but it seemed to me, when we all heard of it in 2008, that few if any ordinary people anywhere knew about it. Otherwise a furore would surely have started sooner to prevent such waste. Why? If it is an innocent scientific investigation, why was there all the apparent secrecy? Yes, it may be on the internet, open to the world so to speak, but you have to know that something is there to look for it in the first place. Let's face it Bert, when anything is for the public domain, the newspapers get the full story and without delay. Who gave permission to spend such vast amounts of money on something that is so ludicrous and wasteful? I would like to know who gave the go ahead to all the scientists."

"Fear not, Brian, man can try to pit his wits against God, to investigate the universe, but will not win. You see, that is not the purpose of life at all. The earth provides everything that man needs and must be taken care of. There is plenty of energy existing naturally, it just needs harnessing. There is 'black' work afoot in many areas, make no mistake, linked with greed and power, but hidden under several umbrellas. Hence many things are not questioned and the practices just carry on. But, nay lad, I shouldn't be tiring you with all this just now."

Bert stopped.

Brian was very interested in what Bert told him. "I feel I am resting and, strangely, being revived as I listen. I didn't know any, of what you are saying, before. It is very different."

"Well, that is because these truths are not known. People don't have the opportunity, usually, to learn them, as you are having just now. I can't tell you more than just a tiny fraction of the truth in a few minutes, of course, as it is very complex. Each individual has to meet his or her own understanding, and there are many and varied ways. But for those, whose behaviour is deliberately to hurt, it is quite simple. They will receive back what they gave. I have given you the general gist to take with you on your way.

"Many in every society are brainwashed at an early age by other people's beliefs and behaviour and so have not the open mind that is needed to understand. Religions try to recruit their devotees young and through fear. Has anyone asked 'why'? If any religion was true, it would not be necessary! It would speak for itself. Nowadays, for many, 'acquiring material things' is the main and seemingly the only goal in life. Learning to love from being loved, and learning to respect from being respected is what is needed."

"Please tell me more. I feel that if I don't learn just now while I am listening to you, then I shall never know."

"Well, if you are sure you are not feeling too tired after your episode down the road."

"No, not at all. I feel I am being restored in some way talking to you, though that may sound rather odd. I always feel as though you have helped me when we have had our conversations and I am most grateful that you spend your time with me."

"It doesn't matter how old we are, we can always need a helping hand or someone to listen to us. I am glad that our paths have crossed. You realise with your own son, Ben, that children are needy and vulnerable. Brian, let me tell you this. Those who hurt children will, after death, feel the pain they caused, but for them it will last for ever. They may act in darkness and secrecy here on earth, but nothing is hidden after death.

"You see children are loved by God and, in dire times of great pain and fear, for whatever reason, they are given help by angels. Angels are always aware if a child, anywhere, has pain. Have you heard any of the opera 'Hansel and Gretel'? There is a song in there about angels watching over children. It's quite beautiful and so true."

"No, I haven't heard that. I don't really know any opera. I will try to find it when I get home, on the internet. I know how to use a search engine. Bert, I hear what you say, but how can there be so many angels?"

"You wouldn't ask, 'How can there be so many children on earth', would you?"

"No, of course not. That would be a silly question, wouldn't it?"

"Well, your question about angels seems that to me, in the same way. But, you should understand that angels are not humans. They do not exist under earthly laws of life. Let me explain, simply, about children. Suppose you have a child who is frightened and in pain. Well, the part of their brain that registers the excessive pain and fear is guided, temporarily and by an angel, to a different level of awareness. A different 'space of existence' is the easiest way to describe it. While there, they don't feel the pain in their body, but neither do they remember, consciously, the experience. When the pain and fear is over, and if they survive, they are guided back again and continue with their lives. Angels cannot alter what is happening, except in rare cases. They are there to help the child progress through the experience."

"Could anyone know if a child is being helped by an angel?" asked Brian.

"If a child is in pain, what usually happens?" asked Bert.

"The child will cry."

"Exactly! If a child is being hurt or is frightened, there should be tears until everything stops or eases. If the tears stop yet the pain continues as bad as ever, then the child isn't feeling the pain. That is when the angel has come to that child's aid. But, of course, the angel is aware of what is happening, on every different level.

"If they have to be taken to a different plane of awareness as a result of someone's cruel actions, then they take a part of those who are hurting them with them. When they come back the memory of that experience stays in that other plane, but is still attached to the child. If the child does not manage to survive and dies, then that experience is stored on the higher plane. When the abuser dies, he or she can never escape justice on the higher plane of existence. Believe me.

"The important fact to remember is that that same memory is also within the person who does the hurting. Those memories match – perfectly. Now, it will be strange for you to understand, but on that 'other' plane time does not exist. The pain and fear 'wait' as if suspended in time. When the person, who has hurt a child deliberately, for personal satisfaction, eventually dies, they have no option but to collect that pain. The memories that match meet, much like the two sides of a torn page being put together again. But, I assure you that once they collect it, and the 'page is made whole again' then they cannot escape from it. It's as though they have set their own trap, and then been caught by it. That is the simplest way that I can explain what happens, but in truth it is very complicated."

Brian remained silent for a while. He was trying very hard to understand. This was all new to him. Bert waited.

"Do you mean that paedophiles will feel the pain that they cause the children they abuse?"

"Yes, indeed, I mean that – absolutely," continued Bert. "Eventually, they will get back exactly the same pain and fear. But felt as the child felt it, not as an adult. Not only that, but it will exist for them for eternity and in hell. Once the action is done, they cannot escape the consequences – ever. When anyone abuses a child they put themselves beyond mercy and there is only one final destination. Never forget, they had choice – as all humans have. They made a decision to hurt."

"I remember hearing of a man who abused young boys. When he was caught he committed suicide as he presumably didn't want to face his punishment."

"But, all he did was to go to hell sooner rather than later." Bert sounded confident that he knew this truth. "And, of course, once there, it is forever. Time stands still in Hell. When pain is taken into Hell it takes its fragment of time with it, but that can then never change. Once people realise all this, believe me, no one will willingly cause hurt to another. At that time children will be safe from harm."

"Is this the same for people from all religions and races?" asked Brian.

"Of course. Brian, tell me why would it be different? It is the same for all humans. There will be no excuses for any reason or whatever the belief. Hurting another deliberately is wrong and has nothing to do with beliefs or religions. Those who abuse a child or adult will feel their agony. Those who torture will feel exactly the pain which they caused. It isn't difficult to understand. No more but no less. The only difference is that it will last forever in Hell."

"People have never known any of this before, have they?"

"No, but the time is coming when all people will understand. Then anyone, young or old, will be able to walk around, day or night, in total safety – except in the jungle of course. This only applies to humans! But, all humans live to the same 'order' of the universe. That order applies to the poorest of the poor, the richest of the rich, the lowliest and the most exalted, all cultures and all creeds. Religious doctrines make people believe differently, I know, but that has no impact outside the earthly plane. None, whatsoever! You do realise, of course, that there is a heaven for the good, there is a hell for the bad and evil, and there are planes for possible eventual understanding between. Heaven is a place of total beauty in every sense. Hell is a place of total pain. It doesn't matter what people believe or say, that is fact."

"I had not realised any of this at all, until now. But, Bert, how can you be certain of this?" replied Brian.

"Because I know," insisted Bert. "But, one day, all will learn. Mark my words."

"Thank you so very much for taking the trouble to talk to me in this way. You have given me such a lot to think about. I have said this before, but I must say it again, I am so grateful for all your help over the past few years."

"It's my pleasure that our paths have crossed," Bert replied. He thought, 'If he changes the course of his life, as a result of our meetings, then I am very glad and my purpose is fulfilled. It was such a pity that he lost his life back then. He deserves a better one this time. A good lad, yes, he's a good, decent lad.'

"Why do you think Princess Diana is still being talked about and many people still trying to tarnish her name?"

"Oh, some people are not satisfied with the verdict, some are still grieving, but some will say anything for publicity, particularly when that person cannot answer back?"

§

'At least she wasn't accused of signing a document giving the order for someone to be beheaded when she couldn't read or write, was she?'

"No, thank goodness. She was spared that," Bert answered.

'I mean, anyone, can be taught to write a name, particularly if imprisoned at the time. I was so scared. I had to do as I was told. You know me, better than anyone. I would never have done anything like that deliberately – never. I never thought, not even for one moment, that those signatures on blank papers would be stored to use at a later date?'

Brian looked round as he thought he had heard someone else. Who had joined them in their conversation? He saw no one.

"Who was that?" asked Brian. "I thought I heard a voice."

"Sorry, yes, I was distracted."

"Bert, can you tell me how you know so much?"

Bert didn't answer. It felt, to Brian, as if the previous conversation hadn't happened.

§

"That collapse, or whatever it was, must have affected me more than I thought. Thank goodness, we are going on holiday in a few weeks." Brian felt that that time could not come soon enough.

"Where are you going?" asked Bert.

"Well, this year we are all going to France to stay with Sarah's mother. Do you remember I told you that she's half French? It's a very romantic story really. Her grandfather was an officer in the English army in France at the end of the Second World War. He fell in love with a French girl. They were billeted in the outhouses of the vineyard and fruit farm that her parents owned.

"Well, to cut a long story short, though it really merits a longer telling, their love lasted. They eventually married and lived in England. Sarah's mother was an only child but she has lots of extended family in France. Her grandmother was one of four girls, all married and all had families who lived near each other. Most of these relatives still live close to each other, in that same village, and their lives continue to revolve around each other and their fruit farm. They grow apples and pears, and, I believe good crops of apricots, plums and damsons. They have a small vineyard which is now opened up to visitors, along with a small coffee house where they sell their own seasonal produce.

"Sarah's grandfather died about twenty to twenty five years ago. Her grandmother moved back to France soon after to be with her sisters and their families. She had settled in England while her husband was alive, but felt she wanted to spend her last years back 'at home' in France. So, Sarah knows them all very well, as she always accompanied her mother at least twice a year to visit her grandmother. Sarah is amazingly fluent in French. She loves it there.

"I think I told you before that Sarah's own father died six years ago of a heart attack, you know, one of those sudden ones without warning, shortly after Ben was born. Anyway, her mother has moved, permanently now, lock, stock and barrel to France. She went for increasingly longer spells. At first it was to stay with her own mother, Sarah's grandmother, and help to look after her. But, since she died, she still wanted to spend several months each year with her relatives there. Of course, she inherited her mother's house.

"Sometime last year she decided to sell her house in England as she was, increasingly, hardly using it. We lived about two hours drive away anyway. I don't think it will actually take much longer to drive to her home in France once we have crossed the channel. Though Sarah could fly there quite quickly, for some reason it seems much worse for her, and she misses her mother very much. It's a daughter/mother thing. They phone most days. So, this year, we are going to stay there for two weeks," Brian paused, for no reason really. He saw that Bert was waiting to hear more.

"We have tended to go on a package to Spain or the Balearics, but I don't care one way or another. We didn't go anywhere last year, because of Jeanette being so ill. It will be a holiday, and a holiday is what I need. I know Ben will just love it as I gather there are lots of other children in their extended family. It will be all quite new to me, as, like her father, I have always felt I might intrude and haven't been before. Sarah says that's very silly and all I have to do is to learn French. But, I ask you, when do I have the time? Anyway, she particularly wants me to go there this year. We set off in twelve days time."

"That should be a very good change for you. Are you recovered now? You are sure you don't want to call a doctor this evening?"

"Yes, I feel fine now. Thanks Bert. I don't know what I would have done if you hadn't found me when you did. But at least it must have been quiet at the time with no traffic as no one else saw me on the floor. It was very odd, as if I didn't quite know where I was and everything looked strange for a while, sort of different. I've walked that way before when I have visited so I know the village fairly well. Very strange!"

"See you sometime."

"You are not coming in tonight?" asked Brian

"No, no need to now," answered Bert.

It was only later that Brian wondered why Bert had 'no need to'. He'd given the same answer once before, he remembered. He decided that Bert's plans were none of his business.

After his dinner, which he enjoyed despite the 'collapse' beforehand, Brian managed to contact Sarah on the mobile phone. After finding out about her day and Ben, he told her what had happened and she started crying. He was surprised, but in a strange way pleased. She had been at the bottom of the garden with Ben and neither had heard when he phoned before.

"Don't cry, Sarah, I'm alright now."

"I'll phone in the morning and make you an appointment to see Dr Gibbs tomorrow evening," promised Sarah, when she had calmed enough. "I'll make it for about five. Can you be back for then? You gave me a real shock telling me you were unwell."

"I'm sorry, but you had to know. Yes, I'll make sure I am back in plenty of time. I am going to have an early night and a late morning and then I'll set off home."

"Take care. I love you."

"I love you too. Bye now."

§

He was just getting ready to leave next morning, having slept very well, considering how he had been, when he remembered the book.

He found Tom and bought one.

"You wouldn't believe the increase in business since that casket was found," Tom told Brian.

"There hasn't been a room in the motel or an empty chair for dinner here since. If it continues like this then we shall have to seek more help. The visitors seem to be mostly historians and the like at present. But I guess people will finally realise the significance of the book. Then who knows what can happen? I keep asking myself, 'How could anyone, let alone someone from this very village, Audrey Coatesworth, write that book?' But I never come up with an answer. Just amazing. Bloody amazing.

"She calls in here, you know, when passing, and brings me a supply of books. I phoned the number in her book and she answered. Now I just let her know when I need more. She has written poetry books too, you know. They are there, on the counter, if you want to buy one of those. Beautiful poems they are, and the pictures in one of them are painted by her brother, who lives locally.

"She's just a down-to-earth Yorkshire woman. She is perfectly normal, you know, whatever anyone may say or think after that book. I understand that her father and mother were just ordinary people, though I never knew them and that they were both very pleasant. Of course, Audrey left the village many years ago. We understand that the book has been proven to be very accurate. No one can explain it. Maybe she will, one day."

"Haven't you asked her? You know, when she calls in with the books?"

"No, funnily enough, I haven't. I don't really have the chance. I mean I'm a landlord and must respect all my customers. If she doesn't want the people to recognise her, then I can't draw attention to her can I, unless she gives me permission? And I think if she wanted people to know all the facts, she'd tell us. She just comes in everyday jeans and jumper, you know, nothing posh and nothing to make her stand out in a crowd."

"Maybe we shall all understand, one day. Anyway, thanks. I shall read this on holiday. I'll buy one of the poetry books, 'Growing Up' for Ben, seeing as how you recommend them. I'll give you my verdict on both when I see you next time. I'll phone to book a room at the motel as usual. And it seems, as you are so busy, it would help if I order a meal at the same time."

Brian was just going out of the door when a thought struck him. He turned back into the inn.

"Tom, I've just had second thoughts. I'll take the 'Coping with Illness and Grief' book as well. Poor Sarah lost her best friend last year and still misses her a lot. It may help her."

"I'm sure it will. Have a safe journey."

Tom was still standing at the door when Brian drove past. He put his hand up to wave. 'What a pleasant man,' Brian thought, 'always the same and never appears stressed. What's his secret, I wonder?'

» Early September

Back at the pub in Stocksmoor after nearly four months, Brian was just settling down to read the local weekly paper, The Express, when he was very pleased to see Bert enter. Bert saw him directly and went over to sit with him.

"I'm really pleased to see you, Bert," he smiled as Bert approached. "It's very busy again, so, no let up in trade I imagine?"

"Indeed, no. The book from the casket has been on sale now for a few months. It came out soon after your last visit, I believe. People are buying that and Audrey Coatesworth's book, 'Beyond Mercy', together to compare and contrast. Some will no doubt want to find a flaw or pick it to pieces and some will try to ridicule it – if they can. But it seems that most are buying just because they want to read for themselves what everyone is talking about. I was walking on the common the other day and there were people holding the books at the site, as if by doing so they could learn more. Some even had their eyes shut, presumably trying to contact someone or absorb the atmosphere they think must be there. That would make Audrey Coatesworth smile, I think, or maybe wonder what they are doing! She's not a bit like that, you know. There's nothing 'airy-fairy' about her. She's quite the opposite really. Have you read the book you bought?"

"Yes. I thought it quite remarkable. It has made me think a great deal about not only 'how' but 'why' she wrote it. I mean, it is really quite profound, isn't it? People cannot help but believe what it says in the book, especially now since the old book and casket and everything has been proven to exist almost exactly as she detailed. Whatever their previous attitude or convictions have been, it will make everyone think. But I believe it will have other, more personal effects."

"What do you mean?"

"Well, we went away on holiday as you know. I had bought 'Beyond Mercy' for a holiday read. When I unpacked my bag on arriving home, I took out the book and, instead of putting it on the book shelf as I normally would, as Sarah likes things kept tidy, I left it on the conservatory table. Don't ask me why, it was not a conscious thing at all. I was then away for a few days, working as usual. Sarah saw it and read it. I'd told her how unusual it was but also that it was such an interesting 'read'. We have widely different interests in literature, so I never expected her to read it. Just my recommendation would normally have put it on Sarah's black list.

"But, I had bought two of Dr Coatesworth's poetry books as well, 'Growing Up', for Ben, and the 'Coping' one for Sarah. Ben apparently always chooses 'Growing Up' for Sarah to read to him at night. She offers him a selection as usual, but, no, he picks that one. Sarah lost her friend, as I told you last time, and that is why I bought her that book. She says that the poems have comforted her in a way that nothing else has. So, I actually think the poetry books are what got Sarah interested in the novel.

"Anyway, to cut a long story short, when I returned home, expecting her friends round as usual, there was no one. She always has someone round on a Wednesday evening. I can't remember when she didn't. She says it just breaks up the week a bit. But this night there was no one. She had actually cooked a meal just for me and it was great. Then, she looked at me directly and asked, 'Brian, are you happy?' I jest not, Bert, but my heart started beating as though it would jump out of my chest and my stomach felt as if cold water had been poured through it."

"My! What did you say to her?" asked Bert.

"I asked her, 'Sarah, shall I be honest?' She looked really worried, and I could hardly hear her reply, 'Yes, please.' I thought, 'If I don't tell her what I feel now, I never will.' So, I told her everything. That I was very tired and felt exhausted a lot of the time, and all I wanted was to be with her and Ben and for us all to be happy. For me, the holiday in France had been so carefree and, yes, I had felt happy again, but only briefly. In fact, once back, all the tiredness seemed even worse and I felt more stressed than before. I know why. The holiday had somehow made me see the big house as a really big millstone round my neck. I've the large mortgage to find month in and month out and I didn't know how long I could keep it all going, you know, the pressures, the stress of driving on the motorway every day. Finally, I thought, 'I'll say everything whatever the reaction'. So I told her that, though I knew she needed her friends and her activities, all the entertaining seemed pointless, and for me it was just a waste of money and energy. Let's face it, I found it rather boring as it had sameness. It was always predictable. It took away our precious time together, considering I have to work such long hours and be away so often. I told her I didn't like where I was 'in my space' at this present time."

"You told it as it was and no mistake. Where did you find the courage?"

"Well, I think that book helped. Those lives made me feel so sad. They had such short times of happiness and even life for them was fragile and a struggle. Yet, even in their grief, they had a calmness and serenity and spent time helping children. And I couldn't get the book out of my mind. Bits kept coming back, uninvited. It is certainly written to give us another message other than what people did back in history. To know that when the casket was actually dug up it matched what Dr Coatesworth wrote, well, it blows most people's beliefs out of the window, doesn't it? It tells us there is something beyond this life. There has to be. Otherwise how could that book have been written? Where and how did she gather all that information?

"Then I thought about me and Sarah. We have so much, but in order to get everything, you know, our big house and all our so-called 'essential' possessions, we seem to have become quite lost. We are travelling on another track altogether and away from the one we intended. That bubble I was talking about, when we met before, is taking us in the wrong direction. We are not going where we shall be happy. I know this is not what I really want. Bert, I am not happy. I thought I would be. I found the girl I want to share my life with, who is still the girl of my dreams. But that dream has slowly faded and another one has taken over."

"Well, you are finding out at last and all I can say is 'better late than never'. What did Sarah say, and what was the outcome of your truthful outpouring?" Bert enquired.

"She started crying. She has cried a lot this year – especially since her mother finally went to France permanently. She even cried when I told her about my collapse last time I was here."

"And then?"

"I feel awful when I say this, but I thought she had asked the question because she was having an affair or had decided that she wanted to leave me. I think I told you before that she had been rather distant for a long while now. I had never questioned her about this as, basically, I was scared to hear her answer. But, it wasn't that at all, thank goodness. No, since we went to France and had such a delightful time together, with her relatives and helping in the vineyard, she has decided that she wants to sell up here, leave it all and move over to live in France. She had apparently talked at length to her mother and she was all for it. Her mother is very happy there and likes being with her relatives, but she likes being with Sarah best of all. She has decided that she would let us live in her house, which would be Sarah's anyway one day, and she would build on a large annexe as soon as possible and move into that."

"What a brilliant solution!"

"Oh, I jumped at the idea. I mean it's not like someone just selling up and hoping to make a 'new life' in France, is it? I always think that is such a risky step to take. No, we are part of that family and we shall be welcomed. No more 'reaching someone else's targets', no more motorway driving and being away from home. Sarah has realised how much her friend's death and her mother moving away has upset her, but the 'light only went on' recently. She had genuinely thought we needed the latest this or that and a big 'keeping up with the Jones's house'. When she read the book she wept at the losses that those young people had had to suffer and the love and devotion shown from other members of the family. In particular she realised that the main anxiety of her life was losing me or Ben. She felt as if she was trying her hardest to push a wedge between us both and run me into an early grave, either to prove it wouldn't happen or so she wouldn't care when it did."

"So?"

"The house is up for sale. We leave in four weeks time, whether it is sold or not. It is in the hands of an estate agent. Sarah's mother has already applied to build the new extension. We shall live with her until it is finished. Her house is a traditional old French building, small windows, thick stone walls and really very cosy. We have agreed we need a new bathroom suite and the kitchen needs a bit of upgrading but otherwise a lick of paint is all it needs. There are enough rooms for us all, even without the extension. We shall live only a stone's throw from Sarah's favourite half cousin and Ben can go to the local school.

"He is so excited. I never realised, and I feel quite ashamed to say this, that by going to a private school he didn't know the local children where we live now. Sarah invited friends round for him but it isn't quite the same as knowing people who live in the same road, is it? Then, with all the pressure to achieve, targets for youngsters and everything, he was becoming like a tender greenhouse plant. Sarah often had to sit up with him for an hour or so in the night as he was awake and didn't want her out of his sight. She was sure that he worried about me when I wasn't home when he went to bed and that he kept awake as long as he could, trying to see me. That thought made me feel really upset. He had also become very picky with his food. To see him running in the vineyard and collecting raspberries with the other children, sleeping like a log at night and clearing his plate every mealtime was just wonderful. In just a few days he seemed to become 'free' somehow. That's the only way I can explain it.

"We sat him down the next morning after our long talk and explained what we wanted to do. He jumped straight out of the chair and made for the door. We looked at each other and didn't know what to think. Sarah, called to him, 'Ben, can you just stop for a moment?' He turned round, grinning. 'What are you doing?' asked Sarah. Do you know what he replied? 'I'm packing Mummy and then I shall be ready when we set off. Are we going today or tomorrow?'"

"So, no problems with Ben then! I am so glad. I have met a lot of people who have become lost, thinking they are getting what they want and need by going down a certain path, only to find that they have taken the wrong turning at some point. At least you have found out and are able to change direction. Would that more people learned that lesson, valued what they have and were content."

"Yes, I understand that now. I shall work on the house in France a bit and my knowledge of IT will be useful in the office. I think I shall be able to contribute, but we shall have no money worries at all. Our mortgage will end when our present house sells, and we'll have no school fees, nothing. Sarah has been roped in to bake some cakes and enlarge the tearoom and has been told, basically, to 'do what she likes'. She has a lot of ideas, but nothing needs her to hurry. I can't believe it really. Sarah says I have to have a complete rest for a while and get fit, then I can join in the business as much or as little as I want. Do you know, I might even study again, just out of interest."

Brian sat quietly for a while. There was something he had puzzled about and wanted to ask Bert.

"Bert, I was told that you were at the site of the sewerage excavations at just the time that the casket was dug up."

"Yes, I was. What a shame it would have been if it had been damaged or if the men had not recognised its importance."

"Did you know it was there? I know it sounds silly, but did you?"

"Put it this way, yes. But, I cannot explain more," he paused for a while. "Well, I'll be off then. I wish the very best to you and your family for the future."

"Bert, just a minute," Brian took out a card from his pocket. "Please take my card. It is our new address in France. I don't know why, as I doubt you'll ever visit France, but I would just like you to have one."

"Thanks." Bert picked it up and read, "Brian T Woolstone. Hmm... I knew some people called Trevore once. Strange how people meet, isn't it? I am certain you will at last enjoy the happiness you deserve. And, Brian, don't worry about Sarah, they will both be fine. Goodbye and may the true God go with you."

As Brian stood up to shake Bert's hand, he accidently knocked a newspaper onto the floor. He bent down to pick it up. But, when he looked up to say goodbye to Bert, he saw that Bert had gone. He hadn't heard him go. 'That was quick,' he thought. Then he noticed his card on the table.

Tom was wiping a table nearby. He decided to ask him to give it to Bert next time he was in the pub.

"Tom, do you know Bert well?" asked Brian.

"Bert? Bert? I don't think I know anyone of that name. What's his surname?"

"I don't know. I mean Bert. He was here, just now. You know, the man I was talking to. I usually see him and have a chat when I'm in here. I only know him as Bert, but he's a local man. He lives somewhere in the village."

"I'm afraid you have been dreaming," replied Tom. "You have just been asleep for the past hour. I didn't want to disturb you. You really do seem to get very tired with your job. Maybe you don't realise, but you always fall asleep after your dinner. I've never seen you speak to anyone while you have been here – Bert or any other name."

Brian thought, 'That's an odd thing for Tom to say'. But, he did not pursue the conversation. He did not want Tom to think him a bit strange but something was not quite as it appeared to be! He changed the subject, quickly.

"I shan't be coming here again," he confided, "so thank you so much for your very kind welcome at all times. Your food is superb and the rooms in the motel are very comfortable. It has been such a pleasure to spend time here."

"Why's that then?"

"I have just left my job today, resigned. My boss wasn't at all pleased. He wanted me to continue, even agreed to 'up my salary' to keep me. But I was adamant. No, I've basically had enough. My wife and I have made a decision. We are taking our son to a different life."

Brian realised how much he was enjoying being able to talk about his new life, repeating his news, this time to Tom. "Yes, we are moving to live in France with Sarah's mother who's half French. We are going to help in the old established family business. It's almost like a community in itself. They are all lovely, friendly people and, of course, Sarah's family. They want us to go to live amongst them. They have a vineyard and make their own wine. Maybe I could send you a crate, and if you like it you can sell it. I have only one problem, learning French. But, I'm sure I shall soon be able to do that. After all I shall hear it all the time. I've bought a CD, 'Learn French the easy way' for my computer. That should help me and my wife is fluent anyway."

"My, goodness me, that will be a big change for you. Well, all the very best, and, getting as tired as you do, I can only think it has to be a move for the better. There's nothing quite beats working at home. Even long hours don't seem stressful somehow when you can go into your own kitchen for a cup of coffee, have a snooze for an hour, or go out into the garden. You never lose track of what you are doing and why."

"I hope we don't ever do that again. We nearly did. Goodnight. I'll see you in the morning before I leave."

"Goodnight."

§

Brian was lying awake, tired, but his thoughts were keeping him awake. He was thinking about Bert's last words to him, 'I am certain you will at last enjoy the happiness you deserve. Goodbye, and may the true God go with you'. The true God? What did he mean? The happiness I deserve. What do I deserve? I've never done anything to deserve anything. He thought, 'Just a minute, I've read the book. Audrey Coatesworth didn't mention exactly 'when' the casket would be found. So, how did Bert know to be there, in the exact place at the exact time?'

What did he mean about Sarah? 'Don't worry, they'll both be fine'? He must have meant Sarah and Ben. How odd!

Then, like a bolt out of the blue, he suddenly sat up in bed, pulled on the light cord, jumped out of bed and went to rummage in his jacket pocket. He pulled out his business card. "Yes, it doesn't say Trevore," he confirmed. "It says Brian T Woolstone. I thought so. In fact, I knew so all along. But Bert definitely told me that he knew some people called Trevore once. I remember, quite clearly. God, there I go again, talking out loud - to no one!"

Feeling very bemused, he climbed back into bed. 'How did he know my middle name? It's not a usual name. I never mentioned Trevore. I know I didn't.' He went over and over his last conversation with Bert. But the conclusion was always the same. Bert knew his middle name.

Finally, he wondered if he would ever know the answers. He was just remembering that he had read the name 'Trevore' in the book 'Beyond Mercy', when he fell asleep, before he had time to make any connection.

§

He would have the 'full Yorkshire' breakfast – bacon, black pudding, egg, sausage, fried bread, toast and marmalade. The full works! After all, he didn't expect to be back at The Dun Cow again. Once back home it would be the usual shredded wheat and banana, so he might as well make the best of his opportunity.

He decided to phone Sarah before breakfast and just have a word or two with Ben before his school. But, before he had chance to phone, a text message arrived.

Phone me as soon as you can.

Immediately he pressed his quick dial, and Sarah answered.

"What is the matter? Is something wrong?" he asked as soon as he heard her voice.

Sarah laughed. "Well, that depends!"

"What do you mean?" asked Brian, feeling agitated - all of a sudden.

"It must have been the French air."

"What must? What are you talking about?"

"I did a test and it is positive. I'm pregnant."

"Oh, that's wonderful." At this point, Brian's legs failed him so that he suddenly had to sit down on the bed.

"Bye, I must get Ben ready for school. See you later."

He sat for a while, jubilant, thinking, planning and in particular glad they were going to France. He wouldn't have to earn extra money to keep another child. He hoped it would be a girl this time, so one of each. "That's what Bert meant," he realised. "How had he known?" But Bert wasn't there to tell him. It was all very strange.

After breakfast and feeling very satisfied, he decided to read through the landlord's collection of papers, from when the casket was found, in July 2012. He was flicking through one of the local papers, as he was eagerly awaiting his food, when his eye caught sight of a headline underneath which was a photograph of two men. They were holding up a large square object.

Who was the mysterious man who stopped the casket being damaged?

He read,

> 'This photograph shows two men holding the amazing fifteenth century find. The casket was found on Stocksmoor common during the excavation of land for the laying of mains drainage. This casket and its protective bindings have all been carbon dated back to somewhere between 1400 and 1550. So, we know that these are genuine.
>
> What is remarkable, and as yet not understood, is that the photographer, the site foreman who happened to be inspecting the work at the time the casket was dug up, expected to see three men in the photograph.
>
> He told me, "I always keep the camera handy. Rules, you know, in case of an accident and if anyone tries to sue for damages and such like. I would swear on the

Bible and my life that I took a photograph of three men."

I have since questioned the two men who are holding the casket and they too are in agreement. There was a man there, assumed to be from Stocksmoor or the locality around, who seemed to be interested in the work they were doing. It was actually he who noticed the casket in its containing shield of willow canes and alerted them to it. Without his intervention they are absolutely certain they would have crushed it with the digger, as it was completely out of their view.

The foreman also agreed that the same man was the first to notice the bones that were dug up just further along the trench the next day. The human bones that were unearthed a few feet from the site have now been carbon dated, and the villagers of today will be very relieved to learn that they too belong to the 15th century, round about the time that the casket was buried. They have no idea where the man, who should be in the photograph went, who he was or why, strangely, the photograph doesn't show him.'

'That was Bert', thought Brian, with a feeling of great relief. 'I'm not going mad after all, thank goodness. They saw him as well.'

The article continued.

Would this man come forward? If anyone knows this individual please contact 'The Express, Wakefield.' We would like to interview him.

'You'll be lucky,' thought Brian. 'But why did Bert meet me?'

(Would he ever realise why Bert had chosen to help him?)

1505

» Richard returns

Richard Shaw, accompanied by Robbie, returned to the village that he still thought of as 'Stocksmoor'. He had seldom spoken during the journey. The day was July 27th, 1505.

This time they rode directly through the village in broad daylight. They saw a workman at the wood mill who carried on with sawing the tree trunk and made no sign of welcome. Richard was sure that he had seen them. He used to know everyone in this village, but he did not recognise this man and vice versa. The doors of the houses were closed and he saw no one with whom to pass the time of day. He heard no children playing. It felt almost like an unknown place. To his eyes it even looked different. He had no wish to visit anyone, not even to talk to Bernard at the inn. He did not know if he was still the innkeeper, but he wouldn't find out, not today. He no longer regarded the villagers as having anything to do with him.

He knew that the problem was from within himself, but he could not shake off the lethargy of his troubled mind. He felt that he had been taken, by stealth and by an unknown force, into a dark and hidden place. He did not know how to escape the cold mantle of dread that pervaded this inner space. He tried his best to see beyond its darkness, but he saw only small flickers of light occasionally. These were so infrequent that they gave him little hope.

They turned left at the top of the hill and rode out of the village past the inn. He wanted to go onto the common land to Simion's corner by the same path as he had taken on the night four years ago when they buried the casket.

There were two reasons for this visit.

Richard had decided that his old home, a few miles away, should finally be given away to a needy family. He had come over from Poppleton with the purpose of arranging this and handing over the front door key. He had enough money and to spare, for his own and for his children's future needs, and he wanted another family to enjoy his old home. For him, having extra riches had no value.

Mary and William Stocks were good, honest and hard working and looked after their three children with kindness and love. William had not been to blame in any way for the accident that had crushed his left arm, but had been a victim of neglect. The owner of the cart, which he had hired for one day, apparently knew the front wheel axle needed repairing. Yet, out of greed or laziness, had ignored the dangers and let it be used. People in the village of Sheepley, and he had asked many, told him that Mary and William were the most deserving of a new home. They had struggled, more than any other family in the village, for the last three years to pay the tithes of their cottage since William's capacity for work had been limited. He found out that they were to be thrown out of their cottage within the month. Though it was just word of mouth, he had heard from a trusty source, that the reason was not just the inability to pay the tithes, but because Mary, a very comely woman, consistently refused the Squire's bed.

'That man will not win,' Richard was determined in this matter. He had his own reasons for disliking this Squire, which stretched back many years. He had seen him, on more than one occasion, after imbibing too much liquor, whip a horse so viciously that Richard had felt physically sick, yet could not intervene. On one occasion, he was told by a friend who witnessed the incident, that the Squire's horse collapsed while travelling through the village, its eyes bulging and mouth frothing. Yet this Squire in his anger had beaten it. Oh no, he, Richard Shaw had other plans for this family whom he had already decided were deserving of a new and decent home. He knew that if a Squire couldn't treat his animals with kindness, his tenants couldn't expect any favours.

He would never forget the sheer delight on their faces when he invited them to his house and then handed them the key, the deeds to the property and all its contents. He hadn't told them his plans and the joy and tears were not just theirs. It had brought a glimmer of light into his present darkness.

§

So he had decided to use this journey to visit Stocksmoor one final time, and, on the way, he had called to see his brother, Ben, whose wife Hannah had also, sadly, died. One of his boys, now newly married was living in their father's old house, his childhood home, but he didn't even want to see inside that house again. No, his life was changed for ever, and he felt that, sadly, so was he. He could sustain no more anguish and had a numbness of spirit which was alien to him, but which he seemed to have no power to change.

Secondly, Richard wanted to visit the place where the casket had been buried. He had something he wanted to do.

§

Robbie had his own reasons for wanting to visit Stocksmoor. Firstly, he wanted to go into the village and say a final 'farewell' to his brother Edward. He had asked Andrew, Uncle George's son, who was now Lord Lieutenant, for permission to plant a sapling of oak on the common in his memory. And he granted that permission. Secondly, he wanted to try to see Simion and thank him for saving his life, and the third reason was simply to accompany Richard, who he sensed was in a very melancholic mood. He did not think he should travel alone and times were still dangerous. He went to Uncle George who agreed.

"You go with him Robbie. It is your turn to look after him. Bring him back as safely as he brought you here. That is all I ask."

§

Richard's children, Gerrard and Sarah, were well settled in the York area and were not interested in his old house, not even to visit or spend a few days there as a respite to normal daily life. In fact, they did not want to see the house. He understood, but that fact had, for a while, saddened him. Richard had no wish to live back in that village, but he had great affection for his old home. When he had asked Gerrard he had simply, but kindly, replied, "Papa, that house means nothing to me. Do with it what you will." Sarah had answered him by saying, "Papa, I never want to go through that door again. This is my home. Here is where I belong. Give it to someone who needs it. It has been empty and unused for too long. Please give it away."

He knew, logically, that he had had very happy times in the house, but could not feel any of that joy any more. Briefly, he remembered his lovely Beatrice, then the years with Rosamund and their children, but those times were now only memory for him and the colour had gone from these images. Those old memories now appeared to have faded and had no value either for his children – but he understood that they had no wish to recall the times that made them leave their old home.

It was bad enough for them to sustain their present grief, without recalling past ones. He understood that they had only been young when they had had to leave their first home. No, he had no regrets in giving it away.

Uncle George was still well, and, quite amazingly, not showing his quite advanced age. A few problems in his back and legs meant that he couldn't move at his usual pace, but little else seemed to bother him. His mind was as active and acute as ever. Richard thought that he and his daughter, Sarah, should move out from the manor stable block that had been their home for eight years after Gerrard left. He didn't really know why or even if he wanted to do so, but thought that maybe changing his walls would bring a different feeling within himself. He had looked at a small cottage that had become vacant just two doors away from where Gerrard was going to live. He was going to be married soon. The houses were in a village close by. It would have been adequate for their needs.

But, Uncle George had particularly requested that he and Sarah, who was also as yet unmarried, should stay within the manor walls after Gerrard was married. Cousin Andrew had also requested that they should stay. Both reassured him, at separate times, that he and Sarah were their family and should they need to visit anywhere, they could have a driver and the small coach, anytime to anywhere, and whatever horse they wished to ride. But please would they stay in the household. Here they would receive whatever future care was needed. None could face more departures. So, that was that. He was staying where he knew he was wanted, though he felt he was not needed anywhere really. What had gone wrong with him to think this way? Deep down, it wasn't difficult. He knew. It was too much grief, just too much for his mind to have any more energy left to enjoy life.

One day, he was sitting in the library with Uncle George. They sat amicably together, sometime in most days. The age and generation difference had never been an issue.

"You are not right, Richard. Not right at all. Is there anything I can do to help you?"

Richard had told him that, after everything that had happened, each day was just an 'endless waiting' day filled with a feeling akin to doom. He felt as though he was waiting for the next tragedy to happen and wondering how much more his tired spirit could survive. His beloved

Rosamund had been dead for over two years now. She had not complained, but her eyes had become black ringed and sunken, her breathing laboured and her actions slow. He had seen these signs before as people moved slowly to their demise. He had watched day by day with dread but could do nothing to help or stop that progress. Could he bear to lose her? Despite time that has passed since that had happened, he was still asking himself that question. Then the other dear losses were still very raw. 'Dear God, why do you treat me so sorely? Have I not lost enough? Could I have done more?' He told Uncle George that these thoughts went round in his head day in and day out and there was little respite.

He wondered if Beatrice and Rosamund would ever meet and who would he be with if and when he went to heaven, as he hoped God Almighty would grant him a place, if so be it there was a heaven. Yes, he had a sad and troubled mind, and it was at its worst when he was quiet and alone.

Uncle George had listened, quietly and without interruption.

"Richard, you have given so freely of yourself to all those in your care. Please understand, you did everything anyone could have done. We have all been sorely hit by grief, but you more than most as you were so close to everyone. We loved them all, but our loss is not quite at the same level as yours. I understand, my son."

Richard wept. Uncle George, he knew, thought of him as his family, but this was the first time he had called him 'son'. It struck a deep chord of love in his lonely heart.

§

Now, as he and Robbie reached the place where Richard and his sisters' children had buried the casket, they dismounted, tethering the horses to the nearby gate post.

"Richard, do you mind if I leave you for a while? I want to plant the sapling on my own, and just sit a while and be with my brother's spirit. If your sisters can find you, then I think he will find me."

"Of course, Robbie. But don't go too far. Keep within shouting distance." So Robbie disappeared down the path. Richard could soon hear him digging with the small spade he had brought. The place had not changed apart from more blackberry tangles, untended bushes which had spread along the base of the wall, a few small self-set aspen trees and bracken. But then, as he walked nearer, he noticed the wild sorrel flourishing in the centre of the casket's burial place. He knew that Simion had planted it. The boys had told him of their meeting when they were talking about the visit a few days after they had returned home.

He sat down on the grass nearby and soon his tears fell.

He knew why he had a need to return to this place. He felt he had to speak to Ann and Emily. As he was reminded of them, he included Catherine in his thoughts. He was sure that their spirits would be drawn towards this place. He had come to ask for their forgiveness. He wanted to explain that he had done his best to continue to look after their children as they had grown into adults and had felt responsible for them in Ann and Emily's places. But, he had not been able to keep the promise he had made and his heart was sore troubled and could find no ease. There was no one around. He spoke aloud, but softly, the words he needed to say.

He talked to Emily.

"Emily, my dear sister, let me tell you about Miranda. She prepared to be married, but sadly that time never came to pass, though she was loved dearly by a good young man. In the winter of the year after we brought your casket here, just before Yuletide, she contracted a very bad inflammation of her lung. She was ill for several weeks. We thought she had recovered. But it must have weakened her. She died of a dreadful complaint of the throat that blocked her breathing late in the spring after Miriam was married. That same illness also took five children in the village, from two families. These children had all been to the house for reading lessons before they knew either Miranda or they were ill. We can only surmise this was related. It happened before she was married. Emily, I am so sorry. Even with my knowledge of potions I could do nothing to save her. It was so cruel. She was looked after well and with great kindness, but none could save her. Her death affected Miriam very badly."

He then spoke to Ann.

"Ann, I want you to know that Miriam had a lovely wedding day during the summer after we buried the casket. She was very happy during the short time she was allowed. Firstly, as I have told Emily, Miranda became ill and later died in the next spring. Then, in the September that followed, the Church Army reared its ugly head again when a few drunken soldiers, passing through, caused a disturbance in their village. Her husband heard there was something amiss and went to see. He was killed in that skirmish. She had just discovered she was to have a child which should be born the following April or May, but though her heart had gone out of her being, she bravely carried on. Finally, something else happened which I shall tell you and, whether that had anything to do with the tragedy or not we shall never know. But, in her seventh month she went into labour. Before the baby could be born Miriam started to bleed and the midwife, who was very skilled in all her confinements, could not stop the dreadful flow. She was buried with the baby still inside her. Ann, I am so sorry.

"Ann, I need you to know what I have now to say about Mark, Miriam's final blow. They were close as children and remained so after you had died.

"Mark fell in love with one of Uncle George's granddaughters and she with Mark. They would have married in due course. She is his Andrew's eldest daughter, a beautiful, gentle girl called Carolina. I can hardly make myself to tell you. She too is very sad. The light has been taken from her life. She still lives quietly at the manor house with Uncle George, her parents and her youngest sister and everything is provided for her. Her Aunt Ann is back there. To the outside world around, little would appear to have changed. But, for her, all has changed. She no longer has Mark in her life.

"Mark had contracted the same inflammation of the lungs as Miranda had done at the same time and survived. The winter after Miriam's husband died, the same thing happened again. He was ill for a week and then, when we all thought he was getting well again, as before, he had a strange spasm, went blue and died. Ann, I am so sorry. What can I say except that I was briefly out of Poppleton visiting a friend? When I arrived home he was dead. I was too late to try to save him. Whether I could have done so or not I shall never know, but I wasn't there.

"Miriam told me, before she too died, that she had been sitting with Mark when he had the inflammation of the lungs. Ann, she was so like you as she did this regardless of her own health. Though he was very ill, he managed to talk about you for the first time and wept. He told her that he had watched you walk down the road to the ducking stool. He had been hidden behind one of the travelling monks who held him and wouldn't let him go to you. He struggled to no avail.

Then he had heard the monk say, 'If that one,' pointing at you with his other hand, 'had not spoken out, they would all be alive now.'

"From that moment on Mark blamed you for your own death and that is why he couldn't write a letter to you to put in the casket and why he never read the book. Everyone thought he had read the book and that he knew the truth. He told Miriam that he had always regretted not writing, just in case you could ever know and that his dearest wish was that you should know that he loved you very much.

"Miriam said that slowly but surely, even though so ill, Mark recounted much of those last days in Stocksmoor. Ann, he said he wanted you to know that he tried so hard to save you all. He had desperately tried to get help from Uncle Wilfred and Uncle Harold and from me, but I was away. He had tried so hard, but could find no help. He wanted you to know that he hadn't abandoned you. He put in so much effort for such a young lad. What sorrow I feel for him.

"He had hoped to rescue you when you went to be ducked, using his father's sword, but the monk held him so he couldn't assist you. He told Miriam that he saw those memories every night in his dreams. He wanted to forget and forgive, but he couldn't. So I feel I have to tell you this for his sake.

"Miriam had wept with him, explaining gently what I had found out and written in the book and that I was sure that your deaths were prearranged. She told him that the words you had spoken had made no difference. None at all. It just added to the army's excuses for killing you. She told him that she and Miranda had been unable to do anything at all, as they had been taken away, and how dreadful they had both felt at not being able to help. He became reconciled. Poor Mark, because of what he believed, he suffered longer and none of us knew as he would never speak of you. That, more than anything truly upsets me and I feel I failed Mark more than the others. I did not know that he blamed you. He told me what he had tried to do, but he didn't tell me that and I never thought to ask.

"But after Mark's death, following as it did her husband's death and that of her best friend and dearest companion, Miranda, Miriam seemed to fade away despite being with child. She had lost everyone she loved by death, except James."

He paused for a while as his sobs wracked his body and took away the words from his mind.

"Emily, as far as we know James is alive. I do not think he can know about Miriam, as he was not around at the time of her death. He packed his belongings and moved away to the east of the county soon after Mark's death. The place, and everything connected with it, haunted him with sadness too great to sustain if he stayed there. In all their years, he and Mark had never spent any time apart and he just couldn't remain at their home. I understood, fully, his need to leave. I haven't seen him yet, but I intend to ride in his direction, to meet him when and if I can. He is a good lad and I am sure he will use his time well, but I fear that he has a 'long and lonely furrow to plough' before he can find happiness. All he loved are gone.

"He is now the last of the Kittle family, and Uncle George has managed to sort out the inheritance. None of the children had any wish to return to Lower Oakington to Sir Reginald's old home and so gradually it was sold – first the cottages, then some land and finally the large house and farm. It was to have been shared, of course, but now James, being the only one to survive, inherits all the money from his father's family and the title.

"Think not Emily that James left alone. His father's trusty servant Will accompanies him. He has promised me that he will take good care of him. Will came with us to Poppleton after the first year and once the Kittle horses had all been sold. Again, Uncle George offered that he became part of his household because of his dedicated devotion for so many years. He has been as faithful in helping to care for your children as he was for Richard and Peter. Like Nell did, he regards them as his family and has suffered much grief.

"To all three of you I want to tell you that Nell, dear, faithful Nell, nursed Miranda, Mark and finally Miriam. But, the loss became too much for her tired heart to sustain. She was getting old.

"A week after Miriam died, Nell, who had moved back to the manor with Uncle George's daughter, Ann, and Marion after Mark's death, did not arrive downstairs for her usual breakfast. Ann went to call on her. She knocked on the door. When she received no reply she went in. At first she thought that Nell was just sleeping and was about to tip toe out of the room, when she saw her arm on the counterpane. Her hand was white. She went nearer and saw that Nell was dead. She had died in her sleep. She had apparently been tired but well. I can tell you that she suffered no physical pain when she died and we were all very grateful.

"Uncle George insisted that she had a coffin made out of the best oak possible, and I want you to know that she was buried in his family vault in the grounds of his garden, alongside Aunt Gwendolyn, Miranda, Mark and Miriam and Rosamund.

"'She was their mother and father, nanny and helpmate, all in one. She belongs with them.' Uncle George decided.

"But, since Rosamund's death, the deaths of your children, and Nell, a malaise of spirit has come upon me. I have done my best, but I can do no more. I will, but just now, I cannot. I have felt compelled to come to this place in my great sorrow and beg your forgiveness."

His messages complete he could not contain his distress any longer and, sitting on the ground, he rocked back and forth in tears.

After a while, he became aware of a hand on his shoulder. He had heard nothing, but looking up he saw Simion's dishevelled hair and thin, gaunt face bending over him. Richard felt warmth coming from his hand. As he looked into his eyes he saw a deep kindness and compassion. At that moment he realised that this poor, outcast man had more riches in his spirit than any man he had ever met, even counting his father and Uncle George. He realised why his sisters had cared for him as they had. Here, in his own desolate wilderness, reviled by society, was a true man of God.

Gradually his tears dried.

Simion stood back, went to the wild sorrel and, touching it, he pretended to pick some leaves. He put them to his mouth, but shook his head and threw them away. Then he pointed to where the casket was and finally he made as if rocking a baby and putting it on the earth. He did this three times. Then, as if he had delivered a message, he put his hand to his forehead, nodded and walked away very slowly.

"Simion, come back. Please come back." But Simion did not come back. Richard knew that he couldn't hear him.

Richard watched him as he disappeared into the undergrowth. He stood up and went to find him. Simion was very unwell. He could see that and he wished to help, but Simion was not someone anyone could find. He had now disappeared. Simion always found him, never the other way round. So, he accepted the inevitable, sat quietly and waited for Robbie to return.

He wondered if his sisters had heard him. Had they forgiven him?

He didn't know how long he sat there, waiting. It didn't really matter. He didn't care what the time was or whether he stayed or left. He had done what he wanted to do.

Just then Robbie appeared.

"Richard! I have seen Simion. He came and sat by my sapling. He looks so very frail now. I was able to thank him once more. I know he can't hear, but I had to try to tell him. I hugged him. I could weep Richard. He is so thin. All his rib bones felt to be standing out, I was fearful I might break one. What can we do for him?"

"Nothing, Robbie. I feel the same. I left money at the inn many moons ago, and they have given him food if he has gone to their back door. Bernard has told me though, that he didn't go very often. I remember we had a good priest, Father Simon, when Simion arrived in the village. He offered Simion a roof and a bed. My father would have given him a room in our house. But Simion would never accept anything but a few clothes and food when he needed it. I fear, as I saw him, that he is now not long for this world. May God understand that he is a very good man. Robbie, let us go home."

They untethered their horses and, were just about to ride up the lane away from Simion's corner when, on impulse, Richard turned his horse in the opposite direction.

"I am determined that I shall never come back this way again, Robbie, so I will also pay my respects to my sisters at the place where they were burned. Come, we shall add little to our journey but much to my peace of mind."

Having turned the horses, they headed across the common top. When they arrived at the place, Richard noticed flowers had been strewn around and that there was a man standing, head down, as if in contemplation. He looked up as the riders approached.

"Cousin Geoffrey, what a surprise to see you here."

Richard dismounted quickly and rushed over to his cousin. They hugged each other briefly.

"I come each year, Richard, to pay my respects and scatter a few flowers. But I come on the day they died, not when they were burned."

"This is a young cousin of ours, Robbie," Richard introduced Robbie. "Uncle George sent him to keep an eye on me as I am not as well as

I should be." Richard did not explain any further, about himself or Robbie, nor did he mention the casket. He could not risk anything, even to Geoffrey.

"Richard, you will not know, but Mama died in May."

"I am sorry to hear that."

"She has had sad and lonely years since Papa died and my sisters went away. They have visited only once each year and then only for an overnight stay. It is very apparent that they do not wish to be at the Hall or round this area at all."

They walked side by side along the road through the village and turned left towards Bretton. Richard was leading his horse and Robbie was walking a short distance behind, to let the cousins speak privately together.

"Where is your horse, Geoffrey?" Richard asked.

"On this day, I always leave my horse behind. It feels better somehow. Richard, I want to tell you something that I would rather not, but in this respect, I must choose between your regard of Papa or of Mama. I can tell you that it was Mama who persuaded Papa not to send help for your sisters. You will not realise, but Mama was determined and strong and what she decided was always the law of the household.

"I couldn't believe it, but I heard her tell the priest. He came to pray with her many times in the weeks before her death. I didn't mean to listen, but no one told me to leave the room or that she was going to have a confessional with him. I sat with her for many hours in a week, occasionally talking, but mostly we were silent. I felt that I was company for her, though she kept the curtain half drawn round her bed, to cut out the sunlight. But, I think she forgot I was sitting in her room by the window reading, so I just stayed. The priest never even noticed I was there."

"Surely, Geoffrey, your mama would not have interfered in a matter of duty."

"That is what I would have thought, but I heard her with my own ears and she was in her right mind. I have been thinking a lot about Mama and Papa, and I realise that Papa was a man who had been used to being told what to do by Grandmama and he continued the same with Mama. Poor Papa, he was so repentant and never forgave himself."

"I never really knew your mama, as she took little notice of me when I was at the Hall. It is a big place in which anyone can be easily overlooked, whether by design or ignorance. But your father, Uncle Wilfred, was always very kind to me. I could not change my regard for him, even before I knew his reasoning about not sending aid to my sisters. I have to say that I tried to be angry, but, somehow, I could not feel it. I just hope that he is reconciled now with them all. As for your mama, she will have to answer for herself. I am sure that she was as frightened for her children as your papa was. It is time for us all to leave the past, Geoffrey. My visit here today was to help me to do just that and I shall not return. I am glad we have met again."

They had reached the path that lead to the parkland of the Hall.

"Farewell, Geoffrey. I hope you may continue to have renewed health and strength for the years ahead. If you visit York then please come to see us. You would always be very welcome."

They hugged each other. Geoffrey reached up to Robbie, on his horse, and shook his hand.

"Farewell to you both."

§

The day after their visit, early in the morning, the stonemason was walking on the path at the upper end of the common. He had been Dorothy's husband. He still lived in Stocksmoor, and Ben ensured that he still had the same cottage, and lived in it free of tithes. He had never remarried. He had been asked by one of the farmers if he would repair the wall at the end of his field, just before the gate leading onto the common top. One of the horses pulling his plough had turned too quickly. The plough had accidentally hit the wall and a good few feet had been damaged.

As he neared the gate, he saw what he thought was a pile of old clothes laying on the ground. As he drew nearer, he saw that it was Simion, dead, cold and stiff. He went back into the village and called at a few of the houses. Finally, three others went with him. They wrapped the body in sacking.

"Where shall we bury him, do you think?"

"Well, this is where he sat, endlessly. So why not just here? Help me to move him and then we can dig in the very same place. At least he'll feel at home, poor thing. What a bloody rotten life! We'd best be careful as he's just skin and bones. It seems that he died yesterday, sometime."

"Yes, he died as he lived, alone."

"I've just realised that today is July 28 th. That means Simion must have died on the same day as Ann, Emily and Catherine were killed, and is being buried on the day when their bodies were burned. It seems the end of that chapter at last."

"Tragic, all of it. That's all I can say. I believe that none of us will ever forget those dreadful days or the actual date, however long we live."

Simion's long, bleak existence was finally over. The place where he was buried was about six feet from the casket. Even at the last, he had made as sure as he could that, when his body was buried, the casket would not be disturbed.

§

A few days after he had returned home, Richard woke one morning and began to realise what Simion's miming had meant. The answer came to him as though it was given to him in his sleep. Simion had pointed to the herb, one he had helped collect for the sisters and in the shake of his head he was telling him that nothing, no herb of any kind, could have saved the lives of Miranda, Mark and Miriam, the babies of Ann and Emily that he mimicked as if being rocked.

That night he had a dream, one that he would recall for the rest of his life.

He was travelling over a lake. How? He did not know. As he looked down, he saw a long, white boat, moving without a ripple, through water of a blue that was more vivid than he had ever seen before. He was taken towards the boat and his vision focussed on different people in the boat. He was shown Ann and Emily with their husbands, Catherine with William, Elizabeth with Andrew, Alend and three little girls, Miranda, Miriam and her husband and Mark. He saw that Miriam was holding two babies, one in each arm. What a lovely surprise, even in a dream. They were all looking upwards and smiling at him, so he knew they could see him. He was then shown a different part of the boat, where four women were sitting with their backs to him.

The first one looked round and smiled. As he looked he thought it was Beatrice, but then he was sure it was Rosamund, as she had been when young. They seemed as if the same person.

He then found himself looking at the second. He had no difficulty knowing Nell, dear, strong Nell. She waved and smiled.

The third turned to face him, waving to him with her right hand. It was Hilda. She was holding a small girl on her lap. She bent her head as if to whisper into the child's ear. The child then looked up and waved. (Even in his dream, Richard wondered why the two boy babies that Hilda had lost were not with Hilda. But Hilda was happy and that was what was important.)

Then, his eyes moved to the fourth lady. She was looking away from him. She wore a cloak of palest green with a scrolled pattern of gold round the edge of the hem. Her hood was over her head, so he couldn't even tell the colour of her hair. Who was she? He didn't know.

He hovered for what seemed like minutes of precious, different time. He wanted to stay to find out more. But he moved and saw a silver boat travelling towards the other, which had stopped, as if to wait. This was just a small boat with only one young man sitting in it. "Who is that?" he asked, aloud. Then, as if the force that carried him heard him, he swooped nearer and the young man, in a white tunic smiled and waved at him. Richard saw the young man stand up in his boat. He watched the very same movements that Simion had mimed the last time he saw him flailing his arms.

Richard then knew that Simion had died and was going to meet those he had loved. At last he was happy and well. He would tell Robbie.

He awoke and found himself crying.

Dreams, even if momentarily remembered on waking, usually fade quickly, unless they have a message for the dreamer. He felt certain now that they were all in heaven, and that they would wait patiently for him. The Church meant only grief to him. He had no need of its preaching. He was confident that there was a life after death. From the beginning of that morning, he started to get well again.

Later that day, he joined Uncle George in his sitting room overlooking the large front courtyard. Richard told him about the visit, the family to whom he had given the house, his time on the common where the casket had been buried and finally he spoke of Simion.

"Uncle George, I had a dream last night. Can I tell you about it?" asked Richard.

"Of course, carry on."

When Richard had related the dream, he stopped for a moment, adding, "Uncle George, I couldn't tell who the lady in the pale green cloak was."

Uncle George didn't speak and Richard saw tears streaming down his face. When his emotion had eased, Uncle George stood up.

"Wait there a moment, Richard, I shan't be long."

He went into his dressing room and returned with something over his arm, wrapped in a white sheet.

"Richard, this belonged to your Aunt Gwendolyn. I bought it for her as a present on her wedding day. I'm sure someone would have a use for it, but I could never give it away after her death." He laid it carefully on the table. "Take a look at it."

Richard took off the white covering and saw, to his amazement, a pale green cloak of pure silk with scrolled gold embroidery round the hem.

"This is the very same that I saw."

This dream brought solace, at last, to two weary hearts.

Final comments

One night, about a year later, Richard woke from his sleep and again remembered a very vivid dream.

He saw someone reading his book but didn't know who it was, man or woman. However, as they were reading, he also saw the images of what they were reading as though it was actual reality. In this way, he knew they were reading the chapter where he meets Hilda and where he sees, for the first time, the ornate eagle just before she throws it in the river. The person reading the book asked, "Who is the author of this book?" He answered whoever, by saying, "It is me. I am the author."

While I was writing this book and had just written the chapter about Hilda and the eagle, I too had that same dream and heard the same question, "Who is the author?"

I answered in my mind, 'I wrote that book.'

When I awoke and remembered what I had heard and seen in my dream, I thought, 'Did I?' On a conscious level, yes, of course I wrote it. My mind recollected the information, bit by bit, over a few years. I thought it all out and gradually and meticulously pieced the fragments together. But, I know that I did not imagine the story. Let me explain a little.

§

One night a few years ago, I was taken 'somewhere' in my mind, though at first I didn't recognise where I had been. I didn't ask for this experience, how could I? It just happened.

I was in bed, wide awake. But it was as if, in my head, I was walking, jerkily, with difficulty and in great pain down a hill with a high stone wall on my left side. I felt very ill and had a great feeling of desperation. But, I knew I had no choice but to walk that road. It was little more than a wide track and in a slight valley as the ground on the right rose gradually for a few feet and was covered in grass. I felt as if I was trying to pull my clothes around me as I walked and I had bare feet. Then all changed.

Now I was looking down the road from higher up the hill. I saw the woman who I thought had been me, struggling. She was swaying down the road about fifty yards ahead and I thought she was about to fall. She was holding her clothes around her, as if in a state of agitation. Her long, over-the-shoulder fair hair was very dishevelled. Her skirt was torn and dirty and her clothes appeared to be covered in blood. I was totally mystified. Who had I seen? Where was this road? I knew that somehow I recognised the woman, the road and the stone wall. They were very familiar. But where were they?

This 'film' replayed in my mind many times for several days. It would just come back into prominence in my inner thoughts and always bring with it the questions 'Where?' and 'When?' It seemed really important to know and it didn't go away until, quite suddenly, one day, the answer was there. I realised it was the road down the same village that I grew up in. The only difference, that had confused me initially, was that the wall was much higher than I have known it this life. In fact, I realised that it was the road, in the past, which was much lower.

The film in my head was a memory from several centuries before. The extra height of the road had been caused by layer upon layer of road material having been added during the many intervening years, thus covering up the wall on the road side and some of the rising slope on the other. Both are still discernible despite modern progress, but much less pronounced. I have found since then, in other past memories, that, unless a massive earth movement, for example to build a motorway, has happened, then original contours of any place remain basically unchanged over centuries.

Gradually, over the next few years, many more images and scenes of that time came into my mind. They were very painful and emotional experiences. I was either 'in the pain and action' or I 'watched' and 'heard' the events. It all came as fragments, jumbled in time, which I slowly pieced together. It was like doing a giant jigsaw, whose overall picture I did not know until it was complete. I made notes as the different events slowly surfaced, until I could write this book.

What took a while to realise was how my whole life has been 'linked', like a kind of memory legacy to those events in the past.

For example, I suffered from asthma and often, when I couldn't breathe but was not ill enough to stay in bed, I would struggle to the top of the hill and sit on the wall near the chapel, to try to find some kind of release from the suffocating feeling. I would always sit facing the woodland, not the valley or the Pennines in the distance. I felt I needed to go there to cope, but that need always seemed strange but real. It had nothing to do with getting near to God's house for God to help – that never entered my thinking – not at all! God, in my mind, wasn't very kind to the child he had created. No, God was for well people. They didn't know what asthma was like so could think that God was good and kind. It was, also, logically, totally unnecessary, as there was always a breeze in the garden. We lived on the hill and wind blew almost constantly directly from the hills in the west. Though I didn't know why at the time, I now know I went to sit at the place where the stocks had stood.

I had an injury inflicted to my neck, which, though not serious, caused great pain for many years so that often it was difficult to hold my head erect. On another occasion I was beaten up in the outside earth toilet of the chapel, which was more or less the site of the soldier's makeshift hut.

I finally understand why I always used to feel rather scared in the front garden of my grandparents' house, Albion Mount, a house I didn't like. I loved my grandmother dearly and visited her each day if possible, so it didn't make sense. In fact I can remember screaming uncontrollably when I was about two years of age at seeing someone in army uniform at my grandparents' front door. It was the place of the mock trial in 1497.

And I made sense of why I used to walk along the path at the upper end of the common ground – as if to a place where I could commune more easily with an inner 'me'. It is the place where the casket was buried. I had a strong feeling that I must get away from the village. That feeling positively encouraged me to work to pass my exams! So not all the 'links' were negative.

On July 28th, 1962, at 12 noon, I married and left that village, as my home, for ever. I now know that day and time was exactly four hundred and sixty five years after the bodies were burned and the fire had died out completely.

I am sure you will by now have guessed, before I tell you, that I was Ann Kittle, Emily Kittle was my twin, and Catherine Shaw our elder sister. I was born and lived in a cottage in almost the same place as in this life. Most of the family and people were different. But I can tell you that my father and my mother were the same and that they came again with me this life. But I came without my twin or elder sister. The Almighty obviously decided that one life in that village was enough for them! In my mind, at the beginning of this journey into the past, I had walked down the main road through Stocksmoor, West Yorkshire on July 27th, 1497. I wrote this poem to their memory.

Suffering

Endless, isn't long enough
To describe the pain I feel
Empty, contains more than me
Of the energy to heal
Desolate has more joy
Than this place wherein I stand
Alone, and beyond the reach
Of any helping hand
I cannot leave or evade
The path which is my own
Unasked for torment
When cruelty was shown
Yet in the end I shall win
I shall love and never hate
All those who caused the pain
Will follow their chosen fate
No Mercy will intercede
Grace looks a different way
They were ignored by evil
When cruelty held sway
Those who thrived on pain
Will find hope and pardon gone
But no one else is to blame
When true Justice will be done

§

I shall be very interested when Richard Shaw's book becomes reality and the casket is eventually found, as I believe it will be, to find out just how accurately I retrieved the information from nearly 500 years ago and how closely it matches his original writing, given the leeway of passing time and the consequent language translation.

I predict that, round about the time that the casket is found, the bejewelled cross of the High Chief of the Church Army, and maybe even his pendant, which Hilda threw into the river, will be found during dredging work on the river Ouse in York.

However, in writing this book, though I have been as accurate as possible in relating the information that has gradually come into my mind, I have done no research, other than to check in the Magna Carta that I had recollected the definition of a 'free man' as correctly as I needed it to be! And I had! I have to say that recalling names and some dates has been difficult and some may not be quite correct. When the truth is found, as I believe it will be, please forgive any minor errors. After all, it was a long time ago.

Are the names, dates and story for the future accurate? I don't know. I shall, like you, have to wait and see!

The enlightenment that Richard Shaw spoke of will come out of the book and, at the same time, this book will make sure that the difficult lives and deaths of those three women were not in vain. The effect at the time was limited only to the Church Army activities, but now there will be a much wider, gradual impact.

Shall I, too, be prosecuted by the Church and religious leaders and denounced by ardent believers or fanatics and those whose minds are closed?

The answer is that, whatever, I have no fear. But, given the behaviour, rigidity and fear emanating from and caused by 'blind' religious belief, I suppose that could be a possibility. Some will merely try to rubbish what I write or others may pick on any small fault or inaccuracy, for reasons 'all their own'. There could be many who are so biased that they will feel unable, unwilling or too frightened to alter their beliefs. But, eventually, the truth will speak for itself.

All have choice or should have choice in how they think or what they believe. Each person's future, whether in eternity or not, is theirs and theirs alone. It would be well if people remembered Bert's words of wisdom. No priest or different doctrinal beliefs of whatever religion, race or creed, however strongly held, can take that individual task from each and every mortal. All adults are responsible, according to their ability on this earth, for their own actions. They will reap what they sow – if not on this plane, then on the next where all actions are known and remembered. That waits for everyone.

I must leave one final message to anyone who might decide to try to find and dig up the casket before its appointed time. I have no doubt in the climate of the present day that many may want or even attempt to do so to win easy fame, fortune or celebrity status.

Remember that Bert is guarding it. I suspect that Simion is also keeping his vigil. There is a 'proper' time waiting to happen. On that day and that day alone will the casket surface. You or anyone else will be unable to forestall that time, so it would be advisable not to attempt fate.

I could have salvaged the casket already, couldn't I? Why do I not do so? The reason is simple. My task is to write this book and it is not yet time for the casket to surface. The book is relevant to and will eventually be read by people throughout the world. When sufficient people know about it, and understand the implications, then, all I can say is ..."wait and see."

I have other lives to describe. These have also had links and played a part in the total 'physical' legacy that has been my present life. I believe, that in each life, evidence of the truth of what I write has been left, hidden. But writing is not something that is instantaneous and I can only do one book at a time.

I nearly died a few years ago and was not expected to live. But, while deeply unconscious I reached a place where I was not allowed to see but could hear. I was told quite clearly, in a male voice I shall always remember, "No, you cannot stay. You are getting cold. You must go back now and write your books. Tell what you have learned." So, after a long and very painful recovery, I am doing as I was instructed. But, I am determined that I shall not hurry as there is a lot I want to see and do!

I completed my story, at least, so I thought, when these words came into my mind...

§

"You thought to finish the book there, didn't you?"

"Why yes, I did."

"Please don't. We want and need you to write a little more. Firstly, can you tell us what happened to Oliver? I believe other people will be interested to know. He was always our favourite cousin, so amusing and debonair, yet serious and hard working. He had such an

interesting mind, always searching for knowledge about his beloved plants. We always understood that he took Richard into some real scrapes, but they always escaped unscathed. He had a knack of being in the wrong place but at the right time, as help always came along. Fortunately!"

Oliver, as you know, lived most of his adult life in and around London. But he lectured in the places of learning around the country, his knowledge of all aspects of plants being second to none.

He had a wife and three children. Camellia was a good mother and dutiful wife, and someone who shared his interest in plants. She learned to love gardening from her own father who had a beautiful garden, and, in particular, she grew many different flowers. Roses were her favourites. It may be assumed her father chose her name.

She, sadly, died just a few months after Rosamund. From then on, Oliver spent more time at the Manor, having kept his own quarters there ever since he was a youth. He and Richard had remained the best of friends, despite the distance between their homes. Gradually, he left London behind as his main home but still spent much time travelling to lecture or visit gardens to give advice and such like. He would always be in demand, somewhere. Such was his nature that people liked to be with him and hear what he had to say, based on knowledge but much humour.

Richard had kept his old travelling covered wagon, and, for many years, at Uncle George's request, it was a feature in a corner of the large garden. Having cleaned it of all medicaments, the youngest son and daughter of Andrew used to play in it and pretend they were going on long journeys.

By now, they had grown past this activity and the wagon was unused, as such was the difference between Andrew and his father that his older children were not allowed to wander the countryside in the wagon. Oliver persuaded Richard that is was time for the two of them to explore the country again. He thought it would be a good idea to travel north, south, east and west and find out what was happening. He had never lost his interest in seeking and gathering new plants, and Richard could never pass a horse that suffered without offering assistance. They were also interested in whether the Church Army was still active or not.

So, for a few weeks at a time in the warm weather, they would be travellers once again. More often than not, having regard for their mature years, they would stay in inns rather than out in the open. Despite their continued enthusiasm, both agreed that, realistically, those times were long since past.

§

"Tell us about, Robbie. You know we never knew him, but have grown to love him while you have been telling the story. Tell me what happened to him."

"You mean you don't know? I thought you would know everything."

"Of course not. We are only just becoming free, as you have travelled your long journey through our pain to your recovery."

"I didn't realise that and don't really understand. Do you mean that if I had not plodded on through all the pain for years, you would never have been a free spirit?"

"Not exactly. You will know all the answers, one day. Please, tell us about Robbie."

Robbie became Uncle George's scribe, working with and for him, increasingly, as the years passed. Uncle George used to dictate to Robbie in the library. From their first few meetings Uncle George, who, as you know had an astute mind, admired Robbie's intellect and learning.

It was common knowledge in the household, and, of course, to Richard and to Uncle George, that Robbie loved Sarah, Richard's daughter. She was a few years younger than he, but of a similar nature. She was intelligent and pretty. Robbie tutored her in Latin and the English language. She liked to write. They would sit together, quietly and companionably, in the library for hours. He would study one of Uncle George's books and she would write her stories or poems.

If Robbie took Sarah out of the manor grounds, they would travel in one of Uncle George's small carriages, with Robbie dressed in the garb of a stable boy or groom. When he was dressed as such, no one would ever question his real status, which was the whole purpose of the disguise.

Sarah loved Robbie and made no secret of that.

However, marriage seemed out of the question. Although Uncle George had documented Robbie's change of name and no one had ever had cause to question further, a wedding in a church involving someone from the manor, would undoubtedly be noted. There was always someone ready to make the Church authorities aware; particularly should Uncle George be involved. His actions when Lord Lieutenant regarding the Church Army meant that his name was not spoken in ecclesiastical circles with enthusiasm.

Even till now, no one could risk Robbie being recognised. Uncle George had had a dark wig made for him to use, for when he accompanied Richard anywhere. At those times, he behaved and dressed as if Richard's valet. If he went with Uncle George to any meeting or even into York, he was always dressed as if he was his legal clerk, and wore a short grey wig. No one noticed anyone's servant, valet or legal clerk, and least of all when Uncle George could be seen instead. Though he was no longer the Lord Lieutenant, his knowledge on all matters relating to the county meant that he was still called upon for advice or to give opinions. He still could be a formidable figure and always took the centre stage, whether he wished it or not. If Robbie went out alone, which was not often necessary, he would wear Richard's old monk's habit and a pendant around his neck, which Uncle George had had specially made in silver for this purpose. Just in case.

Richard was talking to Uncle George one evening.

"Uncle, what do you think we can do to help Robbie and Sarah? They love each other. They should be married and be able to live together. I know they see each other daily and are nearly under the same roof, but you know what I mean. We have had so much sadness. I simply want Sarah to be happy and who knows what can happen."

Uncle George answered him, "Richard, I have thought the very same for some time now. I have already decided what I can do and was merely waiting for you to speak first. Leave it with me. Send them both to me tomorrow morning. I get up later and later these days. Eleven o'clock will be early enough."

Next morning, both Sarah and Robbie dutifully presented themselves before Uncle George. Sarah gave him a hug.

"You want to see us, Uncle George?"

They both loved him dearly, but he had an expression on his face which they could not interpret.

"Indeed! I do. Now, I will come straight to the point," he pretended to speak in a stern voice.

They looked at each other in some consternation.

"I know the problems you face. But, tell me truthfully, do you two want to be married?"

"Oh, Uncle George, that is our dearest wish in the whole world." Sarah's face relaxed into a big smile. "But I want Robbie's continued safety first before anything else. I would rather us remain unmarried for ever, than risk his life."

"I have looked up the legalities. Andrew is now Lord Lieutenant. What he decrees is legally binding. Do you mind if we leave the Church out of it?"

"After what they did to Edward and your nieces? Indeed, Sir, I want nothing to do with the church. Ever," replied Robbie, expressing clearly how he felt.

"You are just wonderful Uncle." An ecstatic Sarah gave Uncle George another hug.

"No, don't thank me. Thank your father. He wants you to be happy," and then added, with a smile, "and legal."

Sarah and Robbie put their arms about each other and danced around. Could their dreams really be coming true?

"Then it is settled. Andrew and I shall marry you," he smiled as he spoke.

Three days later, Uncle George had ordered the whole household to the library. He addressed them and told them that Sarah and Robbie were to be married the next day at eleven o'clock, and, if they wished, they could attend to witness the ceremony. He asked them to wear their best uniforms. He simply told them that he had decided, as a lawyer, that to him and the family it was such a special occasion that he would officiate himself, and Sir Andrew would, as Lord Lieutenant, be witness.

So, on the morrow, the staff, lined up along the long walls of the library. Uncle George's family entered and sat at the far end of the room by the large window, with Uncle George and Andrew in the centre. Gerrard and his wife joined them. Then, Robbie entered alone to silence. Quietly and slowly he walked to stand in front of Uncle George, but some short distance away. Finally, Richard escorted Sarah, dressed in a white gown of silk, quickly made by the housekeeper, who was a skilled dressmaker, and took her to stand beside Robbie. She had flowers in her hair and looked very pretty. He then went to sit with Uncle George.

Marion walked behind her, in a long white dress, and similar flowers threaded in her long hair.

So Sarah married her sweetheart, Robbie. It was a simple ceremony. Uncle George stood and walked a few paces forward to the couple. He asked if each wished to marry the other, and both answered, "Yes."

"Lord Lieutenant of the county of Yorkshire, Sir Andrew Shaw, would you please step forward."

His son Andrew went slowly to his father's side, bringing as much pomp as the circumstances allowed, for the benefit of the watching staff.

"I, Andrew Shaw, Lord Lieutenant of Yorkshire, with due and legal authority, do hereby pronounce that Sarah Shaw and Robbie Cecil be legally man and wife."

Uncle George concluded with the words, "May you live in peace, with good health and happiness, and we humbly ask that our loving God be with you." He went to stand by Richard, his task complete.

Sarah and Robbie kissed each other, then turned and bowed to everyone. All present clapped and cheered. These two were very popular members of Uncle George's household.

"All are welcome to join the happy couple for a wedding breakfast. Please follow us to the large dining room," invited Uncle George.

Uncle George put his arm around Richard's shoulder and whispered,

"Well, that is done and the Church can do nothing about it."

They walked slowly after Sarah and Robbie and the assembled family and staff followed.

"I think Rosamund would be very pleased, don't you?"

"Oh, yes. She would want to thank you, as I do, from the depths of her heart. All she ever wanted was her children to be well and happy. Such happiness as Sarah shows is like a bright ray of sunshine bursting through the dark grey sky. Never can I find sufficient words to describe your kindness or express my gratitude." Richard's eyes brimmed with tears.

"None are ever needed, Richard."

As they left the library, Uncle George put his arm around Richard's shoulder.

"We work well together, don't you think, Richard?"

Richard smiled and nodded in agreement.

"Indeed we do."

§

This book was about to go to print in a few days. I was just 'polishing' the text with a few final words and the occasional correction, when ...

§

Tell us what happened to Ben?

The carriage drew up in the rear courtyard of the Manor. Richard went to the window and saw Ben alight. But, there was something different, a spring in his step. He puzzled. What was it? Then to his surprise, he watched Ben hold out his hand and saw a comely, small woman, with dark hair and dressed simply but stylishly in grey and mid-blue, step down from the carriage. He went to the door to greet them, having no idea who this lady could be.

"Richard, I would like to introduce you to my wife, Eleanor."

Delighted but quite shocked, Richard welcomed Eleanor to his home.

Ben was, by now, in his fifty-first year and had lived alone for several years since Hannah had died prematurely. His sons had married. The eldest lived in his father's old house and the other a few miles distant. After Hannah's death, Ben's enthusiasm for the wood business, started by his father, faded and, as neither of his boys wanted to continue, he sold out to the highest bidder. He was well and decided he must create a different life for himself. He felt shrouded by a dusk, it wasn't quite a darkness, but it would not lift.

He visited the Manor about once every year. On one such visit he discussed with Uncle George his plan to travel around the county and paint the countryside. Assisted by Andrew, Uncle George compiled a list and supplied Ben with the names and addresses around Yorkshire where he could stay overnight and be assured of a clean bed and good food. He gave Ben a letter of introduction, which would ensure he always obtained the best treatment possible.

Ben duly found his courage. One day he woke early, and with no further procrastinating or excusing, he packed some belongings in two large panniers. Taking his two horses, one loaded and one saddled, he departed on his first journey. Without knowing it, he was taking the first steps to a new life. Following that, he regularly travelled from home for several days or even weeks at a time.

On one such occasion he met Eleanor, about eighteen months before they married,. She was a widow, forty-two years of age, and the youngest sister of a local Squire. Her husband had been killed in a riding accident many years ago, soon after the birth of her youngest child. Having private means, she had never considered marrying again and had accepted her situation without protest, until she was introduced to Ben. She had lived a quiet life, with her children, in a house nearby her brother and his family.

When Eleanor was meeting and chatting to Sarah, who had given birth to her baby girl six weeks earlier, Ben told Richard, "I know you will understand, Richard. I still love Hannah, but Eleanor is different. Even from childhood I always accepted what I had to accept. I knew I had no choice. How we all managed to survive the events of 1497, I have never known, and since then I had to face the loss of Hannah. But, you know what that is like. Until I met Eleanor I hadn't realised how lonely I was. It is as though she has opened up a door to emotions that I never knew existed, and it leads to a fragrant garden."

"I am so pleased for you, I cannot find the proper words to express what I want to say," replied Richard. "I have never in our lives seen you so happy, it is wonderful. I wish you many years of joy."

"Richard, I have brought you this picture. I don't need it as I have the very same in my mind at any time. I thought you may like to share it with Uncle George. I will give you a new address where you will find me in the near future, as I shall not live at my home for much longer. We are moving to be near Eleanor's family. I have bought a suitable cottage in the same village. I have given all my other portraits to my sons, who, to be quite truthful, I see very little. I am not sure they approve of my actions but, in any event, they are busy." A shadow temporarily crossed his face. "If people, even your own flesh and blood do not understand, then I have come to the conclusion that the loss is theirs. I cannot nor do I wish to convince them of their error. I feel happy, Richard, in the company of Eleanor. Her children have accepted me without a problem."

It was a portrait of their father, and such a likeness that Richard was overcome with emotion, as was Uncle George later.

"You are very talented, Ben. I feel I could almost talk to him."

"Papa taught me all I know," answered Ben, simply. "I feel he knows my path and he approves."

"That picture takes me back in time. Yes, a very long way," commented Uncle George later. "Do you mind if I keep it in my room for a while? As for Eleanor, she's a grand lass. Ben is still a youngish man and loneliness can last a long time, as both you and I know only too well. I am very happy for him."

Ben lived well into his seventies with his wife Eleanor by his side throughout, giving him love, companionship and humour. As he admitted to Richard, "I could not ask for more."

§

Before you finish can you tell us what happened to Uncle George and Richard. They were such wonderful men and we are eternally grateful to them. We have only a few more steps to take on our journey. Then our journey is over and your book will be complete.

Uncle George lived to an unusually old age, and apart from some joint stiffness and increasing frailty, he remained able to potter around. He faced and accepted each day as it presented, and no one ever heard him moan his advanced years. He had long since stopped travelling, spending most of his day in his sitting room, though he did not give up riding his horse until well into his seventies. Even though he travelled by carriage in his latter years as Lord Lieutenant and was always accompanied by his valet or son, Andrew, he would insist that his horse went along with them, so that he could ride part of the way. He always maintained that travelling for hours in a carriage was more tiring that an hour or two on a horse.

He had always been a busy man, a man of action and movement and would not have been suited to a sedentary life at a younger age. But, even then, when in the company of interesting manuscripts a different side of his being would take over. He never counted the time spent reading. His books increasingly became his solace in his latter years.

His son Andrew was often away from the Manor, serving his county and country as Lord Lieutenant of Yorkshire. Oliver spent much time away. It was Richard who accompanied Uncle George on his daily walk in the grounds, holding his arm to steady his footsteps. Engrossed in their conversations, they would walk up and down in the garden or stroke the horses in the meadow. Neither man tired of the other's company as they always had much to talk about. Uncle George had a wealth of anecdotes and his interest and enthusiasm never faded.

The cruel events of 1497, the subsequent loss of his sister's children and the death of his own dear wife, had taken a huge toll on Richard's stamina, more than anyone had realised. Though much younger in years than Uncle George, the age difference was of no significance.

Richard spent many afternoons with Uncle George, unless Uncle George had a visitor. Most evenings they ate together at six o'clock, prompt, at Uncle George's suggestion and request. "Why have two cooks working in two kitchens, when one can suffice? Anyway, Richard, I enjoy my food much better in company. And, whose better than yours?"

At around seven o'clock, one evening in mid-May in 1512, all changed.

Uncle George and Richard were sitting near the window in Uncle George's first floor sitting room. For the last few years this room had become his sanctuary. He had chosen the adjoining room, with connecting door, as his bedroom. The sitting room was panelled with polished oak, and was easy to keep warm in winter, with a large marble fireplace, which could be fed with logs. There were thick drapes at the windows to keep out any draughts. Comfortable sofas, chairs and his desk provided the furniture, along with a small oak table placed by the window for his meals.

Several large portraits graced the walls and bookshelves contained a few hundred of his chosen books. He was content in these surroundings, knowing that his family and Richard were close by. His favourite portrait was of his wife Gwendolyn standing on the rear terrace, with her beloved garden in the background. He had placed this directly opposite the window. As he often commented, "I can see both the front of the house and the back without leaving this room or even my chair." He confided in Richard that sometimes, when he was tired, he would look at the portrait and almost imagine walking in the garden with Gwendolyn. It was a very good likeness.

The weather had been too blustery and wet for walking outdoors on this day. Richard had been pleased, as for a few days he had felt unwell. He had had twinges of pain in his chest and some unfamiliar shortness of breath. He felt the discomfort was nothing to complain about and he had not mentioned what he believed, and hoped, were minor annoyances. He had never had the nature to make a fuss about his own needs. He remembered his father had had similar problems, but he tried to put these thoughts out of his mind.

His cousin Andrew had told his wife Teresa a few days ago, "Richard looks pale and tired. I hope he isn't ill." Uncle George had said, "Richard, lad, you look as though you haven't slept for a few nights." His condition had not gone unnoticed.

They were now chatting amicably after their dinner. Richard had requested that the cook should prepare something 'light' that evening. He usually retired to his own home around half past seven or eight, at the latest.

As was their habit, they were enjoying a glass of Uncle George's vintage wine. He maintained that his food suited his aging body far better when his stomach was 'encouraged', both before and after a meal! He was by now in his eighty-seventh year and Richard was getting close to his sixtieth. Uncle George's brain was still very acute and it was his belief that his longevity was directly related to his active brain. He discussed his remarkable health with Richard.

"I have been the most fortunate of men in my physical health. But, you know Richard, had I not had such a robust constitution, I would not have been able to start, never mind complete, our task against the Church Army to get some justice and reform. Particularly at the age I was at the time, an age when most men, if even still alive, would have already given up all thought of work or any struggle.

"You may not know, but when Aunt Gwendolyn died I was so affected that I very nearly resigned from being Lord Lieutenant in favour of Andrew. But some small voice inside my head said, 'Carry on, wait. Now is not the time.' I am so glad I listened to that instinct and obeyed. I needed the authority and the backing of the other Lord Lieutenants to fight the Church Army as we did. Though, of course, I must admit that Andrew had done very much work for me in the preceding few years, in preparation for taking over the position. But, I do feel, very deeply, that my robust health was given to me so that I could complete that task."

"I suspect you are right, Uncle. Very few people have had your stamina and energy or been free from illness and pain for this many years. I shall thank God, from the depths of my soul, when I see him. I promise you. Without you, I do not know what we would have done. I have never been able to thank you enough."

"Nay, Richard, it was not only my duty but my great pleasure to have your family living with us. Out of a tragedy came much pain but also joy. Think of your son, Gerrard. He really is the perfect match for my granddaughter Anna-Marie. Sarah and Robbie are so happy together and now they have been blessed with little Rosemary. Their paths wouldn't have crossed otherwise. I can remember Teresa bemoaning that she and Andrew's children were now in their teens but really quite isolated and without suitable friends and acquaintances locally. Then, within a few months, six intelligent, lovely children came into our household. No, Richard, it is me and my family who have gained the most."

"We could argue this for ever." They both laughed.

Uncle George had been reading Latin verse.

"Richard, you remember the quotation that I chose for your book, from these old pages? I have just been reading the poem again. Let me read some further lines. I do believe that the sage was inspired by such a dream as yours. The concept of the 'healing fields' is quite beautiful, very comforting and maybe, even unique. I haven't come across it in any other context, and I have read much diverse text.

He opened the pages.

"Listen and I will translate as best I can. I know the meaning but finding the English to adequately express what is written is sometimes quite difficult. He continued,

> *What message can I send?*
> *To those who cannot know'*
> *'Be kind, use your life well*
> *No friendship to Satan show*
>
> *You may suffer, but better still*
> *To die than hurt another*
> *If all followed that simple task*
> *The world would be our brother*

"It ends with,   *This place would then welcome*
                   Everyone to its welcome light'

"If you remember, this place that the poet speaks about was called the 'healing fields'. This poem makes me believe that when we leave this earthly body we have a spiritual body which carries all the pain of our earthly life and all our grief and sorrow to those 'healing fields'. There the healing takes place. Only after that process and when completely free from all pain can our spirit arrive in heaven. What do you think to that thought? Otherwise suffering on this earth has no meaning. All pain is connected to the mind and, I feel, the spirit. How can it be merely discarded at death? "

"That is very profound and makes such sense, Uncle, but we shall never know, shall we? But we can hope that is so. As I can understand, Uncle, it also infers that only those who are 'kind' will go to the healing fields. At that point in the poem you have just read, it talks in the future about 'everyone' being welcomed. I wonder, will a time come when all people are kind and good? I would like to have been here to witness that."

"Richard. I will underline the appropriate line and make a note in the margin, for further thought. That is a very good point, very good indeed. Thank you. I must confess I had missed that inference last time and even now again, in my enthusiasm for my quotation. I have always believed that all people start their lives equal in the sight of God and, after that, everyone has choice as to whether they are kind or not along their life's journey. Look at Nell, Will or Norman, faithful in their service to us, yet not asking for anything in return. I hope we adequately served them. Wonderful people, yet I know they would not have been allowed to walk through your grandmama's front door. One can only hope that she has learned the error of her ways, wherever she is."

"She was always kind to me."

"Yes, in many other aspects, I know she was kind. But Eve suffered as a result of her beliefs and, indirectly, so did your sisters. Ever stone thrown into a pool causes ripples. You know Richard, all actions are connected, for good or bad. It makes me ask the question, 'Who offers forgiveness?' I know that she was not bad, just misguided in her beliefs, but trained to be so from childhood."

"I like to think that my sisters, Rosamund, Aunt Gwendolyn and all we have loved who suffered, are now free of pain. Since my dream or vision of the boat, I believe that to be true. I could tell that they were quite serene. Maybe they had just left the healing fields when I saw them?"

"I am surprised at myself. Richard, why have I never thought of all this before?" asked Uncle George.

"Maybe it wasn't the time for you to do so," answered Richard.

"What on earth is ..." Uncle George suddenly stopped.

Richard watched with horror. As if time was in slow motion, Uncle George's glass appeared to slip in his hand, spilling the wine onto his coat. His hand fell forward, the glass dropped and shattered on the floor. Uncle George slumped sideways in his chair, his eyes open and staring upwards.

Richard stood up to rush to the bell-pull by the fireplace to summon Uncle George's valet, William. His father, Norman had long since been retired.

He had hardly taken two steps when, strangely, his legs felt heavy, as though he was walking through deep mud. He could not lift his left foot. 'Oh, come on, move,' he panicked, briefly. His vision blurred as if a thick fog had descended. He felt a searing pain in his chest. Richard, though no longer aware, fell to the floor gasping. His colour turned blue, then grey as his breathing gradually stopped. His heart had finally broken.

Their bodies were found when William came to clear the dinner plates. The best of companions, these two kind and dear men had departed together.

§

A spectral Uncle George waited by the large marble fireplace. After a few minutes, Richard's spirit joined him. Together, arm in arm, and, as if their conversation was merely and only temporarily interrupted, they appeared to float across the centre of the room without a backward glance. They disappeared through Uncle George's favourite portrait, as if to greet Aunt Gwendolyn in her beloved garden.

'They are on their way to the healing fields.'

Dr Audrey Coatesworth – for any details go to websites:-

www.audreycoatesworth.com
www.plppublishings.co.uk
www.buybeyondmercybook.com

Other books:-

Poetry
Growing Up - for 7-13 yrs
Coping with Illness and Grief - for 7-13yrs
Choice for Teenagers

All sold via websites

Additional websites
www.primaryschoolpoems.com
www.elementaryschoolpoems.com
www.secondaryschoolpoems.com